HARRY POTTER

AND THE DEATHLY HALLOWS

ALSO BY J. K. ROWLING

Harry Potter and the Sorcerer's Stone
Year One at Hogwarts

Harry Potter and the Chamber of Secrets
Year Two at Hogwarts

Harry Potter and the Prisoner of Azkaban
Year Three at Hogwarts

Harry Potter and the Goblet of Fire
Year Four at Hogwarts

Harry Potter and the Order of the Phoenix
Year Five at Hogwarts

Harry Potter and the Half-Blood Prince
Year Six at Hogwarts

HARRY POTTER

AND THE DEATHLY HALLOWS

BY

J. K. ROWLING

ILLUSTRATIONS BY MARY GRANDPRÉ

ARTHUR A. LEVINE BOOKS

AN IMPRINT OF SCHOLASTIC INC.

Library of Congress Control Number: 2007925449

ISBN-13: 978-0-545-02936-0
ISBN-10: 0-545-02936-8

10 9 8 7 6 5 4 3 2 1   07 08 09 10 11
Printed in the U.S.A.   23
Reinforced library edition, July 2007

THE

DEDICATION

OF THIS BOOK

IS SPLIT

SEVEN WAYS:

TO NEIL,

TO JESSICA,

TO DAVID,

TO KENZIE,

TO DI,

TO ANNE,

AND TO YOU,

IF YOU HAVE

STUCK

WITH HARRY

UNTIL THE

VERY

END.

CONTENTS

ONE
The Dark Lord Ascending · 1

TWO
In Memoriam · 13

THREE
The Dursleys Departing · 30

FOUR
The Seven Potters · 43

FIVE
Fallen Warrior · 63

SIX
The Ghoul in Pajamas · 86

SEVEN
The Will of Albus Dumbledore · 111

EIGHT
The Wedding · 137

NINE
A Place to Hide · 160

TEN

Kreacher's Tale · 176

ELEVEN

The Bribe · 201

TWELVE

Magic Is Might · 223

THIRTEEN

The Muggle-born Registration Commission · 246

FOURTEEN

The Thief · 268

FIFTEEN

The Goblin's Revenge · 284

SIXTEEN

Godric's Hollow · 311

SEVENTEEN

Bathilda's Secret · 330

EIGHTEEN

The Life and Lies of Albus Dumbledore · 350

NINETEEN

The Silver Doe · 363

TWENTY
Xenophilius Lovegood · 388

TWENTY-ONE
The Tale of the Three Brothers · 405

TWENTY-TWO
The Deathly Hallows · 424

TWENTY-THREE
Malfoy Manor · 446

TWENTY-FOUR
The Wandmaker · 477

TWENTY-FIVE
Shell Cottage · 502

TWENTY-SIX
Gringotts · 519

TWENTY-SEVEN
The Final Hiding Place · 544

TWENTY-EIGHT
The Missing Mirror · 554

TWENTY-NINE
The Lost Diadem · 571

THIRTY

The Sacking of Severus Snape · 589

THIRTY–ONE

The Battle of Hogwarts · 608

THIRTY–TWO

The Elder Wand · 638

THIRTY–THREE

The Prince's Tale · 659

THIRTY–FOUR

The Forest Again · 691

THIRTY–FIVE

King's Cross · 705

THIRTY–SIX

The Flaw in the Plan · 724

EPILOGUE

753

Oh, the torment bred in the race,
      the grinding scream of death
          and the stroke that hits the vein,
   the hemorrhage none can staunch, the grief,
the curse no man can bear.

But there is a cure in the house,
      and not outside it, no,
          not from others but from *them*,
   their bloody strife. We sing to you,
dark gods beneath the earth.

Now hear, you blissful powers underground —
   answer the call, send help.
Bless the children, give them triumph now.

          Aeschylus, *The Libation Bearers*

Death is but crossing the world, as friends do the seas; they live in one another still. For they must needs be present, that love and live in that which is omnipresent. In this divine glass, they see face to face; and their converse is free, as well as pure. This is the comfort of friends, that though they may be said to die, yet their friendship and society are, in the best sense, ever present, because immortal.

          William Penn, *More Fruits of Solitude*

HARRY POTTER

AND THE DEATHLY HALLOWS

CHAPTER ONE

THE DARK LORD ASCENDING

The two men appeared out of nowhere, a few yards apart in the narrow, moonlit lane. For a second they stood quite still, wands directed at each other's chests; then, recognizing each other, they stowed their wands beneath their cloaks and started walking briskly in the same direction.

"News?" asked the taller of the two.

"The best," replied Severus Snape.

The lane was bordered on the left by wild, low-growing brambles, on the right by a high, neatly manicured hedge. The men's long cloaks flapped around their ankles as they marched.

"Thought I might be late," said Yaxley, his blunt features sliding in and out of sight as the branches of overhanging trees broke the moonlight. "It was a little trickier than I expected. But I hope he will be satisfied. You sound confident that your reception will be good?"

Snape nodded, but did not elaborate. They turned right, into a wide driveway that led off the lane. The high hedge curved with them, running off into the distance beyond the pair of impressive wrought-iron gates barring the men's way. Neither of them broke step: In silence both raised their left arms in a kind of salute and passed straight through, as though the dark metal were smoke.

The yew hedges muffled the sound of the men's footsteps. There was a rustle somewhere to their right: Yaxley drew his wand again, pointing it over his companion's head, but the source of the noise proved to be nothing more than a pure-white peacock, strutting majestically along the top of the hedge.

"He always did himself well, Lucius. *Peacocks . . .*" Yaxley thrust his wand back under his cloak with a snort.

A handsome manor house grew out of the darkness at the end of the straight drive, lights glinting in the diamond-paned downstairs windows. Somewhere in the dark garden beyond the hedge a fountain was playing. Gravel crackled beneath their feet as Snape and Yaxley sped toward the front door, which swung inward at their approach, though nobody had visibly opened it.

The hallway was large, dimly lit, and sumptuously decorated, with a magnificent carpet covering most of the stone floor. The eyes of the pale-faced portraits on the walls followed Snape and Yaxley as they strode past. The two men halted at a heavy wooden door leading into the next room, hesitated for the space of a heartbeat, then Snape turned the bronze handle.

The drawing room was full of silent people, sitting at a long and ornate table. The room's usual furniture had been pushed carelessly up against the walls. Illumination came from a roaring fire beneath a handsome marble mantelpiece surmounted by a gilded mirror. Snape and Yaxley lingered for a moment on the threshold. As their eyes grew accustomed to the lack of light, they were drawn upward to the strangest feature of the scene: an apparently unconscious human figure hanging upside down over the table, revolving slowly as if suspended by an invisible rope, and reflected in the mirror and in the bare, polished surface of the table below. None of the people seated underneath this singular sight was looking at it except for a pale young man sitting almost directly below it. He seemed unable to prevent himself from glancing upward every minute or so.

"Yaxley. Snape," said a high, clear voice from the head of the table. "You are very nearly late."

The speaker was seated directly in front of the fireplace, so that it was difficult, at first, for the new arrivals to make out more than his silhouette. As they drew nearer, however, his face shone through the gloom, hairless, snakelike, with slits for nostrils and gleaming red eyes whose pupils were vertical. He was so pale that he seemed to emit a pearly glow.

"Severus, here," said Voldemort, indicating the seat on his immediate right. "Yaxley — beside Dolohov."

The two men took their allotted places. Most of the eyes around the table followed Snape, and it was to him that Voldemort spoke first.

"So?"

"My Lord, the Order of the Phoenix intends to move Harry Potter from his current place of safety on Saturday next, at nightfall."

The interest around the table sharpened palpably: Some stiffened, others fidgeted, all gazing at Snape and Voldemort.

"Saturday . . . at nightfall," repeated Voldemort. His red eyes fastened upon Snape's black ones with such intensity that some of the watchers looked away, apparently fearful that they themselves would be scorched by the ferocity of the gaze. Snape, however, looked calmly back into Voldemort's face and, after a moment or two, Voldemort's lipless mouth curved into something like a smile.

"Good. Very good. And this information comes —"

"— from the source we discussed," said Snape.

"My Lord."

Yaxley had leaned forward to look down the long table at Voldemort and Snape. All faces turned to him.

"My Lord, I have heard differently."

Yaxley waited, but Voldemort did not speak, so he went on, "Dawlish, the Auror, let slip that Potter will not be moved until the thirtieth, the night before the boy turns seventeen."

Snape was smiling.

"My source told me that there are plans to lay a false trail; this must be it. No doubt a Confundus Charm has been placed upon Dawlish. It would not be the first time; he is known to be susceptible."

"I assure you, my Lord, Dawlish seemed quite certain," said Yaxley.

"If he has been Confunded, naturally he is certain," said Snape. "I assure *you,* Yaxley, the Auror Office will play no further part in the protection of Harry Potter. The Order believes that we have infiltrated the Ministry."

"The Order's got one thing right, then, eh?" said a squat man sitting a short distance from Yaxley; he gave a wheezy giggle that was echoed here and there along the table.

Voldemort did not laugh. His gaze had wandered upward to the body revolving slowly overhead, and he seemed to be lost in thought.

"My Lord," Yaxley went on, "Dawlish believes an entire party of Aurors will be used to transfer the boy —"

Voldemort held up a large white hand, and Yaxley subsided at once, watching resentfully as Voldemort turned back to Snape.

"Where are they going to hide the boy next?"

"At the home of one of the Order," said Snape. "The place, according to the source, has been given every protection that the Order and Ministry together could provide. I think that there is little chance of taking him once he is there, my Lord, unless, of course, the Ministry has fallen before next Saturday, which might give us the opportunity to discover and undo enough of the enchantments to break through the rest."

"Well, Yaxley?" Voldemort called down the table, the firelight glinting strangely in his red eyes. "*Will* the Ministry have fallen by next Saturday?"

Once again, all heads turned. Yaxley squared his shoulders.

"My Lord, I have good news on that score. I have — with difficulty, and after great effort — suceeded in placing an Imperius Curse upon Pius Thicknesse."

Many of those sitting around Yaxley looked impressed; his neighbor, Dolohov, a man with a long, twisted face, clapped him on the back.

"It is a start," said Voldemort. "But Thicknesse is only one man. Scrimgeour must be surrounded by our people before I act. One failed attempt on the Minister's life will set me back a long way."

"Yes — my Lord, that is true — but you know, as Head of the Department of Magical Law Enforcement, Thicknesse has regular contact not only with the Minister himself, but also with the Heads of all the other Ministry departments. It will, I think, be easy now that we have such a high-ranking official under our control, to subjugate the others, and then they can all work together to bring Scrimgeour down."

"As long as our friend Thicknesse is not discovered before he has converted the rest," said Voldemort. "At any rate, it remains unlikely that the Ministry will be mine before next Saturday. If we cannot touch the boy at his destination, then it must be done while he travels."

"We are at an advantage there, my Lord," said Yaxley, who seemed determined to receive some portion of approval. "We now have several people planted within the Department of Magical Transport. If Potter Apparates or uses the Floo Network, we shall know immediately."

"He will not do either," said Snape. "The Order is eschewing any form of transport that is controlled or regulated by the Ministry; they mistrust everything to do with the place."

"All the better," said Voldemort. "He will have to move in the open. Easier to take, by far."

Again, Voldemort looked up at the slowly revolving body as he went on, "I shall attend to the boy in person. There have been too many mistakes where Harry Potter is concerned. Some of them have been my own. That Potter lives is due more to my errors than to his triumphs."

The company around the table watched Voldemort apprehensively, each of them, by his or her expression, afraid that they might be blamed for Harry Potter's continued existence. Voldemort, however, seemed to be speaking more to himself than to any of them, still addressing the unconscious body above him.

"I have been careless, and so have been thwarted by luck and chance, those wreckers of all but the best-laid plans. But I know better now. I understand those things that I did not understand before. I must be the one to kill Harry Potter, and I shall be."

At these words, seemingly in response to them, a sudden wail sounded, a terrible, drawn-out cry of misery and pain. Many of those at the table looked downward, startled, for the sound had seemed to issue from below their feet.

"Wormtail," said Voldemort, with no change in his quiet, thoughtful tone, and without removing his eyes from the revolving body above, "have I not spoken to you about keeping our prisoner quiet?"

"Yes, m-my Lord," gasped a small man halfway down the table, who had been sitting so low in his chair that it had appeared, at first glance, to be unoccupied. Now he scrambled from his seat and scurried from the room, leaving nothing behind him but a curious gleam of silver.

"As I was saying," continued Voldemort, looking again at the tense faces of his followers, "I understand better now. I shall need, for instance, to borrow a wand from one of you before I go to kill Potter."

The faces around him displayed nothing but shock; he might have announced that he wanted to borrow one of their arms.

"No volunteers?" said Voldemort. "Let's see . . . Lucius, I see no reason for you to have a wand anymore."

Lucius Malfoy looked up. His skin appeared yellowish and waxy in the firelight, and his eyes were sunken and shadowed. When he spoke, his voice was hoarse.

"My Lord?"

"Your wand, Lucius. I require your wand."

"I . . ."

Malfoy glanced sideways at his wife. She was staring straight ahead, quite as pale as he was, her long blonde hair hanging down her back, but beneath the table her slim fingers closed briefly on his wrist. At her touch, Malfoy put his hand into his robes, withdrew a wand, and passed it along to Voldemort, who held it up in front of his red eyes, examining it closely.

"What is it?"

"Elm, my Lord," whispered Malfoy.

"And the core?"

"Dragon — dragon heartstring."

"Good," said Voldemort. He drew out his own wand and compared the lengths. Lucius Malfoy made an involuntary movement; for a fraction of a second, it seemed he expected to receive Voldemort's wand in exchange for his own. The gesture was not missed by Voldemort, whose eyes widened maliciously.

"Give you my wand, Lucius? *My* wand?"

Some of the throng sniggered.

"I have given you your liberty, Lucius, is that not enough for you? But I have noticed that you and your family seem less than happy of late. . . . What is it about my presence in your home that displeases you, Lucius?"

"Nothing — nothing, my Lord!"

"Such *lies*, Lucius . . ."

The soft voice seemed to hiss on even after the cruel mouth had stopped moving. One or two of the wizards barely repressed a shudder as the hissing grew louder; something heavy could be heard sliding across the floor beneath the table.

The huge snake emerged to climb slowly up Voldemort's chair. It rose, seemingly endlessly, and came to rest across Voldemort's shoulders: its neck the thickness of a man's thigh; its eyes, with their vertical slits for pupils, unblinking. Voldemort stroked the creature absently with long thin fingers, still looking at Lucius Malfoy.

"Why do the Malfoys look so unhappy with their lot? Is my return, my rise to power, not the very thing they professed to desire for so many years?"

"Of course, my Lord," said Lucius Malfoy. His hand shook as he wiped sweat from his upper lip. "We did desire it — we do."

To Malfoy's left, his wife made an odd, stiff nod, her eyes averted from Voldemort and the snake. To his right, his son, Draco, who had been gazing up at the inert body overhead, glanced quickly at Voldemort and away again, terrified to make eye contact.

"My Lord," said a dark woman halfway down the table, her voice constricted with emotion, "it is an honor to have you here, in our family's house. There can be no higher pleasure."

She sat beside her sister, as unlike her in looks, with her dark hair and heavily lidded eyes, as she was in bearing and demeanor; where Narcissa sat rigid and impassive, Bellatrix leaned toward Voldemort, for mere words could not demonstrate her longing for closeness.

"No higher pleasure," repeated Voldemort, his head tilted a little to one side as he considered Bellatrix. "That means a great deal, Bellatrix, from you."

Her face flooded with color; her eyes welled with tears of delight.

"My Lord knows I speak nothing but the truth!"

"No higher pleasure . . . even compared with the happy event that, I hear, has taken place in your family this week?"

She stared at him, her lips parted, evidently confused.

"I don't know what you mean, my Lord."

"I'm talking about your niece, Bellatrix. And yours, Lucius and Narcissa. She has just married the werewolf, Remus Lupin. You must be so proud."

There was an eruption of jeering laughter from around the table. Many leaned forward to exchange gleeful looks; a few thumped the table with their fists. The great snake, disliking the disturbance, opened its mouth wide and hissed angrily, but the Death Eaters did not hear it, so jubilant were they at Bellatrix and the Malfoys' humiliation. Bellatrix's face, so recently flushed with happiness, had turned an ugly, blotchy red.

"She is no niece of ours, my Lord," she cried over the outpouring of mirth. "We — Narcissa and I — have never set eyes on our sister since she married the Mudblood. This brat has nothing to do with either of us, nor any beast she marries."

"What say you, Draco?" asked Voldemort, and though his voice was quiet, it carried clearly through the catcalls and jeers. "Will you babysit the cubs?"

The hilarity mounted; Draco Malfoy looked in terror at his father, who was staring down into his own lap, then caught his mother's eye. She shook her head almost imperceptibly, then resumed her own deadpan stare at the opposite wall.

"Enough," said Voldemort, stroking the angry snake. "Enough."

And the laughter died at once.

"Many of our oldest family trees become a little diseased over time," he said as Bellatrix gazed at him, breathless and imploring.

"You must prune yours, must you not, to keep it healthy? Cut away those parts that threaten the health of the rest."

"Yes, my Lord," whispered Bellatrix, and her eyes swam with tears of gratitude again. "At the first chance!"

"You shall have it," said Voldemort. "And in your family, so in the world . . . we shall cut away the canker that infects us until only those of the true blood remain. . . ."

Voldemort raised Lucius Malfoy's wand, pointed it directly at the slowly revolving figure suspended over the table, and gave it a tiny flick. The figure came to life with a groan and began to struggle against invisible bonds.

"Do you recognize our guest, Severus?" asked Voldemort.

Snape raised his eyes to the upside-down face. All of the Death Eaters were looking up at the captive now, as though they had been given permission to show curiosity. As she revolved to face the fire-light, the woman said in a cracked and terrified voice, "Severus! Help me!"

"Ah, yes," said Snape as the prisoner turned slowly away again.

"And you, Draco?" asked Voldemort, stroking the snake's snout with his wand-free hand. Draco shook his head jerkily. Now that the woman had woken, he seemed unable to look at her anymore.

"But you would not have taken her classes," said Voldemort. "For those of you who do not know, we are joined here tonight by Charity Burbage who, until recently, taught at Hogwarts School of Witch-craft and Wizardry."

There were small noises of comprehension around the table. A broad, hunched woman with pointed teeth cackled.

"Yes . . . Professor Burbage taught the children of witches and wizards all about Muggles . . . how they are not so different from us . . ."

One of the Death Eaters spat on the floor. Charity Burbage revolved to face Snape again.

"Severus . . . please . . . please . . ."

"Silence," said Voldemort, with another twitch of Malfoy's wand, and Charity fell silent as if gagged. "Not content with corrupting and polluting the minds of Wizarding children, last week Professor Burbage wrote an impassioned defense of Mudbloods in the *Daily Prophet*. Wizards, she says, must accept these thieves of their knowledge and magic. The dwindling of the purebloods is, says Professor Burbage, a most desirable circumstance. . . . She would have us all mate with Muggles . . . or, no doubt, werewolves. . . ."

Nobody laughed this time: There was no mistaking the anger and contempt in Voldemort's voice. For the third time, Charity Burbage revolved to face Snape. Tears were pouring from her eyes into her hair. Snape looked back at her, quite impassive, as she turned slowly away from him again.

"*Avada Kedavra.*"

The flash of green light illuminated every corner of the room. Charity fell, with a resounding crash, onto the table below, which trembled and creaked. Several of the Death Eaters leapt back in their chairs. Draco fell out of his onto the floor.

"Dinner, Nagini," said Voldemort softly, and the great snake swayed and slithered from his shoulders onto the polished wood.

CHAPTER TWO

IN MEMORIAM

Harry was bleeding. Clutching his right hand in his left and swearing under his breath, he shouldered open his bedroom door. There was a crunch of breaking china: He had trodden on a cup of cold tea that had been sitting on the floor outside his bedroom door.

"What the — ?"

He looked around; the landing of number four, Privet Drive, was deserted. Possibly the cup of tea was Dudley's idea of a clever booby trap. Keeping his bleeding hand elevated, Harry scraped the fragments of cup together with the other hand and threw them into the already crammed bin just visible inside his bedroom door. Then he tramped across to the bathroom to run his finger under the tap.

It was stupid, pointless, irritating beyond belief that he still had four days left of being unable to perform magic . . . but he had to admit to himself that this jagged cut in his finger would have defeated him. He had never learned how to repair wounds, and now he came to think of it — particularly in light of his immediate plans — this seemed a serious flaw in his magical education. Making a mental note to ask Hermione how it was done, he used a large wad of toilet paper to mop up as much of the tea as he could, before returning to his bedroom and slamming the door behind him.

Harry had spent the morning completely emptying his school trunk for the first time since he had packed it six years ago. At the start of the intervening school years, he had merely skimmed off the topmost three quarters of the contents and replaced or updated them, leaving a layer of general debris at the bottom — old quills, desiccated beetle eyes, single socks that no longer fit. Minutes previously, Harry had plunged his hand into this mulch, experienced a stabbing pain in the fourth finger of his right hand, and withdrawn it to see a lot of blood.

He now proceeded a little more cautiously. Kneeling down beside the trunk again, he groped around in the bottom and, after retrieving an old badge that flickered feebly between *Support CEDRIC DIGGORY* and *POTTER STINKS,* a cracked and worn-out Sneakoscope, and a gold locket inside which a note signed R.A.B. had been hidden, he finally discovered the sharp edge that had done the damage. He recognized it at once. It was a two-inch-long fragment of the enchanted mirror that his dead godfather, Sirius, had given him. Harry laid it aside and felt cautiously around the trunk for the rest, but nothing more remained of his godfather's last gift except powdered glass, which clung to the deepest layer of debris like glittering grit.

Harry sat up and examined the jagged piece on which he had cut himself, seeing nothing but his own bright green eye reflected back at him. Then he placed the fragment on top of that morning's

Daily Prophet, which lay unread on the bed, and attempted to stem the sudden upsurge of bitter memories, the stabs of regret and of longing the discovery of the broken mirror had occasioned, by attacking the rest of the rubbish in the trunk.

It took another hour to empty it completely, throw away the useless items, and sort the remainder in piles according to whether or not he would need them from now on. His school and Quidditch robes, cauldron, parchment, quills, and most of his textbooks were piled in a corner, to be left behind. He wondered what his aunt and uncle would do with them; burn them in the dead of night, probably, as if they were the evidence of some dreadful crime. His Muggle clothing, Invisibility Cloak, potion-making kit, certain books, the photograph album Hagrid had once given him, a stack of letters, and his wand had been repacked into an old rucksack. In a front pocket were the Marauder's Map and the locket with the note signed R.A.B. inside it. The locket was accorded this place of honor not because it was valuable — in all usual senses it was worthless — but because of what it had cost to attain it.

This left a sizable stack of newspapers sitting on his desk beside his snowy owl, Hedwig: one for each of the days Harry had spent at Privet Drive this summer.

He got up off the floor, stretched, and moved across to his desk. Hedwig made no movement as he began to flick through the newspapers, throwing them onto the rubbish pile one by one. The owl was asleep, or else faking; she was angry with Harry about the limited amount of time she was allowed out of her cage at the moment.

As he neared the bottom of the pile of newspapers, Harry slowed down, searching for one particular issue that he knew had arrived shortly after he had returned to Privet Drive for the summer; he remembered that there had been a small mention on the front about the resignation of Charity Burbage, the Muggle Studies teacher at Hogwarts. At last he found it. Turning to page ten, he sank into his desk chair and reread the article he had been looking for.

ALBUS DUMBLEDORE REMEMBERED

by Elphias Doge

I met Albus Dumbledore at the age of eleven, on our first day at Hogwarts. Our mutual attraction was undoubtedly due to the fact that we both felt ourselves to be outsiders. I had contracted dragon pox shortly before arriving at school, and while I was no longer contagious, my pockmarked visage and greenish hue did not encourage many to approach me. For his part, Albus had arrived at Hogwarts under the burden of unwanted notoriety. Scarcely a year previously, his father, Percival, had been convicted of a savage and well-publicized attack upon three young Muggles.

Albus never attempted to deny that his father (who was to die in Azkaban) had committed this crime; on the contrary, when I plucked up courage to ask him, he assured me that he knew his father to be guilty. Beyond that, Dumbledore refused to speak of the sad business, though many attempted to make him do so. Some, indeed, were disposed to praise his father's action and assumed that Albus too was a Muggle-hater. They could not have been more mistaken: As anybody who knew Albus would attest, he never revealed the remotest anti-Muggle tendency. Indeed, his determined support for Muggle rights gained him many enemies in subsequent years.

In a matter of months, however, Albus's own fame had begun to eclipse that of his father. By the end of his first year he would never again be known as the son of a Muggle-hater, but as nothing more or less than the most brilliant student ever seen at the school. Those of us who were privileged to be his friends benefited from his example, not to mention his help and encouragement, with which he was always generous. He confessed to me in later life that he knew even then that his greatest pleasure lay in teaching.

He not only won every prize of note that the school offered, he was soon in regular correspondence with the most notable magical names of the day, including Nicolas Flamel, the celebrated alchemist; Bathilda Bagshot, the noted historian; and Adalbert Waffling, the magical theoretician. Several of his papers found their way into learned publications such as *Transfiguration Today, Challenges in Charming,* and *The Practical Potioneer.* Dumbledore's future career seemed likely to be meteoric, and the only question that remained was when he would become Minister of Magic. Though it was often predicted in later years that he was on the point of taking the job, however, he never had Ministerial ambitions.

Three years after we had started at Hogwarts,

Albus's brother, Aberforth, arrived at school. They were not alike; Aberforth was never bookish and, unlike Albus, preferred to settle arguments by dueling rather than through reasoned discussion. However, it is quite wrong to suggest, as some have, that the brothers were not friends. They rubbed along as comfortably as two such different boys could do. In fairness to Aberforth, it must be admitted that living in Albus's shadow cannot have been an altogether comfortable experience. Being continually outshone was an occupational hazard of being his friend and cannot have been any more pleasurable as a brother.

When Albus and I left Hogwarts we intended to take the then-traditional tour of the world together, visiting and observing foreign wizards, before pursuing our separate careers. However, tragedy intervened. On the very eve of our trip, Albus's mother, Kendra, died, leaving Albus the head, and sole breadwinner, of the family. I postponed my departure long enough to pay my respects at Kendra's funeral, then left for what was now to be a solitary journey. With a younger brother and sister to care for, and little gold left to them, there could no longer be any question of Albus accompanying me.

That was the period of our lives when we had least contact. I wrote to Albus, describing, perhaps insensitively, the wonders of my journey, from narrow escapes from chimaeras in Greece to the experiments of the Egyptian alchemists. His letters told me little of his day-to-day life, which I guessed to be frustratingly dull for such a brilliant wizard. Immersed in my own experiences, it was with horror that I heard, toward the end of my year's travels, that yet another tragedy had struck the Dumbledores: the death of his sister, Ariana.

Though Ariana had been in poor health for a long time, the blow, coming so soon after the loss of their mother, had a profound effect on both of her brothers. All those closest to Albus — and I count myself one of that lucky number — agree that Ariana's death, and Albus's feeling of personal responsibility for it (though, of course, he was guiltless), left their mark upon him forevermore.

I returned home to find a young man who had experienced a much older person's suffering. Albus was more reserved than before, and much less lighthearted. To add to his misery, the loss of Ariana had led, not to a renewed closeness between Albus and Aberforth, but to an estrangement. (In time this would lift — in later years they reestablished, if not a close relationship, then certainly a cordial one.) However, he rarely spoke of his parents or of Ariana from then on, and his friends learned not to mention them.

Other quills will describe the triumphs of the following years. Dumbledore's innumerable contributions to the store of Wizarding knowledge, including his discovery of the twelve uses of dragon's blood, will benefit generations to come, as will the wisdom he displayed in the many judgments he made while Chief Warlock of the Wizengamot. They say, still, that no Wizarding duel ever matched that between Dumbledore and Grindelwald in 1945. Those who witnessed it have written of the terror and the awe they felt as they watched these two extraordinary wizards do battle. Dumbledore's triumph, and its consequences for the Wizarding world, are considered a turning point in magical history to match the introduction of the International Statute of Secrecy or the downfall of He-Who-Must-Not-Be-Named.

Albus Dumbledore was never proud or vain; he could find something to value in anyone, however apparently insignificant or wretched, and I believe that his early losses endowed him with great humanity and sympathy. I shall miss his friendship more than I can say, but my loss is as nothing compared to the Wizarding world's. That he was the most inspiring and the best loved of all Hogwarts headmasters cannot be in question. He died as he lived: working always for the greater good and, to his last hour, as willing to stretch out a hand to a small boy with dragon pox as he was on the day that I met him.

Harry finished reading but continued to gaze at the picture accompanying the obituary. Dumbledore was wearing his familiar, kindly smile, but as he peered over the top of his half-moon spec-tacles, he gave the impression, even in newsprint, of X-raying Harry, whose sadness mingled with a sense of humiliation.

He had thought he knew Dumbledore quite well, but ever since reading this obituary he had been forced to recognize that he had barely known him at all. Never once had he imagined Dumbledore's childhood or youth; it was as though he had sprung into being as Harry had known him, venerable and silver-haired and old. The idea of a teenage Dumbledore was simply odd, like trying to imagine a stupid Hermione or a friendly Blast-Ended Skrewt.

He had never thought to ask Dumbledore about his past. No doubt it would have felt strange, impertinent even, but after all, it had been common knowledge that Dumbledore had taken part in that legendary duel with Grindelwald, and Harry had not thought to ask Dumbledore what that had been like, nor about any of his other famous achievements. No, they had always discussed Harry, Harry's past, Harry's future, Harry's plans . . . and it seemed to Harry now, despite the fact that his future was so dangerous and so uncertain, that he had missed irreplaceable opportunities when he had failed to ask Dumbledore more about himself, even though the only personal question he had ever asked his headmaster was also the only one he suspected that Dumbledore had not answered honestly:

"What do you see when you look in the mirror?"

"I? I see myself holding a pair of thick, woolen socks."

After several minutes' thought, Harry tore the obituary out of the *Prophet,* folded it carefully, and tucked it inside the first volume of *Practical Defensive Magic and Its Use Against the Dark Arts.* Then he threw the rest of the newspaper onto the rubbish pile and turned to face the room. It was much tidier. The only things left out of place were today's *Daily Prophet,* still lying on the bed, and on top of it, the piece of broken mirror.

Harry moved across the room, slid the mirror fragment off today's *Prophet,* and unfolded the newspaper. He had merely glanced at the headline when he had taken the rolled-up paper from the delivery owl early that morning and thrown it aside, after noting that it said nothing about Voldemort. Harry was sure that the Ministry was leaning on the *Prophet* to suppress news about Voldemort. It was only now, therefore, that he saw what he had missed.

Across the bottom half of the front page a smaller headline was set over a picture of Dumbledore striding along looking harried:

DUMBLEDORE — THE TRUTH AT LAST?

Coming next week, the shocking story of the flawed genius considered by many to be the greatest wizard of his generation. Stripping away the popular image of serene, silver-bearded wisdom, Rita Skeeter reveals the disturbed childhood, the lawless youth, the life-long feuds, and the guilty secrets that Dumbledore carried to his grave. WHY was the man tipped to be Minister of Magic content to remain a mere head-master? WHAT was the real purpose of the secret organization known as the Order of the Phoenix? HOW did Dumbledore really meet his end?

The answers to these and many more questions are explored in the explosive new biography, *The Life and Lies of Albus Dumbledore,* by Rita Skeeter, exclusively interviewed by Betty Braithwaite, page 13, inside.

Harry ripped open the paper and found page thirteen. The article was topped with a picture showing another familiar face: a woman wearing jeweled glasses with elaborately curled blonde hair, her teeth bared in what was clearly supposed to be a winning smile, wiggling her fingers up at him. Doing his best to ignore this nauseating image, Harry read on.

In person, Rita Skeeter is much warmer and softer than her famously ferocious quill-portraits might suggest. Greeting me in the hallway of her cozy home, she leads me straight into the kitchen for a cup of tea, a slice of pound cake and, it goes without saying, a steaming vat of freshest gossip.

"Well, of course, Dumbledore is a biographer's dream," says Skeeter. "Such a long, full life. I'm sure my book will be the first of very, very many."

Skeeter was certainly quick off the mark. Her nine-hundred-page book was completed a mere four weeks after Dumbledore's mysterious death in June. I ask her how she managed this superfast feat.

"Oh, when you've been a journalist as long as I have, working to a deadline is second nature. I knew that the Wizarding world was clamoring for the full story and I wanted to be the first to meet that need."

I mention the recent, widely publicized remarks

of Elphias Doge, Special Advisor to the Wizengamot and longstanding friend of Albus Dumbledore's, that "Skeeter's book contains less fact than a Chocolate Frog card."

Skeeter throws back her head and laughs.

"Darling Dodgy! I remember interviewing him a few years back about merpeople rights, bless him. Completely gaga, seemed to think we were sitting at the bottom of Lake Windermere, kept telling me to watch out for trout."

And yet Elphias Doge's accusations of inaccuracy have been echoed in many places. Does Skeeter really feel that four short weeks have been enough to gain a full picture of Dumbledore's long and extraordinary life?

"Oh, my dear," beams Skeeter, rapping me affectionately across the knuckles, "you know as well as I do how much information can be generated by a fat bag of Galleons, a refusal to hear the word 'no,' and a nice sharp Quick-Quotes Quill! People were queuing to dish the dirt on Dumbledore anyway. Not everyone thought he was so wonderful, you know — he trod on an awful lot of important toes. But old Dodgy Doge can get off his high hippogriff, because I've had access to a source most journalists would swap their wands for, one who has never spoken in public before and who was close to Dumbledore during the most turbulent and disturbing phase of his youth."

The advance publicity for Skeeter's biography has certainly suggested that there will be shocks in store for those who believe Dumbledore to have led a blameless life. What were the biggest surprises she uncovered, I ask?

"Now, come off it, Betty, I'm not giving away all the highlights before anybody's bought the book!" laughs Skeeter. "But I can promise that anybody who still thinks Dumbledore was white as his beard is in for a rude awakening! Let's just say that nobody hearing him rage against You-Know-Who would have dreamed that he dabbled in the Dark Arts himself in his youth! And for a wizard who spent his later years pleading for tolerance, he wasn't exactly broad-minded when he was younger! Yes, Albus Dumbledore had an extremely murky past, not to mention that very fishy family, which he worked so hard to keep hushed up."

I ask whether Skeeter is referring to Dumbledore's brother, Aberforth, whose conviction by the Wizengamot for misuse of magic caused a minor scandal fifteen years ago.

"Oh, Aberforth is just the tip of the dung heap," laughs Skeeter. "No, no, I'm talking about much worse than a brother with a fondness for fiddling about with goats, worse even than the Muggle-maiming father — Dumbledore couldn't keep either of them quiet anyway, they were both charged by the Wizengamot. No, it's the mother and the sister that intrigued me, and a little digging uncovered a positive nest of nastiness — but, as I say, you'll have to wait for chapters nine to twelve for full details. All I can say now is, it's no wonder Dumbledore never talked about how his nose got broken."

Family skeletons notwithstanding, does Skeeter deny the brilliance that led to Dumbledore's many magical discoveries?

"He had brains," she concedes, "although many now question whether he could really take full credit for all of his supposed achievements. As I reveal in chapter sixteen, Ivor Dillonsby claims he had already discovered eight uses of dragon's blood when Dumbledore 'borrowed' his papers."

But the importance of some of Dumbledore's achievements cannot, I venture, be denied. What of his famous defeat of Grindelwald?

"Oh, now, I'm glad you mentioned Grindelwald," says Skeeter with a tantalizing smile. "I'm afraid those who go dewy-eyed over Dumbledore's spectacular victory must brace themselves for a bombshell — or perhaps a Dungbomb. Very dirty business indeed. All I'll say is, don't be so sure that there really was the spectacular duel of legend. After they've read my book, people may be forced to conclude that Grindelwald simply conjured a white handkerchief from the end of his wand and came quietly!"

Skeeter refuses to give any more away on this intriguing subject, so we turn instead to the relationship that will undoubtedly fascinate her readers more than any other.

"Oh yes," says Skeeter, nodding briskly, "I devote an entire chapter to the whole Potter–Dumbledore relationship. It's been called unhealthy, even sinister. Again, your readers will have to buy my book for the whole story, but there is no question that Dumbledore took an unnatural interest in Potter from the word go. Whether that was really in the boy's best interests — well, we'll see. It's certainly an open secret that Potter has had a most troubled adolescence."

I ask whether Skeeter is still in touch with Harry Potter, whom she so famously interviewed last year: a breakthrough piece in which Potter spoke exclusively of his conviction that You-Know-Who had returned.

"Oh, yes, we've developed a close bond," says Skeeter. "Poor Potter has few real friends, and we met at one of the most testing moments of his life — the Triwizard Tournament. I am probably one of the only people alive who can say that they know the real Harry Potter."

Which leads us neatly to the many rumors still circulating about Dumbledore's final hours. Does Skeeter believe that Potter was there when Dumbledore died?

"Well, I don't want to say too much — it's all in the book — but eyewitnesses inside Hogwarts castle saw Potter running away from the scene moments after Dumbledore fell, jumped, or was pushed. Potter later gave evidence against Severus Snape, a man against whom he has a notorious grudge. Is everything as it seems? That is for the Wizarding community to decide — once they've read my book."

On that intriguing note, I take my leave. There can be no doubt that Skeeter has quilled an instant bestseller. Dumbledore's legions of admirers, meanwhile, may well be trembling at what is soon to emerge about their hero.

Harry reached the bottom of the article, but continued to stare blankly at the page. Revulsion and fury rose in him like vomit; he balled up the newspaper and threw it, with all his force, at the wall, where it joined the rest of the rubbish heaped around his overflowing bin.

He began to stride blindly around the room, opening empty drawers and picking up books only to replace them on the same piles, barely conscious of what he was doing, as random phrases from Rita's article echoed in his head: *An entire chapter to the whole Potter–Dumbledore relationship . . . It's been called unhealthy, even sinister. . . . He dabbled in the Dark Arts himself in his youth . . . I've had access to a source most journalists would swap their wands for . . .*

"Lies!" Harry bellowed, and through the window he saw the next-door neighbor, who had paused to restart his lawn mower, look up nervously.

Harry sat down hard on the bed. The broken bit of mirror danced away from him; he picked it up and turned it over in his fingers, thinking, thinking of Dumbledore and the lies with which Rita Skeeter was defaming him. . . .

A flash of brightest blue. Harry froze, his cut finger slipping on the jagged edge of the mirror again. He had imagined it, he must have done. He glanced over his shoulder, but the wall was a sickly peach color of Aunt Petunia's choosing: There was nothing blue there for the mirror to reflect. He peered into the mirror fragment again, and saw nothing but his own bright green eye looking back at him.

He had imagined it, there was no other explanation; imagined it, because he had been thinking of his dead headmaster. If anything was certain, it was that the bright blue eyes of Albus Dumbledore would never pierce him again.

THE DURSLEYS DEPARTING

The sound of the front door slamming echoed up the stairs and a voice yelled, "Oi! You!"

Sixteen years of being addressed thus left Harry in no doubt whom his uncle was calling; nevertheless, he did not immediately respond. He was still gazing at the mirror fragment in which, for a split second, he had thought he saw Dumbledore's eye. It was not until his uncle bellowed, "BOY!" that Harry got slowly to his feet and headed for the bedroom door, pausing to add the piece of broken mirror to the rucksack filled with things he would be taking with him.

"You took your time!" roared Vernon Dursley when Harry appeared at the top of the stairs. "Get down here, I want a word!"

Harry strolled downstairs, his hands deep in his jeans pockets. When he reached the living room he found all three Dursleys. They were dressed for traveling: Uncle Vernon in a fawn zip-up jacket, Aunt Petunia in a neat salmon-colored coat, and Dudley, Harry's large, blond, muscular cousin, in his leather jacket.

"Yes?" asked Harry.

"Sit down!" said Uncle Vernon. Harry raised his eyebrows. "Please!" added Uncle Vernon, wincing slightly as though the word was sharp in his throat.

Harry sat. He thought he knew what was coming. His uncle began to pace up and down, Aunt Petunia and Dudley following his movements with anxious expressions. Finally, his large purple face crumpled with concentration, Uncle Vernon stopped in front of Harry and spoke.

"I've changed my mind," he said.

"What a surprise," said Harry.

"Don't you take that tone —" began Aunt Petunia in a shrill voice, but Vernon Dursley waved her down.

"It's all a lot of claptrap," said Uncle Vernon, glaring at Harry with piggy little eyes. "I've decided I don't believe a word of it. We're staying put, we're not going anywhere."

Harry looked up at his uncle and felt a mixture of exasperation and amusement. Vernon Dursley had been changing his mind every twenty-four hours for the past four weeks, packing and unpacking and repacking the car with every change of heart. Harry's favorite moment had been the one when Uncle Vernon, unaware that Dudley had added his dumbbells to his case since the last time it had been unpacked, had attempted to hoist it back into the boot and collapsed with roars of pain and much swearing.

"According to you," Vernon Dursley said now, resuming his pacing up and down the living room, "we — Petunia, Dudley, and I — are in danger. From — from —"

"Some of 'my lot,' right," said Harry.

"Well, I don't believe it," repeated Uncle Vernon, coming to a halt in front of Harry again. "I was awake half the night thinking it all over, and I believe it's a plot to get the house."

"The house?" repeated Harry. "What house?"

"*This* house!" shrieked Uncle Vernon, the vein in his forehead starting to pulse. "*Our* house! House prices are skyrocketing around here! You want us out of the way and then you're going to do a bit of hocus-pocus and before we know it the deeds will be in your name and —"

"Are you out of your mind?" demanded Harry. "A plot to get this house? Are you actually as stupid as you look?"

"Don't you dare — !" squealed Aunt Petunia, but again, Vernon waved her down: Slights on his personal appearance were, it seemed, as nothing to the danger he had spotted.

"Just in case you've forgotten," said Harry, "I've already got a house, my godfather left me one. So why would I want this one? All the happy memories?"

There was silence. Harry thought he had rather impressed his uncle with this argument.

"You claim," said Uncle Vernon, starting to pace yet again, "that this Lord Thing —"

"— Voldemort," said Harry impatiently, "and we've been through this about a hundred times already. This isn't a claim, it's fact, Dumbledore told you last year, and Kingsley and Mr. Weasley —"

Vernon Dursley hunched his shoulders angrily, and Harry guessed that his uncle was attempting to ward off recollections of the unannounced visit, a few days into Harry's summer holidays, of two fully grown wizards. The arrival on the doorstep of Kingsley Shacklebolt and Arthur Weasley had come as a most unpleasant shock to the

Dursleys. Harry had to admit, however, that as Mr. Weasley had once demolished half of the living room, his reappearance could not have been expected to delight Uncle Vernon.

"— Kingsley and Mr. Weasley explained it all as well," Harry pressed on remorselessly. "Once I'm seventeen, the protective charm that keeps me safe will break, and that exposes you as well as me. The Order is sure Voldemort will target you, whether to torture you to try and find out where I am, or because he thinks by holding you hostage I'd come and try to rescue you."

Uncle Vernon's and Harry's eyes met. Harry was sure that in that instant they were both wondering the same thing. Then Uncle Vernon walked on and Harry resumed, "You've got to go into hiding and the Order wants to help. You're being offered serious protection, the best there is."

Uncle Vernon said nothing, but continued to pace up and down. Outside the sun hung low over the privet hedges. The next-door neighbor's lawn mower stalled again.

"I thought there was a Ministry of Magic?" asked Vernon Dursley abruptly.

"There is," said Harry, surprised.

"Well, then, why can't they protect us? It seems to me that, as innocent victims, guilty of nothing more than harboring a marked man, we ought to qualify for government protection!"

Harry laughed; he could not help himself. It was so very typical of his uncle to put his hopes in the establishment, even within this world that he despised and mistrusted.

"You heard what Mr. Weasley and Kingsley said," Harry replied. "We think the Ministry has been infiltrated."

Uncle Vernon strode to the fireplace and back, breathing so heavily that his great black mustache rippled, his face still purple with concentration.

"All right," he said, stopping in front of Harry yet again. "All right, let's say, for the sake of argument, we accept this protection. I still don't see why we can't have that Kingsley bloke."

Harry managed not to roll his eyes, but with difficulty. This question had also been addressed half a dozen times.

"As I've told you," he said through gritted teeth, "Kingsley is protecting the Mug — I mean, your Prime Minister."

"Exactly — he's the best!" said Uncle Vernon, pointing at the blank television screen. The Dursleys had spotted Kingsley on the news, walking along discreetly behind the Muggle Prime Minister as he visited a hospital. This, and the fact that Kingsley had mastered the knack of dressing like a Muggle, not to mention a certain reassuring something in his slow, deep voice, had caused the Dursleys to take to Kingsley in a way that they had certainly not done with any other wizard, although it was true that they had never seen him with his earring in.

"Well, he's taken," said Harry. "But Hestia Jones and Dedalus Diggle are more than up to the job —"

"If we'd even seen CVs . . ." began Uncle Vernon, but Harry lost patience. Getting to his feet, he advanced on his uncle, now pointing at the TV set himself.

"These accidents aren't accidents — the crashes and explosions and derailments and whatever else has happened since we last watched the news. People are disappearing and dying and he's behind it — Voldemort. I've told you this over and over again, he kills

Muggles for fun. Even the fogs — they're caused by dementors, and if you can't remember what they are, ask your son!"

Dudley's hands jerked upward to cover his mouth. With his parents' and Harry's eyes upon him, he slowly lowered them again and asked, "There are . . . more of them?"

"More?" laughed Harry. "More than the two that attacked us, you mean? Of course there are, there are hundreds, maybe thousands by this time, seeing as they feed off fear and despair —"

"All right, all right," blustered Vernon Dursley. "You've made your point —"

"I hope so," said Harry, "because once I'm seventeen, all of them — Death Eaters, dementors, maybe even Inferi — which means dead bodies enchanted by a Dark wizard — will be able to find you and will certainly attack you. And if you remember the last time you tried to outrun wizards, I think you'll agree you need help."

There was a brief silence in which the distant echo of Hagrid smashing down a wooden front door seemed to reverberate through the intervening years. Aunt Petunia was looking at Uncle Vernon; Dudley was staring at Harry. Finally Uncle Vernon blurted out, "But what about my work? What about Dudley's school? I don't suppose those things matter to a bunch of layabout wizards —"

"Don't you understand?" shouted Harry. *"They will torture and kill you like they did my parents!"*

"Dad," said Dudley in a loud voice, "Dad — I'm going with these Order people."

"Dudley," said Harry, "for the first time in your life, you're talking sense."

He knew that the battle was won. If Dudley was frightened

enough to accept the Order's help, his parents would accompany him: There could be no question of being separated from their Diddykins. Harry glanced at the carriage clock on the mantelpiece.

"They'll be here in about five minutes," he said, and when none of the Dursleys replied, he left the room. The prospect of parting — probably forever — from his aunt, uncle, and cousin was one that he was able to contemplate quite cheerfully, but there was nevertheless a certain awkwardness in the air. What did you say to one another at the end of sixteen years' solid dislike?

Back in his bedroom, Harry fiddled aimlessly with his rucksack, then poked a couple of owl nuts through the bars of Hedwig's cage. They fell with dull thuds to the bottom, where she ignored them.

"We're leaving soon, really soon," Harry told her. "And then you'll be able to fly again."

The doorbell rang. Harry hesitated, then headed back out of his room and downstairs. It was too much to expect Hestia and Dedalus to cope with the Dursleys on their own.

"Harry Potter!" squeaked an excited voice, the moment Harry had opened the door; a small man in a mauve top hat was sweeping him a deep bow. "An honor, as ever!"

"Thanks, Dedalus," said Harry, bestowing a small and embarrassed smile upon the dark-haired Hestia. "It's really good of you to do this. . . . They're through here, my aunt and uncle and cousin. . . ."

"Good day to you, Harry Potter's relatives!" said Dedalus happily, striding into the living room. The Dursleys did not look at all happy to be addressed thus; Harry half expected another change of mind. Dudley shrank nearer to his mother at the sight of the witch and wizard.

"I see you are packed and ready. Excellent! The plan, as Harry has told you, is a simple one," said Dedalus, pulling an immense pocket watch out of his waistcoat and examining it. "We shall be leaving before Harry does. Due to the danger of using magic in your house — Harry being still underage, it could provide the Ministry with an excuse to arrest him — we shall be driving, say, ten miles or so, before Disapparating to the safe location we have picked out for you. You know how to drive, I take it?" he asked Uncle Vernon politely.

"Know how to — ? Of course I ruddy well know how to drive!" spluttered Uncle Vernon.

"Very clever of you, sir, very clever, I personally would be utterly bamboozled by all those buttons and knobs," said Dedalus. He was clearly under the impression that he was flattering Vernon Dursley, who was visibly losing confidence in the plan with every word Dedalus spoke.

"Can't even drive," he muttered under his breath, his mustache rippling indignantly, but fortunately neither Dedalus nor Hestia seemed to hear him.

"You, Harry," Dedalus continued, "will wait here for your guard. There has been a little change in the arrangements —"

"What d'you mean?" said Harry at once. "I thought Mad-Eye was going to come and take me by Side-Along-Apparition?"

"Can't do it," said Hestia tersely. "Mad-Eye will explain."

The Dursleys, who had listened to all of this with looks of utter incomprehension on their faces, jumped as a loud voice screeched, *"Hurry up!"* Harry looked all around the room before realizing that the voice had issued from Dedalus's pocket watch.

"Quite right, we're operating to a very tight schedule," said

Dedalus, nodding at his watch and tucking it back into his waist-coat. "We are attempting to time your departure from the house with your family's Disapparition, Harry; thus, the charm breaks at the moment you all head for safety." He turned to the Dursleys. "Well, are we all packed and ready to go?"

None of them answered him. Uncle Vernon was still staring, ap-palled, at the bulge in Dedalus's waistcoat pocket.

"Perhaps we should wait outside in the hall, Dedalus," murmured Hestia. She clearly felt that it would be tactless for them to remain in the room while Harry and the Dursleys exchanged loving, pos-sibly tearful farewells.

"There's no need," Harry muttered, but Uncle Vernon made any further explanation unnecessary by saying loudly,

"Well, this is good-bye, then, boy."

He swung his right arm upward to shake Harry's hand, but at the last moment seemed unable to face it, and merely closed his fist and began swinging it backward and forward like a metronome.

"Ready, Diddy?" asked Aunt Petunia, fussily checking the clasp of her handbag so as to avoid looking at Harry altogether.

Dudley did not answer, but stood there with his mouth slightly ajar, reminding Harry a little of the giant, Grawp.

"Come along, then," said Uncle Vernon.

He had already reached the living room door when Dudley mum-bled, "I don't understand."

"What don't you understand, popkin?" asked Aunt Petunia, look-ing up at her son.

Dudley raised a large, hamlike hand to point at Harry.

"Why isn't he coming with us?"

Uncle Vernon and Aunt Petunia froze where they stood, staring at Dudley as though he had just expressed a desire to become a ballerina.

"What?" said Uncle Vernon loudly.

"Why isn't he coming too?" asked Dudley.

"Well, he — he doesn't want to," said Uncle Vernon, turning to glare at Harry and adding, "You don't want to, do you?"

"Not in the slightest," said Harry.

"There you are," Uncle Vernon told Dudley. "Now come on, we're off."

He marched out of the room. They heard the front door open, but Dudley did not move and after a few faltering steps Aunt Petunia stopped too.

"What now?" barked Uncle Vernon, reappearing in the doorway.

It seemed that Dudley was struggling with concepts too difficult to put into words. After several moments of apparently painful internal struggle he said, "But where's he going to go?"

Aunt Petunia and Uncle Vernon looked at each other. It was clear that Dudley was frightening them. Hestia Jones broke the silence.

"But . . . surely you know where your nephew is going?" she asked, looking bewildered.

"Certainly we know," said Vernon Dursley. "He's off with some of your lot, isn't he? Right, Dudley, let's get in the car, you heard the man, we're in a hurry."

Again, Vernon Dursley marched as far as the front door, but Dudley did not follow.

"Off with some of *our* lot?"

Hestia looked outraged. Harry had met this attitude before: Witches and wizards seemed stunned that his closest living relatives took so little interest in the famous Harry Potter.

"It's fine," Harry assured her. "It doesn't matter, honestly."

"Doesn't matter?" repeated Hestia, her voice rising ominously. "Don't these people realize what you've been through? What danger you are in? The unique position you hold in the hearts of the anti-Voldemort movement?"

"Er — no, they don't," said Harry. "They think I'm a waste of space, actually, but I'm used to —"

"I don't think you're a waste of space."

If Harry had not seen Dudley's lips move, he might not have believed it. As it was, he stared at Dudley for several seconds before accepting that it must have been his cousin who had spoken; for one thing, Dudley had turned red. Harry was embarrassed and astonished himself.

"Well . . . er . . . thanks, Dudley."

Again, Dudley appeared to grapple with thoughts too unwieldy for expression before mumbling, "You saved my life."

"Not really," said Harry. "It was your soul the dementor would have taken. . . ."

He looked curiously at his cousin. They had had virtually no contact during this summer or last, as Harry had come back to Privet Drive so briefly and kept to his room so much. It now dawned on Harry, however, that the cup of cold tea on which he had trodden that morning might not have been a booby trap at all. Although rather touched, he was nevertheless quite relieved that Dudley appeared to have exhausted his ability to express his feelings. After opening his mouth once or twice more, Dudley subsided into scarlet-faced silence.

Aunt Petunia burst into tears. Hestia Jones gave her an approving look that changed to outrage as Aunt Petunia ran forward and embraced Dudley rather than Harry.

"S-so sweet, Dudders . . ." she sobbed into his massive chest. "S-such a lovely b-boy . . . s-saying thank you . . ."

"But he hasn't said thank you at all!" said Hestia indignantly. "He only said he didn't think Harry was a waste of space!"

"Yeah, but coming from Dudley that's like 'I love you,'" said Harry, torn between annoyance and a desire to laugh as Aunt Petunia continued to clutch at Dudley as if he had just saved Harry from a burning building.

"Are we going or not?" roared Uncle Vernon, reappearing yet again at the living room door. "I thought we were on a tight schedule!"

"Yes — yes, we are," said Dedalus Diggle, who had been watching these exchanges with an air of bemusement and now seemed to pull himself together. "We really must be off. Harry —"

He tripped forward and wrung Harry's hand with both of his own.

"— good luck. I hope we meet again. The hopes of the Wizarding world rest upon your shoulders."

"Oh," said Harry, "right. Thanks."

"Farewell, Harry," said Hestia, also clasping his hand. "Our thoughts go with you."

"I hope everything's okay," said Harry with a glance toward Aunt Petunia and Dudley.

"Oh, I'm sure we shall end up the best of chums," said Diggle brightly, waving his hat as he left the room. Hestia followed him.

Dudley gently released himself from his mother's clutches and walked toward Harry, who had to repress an urge to threaten him with magic. Then Dudley held out his large, pink hand.

"Blimey, Dudley," said Harry over Aunt Petunia's renewed sobs, "did the dementors blow a different personality into you?"

"Dunno," muttered Dudley. "See you, Harry."

"Yeah . . ." said Harry, taking Dudley's hand and shaking it. "Maybe. Take care, Big D."

Dudley nearly smiled, then lumbered from the room. Harry heard his heavy footfalls on the graveled drive, and then a car door slammed.

Aunt Petunia, whose face had been buried in her handkerchief, looked around at the sound. She did not seem to have expected to find herself alone with Harry. Hastily stowing her wet handkerchief into her pocket, she said, "Well — good-bye," and marched toward the door without looking at him.

"Good-bye," said Harry.

She stopped and looked back. For a moment Harry had the strangest feeling that she wanted to say something to him: She gave him an odd, tremulous look and seemed to teeter on the edge of speech, but then, with a little jerk of her head, she bustled out of the room after her husband and son.

CHAPTER FOUR

THE SEVEN POTTERS

Harry ran back upstairs to his bedroom, arriving at the window just in time to see the Dursleys' car swinging out of the drive and off up the road. Dedalus's top hat was visible between Aunt Petunia and Dudley in the backseat. The car turned right at the end of Privet Drive, its windows burned scarlet for a moment in the now setting sun, and then it was gone.

Harry picked up Hedwig's cage, his Firebolt, and his rucksack, gave his unnaturally tidy bedroom one last sweeping look, and then made his ungainly way back downstairs to the hall, where he deposited cage, broomstick, and bag near the foot of the stairs. The light was fading rapidly now, the hall full of shadows in the evening light. It felt most strange to stand here in the silence and know that he was about to leave the house for the last time. Long ago, when he had been left alone while the Dursleys went out to enjoy themselves, the hours of solitude had been a rare treat: Pausing only to sneak something tasty from the fridge, he had rushed upstairs to play on

Dudley's computer, or put on the television and flicked through the channels to his heart's content. It gave him an odd, empty feeling to remember those times; it was like remembering a younger brother whom he had lost.

"Don't you want to take a last look at the place?" he asked Hedwig, who was still sulking with her head under her wing. "We'll never be here again. Don't you want to remember all the good times? I mean, look at this doormat. What memories . . . Dudley puked on it after I saved him from the dementors. . . . Turns out he was grateful after all, can you believe it? . . . And last summer, Dumbledore walked through that front door. . . ."

Harry lost the thread of his thoughts for a moment and Hedwig did nothing to help him retrieve it, but continued to sit with her head under her wing. Harry turned his back on the front door.

"And under here, Hedwig" — Harry pulled open a door under the stairs — "is where I used to sleep! You never knew me then — Blimey, it's small, I'd forgotten. . . ."

Harry looked around at the stacked shoes and umbrellas, remembering how he used to wake every morning looking up at the underside of the staircase, which was more often than not adorned with a spider or two. Those had been the days before he had known anything about his true identity; before he had found out how his parents had died or why such strange things often happened around him. But Harry could still remember the dreams that had dogged him, even in those days: confused dreams involving flashes of green light and once — Uncle Vernon had nearly crashed the car when Harry had recounted it — a flying motorbike . . .

There was a sudden, deafening roar from somewhere nearby. Harry straightened up with a jerk and smacked the top of his head on the low door frame. Pausing only to employ a few of Uncle Vernon's choicest swear words, he staggered back into the kitchen, clutching his head and staring out of the window into the back garden.

The darkness seemed to be rippling, the air itself quivering. Then, one by one, figures began to pop into sight as their Disillusionment Charms lifted. Dominating the scene was Hagrid, wearing a helmet and goggles and sitting astride an enormous motorbike with a black sidecar attached. All around him other people were dismounting from brooms and, in two cases, skeletal, black winged horses.

Wrenching open the back door, Harry hurtled into their midst. There was a general cry of greeting as Hermione flung her arms around him, Ron clapped him on the back, and Hagrid said, "All righ', Harry? Ready fer the off?"

"Definitely," said Harry, beaming around at them all. "But I wasn't expecting this many of you!"

"Change of plan," growled Mad-Eye, who was holding two enormous, bulging sacks, and whose magical eye was spinning from darkening sky to house to garden with dizzying rapidity. "Let's get undercover before we talk you through it."

Harry led them all back into the kitchen where, laughing and chattering, they settled on chairs, sat themselves upon Aunt Petunia's gleaming work surfaces, or leaned up against her spotless appliances: Ron, long and lanky; Hermione, her bushy hair tied back in a long plait; Fred and George, grinning identically; Bill, badly scarred and long-haired; Mr. Weasley, kind-faced, balding, his spectacles a little awry; Mad-Eye, battle-worn, one-legged, his bright blue magical eye whizzing in its socket; Tonks, whose short hair was her favorite shade of bright pink; Lupin, grayer, more lined; Fleur, slender and beautiful, with her long silvery blonde hair; Kingsley, bald, black, broad-shouldered; Hagrid, with his wild hair and beard, standing hunchbacked to avoid hitting his head on the ceiling; and Mundungus Fletcher, small, dirty, and hangdog, with his droopy basset hound's eyes and matted hair. Harry's heart seemed to expand and glow at the sight: He felt incredibly fond of all of them, even Mundungus, whom he had tried to strangle the last time they had met.

"Kingsley, I thought you were looking after the Muggle Prime Minister?" he called across the room.

"He can get along without me for one night," said Kingsley. "You're more important."

"Harry, guess what?" said Tonks from her perch on top of the washing machine, and she wiggled her left hand at him; a ring glittered there.

"You got married?" Harry yelped, looking from her to Lupin.

"I'm sorry you couldn't be there, Harry, it was very quiet."

"That's brilliant, congrat —"

"All right, all right, we'll have time for a cozy catch-up later!" roared Moody over the hubbub, and silence fell in the kitchen. Moody dropped his sacks at his feet and turned to Harry. "As Dedalus probably told you, we had to abandon Plan A. Pius Thicknesse has gone over, which gives us a big problem. He's made it an imprisonable offense to connect this house to the Floo Network, place a Portkey here, or Apparate in or out. All done in the name of your protection, to prevent You-Know-Who getting in at you. Absolutely pointless, seeing as your mother's charm does that already. What he's really done is to stop you getting out of here safely.

"Second problem: You're underage, which means you've still got the Trace on you."

"I don't —"

"The Trace, the Trace!" said Mad-Eye impatiently. "The charm that detects magical activity around under-seventeens, the way the Ministry finds out about underage magic! If you, or anyone around you, casts a spell to get you out of here, Thicknesse is going to know about it, and so will the Death Eaters.

"We can't wait for the Trace to break, because the moment you turn seventeen you'll lose all the protection your mother gave you. In short: Pius Thicknesse thinks he's got you cornered good and proper."

Harry could not help but agree with the unknown Thicknesse.

"So what are we going to do?"

"We're going to use the only means of transport left to us, the only ones the Trace can't detect, because we don't need to cast spells to use them: brooms, thestrals, and Hagrid's motorbike."

Harry could see flaws in this plan; however, he held his tongue to give Mad-Eye the chance to address them.

"Now, your mother's charm will only break under two conditions: when you come of age, or" — Moody gestured around the pristine kitchen — "you no longer call this place home. You and your aunt and uncle are going your separate ways tonight, in the full understanding that you're never going to live together again, correct?"

Harry nodded.

"So this time, when you leave, there'll be no going back, and the charm will break the moment you get outside its range. We're choosing to break it early, because the alternative is waiting for You-Know-Who to come and seize you the moment you turn seventeen.

"The one thing we've got on our side is that You-Know-Who doesn't know we're moving you tonight. We've leaked a fake trail to the Ministry: They think you're not leaving until the thirtieth. However, this is You-Know-Who we're dealing with, so we can't just rely on him getting the date wrong; he's bound to have a couple of Death Eaters patrolling the skies in this general area, just in case. So, we've given a dozen different houses every protection we can throw at them. They all look like they could be the place we're going to hide you, they've all got some connection with the Order: my house, Kingsley's place, Molly's Auntie Muriel's — you get the idea."

"Yeah," said Harry, not entirely truthfully, because he could still spot a gaping hole in the plan.

"You'll be going to Tonks's parents. Once you're within the boundaries of the protective enchantments we've put on their house, you'll be able to use a Portkey to the Burrow. Any questions?"

"Er — yes," said Harry. "Maybe they won't know which of the twelve secure houses I'm heading for at first, but won't it be sort of obvious once" — he performed a quick headcount — "fourteen of us fly off toward Tonks's parents'?"

"Ah," said Moody, "I forgot to mention the key point. Fourteen of us won't be flying to Tonks's parents'. There will be seven Harry Potters moving through the skies tonight, each of them with a companion, each pair heading for a different safe house."

From inside his cloak Moody now withdrew a flask of what looked like mud. There was no need for him to say another word; Harry understood the rest of the plan immediately.

"No!" he said loudly, his voice ringing through the kitchen. "No way!"

"I told them you'd take it like this," said Hermione with a hint of complacency.

"If you think I'm going to let six people risk their lives — !"

"— because it's the first time for all of us," said Ron.

"This is different, pretending to be me —"

"Well, none of us really fancy it, Harry," said Fred earnestly. "Imagine if something went wrong and we were stuck as specky, scrawny gits forever."

Harry did not smile.

"You can't do it if I don't cooperate, you need me to give you some hair."

"Well, that's that plan scuppered," said George. "Obviously there's no chance at all of us getting a bit of your hair unless you cooperate."

"Yeah, thirteen of us against one bloke who's not allowed to use magic; we've got no chance," said Fred.

"Funny," said Harry, "really amusing."

"If it has to come to force, then it will," growled Moody, his magical eye now quivering a little in its socket as he glared at Harry. "Everyone here's overage, Potter, and they're all prepared to take the risk."

Mundungus shrugged and grimaced; the magical eye swerved sideways to glare at him out of the side of Moody's head.

"Let's have no more arguments. Time's wearing on. I want a few of your hairs, boy, now."

"But this is mad, there's no need —"

"No need!" snarled Moody. "With You-Know-Who out there and half the Ministry on his side? Potter, if we're lucky he'll have swallowed the fake bait and he'll be planning to ambush you on the thirtieth, but he'd be mad not to have a Death Eater or two keeping an eye out, it's what I'd do. They might not be able to get at you or this house while your mother's charm holds, but it's about to break and they know the rough position of the place. Our only chance is to use decoys. Even You-Know-Who can't split himself into seven."

Harry caught Hermione's eye and looked away at once.

"So, Potter — some of your hair, if you please."

Harry glanced at Ron, who grimaced at him in a just-do-it sort of way.

"Now!" barked Moody.

With all of their eyes upon him, Harry reached up to the top of his head, grabbed a hank of hair, and pulled.

"Good," said Moody, limping forward as he pulled the stopper out of the flask of potion. "Straight in here, if you please."

Harry dropped the hair into the mudlike liquid. The moment it made contact with its surface, the potion began to froth and smoke, then, all at once, it turned a clear, bright gold.

"Ooh, you look much tastier than Crabbe and Goyle, Harry," said Hermione, before catching sight of Ron's raised eyebrows, blushing slightly, and saying, "Oh, you know what I mean — Goyle's potion looked like bogies."

"Right then, fake Potters line up over here, please," said Moody.

Ron, Hermione, Fred, George, and Fleur lined up in front of Aunt Petunia's gleaming sink.

"We're one short," said Lupin.

"Here," said Hagrid gruffly, and he lifted Mundungus by the scruff of the neck and dropped him down beside Fleur, who wrinkled her nose pointedly and moved along to stand between Fred and George instead.

"I've toldjer, I'd sooner be a protector," said Mundungus.

"Shut it," growled Moody. "As I've already told you, you spineless worm, any Death Eaters we run into will be aiming to capture Potter, not kill him. Dumbledore always said You-Know-Who would want to finish Potter in person. It'll be the protectors who have got the most to worry about, the Death Eaters'll want to kill them."

Mundungus did not look particularly reassured, but Moody was already pulling half a dozen eggcup-sized glasses from inside his cloak, which he handed out, before pouring a little Polyjuice Potion into each one.

"Altogether, then . . ."

Ron, Hermione, Fred, George, Fleur, and Mundungus drank. All of them gasped and grimaced as the potion hit their throats: At once, their features began to bubble and distort like hot wax. Hermione and Mundungus were shooting upward; Ron, Fred, and George were shrinking; their hair was darkening, Hermione's and Fleur's appearing to shoot backward into their skulls.

Moody, quite unconcerned, was now loosening the ties of the large sacks he had brought with him. When he straightened up again, there were six Harry Potters gasping and panting in front of him.

Fred and George turned to each other and said together, "Wow — we're identical!"

"I dunno, though, I think I'm still better-looking," said Fred, examining his reflection in the kettle.

"Bah," said Fleur, checking herself in the microwave door, "Bill, don't look at me — I'm 'ideous."

"Those whose clothes are a bit roomy, I've got smaller here," said Moody, indicating the first sack, "and vice versa. Don't forget the glasses, there's six pairs in the side pocket. And when you're dressed, there's luggage in the other sack."

The real Harry thought that this might just be the most bizarre thing he had ever seen, and he had seen some extremely odd things. He watched as his six doppelgangers rummaged in the sacks, pulling out sets of clothes, putting on glasses, stuffing their own things away. He felt like asking them to show a little more respect for his privacy as they all began stripping off with impunity, clearly much more at ease with displaying his body than they would have been with their own.

"I knew Ginny was lying about that tattoo," said Ron, looking down at his bare chest.

"Harry, your eyesight really is awful," said Hermione, as she put on glasses.

Once dressed, the fake Harrys took rucksacks and owl cages, each containing a stuffed snowy owl, from the second sack.

"Good," said Moody, as at last seven dressed, bespectacled, and luggage-laden Harrys faced him. "The pairs will be as follows: Mundungus will be traveling with me, by broom —"

"Why'm I with you?" grunted the Harry nearest the back door.

"Because you're the one that needs watching," growled Moody, and sure enough, his magical eye did not waver from Mundungus as he continued, "Arthur and Fred —"

"I'm George," said the twin at whom Moody was pointing. "Can't you even tell us apart when we're Harry?"

"Sorry, George —"

"I'm only yanking your wand, I'm Fred really —"

"Enough messing around!" snarled Moody. "The other one — George or Fred or whoever you are — you're with Remus. Miss Delacour —"

"I'm taking Fleur on a thestral," said Bill. "She's not that fond of brooms."

Fleur walked over to stand beside him, giving him a soppy, slavish look that Harry hoped with all his heart would never appear on his face again.

"Miss Granger with Kingsley, again by thestral —"

Hermione looked reassured as she answered Kingsley's smile; Harry knew that Hermione too lacked confidence on a broomstick.

"Which leaves you and me, Ron!" said Tonks brightly, knocking over a mug tree as she waved at him.

Ron did not look quite as pleased as Hermione.

"An' you're with me, Harry. That all righ'?" said Hagrid, looking a little anxious. "We'll be on the bike, brooms an' thestrals can't take me weight, see. Not a lot o' room on the seat with me on it, though, so you'll be in the sidecar."

"That's great," said Harry, not altogether truthfully.

"We think the Death Eaters will expect you to be on a broom," said Moody, who seemed to guess how Harry was feeling. "Snape's had plenty of time to tell them everything about you he's never mentioned before, so if we do run into any Death Eaters, we're betting they'll choose one of the Potters who look at home on a broomstick. All right then," he went on, tying up the sack with the fake Potters' clothes in it and leading the way back to the door, "I make it three minutes until we're supposed to leave. No point locking the back door, it won't keep the Death Eaters out when they come looking. . . . Come on. . . ."

Harry hurried into the hall to fetch his rucksack, Firebolt, and Hedwig's cage before joining the others in the dark back garden.

On every side broomsticks were leaping into hands; Hermione had already been helped up onto a great black thestral by Kingsley, Fleur onto the other by Bill. Hagrid was standing ready beside the motorbike, goggles on.

"Is this it? Is this Sirius's bike?"

"The very same," said Hagrid, beaming down at Harry. "An' the last time yeh was on it, Harry, I could fit yeh in one hand!"

Harry could not help but feel a little humiliated as he got into the sidecar. It placed him several feet below everybody else: Ron smirked at the sight of him sitting there like a child in a bumper car. Harry stuffed his rucksack and broomstick down by his feet and rammed Hedwig's cage between his knees. It was extremely uncomfortable.

"Arthur's done a bit o' tinkerin'," said Hagrid, quite oblivious to Harry's discomfort. He settled himself astride the motorcycle, which creaked slightly and sank inches into the ground. "It's got a few tricks up its handlebars now. Tha' one was my idea."

He pointed a thick finger at a purple button near the speedometer.

"Please be careful, Hagrid," said Mr. Weasley, who was standing beside them, holding his broomstick. "I'm still not sure that was advisable and it's certainly only to be used in emergencies."

"All right then," said Moody. "Everyone ready, please; I want us all to leave at exactly the same time or the whole point of the diversion's lost."

Everybody mounted their brooms.

"Hold tight now, Ron," said Tonks, and Harry saw Ron throw a furtive, guilty look at Lupin before placing his hands on either side of her waist. Hagrid kicked the motorbike into life: It roared like a dragon, and the sidecar began to vibrate.

"Good luck, everyone," shouted Moody. "See you all in about an hour at the Burrow. On the count of three. One . . . two . . . THREE."

There was a great roar from the motorbike, and Harry felt the sidecar give a nasty lurch: He was rising through the air fast, his eyes watering slightly, hair whipped back off his face. Around him brooms were soaring upward too; the long black tail of a thestral flicked past. His legs, jammed into the sidecar by Hedwig's cage and his rucksack, were already sore and starting to go numb. So great was his discomfort that he almost forgot to take a last glimpse of number four, Privet Drive; by the time he looked over the edge of the sidecar he could no longer tell which one it was. Higher and higher they climbed into the sky —

And then, out of nowhere, out of nothing, they were surrounded. At least thirty hooded figures, suspended in midair, formed a vast circle in the midst of which the Order members had risen, oblivious —

Screams, a blaze of green light on every side: Hagrid gave a yell and the motorbike rolled over. Harry lost any sense of where they were: Streetlights above him, yells around him, he was clinging to the sidecar for dear life. Hedwig's cage, the Firebolt, and his rucksack slipped from beneath his knees —

"No — HEDWIG!"

The broomstick spun to earth, but he just managed to seize the strap of his rucksack and the top of the cage as the motorbike swung the right way up again. A second's relief, and then another burst of green light. The owl screeched and fell to the floor of the cage.

"No — NO!"

The motorbike zoomed forward; Harry glimpsed hooded Death Eaters scattering as Hagrid blasted through their circle.

"Hedwig — *Hedwig* —"

But the owl lay motionless and pathetic as a toy on the floor of her cage. He could not take it in, and his terror for the others was paramount. He glanced over his shoulder and saw a mass of people moving, flares of green light, two pairs of people on brooms soaring off into the distance, but he could not tell who they were —

"Hagrid, we've got to go back, we've got to go back!" he yelled over the thunderous roar of the engine, pulling out his wand, ramming Hedwig's cage onto the floor, refusing to believe that she was dead. "Hagrid, TURN AROUND!"

"My job's ter get you there safe, Harry!" bellowed Hagrid, and he opened the throttle.

"Stop — STOP!" Harry shouted, but as he looked back again two jets of green light flew past his left ear: Four Death Eaters had broken away from the circle and were pursuing them, aiming for Hagrid's broad back. Hagrid swerved, but the Death Eaters were keeping up with the bike; more curses shot after them, and Harry had to sink low into the sidecar to avoid them. Wriggling around he cried, *"Stupefy!"* and a red bolt of light shot from his own wand, cleaving a gap between the four pursuing Death Eaters as they scattered to avoid it.

"Hold on, Harry, this'll do for 'em!" roared Hagrid, and Harry looked up just in time to see Hagrid slamming a thick finger into a green button near the fuel gauge.

A wall, a solid brick wall, erupted out of the exhaust pipe. Craning his neck, Harry saw it expand into being in midair. Three of the Death Eaters swerved and avoided it, but the fourth was not so lucky: He vanished from view and then dropped like a boulder from behind it, his broomstick broken into pieces. One of his fellows slowed up to save him, but they and the airborne wall were swallowed by darkness as Hagrid leaned low over the handlebars and sped up.

More Killing Curses flew past Harry's head from the two remaining Death Eaters' wands; they were aiming for Hagrid. Harry responded with further Stunning Spells: Red and green collided in midair in a shower of multicolored sparks, and Harry thought wildly of fireworks, and the Muggles below who would have no idea what was happening —

"Here we go again, Harry, hold on!" yelled Hagrid, and he jabbed at a second button. This time a great net burst from the bike's exhaust, but the Death Eaters were ready for it. Not only did they swerve to avoid it, but the companion who had slowed to save their unconscious friend had caught up. He bloomed suddenly out of darkness and now three of them were pursuing the motorbike, all shooting curses after it.

"This'll do it, Harry, hold on tight!" yelled Hagrid, and Harry saw him slam his whole hand onto the purple button beside the speedometer.

With an unmistakable bellowing roar, dragon fire burst from the exhaust, white-hot and blue, and the motorbike shot forward like a bullet with a sound of wrenching metal. Harry saw the Death Eaters swerve out of sight to avoid the deadly trail of flame, and at the same time felt the sidecar sway ominously: Its metal connections to the bike had splintered with the force of acceleration.

"It's all righ', Harry!" bellowed Hagrid, now thrown flat onto his back by the surge of speed; nobody was steering now, and the sidecar was starting to twist violently in the bike's slipstream.

"I'm on it, Harry, don' worry!" Hagrid yelled, and from inside his jacket pocket he pulled his flowery pink umbrella.

"Hagrid! No! Let me!"

"REPARO!"

There was a deafening bang and the sidecar broke away from the bike completely: Harry sped forward, propelled by the impetus of the bike's flight, then the sidecar began to lose height —

In desperation Harry pointed his wand at the sidecar and shouted, *"Wingardium Leviosa!"*

The sidecar rose like a cork, unsteerable but at least still airborne: He had but a split second's relief, however, as more curses streaked past him: The three Death Eaters were closing in.

"I'm comin', Harry!" Hagrid yelled from out of the darkness, but Harry could feel the sidecar beginning to sink again: Crouching as low as he could, he pointed at the middle of the oncoming figures and yelled, *"Impedimenta!"*

The jinx hit the middle Death Eater in the chest: For a moment the man was absurdly spread-eagled in midair as though he had hit an invisible barrier: One of his fellows almost collided with him —

Then the sidecar began to fall in earnest, and the remaining Death Eater shot a curse so close to Harry that he had to duck below the rim of the car, knocking out a tooth on the edge of his seat —

"I'm comin', Harry, I'm comin'!"

A huge hand seized the back of Harry's robes and hoisted him out of the plummeting sidecar; Harry pulled his rucksack with him as he dragged himself onto the motorbike's seat and found himself back-to-back with Hagrid. As they soared upward, away from the two remaining Death Eaters, Harry spat blood out of his mouth, pointed his wand at the falling sidecar, and yelled, *"Confringo!"*

He knew a dreadful, gut-wrenching pang for Hedwig as it exploded; the Death Eater nearest it was blasted off his broom and fell from sight; his companion fell back and vanished.

"Harry, I'm sorry, I'm sorry," moaned Hagrid, "I shouldn'ta tried ter repair it meself — yeh've got no room —"

"It's not a problem, just keep flying!" Harry shouted back, as two more Death Eaters emerged out of the darkness, drawing closer.

As the curses came shooting across the intervening space again, Hagrid swerved and zigzagged: Harry knew that Hagrid did not dare use the dragon-fire button again, with Harry seated so insecurely. Harry sent Stunning Spell after Stunning Spell back at their pursuers, barely holding them off. He shot another blocking jinx at them: The closest Death Eater swerved to avoid it and his hood slipped, and by the red light of his next Stunning Spell, Harry saw the strangely blank face of Stanley Shunpike — Stan —

"Expelliarmus!" Harry yelled.

"That's him, it's him, it's the real one!"

The hooded Death Eater's shout reached Harry even above the thunder of the motorbike's engine: Next moment, both pursuers had fallen back and disappeared from view.

"Harry, what's happened?" bellowed Hagrid. "Where've they gone?"

"I don't know!"

But Harry was afraid: The hooded Death Eater had shouted "It's the real one!"; how had he known? He gazed around at the apparently empty darkness and felt its menace. Where were they?

He clambered around on the seat to face forward and seized hold of the back of Hagrid's jacket.

"Hagrid, do the dragon-fire thing again, let's get out of here!"

"Hold on tight, then, Harry!"

There was a deafening, screeching roar again and the white-blue fire shot from the exhaust: Harry felt himself slipping backward off what little of the seat he had, Hagrid flung backward upon him, barely maintaining his grip on the handlebars —

"I think we've lost 'em Harry, I think we've done it!" yelled Hagrid.

But Harry was not convinced: Fear lapped at him as he looked left and right for pursuers he was sure would come. . . . Why had they fallen back? One of them had still had a wand. . . . *It's him* . . . *it's the real one.* . . . They had said it right after he had tried to Disarm Stan. . . .

"We're nearly there, Harry, we've nearly made it!" shouted Hagrid.

Harry felt the bike drop a little, though the lights down on the ground still seemed remote as stars.

Then the scar on his forehead burned like fire; as a Death Eater appeared on either side of the bike, two Killing Curses missed Harry by millimeters, cast from behind —

And then Harry saw him. Voldemort was flying like smoke on the wind, without broomstick or thestral to hold him, his snake-like face gleaming out of the blackness, his white fingers raising his wand again —

Hagrid let out a bellow of fear and steered the motorbike into a vertical dive. Clinging on for dear life, Harry sent Stunning Spells flying at random into the whirling night. He saw a body fly past him and knew he had hit one of them, but then he heard a bang and saw sparks from the engine; the motorbike spiraled through the air, completely out of control —

Green jets of light shot past them again. Harry had no idea which way was up, which down: His scar was still burning; he expected to die at any second. A hooded figure on a broomstick was feet from him, he saw it raise its arm —

"NO!"

With a shout of fury Hagrid launched himself off the bike at the Death Eater; to his horror, Harry saw both Hagrid and the Death Eater falling out of sight, their combined weight too much for the broomstick —

Barely gripping the plummeting bike with his knees, Harry heard Voldemort scream, *"Mine!"*

It was over: He could not see or hear where Voldemort was; he glimpsed another Death Eater swooping out of the way and heard, *"Avada —"*

As the pain from Harry's scar forced his eyes shut, his wand acted of its own accord. He felt it drag his hand around like some great magnet, saw a spurt of golden fire through his half-closed eyelids, heard a crack and a scream of fury. The remaining Death Eater yelled; Voldemort screamed, *"No!"*: Somehow, Harry found his nose an inch from the dragon-fire button. He punched it with his wand-free hand and the bike shot more flames into the air, hurtling straight toward the ground.

"Hagrid!" Harry called, holding on to the bike for dear life. "Hagrid — *Accio Hagrid!*"

The motorbike sped up, sucked toward the earth. Face level with the handlebars, Harry could see nothing but distant lights growing nearer and nearer: He was going to crash and there was nothing he could do about it. Behind him came another scream, *"Your wand, Selwyn, give me your wand!"*

He felt Voldemort before he saw him. Looking sideways, he stared into the red eyes and was sure they would be the last thing he ever saw: Voldemort preparing to curse him once more —

And then Voldemort vanished. Harry looked down and saw Hagrid spread-eagled on the ground below him. He pulled hard at the handlebars to avoid hitting him, groped for the brake, but with an earsplitting, ground-trembling crash, he smashed into a muddy pond.

FALLEN WARRIOR

"Hagrid?"

Harry struggled to raise himself out of the debris of metal and leather that surrounded him; his hands sank into inches of muddy water as he tried to stand. He could not understand where Voldemort had gone and expected him to swoop out of the darkness at any moment. Something hot and wet was trickling down his chin and from his forehead. He crawled out of the pond and stumbled toward the great dark mass on the ground that was Hagrid.

"Hagrid? Hagrid, talk to me —"

But the dark mass did not stir.

"Who's there? Is it Potter? Are you Harry Potter?"

Harry did not recognize the man's voice. Then a woman shouted, "They've crashed, Ted! Crashed in the garden!"

Harry's head was swimming.

"Hagrid," he repeated stupidly, and his knees buckled.

The next thing he knew, he was lying on his back on what felt like cushions, with a burning sensation in his ribs and right arm. His missing tooth had been regrown. The scar on his forehead was still throbbing.

"Hagrid?"

He opened his eyes and saw that he was lying on a sofa in an unfamiliar, lamplit sitting room. His rucksack lay on the floor a short distance away, wet and muddy. A fair-haired, big-bellied man was watching Harry anxiously.

"Hagrid's fine, son," said the man, "the wife's seeing to him now. How are you feeling? Anything else broken? I've fixed your ribs, your tooth, and your arm. I'm Ted, by the way, Ted Tonks — Dora's father."

Harry sat up too quickly: Lights popped in front of his eyes and he felt sick and giddy.

"Voldemort —"

"Easy, now," said Ted Tonks, placing a hand on Harry's shoulder and pushing him back against the cushions. "That was a nasty crash you just had. What happened, anyway? Something go wrong with the bike? Arthur Weasley overstretch himself again, him and his Muggle contraptions?"

"No," said Harry, as his scar pulsed like an open wound. "Death Eaters, loads of them — we were chased —"

"Death Eaters?" said Ted sharply. "What d'you mean, Death Eaters? I thought they didn't know you were being moved tonight, I thought —"

"They knew," said Harry.

Ted Tonks looked up at the ceiling as though he could see through it to the sky above.

"Well, we know our protective charms hold, then, don't we? They shouldn't be able to get within a hundred yards of the place in any direction."

Now Harry understood why Voldemort had vanished; it had been at the point when the motorbike crossed the barrier of the Order's charms. He only hoped they would continue to work: He imagined Voldemort, a hundred yards above them as they spoke, looking for a way to penetrate what Harry visualized as a great transparent bubble.

He swung his legs off the sofa; he needed to see Hagrid with his own eyes before he would believe that he was alive. He had barely stood up, however, when a door opened and Hagrid squeezed through it, his face covered in mud and blood, limping a little but miraculously alive.

"Harry!"

Knocking over two delicate tables and an aspidistra, he covered the floor between them in two strides and pulled Harry into a hug that nearly cracked his newly repaired ribs. "Blimey, Harry, how did yeh get out o' that? I thought we were both goners."

"Yeah, me too. I can't believe —"

Harry broke off. He had just noticed the woman who had entered the room behind Hagrid.

"You!" he shouted, and he thrust his hand into his pocket, but it was empty.

"Your wand's here, son," said Ted, tapping it on Harry's arm. "It fell right beside you, I picked it up. And that's my wife you're shouting at."

"Oh, I'm — I'm sorry."

As she moved forward into the room, Mrs. Tonks's resemblance to her sister Bellatrix became much less pronounced: Her hair was a light, soft brown and her eyes were wider and kinder. Nevertheless, she looked a little haughty after Harry's exclamation.

"What happened to our daughter?" she asked. "Hagrid said you were ambushed; where is Nymphadora?"

"I don't know," said Harry. "We don't know what happened to anyone else."

She and Ted exchanged looks. A mixture of fear and guilt gripped Harry at the sight of their expressions; if any of the others had died, it was his fault, all his fault. He had consented to the plan, given them his hair. . . .

"The Portkey," he said, remembering all of a sudden. "We've got to get back to the Burrow and find out — then we'll be able to send you word, or — or Tonks will, once she's —"

"Dora'll be okay, 'Dromeda," said Ted. "She knows her stuff, she's been in plenty of tight spots with the Aurors. The Portkey's through here," he added to Harry. "It's supposed to leave in three minutes, if you want to take it."

"Yeah, we do," said Harry. He seized his rucksack, swung it onto his shoulders. "I —"

He looked at Mrs. Tonks, wanting to apologize for the state of fear in which he left her and for which he felt so terribly responsible, but no words occurred to him that did not seem hollow and insincere.

"I'll tell Tonks — Dora — to send word, when she . . . Thanks for patching us up, thanks for everything. I —"

He was glad to leave the room and follow Ted Tonks along a short hallway and into a bedroom. Hagrid came after them, bending low to avoid hitting his head on the door lintel.

"There you go, son. That's the Portkey."

Mr. Tonks was pointing to a small, silver-backed hairbrush lying on the dressing table.

"Thanks," said Harry, reaching out to place a finger on it, ready to leave.

"Wait a moment," said Hagrid, looking around. "Harry, where's Hedwig?"

"She . . . she got hit," said Harry.

The realization crashed over him: He felt ashamed of himself as the tears stung his eyes. The owl had been his companion, his one great link with the magical world whenever he had been forced to return to the Dursleys.

Hagrid reached out a great hand and patted him painfully on the shoulder.

"Never mind," he said gruffly. "Never mind. She had a great old life —"

"Hagrid!" said Ted Tonks warningly, as the hairbrush glowed bright blue, and Hagrid only just got his forefinger to it in time.

With a jerk behind the navel as though an invisible hook and line had dragged him forward, Harry was pulled into nothingness, spinning uncontrollably, his finger glued to the Portkey as he and Hagrid hurtled away from Mr. Tonks. Seconds later Harry's feet slammed onto hard ground and he fell onto his hands and knees in the yard of the Burrow. He heard screams. Throwing aside the no longer glowing hairbrush, Harry stood up, swaying slightly, and saw Mrs. Weasley and Ginny running down the steps by the back door as Hagrid, who had also collapsed on landing, clambered laboriously to his feet.

"Harry? You are the real Harry? What happened? Where are the others?" cried Mrs. Weasley.

"What d'you mean? Isn't anyone else back?" Harry panted.

The answer was clearly etched in Mrs. Weasley's pale face.

"The Death Eaters were waiting for us," Harry told her. "We were surrounded the moment we took off — they knew it was to-night — I don't know what happened to anyone else, four of them chased us, it was all we could do to get away, and then Voldemort caught up with us —"

He could hear the self-justifying note in his voice, the plea for her to understand why he did not know what had happened to her sons, but —

"Thank goodness you're all right," she said, pulling him into a hug he did not feel he deserved.

"Haven't go' any brandy, have yeh, Molly?" asked Hagrid a little shakily. "Fer medicinal purposes?"

She could have summoned it by magic, but as she hurried back toward the crooked house, Harry knew that she wanted to hide her face. He turned to Ginny and she answered his unspoken plea for information at once.

"Ron and Tonks should have been back first, but they missed their Portkey, it came back without them," she said, pointing at a rusty oil can lying on the ground nearby. "And that one," she pointed at an ancient sneaker, "should have been Dad and Fred's, they were supposed to be second. You and Hagrid were third and," she checked her watch, "if they made it, George and Lupin ought to be back in about a minute."

Mrs. Weasley reappeared carrying a bottle of brandy, which she handed to Hagrid. He uncorked it and drank it straight down in one.

"Mum!" shouted Ginny, pointing to a spot several feet away.

A blue light had appeared in the darkness: It grew larger and brighter, and Lupin and George appeared, spinning and then falling. Harry knew immediately that there was something wrong: Lupin was supporting George, who was unconscious and whose face was covered in blood.

Harry ran forward and seized George's legs. Together, he and Lupin carried George into the house and through the kitchen to the sitting room, where they laid him on the sofa. As the lamplight fell across George's head, Ginny gasped and Harry's stomach lurched: One of George's ears was missing. The side of his head and neck were drenched in wet, shockingly scarlet blood.

No sooner had Mrs. Weasley bent over her son than Lupin grabbed Harry by the upper arm and dragged him, none too gently, back into the kitchen, where Hagrid was still attempting to ease his bulk through the back door.

"Oi!" said Hagrid indignantly. "Le' go of him! Le' go of Harry!"

Lupin ignored him.

"What creature sat in the corner the first time that Harry Potter visited my office at Hogwarts?" he said, giving Harry a small shake. "Answer me!"

"A — a grindylow in a tank, wasn't it?"

Lupin released Harry and fell back against a kitchen cupboard.

"Wha' was tha' about?" roared Hagrid.

"I'm sorry, Harry, but I had to check," said Lupin tersely. "We've been betrayed. Voldemort knew that you were being moved tonight and the only people who could have told him were directly involved in the plan. You might have been an impostor."

"So why aren' you checkin' me?" panted Hagrid, still struggling to fit through the door.

"You're half-giant," said Lupin, looking up at Hagrid. "The Polyjuice Potion is designed for human use only."

"None of the Order would have told Voldemort we were moving tonight," said Harry. The idea was dreadful to him, he could not believe it of any of them. "Voldemort only caught up with me toward the end, he didn't know which one I was in the beginning. If he'd been in on the plan he'd have known from the start I was the one with Hagrid."

"Voldemort caught up with you?" said Lupin sharply. "What happened? How did you escape?"

Harry explained briefly how the Death Eaters pursuing them had seemed to recognize him as the true Harry, how they had abandoned the chase, how they must have summoned Voldemort, who had appeared just before he and Hagrid had reached the sanctuary of Tonks's parents.

"They recognized you? But how? What had you done?"

"I . . ." Harry tried to remember; the whole journey seemed like a blur of panic and confusion. "I saw Stan Shunpike. . . . You know, the bloke who was the conductor on the Knight Bus? And I tried to Disarm him instead of — well, he doesn't know what he's doing, does he? He must be Imperiused!"

Lupin looked aghast.

"Harry, the time for Disarming is past! These people are trying to capture and kill you! At least Stun if you aren't prepared to kill!"

"We were hundreds of feet up! Stan's not himself, and if I Stunned him and he'd fallen, he'd have died the same as if I'd used Avada Kedavra! Expelliarmus saved me from Voldemort two years ago," Harry added defiantly. Lupin was reminding him of the sneering

Hufflepuff Zacharias Smith, who had jeered at Harry for wanting to teach Dumbledore's Army how to Disarm.

"Yes, Harry," said Lupin with painful restraint, "and a great number of Death Eaters witnessed that happening! Forgive me, but it was a very unusual move then, under imminent threat of death. Repeating it tonight in front of Death Eaters who either witnessed or heard about the first occasion was close to suicidal!"

"So you think I should have killed Stan Shunpike?" said Harry angrily.

"Of course not," said Lupin, "but the Death Eaters — frankly, most people! — would have expected you to attack back! Expelliarmus is a useful spell, Harry, but the Death Eaters seem to think it is your signature move, and I urge you not to let it become so!"

Lupin was making Harry feel idiotic, and yet there was still a grain of defiance inside him.

"I won't blast people out of my way just because they're there," said Harry. "That's Voldemort's job."

Lupin's retort was lost: Finally succeeding in squeezing through the door, Hagrid staggered to a chair and sat down; it collapsed beneath him. Ignoring his mingled oaths and apologies, Harry addressed Lupin again.

"Will George be okay?"

All Lupin's frustration with Harry seemed to drain away at the question.

"I think so, although there's no chance of replacing his ear, not when it's been cursed off —"

There was a scuffling from outside. Lupin dived for the back door; Harry leapt over Hagrid's legs and sprinted into the yard.

Two figures had appeared in the yard, and as Harry ran toward them he realized they were Hermione, now returning to her normal appearance, and Kingsley, both clutching a bent coat hanger. Hermione flung herself into Harry's arms, but Kingsley showed no pleasure at the sight of any of them. Over Hermione's shoulder Harry saw him raise his wand and point it at Lupin's chest.

"The last words Albus Dumbledore spoke to the pair of us?"

"'Harry is the best hope we have. Trust him,'" said Lupin calmly.

Kingsley turned his wand on Harry, but Lupin said, "It's him, I've checked!"

"All right, all right!" said Kingsley, stowing his wand back beneath his cloak. "But somebody betrayed us! They knew, they knew it was tonight!"

"So it seems," replied Lupin, "but apparently they did not realize that there would be seven Harrys."

"Small comfort!" snarled Kingsley. "Who else is back?"

"Only Harry, Hagrid, George, and me."

Hermione stifled a little moan behind her hand.

"What happened to you?" Lupin asked Kingsley.

"Followed by five, injured two, might've killed one," Kingsley reeled off, "and we saw You-Know-Who as well, he joined the chase halfway through but vanished pretty quickly. Remus, he can —"

"Fly," supplied Harry. "I saw him too, he came after Hagrid and me."

"So that's why he left, to follow you!" said Kingsley. "I couldn't understand why he'd vanished. But what made him change targets?"

"Harry behaved a little too kindly to Stan Shunpike," said Lupin.

"Stan?" repeated Hermione. "But I thought he was in Azkaban?"

Kingsley let out a mirthless laugh.

"Hermione, there's obviously been a mass breakout which the Ministry has hushed up. Travers's hood fell off when I cursed him, he's supposed to be inside too. But what happened to you, Remus? Where's George?"

"He lost an ear," said Lupin.

"Lost an — ?" repeated Hermione in a high voice.

"Snape's work," said Lupin.

"*Snape?*" shouted Harry. "You didn't say —"

"He lost his hood during the chase. Sectumsempra was always a speciality of Snape's. I wish I could say I'd paid him back in kind, but it was all I could do to keep George on the broom after he was injured, he was losing so much blood."

Silence fell between the four of them as they looked up at the sky. There was no sign of movement; the stars stared back, unblinking, indifferent, unobscured by flying friends. Where was Ron? Where were Fred and Mr. Weasley? Where were Bill, Fleur, Tonks, Mad-Eye, and Mundungus?

"Harry, give us a hand!" called Hagrid hoarsely from the door, in which he was stuck again. Glad of something to do, Harry pulled him free, then headed through the empty kitchen and back into the sitting room, where Mrs. Weasley and Ginny were still tending to George. Mrs. Weasley had staunched his bleeding now, and by the lamplight Harry saw a clean, gaping hole where George's ear had been.

"How is he?"

Mrs. Weasley looked around and said, "I can't make it grow back, not when it's been removed by Dark Magic. But it could have been so much worse. . . . He's alive."

"Yeah," said Harry. "Thank God."

"Did I hear someone else in the yard?" Ginny asked.

"Hermione and Kingsley," said Harry.

"Thank goodness," Ginny whispered. They looked at each other; Harry wanted to hug her, hold on to her; he did not even care much that Mrs. Weasley was there, but before he could act on the impulse there was a great crash from the kitchen.

"I'll prove who I am, Kingsley, after I've seen my son, now back off if you know what's good for you!"

Harry had never heard Mr. Weasley shout like that before. He burst into the living room, his bald patch gleaming with sweat, his spectacles askew, Fred right behind him, both pale but uninjured.

"Arthur!" sobbed Mrs. Weasley. "Oh thank goodness!"

"How is he?"

Mr. Weasley dropped to his knees beside George. For the first time since Harry had known him, Fred seemed to be lost for words. He gaped over the back of the sofa at his twin's wound as if he could not believe what he was seeing.

Perhaps roused by the sound of Fred and their father's arrival, George stirred.

"How do you feel, Georgie?" whispered Mrs. Weasley.

George's fingers groped for the side of his head.

"Saintlike," he murmured.

"What's wrong with him?" croaked Fred, looking terrified. "Is his mind affected?"

"Saintlike," repeated George, opening his eyes and looking up at his brother. "You see . . . I'm holy. *Holey,* Fred, geddit?"

Mrs. Weasley sobbed harder than ever. Color flooded Fred's pale face.

"Pathetic," he told George. "Pathetic! With the whole wide world of ear-related humor before you, you go for *holey*?"

"Ah well," said George, grinning at his tear-soaked mother. "You'll be able to tell us apart now, anyway, Mum."

He looked around.

"Hi, Harry — you are Harry, right?"

"Yeah, I am," said Harry, moving closer to the sofa.

"Well, at least we got you back okay," said George. "Why aren't Ron and Bill huddled round my sickbed?"

"They're not back yet, George," said Mrs. Weasley. George's grin faded. Harry glanced at Ginny and motioned to her to accompany him back outside. As they walked through the kitchen she said in a low voice,

"Ron and Tonks should be back by now. They didn't have a long journey; Auntie Muriel's not that far from here."

Harry said nothing. He had been trying to keep fear at bay ever since reaching the Burrow, but now it enveloped him, seeming to crawl over his skin, throbbing in his chest, clogging his throat. As they walked down the back steps into the dark yard, Ginny took his hand.

Kingsley was striding backward and forward, glancing up at the sky every time he turned. Harry was reminded of Uncle Vernon pacing the living room a million years ago. Hagrid, Hermione, and Lupin stood shoulder to shoulder, gazing upward in silence. None of them looked around when Harry and Ginny joined their silent vigil.

The minutes stretched into what might as well have been years. The slightest breath of wind made them all jump and turn toward the whispering bush or tree in the hope that one of the missing Order members might leap unscathed from its leaves —

And then a broom materialized directly above them and streaked toward the ground —

"It's them!" screamed Hermione.

Tonks landed in a long skid that sent earth and pebbles everywhere.

"Remus!" Tonks cried as she staggered off the broom into Lupin's arms. His face was set and white: He seemed unable to speak. Ron tripped dazedly toward Harry and Hermione.

"You're okay," he mumbled, before Hermione flew at him and hugged him tightly.

"I thought — I thought —"

"'M all right," said Ron, patting her on the back. "'M fine."

"Ron was great," said Tonks warmly, relinquishing her hold on Lupin. "Wonderful. Stunned one of the Death Eaters, straight to the head, and when you're aiming at a moving target from a flying broom —"

"You did?" said Hermione, gazing up at Ron with her arms still around his neck.

"Always the tone of surprise," he said a little grumpily, breaking free. "Are we the last back?"

"No," said Ginny, "we're still waiting for Bill and Fleur and Mad-Eye and Mundungus. I'm going to tell Mum and Dad you're okay, Ron —"

She ran back inside.

"So what kept you? What happened?" Lupin sounded almost angry at Tonks.

"Bellatrix," said Tonks. "She wants me quite as much as she wants Harry, Remus, she tried very hard to kill me. I just wish I'd got her, I owe Bellatrix. But we definitely injured Rodolphus. . . . Then we got to Ron's Auntie Muriel's and we'd missed our Portkey and she was fussing over us —"

A muscle was jumping in Lupin's jaw. He nodded, but seemed unable to say anything else.

"So what happened to you lot?" Tonks asked, turning to Harry, Hermione, and Kingsley.

They recounted the stories of their own journeys, but all the time the continued absence of Bill, Fleur, Mad-Eye, and Mundungus seemed to lie upon them like a frost, its icy bite harder and harder to ignore.

"I'm going to have to get back to Downing Street, I should have been there an hour ago," said Kingsley finally, after a last sweeping gaze at the sky. "Let me know when they're back."

Lupin nodded. With a wave to the others, Kingsley walked away into the darkness toward the gate. Harry thought he heard the faintest *pop* as Kingsley Disapparated just beyond the Burrow's boundaries.

Mr. and Mrs. Weasley came racing down the back steps, Ginny behind them. Both parents hugged Ron before turning to Lupin and Tonks.

"Thank you," said Mrs. Weasley, "for our sons."

"Don't be silly, Molly," said Tonks at once.

"How's George?" asked Lupin.

"What's wrong with him?" piped up Ron.

"He's lost —"

But the end of Mrs. Weasley's sentence was drowned in a general outcry: A thestral had just soared into sight and landed a few feet from them. Bill and Fleur slid from its back, windswept but unhurt.

"Bill! Thank God, thank God —"

Mrs. Weasley ran forward, but the hug Bill bestowed upon her was perfunctory. Looking directly at his father, he said, "Mad-Eye's dead."

Nobody spoke, nobody moved. Harry felt as though something inside him was falling, falling through the earth, leaving him forever.

"We saw it," said Bill; Fleur nodded, tear tracks glittering on her cheeks in the light from the kitchen window. "It happened just after we broke out of the circle: Mad-Eye and Dung were close by us, they were heading north too. Voldemort — he can fly — went straight for them. Dung panicked, I heard him cry out, Mad-Eye tried to stop him, but he Disapparated. Voldemort's curse hit Mad-Eye full in the face, he fell backward off his broom and — there was nothing we could do, nothing, we had half a dozen of them on our own tail —"

Bill's voice broke.

"Of course you couldn't have done anything," said Lupin.

They all stood looking at each other. Harry could not quite comprehend it. Mad-Eye dead; it could not be. . . . Mad-Eye, so tough, so brave, the consummate survivor . . .

At last it seemed to dawn on everyone, though nobody said it, that there was no point waiting in the yard anymore, and in silence they followed Mr. and Mrs. Weasley back into the Burrow, and into the living room, where Fred and George were laughing together.

"What's wrong?" said Fred, scanning their faces as they entered. "What's happened? Who's — ?"

"Mad-Eye," said Mr. Weasley. "Dead."

The twins' grins turned to grimaces of shock. Nobody seemed

to know what to do. Tonks was crying silently into a handkerchief: She had been close to Mad-Eye, Harry knew, his favorite and his protégée at the Ministry of Magic. Hagrid, who had sat down on the floor in the corner where he had most space, was dabbing at his eyes with his tablecloth-sized handkerchief.

Bill walked over to the sideboard and pulled out a bottle of firewhisky and some glasses.

"Here," he said, and with a wave of his wand he sent twelve full glasses soaring through the room to each of them, holding the thirteenth aloft. "Mad-Eye."

"Mad-Eye," they all said, and drank.

"Mad-Eye," echoed Hagrid, a little late, with a hiccup.

The firewhisky seared Harry's throat. It seemed to burn feeling back into him, dispelling the numbness and sense of unreality, firing him with something that was like courage.

"So Mundungus disappeared?" said Lupin, who had drained his own glass in one.

The atmosphere changed at once. Everybody looked tense, watching Lupin, both wanting him to go on, it seemed to Harry, and slightly afraid of what they might hear.

"I know what you're thinking," said Bill, "and I wondered that too, on the way back here, because they seemed to be expecting us, didn't they? But Mundungus can't have betrayed us. They didn't know there would be seven Harrys, that confused them the moment we appeared, and in case you've forgotten, it was Mundungus who suggested that little bit of skullduggery. Why wouldn't he have told them the essential point? I think Dung panicked, it's as simple as that. He didn't want to come in the first place, but Mad-Eye made him, and You-Know-Who went straight for them. It was enough to make anyone panic."

"You-Know-Who acted exactly as Mad-Eye expected him to," sniffed Tonks. "Mad-Eye said he'd expect the real Harry to be with the toughest, most skilled Aurors. He chased Mad-Eye first, and when Mundungus gave them away he switched to Kingsley. . . ."

"Yes, and zat eez all very good," snapped Fleur, "but still eet does not explain 'ow zey knew we were moving 'Arry tonight, does eet? Somebody must 'ave been careless. Somebody let slip ze date to an outsider. It is ze only explanation for zem knowing ze date but not ze 'ole plan."

She glared around at them all, tear tracks still etched on her beautiful face, silently daring any of them to contradict her. Nobody did. The only sound to break the silence was that of Hagrid hiccuping from behind his handkerchief. Harry glanced at Hagrid, who had just risked his own life to save Harry's — Hagrid, whom he loved, whom he trusted, who had once been tricked into giving Voldemort crucial information in exchange for a dragon's egg. . . .

"No," Harry said aloud, and they all looked at him, surprised: The firewhisky seemed to have amplified his voice. "I mean . . . if somebody made a mistake," Harry went on, "and let something slip, I know they didn't mean to do it. It's not their fault," he repeated, again a little louder than he would usually have spoken. "We've got to trust each other. I trust all of you, I don't think anyone in this room would ever sell me to Voldemort."

More silence followed his words. They were all looking at him; Harry felt a little hot again, and drank some more firewhisky for something to do. As he drank, he thought of Mad-Eye. Mad-Eye had always been scathing about Dumbledore's willingness to trust people.

"Well said, Harry," said Fred unexpectedly.

"Yeah, 'ear, 'ear," said George, with half a glance at Fred, the corner of whose mouth twitched.

Lupin was wearing an odd expression as he looked at Harry. It was close to pitying.

"You think I'm a fool?" demanded Harry.

"No, I think you're like James," said Lupin, "who would have regarded it as the height of dishonor to mistrust his friends."

Harry knew what Lupin was getting at: that his father had been betrayed by his friend, Peter Pettigrew. He felt irrationally angry. He wanted to argue, but Lupin had turned away from him, set down his glass upon a side table, and addressed Bill, "There's work to do. I can ask Kingsley whether —"

"No," said Bill at once, "I'll do it, I'll come."

"Where are you going?" said Tonks and Fleur together.

"Mad-Eye's body," said Lupin. "We need to recover it."

"Can't it — ?" began Mrs. Weasley with an appealing look at Bill.

"Wait?" said Bill. "Not unless you'd rather the Death Eaters took it?"

Nobody spoke. Lupin and Bill said good-bye and left.

The rest of them now dropped into chairs, all except for Harry, who remained standing. The suddenness and completeness of death was with them like a presence.

"I've got to go too," said Harry.

Ten pairs of startled eyes looked at him.

"Don't be silly, Harry," said Mrs. Weasley. "What are you talking about?"

"I can't stay here."

He rubbed his forehead; it was prickling again, it had not hurt like this for more than a year.

"You're all in danger while I'm here. I don't want —"

"But don't be so silly!" said Mrs. Weasley. "The whole point of tonight was to get you here safely, and thank goodness it worked. And Fleur's agreed to get married here rather than in France, we've arranged everything so that we can all stay together and look after you —"

She did not understand; she was making him feel worse, not better.

"If Voldemort finds out I'm here —"

"But why should he?" asked Mrs. Weasley.

"There are a dozen places you might be now, Harry," said Mr. Weasley. "He's got no way of knowing which safe house you're in."

"It's not me I'm worried for!" said Harry.

"We know that," said Mr. Weasley quietly, "but it would make our efforts tonight seem rather pointless if you left."

"Yer not goin' anywhere," growled Hagrid. "Blimey, Harry, after all we wen' through ter get you here?"

"Yeah, what about my bleeding ear?" said George, hoisting himself up on his cushions.

"I know that —"

"Mad-Eye wouldn't want —"

"I KNOW!" Harry bellowed.

He felt beleaguered and blackmailed: Did they think he did not know what they had done for him, didn't they understand that it was for precisely that reason that he wanted to go now, before they had to suffer any more on his behalf? There was a long and awkward silence in which his scar continued to prickle and throb, and which was broken at last by Mrs. Weasley.

"Where's Hedwig, Harry?" she said coaxingly. "We can put her up with Pigwidgeon and give her something to eat."

His insides clenched like a fist. He could not tell her the truth. He drank the last of his firewhisky to avoid answering.

"Wait till it gets out yeh did it again, Harry," said Hagrid. "Escaped him, fought him off when he was right on top of yeh!"

"It wasn't me," said Harry flatly. "It was my wand. My wand acted of its own accord."

After a few moments, Hermione said gently, "But that's impossible, Harry. You mean that you did magic without meaning to; you reacted instinctively."

"No," said Harry. "The bike was falling, I couldn't have told you where Voldemort was, but my wand spun in my hand and found him and shot a spell at him, and it wasn't even a spell I recognized. I've never made gold flames appear before."

"Often," said Mr. Weasley, "when you're in a pressured situation you can produce magic you never dreamed of. Small children often find, before they're trained —"

"It wasn't like that," said Harry through gritted teeth. His scar was burning: He felt angry and frustrated; he hated the idea that they were all imagining him to have power to match Voldemort's.

No one said anything. He knew that they did not believe him. Now that he came to think of it, he had never heard of a wand performing magic on its own before.

His scar seared with pain; it was all he could do not to moan aloud. Muttering about fresh air, he set down his glass and left the room.

As he crossed the dark yard, the great skeletal thestral looked up, rustled its enormous batlike wings, then resumed its grazing. Harry stopped at the gate into the garden, staring out at its overgrown plants, rubbing his pounding forehead and thinking of Dumbledore.

Dumbledore would have believed him, he knew it. Dumbledore would have known how and why Harry's wand had acted independently, because Dumbledore always had the answers; he had known about wands, had explained to Harry the strange connection that existed between his wand and Voldemort's. . . . But Dumbledore, like Mad-Eye, like Sirius, like his parents, like his poor owl, all were gone where Harry could never talk to them again. He felt a burning in his throat that had nothing to do with firewhisky. . . .

And then, out of nowhere, the pain in his scar peaked. As he clutched his forehead and closed his eyes, a voice screamed inside his head.

"You told me the problem would be solved by using another's wand!"

And into his mind burst the vision of an emaciated old man lying in rags upon a stone floor, screaming, a horrible, drawn-out scream, a scream of unendurable agony. . . .

"No! No! I beg you, I beg you. . . ."

"You lied to Lord Voldemort, Ollivander!"

"I did not. . . . I swear I did not. . . ."

"You sought to help Potter, to help him escape me!"

"I swear I did not. . . . I believed a different wand would work. . . ."

"Explain, then, what happened. Lucius's wand is destroyed!"

"I cannot understand. . . . The connection . . . exists only . . . between your two wands. . . ."

"*Lies!*"

"Please . . . I beg you. . . ."

And Harry saw the white hand raise its wand and felt Voldemort's surge of vicious anger, saw the frail old man on the floor writhe in agony —

"Harry?"

It was over as quickly as it had come: Harry stood shaking in the darkness, clutching the gate into the garden, his heart racing, his scar still tingling. It was several moments before he realized that Ron and Hermione were at his side.

"Harry, come back in the house," Hermione whispered. "You aren't still thinking of leaving?"

"Yeah, you've got to stay, mate," said Ron, thumping Harry on the back.

"Are you all right?" Hermione asked, close enough now to look into Harry's face. "You look awful!"

"Well," said Harry shakily, "I probably look better than Ollivander. . . ."

When he had finished telling them what he had seen, Ron looked appalled, but Hermione downright terrified.

"But it was supposed to have stopped! Your scar — it wasn't supposed to do this anymore! You mustn't let that connection open up again — Dumbledore wanted you to close your mind!"

When he did not reply, she gripped his arm.

"Harry, he's taking over the Ministry and the newspapers and half the Wizarding world! Don't let him inside your head too!"

THE GHOUL IN PAJAMAS

The shock of losing Mad-Eye hung over the house in the days that followed; Harry kept expecting to see him stumping in through the back door like the other Order members, who passed in and out to relay news. Harry felt that nothing but action would assuage his feelings of guilt and grief and that he ought to set out on his mission to find and destroy Horcruxes as soon as possible.

"Well, you can't do anything about the" — Ron mouthed the word *Horcruxes* — "till you're seventeen. You've still got the Trace on you. And we can plan here as well as anywhere, can't we? Or," he dropped his voice to a whisper, "d'you reckon you already know where the You-Know-Whats are?"

"No," Harry admitted.

"I think Hermione's been doing a bit of research," said Ron. "She said she was saving it for when you got here."

They were sitting at the breakfast table; Mr. Weasley and Bill had

just left for work. Mrs. Weasley had gone upstairs to wake Hermione
and Ginny, while Fleur had drifted off to take a bath.

"The Trace'll break on the thirty-first," said Harry. "That means
I only need to stay here four days. Then I can —"

"Five days," Ron corrected him firmly. "We've got to stay for the
wedding. They'll kill us if we miss it."

Harry understood "they" to mean Fleur and Mrs. Weasley.

"It's one extra day," said Ron, when Harry looked mutinous.

"Don't they realize how important — ?"

"'Course they don't," said Ron. "They haven't got a clue. And now
you mention it, I wanted to talk to you about that."

Ron glanced toward the door into the hall to check that Mrs.
Weasley was not returning yet, then leaned in closer to Harry.

"Mum's been trying to get it out of Hermione and me. What
we're off to do. She'll try you next, so brace yourself. Dad and
Lupin've both asked as well, but when we said Dumbledore told you
not to tell anyone except us, they dropped it. Not Mum, though.
She's determined."

Ron's prediction came true within hours. Shortly before lunch,
Mrs. Weasley detached Harry from the others by asking him to help
identify a lone man's sock that she thought might have come out
of his rucksack. Once she had him cornered in the tiny scullery off
the kitchen, she started.

"Ron and Hermione seem to think that the three of you are dropping out of Hogwarts," she began in a light, casual tone.

"Oh," said Harry. "Well, yeah. We are."

The mangle turned of its own accord in a corner, wringing out
what looked like one of Mr. Weasley's vests.

"May I ask *why* you are abandoning your education?" said Mrs. Weasley.

"Well, Dumbledore left me . . . stuff to do," mumbled Harry. "Ron and Hermione know about it, and they want to come too."

"What sort of 'stuff'?"

"I'm sorry, I can't —"

"Well, frankly, I think Arthur and I have a right to know, and I'm sure Mr. and Mrs. Granger would agree!" said Mrs. Weasley. Harry had been afraid of the "concerned parent" attack. He forced himself to look directly into her eyes, noticing as he did so that they were precisely the same shade of brown as Ginny's. This did not help.

"Dumbledore didn't want anyone else to know, Mrs. Weasley. I'm sorry. Ron and Hermione don't have to come, it's their choice —"

"I don't see that *you* have to go either!" she snapped, dropping all pretense now. "You're barely of age, any of you! It's utter nonsense, if Dumbledore needed work doing, he had the whole Order at his command! Harry, you must have misunderstood him. Probably he was telling you something he *wanted* done, and you took it to mean that he wanted *you* —"

"I didn't misunderstand," said Harry flatly. "It's got to be me."

He handed her back the single sock he was supposed to be identifying, which was patterned with golden bulrushes.

"And that's not mine, I don't support Puddlemere United."

"Oh, of course not," said Mrs. Weasley with a sudden and rather unnerving return to her casual tone. "I should have realized. Well, Harry, while we've still got you here, you won't mind helping with the preparations for Bill and Fleur's wedding, will you? There's still so much to do."

"No — I — of course not," said Harry, disconcerted by this sudden change of subject.

"Sweet of you," she replied, and she smiled as she left the scullery.

From that moment on, Mrs. Weasley kept Harry, Ron, and Hermione so busy with preparations for the wedding that they hardly had any time to think. The kindest explanation of this behavior would have been that Mrs. Weasley wanted to distract them all from thoughts of Mad-Eye and the terrors of their recent journey. After two days of nonstop cutlery cleaning, of color-matching favors, ribbons, and flowers, of de-gnoming the garden and helping Mrs. Weasley cook vast batches of canapés, however, Harry started to suspect her of a different motive. All the jobs she handed out seemed to keep him, Ron, and Hermione away from one another; he had not had a chance to speak to the two of them alone since the first night, when he had told them about Voldemort torturing Ollivander.

"I think Mum thinks that if she can stop the three of you getting together and planning, she'll be able to delay you leaving," Ginny told Harry in an undertone, as they laid the table for dinner on the third night of his stay.

"And then what does she think's going to happen?" Harry muttered. "Someone else might kill off Voldemort while she's holding us here making vol-au-vents?"

He had spoken without thinking, and saw Ginny's face whiten.

"So it's true?" she said. "That's what you're trying to do?"

"I — not — I was joking," said Harry evasively.

They stared at each other, and there was something more than shock in Ginny's expression. Suddenly Harry became aware that this was the first time that he had been alone with her since those stolen hours in secluded corners of the Hogwarts grounds. He was sure she was remembering them too. Both of them jumped as the door opened, and Mr. Weasley, Kingsley, and Bill walked in.

They were often joined by other Order members for dinner now, because the Burrow had replaced number twelve, Grimmauld Place as the headquarters. Mr. Weasley had explained that after the death of Dumbledore, their Secret-Keeper, each of the people to whom Dumbledore had confided Grimmauld Place's location had become a Secret-Keeper in turn.

"And as there are around twenty of us, that greatly dilutes the power of the Fidelius Charm. Twenty times as many opportunities for the Death Eaters to get the secret out of somebody. We can't expect it to hold much longer."

"But surely Snape will have told the Death Eaters the address by now?" asked Harry.

"Well, Mad-Eye set up a couple of curses against Snape in case he turns up there again. We hope they'll be strong enough both to keep him out and to bind his tongue if he tries to talk about the place, but we can't be sure. It would have been insane to keep using the place as headquarters now that its protection has become so shaky."

The kitchen was so crowded that evening it was difficult to maneuver knives and forks. Harry found himself crammed beside Ginny; the unsaid things that had just passed between them made him wish they had been separated by a few more people. He was trying so hard to avoid brushing her arm he could barely cut his chicken.

"No news about Mad-Eye?" Harry asked Bill.

"Nothing," replied Bill.

They had not been able to hold a funeral for Moody, because Bill and Lupin had failed to recover his body. It had been difficult to know where he might have fallen, given the darkness and the confusion of the battle.

"The *Daily Prophet* hasn't said a word about him dying or about finding the body," Bill went on. "But that doesn't mean much. It's keeping a lot quiet these days."

"And they still haven't called a hearing about all the underage magic I used escaping the Death Eaters?" Harry called across the table to Mr. Weasley, who shook his head.

"Because they know I had no choice or because they don't want me to tell the world Voldemort attacked me?"

"The latter, I think. Scrimgeour doesn't want to admit that You-Know-Who is as powerful as he is, nor that Azkaban's seen a mass breakout."

"Yeah, why tell the public the truth?" said Harry, clenching his knife so tightly that the faint scars on the back of his right hand stood out, white against his skin: *I must not tell lies.*

"Isn't anyone at the Ministry prepared to stand up to him?" asked Ron angrily.

"Of course, Ron, but people are terrified," Mr. Weasley replied, "terrified that they will be next to disappear, their children the next to be attacked! There are nasty rumors going around; I for one don't believe the Muggle Studies professor at Hogwarts resigned. She hasn't been seen for weeks now. Meanwhile Scrimgeour remains shut up in his office all day: I just hope he's working on a plan."

There was a pause in which Mrs. Weasley magicked the empty plates onto the work surface and served apple tart.

"We must decide 'ow you will be disguised, 'Arry," said Fleur, once everyone had pudding. "For ze wedding," she added, when he looked confused. "Of course, none of our guests are Death Eaters, but we cannot guarantee zat zey will not let something slip after zey 'ave 'ad champagne."

From this, Harry gathered that she still suspected Hagrid.

"Yes, good point," said Mrs. Weasley from the top of the table, where she sat, spectacles perched on the end of her nose, scanning an immense list of jobs that she had scribbled on a very long piece of parchment. "Now, Ron, have you cleaned out your room yet?"

"*Why?*" exclaimed Ron, slamming his spoon down and glaring at his mother. "Why does my room have to be cleaned out? Harry and I are fine with it the way it is!"

"We are holding your brother's wedding here in a few days' time, young man —"

"And are they getting married in my bedroom?" asked Ron furiously. "No! So why in the name of Merlin's saggy left —"

"Don't talk to your mother like that," said Mr. Weasley firmly. "And do as you're told."

Ron scowled at both his parents, then picked up his spoon and attacked the last few mouthfuls of his apple tart.

"I can help, some of it's my mess," Harry told Ron, but Mrs. Weasley cut across him.

"No, Harry, dear, I'd much rather you helped Arthur muck out the chickens, and Hermione, I'd be ever so grateful if you'd change the sheets for Monsieur and Madame Delacour; you know they're arriving at eleven tomorrow morning."

But as it turned out, there was very little to do for the chickens.

"There's no need to, er, mention it to Molly," Mr. Weasley told Harry, blocking his access to the coop, "but, er, Ted Tonks sent me most of what was left of Sirius's bike and, er, I'm hiding — that's to say, keeping — it in here. Fantastic stuff: There's an exhaust gaskin, as I believe it's called, the most magnificent battery, and it'll be a great opportunity to find out how brakes work. I'm going to try and put it all back together again when Molly's not — I mean, when I've got time."

When they returned to the house, Mrs. Weasley was nowhere to be seen, so Harry slipped upstairs to Ron's attic bedroom.

"I'm doing it, I'm doing — ! Oh, it's you," said Ron in relief, as Harry entered the room. Ron lay back down on the bed, which he had evidently just vacated. The room was just as messy as it had been all week; the only change was that Hermione was now sitting in the far corner, her fluffy ginger cat, Crookshanks, at her feet, sorting books, some of which Harry recognized as his own, into two enormous piles.

"Hi, Harry," she said, as he sat down on his camp bed.

"And how did you manage to get away?"

"Oh, Ron's mum forgot that she asked Ginny and me to change the sheets yesterday," said Hermione. She threw *Numerology and Grammatica* onto one pile and *The Rise and Fall of the Dark Arts* onto the other.

"We were just talking about Mad-Eye," Ron told Harry. "I reckon he might have survived."

"But Bill saw him hit by the Killing Curse," said Harry.

"Yeah, but Bill was under attack too," said Ron. "How can he be sure what he saw?"

"Even if the Killing Curse missed, Mad-Eye still fell about a thousand feet," said Hermione, now weighing *Quidditch Teams of Britain and Ireland* in her hand.

"He could have used a Shield Charm —"

"Fleur said his wand was blasted out of his hand," said Harry.

"Well, all right, if you want him to be dead," said Ron grumpily, punching his pillow into a more comfortable shape.

"Of course we don't want him to be dead!" said Hermione, looking shocked. "It's dreadful that he's dead! But we're being realistic!"

For the first time, Harry imagined Mad-Eye's body, broken as Dumbledore's had been, yet with that one eye still whizzing in its socket. He felt a stab of revulsion mixed with a bizarre desire to laugh.

"The Death Eaters probably tidied up after themselves, that's why no one's found him," said Ron wisely.

"Yeah," said Harry. "Like Barty Crouch, turned into a bone and buried in Hagrid's front garden. They probably transfigured Moody and stuffed him —"

"Don't!" squealed Hermione. Startled, Harry looked over just in time to see her burst into tears over her copy of *Spellman's Syllabary.*

"Oh no," said Harry, struggling to get up from the old camp bed. "Hermione, I wasn't trying to upset —"

But with a great creaking of rusty bedsprings, Ron bounded off the bed and got there first. One arm around Hermione, he fished in his jeans pocket and withdrew a revolting-looking handkerchief that he had used to clean out the oven earlier. Hastily pulling out his wand, he pointed it at the rag and said, *"Tergeo."*

The wand siphoned off most of the grease. Looking rather pleased with himself, Ron handed the slightly smoking handkerchief to Hermione.

"Oh . . . thanks, Ron. . . . I'm sorry. . . ." She blew her nose and hiccuped. "It's just so awf-ful, isn't it? R-right after Dumbledore . . . I j-just n-never imagined Mad-Eye dying, somehow, he seemed so tough!"

"Yeah, I know," said Ron, giving her a squeeze. "But you know what he'd say to us if he was here?"

"'C-constant vigilance,'" said Hermione, mopping her eyes.

"That's right," said Ron, nodding. "He'd tell us to learn from what happened to him. And what I've learned is not to trust that cowardly little squit, Mundungus."

Hermione gave a shaky laugh and leaned forward to pick up two more books. A second later, Ron had snatched his arm back from around her shoulders; she had dropped *The Monster Book of Monsters* on his foot. The book had broken free from its restraining belt and snapped viciously at Ron's ankle.

"I'm sorry, I'm sorry!" Hermione cried as Harry wrenched the book from Ron's leg and retied it shut.

"What are you doing with all those books anyway?" Ron asked, limping back to his bed.

"Just trying to decide which ones to take with us," said Hermione. "When we're looking for the Horcruxes."

"Oh, of course," said Ron, clapping a hand to his forehead. "I forgot we'll be hunting down Voldemort in a mobile library."

"Ha ha," said Hermione, looking down at *Spellman's Syllabary.* "I wonder . . . will we need to translate runes? It's possible. . . . I think we'd better take it, to be safe."

She dropped the syllabary onto the larger of the two piles and picked up *Hogwarts, A History*.

"Listen," said Harry.

He had sat up straight. Ron and Hermione looked at him with similar mixtures of resignation and defiance.

"I know you said after Dumbledore's funeral that you wanted to come with me," Harry began.

"Here he goes," Ron said to Hermione, rolling his eyes.

"As we knew he would," she sighed, turning back to the books. "You know, I think I *will* take *Hogwarts, A History*. Even if we're not going back there, I don't think I'd feel right if I didn't have it with —"

"Listen!" said Harry again.

"No, Harry, *you* listen," said Hermione. "We're coming with you. That was decided months ago — years, really."

"But —"

"Shut up," Ron advised him.

"— are you sure you've thought this through?" Harry persisted.

"Let's see," said Hermione, slamming *Travels with Trolls* onto the discarded pile with a rather fierce look. "I've been packing for days, so we're ready to leave at a moment's notice, which for your information has included doing some pretty difficult magic, not to mention smuggling Mad-Eye's whole stock of Polyjuice Potion right under Ron's mum's nose.

"I've also modified my parents' memories so that they're convinced they're really called Wendell and Monica Wilkins, and that their life's ambition is to move to Australia, which they have now done. That's to make it more difficult for Voldemort to track them down and interrogate them about me — or you, because unfortunately, I've told them quite a bit about you.

"Assuming I survive our hunt for the Horcruxes, I'll find Mum and Dad and lift the enchantment. If I don't — well, I think I've cast a good enough charm to keep them safe and happy. Wendell and Monica Wilkins don't know that they've got a daughter, you see."

Hermione's eyes were swimming with tears again. Ron got back off the bed, put his arm around her once more, and frowned at Harry as though reproaching him for lack of tact. Harry could not think of anything to say, not least because it was highly unusual for Ron to be teaching anyone else tact.

"I — Hermione, I'm sorry — I didn't —"

"Didn't realize that Ron and I know perfectly well what might happen if we come with you? Well, we do. Ron, show Harry what you've done."

"Nah, he's just eaten," said Ron.

"Go on, he needs to know!"

"Oh, all right. Harry, come here."

For the second time Ron withdrew his arm from around Hermione and stumped over to the door.

"C'mon."

"Why?" Harry asked, following Ron out of the room onto the tiny landing.

Descendo, muttered Ron, pointing his wand at the low ceiling. A hatch opened right over their heads and a ladder slid down to their feet. A horrible, half-sucking, half-moaning sound came out of the square hole, along with an unpleasant smell like open drains.

"That's your ghoul, isn't it?" asked Harry, who had never actually met the creature that sometimes disrupted the nightly silence.

"Yeah, it is," said Ron, climbing the ladder. "Come and have a look at him."

Harry followed Ron up the few short steps into the tiny attic space. His head and shoulders were in the room before he caught sight of the creature curled up a few feet from him, fast asleep in the gloom with its large mouth wide open.

"But it . . . it looks . . . do ghouls normally wear pajamas?"

"No," said Ron. "Nor have they usually got red hair or that number of pustules."

Harry contemplated the thing, slightly revolted. It was human in shape and size, and was wearing what, now that Harry's eyes became used to the darkness, was clearly an old pair of Ron's pajamas. He was also sure that ghouls were generally rather slimy and bald, rather than distinctly hairy and covered in angry purple blisters.

"He's me, see?" said Ron.

"No," said Harry. "I don't."

"I'll explain it back in my room, the smell's getting to me," said Ron. They climbed back down the ladder, which Ron returned to the ceiling, and rejoined Hermione, who was still sorting books.

"Once we've left, the ghoul's going to come and live down here in my room," said Ron. "I think he's really looking forward to it — well, it's hard to tell, because all he can do is moan and drool — but he nods a lot when you mention it. Anyway, he's going to be me with spattergroit. Good, eh?"

Harry merely looked his confusion.

"It is!" said Ron, clearly frustrated that Harry had not grasped the brilliance of the plan. "Look, when we three don't turn up at

Hogwarts again, everyone's going to think Hermione and I must be with you, right? Which means the Death Eaters will go straight for our families to see if they've got information on where you are."

"But hopefully it'll look like I've gone away with Mum and Dad; a lot of Muggle-borns are talking about going into hiding at the moment," said Hermione.

"We can't hide my whole family, it'll look too fishy and they can't all leave their jobs," said Ron. "So we're going to put out the story that I'm seriously ill with spattergroit, which is why I can't go back to school. If anyone comes calling to investigate, Mum or Dad can show them the ghoul in my bed, covered in pustules. Spattergroit's really contagious, so they're not going to want to go near him. It won't matter that he can't say anything, either, because apparently you can't once the fungus has spread to your uvula."

"And your mum and dad are in on this plan?" asked Harry.

"Dad is. He helped Fred and George transform the ghoul. Mum . . . well, you've seen what she's like. She won't accept we're going till we've gone."

There was silence in the room, broken only by gentle thuds as Hermione continued to throw books onto one pile or the other. Ron sat watching her, and Harry looked from one to the other, unable to say anything. The measures they had taken to protect their families made him realize, more than anything else could have done, that they really were going to come with him and that they knew exactly how dangerous that would be. He wanted to tell them what that meant to him, but he simply could not find words important enough.

Through the silence came the muffled sounds of Mrs. Weasley shouting from four floors below.

"Ginny's probably left a speck of dust on a poxy napkin ring," said Ron. "I dunno why the Delacours have got to come two days before the wedding."

"Fleur's sister's a bridesmaid, she needs to be here for the rehearsal, and she's too young to come on her own," said Hermione, as she pored indecisively over *Break with a Banshee.*

"Well, guests aren't going to help Mum's stress levels," said Ron.

"What we really need to decide," said Hermione, tossing *Defensive Magical Theory* into the bin without a second glance and picking up *An Appraisal of Magical Education in Europe,* "is where we're going after we leave here. I know you said you wanted to go to Godric's Hollow first, Harry, and I understand why, but . . . well . . . shouldn't we make the Horcruxes our priority?"

"If we knew where any of the Horcruxes were, I'd agree with you," said Harry, who did not believe that Hermione really understood his desire to return to Godric's Hollow. His parents' graves were only part of the attraction: He had a strong, though inexplicable, feeling that the place held answers for him. Perhaps it was simply because it was there that he had survived Voldemort's Killing Curse; now that he was facing the challenge of repeating the feat, Harry was drawn to the place where it had happened, wanting to understand.

"Don't you think there's a possibility that Voldemort's keeping a watch on Godric's Hollow?" Hermione asked. "He might expect you to go back and visit your parents' graves once you're free to go wherever you like?"

This had not occurred to Harry. While he struggled to find a counterargument, Ron spoke up, evidently following his own train of thought.

"This R.A.B. person," he said. "You know, the one who stole the real locket?"

Hermione nodded.

"He said in his note he was going to destroy it, didn't he?"

Harry dragged his rucksack toward him and pulled out the fake Horcrux in which R.A.B.'s note was still folded.

"'*I have stolen the real Horcrux and intend to destroy it as soon as I can,*'" Harry read out.

"Well, what if he *did* finish it off?" said Ron.

"Or she," interposed Hermione.

"Whichever," said Ron, "it'd be one less for us to do!"

"Yes, but we're still going to have to try and trace the real locket, aren't we?" said Hermione, "to find out whether or not it's destroyed."

"And once we get hold of it, how *do* you destroy a Horcrux?" asked Ron.

"Well," said Hermione, "I've been researching that."

"How?" asked Harry. "I didn't think there were any books on Horcruxes in the library?"

"There weren't," said Hermione, who had turned pink. "Dumbledore removed them all, but he — he didn't destroy them."

Ron sat up straight, wide-eyed.

"How in the name of Merlin's pants have you managed to get your hands on those Horcrux books?"

"It — it wasn't stealing!" said Hermione, looking from Harry to Ron with a kind of desperation. "They were still library books, even if Dumbledore had taken them off the shelves. Anyway, if he *really* didn't want anyone to get at them, I'm sure he would have made it much harder to —"

"Get to the point!" said Ron.

"Well . . . it was easy," said Hermione in a small voice. "I just did a Summoning Charm. You know — Accio. And — they zoomed out of Dumbledore's study window right into the girls' dormitory."

"But when did you do this?" Harry asked, regarding Hermione with a mixture of admiration and incredulity.

"Just after his — Dumbledore's — funeral," said Hermione in an even smaller voice. "Right after we agreed we'd leave school and go and look for the Horcruxes. When I went back upstairs to get my things it — it just occurred to me that the more we knew about them, the better it would be . . . and I was alone in there . . . so I tried . . . and it worked. They flew straight in through the open window and I — I packed them."

She swallowed and then said imploringly, "I can't believe Dumbledore would have been angry, it's not as though we're going to use the information to make a Horcrux, is it?"

"Can you hear us complaining?" said Ron. "Where are these books anyway?"

Hermione rummaged for a moment and then extracted from the pile a large volume, bound in faded black leather. She looked a little nauseated and held it as gingerly as if it were something recently dead.

"This is the one that gives explicit instructions on how to make a Horcrux. *Secrets of the Darkest Art* — it's a horrible book, really awful, full of evil magic. I wonder when Dumbledore removed it from the library. . . . If he didn't do it until he was headmaster, I bet Voldemort got all the instruction he needed from here."

"Why did he have to ask Slughorn how to make a Horcrux, then, if he'd already read that?" asked Ron.

"He only approached Slughorn to find out what would happen if you split your soul into seven," said Harry. "Dumbledore was sure Riddle already knew how to make a Horcrux by the time he asked Slughorn about them. I think you're right, Hermione, that could easily have been where he got the information."

"And the more I've read about them," said Hermione, "the more horrible they seem, and the less I can believe that he actually made six. It warns in this book how unstable you make the rest of your soul by ripping it, and that's just by making one Horcrux!"

Harry remembered what Dumbledore had said about Voldemort moving beyond "usual evil."

"Isn't there any way of putting yourself back together?" Ron asked.

"Yes," said Hermione with a hollow smile, "but it would be excruciatingly painful."

"Why? How do you do it?" asked Harry.

"Remorse," said Hermione. "You've got to really feel what you've done. There's a footnote. Apparently the pain of it can destroy you. I can't see Voldemort attempting it somehow, can you?"

"No," said Ron, before Harry could answer. "So does it say how to destroy Horcruxes in that book?"

"Yes," said Hermione, now turning the fragile pages as if examining rotting entrails, "because it warns Dark wizards how strong they have to make the enchantments on them. From all that I've read, what Harry did to Riddle's diary was one of the few really foolproof ways of destroying a Horcrux."

"What, stabbing it with a basilisk fang?" asked Harry.

"Oh well, lucky we've got such a large supply of basilisk fangs, then," said Ron. "I was wondering what we were going to do with them."

"It doesn't have to be a basilisk fang," said Hermione patiently. "It has to be something so destructive that the Horcrux can't repair itself. Basilisk venom only has one antidote, and it's incredibly rare —"

"— phoenix tears," said Harry, nodding.

"Exactly," said Hermione. "Our problem is that there are very few substances as destructive as basilisk venom, and they're all dangerous to carry around with you. That's a problem we're going to have to solve, though, because ripping, smashing, or crushing a Horcrux won't do the trick. You've got to put it beyond magical repair."

"But even if we wreck the thing it lives in," said Ron, "why can't the bit of soul in it just go and live in something else?"

"Because a Horcrux is the complete opposite of a human being."

Seeing that Harry and Ron looked thoroughly confused, Hermione hurried on, "Look, if I picked up a sword right now, Ron, and ran you through with it, I wouldn't damage your soul at all."

"Which would be a real comfort to me, I'm sure," said Ron. Harry laughed.

"It should be, actually! But my point is that whatever happens to your body, your soul will survive, untouched," said Hermione. "But it's the other way round with a Horcrux. The fragment of soul inside it depends on its container, its enchanted body, for survival. It can't exist without it."

"That diary sort of died when I stabbed it," said Harry, remembering ink pouring like blood from the punctured pages, and the screams of the piece of Voldemort's soul as it vanished.

"And once the diary was properly destroyed, the bit of soul trapped in it could no longer exist. Ginny tried to get rid of the diary before you did, flushing it away, but obviously it came back good as new."

"Hang on," said Ron, frowning. "The bit of soul in that diary was possessing Ginny, wasn't it? How does that work, then?"

"While the magical container is still intact, the bit of soul inside it can flit in and out of someone if they get too close to the object. I don't mean holding it for too long, it's nothing to do with touching it," she added before Ron could speak. "I mean close emotionally. Ginny poured her heart out into that diary, she made herself incredibly vulnerable. You're in trouble if you get too fond of or dependent on the Horcrux."

"I wonder how Dumbledore destroyed the ring?" said Harry. "Why didn't I ask him? I never really . . ."

His voice tailed away: He was thinking of all the things he should have asked Dumbledore, and of how, since the headmaster had died, it seemed to Harry that he had wasted so many opportunities when Dumbledore had been alive, to find out more . . . to find out everything. . . .

The silence was shattered as the bedroom door flew open with a wall-shaking crash. Hermione shrieked and dropped *Secrets of the Darkest Art*; Crookshanks streaked under the bed, hissing indignantly; Ron jumped off the bed, skidded on a discarded Chocolate Frog wrapper, and smacked his head on the opposite wall; and Harry instinctively dived for his wand before realizing that he was looking up at Mrs. Weasley, whose hair was disheveled and whose face was contorted with rage.

"I'm so sorry to break up this cozy little gathering," she said, her voice trembling. "I'm sure you all need your rest . . . but there are wedding presents stacked in my room that need sorting out and I was under the impression that you had agreed to help."

"Oh yes," said Hermione, looking terrified as she leapt to her feet, sending books flying in every direction, "we will . . . we're sorry . . ."

With an anguished look at Harry and Ron, Hermione hurried out of the room after Mrs. Weasley.

"It's like being a house-elf," complained Ron in an undertone, still massaging his head as he and Harry followed. "Except without the job satisfaction. The sooner this wedding's over, the happier I'll be."

"Yeah," said Harry, "then we'll have nothing to do except find Horcruxes. . . . It'll be like a holiday, won't it?"

Ron started to laugh, but at the sight of the enormous pile of wedding presents waiting for them in Mrs. Weasley's room, stopped quite abruptly.

The Delacours arrived the following morning at eleven o'clock. Harry, Ron, Hermione, and Ginny were feeling quite resentful toward Fleur's family by this time, and it was with ill grace that Ron stumped back upstairs to put on matching socks, and Harry attempted to flatten his hair. Once they had all been deemed smart enough, they trooped out into the sunny backyard to await the visitors.

Harry had never seen the place looking so tidy. The rusty cauldrons and old Wellington boots that usually littered the steps by the back door were gone, replaced by two new Flutterby bushes standing either side of the door in large pots; though there was no breeze, the leaves waved lazily, giving an attractive rippling effect. The chickens had been shut away, the yard had been swept, and the nearby garden had been pruned, plucked, and generally spruced up, although Harry, who liked it in its overgrown state, thought that it looked rather forlorn without its usual contingent of capering gnomes.

He had lost track of how many security enchantments had been placed upon the Burrow by both the Order and the Ministry; all he knew was that it was no longer possible for anybody to travel by magic directly into the place. Mr. Weasley had therefore gone to meet the Delacours on top of a nearby hill, where they were to arrive by Portkey. The first sound of their approach was an unusually high-pitched laugh, which turned out to be coming from Mr. Weasley, who appeared at the gate moments later, laden with luggage and leading a beautiful blonde woman in long, leaf-green robes, who could only be Fleur's mother.

"Maman!" cried Fleur, rushing forward to embrace her. "Papa!"

Monsieur Delacour was nowhere near as attractive as his wife; he was a head shorter and extremely plump, with a little, pointed black beard. However, he looked good-natured. Bouncing toward Mrs. Weasley on high-heeled boots, he kissed her twice on each cheek, leaving her flustered.

"You 'ave been to much trouble," he said in a deep voice. "Fleur tells us you 'ave been working very 'ard."

"Oh, it's been nothing, nothing!" trilled Mrs. Weasley. "No trouble at all!"

Ron relieved his feelings by aiming a kick at a gnome who was peering out from behind one of the new Flutterby bushes.

"Dear lady!" said Monsieur Delacour, still holding Mrs. Weasley's hand between his own two plump ones and beaming. "We are most honored at the approaching union of our two families! Let me present my wife, Apolline."

Madame Delacour glided forward and stooped to kiss Mrs. Weasley too.

"Enchantée," she said. "Your 'usband 'as been telling us such amusing stories!"

Mr. Weasley gave a maniacal laugh; Mrs. Weasley threw him a look, upon which he became immediately silent and assumed an expression appropriate to the sickbed of a close friend.

"And, of course, you 'ave met my leetle daughter, Gabrielle!" said Monsieur Delacour. Gabrielle was Fleur in miniature; eleven years old, with waist-length hair of pure, silvery blonde, she gave Mrs. Weasley a dazzling smile and hugged her, then threw Harry a glowing look, batting her eyelashes. Ginny cleared her throat loudly.

"Well, come in, do!" said Mrs. Weasley brightly, and she ushered the Delacours into the house, with many "No, please!"s and "After you!"s and "Not at all!"s.

The Delacours, it soon transpired, were helpful, pleasant guests. They were pleased with everything and keen to assist with the preparations for the wedding. Monsieur Delacour pronounced everything from the seating plan to the bridesmaids' shoes *"Charmant!"* Madame Delacour was most accomplished at household spells and had the oven properly cleaned in a trice; Gabrielle followed her elder sister around, trying to assist in any way she could and jabbering away in rapid French.

On the downside, the Burrow was not built to accommodate so many people. Mr. and Mrs. Weasley were now sleeping in the sitting room, having shouted down Monsieur and Madame Delacour's protests and insisted they take their bedroom. Gabrielle was sleeping with Fleur in Percy's old room, and Bill would be sharing with Charlie, his best man, once Charlie arrived from Romania. Opportunities to make plans together became virtually nonexistent, and it was in desperation that Harry, Ron, and Hermione took to volunteering to feed the chickens just to escape the overcrowded house.

"But she *still* won't leave us alone!" snarled Ron, as their second attempt at a meeting in the yard was foiled by the appearance of Mrs. Weasley carrying a large basket of laundry in her arms.

"Oh, good, you've fed the chickens," she called as she approached them. "We'd better shut them away again before the men arrive tomorrow . . . to put up the tent for the wedding," she explained, pausing to lean against the henhouse. She looked exhausted. "Millamant's Magic Marquees . . . they're very good, Bill's escorting them. . . . You'd better stay inside while they're here, Harry. I must say it does complicate organizing a wedding, having all these security spells around the place."

"I'm sorry," said Harry humbly.

"Oh, don't be silly, dear!" said Mrs. Weasley at once. "I didn't mean — well, your safety's much more important! Actually, I've been wanting to ask you how you want to celebrate your birthday, Harry. Seventeen, after all, it's an important day. . . ."

"I don't want a fuss," said Harry quickly, envisaging the additional strain this would put on them all. "Really, Mrs. Weasley, just a normal dinner would be fine. . . . It's the day before the wedding. . . ."

"Oh, well, if you're sure, dear. I'll invite Remus and Tonks, shall I? And how about Hagrid?"

"That'd be great," said Harry. "But please don't go to loads of trouble."

"Not at all, not at all . . . It's no trouble. . . ."

She looked at him, a long, searching look, then smiled a little sadly, straightened up, and walked away. Harry watched as she waved her wand near the washing line, and the damp clothes rose into the air to hang themselves up, and suddenly he felt a great wave of remorse for the inconvenience and the pain he was giving her.

THE WILL OF
ALBUS DUMBLEDORE

He was walking along a mountain road in the cool blue light of dawn. Far below, swathed in mist, was the shadow of a small town. Was the man he sought down there, the man he needed so badly he could think of little else, the man who held the answer, the answer to his problem . . . ?

"Oi, wake up."

Harry opened his eyes. He was lying again on the camp bed in Ron's dingy attic room. The sun had not yet risen and the room was still shadowy. Pigwidgeon was asleep with his head under his tiny wing. The scar on Harry's forehead was prickling.

"You were muttering in your sleep."

"Was I?"

"Yeah. 'Gregorovitch.' You kept saying 'Gregorovitch.'"

Harry was not wearing his glasses; Ron's face appeared slightly blurred.

"Who's Gregorovitch?"

"I dunno, do I? You were the one saying it."

Harry rubbed his forehead, thinking. He had a vague idea he had heard the name before, but he could not think where.

"I think Voldemort's looking for him."

"Poor bloke," said Ron fervently.

Harry sat up, still rubbing his scar, now wide awake. He tried to remember exactly what he had seen in the dream, but all that came back was a mountainous horizon and the outline of the little village cradled in a deep valley.

"I think he's abroad."

"Who, Gregorovitch?"

"Voldemort. I think he's somewhere abroad, looking for Gregorovitch. It didn't look like anywhere in Britain."

"You reckon you were seeing into his mind again?"

Ron sounded worried.

"Do me a favor and don't tell Hermione," said Harry. "Although how she expects me to stop seeing stuff in my sleep . . ."

He gazed up at little Pigwidgeon's cage, thinking . . . Why was the name "Gregorovitch" familiar?

"I think," he said slowly, "he's got something to do with Quidditch. There's some connection, but I can't — I can't think what it is."

"Quidditch?" said Ron. "Sure you're not thinking of Gorgovitch?"

"Who?"

"Dragomir Gorgovitch, Chaser, transferred to the Chudley Cannons for a record fee two years ago. Record holder for most Quaffle drops in a season."

"No," said Harry. "I'm definitely not thinking of Gorgovitch."

"I try not to either," said Ron. "Well, happy birthday anyway."

"Wow — that's right, I forgot! I'm seventeen!"

Harry seized the wand lying beside his camp bed, pointed it at the cluttered desk where he had left his glasses, and said, *"Accio Glasses!"* Although they were only around a foot away, there was something immensely satisfying about seeing them zoom toward him, at least until they poked him in the eye.

"Slick," snorted Ron.

Reveling in the removal of his Trace, Harry sent Ron's possessions flying around the room, causing Pigwidgeon to wake up and flutter excitedly around his cage. Harry also tried tying the laces of his trainers by magic (the resultant knot took several minutes to untie by hand) and, purely for the pleasure of it, turned the orange robes on Ron's Chudley Cannons posters bright blue.

"I'd do your fly by hand, though," Ron advised Harry, sniggering when Harry immediately checked it. "Here's your present. Unwrap it up here, it's not for my mother's eyes."

"A book?" said Harry as he took the rectangular parcel. "Bit of a departure from tradition, isn't it?"

"This isn't your average book," said Ron. "It's pure gold: *Twelve Fail-Safe Ways to Charm Witches.* Explains everything you need to know about girls. If only I'd had this last year I'd have known exactly how to get rid of Lavender and I would've known how to get going with . . . Well, Fred and George gave me a copy, and I've learned a lot. You'd be surprised, it's not all about wandwork, either."

When they arrived in the kitchen they found a pile of presents waiting on the table. Bill and Monsieur Delacour were finishing their breakfasts, while Mrs. Weasley stood chatting to them over the frying pan.

"Arthur told me to wish you a happy seventeenth, Harry," said Mrs. Weasley, beaming at him. "He had to leave early for work, but he'll be back for dinner. That's our present on top."

Harry sat down, took the square parcel she had indicated, and unwrapped it. Inside was a watch very like the one Mr. and Mrs. Weasley had given Ron for his seventeenth; it was gold, with stars circling around the face instead of hands.

"It's traditional to give a wizard a watch when he comes of age," said Mrs. Weasley, watching him anxiously from beside the cooker. "I'm afraid that one isn't new like Ron's, it was actually my brother Fabian's and he wasn't terribly careful with his possessions, it's a bit dented on the back, but —"

The rest of her speech was lost; Harry had got up and hugged her. He tried to put a lot of unsaid things into the hug and perhaps she understood them, because she patted his cheek clumsily when he released her, then waved her wand in a slightly random way, causing half a pack of bacon to flop out of the frying pan onto the floor.

"Happy birthday, Harry!" said Hermione, hurrying into the kitchen and adding her own present to the top of the pile. "It's not much, but I hope you like it. What did you get him?" she added to Ron, who seemed not to hear her.

"Come on, then, open Hermione's!" said Ron.

She had bought him a new Sneakoscope. The other packages contained an enchanted razor from Bill and Fleur ("Ah yes, zis will give you ze smoothest shave you will ever 'ave," Monsieur Delacour assured him, "but you must tell it clearly what you want . . . ozzerwise you might find you 'ave a leetle less hair zan you would like. . . ."), chocolates from the Delacours, and an enormous box of the latest Weasleys' Wizard Wheezes merchandise from Fred and George.

Harry, Ron, and Hermione did not linger at the table, as the arrival of Madame Delacour, Fleur, and Gabrielle made the kitchen uncomfortably crowded.

"I'll pack these for you," Hermione said brightly, taking Harry's presents out of his arms as the three of them headed back upstairs. "I'm nearly done, I'm just waiting for the rest of your underpants to come out of the wash, Ron —"

Ron's splutter was interrupted by the opening of a door on the first-floor landing.

"Harry, will you come in here a moment?"

It was Ginny. Ron came to an abrupt halt, but Hermione took him by the elbow and tugged him on up the stairs. Feeling nervous, Harry followed Ginny into her room.

He had never been inside it before. It was small, but bright. There was a large poster of the Wizarding band the Weird Sisters on one wall, and a picture of Gwenog Jones, Captain of the all-witch Quidditch team the Holyhead Harpies, on the other. A desk stood facing the open window, which looked out over the orchard where he and Ginny had once played two-a-side Quidditch with Ron and Hermione, and which now housed a large, pearly white marquee. The golden flag on top was level with Ginny's window.

Ginny looked up into Harry's face, took a deep breath, and said, "Happy seventeenth."

"Yeah . . . thanks."

She was looking at him steadily; he, however, found it difficult to look back at her; it was like gazing into a brilliant light.

"Nice view," he said feebly, pointing toward the window.

She ignored this. He could not blame her.

"I couldn't think what to get you," she said.

"You didn't have to get me anything."

She disregarded this too.

"I didn't know what would be useful. Nothing too big, because you wouldn't be able to take it with you."

He chanced a glance at her. She was not tearful; that was one of the many wonderful things about Ginny, she was rarely weepy. He had sometimes thought that having six brothers must have toughened her up.

She took a step closer to him.

"So then I thought, I'd like you to have something to remember me by, you know, if you meet some veela when you're off doing whatever you're doing."

"I think dating opportunities are going to be pretty thin on the ground, to be honest."

"There's the silver lining I've been looking for," she whispered, and then she was kissing him as she had never kissed him before, and Harry was kissing her back, and it was blissful oblivion, better than firewhisky; she was the only real thing in the world, Ginny, the feel of her, one hand at her back and one in her long, sweet-smelling hair —

The door banged open behind them and they jumped apart.

"Oh," said Ron pointedly. "Sorry."

"Ron!" Hermione was just behind him, slightly out of breath. There was a strained silence, then Ginny said in a flat little voice,

"Well, happy birthday anyway, Harry."

Ron's ears were scarlet; Hermione looked nervous. Harry wanted to slam the door in their faces, but it felt as though a cold draft had entered the room when the door opened, and his shining moment had popped like a soap bubble. All the reasons for ending his relationship with Ginny, for staying well away from her, seemed to have slunk inside the room with Ron, and all happy forgetfulness was gone.

He looked at Ginny, wanting to say something, though he hardly knew what, but she had turned her back on him. He thought that she might have succumbed, for once, to tears. He could not do anything to comfort her in front of Ron.

"I'll see you later," he said, and followed the other two out of the bedroom.

Ron marched downstairs, through the still-crowded kitchen and into the yard, and Harry kept pace with him all the way, Hermione trotting along behind them looking scared.

Once he reached the seclusion of the freshly mown lawn, Ron rounded on Harry.

"You ditched her. What are you doing now, messing her around?"

"I'm not messing her around," said Harry, as Hermione caught up with them.

"Ron —"

But Ron held up a hand to silence her.

"She was really cut up when you ended it —"

"So was I. You know why I stopped it, and it wasn't because I wanted to."

"Yeah, but you go snogging her now and she's just going to get her hopes up again —"

"She's not an idiot, she knows it can't happen, she's not expecting us to — to end up married, or —"

As he said it, a vivid picture formed in Harry's mind of Ginny in a white dress, marrying a tall, faceless, and unpleasant stranger.

In one spiraling moment it seemed to hit him: Her future was free and unencumbered, whereas his . . . he could see nothing but Voldemort ahead.

"If you keep groping her every chance you get —"

"It won't happen again," said Harry harshly. The day was cloudless, but he felt as though the sun had gone in. "Okay?"

Ron looked half resentful, half sheepish; he rocked backward and forward on his feet for a moment, then said, "Right then, well, that's . . . yeah."

Ginny did not seek another one-to-one meeting with Harry for the rest of the day, nor by any look or gesture did she show that they had shared more than polite conversation in her room. Nevertheless, Charlie's arrival came as a relief to Harry. It provided a distraction, watching Mrs. Weasley force Charlie into a chair, raise her wand threateningly, and announce that he was about to get a proper haircut.

As Harry's birthday dinner would have stretched the Burrow's kitchen to breaking point even before the arrival of Charlie, Lupin, Tonks, and Hagrid, several tables were placed end to end in the garden. Fred and George bewitched a number of purple lanterns, all emblazoned with a large number 17, to hang in midair over the guests. Thanks to Mrs. Weasley's ministrations, George's wound was neat and clean, but Harry was not yet used to the dark hole in the side of his head, despite the twins' many jokes about it.

Hermione made purple and gold streamers erupt from the end of her wand and drape themselves artistically over the trees and bushes.

"Nice," said Ron, as with one final flourish of her wand, Hermione turned the leaves on the crabapple tree to gold. "You've really got an eye for that sort of thing."

"Thank you, Ron!" said Hermione, looking both pleased and a little confused. Harry turned away, smiling to himself. He had a funny notion that he would find a chapter on compliments when he found time to peruse his copy of *Twelve Fail-Safe Ways to Charm Witches*; he caught Ginny's eye and grinned at her before remembering his promise to Ron and hurriedly striking up a conversation with Monsieur Delacour.

"Out of the way, out of the way!" sang Mrs. Weasley, coming through the gate with what appeared to be a giant, beach-ball-sized Snitch floating in front of her. Seconds later Harry realized that it was his birthday cake, which Mrs. Weasley was suspending with her wand, rather than risk carrying it over the uneven ground. When the cake had finally landed in the middle of the table, Harry said,

"That looks amazing, Mrs. Weasley."

"Oh, it's nothing, dear," she said fondly. Over her shoulder, Ron gave Harry the thumbs-up and mouthed, *Good one.*

By seven o'clock all the guests had arrived, led into the house by Fred and George, who had waited for them at the end of the lane. Hagrid had honored the occasion by wearing his best, and horrible, hairy brown suit. Although Lupin smiled as he shook Harry's hand, Harry thought he looked rather unhappy. It was all very odd; Tonks, beside him, looked simply radiant.

"Happy birthday, Harry," she said, hugging him tightly.

"Seventeen, eh!" said Hagrid as he accepted a bucket-sized glass of wine from Fred. "Six years ter the day since we met, Harry, d'yeh remember it?"

"Vaguely," said Harry, grinning up at him. "Didn't you smash down the front door, give Dudley a pig's tail, and tell me I was a wizard?"

"I forge' the details," Hagrid chortled. "All righ', Ron, Hermione?"

"We're fine," said Hermione. "How are you?"

"Ar, not bad. Bin busy, we got some newborn unicorns, I'll show yeh when yeh get back —" Harry avoided Ron's and Hermione's gazes as Hagrid rummaged in his pocket. "Here, Harry — couldn' think what ter get yeh, but then I remembered this." He pulled out a small, slightly furry drawstring pouch with a long string, evidently intended to be worn around the neck. "Mokeskin. Hide anythin' in there an' no one but the owner can get it out. They're rare, them."

"Hagrid, thanks!"

"'S'nothin'," said Hagrid with a wave of a dustbin-lid-sized hand. "An' there's Charlie! Always liked him — hey! Charlie!"

Charlie approached, running his hand slightly ruefully over his new, brutally short haircut. He was shorter than Ron, thickset, with a number of burns and scratches up his muscley arms.

"Hi, Hagrid, how's it going?"

"Bin meanin' ter write fer ages. How's Norbert doin'?"

"Norbert?" Charlie laughed. "The Norwegian Ridgeback? We call her Norberta now."

"Wha — Norbert's a girl?"

"Oh yeah," said Charlie.

"How can you tell?" asked Hermione.

"They're a lot more vicious," said Charlie. He looked over his shoulder and dropped his voice. "Wish Dad would hurry up and get here. Mum's getting edgy."

They all looked over at Mrs. Weasley. She was trying to talk to Madame Delacour while glancing repeatedly at the gate.

"I think we'd better start without Arthur," she called to the garden at large after a moment or two. "He must have been held up at — oh!"

They all saw it at the same time: a streak of light that came flying across the yard and onto the table, where it resolved itself into a bright silver weasel, which stood on its hind legs and spoke with Mr. Weasley's voice.

"Minister of Magic coming with me."

The Patronus dissolved into thin air, leaving Fleur's family peering in astonishment at the place where it had vanished.

"We shouldn't be here," said Lupin at once. "Harry — I'm sorry — I'll explain another time —"

He seized Tonks's wrist and pulled her away; they reached the fence, climbed over it, and vanished from sight. Mrs. Weasley looked bewildered.

"The Minister — but why — ? I don't understand —"

But there was no time to discuss the matter; a second later, Mr. Weasley had appeared out of thin air at the gate, accompanied by Rufus Scrimgeour, instantly recognizable by his mane of grizzled hair.

The two newcomers marched across the yard toward the garden and the lantern-lit table, where everybody sat in silence, watching them draw closer. As Scrimgeour came within range of the lantern light, Harry saw that he looked much older than the last time they had met, scraggy and grim.

"Sorry to intrude," said Scrimgeour, as he limped to a halt before the table. "Especially as I can see that I am gate-crashing a party."

His eyes lingered for a moment on the giant Snitch cake.

"Many happy returns."

"Thanks," said Harry.

"I require a private word with you," Scrimgeour went on. "Also with Mr. Ronald Weasley and Miss Hermione Granger."

"Us?" said Ron, sounding surprised. "Why us?"

"I shall tell you that when we are somewhere more private," said Scrimgeour. "Is there such a place?" he demanded of Mr. Weasley.

"Yes, of course," said Mr. Weasley, who looked nervous. "The, er, sitting room, why don't you use that?"

"You can lead the way," Scrimgeour said to Ron. "There will be no need for you to accompany us, Arthur."

Harry saw Mr. Weasley exchange a worried look with Mrs. Weasley as he, Ron, and Hermione stood up. As they led the way back to the house in silence, Harry knew that the other two were thinking the same as he was: Scrimgeour must, somehow, have learned that the three of them were planning to drop out of Hogwarts.

Scrimgeour did not speak as they all passed through the messy kitchen and into the Burrow's sitting room. Although the garden had been full of soft golden evening light, it was already dark in here: Harry flicked his wand at the oil lamps as he entered and they illuminated the shabby but cozy room. Scrimgeour sat himself in the sagging armchair that Mr. Weasley normally occupied, leaving Harry, Ron, and Hermione to squeeze side by side onto the sofa. Once they had done so, Scrimgeour spoke.

"I have some questions for the three of you, and I think it will be best if we do it individually. If you two" — he pointed at Harry and Hermione — "can wait upstairs, I will start with Ronald."

"We're not going anywhere," said Harry, while Hermione nodded vigorously. "You can speak to us together, or not at all."

Scrimgeour gave Harry a cold, appraising look. Harry had the impression that the Minister was wondering whether it was worthwhile opening hostilities this early.

"Very well then, together," he said, shrugging. He cleared his throat. "I am here, as I'm sure you know, because of Albus Dumbledore's will."

Harry, Ron, and Hermione looked at one another.

"A surprise, apparently! You were not aware then that Dumbledore had left you anything?"

"A-all of us?" said Ron. "Me and Hermione too?"

"Yes, all of —"

But Harry interrupted.

"Dumbledore died over a month ago. Why has it taken this long to give us what he left us?"

"Isn't it obvious?" said Hermione, before Scrimgeour could answer. "They wanted to examine whatever he's left us. You had no right to do that!" she said, and her voice trembled slightly.

"I had every right," said Scrimgeour dismissively. "The Decree for Justifiable Confiscation gives the Ministry the power to confiscate the contents of a will —"

"That law was created to stop wizards passing on Dark artifacts," said Hermione, "and the Ministry is supposed to have powerful evidence that the deceased's possessions are illegal before seizing them! Are you telling me that you thought Dumbledore was trying to pass us something cursed?"

"Are you planning to follow a career in Magical Law, Miss Granger?" asked Scrimgeour.

"No, I'm not," retorted Hermione. "I'm hoping to do some good in the world!"

Ron laughed. Scrimgeour's eyes flickered toward him and away again as Harry spoke.

"So why have you decided to let us have our things now? Can't think of a pretext to keep them?"

"No, it'll be because the thirty-one days are up," said Hermione at once. "They can't keep the objects longer than that unless they can prove they're dangerous. Right?"

"Would you say you were close to Dumbledore, Ronald?" asked Scrimgeour, ignoring Hermione. Ron looked startled.

"Me? Not — not really . . . It was always Harry who . . ."

Ron looked around at Harry and Hermione, to see Hermione giving him a *stop-talking-now!* sort of look, but the damage was done: Scrimgeour looked as though he had heard exactly what he had expected, and wanted, to hear. He swooped like a bird of prey upon Ron's answer.

"If you were not very close to Dumbledore, how do you account for the fact that he remembered you in his will? He made exceptionally few personal bequests. The vast majority of his possessions — his private library, his magical instruments, and other personal effects — were left to Hogwarts. Why do you think you were singled out?"

"I . . . dunno," said Ron. "I . . . when I say we weren't close . . . I mean, I think he liked me. . . ."

"You're being modest, Ron," said Hermione. "Dumbledore was very fond of you."

This was stretching the truth to breaking point; as far as Harry knew, Ron and Dumbledore had never been alone together, and direct contact between them had been negligible. However, Scrimgeour did not seem to be listening. He put his hand inside his cloak and drew out a drawstring pouch much larger than the one Hagrid had given Harry. From it, he removed a scroll of parchment which he unrolled and read aloud.

"'The Last Will and Testament of Albus Percival Wulfric Brian Dumbledore' . . . Yes, here we are. . . . 'To Ronald Bilius Weasley, I leave my Deluminator, in the hope that he will remember me when he uses it.'"

Scrimgeour took from the bag an object that Harry had seen before: It looked something like a silver cigarette lighter, but it had, he knew, the power to suck all light from a place, and restore it, with a simple click. Scrimgeour leaned forward and passed the Deluminator to Ron, who took it and turned it over in his fingers, looking stunned.

"That is a valuable object," said Scrimgeour, watching Ron. "It may even be unique. Certainly it is of Dumbledore's own design. Why would he have left you an item so rare?"

Ron shook his head, looking bewildered.

"Dumbledore must have taught thousands of students," Scrimgeour persevered. "Yet the only ones he remembered in his will are you three. Why is that? To what use did he think you would put his Deluminator, Mr. Weasley?"

"Put out lights, I s'pose," mumbled Ron. "What else could I do with it?"

Evidently Scrimgeour had no suggestions. After squinting at Ron for a moment or two, he turned back to Dumbledore's will.

"'To Miss Hermione Jean Granger, I leave my copy of The Tales of Beedle the Bard, *in the hope that she will find it entertaining and instructive.'"*

Scrimgeour now pulled out of the bag a small book that looked as ancient as the copy of *Secrets of the Darkest Art* upstairs. Its binding was stained and peeling in places. Hermione took it from Scrimgeour without a word. She held the book in her lap and gazed at it. Harry saw that the title was in runes; he had never learned to read them. As he looked, a tear splashed onto the embossed symbols.

"Why do you think Dumbledore left you that book, Miss Granger?" asked Scrimgeour.

"He . . . he knew I liked books," said Hermione in a thick voice, mopping her eyes with her sleeve.

"But why that particular book?"

"I don't know. He must have thought I'd enjoy it."

"Did you ever discuss codes, or any means of passing secret messages, with Dumbledore?"

"No, I didn't," said Hermione, still wiping her eyes on her sleeve. "And if the Ministry hasn't found any hidden codes in this book in thirty-one days, I doubt that I will."

She suppressed a sob. They were wedged together so tightly that Ron had difficulty extracting his arm to put it around Hermione's shoulders. Scrimgeour turned back to the will.

"*'To Harry James Potter,'*" he read, and Harry's insides contracted with a sudden excitement, "*'I leave the Snitch he caught in his first Quidditch match at Hogwarts, as a reminder of the rewards of perseverance and skill.'"*

As Scrimgeour pulled out the tiny, walnut-sized golden ball, its silver wings fluttered rather feebly, and Harry could not help feeling a definite sense of anticlimax.

"Why did Dumbledore leave you this Snitch?" asked Scrimgeour.

"No idea," said Harry. "For the reasons you just read out, I suppose . . . to remind me what you can get if you . . . persevere and whatever it was."

"You think this a mere symbolic keepsake, then?"

"I suppose so," said Harry. "What else could it be?"

"I'm asking the questions," said Scrimgeour, shifting his chair a little closer to the sofa. Dusk was really falling outside now; the marquee beyond the windows towered ghostly white over the hedge.

"I notice that your birthday cake is in the shape of a Snitch," Scrimgeour said to Harry. "Why is that?"

Hermione laughed derisively.

"Oh, it can't be a reference to the fact Harry's a great Seeker, that's way too obvious," she said. "There must be a secret message from Dumbledore hidden in the icing!"

"I don't think there's anything hidden in the icing," said Scrimgeour, "but a Snitch would be a very good hiding place for a small object. You know why, I'm sure?"

Harry shrugged. Hermione, however, answered: Harry thought that answering questions correctly was such a deeply ingrained habit she could not suppress the urge.

"Because Snitches have flesh memories," she said.

"What?" said Harry and Ron together; both considered Hermione's Quidditch knowledge negligible.

"Correct," said Scrimgeour. "A Snitch is not touched by bare skin before it is released, not even by the maker, who wears gloves. It carries an enchantment by which it can identify the first human to lay hands upon it, in case of a disputed capture. This Snitch" — he held up the tiny golden ball — "will remember your touch, Potter.

It occurs to me that Dumbledore, who had prodigious magical skill, whatever his other faults, might have enchanted this Snitch so that it will open only for you."

Harry's heart was beating rather fast. He was sure that Scrimgeour was right. How could he avoid taking the Snitch with his bare hand in front of the Minister?

"You don't say anything," said Scrimgeour. "Perhaps you already know what the Snitch contains?"

"No," said Harry, still wondering how he could appear to touch the Snitch without really doing so. If only he knew Legilimency, really knew it, and could read Hermione's mind; he could practically hear her brain whirring beside him.

"Take it," said Scrimgeour quietly.

Harry met the Minister's yellow eyes and knew he had no option but to obey. He held out his hand, and Scrimgeour leaned forward again and placed the Snitch, slowly and deliberately, into Harry's palm.

Nothing happened. As Harry's fingers closed around the Snitch, its tired wings fluttered and were still. Scrimgeour, Ron, and Hermione continued to gaze avidly at the now partially concealed ball, as if still hoping it might transform in some way.

"That was dramatic," said Harry coolly. Both Ron and Hermione laughed.

"That's all, then, is it?" asked Hermione, making to prise herself off the sofa.

"Not quite," said Scrimgeour, who looked bad-tempered now. "Dumbledore left you a second bequest, Potter."

"What is it?" asked Harry, excitement rekindling.

Scrimgeour did not bother to read from the will this time.

"The sword of Godric Gryffindor," he said.

Hermione and Ron both stiffened. Harry looked around for a sign of the ruby-encrusted hilt, but Scrimgeour did not pull the sword from the leather pouch, which in any case looked much too small to contain it.

"So where is it?" Harry asked suspiciously.

"Unfortunately," said Scrimgeour, "that sword was not Dumbledore's to give away. The sword of Godric Gryffindor is an important historical artifact, and as such, belongs —"

"It belongs to Harry!" said Hermione hotly. "It chose him, he was the one who found it, it came to him out of the Sorting Hat —"

"According to reliable historical sources, the sword may present itself to any worthy Gryffindor," said Scrimgeour. "That does not make it the exclusive property of Mr. Potter, whatever Dumbledore may have decided." Scrimgeour scratched his badly shaven cheek, scrutinizing Harry. "Why do you think — ?"

"— Dumbledore wanted to give me the sword?" said Harry, struggling to keep his temper. "Maybe he thought it would look nice on my wall."

"This is not a joke, Potter!" growled Scrimgeour. "Was it because Dumbledore believed that only the sword of Godric Gryffindor could defeat the Heir of Slytherin? Did he wish to give you that sword, Potter, because he believed, as do many, that you are the one destined to destroy He-Who-Must-Not-Be-Named?"

"Interesting theory," said Harry. "Has anyone ever tried sticking a sword in Voldemort? Maybe the Ministry should put some people onto that, instead of wasting their time stripping down Deluminators or covering up breakouts from Azkaban. So is this what you've been doing, Minister, shut up in your office, trying to break open

a Snitch? People are dying — I was nearly one of them — Voldemort chased me across three counties, he killed Mad-Eye Moody,
but there's been no word about any of that from the Ministry, has
there? And you still expect us to cooperate with you!"

"You go too far!" shouted Scrimgeour, standing up; Harry jumped
to his feet too. Scrimgeour limped toward Harry and jabbed him
hard in the chest with the point of his wand: It singed a hole in
Harry's T-shirt like a lit cigarette.

"Oi!" said Ron, jumping up and raising his own wand, but Harry
said,

"No! D'you want to give him an excuse to arrest us?"

"Remembered you're not at school, have you?" said Scrimgeour,
breathing hard into Harry's face. "Remembered that I am not Dumbledore, who forgave your insolence and insubordination? You may
wear that scar like a crown, Potter, but it is not up to a seventeen-
year-old boy to tell me how to do my job! It's time you learned some
respect!"

"It's time you earned it," said Harry.

The floor trembled; there was a sound of running footsteps, then
the door to the sitting room burst open and Mr. and Mrs. Weasley
ran in.

"We — we thought we heard —" began Mr. Weasley, looking
thoroughly alarmed at the sight of Harry and the Minister virtually nose to nose.

"— raised voices," panted Mrs. Weasley.

Scrimgeour took a couple of steps back from Harry, glancing at
the hole he had made in Harry's T-shirt. He seemed to regret his
loss of temper.

"It — it was nothing," he growled. "I . . . regret your attitude," he said, looking Harry full in the face once more. "You seem to think that the Ministry does not desire what you — what Dumbledore — desired. We ought to be working together."

"I don't like your methods, Minister," said Harry. "Remember?"

For the second time, he raised his right fist and displayed to Scrimgeour the scars that still showed white on the back of it, spelling *I must not tell lies.* Scrimgeour's expression hardened. He turned away without another word and limped from the room. Mrs. Weasley hurried after him; Harry heard her stop at the back door. After a minute or so she called, "He's gone!"

"What did he want?" Mr. Weasley asked, looking around at Harry, Ron, and Hermione as Mrs. Weasley came hurrying back to them.

"To give us what Dumbledore left us," said Harry. "They've only just released the contents of his will."

Outside in the garden, over the dinner tables, the three objects Scrimgeour had given them were passed from hand to hand. Everyone exclaimed over the Deluminator and *The Tales of Beedle the Bard* and lamented the fact that Scrimgeour had refused to pass on the sword, but none of them could offer any suggestion as to why Dumbledore would have left Harry an old Snitch. As Mr. Weasley examined the Deluminator for the third or fourth time, Mrs. Weasley said tentatively, "Harry, dear, everyone's awfully hungry, we didn't like to start without you. . . . Shall I serve dinner now?"

They all ate rather hurriedly and then, after a hasty chorus of "Happy Birthday" and much gulping of cake, the party broke up. Hagrid, who was invited to the wedding the following day, but was far too bulky to sleep in the overstretched Burrow, left to set up a tent for himself in a neighboring field.

"Meet us upstairs," Harry whispered to Hermione, while they helped Mrs. Weasley restore the garden to its normal state. "After everyone's gone to bed."

Up in the attic room, Ron examined his Deluminator, and Harry filled Hagrid's mokeskin purse, not with gold, but with those items he most prized, apparently worthless though some of them were: the Marauder's Map, the shard of Sirius's enchanted mirror, and R.A.B.'s locket. He pulled the strings tight and slipped the purse around his neck, then sat holding the old Snitch and watching its wings flutter feebly. At last, Hermione tapped on the door and tiptoed inside.

"Muffliato," she whispered, waving her wand in the direction of the stairs.

"Thought you didn't approve of that spell?" said Ron.

"Times change," said Hermione. "Now, show us that Deluminator."

Ron obliged at once. Holding it up in front of him, he clicked it. The solitary lamp they had lit went out at once.

"The thing is," whispered Hermione through the dark, "we could have achieved that with Peruvian Instant Darkness Powder."

There was a small *click,* and the ball of light from the lamp flew back to the ceiling and illuminated them all once more.

"Still, it's cool," said Ron, a little defensively. "And from what they said, Dumbledore invented it himself!"

"I know, but surely he wouldn't have singled you out in his will just to help us turn out the lights!"

"D'you think he knew the Ministry would confiscate his will and examine everything he'd left us?" asked Harry.

"Definitely," said Hermione. "He couldn't tell us in the will why he was leaving us these things, but that still doesn't explain . . ."

". . . why he couldn't have given us a hint when he was alive?" asked Ron.

"Well, exactly," said Hermione, now flicking through *The Tales of Beedle the Bard*. "If these things are important enough to pass on right under the nose of the Ministry, you'd think he'd have let us know why . . . unless he thought it was obvious?"

"Thought wrong, then, didn't he?" said Ron. "I always said he was mental. Brilliant and everything, but cracked. Leaving Harry an old Snitch — what the hell was that about?"

"I've no idea," said Hermione. "When Scrimgeour made you take it, Harry, I was so sure that something was going to happen!"

"Yeah, well," said Harry, his pulse quickening as he raised the Snitch in his fingers. "I wasn't going to try too hard in front of Scrimgeour, was I?"

"What do you mean?" asked Hermione.

"The Snitch I caught in my first ever Quidditch match?" said Harry. "Don't you remember?"

Hermione looked simply bemused. Ron, however, gasped, pointing frantically from Harry to the Snitch and back again until he found his voice.

"That was the one you nearly swallowed!"

"Exactly," said Harry, and with his heart beating fast, he pressed his mouth to the Snitch.

It did not open. Frustration and bitter disappointment welled up inside him: He lowered the golden sphere, but then Hermione cried out.

"Writing! There's writing on it, quick, look!"

He nearly dropped the Snitch in surprise and excitement. Hermione was quite right. Engraved upon the smooth golden surface, where seconds before there had been nothing, were five words written in the thin, slanting handwriting that Harry recognized as Dumbledore's:

I open at the close.

He had barely read them when the words vanished again.

"'I open at the close . . .' What's that supposed to mean?"

Hermione and Ron shook their heads, looking blank.

"I open at the close . . . at the *close* . . . I open at the close . . ."

But no matter how often they repeated the words, with many different inflections, they were unable to wring any more meaning from them.

"And the sword," said Ron finally, when they had at last abandoned their attempts to divine meaning in the Snitch's inscription. "Why did he want Harry to have the sword?"

"And why couldn't he just have told me?" Harry said quietly. "It was *there,* it was right there on the wall of his office during all our talks last year! If he wanted me to have it, why didn't he just give it to me then?"

He felt as though he were sitting in an examination with a question he ought to have been able to answer in front of him, his brain slow and unresponsive. Was there something he had missed in the long talks with Dumbledore last year? Ought he to know what it all meant? Had Dumbledore expected him to understand?

"And as for this book," said Hermione, "*The Tales of Beedle the Bard* . . . I've never even heard of them!"

"You've never heard of *The Tales of Beedle the Bard*?" said Ron incredulously. "You're kidding, right?"

"No, I'm not!" said Hermione in surprise. "Do you know them, then?"

"Well, of course I do!"

Harry looked up, diverted. The circumstance of Ron having read a book that Hermione had not was unprecedented. Ron, however, looked bemused by their surprise.

"Oh come on! All the old kids' stories are supposed to be Beedle's, aren't they? 'The Fountain of Fair Fortune' . . . 'The Wizard and the Hopping Pot' . . . 'Babbitty Rabbitty and her Cackling Stump' . . ."

"Excuse me?" said Hermione, giggling. "What was that last one?"

"Come off it!" said Ron, looking in disbelief from Harry to Hermione. "You must've heard of Babbitty Rabbitty —"

"Ron, you know full well Harry and I were brought up by Muggles!" said Hermione. "We didn't hear stories like that when we were little, we heard 'Snow White and the Seven Dwarfs' and 'Cinderella' —"

"What's that, an illness?" asked Ron.

"So these are children's stories?" asked Hermione, bending again over the runes.

"Yeah," said Ron uncertainly, "I mean, that's just what you hear, you know, that all these old stories came from Beedle. I dunno what they're like in the original versions."

"But I wonder why Dumbledore thought I should read them?"

Something creaked downstairs.

"Probably just Charlie, now Mum's asleep, sneaking off to regrow his hair," said Ron nervously.

"All the same, we should get to bed," whispered Hermione. "It wouldn't do to oversleep tomorrow."

"No," agreed Ron. "A brutal triple murder by the bridegroom's mother might put a bit of a damper on the wedding. I'll get the lights."

And he clicked the Deluminator once more as Hermione left the room.

THE WEDDING

Three o'clock on the following afternoon found Harry, Ron, Fred, and George standing outside the great white marquee in the orchard, awaiting the arrival of the wedding guests. Harry had taken a large dose of Polyjuice Potion and was now the double of a redheaded Muggle boy from the local village, Ottery St. Catchpole, from whom Fred had stolen hairs using a Summoning Charm. The plan was to introduce Harry as "Cousin Barny" and trust to the great number of Weasley relatives to camouflage him.

All four of them were clutching seating plans, so that they could help show people to the right seats. A host of white-robed waiters had arrived an hour earlier, along with a golden-jacketed band, and all of these wizards were currently sitting a short distance away under a tree; Harry could see a blue haze of pipe smoke issuing from the spot.

Behind Harry, the entrance to the marquee revealed rows and rows of fragile golden chairs set on either side of a long purple carpet.

The supporting poles were entwined with white and gold flowers. Fred and George had fastened an enormous bunch of golden balloons over the exact point where Bill and Fleur would shortly become husband and wife. Outside, butterflies and bees were hovering lazily over the grass and hedgerow. Harry was rather uncomfortable. The Muggle boy whose appearance he was affecting was slightly fatter than him, and his dress robes felt hot and tight in the full glare of a summer's day.

"When I get married," said Fred, tugging at the collar of his own robes, "I won't be bothering with any of this nonsense. You can all wear what you like, and I'll put a full Body-Bind Curse on Mum until it's all over."

"She wasn't too bad this morning, considering," said George. "Cried a bit about Percy not being here, but who wants him? Oh blimey, brace yourselves — here they come, look."

Brightly colored figures were appearing, one by one, out of nowhere at the distant boundary of the yard. Within minutes a procession had formed, which began to snake its way up through the garden toward the marquee. Exotic flowers and bewitched birds fluttered on the witches' hats, while precious gems glittered from many of the wizards' cravats; a hum of excited chatter grew louder and louder, drowning the sound of the bees as the crowd approached the tent.

"Excellent, I think I see a few veela cousins," said George, craning his neck for a better look. "They'll need help understanding our English customs, I'll look after them. . . ."

"Not so fast, Your Holeyness," said Fred, and darting past the gaggle of middle-aged witches heading the procession, he said, "Here — *permettez-moi* to *assister vous*," to a pair of pretty French girls, who giggled and allowed him to escort them inside. George was left to deal with the middle-aged witches and Ron took charge of Mr. Weasley's old Ministry colleague Perkins, while a rather deaf old couple fell to Harry's lot.

"Wotcher," said a familiar voice as he came out of the marquee again and found Tonks and Lupin at the front of the queue. She had turned blonde for the occasion. "Arthur told us you were the one with the curly hair. Sorry about last night," she added in a whisper as Harry led them up the aisle. "The Ministry's being very anti-werewolf at the moment and we thought our presence might not do you any favors."

"It's fine, I understand," said Harry, speaking more to Lupin than Tonks. Lupin gave him a swift smile, but as they turned away, Harry saw Lupin's face fall again into lines of misery. He did not understand it, but there was no time to dwell on the matter: Hagrid was causing a certain amount of disruption. Having misunderstood Fred's directions he had sat himself, not upon the magically enlarged and reinforced seat set aside for him in the back row, but on five seats that now resembled a large pile of golden matchsticks.

While Mr. Weasley repaired the damage and Hagrid shouted apologies to anybody who would listen, Harry hurried back to the entrance to find Ron face-to-face with a most eccentric-looking wizard. Slightly cross-eyed, with shoulder-length white hair the texture of candyfloss, he wore a cap whose tassel dangled in front of his nose and robes of an eye-watering shade of egg-yolk yellow. An odd symbol, rather like a triangular eye, glistened from a golden chain around his neck.

"Xenophilius Lovegood," he said, extending a hand to Harry, "my daughter and I live just over the hill, so kind of the good Weasleys to invite us. But I think you know my Luna?" he added to Ron.

"Yes," said Ron. "Isn't she with you?"

"She lingered in that charming little garden to say hello to the gnomes, such a glorious infestation! How few wizards realize just how much we can learn from the wise little gnomes — or, to give them their correct name, the *Gernumbli gardensi*."

"Ours do know a lot of excellent swear words," said Ron, "but I think Fred and George taught them those."

He led a party of warlocks into the marquee as Luna rushed up.

"Hello, Harry!" she said.

"Er — my name's Barny," said Harry, flummoxed.

"Oh, have you changed that too?" she asked brightly.

"How did you know — ?"

"Oh, just your expression," she said.

Like her father, Luna was wearing bright yellow robes, which she had accessorized with a large sunflower in her hair. Once you got over the brightness of it all, the general effect was quite pleasant. At least there were no radishes dangling from her ears.

Xenophilius, who was deep in conversation with an acquaintance, had missed the exchange between Luna and Harry. Bidding the wizard farewell, he turned to his daughter, who held up her finger and said, "Daddy, look — one of the gnomes actually bit me!"

"How wonderful! Gnome saliva is enormously beneficial!" said Mr. Lovegood, seizing Luna's outstretched finger and examining the bleeding puncture marks. "Luna, my love, if you should feel any burgeoning talent today — perhaps an unexpected urge to sing opera or to declaim in Mermish — do not repress it! You may have been gifted by the Gernumblies!"

Ron, passing them in the opposite direction, let out a loud snort.

"Ron can laugh," said Luna serenely as Harry led her and Xenophilius toward their seats, "but my father has done a lot of research
on Gernumbli magic."

"Really?" said Harry, who had long since decided not to challenge
Luna or her father's peculiar views. "Are you sure you don't want to
put anything on that bite, though?"

"Oh, it's fine," said Luna, sucking her finger in a dreamy fashion
and looking Harry up and down. "You look smart. I told Daddy
most people would probably wear dress robes, but he believes you
ought to wear sun colors to a wedding, for luck, you know."

As she drifted off after her father, Ron reappeared with an elderly
witch clutching his arm. Her beaky nose, red-rimmed eyes, and
feathery pink hat gave her the look of a bad-tempered flamingo.

". . . and your hair's much too long, Ronald, for a moment I
thought you were Ginevra. Merlin's beard, what is Xenophilius
Lovegood wearing? He looks like an omelet. And who are you?"
she barked at Harry.

"Oh yeah, Auntie Muriel, this is our cousin Barny."

"Another Weasley? You breed like gnomes. Isn't Harry Potter
here? I was hoping to meet him. I thought he was a friend of yours,
Ronald, or have you merely been boasting?"

"No — he couldn't come —"

"Hmm. Made an excuse, did he? Not as gormless as he looks in
press photographs, then. I've just been instructing the bride on how
best to wear my tiara," she shouted at Harry. "Goblin-made, you
know, and been in my family for centuries. She's a good-looking
girl, but still — *French.* Well, well, find me a good seat, Ronald,
I am a hundred and seven and I ought not to be on my feet too
long."

Ron gave Harry a meaningful look as he passed and did not reappear for some time: When next they met at the entrance, Harry had shown a dozen more people to their places. The marquee was nearly full now, and for the first time there was no queue outside.

"Nightmare, Muriel is," said Ron, mopping his forehead on his sleeve. "She used to come for Christmas every year, then, thank God, she took offense because Fred and George set off a Dungbomb under her chair at dinner. Dad always says she'll have written them out of her will — like they care, they're going to end up richer than anyone in the family, rate they're going. . . . Wow," he added, blinking rather rapidly as Hermione came hurrying toward them. "You look great!"

"Always the tone of surprise," said Hermione, though she smiled. She was wearing a floaty, lilac-colored dress with matching high heels; her hair was sleek and shiny. "Your Great-Aunt Muriel doesn't agree, I just met her upstairs while she was giving Fleur the tiara. She said, 'Oh dear, is this the Muggle-born?' and then, 'Bad posture and skinny ankles.'"

"Don't take it personally, she's rude to everyone," said Ron.

"Talking about Muriel?" inquired George, reemerging from the marquee with Fred. "Yeah, she's just told me my ears are lopsided. Old bat. I wish old Uncle Bilius was still with us, though; he was a right laugh at weddings."

"Wasn't he the one who saw a Grim and died twenty-four hours later?" asked Hermione.

"Well, yeah, he went a bit odd toward the end," conceded George.

"But before he went loopy he was the life and soul of the party," said Fred. "He used to down an entire bottle of firewhisky, then run onto the dance floor, hoist up his robes, and start pulling bunches of flowers out of his —"

"Yes, he sounds a real charmer," said Hermione, while Harry roared with laughter.

"Never married, for some reason," said Ron.

"You amaze me," said Hermione.

They were all laughing so much that none of them noticed the latecomer, a dark-haired young man with a large, curved nose and thick black eyebrows, until he held out his invitation to Ron and said, with his eyes on Hermione, "You look vunderful."

"Viktor!" she shrieked, and dropped her small beaded bag, which made a loud thump quite disproportionate to its size. As she scrambled, blushing, to pick it up, she said, "I didn't know you were — goodness — it's lovely to see — how are you?"

Ron's ears had turned bright red again. After glancing at Krum's invitation as if he did not believe a word of it, he said, much too loudly, "How come you're here?"

"Fleur invited me," said Krum, eyebrows raised.

Harry, who had no grudge against Krum, shook hands; then, feeling that it would be prudent to remove Krum from Ron's vicinity, offered to show him his seat.

"Your friend is not pleased to see me," said Krum as they entered the now packed marquee. "Or is he a relative?" he added with a glance at Harry's red curly hair.

"Cousin," Harry muttered, but Krum was not really listening. His appearance was causing a stir, particularly amongst the veela cousins: He was, after all, a famous Quidditch player. While people were still craning their necks to get a good look at him, Ron, Hermione, Fred, and George came hurrying down the aisle.

"Time to sit down," Fred told Harry, "or we're going to get run over by the bride."

Harry, Ron, and Hermione took their seats in the second row behind Fred and George. Hermione looked rather pink and Ron's ears were still scarlet. After a few moments he muttered to Harry, "Did you see he's grown a stupid little beard?"

Harry gave a noncommittal grunt.

A sense of jittery anticipation had filled the warm tent, the general murmuring broken by occasional spurts of excited laughter. Mr. and Mrs. Weasley strolled up the aisle, smiling and waving at relatives; Mrs. Weasley was wearing a brand-new set of amethyst-colored robes with a matching hat.

A moment later Bill and Charlie stood up at the front of the marquee, both wearing dress robes, with large white roses in their buttonholes; Fred wolf-whistled and there was an outbreak of giggling from the veela cousins. Then the crowd fell silent as music swelled from what seemed to be the golden balloons.

"Ooooh!" said Hermione, swiveling around in her seat to look at the entrance.

A great collective sigh issued from the assembled witches and wizards as Monsieur Delacour and Fleur came walking up the aisle, Fleur gliding, Monsieur Delacour bouncing and beaming. Fleur was wearing a very simple white dress and seemed to be emitting a strong, silvery glow. While her radiance usually dimmed everyone else by comparison, today it beautified everybody it fell upon. Ginny and Gabrielle, both wearing golden dresses, looked even prettier than usual, and once Fleur had reached him, Bill did not look as though he had ever met Fenrir Greyback.

"Ladies and gentlemen," said a slightly singsong voice, and with a slight shock, Harry saw the same small, tufty-haired wizard who had presided at Dumbledore's funeral, now standing in front of Bill and Fleur. "We are gathered here today to celebrate the union of two faithful souls . . ."

"Yes, my tiara sets off the whole thing nicely," said Auntie Muriel in a rather carrying whisper. "But I must say, Ginevra's dress is far too low cut."

Ginny glanced around, grinning, winked at Harry, then quickly faced the front again. Harry's mind wandered a long way from the marquee, back to afternoons spent alone with Ginny in lonely parts of the school grounds. They seemed so long ago; they had always seemed too good to be true, as though he had been stealing shining hours from a normal person's life, a person without a lightning-shaped scar on his forehead. . . .

"Do you, William Arthur, take Fleur Isabelle . . . ?"

In the front row, Mrs. Weasley and Madame Delacour were both sobbing quietly into scraps of lace. Trumpetlike sounds from the back of the marquee told everyone that Hagrid had taken out one of his own tablecloth-sized handkerchiefs. Hermione turned and beamed at Harry; her eyes too were full of tears.

". . . then I declare you bonded for life."

The tufty-haired wizard waved his wand high over the heads of Bill and Fleur and a shower of silver stars fell upon them, spiraling around their now entwined figures. As Fred and George led a round of applause, the golden balloons overhead burst: Birds of paradise and tiny golden bells flew and floated out of them, adding their songs and chimes to the din.

"Ladies and gentlemen!" called the tufty-haired wizard. "If you would please stand up!"

They all did so, Auntie Muriel grumbling audibly; he waved his wand again. The seats on which they had been sitting rose gracefully into the air as the canvas walls of the marquee vanished, so that they stood beneath a canopy supported by golden poles, with a glorious view of the sunlit orchard and surrounding countryside. Next, a pool of molten gold spread from the center of the tent to form a gleaming dance floor; the hovering chairs grouped themselves around small, white-clothed tables, which all floated gracefully back to earth around it, and the golden-jacketed band trooped toward a podium.

"Smooth," said Ron approvingly as the waiters popped up on all sides, some bearing silver trays of pumpkin juice, butterbeer, and firewhisky, others tottering piles of tarts and sandwiches.

"We should go and congratulate them!" said Hermione, standing on tiptoe to see the place where Bill and Fleur had vanished amid a crowd of well-wishers.

"We'll have time later," shrugged Ron, snatching three butterbeers from a passing tray and handing one to Harry. "Hermione, cop hold, let's grab a table. . . . Not there! Nowhere near Muriel —"

Ron led the way across the empty dance floor, glancing left and right as he went: Harry felt sure that he was keeping an eye out for Krum. By the time they had reached the other side of the marquee, most of the tables were occupied: The emptiest was the one where Luna sat alone.

"All right if we join you?" asked Ron.

"Oh yes," she said happily. "Daddy's just gone to give Bill and Fleur our present."

"What is it, a lifetime's supply of Gurdyroots?" asked Ron.

Hermione aimed a kick at him under the table, but caught Harry instead. Eyes watering in pain, Harry lost track of the conversation for a few moments.

The band had begun to play. Bill and Fleur took to the dance floor first, to great applause; after a while, Mr. Weasley led Madame Delacour onto the floor, followed by Mrs. Weasley and Fleur's father.

"I like this song," said Luna, swaying in time to the waltzlike tune, and a few seconds later she stood up and glided onto the dance floor, where she revolved on the spot, quite alone, eyes closed and waving her arms.

"She's great, isn't she?" said Ron admiringly. "Always good value."

But the smile vanished from his face at once: Viktor Krum had dropped into Luna's vacant seat. Hermione looked pleasurably flustered, but this time Krum had not come to compliment her. With a scowl on his face he said, "Who is that man in the yellow?"

"That's Xenophilius Lovegood, he's the father of a friend of ours," said Ron. His pugnacious tone indicated that they were not about to laugh at Xenophilius, despite the clear provocation. "Come and dance," he added abruptly to Hermione.

She looked taken aback, but pleased too, and got up. They vanished together into the growing throng on the dance floor.

"Ah, they are together now?" asked Krum, momentarily distracted.

"Er — sort of," said Harry.

"Who are you?" Krum asked.

"Barny Weasley."

They shook hands.

"You, Barny — you know this man Lovegood vell?"

"No, I only met him today. Why?"

Krum glowered over the top of his drink, watching Xenophilius, who was chatting to several warlocks on the other side of the dance floor.

"Because," said Krum, "if he vos not a guest of Fleur's, I vould duel him, here and now, for vearing that filthy sign upon his chest."

"Sign?" said Harry, looking over at Xenophilius too. The strange triangular eye was gleaming on his chest. "Why? What's wrong with it?"

"Grindelvald. That is Grindelvald's sign."

"Grindelwald . . . the Dark wizard Dumbledore defeated?"

"Exactly."

Krum's jaw muscles worked as if he were chewing, then he said, "Grindelvald killed many people, my grandfather, for instance. Of course, he vos never poverful in this country, they said he feared Dumbledore — and rightly, seeing how he vos finished. But this" — he pointed a finger at Xenophilius — "this is his symbol, I recognized it at vunce: Grindelvald carved it into a vall at Durmstrang ven he vos a pupil there. Some idiots copied it onto their books and clothes, thinking to shock, make themselves impressive — until those of us who had lost family members to Grindelvald taught them better."

Krum cracked his knuckles menacingly and glowered at Xenophilius. Harry felt perplexed. It seemed incredibly unlikely that Luna's father was a supporter of the Dark Arts, and nobody else in the tent seemed to have recognized the triangular, runelike shape.

"Are you — er — quite sure it's Grindelwald's — ?"

"I am not mistaken," said Krum coldly. "I valked past that sign for several years, I know it vell."

"Well, there's a chance," said Harry, "that Xenophilius doesn't actually know what the symbol means. The Lovegoods are quite . . .

unusual. He could easily have picked it up somewhere and think it's a cross section of the head of a Crumple-Horned Snorkack or something."

"The cross section of a vot?"

"Well, I don't know what they are, but apparently he and his daughter go on holiday looking for them. . . ."

Harry felt he was doing a bad job explaining Luna and her father.

"That's her," he said, pointing at Luna, who was still dancing alone, waving her arms around her head like someone attempting to beat off midges.

"Vy is she doing that?" asked Krum.

"Probably trying to get rid of a Wrackspurt," said Harry, who recognized the symptoms.

Krum did not seem to know whether or not Harry was making fun of him. He drew his wand from inside his robes and tapped it menacingly on his thigh; sparks flew out of the end.

"Gregorovitch!" said Harry loudly, and Krum started, but Harry was too excited to care; the memory had come back to him at the sight of Krum's wand: Ollivander taking it and examining it carefully before the Triwizard Tournament.

"Vot about him?" asked Krum suspiciously.

"He's a wandmaker!"

"I know that," said Krum.

"He made your wand! That's why I thought — Quidditch —"

Krum was looking more and more suspicious.

"How do you know Gregorovitch made my vand?"

"I . . . I read it somewhere, I think," said Harry. "In a — a fan magazine," he improvised wildly and Krum looked mollified.

"I had not realized I ever discussed my vand with fans," he said.

"So . . . er . . . where is Gregorovitch these days?"

Krum looked puzzled.

"He retired several years ago. I vos one of the last to purchase a Gregorovitch vand. They are the best — although I know, of course, that you Britons set much store by Ollivander."

Harry did not answer. He pretended to watch the dancers, like Krum, but he was thinking hard. So Voldemort was looking for a celebrated wandmaker, and Harry did not have to search far for a reason: It was surely because of what Harry's wand had done on the night that Voldemort had pursued him across the skies. The holly and phoenix feather wand had conquered the borrowed wand, something that Ollivander had not anticipated or understood. Would Gregorovitch know better? Was he truly more skilled than Ollivander, did he know secrets of wands that Ollivander did not?

"This girl is very nice-looking," Krum said, recalling Harry to his surroundings. Krum was pointing at Ginny, who had just joined Luna. "She is also a relative of yours?"

"Yeah," said Harry, suddenly irritated, "and she's seeing someone. Jealous type. Big bloke. You wouldn't want to cross him."

Krum grunted.

"Vot," he said, draining his goblet and getting to his feet again, "is the point of being an international Quidditch player if all the good-looking girls are taken?"

And he strode off, leaving Harry to take a sandwich from a passing waiter and make his way around the edge of the crowded dance floor. He wanted to find Ron, to tell him about Gregorovitch, but Ron was dancing with Hermione out in the middle of the floor.

Harry leaned up against one of the golden pillars and watched Ginny, who was now dancing with Fred and George's friend Lee Jordan, trying not to feel resentful about the promise he had given Ron.

He had never been to a wedding before, so he could not judge how Wizarding celebrations differed from Muggle ones, though he was pretty sure that the latter would not involve a wedding cake topped with two model phoenixes that took flight when the cake was cut, or bottles of champagne that floated unsupported through the crowd. As evening drew in, and moths began to swoop under the canopy, now lit with floating golden lanterns, the revelry became more and more uncontained. Fred and George had long since disappeared into the darkness with a pair of Fleur's cousins; Charlie, Hagrid, and a squat wizard in a purple porkpie hat were singing "Odo the Hero" in a corner.

Wandering through the crowd so as to escape a drunken uncle of Ron's who seemed unsure whether or not Harry was his son, Harry spotted an old wizard sitting alone at a table. His cloud of white hair made him look rather like an aged dandelion clock and was topped by a moth-eaten fez. He was vaguely familiar: Racking his brains, Harry suddenly realized that this was Elphias Doge, member of the Order of the Phoenix and the writer of Dumbledore's obituary.

Harry approached him.

"May I sit down?"

"Of course, of course," said Doge; he had a rather high-pitched, wheezy voice.

Harry leaned in.

"Mr. Doge, I'm Harry Potter."

Doge gasped.

"My dear boy! Arthur told me you were here, disguised. . . . I am so glad, so honored!"

In a flutter of nervous pleasure Doge poured Harry a goblet of champagne.

"I thought of writing to you," he whispered, "after Dumbledore . . . the shock . . . and for you, I am sure . . ."

Doge's tiny eyes filled with sudden tears.

"I saw the obituary you wrote for the *Daily Prophet*," said Harry. "I didn't realize you knew Professor Dumbledore so well."

"As well as anyone," said Doge, dabbing his eyes with a napkin. "Certainly I knew him longest, if you don't count Aberforth — and somehow, people never *do* seem to count Aberforth."

"Speaking of the *Daily Prophet* . . . I don't know whether you saw, Mr. Doge — ?"

"Oh, please call me Elphias, dear boy."

"Elphias, I don't know whether you saw the interview Rita Skeeter gave about Dumbledore?"

Doge's face flooded with angry color.

"Oh yes, Harry, I saw it. That woman, or vulture might be a more accurate term, positively pestered me to talk to her. I am ashamed to say that I became rather rude, called her an interfering trout, which resulted, as you may have seen, in aspersions cast upon my sanity."

"Well, in that interview," Harry went on, "Rita Skeeter hinted that Professor Dumbledore was involved in the Dark Arts when he was young."

"Don't believe a word of it!" said Doge at once. "Not a word, Harry! Let nothing tarnish your memories of Albus Dumbledore!"

Harry looked into Doge's earnest, pained face and felt, not reassured, but frustrated. Did Doge really think it was that easy, that

Harry could simply *choose* not to believe? Didn't Doge understand Harry's need to be sure, to know *everything*?

Perhaps Doge suspected Harry's feelings, for he looked concerned and hurried on, "Harry, Rita Skeeter is a dreadful —"

But he was interrupted by a shrill cackle.

"Rita Skeeter? Oh, I love her, always read her!"

Harry and Doge looked up to see Auntie Muriel standing there, the plumes dancing on her hat, a goblet of champagne in her hand. "She's written a book about Dumbledore, you know!"

"Hello, Muriel," said Doge. "Yes, we were just discussing —"

"You there! Give me your chair, I'm a hundred and seven!"

Another redheaded Weasley cousin jumped off his seat, looking alarmed, and Auntie Muriel swung it around with surprising strength and plopped herself down upon it between Doge and Harry.

"Hello again, Barry, or whatever your name is," she said to Harry. "Now, what were you saying about Rita Skeeter, Elphias? You know she's written a biography of Dumbledore? I can't wait to read it, I must remember to place an order at Flourish and Blotts!"

Doge looked stiff and solemn at this, but Auntie Muriel drained her goblet and clicked her bony fingers at a passing waiter for a replacement. She took another large gulp of champagne, belched, and then said, "There's no need to look like a pair of stuffed frogs! Before he became so respected and respectable and all that tosh, there were some mighty funny rumors about Albus!"

"Ill-informed sniping," said Doge, turning radish-colored again.

"You would say that, Elphias," cackled Auntie Muriel. "I noticed how you skated over the sticky patches in that obituary of yours!"

"I'm sorry you think so," said Doge, more coldly still. "I assure you I was writing from the heart."

"Oh, we all know you worshipped Dumbledore; I daresay you'll still think he was a saint even if it does turn out that he did away with his Squib sister!"

"Muriel!" exclaimed Doge.

A chill that had nothing to do with the iced champagne was stealing through Harry's chest.

"What do you mean?" he asked Muriel. "Who said his sister was a Squib? I thought she was ill?"

"Thought wrong, then, didn't you, Barry!" said Auntie Muriel, looking delighted at the effect she had produced. "Anyway, how could you expect to know anything about it? It all happened years and years before you were even thought of, my dear, and the truth is that those of us who were alive then never knew what really happened. That's why I can't wait to find out what Skeeter's unearthed! Dumbledore kept that sister of his quiet for a long time!"

"Untrue!" wheezed Doge. "Absolutely untrue!"

"He never told me his sister was a Squib," said Harry, without thinking, still cold inside.

"And why on earth would he tell you?" screeched Muriel, swaying a little in her seat as she attempted to focus upon Harry.

"The reason Albus never spoke about Ariana," began Elphias in a voice stiff with emotion, "is, I should have thought, quite clear. He was so devastated by her death —"

"Why did nobody ever see her, Elphias?" squawked Muriel. "Why did half of us never even know she existed, until they carried the coffin out of the house and held a funeral for her? Where was saintly Albus while Ariana was locked in the cellar? Off being brilliant at Hogwarts, and never mind what was going on in his own house!"

"What d'you mean, locked in the cellar?" asked Harry. "What is this?"

Doge looked wretched. Auntie Muriel cackled again and answered Harry.

"Dumbledore's mother was a terrifying woman, simply terrifying. Muggle-born, though I heard she pretended otherwise —"

"She never pretended anything of the sort! Kendra was a fine woman," whispered Doge miserably, but Auntie Muriel ignored him.

"— proud and very domineering, the sort of witch who would have been mortified to produce a Squib —"

"Ariana was not a Squib!" wheezed Doge.

"So you say, Elphias, but explain, then, why she never attended Hogwarts!" said Auntie Muriel. She turned back to Harry. "In our day, Squibs were often hushed up, though to take it to the extreme of actually imprisoning a little girl in the house and pretending she didn't exist —"

"I tell you, that's not what happened!" said Doge, but Auntie Muriel steamrollered on, still addressing Harry.

"Squibs were usually shipped off to Muggle schools and encouraged to integrate into the Muggle community . . . much kinder than trying to find them a place in the Wizarding world, where they must always be second class; but naturally Kendra Dumbledore wouldn't have dreamed of letting her daughter go to a Muggle school —"

"Ariana was delicate!" said Doge desperately. "Her health was always too poor to permit her —"

"— to permit her to leave the house?" cackled Muriel. "And yet she was never taken to St. Mungo's and no Healer was ever summoned to see her!"

"Really, Muriel, how you can possibly know whether —"

"For your information, Elphias, my cousin Lancelot was a Healer at St. Mungo's at the time, and he told my family in strictest confidence that Ariana had never been seen there. All most suspicious, Lancelot thought!"

Doge looked to be on the verge of tears. Auntie Muriel, who seemed to be enjoying herself hugely, snapped her fingers for more champagne. Numbly Harry thought of how the Dursleys had once shut him up, locked him away, kept him out of sight, all for the crime of being a wizard. Had Dumbledore's sister suffered the same fate in reverse: imprisoned for her lack of magic? And had Dumbledore truly left her to her fate while he went off to Hogwarts, to prove himself brilliant and talented?

"Now, if Kendra hadn't died first," Muriel resumed, "I'd have said that it was she who finished off Ariana —"

"How can you, Muriel?" groaned Doge. "A mother kill her own daughter? Think what you are saying!"

"If the mother in question was capable of imprisoning her daughter for years on end, why not?" shrugged Auntie Muriel. "But as I say, it doesn't fit, because Kendra died before Ariana — of what, nobody ever seemed sure —"

"Oh, no doubt Ariana murdered her," said Doge with a brave attempt at scorn. "Why not?"

"Yes, Ariana might have made a desperate bid for freedom and killed Kendra in the struggle," said Auntie Muriel thoughtfully. "Shake your head all you like, Elphias! You were at Ariana's funeral, were you not?"

"Yes I was," said Doge, through trembling lips. "And a more desperately sad occasion I cannot remember. Albus was heartbroken —"

"His heart wasn't the only thing. Didn't Aberforth break Albus's nose halfway through the service?"

If Doge had looked horrified before this, it was nothing to how he looked now. Muriel might have stabbed him. She cackled loudly and took another swig of champagne, which dribbled down her chin.

"How do you — ?" croaked Doge.

"My mother was friendly with old Bathilda Bagshot," said Auntie Muriel happily. "Bathilda described the whole thing to Mother while I was listening at the door. A coffin-side brawl! The way Bathilda told it, Aberforth shouted that it was all Albus's fault that Ariana was dead and then punched him in the face. According to Bathilda, Albus did not even defend himself, and that's odd enough in itself, Albus could have destroyed Aberforth in a duel with both hands tied behind his back."

Muriel swigged yet more champagne. The recitation of these old scandals seemed to elate her as much as they horrified Doge. Harry did not know what to think, what to believe: He wanted the truth, and yet all Doge did was sit there and bleat feebly that Ariana had been ill. Harry could hardly believe that Dumbledore would not have intervened if such cruelty was happening inside his own house, and yet there was undoubtedly something odd about the story.

"And I'll tell you something else," Muriel said, hiccuping slightly as she lowered her goblet. "I think Bathilda has spilled the beans to Rita Skeeter. All those hints in Skeeter's interview about an important source close to the Dumbledores — goodness knows she was there all through the Ariana business, and it would fit!"

"Bathilda would never talk to Rita Skeeter!" whispered Doge.

"Bathilda Bagshot?" Harry said. "The author of *A History of Magic*?"

The name was printed on the front of one of Harry's textbooks, though admittedly not one of the ones he had read most attentively.

"Yes," said Doge, clutching at Harry's question like a drowning man at a life belt. "A most gifted magical historian and an old friend of Albus's."

"Quite gaga these days, I've heard," said Auntie Muriel cheerfully.

"If that is so, it is even more dishonorable for Skeeter to have taken advantage of her," said Doge, "and no reliance can be placed on anything Bathilda may have said!"

"Oh, there are ways of bringing back memories, and I'm sure Rita Skeeter knows them all," said Auntie Muriel. "But even if Bathilda's completely cuckoo, I'm sure she'd still have old photographs, maybe even letters. She knew the Dumbledores for years. . . . Well worth a trip to Godric's Hollow, I'd have thought."

Harry, who had been taking a sip of butterbeer, choked. Doge banged him on the back as Harry coughed, looking at Auntie Muriel through streaming eyes. Once he had control of his voice again, he asked, "Bathilda Bagshot lives in Godric's Hollow?"

"Oh yes, she's been there forever! The Dumbledores moved there after Percival was imprisoned, and she was their neighbor."

"The Dumbledores lived in Godric's Hollow?"

"Yes, Barry, that's what I just said," said Auntie Muriel testily.

Harry felt drained, empty. Never once, in six years, had Dumbledore told Harry that they had both lived and lost loved ones in Godric's Hollow. Why? Were Lily and James buried close to

Dumbledore's mother and sister? Had Dumbledore visited their graves, perhaps walked past Lily's and James's to do so? And he had never once told Harry . . . never bothered to say . . .

And why it was so important, Harry could not explain even to himself, yet he felt it had been tantamount to a lie not to tell him that they had this place and these experiences in common. He stared ahead of him, barely noticing what was going on around him, and did not realize that Hermione had appeared out of the crowd until she drew up a chair beside him.

"I simply can't dance anymore," she panted, slipping off one of her shoes and rubbing the sole of her foot. "Ron's gone looking to find more butterbeers. It's a bit odd, I've just seen Viktor storming away from Luna's father, it looked like they'd been arguing —" She dropped her voice, staring at him. "Harry, are you okay?"

Harry did not know where to begin, but it did not matter. At that moment, something large and silver came falling through the canopy over the dance floor. Graceful and gleaming, the lynx landed lightly in the middle of the astonished dancers. Heads turned, as those nearest it froze absurdly in mid-dance. Then the Patronus's mouth opened wide and it spoke in the loud, deep, slow voice of Kingsley Shacklebolt.

"The Ministry has fallen. Scrimgeour is dead. They are coming."

A PLACE TO HIDE

Everything seemed fuzzy, slow. Harry and Hermione jumped to their feet and drew their wands. Many people were only just realizing that something strange had happened; heads were still turning toward the silver cat as it vanished. Silence spread outward in cold ripples from the place where the Patronus had landed. Then somebody screamed.

Harry and Hermione threw themselves into the panicking crowd. Guests were sprinting in all directions; many were Disapparating; the protective enchantments around the Burrow had broken.

"Ron!" Hermione cried. "Ron, where are you?"

As they pushed their way across the dance floor, Harry saw cloaked and masked figures appearing in the crowd; then he saw Lupin and Tonks, their wands raised, and heard both of them shout, *"Protego!"*, a cry that was echoed on all sides —

"Ron! Ron!" Hermione called, half sobbing as she and Harry were buffeted by terrified guests: Harry seized her hand to make sure they weren't separated as a streak of light whizzed over their heads, whether a protective charm or something more sinister he did not know —

And then Ron was there. He caught hold of Hermione's free arm, and Harry felt her turn on the spot; sight and sound were extinguished as darkness pressed in upon him; all he could feel was Hermione's hand as he was squeezed through space and time, away from the Burrow, away from the descending Death Eaters, away, perhaps, from Voldemort himself. . . .

"Where are we?" said Ron's voice.

Harry opened his eyes. For a moment he thought they had not left the wedding after all: They still seemed to be surrounded by people.

"Tottenham Court Road," panted Hermione. "Walk, just walk, we need to find somewhere for you to change."

Harry did as she asked. They half walked, half ran up the wide dark street thronged with late-night revelers and lined with closed shops, stars twinkling above them. A double-decker bus rumbled by and a group of merry pub-goers ogled them as they passed; Harry and Ron were still wearing dress robes.

"Hermione, we haven't got anything to change into," Ron told her, as a young woman burst into raucous giggles at the sight of him.

"Why didn't I make sure I had the Invisibility Cloak with me?" said Harry, inwardly cursing his own stupidity. "All last year I kept it on me and —"

"It's okay, I've got the Cloak, I've got clothes for both of you," said Hermione. "Just try and act naturally until — this will do."

She led them down a side street, then into the shelter of a shadowy alleyway.

"When you say you've got the Cloak, and clothes . . ." said Harry, frowning at Hermione, who was carrying nothing except her small beaded handbag, in which she was now rummaging.

"Yes, they're here," said Hermione, and to Harry and Ron's utter astonishment, she pulled out a pair of jeans, a sweatshirt, some maroon socks, and finally the silvery Invisibility Cloak.

"How the ruddy hell — ?"

"Undetectable Extension Charm," said Hermione. "Tricky, but I think I've done it okay; anyway, I managed to fit everything we need in here." She gave the fragile-looking bag a little shake and it echoed like a cargo hold as a number of heavy objects rolled around inside it. "Oh, damn, that'll be the books," she said, peering into it, "and I had them all stacked by subject. . . . Oh well. . . . Harry, you'd better take the Invisibility Cloak. Ron, hurry up and change. . . ."

"When did you do all this?" Harry asked as Ron stripped off his robes.

"I told you at the Burrow, I've had the essentials packed for days, you know, in case we needed to make a quick getaway. I packed your rucksack this morning, Harry, after you changed, and put it in here. . . . I just had a feeling. . . ."

"You're amazing, you are," said Ron, handing her his bundled-up robes.

"Thank you," said Hermione, managing a small smile as she pushed the robes into the bag. "Please, Harry, get that Cloak on!"

Harry threw the Invisibility Cloak around his shoulders and pulled it up over his head, vanishing from sight. He was only just beginning to appreciate what had happened.

"The others — everyone at the wedding —"

"We can't worry about that now," whispered Hermione. "It's you they're after, Harry, and we'll just put everyone in even more danger by going back."

"She's right," said Ron, who seemed to know that Harry was about to argue, even if he could not see his face. "Most of the Order was there, they'll look after everyone."

Harry nodded, then remembered that they could not see him, and said, "Yeah." But he thought of Ginny, and fear bubbled like acid in his stomach.

"Come on, I think we ought to keep moving," said Hermione.

They moved back up the side street and onto the main road again, where a group of men on the opposite side was singing and weaving across the pavement.

"Just as a matter of interest, why Tottenham Court Road?" Ron asked Hermione.

"I've no idea, it just popped into my head, but I'm sure we're safer out in the Muggle world, it's not where they'll expect us to be."

"True," said Ron, looking around, "but don't you feel a bit — exposed?"

"Where else is there?" asked Hermione, cringing as the men on the other side of the road started wolf-whistling at her. "We can hardly book rooms at the Leaky Cauldron, can we? And Grimmauld Place is out if Snape can get in there. . . . I suppose we could try my parents' house, though I think there's a chance they might check there. . . . Oh, I wish they'd shut up!"

"All right, darling?" the drunkest of the men on the other pavement was yelling. "Fancy a drink? Ditch ginger and come and have a pint!"

"Let's sit down somewhere," Hermione said hastily as Ron opened his mouth to shout back across the road. "Look, this will do, in here!"

It was a small and shabby all-night café. A light layer of grease lay on all the Formica-topped tables, but it was at least empty. Harry slipped into a booth first and Ron sat next to him opposite Hermione, who had her back to the entrance and did not like it: She glanced over her shoulder so frequently she appeared to have a twitch. Harry did not like being stationary; walking had given the illusion that they had a goal. Beneath the Cloak he could feel the last vestiges of Polyjuice leaving him, his hands returning to their usual length and shape. He pulled his glasses out of his pocket and put them on again.

After a minute or two, Ron said, "You know, we're not far from the Leaky Cauldron here, it's only in Charing Cross —"

"Ron, we can't!" said Hermione at once.

"Not to stay there, but to find out what's going on!"

"We know what's going on! Voldemort's taken over the Ministry, what else do we need to know?"

"Okay, okay, it was just an idea!"

They relapsed into a prickly silence. The gum-chewing waitress shuffled over and Hermione ordered two cappuccinos: As Harry was invisible, it would have looked odd to order him one. A pair of burly workmen entered the café and squeezed into the next booth. Hermione dropped her voice to a whisper.

"I say we find a quiet place to Disapparate and head for the countryside. Once we're there, we could send a message to the Order."

"Can you do that talking Patronus thing, then?" asked Ron.

"I've been practicing and I think so," said Hermione.

"Well, as long as it doesn't get them into trouble, though they might've been arrested already. God, that's revolting," Ron added after one sip of the foamy, grayish coffee. The waitress had heard; she shot Ron a nasty look as she shuffled off to take the new customers' orders. The larger of the two workmen, who was blond and quite huge, now that Harry came to look at him, waved her away. She stared, affronted.

"Let's get going, then, I don't want to drink this muck," said Ron. "Hermione, have you got Muggle money to pay for this?"

"Yes, I took out all my Building Society savings before I came to the Burrow. I'll bet all the change is at the bottom," sighed Hermione, reaching for her beaded bag.

The two workmen made identical movements, and Harry mirrored them without conscious thought: All three of them drew their wands. Ron, a few seconds late in realizing what was going on, lunged across the table, pushing Hermione sideways onto her bench. The force of the Death Eaters' spells shattered the tiled wall where Ron's head had just been, as Harry, still invisible, yelled, *"Stupefy!"*

The great blond Death Eater was hit in the face by a jet of red light: He slumped sideways, unconscious. His companion, unable to see who had cast the spell, fired another at Ron: Shining black ropes flew from his wand-tip and bound Ron head to foot — the waitress screamed and ran for the door — Harry sent another Stunning Spell at the Death Eater with the twisted face who had tied up Ron, but the spell missed, rebounded on the window, and hit the waitress, who collapsed in front of the door.

"Expulso!" bellowed the Death Eater, and the table behind which Harry was standing blew up: The force of the explosion slammed

him into the wall and he felt his wand leave his hand as the Cloak slipped off him.

"*Petrificus Totalus!*" screamed Hermione from out of sight, and the Death Eater fell forward like a statue to land with a crunching thud on the mess of broken china, table, and coffee. Hermione crawled out from underneath the bench, shaking bits of glass ashtray out of her hair and trembling all over.

"*D-diffindo,*" she said, pointing her wand at Ron, who roared in pain as she slashed open the knee of his jeans, leaving a deep cut. "Oh, I'm so sorry, Ron, my hand's shaking! *Diffindo!*"

The severed ropes fell away. Ron got to his feet, shaking his arms to regain feeling in them. Harry picked up his wand and climbed over all the debris to where the large blond Death Eater was sprawled across the bench.

"I should've recognized him, he was there the night Dumbledore died," he said. He turned over the darker Death Eater with his foot; the man's eyes moved rapidly between Harry, Ron, and Hermione.

"That's Dolohov," said Ron. "I recognize him from the old wanted posters. I think the big one's Thorfinn Rowle."

"Never mind what they're called!" said Hermione a little hysterically. "How did they find us? What are we going to do?"

Somehow her panic seemed to clear Harry's head.

"Lock the door," he told her, "and Ron, turn out the lights."

He looked down at the paralyzed Dolohov, thinking fast as the lock clicked and Ron used the Deluminator to plunge the café into darkness. Harry could hear the men who had jeered at Hermione earlier, yelling at another girl in the distance.

"What are we going to do with them?" Ron whispered to Harry

through the dark; then, even more quietly, "Kill them? They'd kill us. They had a good go just now."

Hermione shuddered and took a step backward. Harry shook his head.

"We just need to wipe their memories," said Harry. "It's better like that, it'll throw them off the scent. If we killed them it'd be obvious we were here."

"You're the boss," said Ron, sounding profoundly relieved. "But I've never done a Memory Charm."

"Nor have I," said Hermione, "but I know the theory."

She took a deep, calming breath, then pointed her wand at Dolohov's forehead and said, *"Obliviate."*

At once, Dolohov's eyes became unfocused and dreamy.

"Brilliant!" said Harry, clapping her on the back. "Take care of the other one and the waitress while Ron and I clear up."

"Clear up?" said Ron, looking around at the partly destroyed café. "Why?"

"Don't you think they might wonder what's happened if they wake up and find themselves in a place that looks like it's just been bombed?"

"Oh right, yeah . . ."

Ron struggled for a moment before managing to extract his wand from his pocket.

"It's no wonder I can't get it out, Hermione, you packed my old jeans, they're tight."

"Oh, I'm so sorry," hissed Hermione, and as she dragged the waitress out of sight of the windows, Harry heard her mutter a suggestion as to where Ron could stick his wand instead.

Once the café was restored to its previous condition, they heaved the Death Eaters back into their booth and propped them up facing each other.

"But how did they find us?" Hermione asked, looking from one inert man to the other. "How did they know where we were?"

She turned to Harry.

"You — you don't think you've still got your Trace on you, do you, Harry?"

"He can't have," said Ron. "The Trace breaks at seventeen, that's Wizarding law, you can't put it on an adult."

"As far as you know," said Hermione. "What if the Death Eaters have found a way to put it on a seventeen-year-old?"

"But Harry hasn't been near a Death Eater in the last twenty-four hours. Who's supposed to have put a Trace back on him?"

Hermione did not reply. Harry felt contaminated, tainted: Was that really how the Death Eaters had found them?

"If I can't use magic, and you can't use magic near me, without us giving away our position —" he began.

"We're not splitting up!" said Hermione firmly.

"We need a safe place to hide," said Ron. "Give us time to think things through."

"Grimmauld Place," said Harry.

The other two gaped.

"Don't be silly, Harry, Snape can get in there!"

"Ron's dad said they've put up jinxes against him — and even if they haven't worked," he pressed on as Hermione began to argue, "so what? I swear, I'd like nothing better than to meet Snape!"

"But —"

"Hermione, where else is there? It's the best chance we've got.

Snape's only one Death Eater. If I've still got the Trace on me, we'll have whole crowds of them on us wherever else we go."

She could not argue, though she looked as if she would have liked to. While she unlocked the café door, Ron clicked the Deluminator to release the café's light. Then, on Harry's count of three, they reversed the spells upon their three victims, and before the waitress or either of the Death Eaters could do more than stir sleepily, Harry, Ron, and Hermione had turned on the spot and vanished into the compressing darkness once more.

Seconds later Harry's lungs expanded gratefully and he opened his eyes: They were now standing in the middle of a familiar small and shabby square. Tall, dilapidated houses looked down on them from every side. Number twelve was visible to them, for they had been told of its existence by Dumbledore, its Secret-Keeper, and they rushed toward it, checking every few yards that they were not being followed or observed. They raced up the stone steps, and Harry tapped the front door once with his wand. They heard a series of metallic clicks and the clatter of a chain, then the door swung open with a creak and they hurried over the threshold.

As Harry closed the door behind them, the old-fashioned gas lamps sprang into life, casting flickering light along the length of the hallway. It looked just as Harry remembered it: eerie, cobwebbed, the outlines of the house-elf heads on the wall throwing odd shadows up the staircase. Long dark curtains concealed the portrait of Sirius's mother. The only thing that was out of place was the troll's leg umbrella stand, which was lying on its side as if Tonks had just knocked it over again.

"I think somebody's been in here," Hermione whispered, pointing toward it.

"That could've happened as the Order left," Ron murmured back.

"So where are these jinxes they put up against Snape?" Harry asked.

"Maybe they're only activated if he shows up?" suggested Ron.

Yet they remained close together on the doormat, backs against the door, scared to move farther into the house.

"Well, we can't stay here forever," said Harry, and he took a step forward.

"Severus Snape?"

Mad-Eye Moody's voice whispered out of the darkness, making all three of them jump back in fright. "We're not Snape!" croaked Harry, before something whooshed over him like cold air and his tongue curled backward on itself, making it impossible to speak. Before he had time to feel inside his mouth, however, his tongue had unraveled again.

The other two seemed to have experienced the same unpleasant sensation. Ron was making retching noises; Hermione stammered, "That m-must have b-been the T-Tongue-Tying Curse Mad-Eye set up for Snape!"

Gingerly Harry took another step forward. Something shifted in the shadows at the end of the hall, and before any of them could say another word, a figure had risen up out of the carpet, tall, dust-colored, and terrible: Hermione screamed and so did Mrs. Black, her curtains flying open; the gray figure was gliding toward them, faster and faster, its waist-length hair and beard streaming behind it, its face sunken, fleshless, with empty eye sockets: Horribly familiar, dreadfully altered, it raised a wasted arm, pointing at Harry.

"No!" Harry shouted, and though he had raised his wand no spell occurred to him. "No! It wasn't us! We didn't kill you —"

On the word *kill,* the figure exploded in a great cloud of dust: Coughing, his eyes watering, Harry looked around to see Hermione crouched on the floor by the door with her arms over her head, and Ron, who was shaking from head to foot, patting her clumsily on the shoulder and saying, "It's all r-right. . . . It's g-gone. . . ."

Dust swirled around Harry like mist, catching the blue gaslight, as Mrs. Black continued to scream.

"Mudbloods, filth, stains of dishonor, taint of shame on the house of my fathers —"

"SHUT UP!" Harry bellowed, directing his wand at her, and with a bang and a burst of red sparks, the curtains swung shut again, silencing her.

"That . . . that was . . ." Hermione whimpered, as Ron helped her to her feet.

"Yeah," said Harry, "but it wasn't really him, was it? Just something to scare Snape."

Had it worked, Harry wondered, or had Snape already blasted the horror-figure aside as casually as he had killed the real Dumbledore? Nerves still tingling, he led the other two up the hall, half-expecting some new terror to reveal itself, but nothing moved except for a mouse skittering along the skirting board.

"Before we go any farther, I think we'd better check," whispered Hermione, and she raised her wand and said, *"Homenum revelio."*

Nothing happened.

"Well, you've just had a big shock," said Ron kindly. "What was that supposed to do?"

"It did what I meant it to do!" said Hermione rather crossly. "That was a spell to reveal human presence, and there's nobody here except us!"

"And old Dusty," said Ron, glancing at the patch of carpet from which the corpse-figure had risen.

"Let's go up," said Hermione with a frightened look at the same spot, and she led the way up the creaking stairs to the drawing room on the first floor.

Hermione waved her wand to ignite the old gas lamps, then, shivering slightly in the drafty room, she perched on the sofa, her arms wrapped tightly around her. Ron crossed to the window and moved the heavy velvet curtain aside an inch.

"Can't see anyone out there," he reported. "And you'd think, if Harry still had a Trace on him, they'd have followed us here. I know they can't get in the house, but — what's up, Harry?"

Harry had given a cry of pain: His scar had burned again as something flashed across his mind like a bright light on water. He saw a large shadow and felt a fury that was not his own pound through his body, violent and brief as an electric shock.

"What did you see?" Ron asked, advancing on Harry. "Did you see him at my place?"

"No, I just felt anger — he's really angry —"

"But that could be at the Burrow," said Ron loudly. "What else? Didn't you see anything? Was he cursing someone?"

"No, I just felt anger — I couldn't tell —"

Harry felt badgered, confused, and Hermione did not help as she said in a frightened voice, "Your scar, again? But what's going on? I thought that connection had closed!"

"It did, for a while," muttered Harry; his scar was still painful, which made it hard to concentrate. "I — I think it's started opening again whenever he loses control, that's how it used to —"

"But then you've got to close your mind!" said Hermione shrilly. "Harry, Dumbledore didn't want you to use that connection, he wanted you to shut it down, that's why you were supposed to use Occlumency! Otherwise Voldemort can plant false images in your mind, remember —"

"Yeah, I do remember, thanks," said Harry through gritted teeth; he did not need Hermione to tell him that Voldemort had once used this selfsame connection between them to lead him into a trap, nor that it had resulted in Sirius's death. He wished that he had not told them what he had seen and felt; it made Voldemort more threatening, as though he were pressing against the window of the room, and still the pain in his scar was building and he fought it: It was like resisting the urge to be sick.

He turned his back on Ron and Hermione, pretending to examine the old tapestry of the Black family tree on the wall. Then Hermione shrieked: Harry drew his wand again and spun around to see a silver Patronus soar through the drawing room window and land upon the floor in front of them, where it solidified into the weasel that spoke with the voice of Ron's father.

"Family safe, do not reply, we are being watched."

The Patronus dissolved into nothingness. Ron let out a noise between a whimper and a groan and dropped onto the sofa: Hermione joined him, gripping his arm.

"They're all right, they're all right!" she whispered, and Ron half laughed and hugged her.

"Harry," he said over Hermione's shoulder, "I —"

"It's not a problem," said Harry, sickened by the pain in his head.

"It's your family, 'course you're worried. I'd feel the same way." He thought of Ginny. "I *do* feel the same way."

The pain in his scar was reaching a peak, burning as it had done in the garden of the Burrow. Faintly he heard Hermione say, "I don't want to be on my own. Could we use the sleeping bags I've brought and camp in here tonight?"

He heard Ron agree. He could not fight the pain much longer: He had to succumb.

"Bathroom," he muttered, and he left the room as fast as he could without running.

He barely made it: Bolting the door behind him with trembling hands, he grasped his pounding head and fell to the floor, then in an explosion of agony, he felt the rage that did not belong to him possess his soul, saw a long room lit only by firelight, and the great blond Death Eater on the floor, screaming and writhing, and a slighter figure standing over him, wand outstretched, while Harry spoke in a high, cold, merciless voice.

"More, Rowle, or shall we end it and feed you to Nagini? Lord Voldemort is not sure that he will forgive this time. . . . You called me back for this, to tell me that Harry Potter has escaped again? Draco, give Rowle another taste of our displeasure. . . . Do it, or feel my wrath yourself!"

A log fell in the fire: Flames reared, their light darting across a terrified, pointed white face — with a sense of emerging from deep water, Harry drew heaving breaths and opened his eyes.

He was spread-eagled on the cold black marble floor, his nose inches from one of the silver serpent tails that supported the large bathtub. He sat up. Malfoy's gaunt, petrified face seemed branded on the inside of his eyes. Harry felt sickened by what he had seen, by the use to which Draco was now being put by Voldemort.

There was a sharp rap on the door, and Harry jumped as Hermione's voice rang out.

"Harry, do you want your toothbrush? I've got it here."

"Yeah, great, thanks," he said, fighting to keep his voice casual as he stood up to let her in.

KREACHER'S TALE

arry woke early next morning, wrapped in a sleeping
bag on the drawing room floor. A chink of sky was visible between the heavy curtains: It was the cool, clear blue of watered
ink, somewhere between night and dawn, and everything was quiet
except for Ron and Hermione's slow, deep breathing. Harry glanced
over at the dark shapes they made on the floor beside him. Ron
had had a fit of gallantry and insisted that Hermione sleep on the
cushions from the sofa, so that her silhouette was raised above his.
Her arm curved to the floor, her fingers inches from Ron's. Harry
wondered whether they had fallen asleep holding hands. The idea
made him feel strangely lonely.

He looked up at the shadowy ceiling, the cobwebbed chandelier. Less than twenty-four hours ago, he had been standing in the
sunlight at the entrance to the marquee, waiting to show in wedding guests. It seemed a lifetime away. What was going to happen
now? He lay on the floor and he thought of the Horcruxes, of the

daunting, complex mission Dumbledore had left him. . . . Dumbledore . . .

The grief that had possessed him since Dumbledore's death felt
different now. The accusations he had heard from Muriel at the
wedding seemed to have nested in his brain like diseased things,
infecting his memories of the wizard he had idolized. Could Dumbledore have let such things happen? Had he been like Dudley,
content to watch neglect and abuse as long as it did not affect him?
Could he have turned his back on a sister who was being imprisoned and hidden?

Harry thought of Godric's Hollow, of graves Dumbledore had
never mentioned there; he thought of mysterious objects left without explanation in Dumbledore's will, and resentment swelled in
the darkness. Why hadn't Dumbledore told him? Why hadn't he
explained? Had Dumbledore actually cared about Harry at all? Or
had Harry been nothing more than a tool to be polished and honed,
but not trusted, never confided in?

Harry could not stand lying there with nothing but bitter
thoughts for company. Desperate for something to do, for distraction, he slipped out of his sleeping bag, picked up his wand, and
crept out of the room. On the landing he whispered, *"Lumos,"* and
started to climb the stairs by wandlight.

On the second landing was the bedroom in which he and Ron
had slept last time they had been here; he glanced into it. The wardrobe doors stood open and the bedclothes had been ripped back.
Harry remembered the overturned troll leg downstairs. Somebody
had searched the house since the Order had left. Snape? Or perhaps
Mundungus, who had pilfered plenty from this house both before
and after Sirius died? Harry's gaze wandered to the portrait that

sometimes contained Phineas Nigellus Black, Sirius's great-great-grandfather, but it was empty, showing nothing but a stretch of muddy backdrop. Phineas Nigellus was evidently spending the night in the headmaster's study at Hogwarts.

Harry continued up the stairs until he reached the topmost landing, where there were only two doors. The one facing him bore a nameplate reading SIRIUS. Harry had never entered his godfather's bedroom before. He pushed open the door, holding his wand high to cast light as widely as possible. The room was spacious and must once have been handsome. There was a large bed with a carved wooden headboard, a tall window obscured by long velvet curtains, and a chandelier thickly coated in dust with candle stubs still resting in its sockets, solid wax hanging in frostlike drips. A fine film of dust covered the pictures on the walls and the bed's headboard; a spider's web stretched between the chandelier and the top of the large wooden wardrobe, and as Harry moved deeper into the room, he heard a scurrying of disturbed mice.

The teenage Sirius had plastered the walls with so many posters and pictures that little of the walls' silvery-gray silk was visible. Harry could only assume that Sirius's parents had been unable to remove the Permanent Sticking Charm that kept them on the wall, because he was sure they would not have appreciated their eldest son's taste in decoration. Sirius seemed to have gone out of his way to annoy his parents. There were several large Gryffindor banners, faded scarlet and gold, just to underline his difference from all the rest of the Slytherin family. There were many pictures of Muggle motorcycles, and also (Harry had to admire Sirius's nerve) several posters of bikini-clad Muggle girls; Harry could tell that they were Muggles because they remained quite stationary within their pictures, faded smiles and glazed eyes frozen on the paper. This was in contrast to the only Wizarding photograph on the walls, which was a picture of four Hogwarts students standing arm in arm, laughing at the camera.

With a leap of pleasure, Harry recognized his father; his untidy black hair stuck up at the back like Harry's, and he too wore glasses. Beside him was Sirius, carelessly handsome, his slightly arrogant face so much younger and happier than Harry had ever seen it alive. To Sirius's right stood Pettigrew, more than a head shorter, plump and watery-eyed, flushed with pleasure at his inclusion in this coolest of gangs, with the much-admired rebels that James and Sirius had been. On James's left was Lupin, even then a little shabby-looking, but he had the same air of delighted surprise at finding himself liked and included . . . or was it simply because Harry knew how it had been, that he saw these things in the picture? He tried to take it from the wall; it was his now, after all, Sirius had left him everything, but it would not budge. Sirius had taken no chances in preventing his parents from redecorating his room.

Harry looked around at the floor. The sky outside was growing brighter: A shaft of light revealed bits of paper, books, and small objects scattered over the carpet. Evidently Sirius's bedroom had been searched too, although its contents seemed to have been judged mostly, if not entirely, worthless. A few of the books had been shaken roughly enough to part company with their covers, and sundry pages littered the floor.

Harry bent down, picked up a few of the pieces of paper, and examined them. He recognized one as part of an old edition of *A History of Magic,* by Bathilda Bagshot, and another as belonging to a motorcycle maintenance manual. The third was handwritten and crumpled. He smoothed it out.

Dear Padfoot,

Thank you, thank you, for Harry's birthday present! It was his favorite by far. One year old and already zooming along on a toy broomstick, he looked so pleased with himself, I'm enclosing a picture so you can see. You know it only rises about two feet off the ground, but he nearly killed the cat and he smashed a horrible vase Petunia sent me for Christmas (no complaints there). Of course, James thought it was so funny, says he's going to be a great Quidditch player, but we've had to pack away all the ornaments and make sure we don't take our eyes off him when he gets going.

We had a very quiet birthday tea, just us and old Bathilda, who has always been sweet to us and who dotes on Harry. We were so sorry you couldn't come, but the Order's got to come first, and Harry's not old enough to know it's his birthday anyway! James is getting a bit frustrated shut up here, he tries not to show it but I can tell — also, Dumbledore's still got his Invisibility Cloak, so no chance of little excursions. If you could visit, it would cheer him up so much. Wormy was here last weekend, I thought he seemed down, but that was probably the news about the McKinnons; I cried all evening when I heard.

Bathilda drops in most days, she's a fascinating old thing with the most amazing stories about Dumbledore, I'm not

sure he'd be pleased if he knew! I don't know how much to
believe, actually, because it seems incredible that Dumbledore

Harry's extremities seemed to have gone numb. He stood quite still, holding the miraculous paper in his nerveless fingers while inside him a kind of quiet eruption sent joy and grief thundering in equal measure through his veins. Lurching to the bed, he sat down.

He read the letter again, but could not take in any more meaning than he had done the first time, and was reduced to staring at the handwriting itself. She had made her "g"s the same way he did: He searched through the letter for every one of them, and each felt like a friendly little wave glimpsed from behind a veil. The letter was an incredible treasure, proof that Lily Potter had lived, really lived, that her warm hand had once moved across this parchment, tracing ink into these letters, these words, words about him, Harry, her son.

Impatiently brushing away the wetness in his eyes, he reread the letter, this time concentrating on the meaning. It was like listening to a half-remembered voice.

They had had a cat . . . perhaps it had perished, like his parents, at Godric's Hollow . . . or else fled when there was nobody left to feed it. . . . Sirius had bought him his first broomstick. . . . His parents had known Bathilda Bagshot; had Dumbledore introduced them? *Dumbledore's still got his Invisibility Cloak* . . . There was something funny there. . . .

Harry paused, pondering his mother's words. Why had Dumbledore taken James's Invisibility Cloak? Harry distinctly remembered his headmaster telling him years before, "I don't need a cloak to become invisible." Perhaps some less gifted Order member had needed its assistance, and Dumbledore had acted as carrier? Harry passed on. . . .

Wormy was here . . . Pettigrew, the traitor, had seemed "down," had he? Was he aware that he was seeing James and Lily alive for the last time?

And finally Bathilda again, who told incredible stories about Dumbledore. *It seems incredible that Dumbledore —*

That Dumbledore what? But there were any number of things that would seem incredible about Dumbledore; that he had once received bottom marks in a Transfiguration test, for instance, or had taken up goat-charming like Aberforth. . . .

Harry got to his feet and scanned the floor: Perhaps the rest of the letter was here somewhere. He seized papers, treating them, in his eagerness, with as little consideration as the original searcher; he pulled open drawers, shook out books, stood on a chair to run his hand over the top of the wardrobe, and crawled under the bed and armchair.

At last, lying facedown on the floor, he spotted what looked like a torn piece of paper under the chest of drawers. When he pulled it out, it proved to be most of the photograph Lily had described in her letter. A black-haired baby was zooming in and out of the picture on a tiny broom, roaring with laughter, and a pair of legs that must have belonged to James was chasing after him. Harry tucked the photograph into his pocket with Lily's letter and continued to look for the second sheet.

After another quarter of an hour, however, he was forced to conclude that the rest of his mother's letter was gone. Had it simply been lost in the sixteen years that had elapsed since it had been written, or had it been taken by whoever had searched the room? Harry read the first sheet again, this time looking for clues as to what might have made the second sheet valuable. His toy broomstick could hardly be considered interesting to the Death Eaters. . . . The only potentially useful thing he could see here was possible information on Dumbledore. *It seems incredible that Dumbledore* — what?

"Harry? Harry! *Harry!*"

"I'm here!" he called. "What's happened?"

There was a clatter of footsteps outside the door, and Hermione burst inside.

"We woke up and didn't know where you were!" she said breathlessly. She turned and shouted over her shoulder, "Ron! I've found him!"

Ron's annoyed voice echoed distantly from several floors below.

"Good! Tell him from me he's a git!"

"Harry, don't just disappear, please, we were terrified! Why did you come up here anyway?" She gazed around the ransacked room. "What have you been doing?"

"Look what I've just found."

He held out his mother's letter. Hermione took it and read it while Harry watched her. When she reached the end of the page she looked up at him.

"Oh, Harry . . ."

"And there's this too."

He handed her the torn photograph, and Hermione smiled at the baby zooming in and out of sight on the toy broom.

"I've been looking for the rest of the letter," Harry said, "but it's not here."

Hermione glanced around.

"Did you make all this mess, or was some of it done when you got here?"

"Someone had searched before me," said Harry.

"I thought so. Every room I looked into on the way up had been disturbed. What were they after, do you think?"

"Information on the Order, if it was Snape."

"But you'd think he'd already have all he needed, I mean, he was *in* the Order, wasn't he?"

"Well then," said Harry, keen to discuss his theory, "what about information on Dumbledore? The second page of this letter, for instance. You know this Bathilda my mum mentions, you know who she is?"

"Who?"

"Bathilda Bagshot, the author of —"

"*A History of Magic,*" said Hermione, looking interested. "So your parents knew her? She was an incredible magical historian."

"And she's still alive," said Harry, "and she lives in Godric's Hollow, Ron's Auntie Muriel was talking about her at the wedding. She knew Dumbledore's family too. Be pretty interesting to talk to, wouldn't she?"

There was a little too much understanding in the smile Hermione gave him for Harry's liking. He took back the letter and the photograph and tucked them inside the pouch around his neck, so as not to have to look at her and give himself away.

"I understand why you'd love to talk to her about your mum and dad, and Dumbledore too," said Hermione. "But that wouldn't really help us in our search for the Horcruxes, would it?" Harry did not answer, and she rushed on, "Harry, I know you really want to go to Godric's Hollow, but I'm scared, I'm scared at how easily those

Death Eaters found us yesterday. It just makes me feel more than ever that we ought to avoid the place where your parents are buried, I'm sure they'd be expecting you to visit it."

"It's not just that," Harry said, still avoiding looking at her. "Muriel said stuff about Dumbledore at the wedding. I want to know the truth. . . ."

He told Hermione everything that Muriel had told him. When he had finished, Hermione said, "Of course, I can see why that's upset you, Harry —"

"I'm not upset," he lied, "I'd just like to know whether or not it's true or —"

"Harry, do you really think you'll get the truth from a malicious old woman like Muriel, or from Rita Skeeter? How can you believe them? You knew Dumbledore!"

"I thought I did," he muttered.

"But you know how much truth there was in everything Rita wrote about you! Doge is right, how can you let these people tarnish your memories of Dumbledore?"

He looked away, trying not to betray the resentment he felt. There it was again: Choose what to believe. He wanted the truth. Why was everybody so determined that he should not get it?

"Shall we go down to the kitchen?" Hermione suggested after a little pause. "Find something for breakfast?"

He agreed, but grudgingly, and followed her out onto the landing and past the second door that led off it. There were deep scratch marks in the paintwork below a small sign that he had not noticed in the dark. He paused at the top of the stairs to read it. It was a pompous little sign, neatly lettered by hand, the sort of thing that Percy Weasley might have stuck on his bedroom door:

Do Not Enter
Without the Express Permission of
Regulus Arcturus Black

Excitement trickled through Harry, but he was not immediately sure why. He read the sign again. Hermione was already a flight of stairs below him.

"Hermione," he said, and he was surprised that his voice was so calm. "Come back up here."

"What's the matter?"

"R.A.B. I think I've found him."

There was a gasp, and then Hermione ran back up the stairs.

"In your mum's letter? But I didn't see —"

Harry shook his head, pointing at Regulus's sign. She read it, then clutched Harry's arm so tightly that he winced.

"Sirius's brother?" she whispered.

"He was a Death Eater," said Harry, "Sirius told me about him, he joined up when he was really young and then got cold feet and tried to leave — so they killed him."

"That fits!" gasped Hermione. "If he was a Death Eater he had access to Voldemort, and if he became disenchanted, then he would have wanted to bring Voldemort down!"

She released Harry, leaned over the banister, and screamed, "Ron! RON! Get up here, quick!"

Ron appeared, panting, a minute later, his wand ready in his hand.

"What's up? If it's massive spiders again I want breakfast before I —"

He frowned at the sign on Regulus's door, to which Hermione was silently pointing.

"What? That was Sirius's brother, wasn't it? Regulus Arcturus . . . Regulus . . . *R.A.B.*! The locket — you don't reckon — ?"

"Let's find out," said Harry. He pushed the door: It was locked. Hermione pointed her wand at the handle and said, *"Alohomora."* There was a click, and the door swung open.

They moved over the threshold together, gazing around. Regulus's bedroom was slightly smaller than Sirius's, though it had the same sense of former grandeur. Whereas Sirius had sought to advertise his difference from the rest of the family, Regulus had striven to emphasize the opposite. The Slytherin colors of emerald and silver were everywhere, draping the bed, the walls, and the windows. The Black family crest was painstakingly painted over the bed, along with its motto, TOUJOURS PUR. Beneath this was a collection of yellow newspaper cuttings, all stuck together to make a ragged collage. Hermione crossed the room to examine them.

"They're all about Voldemort," she said. "Regulus seems to have been a fan for a few years before he joined the Death Eaters. . . ."

A little puff of dust rose from the bedcovers as she sat down to read the clippings. Harry, meanwhile, had noticed another photograph; a Hogwarts Quidditch team was smiling and waving out of the frame. He moved closer and saw the snakes emblazoned on their chests: Slytherins. Regulus was instantly recognizable as the boy sitting in the middle of the front row: He had the same dark hair and slightly haughty look of his brother, though he was smaller, slighter, and rather less handsome than Sirius had been.

"He played Seeker," said Harry.

"What?" said Hermione vaguely; she was still immersed in Voldemort's press clippings.

"He's sitting in the middle of the front row, that's where the Seeker . . . Never mind," said Harry, realizing that nobody was listening: Ron was on his hands and knees, searching under the wardrobe. Harry looked around the room for likely hiding places and approached the desk. Yet again, somebody had searched before them. The drawers' contents had been turned over recently, the dust disturbed, but there was nothing of value there: old quills, out-of-date textbooks that bore evidence of being roughly handled, a recently smashed ink bottle, its sticky residue covering the contents of the drawer.

"There's an easier way," said Hermione, as Harry wiped his inky fingers on his jeans. She raised her wand and said, *"Accio Locket!"*

Nothing happened. Ron, who had been searching the folds of the faded curtains, looked disappointed.

"Is that it, then? It's not here?"

"Oh, it could still be here, but under counter-enchantments," said Hermione. "Charms to prevent it being summoned magically, you know."

"Like Voldemort put on the stone basin in the cave," said Harry, remembering how he had been unable to Summon the fake locket.

"How are we supposed to find it then?" asked Ron.

"We search manually," said Hermione.

"That's a good idea," said Ron, rolling his eyes, and he resumed his examination of the curtains.

They combed every inch of the room for more than an hour, but were forced, finally, to conclude that the locket was not there.

The sun had risen now; its light dazzled them even through the grimy landing windows.

"It could be somewhere else in the house, though," said Hermione in a rallying tone as they walked back downstairs: As Harry and Ron had become more discouraged, she seemed to have become more determined. "Whether he'd managed to destroy it or not, he'd want to keep it hidden from Voldemort, wouldn't he? Remember all those awful things we had to get rid of when we were here last time? That clock that shot bolts at everyone and those old robes that tried to strangle Ron; Regulus might have put them there to protect the locket's hiding place, even though we didn't realize it at . . . at . . ."

Harry and Ron looked at her. She was standing with one foot in midair, with the dumbstruck look of one who had just been Obliviated; her eyes had even drifted out of focus.

". . . at the time," she finished in a whisper.

"Something wrong?" asked Ron.

"There was a locket."

"What?" said Harry and Ron together.

"In the cabinet in the drawing room. Nobody could open it. And we . . . we . . ."

Harry felt as though a brick had slid down through his chest into his stomach. He remembered: He had even handled the thing as they passed it around, each trying in turn to prise it open. It had been tossed into a sack of rubbish, along with the snuffbox of Wartcap powder and the music box that had made everyone sleepy. . . .

"Kreacher nicked loads of things back from us," said Harry. It was the only chance, the only slender hope left to them, and he was going to cling to it until forced to let go. "He had a whole stash of stuff in his cupboard in the kitchen. C'mon."

He ran down the stairs taking two steps at a time, the other two thundering along in his wake. They made so much noise that they woke the portrait of Sirius's mother as they passed through the hall.

"Filth! Mudbloods! Scum!" she screamed after them as they dashed down into the basement kitchen and slammed the door behind them.

Harry ran the length of the room, skidded to a halt at the door of Kreacher's cupboard, and wrenched it open. There was the nest of dirty old blankets in which the house-elf had once slept, but they were no longer glittering with the trinkets Kreacher had salvaged. The only thing there was an old copy of *Nature's Nobility: A Wizarding Genealogy.* Refusing to believe his eyes, Harry snatched up the blankets and shook them. A dead mouse fell out and rolled dismally across the floor. Ron groaned as he threw himself into a kitchen chair; Hermione closed her eyes.

"It's not over yet," said Harry, and he raised his voice and called, *"Kreacher!"*

There was a loud *crack* and the house-elf that Harry had so reluctantly inherited from Sirius appeared out of nowhere in front of the cold and empty fireplace: tiny, half human-sized, his pale skin hanging off him in folds, white hair sprouting copiously from his batlike ears. He was still wearing the filthy rag in which they had first met him, and the contemptuous look he bent upon Harry showed that his attitude to his change of ownership had altered no more than his outfit.

"Master," croaked Kreacher in his bullfrog's voice, and he bowed low, muttering to his knees, "back in my Mistress's old house with the blood-traitor Weasley and the Mudblood —"

"I forbid you to call anyone 'blood traitor' or 'Mudblood,'" growled Harry. He would have found Kreacher, with his snoutlike nose and bloodshot eyes, a distinctly unlovable object even if the elf had not betrayed Sirius to Voldemort.

"I've got a question for you," said Harry, his heart beating rather fast as he looked down at the elf, "and I order you to answer it truthfully. Understand?"

"Yes, Master," said Kreacher, bowing low again: Harry saw his lips moving soundlessly, undoubtedly framing the insults he was now forbidden to utter.

"Two years ago," said Harry, his heart now hammering against his ribs, "there was a big gold locket in the drawing room upstairs. We threw it out. Did you steal it back?"

There was a moment's silence, during which Kreacher straightened up to look Harry full in the face. Then he said, "Yes."

"Where is it now?" asked Harry jubilantly as Ron and Hermione looked gleeful.

Kreacher closed his eyes as though he could not bear to see their reactions to his next word.

"Gone."

"Gone?" echoed Harry, elation flooding out of him. "What do you mean, it's gone?"

The elf shivered. He swayed.

"Kreacher," said Harry fiercely, "I order you —"

"Mundungus Fletcher," croaked the elf, his eyes still tight shut. "Mundungus Fletcher stole it all: Miss Bella's and Miss Cissy's pictures, my Mistress's gloves, the Order of Merlin, First Class, the goblets with the family crest, and — and —"

Kreacher was gulping for air: His hollow chest was rising and falling rapidly, then his eyes flew open and he uttered a bloodcurdling scream.

"— *and the locket, Master Regulus's locket, Kreacher did wrong, Kreacher failed in his orders!*"

Harry reacted instinctively: As Kreacher lunged for the poker standing in the grate, he launched himself upon the elf, flattening him. Hermione's scream mingled with Kreacher's, but Harry bellowed louder than both of them: "Kreacher, I order you to stay still!"

He felt the elf freeze and released him. Kreacher lay flat on the cold stone floor, tears gushing from his sagging eyes.

"Harry, let him up!" Hermione whispered.

"So he can beat himself up with the poker?" snorted Harry, kneeling beside the elf. "I don't think so. Right, Kreacher, I want the truth: How do you know Mundungus Fletcher stole the locket?"

"Kreacher saw him!" gasped the elf as tears poured over his snout and into his mouth full of graying teeth. "Kreacher saw him coming out of Kreacher's cupboard with his hands full of Kreacher's treasures. Kreacher told the sneak thief to stop, but Mundungus Fletcher laughed and r-ran. . . ."

"You called the locket 'Master Regulus's,'" said Harry. "Why? Where did it come from? What did Regulus have to do with it? Kreacher, sit up and tell me everything you know about that locket, and everything Regulus had to do with it!"

The elf sat up, curled into a ball, placed his wet face between his knees, and began to rock backward and forward. When he spoke, his voice was muffled but quite distinct in the silent, echoing kitchen.

"Master Sirius ran away, good riddance, for he was a bad boy and broke my Mistress's heart with his lawless ways. But Master Regulus had proper pride; he knew what was due to the name of Black and the dignity of his pure blood. For years he talked of the Dark Lord, who was going to bring the wizards out of hiding to rule the Muggles and the Muggle-borns . . . and when he was sixteen years old, Master Regulus joined the Dark Lord. So proud, so proud, so happy to serve . . .

"And one day, a year after he had joined, Master Regulus came down to the kitchen to see Kreacher. Master Regulus always liked Kreacher. And Master Regulus said . . . he said . . ."

The old elf rocked faster than ever.

". . . he said that the Dark Lord required an elf."

"Voldemort needed an *elf*?" Harry repeated, looking around at Ron and Hermione, who looked just as puzzled as he did.

"Oh yes," moaned Kreacher. "And Master Regulus had volunteered Kreacher. It was an honor, said Master Regulus, an honor for him and for Kreacher, who must be sure to do whatever the Dark Lord ordered him to do . . . and then to c-come home."

Kreacher rocked still faster, his breath coming in sobs.

"So Kreacher went to the Dark Lord. The Dark Lord did not tell Kreacher what they were to do, but took Kreacher with him to a cave beside the sea. And beyond the cave there was a cavern, and in the cavern was a great black lake . . ."

The hairs on the back of Harry's neck stood up. Kreacher's croaking voice seemed to come to him from across that dark water. He saw what had happened as clearly as though he had been present.

". . . There was a boat . . ."

Of course there had been a boat; Harry knew the boat, ghostly green and tiny, bewitched so as to carry one wizard and one victim toward the island in the center. This, then, was how Voldemort had tested the defenses surrounding the Horcrux: by borrowing a disposable creature, a house-elf . . .

"There was a b-basin full of potion on the island. The D-Dark Lord made Kreacher drink it. . . ."

The elf quaked from head to foot.

"Kreacher drank, and as he drank, he saw terrible things. . . . Kreacher's insides burned. . . . Kreacher cried for Master Regulus to save him, he cried for his Mistress Black, but the Dark Lord only laughed. . . . He made Kreacher drink all the potion. . . . He dropped a locket into the empty basin. . . . He filled it with more potion.

"And then the Dark Lord sailed away, leaving Kreacher on the island. . . ."

Harry could see it happening. He watched Voldemort's white, snakelike face vanishing into darkness, those red eyes fixed pitilessly on the thrashing elf whose death would occur within minutes, whenever he succumbed to the desperate thirst that the burning potion caused its victim. . . . But here, Harry's imagination could go no further, for he could not see how Kreacher had escaped.

"Kreacher needed water, he crawled to the island's edge and he drank from the black lake . . . and hands, dead hands, came out of the water and dragged Kreacher under the surface. . . ."

"How did you get away?" Harry asked, and he was not surprised to hear himself whispering.

Kreacher raised his ugly head and looked at Harry with his great, bloodshot eyes.

"Master Regulus told Kreacher to come back," he said.

"I know — but how did you escape the Inferi?"

Kreacher did not seem to understand.

"Master Regulus told Kreacher to come back," he repeated.

"I know, but —"

"Well, it's obvious, isn't it, Harry?" said Ron. "He Disapparated!"

"But . . . you couldn't Apparate in and out of that cave," said Harry, "otherwise Dumbledore —"

"Elf magic isn't like wizard's magic, is it?" said Ron. "I mean, they can Apparate and Disapparate in and out of Hogwarts when we can't."

There was silence as Harry digested this. How could Voldemort have made such a mistake? But even as he thought this, Hermione spoke, and her voice was icy.

"Of course, Voldemort would have considered the ways of house-elves far beneath his notice, just like all the purebloods who treat them like animals. . . . It would never have occurred to him that they might have magic that he didn't."

"The house-elf's highest law is his Master's bidding," intoned Kreacher. "Kreacher was told to come home, so Kreacher came home. . . ."

"Well, then, you did what you were told, didn't you?" said Hermione kindly. "You didn't disobey orders at all!"

Kreacher shook his head, rocking as fast as ever.

"So what happened when you got back?" Harry asked. "What did Regulus say when you told him what had happened?"

"Master Regulus was very worried, very worried," croaked Kreacher. "Master Regulus told Kreacher to stay hidden and not to leave the house. And then . . . it was a little while later . . . Master Regulus came to find Kreacher in his cupboard one night, and Master Regulus was strange, not as he usually was, disturbed in his mind, Kreacher could tell . . . and he asked Kreacher to take him to the cave, the cave where Kreacher had gone with the Dark Lord. . . ."

And so they had set off. Harry could visualize them quite clearly, the frightened old elf and the thin, dark Seeker who had so resembled Sirius. . . . Kreacher knew how to open the concealed entrance to the underground cavern, knew how to raise the tiny boat; this time it was his beloved Regulus who sailed with him to the island with its basin of poison. . . .

"And he made you drink the potion?" said Harry, disgusted.

But Kreacher shook his head and wept. Hermione's hands leapt to her mouth: She seemed to have understood something.

"M-Master Regulus took from his pocket a locket like the one the Dark Lord had," said Kreacher, tears pouring down either side of his snoutlike nose. "And he told Kreacher to take it and, when the basin was empty, to switch the lockets. . . ."

Kreacher's sobs came in great rasps now; Harry had to concentrate hard to understand him.

"And he ordered — Kreacher to leave — without him. And he told Kreacher — to go home — and never to tell my Mistress — what he had done — but to destroy — the first locket. And he drank — all the potion — and Kreacher swapped the lockets — and watched . . . as Master Regulus . . . was dragged beneath the water . . . and . . ."

"Oh, Kreacher!" wailed Hermione, who was crying. She dropped to her knees beside the elf and tried to hug him. At once he was on his feet, cringing away from her, quite obviously repulsed.

"The Mudblood touched Kreacher, he will not allow it, what would his Mistress say?"

"I told you not to call her 'Mudblood'!" snarled Harry, but the elf was already punishing himself: He fell to the ground and banged his forehead on the floor.

"Stop him — stop him!" Hermione cried. "Oh, don't you see now how sick it is, the way they've got to obey?"

"Kreacher — stop, stop!" shouted Harry.

The elf lay on the floor, panting and shivering, green mucus glistening around his snout, a bruise already blooming on his pallid forehead where he had struck himself, his eyes swollen and bloodshot and swimming in tears. Harry had never seen anything so pitiful.

"So you brought the locket home," he said relentlessly, for he was determined to know the full story. "And you tried to destroy it?"

"Nothing Kreacher did made any mark upon it," moaned the elf. "Kreacher tried everything, everything he knew, but nothing, nothing would work. . . . So many powerful spells upon the casing, Kreacher was sure the way to destroy it was to get inside it, but it would not open. . . . Kreacher punished himself, he tried again, he punished himself, he tried again. Kreacher failed to obey orders, Kreacher could not destroy the locket! And his Mistress was mad with grief, because Master Regulus had disappeared, and Kreacher could not tell her what had happened, no, because Master Regulus had f-f-forbidden him to tell any of the f-f-family what happened in the c-cave. . . ."

Kreacher began to sob so hard that there were no more coherent words. Tears flowed down Hermione's cheeks as she watched Kreacher, but she did not dare touch him again. Even Ron, who was no fan of Kreacher's, looked troubled. Harry sat back on his heels and shook his head, trying to clear it.

"I don't understand you, Kreacher," he said finally. "Voldemort tried to kill you, Regulus died to bring Voldemort down, but you were still happy to betray Sirius to Voldemort? You were happy to go to Narcissa and Bellatrix, and pass information to Voldemort through them. . . ."

"Harry, Kreacher doesn't think like that," said Hermione, wiping her eyes on the back of her hand. "He's a slave; house-elves are used to bad, even brutal treatment; what Voldemort did to Kreacher wasn't that far out of the common way. What do wizard wars mean to an elf like Kreacher? He's loyal to people who are kind to him, and Mrs. Black must have been, and Regulus certainly was, so he served them willingly and parroted their beliefs. I know what you're going to say," she went on as Harry began to protest, "that Regulus changed his mind . . . but he doesn't seem to have explained that to Kreacher, does he? And I think I know why. Kreacher and Regulus's family were all safer if they kept to the old pure-blood line. Regulus was trying to protect them all."

"Sirius —"

"Sirius was horrible to Kreacher, Harry, and it's no good looking like that, you know it's true. Kreacher had been alone for a long time when Sirius came to live here, and he was probably starving for a bit of affection. I'm sure 'Miss Cissy' and 'Miss Bella' were perfectly lovely to Kreacher when he turned up, so he did them a favor and told them everything they wanted to know. I've said all along that wizards would pay for how they treat house-elves. Well, Voldemort did . . . and so did Sirius."

Harry had no retort. As he watched Kreacher sobbing on the

floor, he remembered what Dumbledore had said to him, mere hours after Sirius's death: *I do not think Sirius ever saw Kreacher as a being with feelings as acute as a human's. . . .*

"Kreacher," said Harry after a while, "when you feel up to it, er . . . please sit up."

It was several minutes before Kreacher hiccuped himself into silence. Then he pushed himself into a sitting position again, rubbing his knuckles into his eyes like a small child.

"Kreacher, I am going to ask you to do something," said Harry. He glanced at Hermione for assistance. He wanted to give the order kindly, but at the same time, he could not pretend that it was not an order. However, the change in his tone seemed to have gained her approval: She smiled encouragingly.

"Kreacher, I want you, please, to go and find Mundungus Fletcher. We need to find out where the locket — where Master Regulus's locket is. It's really important. We want to finish the work Master Regulus started, we want to — er — ensure that he didn't die in vain."

Kreacher dropped his fists and looked up at Harry.

"Find Mundungus Fletcher?" he croaked.

"And bring him here, to Grimmauld Place," said Harry. "Do you think you could do that for us?"

As Kreacher nodded and got to his feet, Harry had a sudden inspiration. He pulled out Hagrid's purse and took out the fake Horcrux, the substitute locket in which Regulus had placed the note to Voldemort.

"Kreacher, I'd, er, like you to have this," he said, pressing the locket into the elf's hand. "This belonged to Regulus and I'm sure he'd want you to have it as a token of gratitude for what you —"

"Overkill, mate," said Ron as the elf took one look at the locket, let out a howl of shock and misery, and threw himself back onto the ground.

It took them nearly half an hour to calm down Kreacher, who was so overcome to be presented with a Black family heirloom for his very own that he was too weak at the knees to stand properly. When finally he was able to totter a few steps they all accompanied him to his cupboard, watched him tuck up the locket safely in his dirty blankets, and assured him that they would make its protection their first priority while he was away. He then made two low bows to Harry and Ron, and even gave a funny little spasm in Hermione's direction that might have been an attempt at a respectful salute, before Disapparating with the usual loud *crack*.

THE BRIBE

I f Kreacher could escape a lake full of Inferi, Harry was confident that the capture of Mundungus would take a few hours at most, and he prowled the house all morning in a state of high anticipation. However, Kreacher did not return that morning or even that afternoon. By nightfall, Harry felt discouraged and anxious, and a supper composed largely of moldy bread, upon which Hermione had tried a variety of unsuccessful Transfigurations, did nothing to help.

Kreacher did not return the following day, nor the day after that. However, two cloaked men had appeared in the square outside number twelve, and they remained there into the night, gazing in the direction of the house that they could not see.

"Death Eaters, for sure," said Ron, as he, Harry, and Hermione watched from the drawing room windows. "Reckon they know we're in here?"

"I don't think so," said Hermione, though she looked frightened, "or they'd have sent Snape in after us, wouldn't they?"

"D'you reckon he's been in here and had his tongue tied by Moody's curse?" asked Ron.

"Yes," said Hermione, "otherwise he'd have been able to tell that lot how to get in, wouldn't he? But they're probably watching to see whether we turn up. They know that Harry owns the house, after all."

"How do they — ?" began Harry.

"Wizarding wills are examined by the Ministry, remember? They'll know Sirius left you the place."

The presence of the Death Eaters outside increased the ominous mood inside number twelve. They had not heard a word from anyone beyond Grimmauld Place since Mr. Weasley's Patronus, and the strain was starting to tell. Restless and irritable, Ron had developed an annoying habit of playing with the Deluminator in his pocket: This particularly infuriated Hermione, who was whiling away the wait for Kreacher by studying *The Tales of Beedle the Bard* and did not appreciate the way the lights kept flashing on and off.

"Will you stop it!" she cried on the third evening of Kreacher's absence, as all light was sucked from the drawing room yet again.

"Sorry, sorry!" said Ron, clicking the Deluminator and restoring the lights. "I don't know I'm doing it!"

"Well, can't you find something useful to occupy yourself?"

"What, like reading kids' stories?"

"Dumbledore left me this book, Ron —"

"— and he left me the Deluminator, maybe I'm supposed to use it!"

Unable to stand the bickering, Harry slipped out of the room unnoticed by either of them. He headed downstairs toward the kitchen, which he kept visiting because he was sure that was where

Kreacher was most likely to reappear. Halfway down the flight of stairs into the hall, however, he heard a tap on the front door, then metallic clicks and the grinding of the chain.

Every nerve in his body seemed to tauten: He pulled out his wand, moved into the shadows beside the decapitated elf heads, and waited. The door opened: He saw a glimpse of the lamplit square outside, and a cloaked figure edged into the hall and closed the door behind it. The intruder took a step forward, and Moody's voice asked, *"Severus Snape?"* Then the dust figure rose from the end of the hall and rushed him, raising its dead hand.

"It was not I who killed you, Albus," said a quiet voice.

The jinx broke: The dust-figure exploded again, and it was impossible to make out the newcomer through the dense gray cloud it left behind.

Harry pointed his wand into the middle of it.

"Don't move!"

He had forgotten the portrait of Mrs. Black: At the sound of his yell, the curtains hiding her flew open and she began to scream, *"Mudbloods and filth dishonoring my house —"*

Ron and Hermione came crashing down the stairs behind Harry, wands pointing, like his, at the unknown man now standing with his arms raised in the hall below.

"Hold your fire, it's me, Remus!"

"Oh, thank goodness," said Hermione weakly, pointing her wand at Mrs. Black instead; with a bang, the curtains swished shut again and silence fell. Ron too lowered his wand, but Harry did not.

"Show yourself!" he called back.

Lupin moved forward into the lamplight, hands still held high in a gesture of surrender.

"I am Remus John Lupin, werewolf, sometimes known as Moony, one of the four creators of the Marauder's Map, married to Nymphadora, usually known as Tonks, and I taught you how to produce a Patronus, Harry, which takes the form of a stag."

"Oh, all right," said Harry, lowering his wand, "but I had to check, didn't I?"

"Speaking as your ex-Defense Against the Dark Arts teacher, I quite agree that you had to check. Ron, Hermione, you shouldn't be quite so quick to lower your defenses."

They ran down the stairs toward him. Wrapped in a thick black traveling cloak, he looked exhausted, but pleased to see them.

"No sign of Severus, then?" he asked.

"No," said Harry. "What's going on? Is everyone okay?"

"Yes," said Lupin, "but we're all being watched. There are a couple of Death Eaters in the square outside —"

"We know —"

"I had to Apparate very precisely onto the top step outside the front door to be sure that they would not see me. They can't know you're in here or I'm sure they'd have more people out there; they're staking out everywhere that's got any connection with you, Harry. Let's go downstairs, there's a lot to tell you, and I want to know what happened after you left the Burrow."

They descended into the kitchen, where Hermione pointed her wand at the grate. A fire sprang up instantly: It gave the illusion of coziness to the stark stone walls and glistened off the long wooden table. Lupin pulled a few butterbeers from beneath his traveling cloak and they sat down.

"I'd have been here three days ago but I needed to shake off the

Death Eater tailing me," said Lupin. "So, you came straight here after the wedding?"

"No," said Harry, "only after we ran into a couple of Death Eaters in a café on Tottenham Court Road."

Lupin slopped most of his butterbeer down his front.

"What?"

They explained what had happened; when they had finished, Lupin looked aghast.

"But how did they find you so quickly? It's impossible to track anyone who Apparates, unless you grab hold of them as they disappear!"

"And it doesn't seem likely they were just strolling down Tottenham Court Road at the time, does it?" said Harry.

"We wondered," said Hermione tentatively, "whether Harry could still have the Trace on him?"

"Impossible," said Lupin. Ron looked smug, and Harry felt hugely relieved. "Apart from anything else, they'd know for sure Harry was here if he still had the Trace on him, wouldn't they? But I can't see how they could have tracked you to Tottenham Court Road, that's worrying, really worrying."

He looked disturbed, but as far as Harry was concerned, that question could wait.

"Tell us what happened after we left, we haven't heard a thing since Ron's dad told us the family were safe."

"Well, Kingsley saved us," said Lupin. "Thanks to his warning most of the wedding guests were able to Disapparate before they arrived."

"Were they Death Eaters or Ministry people?" interjected Hermione.

"A mixture; but to all intents and purposes they're the same thing now," said Lupin. "There were about a dozen of them, but they didn't know you were there, Harry. Arthur heard a rumor that they tried to torture your whereabouts out of Scrimgeour before they killed him; if it's true, he didn't give you away."

Harry looked at Ron and Hermione; their expressions reflected the mingled shock and gratitude he felt. He had never liked Scrimgeour much, but if what Lupin said was true, the man's final act had been to try to protect Harry.

"The Death Eaters searched the Burrow from top to bottom," Lupin went on. "They found the ghoul, but didn't want to get too close — and then they interrogated those of us who remained for hours. They were trying to get information on you, Harry, but of course nobody apart from the Order knew that you had been there.

"At the same time that they were smashing up the wedding, more Death Eaters were forcing their way into every Order-connected house in the country. No deaths," he added quickly, forestalling the question, "but they were rough. They burned down Dedalus Diggle's house, but as you know he wasn't there, and they used the Cruciatus Curse on Tonks's family. Again, trying to find out where you went after you visited them. They're all right — shaken, obviously, but otherwise okay."

"The Death Eaters got through all those protective charms?" Harry asked, remembering how effective these had been on the night he had crashed in Tonks's parents' garden.

"What you've got to realize, Harry, is that the Death Eaters have got the full might of the Ministry on their side now," said Lupin. "They've got the power to perform brutal spells without fear of identification or arrest. They managed to penetrate every defensive spell we'd cast against them, and once inside, they were completely open about why they'd come."

"And are they bothering to give an excuse for torturing Harry's whereabouts out of people?" asked Hermione, an edge to her voice.

"Well," said Lupin. He hesitated, then pulled out a folded copy of the *Daily Prophet.*

"Here," he said, pushing it across the table to Harry, "you'll know sooner or later anyway. That's their pretext for going after you."

Harry smoothed out the paper. A huge photograph of his own face filled the front page. He read the headline over it:

WANTED FOR QUESTIONING ABOUT
THE DEATH OF ALBUS DUMBLEDORE

Ron and Hermione gave roars of outrage, but Harry said nothing. He pushed the newspaper away; he did not want to read any more: He knew what it would say. Nobody but those who had been on top of the tower when Dumbledore died knew who had really killed him and, as Rita Skeeter had already told the Wizarding world, Harry had been seen running from the place moments after Dumbledore had fallen.

"I'm sorry, Harry," Lupin said.

"So Death Eaters have taken over the *Daily Prophet* too?" asked Hermione furiously.

Lupin nodded.

"But surely people realize what's going on?"

"The coup has been smooth and virtually silent," said Lupin.

"The official version of Scrimgeour's murder is that he resigned; he has been replaced by Pius Thicknesse, who is under the Imperius Curse."

"Why didn't Voldemort declare himself Minister of Magic?" asked Ron.

Lupin laughed.

"He doesn't need to, Ron. Effectively he *is* the Minister, but why should he sit behind a desk at the Ministry? His puppet, Thicknesse, is taking care of everyday business, leaving Voldemort free to extend his power beyond the Ministry.

"Naturally many people have deduced what has happened: There has been such a dramatic change in Ministry policy in the last few days, and many are whispering that Voldemort must be behind it. However, that is the point: They whisper. They daren't confide in each other, not knowing whom to trust; they are scared to speak out, in case their suspicions are true and their families are targeted. Yes, Voldemort is playing a very clever game. Declaring himself might have provoked open rebellion: Remaining masked has created confusion, uncertainty, and fear."

"And this dramatic change in Ministry policy," said Harry, "involves warning the Wizarding world against me instead of Voldemort?"

"That's certainly part of it," said Lupin, "and it is a masterstroke. Now that Dumbledore is dead, you — the Boy Who Lived — were sure to be the symbol and rallying point for any resistance to Voldemort. But by suggesting that you had a hand in the old hero's death, Voldemort has not only set a price upon your head, but sown doubt and fear amongst many who would have defended you.

"Meanwhile, the Ministry has started moving against Muggle-borns."

Lupin pointed at the *Daily Prophet*.

"Look at page two."

Hermione turned the pages with much the same expression of distaste she had worn when handling *Secrets of the Darkest Art*.

"'*Muggle-born Register,*'" she read aloud. "'*The Ministry of Magic is undertaking a survey of so-called "Muggle-borns," the better to understand how they came to possess magical secrets.*

"'*Recent research undertaken by the Department of Mysteries reveals that magic can only be passed from person to person when Wizards reproduce. Where no proven Wizarding ancestry exists, therefore, the so-called Muggle-born is likely to have obtained magical power by theft or force.*

"'*The Ministry is determined to root out such usurpers of magical power, and to this end has issued an invitation to every so-called Muggle-born to present themselves for interview by the newly appointed Muggle-born Registration Commission.*'"

"People won't let this happen," said Ron.

"It *is* happening, Ron," said Lupin. "Muggle-borns are being rounded up as we speak."

"But how are they supposed to have 'stolen' magic?" said Ron. "It's mental, if you could steal magic there wouldn't be any Squibs, would there?"

"I know," said Lupin. "Nevertheless, unless you can prove that you have at least one close Wizarding relative, you are now deemed to have obtained your magical power illegally and must suffer the punishment."

Ron glanced at Hermione, then said, "What if purebloods and half-bloods swear a Muggle-born's part of their family? I'll tell everyone Hermione's my cousin —"

Hermione covered Ron's hand with hers and squeezed it.

"Thank you, Ron, but I couldn't let you —"

"You won't have a choice," said Ron fiercely, gripping her hand back. "I'll teach you my family tree so you can answer questions on it."

Hermione gave a shaky laugh.

"Ron, as we're on the run with Harry Potter, the most wanted person in the country, I don't think it matters. If I was going back to school it would be different. What's Voldemort planning for Hogwarts?" she asked Lupin.

"Attendance is now compulsory for every young witch and wizard," he replied. "That was announced yesterday. It's a change, because it was never obligatory before. Of course, nearly every witch and wizard in Britain has been educated at Hogwarts, but their parents had the right to teach them at home or send them abroad if they preferred. This way, Voldemort will have the whole Wizarding population under his eye from a young age. And it's also another way of weeding out Muggle-borns, because students must be given Blood Status — meaning that they have proven to the Ministry that they are of Wizard descent — before they are allowed to attend."

Harry felt sickened and angry: At this moment, excited eleven-year-olds would be poring over stacks of newly purchased spellbooks, unaware that they would never see Hogwarts, perhaps never see their families again either.

"It's . . . it's . . ." he muttered, struggling to find words that did justice to the horror of his thoughts, but Lupin said quietly,

"I know."

Lupin hesitated.

"I'll understand if you can't confirm this, Harry, but the Order is under the impression that Dumbledore left you a mission."

"He did," Harry replied, "and Ron and Hermione are in on it and they're coming with me."

"Can you confide in me what the mission is?"

Harry looked into the prematurely lined face, framed in thick but graying hair, and wished that he could return a different answer.

"I can't, Remus, I'm sorry. If Dumbledore didn't tell you I don't think I can."

"I thought you'd say that," said Lupin, looking disappointed. "But I might still be of some use to you. You know what I am and what I can do. I could come with you to provide protection. There would be no need to tell me exactly what you were up to."

Harry hesitated. It was a very tempting offer, though how they would be able to keep their mission secret from Lupin if he were with them all the time he could not imagine.

Hermione, however, looked puzzled.

"But what about Tonks?" she asked.

"What about her?" said Lupin.

"Well," said Hermione, frowning, "you're married! How does she feel about you going away with us?"

"Tonks will be perfectly safe," said Lupin. "She'll be at her parents' house."

There was something strange in Lupin's tone; it was almost cold. There was also something odd in the idea of Tonks remaining hidden at her parents' house; she was, after all, a member of the Order and, as far as Harry knew, was likely to want to be in the thick of the action.

"Remus," said Hermione tentatively, "is everything all right . . . you know . . . between you and —"

"Everything is fine, thank you," said Lupin pointedly.

Hermione turned pink. There was another pause, an awkward and embarrassed one, and then Lupin said, with an air of forcing himself to admit something unpleasant, "Tonks is going to have a baby."

"Oh, how wonderful!" squealed Hermione.

"Excellent!" said Ron enthusiastically.

"Congratulations," said Harry.

Lupin gave an artificial smile that was more like a grimace, then said, "So . . . do you accept my offer? Will three become four? I cannot believe that Dumbledore would have disapproved, he appointed me your Defense Against the Dark Arts teacher, after all. And I must tell you that I believe that we are facing magic many of us have never encountered or imagined."

Ron and Hermione both looked at Harry.

"Just — just to be clear," he said. "You want to leave Tonks at her parents' house and come away with us?"

"She'll be perfectly safe there, they'll look after her," said Lupin. He spoke with a finality bordering on indifference. "Harry, I'm sure James would have wanted me to stick with you."

"Well," said Harry slowly, "I'm not. I'm pretty sure my father would have wanted to know why you aren't sticking with your own kid, actually."

Lupin's face drained of color. The temperature in the kitchen might have dropped ten degrees. Ron stared around the room as though he had been bidden to memorize it, while Hermione's eyes swiveled backward and forward from Harry to Lupin.

"You don't understand," said Lupin at last.

"Explain, then," said Harry.

Lupin swallowed.

"I — I made a grave mistake in marrying Tonks. I did it against my better judgment and I have regretted it very much ever since."

"I see," said Harry, "so you're just going to dump her and the kid and run off with us?"

Lupin sprang to his feet: His chair toppled over backward, and he glared at them so fiercely that Harry saw, for the first time ever, the shadow of the wolf upon his human face.

"Don't you understand what I've done to my wife and my unborn child? I should never have married her, I've made her an outcast!"

Lupin kicked aside the chair he had overturned.

"You have only ever seen me amongst the Order, or under Dumbledore's protection at Hogwarts! You don't know how most of the Wizarding world sees creatures like me! When they know of my affliction, they can barely talk to me! Don't you see what I've done? Even her own family is disgusted by our marriage, what parents want their only daughter to marry a werewolf? And the child — the child —"

Lupin actually seized handfuls of his own hair; he looked quite deranged.

"My kind don't usually breed! It will be like me, I am convinced of it — how can I forgive myself, when I knowingly risked passing on my own condition to an innocent child? And if, by some miracle, it is not like me, then it will be better off, a hundred times so, without a father of whom it must always be ashamed!"

"Remus!" whispered Hermione, tears in her eyes. "Don't say that — how could any child be ashamed of you?"

"Oh, I don't know, Hermione," said Harry. "I'd be pretty ashamed of him."

Harry did not know where his rage was coming from, but it had propelled him to his feet too. Lupin looked as though Harry had hit him.

"If the new regime thinks Muggle-borns are bad," Harry said, "what will they do to a half-werewolf whose father's in the Order? My father died trying to protect my mother and me, and you reckon he'd tell you to abandon your kid to go on an adventure with us?"

"How — how dare you?" said Lupin. "This is not about a desire for — for danger or personal glory — how dare you suggest such a —"

"I think you're feeling a bit of a daredevil," Harry said. "You fancy stepping into Sirius's shoes —"

"Harry, no!" Hermione begged him, but he continued to glare into Lupin's livid face.

"I'd never have believed this," Harry said. "The man who taught me to fight dementors — a coward."

Lupin drew his wand so fast that Harry had barely reached for his own; there was a loud bang and he felt himself flying backward as if punched; as he slammed into the kitchen wall and slid to the floor, he glimpsed the tail of Lupin's cloak disappearing around the door.

"Remus, Remus, come back!" Hermione cried, but Lupin did not respond. A moment later they heard the front door slam.

"Harry!" wailed Hermione. "How could you?"

"It was easy," said Harry. He stood up; he could feel a lump swelling where his head had hit the wall. He was still so full of anger he was shaking.

"Don't look at me like that!" he snapped at Hermione.

"Don't you start on her!" snarled Ron.

"No — no — we mustn't fight!" said Hermione, launching herself between them.

"You shouldn't have said that stuff to Lupin," Ron told Harry.

"He had it coming to him," said Harry. Broken images were racing each other through his mind: Sirius falling through the veil; Dumbledore suspended, broken, in midair; a flash of green light and his mother's voice, begging for mercy . . .

"Parents," said Harry, "shouldn't leave their kids unless — unless they've got to."

"Harry —" said Hermione, stretching out a consoling hand, but he shrugged it off and walked away, his eyes on the fire Hermione had conjured. He had once spoken to Lupin out of that fireplace, seeking reassurance about James, and Lupin had consoled him. Now Lupin's tortured white face seemed to swim in the air before him. He felt a sickening surge of remorse. Neither Ron nor Hermione spoke, but Harry felt sure that they were looking at each other behind his back, communicating silently.

He turned around and caught them turning hurriedly away from each other.

"I know I shouldn't have called him a coward."

"No, you shouldn't," said Ron at once.

"But he's acting like one."

"All the same . . ." said Hermione.

"I know," said Harry. "But if it makes him go back to Tonks, it'll be worth it, won't it?"

He could not keep the plea out of his voice. Hermione looked sympathetic, Ron uncertain. Harry looked down at his feet, thinking of his father. Would James have backed Harry in what he had said to Lupin, or would he have been angry at how his son had treated his old friend?

The silent kitchen seemed to hum with the shock of the recent scene and with Ron and Hermione's unspoken reproaches. The *Daily Prophet* Lupin had brought was still lying on the table, Harry's own face staring up at the ceiling from the front page. He walked over to it and sat down, opened the paper at random, and pretended to read. He could not take in the words; his mind was still too full of the encounter with Lupin. He was sure that Ron and Hermione had resumed their silent communications on the other side of the *Prophet*. He turned a page loudly, and Dumbledore's name leapt out at him. It was a moment or two before he took in the meaning of the photograph, which showed a family group. Beneath the photograph were the words: *The Dumbledore family, left to right: Albus; Percival, holding newborn Ariana; Kendra; and Aberforth.*

His attention caught, Harry examined the picture more carefully. Dumbledore's father, Percival, was a good-looking man with eyes that seemed to twinkle even in this faded old photograph. The baby, Ariana, was little longer than a loaf of bread and no more distinctive-looking. The mother, Kendra, had jet-black hair pulled into a high bun. Her face had a carved quality about it. Harry thought of photos of Native Americans he'd seen as he studied her dark eyes, high cheekbones, and straight nose, formally composed above a high-necked silk gown. Albus and Aberforth wore matching lacy collared jackets and had identical, shoulder-length hairstyles. Albus looked several years older, but otherwise the two boys looked very alike, for this was before Albus's nose had been broken and before he started wearing glasses.

The family looked quite happy and normal, smiling serenely up out of the newspaper. Baby Ariana's arm waved vaguely out of her shawl. Harry looked above the picture and saw the headline:

EXCLUSIVE EXTRACT FROM THE UPCOMING BIOGRAPHY OF ALBUS DUMBLEDORE
by Rita Skeeter

Thinking that it could hardly make him feel any worse than he already did, Harry began to read:

> Proud and haughty, Kendra Dumbledore could not bear to remain in Mould-on-the-Wold after her husband Percival's well-publicized arrest and imprisonment in Azkaban. She therefore decided to uproot the family and relocate to Godric's Hollow, the village that was later to gain fame as the scene of Harry Potter's strange escape from You-Know-Who.
>
> Like Mould-on-the-Wold, Godric's Hollow was home to a number of Wizarding families, but as Kendra knew none of them, she would be spared the curiosity about her husband's crime she had faced in her former village. By repeatedly rebuffing the friendly advances of her new Wizarding neighbors, she soon ensured that her family was left well alone.
>
> "Slammed the door in my face when I went around to welcome her with a batch of homemade Cauldron Cakes," says Bathilda Bagshot. "The first

year they were there I only ever saw the two boys. Wouldn't have known there was a daughter if I hadn't been picking Plangentines by moonlight the winter after they moved in, and saw Kendra leading Ariana out into the back garden. Walked her round the lawn once, keeping a firm grip on her, then took her back inside. Didn't know what to make of it."

It seems that Kendra thought the move to Godric's Hollow was the perfect opportunity to hide Ariana once and for all, something she had probably been planning for years. The timing was significant. Ariana was barely seven years old when she vanished from sight, and seven is the age by which most experts agree that magic will have revealed itself, if present. Nobody now alive remembers Ariana ever demonstrating even the slightest sign of magical ability. It seems clear, therefore, that Kendra made a decision to hide her daughter's existence rather than suffer the shame of admitting that she had produced a Squib. Moving away from the friends and neighbors who knew Ariana would, of course, make imprisoning her all the easier. The tiny number of people who henceforth knew of Ariana's existence could be counted upon to keep the secret, including her two brothers, who deflected awkward questions with the answer their mother had taught them: "My sister is too frail for school."

Next week: Albus Dumbledore at Hogwarts — the Prizes and the Pretense.

Harry had been wrong: What he had read had indeed made him feel worse. He looked back at the photograph of the apparently happy family. Was it true? How could he find out? He wanted to go to Godric's Hollow, even if Bathilda was in no fit state to talk to him; he wanted to visit the place where he and Dumbledore had both lost loved ones. He was in the process of lowering the newspaper, to ask Ron's and Hermione's opinions, when a deafening *crack* echoed around the kitchen.

For the first time in three days Harry had forgotten all about Kreacher. His immediate thought was that Lupin had burst back into the room, and for a split second, he did not take in the mass of struggling limbs that had appeared out of thin air right beside his chair. He hurried to his feet as Kreacher disentangled himself and, bowing low to Harry, croaked, "Kreacher has returned with the thief Mundungus Fletcher, Master."

Mundungus scrambled up and pulled out his wand; Hermione, however, was too quick for him.

"*Expelliarmus!*"

Mundungus's wand soared into the air, and Hermione caught it. Wild-eyed, Mundungus dived for the stairs: Ron rugby-tackled him and Mundungus hit the stone floor with a muffled crunch.

"What?" he bellowed, writhing in his attempts to free himself from Ron's grip. "Wha've I done? Setting a bleedin' 'ouse-elf on me, what are you playing at, wha've I done, lemme go, lemme go, or —"

"You're not in much of a position to make threats," said Harry. He threw aside the newspaper, crossed the kitchen in a few strides, and dropped to his knees beside Mundungus, who stopped struggling and looked terrified. Ron got up, panting, and watched as Harry pointed his wand deliberately at Mundungus's nose. Mundungus stank of stale sweat and tobacco smoke: His hair was matted and his robes stained.

"Kreacher apologizes for the delay in bringing the thief, Master," croaked the elf. "Fletcher knows how to avoid capture, has many hidey-holes and accomplices. Nevertheless, Kreacher cornered the thief in the end."

"You've done really well, Kreacher," said Harry, and the elf bowed low.

"Right, we've got a few questions for you," Harry told Mundungus, who shouted at once,

"I panicked, okay? I never wanted to come along, no offense, mate, but I never volunteered to die for you, an' that was bleedin' You-Know-Who come flying at me, anyone woulda got outta there, I said all along I didn't wanna do it —"

"For your information, none of the rest of us Disapparated," said Hermione.

"Well, you're a bunch of bleedin' 'eroes then, aren't you, but I never pretended I was up for killing meself —"

"We're not interested in why you ran out on Mad-Eye," said Harry, moving his wand a little closer to Mundungus's baggy, bloodshot eyes. "We already knew you were an unreliable bit of scum."

"Well then, why the 'ell am I being 'unted down by 'ouse-elves? Or is this about them goblets again? I ain't got none of 'em left, or you could 'ave 'em —"

"It's not about the goblets either, although you're getting warmer," said Harry. "Shut up and listen."

It felt wonderful to have something to do, someone of whom he could demand some small portion of truth. Harry's wand was now so close to the bridge of Mundungus's nose that Mundungus had gone cross-eyed trying to keep it in view.

"When you cleaned out this house of anything valuable," Harry began, but Mundungus interrupted him again.

"Sirius never cared about any of the junk —"

There was the sound of pattering feet, a blaze of shining copper, an echoing clang, and a shriek of agony: Kreacher had taken a run at Mundungus and hit him over the head with a saucepan.

"Call 'im off, call 'im off, 'e should be locked up!" screamed Mundungus, cowering as Kreacher raised the heavy-bottomed pan again.

"Kreacher, no!" shouted Harry.

Kreacher's thin arms trembled with the weight of the pan, still held aloft.

"Perhaps just one more, Master Harry, for luck?"

Ron laughed.

"We need him conscious, Kreacher, but if he needs persuading you can do the honors," said Harry.

"Thank you very much, Master," said Kreacher with a bow, and he retreated a short distance, his great pale eyes still fixed upon Mundungus with loathing.

"When you stripped this house of all the valuables you could find," Harry began again, "you took a bunch of stuff from the kitchen cupboard. There was a locket there." Harry's mouth was suddenly dry: He could sense Ron and Hermione's tension and excitement too. "What did you do with it?"

"Why?" asked Mundungus. "Is it valuable?"

"You've still got it!" cried Hermione.

"No, he hasn't," said Ron shrewdly. "He's wondering whether he should have asked more money for it."

"More?" said Mundungus. "That wouldn't have been effing difficult . . . bleedin' gave it away, di'n' I? No choice."

"What do you mean?"

"I was selling in Diagon Alley and she come up to me and asks if I've got a license for trading in magical artifacts. Bleedin' snoop. She was gonna fine me, but she took a fancy to the locket an' told me she'd take it and let me off that time, and to fink meself lucky."

"Who was this woman?" asked Harry.

"I dunno, some Ministry hag."

Mundungus considered for a moment, brow wrinkled.

"Little woman. Bow on top of 'er head."

He frowned and then added, "Looked like a toad."

Harry dropped his wand: It hit Mundungus on the nose and shot red sparks into his eyebrows, which ignited.

"Aguamenti!" screamed Hermione, and a jet of water streamed from her wand, engulfing a spluttering and choking Mundungus.

Harry looked up and saw his own shock reflected in Ron's and Hermione's faces. The scars on the back of his right hand seemed to be tingling again.

MAGIC IS MIGHT

As August wore on, the square of unkempt grass in the middle of Grimmauld Place shriveled in the sun until it was brittle and brown. The inhabitants of number twelve were never seen by anybody in the surrounding houses, and nor was number twelve itself. The Muggles who lived in Grimmauld Place had long since accepted the amusing mistake in the numbering that had caused number eleven to sit beside number thirteen.

And yet the square was now attracting a trickle of visitors who seemed to find the anomaly most intriguing. Barely a day passed without one or two people arriving in Grimmauld Place with no other purpose, or so it seemed, than to lean against the railings facing numbers eleven and thirteen, watching the join between the two houses. The lurkers were never the same two days running, although they all seemed to share a dislike for normal clothing. Most of the Londoners who passed them were used to eccentric dressers and took little notice, though occasionally one of them might glance back, wondering why anyone would wear such long cloaks in this heat.

The watchers seemed to be gleaning little satisfaction from their vigil. Occasionally one of them started forward excitedly, as if they had seen something interesting at last, only to fall back looking disappointed.

On the first day of September there were more people lurking in the square than ever before. Half a dozen men in long cloaks stood silent and watchful, gazing as ever at houses eleven and thirteen, but the thing for which they were waiting still appeared elusive. As evening drew in, bringing with it an unexpected gust of chilly rain for the first time in weeks, there occurred one of those inexplicable moments when they appeared to have seen something interesting. The man with the twisted face pointed and his closest companion, a podgy, pallid man, started forward, but a moment later they had relaxed into their previous state of inactivity, looking frustrated and disappointed.

Meanwhile, inside number twelve, Harry had just entered the hall. He had nearly lost his balance as he Apparated onto the top step just outside the front door, and thought that the Death Eaters might have caught a glimpse of his momentarily exposed elbow. Shutting the front door carefully behind him, he pulled off the Invisibility Cloak, draped it over his arm, and hurried along the gloomy hallway toward the door that led to the basement, a stolen copy of the *Daily Prophet* clutched in his hand.

The usual low whisper of *"Severus Snape?"* greeted him, the chill wind swept him, and his tongue rolled up for a moment.

"I didn't kill you," he said, once it had unrolled, then held his breath as the dusty jinx-figure exploded. He waited until he was halfway down the stairs to the kitchen, out of earshot of Mrs. Black and clear of the dust cloud, before calling, "I've got news, and you won't like it."

The kitchen was almost unrecognizable. Every surface now shone: Copper pots and pans had been burnished to a rosy glow; the wooden tabletop gleamed; the goblets and plates already laid for dinner glinted in the light from a merrily blazing fire, on which a cauldron was simmering. Nothing in the room, however, was more dramatically different than the house-elf who now came hurrying toward Harry, dressed in a snowy-white towel, his ear hair as clean and fluffy as cotton wool, Regulus's locket bouncing on his thin chest.

"Shoes off, if you please, Master Harry, and hands washed before dinner," croaked Kreacher, seizing the Invisibility Cloak and slouching off to hang it on a hook on the wall, beside a number of old-fashioned robes that had been freshly laundered.

"What's happened?" Ron asked apprehensively. He and Hermione had been poring over a sheaf of scribbled notes and hand-drawn maps that littered the end of the long kitchen table, but now they watched Harry as he strode toward them and threw down the newspaper on top of their scattered parchment.

A large picture of a familiar, hook-nosed, black-haired man stared up at them all, beneath a headline that read:

SEVERUS SNAPE CONFIRMED AS HOGWARTS HEADMASTER

"No!" said Ron and Hermione loudly.

Hermione was quickest; she snatched up the newspaper and began to read the accompanying story out loud.

"'*Severus Snape, long-standing Potions master at Hogwarts School of Witchcraft and Wizardry, was today appointed headmaster in the most important of several staffing changes at the ancient school. Following the resignation of the previous Muggle Studies teacher, Alecto Carrow will take over the post while her brother, Amycus, fills the position of Defense Against the Dark Arts professor.*

"' *I welcome the opportunity to uphold our finest Wizarding traditions and values —*' Like committing murder and cutting off people's ears, I suppose! Snape, headmaster! Snape in Dumbledore's study — Merlin's pants!" she shrieked, making both Harry and Ron jump. She leapt up from the table and hurtled from the room, shouting as she went, "I'll be back in a minute!"

"'Merlin's pants'?" repeated Ron, looking amused. "She must be upset." He pulled the newspaper toward him and perused the article about Snape.

"The other teachers won't stand for this. McGonagall and Flitwick and Sprout all know the truth, they know how Dumbledore died. They won't accept Snape as headmaster. And who are these Carrows?"

"Death Eaters," said Harry. "There are pictures of them inside. They were at the top of the tower when Snape killed Dumbledore, so it's all friends together. And," Harry went on bitterly, drawing up a chair, "I can't see that the other teachers have got any choice but to stay. If the Ministry and Voldemort are behind Snape it'll be a choice between staying and teaching, or a nice few years in Azkaban — and that's if they're lucky. I reckon they'll stay to try and protect the students."

Kreacher came bustling to the table with a large tureen in his hands, and ladled out soup into pristine bowls, whistling between his teeth as he did so.

"Thanks, Kreacher," said Harry, flipping over the *Prophet* so as not to have to look at Snape's face. "Well, at least we know exactly where Snape is now."

He began to spoon soup into his mouth. The quality of Kreacher's cooking had improved dramatically ever since he had been given Regulus's locket: Today's French onion was as good as Harry had ever tasted.

"There are still a load of Death Eaters watching the house," he told Ron as he ate, "more than usual. It's like they're hoping we'll march out carrying our school trunks and head off for the Hogwarts Express."

Ron glanced at his watch.

"I've been thinking about that all day. It left nearly six hours ago. Weird, not being on it, isn't it?"

In his mind's eye Harry seemed to see the scarlet steam engine as he and Ron had once followed it by air, shimmering between fields and hills, a rippling scarlet caterpillar. He was sure Ginny, Neville, and Luna were sitting together at this moment, perhaps wondering where he, Ron, and Hermione were, or debating how best to undermine Snape's new regime.

"They nearly saw me coming back in just now," Harry said. "I landed badly on the top step, and the Cloak slipped."

"I do that every time. Oh, here she is," Ron added, craning around in his seat to watch Hermione reentering the kitchen. "And what in the name of Merlin's most baggy Y Fronts was that about?"

"I remembered this," Hermione panted.

She was carrying a large, framed picture, which she now lowered to the floor before seizing her small, beaded bag from the kitchen sideboard. Opening it, she proceeded to force the painting inside, and despite the fact that it was patently too large to fit inside the tiny bag, within a few seconds it had vanished, like so much else, into the bag's capacious depths.

"Phineas Nigellus," Hermione explained as she threw the bag onto the kitchen table with the usual sonorous, clanking crash.

"Sorry?" said Ron, but Harry understood. The painted image of Phineas Nigellus Black was able to flit between his portrait in Grimmauld Place and the one that hung in the headmaster's office at Hogwarts: the circular tower-top room where Snape was no doubt sitting right now, in triumphant possession of Dumbledore's collection of delicate, silver magical instruments, the stone Pensieve, the Sorting Hat and, unless it had been moved elsewhere, the sword of Gryffindor.

"Snape could send Phineas Nigellus to look inside this house for him," Hermione explained to Ron as she resumed her seat. "But let him try it now, all Phineas Nigellus will be able to see is the inside of my handbag."

"Good thinking!" said Ron, looking impressed.

"Thank you," smiled Hermione, pulling her soup toward her. "So, Harry, what else happened today?"

"Nothing," said Harry. "Watched the Ministry entrance for seven hours. No sign of her. Saw your dad, though, Ron. He looks fine."

Ron nodded his appreciation of this news. They had agreed that it was far too dangerous to try and communicate with Mr. Weasley while he walked in and out of the Ministry, because he was always surrounded by other Ministry workers. It was, however, reassuring to catch these glimpses of him, even if he did look very strained and anxious.

"Dad always told us most Ministry people use the Floo Network to get to work," Ron said. "That's why we haven't seen Umbridge, she'd never walk, she'd think she's too important."

"And what about that funny old witch and that little wizard in the navy robes?" Hermione asked.

"Oh yeah, the bloke from Magical Maintenance," said Ron.

"How do you know he works for Magical Maintenance?" Hermione asked, her soupspoon suspended in midair.

"Dad said everyone from Magical Maintenance wears navy blue robes."

"But you never told us that!"

Hermione dropped her spoon and pulled toward her the sheaf of notes and maps that she and Ron had been examining when Harry had entered the kitchen.

"There's nothing in here about navy blue robes, nothing!" she said, flipping feverishly through the pages.

"Well, does it really matter?"

"Ron, it *all* matters! If we're going to get into the Ministry and not give ourselves away when they're *bound* to be on the lookout for intruders, every little detail matters! We've been over and over this, I mean, what's the point of all these reconnaissance trips if you aren't even bothering to tell us —"

"Blimey, Hermione, I forget one little thing —"

"You do realize, don't you, that there's probably no more dangerous place in the whole world for us to be right now than the Ministry of —"

"I think we should do it tomorrow," said Harry.

Hermione stopped dead, her jaw hanging; Ron choked a little over his soup.

"Tomorrow?" repeated Hermione. "You aren't serious, Harry?"

"I am," said Harry. "I don't think we're going to be much better prepared than we are now even if we skulk around the Ministry entrance for another month. The longer we put it off, the farther away that locket could be. There's already a good chance Umbridge has chucked it away; the thing doesn't open."

"Unless," said Ron, "she's found a way of opening it and she's now possessed."

"Wouldn't make any difference to her, she was so evil in the first place," Harry shrugged.

Hermione was biting her lip, deep in thought.

"We know everything important," Harry went on, addressing Hermione. "We know they've stopped Apparition in and out of the Ministry. We know only the most senior Ministry members are allowed to connect their homes to the Floo Network now, because Ron heard those two Unspeakables complaining about it. And we know roughly where Umbridge's office is, because of what you heard that bearded bloke saying to his mate —"

"'I'll be up on level one, Dolores wants to see me,'" Hermione recited immediately.

"Exactly," said Harry. "And we know you get in using those funny coins, or tokens, or whatever they are, because I saw that witch borrowing one from her friend —"

"But we haven't got any!"

"If the plan works, we will have," Harry continued calmly.

"I don't know, Harry, I don't know. . . . There are an awful lot of things that could go wrong, so much relies on chance. . . ."

"That'll be true even if we spend another three months preparing," said Harry. "It's time to act."

He could tell from Ron's and Hermione's faces that they were scared; he was not particularly confident himself, and yet he was sure the time had come to put their plan into operation.

They had spent the previous four weeks taking it in turns to don the Invisibility Cloak and spy on the official entrance to the Ministry, which Ron, thanks to Mr. Weasley, had known since childhood. They had tailed Ministry workers on their way in, eavesdropped on their conversations, and learned by careful observation which of them could be relied upon to appear, alone, at the same time every day. Occasionally there had been a chance to sneak a *Daily Prophet* out of somebody's briefcase. Slowly they had built up the sketchy maps and notes now stacked in front of Hermione.

"All right," said Ron slowly, "let's say we go for it tomorrow. . . . I think it should just be me and Harry."

"Oh, don't start that again!" sighed Hermione. "I thought we'd settled this."

"It's one thing hanging around the entrances under the Cloak, but this is different, Hermione." Ron jabbed a finger at a copy of the *Daily Prophet* dated ten days previously. "You're on the list of Muggle-borns who didn't present themselves for interrogation!"

"And you're supposed to be dying of spattergroit at the Burrow! If anyone shouldn't go, it's Harry, he's got a ten-thousand-Galleon price on his head —"

"Fine, I'll stay here," said Harry. "Let me know if you ever defeat Voldemort, won't you?"

As Ron and Hermione laughed, pain shot through the scar on Harry's forehead. His hand jumped to it: He saw Hermione's eyes narrow, and he tried to pass off the movement by brushing his hair out of his eyes.

"Well, if all three of us go we'll have to Disapparate separately," Ron was saying. "We can't all fit under the Cloak anymore."

Harry's scar was becoming more and more painful. He stood up. At once, Kreacher hurried forward.

"Master has not finished his soup, would Master prefer the savory stew, or else the treacle tart to which Master is so partial?"

"Thanks, Kreacher, but I'll be back in a minute — er — bathroom."

Aware that Hermione was watching him suspiciously, Harry hurried up the stairs to the hall and then to the first landing, where he dashed into the bathroom and bolted the door again. Grunting with pain, he slumped over the black basin with its taps in the form of open-mouthed serpents and closed his eyes. . . .

He was gliding along a twilit street. The buildings on either side of him had high, timbered gables; they looked like gingerbread houses.

He approached one of them, then saw the whiteness of his own long-fingered hand against the door. He knocked. He felt a mounting excitement. . . .

The door opened: A laughing woman stood there. Her face fell as she looked into Harry's face: humor gone, terror replacing it. . . .

"Gregorovitch?" said a high, cold voice.

She shook her head: She was trying to close the door. A white hand held it steady, prevented her shutting him out. . . .

"I want Gregorovitch."

"Er wohnt hier nicht mehr!" she cried, shaking her head. "He no live here! He no live here! I know him not!"

Abandoning the attempt to close the door, she began to back away down the dark hall, and Harry followed, gliding toward her, and his long-fingered hand had drawn his wand.

"Where is he?"

"*Das weiß ich nicht!* He move! I know not, I know not!"

He raised the wand. She screamed. Two young children came running into the hall. She tried to shield them with her arms. There was a flash of green light —

"Harry! HARRY!"

He opened his eyes; he had sunk to the floor. Hermione was pounding on the door again.

"Harry, open up!"

He had shouted out, he knew it. He got up and unbolted the door; Hermione toppled inside at once, regained her balance, and looked around suspiciously. Ron was right behind her, looking unnerved as he pointed his wand into the corners of the chilly bathroom.

"What were you doing?" asked Hermione sternly.

"What d'you think I was doing?" asked Harry with feeble bravado.

"You were yelling your head off!" said Ron.

"Oh yeah . . . I must've dozed off or —"

"Harry, please don't insult our intelligence," said Hermione, taking deep breaths. "We know your scar hurt downstairs, and you're white as a sheet."

Harry sat down on the edge of the bath.

"Fine. I've just seen Voldemort murdering a woman. By now he's probably killed her whole family. And he didn't need to. It was Cedric all over again, they were just *there*. . . ."

"Harry, you aren't supposed to let this happen anymore!"

Hermione cried, her voice echoing through the bathroom. "Dumbledore wanted you to use Occlumency! He thought the connection was dangerous — Voldemort can *use* it, Harry! What good is it to watch him kill and torture, how can it help?"

"Because it means I know what he's doing," said Harry.

"So you're not even going to *try* to shut him out?"

"Hermione, I can't. You know I'm lousy at Occlumency, I never got the hang of it."

"You never really tried!" she said hotly. "I don't get it, Harry — do you *like* having this special connection or relationship or what — whatever —"

She faltered under the look he gave her as he stood up.

"Like it?" he said quietly. "Would *you* like it?"

"I — no — I'm sorry, Harry, I didn't mean —"

"I hate it, I hate the fact that he can get inside me, that I have to watch him when he's most dangerous. But I'm going to use it."

"Dumbledore —"

"Forget Dumbledore. This is my choice, nobody else's. I want to know why he's after Gregorovitch."

"Who?"

"He's a foreign wandmaker," said Harry. "He made Krum's wand and Krum reckons he's brilliant."

"But according to you," said Ron, "Voldemort's got Ollivander locked up somewhere. If he's already got a wandmaker, what does he need another one for?"

"Maybe he agrees with Krum, maybe he thinks Gregorovitch is better . . . or else he thinks Gregorovitch will be able to explain what my wand did when he was chasing me, because Ollivander didn't know."

Harry glanced into the cracked, dusty mirror and saw Ron and Hermione exchanging skeptical looks behind his back.

"Harry, you keep talking about what your wand did," said Hermione, "but *you* made it happen! Why are you so determined not to take responsibility for your own power?"

"Because I know it wasn't me! And so does Voldemort, Hermione! We both know what really happened!"

They glared at each other: Harry knew that he had not convinced Hermione and that she was marshaling counterarguments, against both his theory on his wand and the fact that he was permitting himself to see into Voldemort's mind. To his relief, Ron intervened.

"Drop it," he advised her. "It's up to him. And if we're going to the Ministry tomorrow, don't you reckon we should go over the plan?"

Reluctantly, as the other two could tell, Hermione let the matter rest, though Harry was quite sure she would attack again at the first opportunity. In the meantime, they returned to the basement kitchen, where Kreacher served them all stew and treacle tart.

They did not get to bed until late that night, after spending hours going over and over their plan until they could recite it, word perfect, to each other. Harry, who was now sleeping in Sirius's room, lay in bed with his wandlight trained on the old photograph of his father, Sirius, Lupin, and Pettigrew, and muttered the plan to himself for another ten minutes. As he extinguished his wand, however, he was thinking not of Polyjuice Potion, Puking Pastilles, or the navy blue robes of Magical Maintenance; he thought of Gregorovitch the wandmaker, and how long he could hope to remain hidden while Voldemort sought him so determinedly.

Dawn seemed to follow midnight with indecent haste.

"You look terrible," was Ron's greeting as he entered the room to wake Harry.

"Not for long," said Harry, yawning.

They found Hermione downstairs in the kitchen. She was being served coffee and hot rolls by Kreacher and wearing the slightly manic expression that Harry associated with exam review.

"Robes," she said under her breath, acknowledging their presence with a nervous nod and continuing to poke around in her beaded bag, "Polyjuice Potion . . . Invisibility Cloak . . . Decoy Detonators . . . You should each take a couple just in case. . . . Puking Pastilles, Nosebleed Nougat, Extendable Ears . . ."

They gulped down their breakfast, then set off upstairs, Kreacher bowing them out and promising to have a steak-and-kidney pie ready for them when they returned.

"Bless him," said Ron fondly, "and when you think I used to fantasize about cutting off his head and sticking it on the wall."

They made their way onto the front step with immense caution: They could see a couple of puffy-eyed Death Eaters watching the house from across the misty square.

Hermione Disapparated with Ron first, then came back for Harry.

After the usual brief spell of darkness and near suffocation, Harry found himself in the tiny alleyway where the first phase of their plan was scheduled to take place. It was as yet deserted, except for a couple of large bins; the first Ministry workers did not usually appear here until at least eight o'clock.

"Right then," said Hermione, checking her watch. "She ought to be here in about five minutes. When I've Stunned her —"

"Hermione, we know," said Ron sternly. "And I thought we were supposed to open the door before she got here?"

Hermione squealed.

"I nearly forgot! Stand back —"

She pointed her wand at the padlocked and heavily graffitied fire door beside them, which burst open with a crash. The dark corridor behind it led, as they knew from their careful scouting trips, into an empty theater. Hermione pulled the door back toward her, to make it look as though it was still closed.

"And now," she said, turning back to face the other two in the alleyway, "we put on the Cloak again —"

"— and we wait," Ron finished, throwing it over Hermione's head like a blanket over a birdcage and rolling his eyes at Harry.

Little more than a minute later, there was a tiny *pop* and a little Ministry witch with flyaway gray hair Apparated feet from them, blinking a little in the sudden brightness; the sun had just come out from behind a cloud. She barely had time to enjoy the unexpected warmth, however, before Hermione's silent Stunning Spell hit her in the chest and she toppled over.

"Nicely done, Hermione," said Ron, emerging from behind a bin beside the theater door as Harry took off the Invisibility Cloak. Together they carried the little witch into the dark passageway that led backstage. Hermione plucked a few hairs from the witch's head and added them to a flask of muddy Polyjuice Potion she had taken from the beaded bag. Ron was rummaging through the little witch's handbag.

"She's Mafalda Hopkirk," he said, reading a small card that identified their victim as an assistant in the Improper Use of Magic Office. "You'd better take this, Hermione, and here are the tokens."

He passed her several small golden coins, all embossed with the letters M.O.M., which he had taken from the witch's purse.

Hermione drank the Polyjuice Potion, which was now a pleasant heliotrope color, and within seconds stood before them, the double of Mafalda Hopkirk. As she removed Mafalda's spectacles and put them on, Harry checked his watch.

"We're running late, Mr. Magical Maintenance will be here any second."

They hurried to close the door on the real Mafalda; Harry and Ron threw the Invisibility Cloak over themselves but Hermione remained in view, waiting. Seconds later there was another *pop,* and a small, ferrety-looking wizard appeared before them.

"Oh, hello, Mafalda."

"Hello!" said Hermione in a quavery voice. "How are you today?"

"Not so good, actually," replied the little wizard, who looked thoroughly downcast.

As Hermione and the wizard headed for the main road, Harry and Ron crept along behind them.

"I'm sorry to hear you're under the weather," said Hermione, talking firmly over the little wizard as he tried to expound upon his problems; it was essential to stop him from reaching the street. "Here, have a sweet."

"Eh? Oh, no thanks —"

"I insist!" said Hermione aggressively, shaking the bag of pastilles in his face. Looking rather alarmed, the little wizard took one.

The effect was instantaneous. The moment the pastille touched his tongue, the little wizard started vomiting so hard that he did not even notice as Hermione yanked a handful of hairs from the top of his head.

"Oh dear!" she said, as he splattered the alley with sick. "Perhaps you'd better take the day off!"

"No — no!" He choked and retched, trying to continue on his way despite being unable to walk straight. "I must — today — must go —"

"But that's just silly!" said Hermione, alarmed. "You can't go to work in this state — I think you ought to go to St. Mungo's and get them to sort you out!"

The wizard had collapsed, heaving, onto all fours, still trying to crawl toward the main street.

"You simply can't go to work like this!" cried Hermione.

At last he seemed to accept the truth of her words. Using a repulsed Hermione to claw his way back into a standing position, he turned on the spot and vanished, leaving nothing behind but the bag Ron had snatched from his hand as he went and some flying chunks of vomit.

"Urgh," said Hermione, holding up the skirts of her robe to avoid the puddles of sick. "It would have made much less mess to Stun him too."

"Yeah," said Ron, emerging from under the cloak holding the wizard's bag, "but I still think a whole pile of unconscious bodies would have drawn more attention. Keen on his job, though, isn't he? Chuck us the hair and the potion, then."

Within two minutes, Ron stood before them, as small and ferrety as the sick wizard, and wearing the navy blue robes that had been folded in his bag.

"Weird he wasn't wearing them today, wasn't it, seeing how much he wanted to go? Anyway, I'm Reg Cattermole, according to the label in the back."

"Now wait here," Hermione told Harry, who was still under the Invisibility Cloak, "and we'll be back with some hairs for you."

He had to wait ten minutes, but it seemed much longer to Harry, skulking alone in the sick-splattered alleyway beside the door concealing the Stunned Mafalda. Finally Ron and Hermione reappeared.

"We don't know who he is," Hermione said, passing Harry several curly black hairs, "but he's gone home with a dreadful nosebleed! Here, he's pretty tall, you'll need bigger robes. . . ."

She pulled out a set of the old robes Kreacher had laundered for them, and Harry retired to take the potion and change.

Once the painful transformation was complete he was more than six feet tall and, from what he could tell from his well-muscled arms, powerfully built. He also had a beard. Stowing the Invisibility Cloak and his glasses inside his new robes, he rejoined the other two.

"Blimey, that's scary," said Ron, looking up at Harry, who now towered over him.

"Take one of Mafalda's tokens," Hermione told Harry, "and let's go, it's nearly nine."

They stepped out of the alleyway together. Fifty yards along the crowded pavement there were spiked black railings flanking two flights of steps, one labeled GENTLEMEN, the other LADIES.

"See you in a moment, then," said Hermione nervously, and she tottered off down the steps to LADIES. Harry and Ron joined a number of oddly dressed men descending into what appeared to be an ordinary underground public toilet, tiled in grimy black and white.

"Morning, Reg!" called another wizard in navy blue robes as he let himself into a cubicle by inserting his golden token into a slot in the door. "Blooming pain in the bum, this, eh? Forcing us all to get to work this way! Who are they expecting to turn up, Harry Potter?"

The wizard roared with laughter at his own wit. Ron gave a forced chuckle.

"Yeah," he said, "stupid, isn't it?"

And he and Harry let themselves into adjoining cubicles.

To Harry's left and right came the sound of flushing. He crouched down and peered through the gap at the bottom of the cubicle, just in time to see a pair of booted feet climbing into the toilet next door. He looked left and saw Ron blinking at him.

"We have to flush ourselves in?" he whispered.

"Looks like it," Harry whispered back; his voice came out deep and gravelly.

They both stood up. Feeling exceptionally foolish, Harry clambered into the toilet.

He knew at once that he had done the right thing; though he appeared to be standing in water, his shoes, feet, and robes remained quite dry. He reached up, pulled the chain, and next moment had zoomed down a short chute, emerging out of a fireplace into the Ministry of Magic.

He got up clumsily; there was a lot more of his body than he was accustomed to. The great Atrium seemed darker than Harry remembered it. Previously a golden fountain had filled the center of the hall, casting shimmering spots of light over the polished wooden floor and walls. Now a gigantic statue of black stone dominated the scene. It was rather frightening, this vast sculpture of a witch and a wizard sitting on ornately carved thrones, looking down at the Ministry workers toppling out of fireplaces below them. Engraved in foot-high letters at the base of the statue were the words MAGIC IS MIGHT.

Harry received a heavy blow on the back of the legs: Another wizard had just flown out of the fireplace behind him.

"Out of the way, can't y — oh, sorry, Runcorn!"

Clearly frightened, the balding wizard hurried away. Apparently the man whom Harry was impersonating, Runcorn, was intimidating.

"Psst!" said a voice, and he looked around to see a wispy little witch and the ferrety wizard from Magical Maintenance gesturing to him from over beside the statue. Harry hastened to join them.

"You got in all right, then?" Hermione whispered to Harry.

"No, he's still stuck in the bog," said Ron.

"Oh, very funny . . . It's horrible, isn't it?" she said to Harry, who was staring up at the statue. "Have you seen what they're sitting on?"

Harry looked more closely and realized that what he had thought were decoratively carved thrones were actually mounds of carved humans: hundreds and hundreds of naked bodies, men, women, and children, all with rather stupid, ugly faces, twisted and pressed together to support the weight of the handsomely robed wizards.

"Muggles," whispered Hermione. "In their rightful place. Come on, let's get going."

They joined the stream of witches and wizards moving toward the golden gates at the end of the hall, looking around as surreptitiously as possible, but there was no sign of the distinctive figure of Dolores Umbridge. They passed through the gates and into a smaller hall, where queues were forming in front of twenty golden grilles housing as many lifts. They had barely joined the nearest one when a voice said, "Cattermole!"

They looked around: Harry's stomach turned over. One of the Death Eaters who had witnessed Dumbledore's death was striding toward them. The Ministry workers beside them fell silent, their eyes downcast; Harry could feel fear rippling through them. The man's scowling, slightly brutish face was somehow at odds with his magnificent, sweeping robes, which were embroidered with much gold thread. Someone in the crowd around the lifts called sycophantically, "Morning, Yaxley!" Yaxley ignored them.

"I requested somebody from Magical Maintenance to sort out my office, Cattermole. It's still raining in there."

Ron looked around as though hoping somebody else would intervene, but nobody spoke.

"Raining . . . in your office? That's — that's not good, is it?"

Ron gave a nervous laugh. Yaxley's eyes widened.

"You think it's funny, Cattermole, do you?"

A pair of witches broke away from the queue for the lift and bustled off.

"No," said Ron, "no, of course —"

"You realize that I am on my way downstairs to interrogate your wife, Cattermole? In fact, I'm quite surprised you're not down there holding her hand while she waits. Already given her up as a bad job, have you? Probably wise. Be sure and marry a pureblood next time."

Hermione had let out a little squeak of horror. Yaxley looked at her. She coughed feebly and turned away.

"I — I —" stammered Ron.

"But if *my* wife were accused of being a Mudblood," said Yaxley, "— not that any woman I married would ever be mistaken for such filth — and the Head of the Department of Magical Law Enforcement needed a job doing, I would make it my priority to do that job, Cattermole. Do you understand me?"

"Yes," whispered Ron.

"Then attend to it, Cattermole, and if my office is not completely dry within an hour, your wife's Blood Status will be in even graver doubt than it is now."

The golden grille before them clattered open. With a nod and unpleasant smile to Harry, who was evidently expected to appreciate this treatment of Cattermole, Yaxley swept away toward another lift. Harry, Ron, and Hermione entered theirs, but nobody followed them: It was as if they were infectious. The grilles shut with a clang and the lift began to move upward.

"What am I going to do?" Ron asked the other two at once; he looked stricken. "If I don't turn up, my wife — I mean, Cattermole's wife —"

"We'll come with you, we should stick together —" began Harry, but Ron shook his head feverishly.

"That's mental, we haven't got much time. You two find Umbridge, I'll go and sort out Yaxley's office — but how do I stop it raining?"

"Try Finite Incantatem," said Hermione at once, "that should stop the rain if it's a hex or curse; if it doesn't, something's gone wrong with an Atmospheric Charm, which will be more difficult to fix, so as an interim measure try Impervius to protect his belongings —"

"Say it again, slowly —" said Ron, searching his pockets desperately for a quill, but at that moment the lift juddered to a halt.

A disembodied female voice said, "Level four, Department for the Regulation and Control of Magical Creatures, incorporating Beast, Being, and Spirit Divisions, Goblin Liaison Office, and Pest Advisory Bureau," and the grilles slid open again, admitting a couple of wizards and several pale violet paper airplanes that fluttered around the lamp in the ceiling of the lift.

"Morning, Albert," said a bushily whiskered man, smiling at Harry. He glanced over at Ron and Hermione as the lift creaked upward once more; Hermione was now whispering frantic instructions to Ron. The wizard leaned toward Harry, leering, and muttered, "Dirk Cresswell, eh? From Goblin Liaison? Nice one, Albert. I'm pretty confident I'll get his job now!"

He winked. Harry smiled back, hoping that this would suffice. The lift stopped; the grilles opened once more.

"Level two, Department of Magical Law Enforcement, including the Improper Use of Magic Office, Auror Headquarters, and Wizengamot Administration Services," said the disembodied witch's voice.

Harry saw Hermione give Ron a little push and he hurried out of the lift, followed by the other wizards, leaving Harry and Hermione alone. The moment the golden door had closed Hermione said, very fast, "Actually, Harry, I think I'd better go after him, I don't think he knows what he's doing and if he gets caught the whole thing —"

"Level one, Minister of Magic and Support Staff."

The golden grilles slid apart again and Hermione gasped. Four people stood before them, two of them deep in conversation: a long-haired wizard wearing magnificent robes of black and gold, and a squat, toadlike witch wearing a velvet bow in her short hair and clutching a clipboard to her chest.

THE MUGGLE-BORN REGISTRATION COMMISSION

Ah, Mafalda!" said Umbridge, looking at Hermione. "Travers sent you, did he?"

"Y-yes," squeaked Hermione.

"Good, you'll do perfectly well." Umbridge spoke to the wizard in black and gold. "That's that problem solved, Minister, if Mafalda can be spared for record-keeping we shall be able to start straightaway." She consulted her clipboard. "Ten people today and one of them the wife of a Ministry employee! Tut, tut . . . even here, in the heart of the Ministry!" She stepped into the lift beside Hermione, as did the two wizards who had been listening to Umbridge's conversation with the Minister. "We'll go straight down, Mafalda, you'll find everything you need in the courtroom. Good morning, Albert, aren't you getting out?"

"Yes, of course," said Harry in Runcorn's deep voice.

Harry stepped out of the lift. The golden grilles clanged shut behind him. Glancing over his shoulder, Harry saw Hermione's anxious face sinking back out of sight, a tall wizard on either side of her, Umbridge's velvet hair-bow level with her shoulder.

"What brings you up here, Runcorn?" asked the new Minister of Magic. His long black hair and beard were streaked with silver, and a great overhanging forehead shadowed his glinting eyes, putting Harry in mind of a crab looking out from beneath a rock.

"Needed a quick word with," Harry hesitated for a fraction of a second, "Arthur Weasley. Someone said he was up on level one."

"Ah," said Pius Thicknesse. "Has he been caught having contact with an Undesirable?"

"No," said Harry, his throat dry. "No, nothing like that."

"Ah, well. It's only a matter of time," said Thicknesse. "If you ask me, the blood traitors are as bad as the Mudbloods. Good day, Runcorn."

"Good day, Minister."

Harry watched Thicknesse march away along the thickly carpeted corridor. The moment the Minister had passed out of sight, Harry tugged the Invisibility Cloak out from under his heavy black cloak, threw it over himself, and set off along the corridor in the opposite direction. Runcorn was so tall that Harry was forced to stoop to make sure his big feet were hidden.

Panic pulsed in the pit of his stomach. As he passed gleaming wooden door after gleaming wooden door, each bearing a small plaque with the owner's name and occupation upon it, the might of the Ministry, its complexity, its impenetrability, seemed to force itself upon him so that the plan he had been carefully concocting with Ron and Hermione over the past four weeks seemed laughably childish. They had concentrated all their efforts on getting inside without being detected: They had not given a moment's thought to what they would do if they were forced to separate. Now Hermione was stuck in court proceedings, which would undoubtedly last hours; Ron was struggling to do magic that Harry was sure was beyond him, a woman's liberty possibly depending on the outcome; and he, Harry, was wandering around on the top floor when he knew perfectly well that his quarry had just gone down in the lift.

He stopped walking, leaned against a wall, and tried to decide what to do. The silence pressed upon him: There was no bustling or talk or swift footsteps here; the purple-carpeted corridors were as hushed as though the *Muffliato* charm had been cast over the place.

Her office must be up here, Harry thought.

It seemed most unlikely that Umbridge would keep her jewelry in her office, but on the other hand it seemed foolish not to search it to make sure. He therefore set off along the corridor again, passing nobody but a frowning wizard who was murmuring instructions to a quill that floated in front of him, scribbling on a trail of parchment.

Now paying attention to the names on the doors, Harry turned a corner. Halfway along the next corridor he emerged into a wide, open space where a dozen witches and wizards sat in rows at small desks not unlike school desks, though much more highly polished and free from graffiti. Harry paused to watch them, for the effect was quite mesmerizing. They were all waving and twiddling their wands in unison, and squares of colored paper were flying in every direction like little pink kites. After a few seconds, Harry realized that there was a rhythm to the proceedings, that the papers all formed the same pattern; and after a few more seconds he realized that what he was watching was the creation of pamphlets — that the paper squares were pages, which, when assembled, folded, and magicked into place, fell into neat stacks beside each witch or wizard.

Harry crept closer, although the workers were so intent on what they were doing that he doubted they would notice a carpet-muffled footstep, and he slid a completed pamphlet from the pile beside a young witch. He examined it beneath the Invisibility Cloak. Its pink cover was emblazoned with a golden title:

MUDBLOODS
and the Dangers They Pose to
a Peaceful Pure-Blood Society

Beneath the title was a picture of a red rose with a simpering face in the middle of its petals, being strangled by a green weed with fangs and a scowl. There was no author's name upon the pamphlet, but again, the scars on the back of his right hand seemed to tingle as he examined it. Then the young witch beside him confirmed his suspicion as she said, still waving and twirling her wand, "Will the old hag be interrogating Mudbloods all day, does anyone know?"

"Careful," said the wizard beside her, glancing around nervously; one of his pages slipped and fell to the floor.

"What, has she got magic ears as well as an eye, now?"

The witch glanced toward the shining mahogany door facing the space full of pamphlet-makers; Harry looked too, and rage reared in him like a snake. Where there might have been a peephole on a Muggle front door, a large, round eye with a bright blue iris had been set into the wood — an eye that was shockingly familiar to anybody who had known Alastor Moody.

For a split second Harry forgot where he was and what he was doing there: He even forgot that he was invisible. He strode straight over to the door to examine the eye. It was not moving: It gazed blindly upward, frozen. The plaque beneath it read:

DOLORES UMBRIDGE
SENIOR UNDERSECRETARY TO THE MINISTER

Below that, a slightly shinier new plaque read:

HEAD OF THE MUGGLE-BORN
REGISTRATION COMMISSION

Harry looked back at the dozen pamphlet-makers: Though they were intent upon their work, he could hardly suppose that they would not notice if the door of an empty office opened in front of them. He therefore withdrew from an inner pocket an odd object with little waving legs and a rubber-bulbed horn for a body. Crouching down beneath the Cloak, he placed the Decoy Detonator on the ground.

It scuttled away at once through the legs of the witches and wizards in front of him. A few moments later, during which Harry waited with his hand upon the doorknob, there came a loud bang and a great deal of acrid black smoke billowed from a corner. The young witch in the front row shrieked: Pink pages flew everywhere as she and her fellows jumped up, looking around for the source of the commotion. Harry turned the doorknob, stepped into Umbridge's office, and closed the door behind him.

He felt he had stepped back in time. The room was exactly like Umbridge's office at Hogwarts: Lace draperies, doilies, and dried flowers covered every available surface. The walls bore the same ornamental plates, each featuring a highly colored, beribboned kitten, gamboling and frisking with sickening cuteness. The desk was covered with a flouncy, flowered cloth. Behind Mad-Eye's eye, a telescopic attachment enabled Umbridge to spy on the workers on the other side of the door. Harry took a look through it and saw that they were all still gathered around the Decoy Detonator. He wrenched the telescope out of the door, leaving a hole behind, pulled the magical eyeball out of it, and placed it in his pocket. Then he turned to face the room again, raised his wand, and murmured, *"Accio Locket."*

Nothing happened, but he had not expected it to; no doubt Umbridge knew all about protective charms and spells. He therefore hurried behind her desk and began pulling open the drawers. He saw quills and notebooks and Spellotape; enchanted paper clips that coiled snakelike from their drawer and had to be beaten back; a fussy little lace box full of spare hair bows and clips; but no sign of a locket.

There was a filing cabinet behind the desk: Harry set to searching it. Like Filch's filing cabinets at Hogwarts, it was full of folders, each labeled with a name. It was not until Harry reached the bottommost drawer that he saw something to distract him from his search: Mr. Weasley's file.

He pulled it out and opened it.

ARTHUR WEASLEY

BLOOD STATUS:	Pureblood, but with unacceptable pro-Muggle leanings. Known member of the Order of the Phoenix.

FAMILY:	Wife (pureblood), seven children, two youngest at Hogwarts. NB: Youngest son currently at home, seriously ill, Ministry inspectors have confirmed.
SECURITY STATUS:	TRACKED. All movements are being monitored. Strong likelihood Undesirable No. 1 will contact (has stayed with Weasley family previously)

"Undesirable Number One," Harry muttered under his breath as he replaced Mr. Weasley's folder and shut the drawer. He had an idea he knew who that was, and sure enough, as he straightened up and glanced around the office for fresh hiding places, he saw a poster of himself on the wall, with the words UNDESIRABLE NO. 1 emblazoned across his chest. A little pink note was stuck to it with a picture of a kitten in the corner. Harry moved across to read it and saw that Umbridge had written, *"To be punished."*

Angrier than ever, he proceeded to grope in the bottoms of the vases and baskets of dried flowers, but was not at all surprised that the locket was not there. He gave the office one last sweeping look, and his heart skipped a beat. Dumbledore was staring at him from a small rectangular mirror, propped up on a bookcase beside the desk.

Harry crossed the room at a run and snatched it up, but realized the moment he touched it that it was not a mirror at all. Dumbledore was smiling wistfully out of the front cover of a glossy book. Harry had not immediately noticed the curly green writing across his hat — *The Life and Lies of Albus Dumbledore* — nor the slightly smaller writing across his chest: "by Rita Skeeter, bestselling author of *Armando Dippet: Master or Moron?*"

Harry opened the book at random and saw a full-page photo-graph of two teenage boys, both laughing immoderately with their arms around each other's shoulders. Dumbledore, now with elbow-length hair, had grown a tiny wispy beard that recalled the one on Krum's chin that had so annoyed Ron. The boy who roared in si-lent amusement beside Dumbledore had a gleeful, wild look about him. His golden hair fell in curls to his shoulders. Harry wondered whether it was a young Doge, but before he could check the caption, the door of the office opened.

If Thicknesse had not been looking over his shoulder as he en-tered, Harry would not have had time to pull the Invisibility Cloak over himself. As it was, he thought Thicknesse might have caught a glimpse of movement, because for a moment or two he remained quite still, staring curiously at the place where Harry had just vanished. Perhaps deciding that all he had seen was Dumbledore scratching his nose on the front of the book, for Harry had hastily replaced it upon the shelf, Thicknesse finally walked to the desk and pointed his wand at the quill standing ready in the ink pot. It sprang out and began scribbling a note to Umbridge. Very slowly, hardly daring to breathe, Harry backed out of the office into the open area beyond.

The pamphlet-makers were still clustered around the remains of the Decoy Detonator, which continued to hoot feebly as it smoked. Harry hurried off up the corridor as the young witch said, "I bet it sneaked up here from Experimental Charms, they're so careless, remember that poisonous duck?"

Speeding back toward the lifts, Harry reviewed his options. It had never been likely that the locket was here at the Ministry, and there was no hope of bewitching its whereabouts out of Umbridge while she was sitting in a crowded court. Their priority now had to be to leave the Ministry before they were exposed, and try again another day. The first thing to do was to find Ron, and then they could work out a way of extracting Hermione from the courtroom.

The lift was empty when it arrived. Harry jumped in and pulled off the Invisibility Cloak as it started its descent. To his enormous relief, when it rattled to a halt at level two, a soaking-wet and wild-eyed Ron got in.

"M-morning," he stammered to Harry as the lift set off again.

"Ron, it's me, Harry!"

"Harry! Blimey, I forgot what you looked like — why isn't Hermione with you?"

"She had to go down to the courtrooms with Umbridge, she couldn't refuse, and —"

But before Harry could finish the lift had stopped again: The doors opened and Mr. Weasley walked inside, talking to an elderly witch whose blonde hair was teased so high it resembled an anthill.

". . . I quite understand what you're saying, Wakanda, but I'm afraid I cannot be party to —"

Mr. Weasley broke off; he had noticed Harry. It was very strange to have Mr. Weasley glare at him with that much dislike. The lift doors closed and the four of them trundled downward once more.

"Oh, hello, Reg," said Mr. Weasley, looking around at the sound of steady dripping from Ron's robes. "Isn't your wife in for questioning today? Er — what's happened to you? Why are you so wet?"

"Yaxley's office is raining," said Ron. He addressed Mr. Weasley's shoulder, and Harry felt sure he was scared that his father might recognize him if they looked directly into each other's eyes. "I couldn't stop it, so they've sent me to get Bernie — Pillsworth, I think they said —"

"Yes, a lot of offices have been raining lately," said Mr. Weasley. "Did you try Meteolojinx Recanto? It worked for Bletchley."

"Meteolojinx Recanto?" whispered Ron. "No, I didn't. Thanks, D — I mean, thanks, Arthur."

The lift doors opened; the old witch with the anthill hair left, and Ron darted past her out of sight. Harry made to follow him, but found his path blocked as Percy Weasley strode into the lift, his nose buried in some papers he was reading.

Not until the doors had clanged shut again did Percy realize he was in a lift with his father. He glanced up, saw Mr. Weasley, turned radish red, and left the lift the moment the doors opened again. For the second time, Harry tried to get out, but this time found his way blocked by Mr. Weasley's arm.

"One moment, Runcorn."

The lift doors closed and as they clanked down another floor, Mr. Weasley said, "I hear you laid information about Dirk Cresswell."

Harry had the impression that Mr. Weasley's anger was no less because of the brush with Percy. He decided his best chance was to act stupid.

"Sorry?" he said.

"Don't pretend, Runcorn," said Mr. Weasley fiercely. "You tracked down the wizard who faked his family tree, didn't you?"

"I — so what if I did?" said Harry.

"So Dirk Cresswell is ten times the wizard you are," said Mr. Weasley quietly, as the lift sank ever lower. "And if he survives Azkaban, you'll have to answer to him, not to mention his wife, his sons, and his friends —"

"Arthur," Harry interrupted, "you know you're being tracked, don't you?"

"Is that a threat, Runcorn?" said Mr. Weasley loudly.

"No," said Harry, "it's a fact! They're watching your every move —"

The lift doors opened. They had reached the Atrium. Mr. Weasley gave Harry a scathing look and swept from the lift. Harry stood there, shaken. He wished he was impersonating somebody other than Runcorn. . . . The lift doors clanged shut.

Harry pulled out the Invisibility Cloak and put it back on. He would try to extricate Hermione on his own while Ron was dealing with the raining office. When the doors opened, he stepped out into a torch-lit stone passageway quite different from the wood-paneled and carpeted corridors above. As the lift rattled away again, Harry shivered slightly, looking toward the distant black door that marked the entrance to the Department of Mysteries.

He set off, his destination not the black door, but the doorway he remembered on the left-hand side, which opened onto the flight of stairs down to the court chambers. His mind grappled with possibilities as he crept down them: He still had a couple of Decoy Detonators, but perhaps it would be better to simply knock on the courtroom door, enter as Runcorn, and ask for a quick word with Mafalda? Of course, he did not know whether Runcorn was sufficiently important to get away with this, and even if he managed it, Hermione's non-reappearance might trigger a search before they were clear of the Ministry. . . .

Lost in thought, he did not immediately register the unnatural chill that was creeping over him, as if he were descending into fog. It was becoming colder and colder with every step he took: a cold that reached right down into his throat and tore at his lungs. And then he felt that stealing sense of despair, of hopelessness, filling him, expanding inside him. . . .

Dementors, he thought.

And as he reached the foot of the stairs and turned to his right he saw a dreadful scene. The dark passage outside the courtrooms was packed with tall, black-hooded figures, their faces completely hidden, their ragged breathing the only sound in the place. The petrified Muggle-borns brought in for questioning sat huddled and shivering on hard wooden benches. Most of them were hiding their faces in their hands, perhaps in an instinctive attempt to shield themselves from the dementors' greedy mouths. Some were accompanied by families, others sat alone. The dementors were gliding up and down in front of them, and the cold, and the hopelessness, and the despair of the place laid themselves upon Harry like a curse. . . .

Fight it, he told himself, but he knew that he could not conjure a Patronus here without revealing himself instantly. So he moved forward as silently as he could, and with every step he took numbness seemed to steal over his brain, but he forced himself to think of Hermione and of Ron, who needed him.

Moving through the towering black figures was terrifying: The eyeless faces hidden beneath their hoods turned as he passed, and he felt sure that they sensed him, sensed, perhaps, a human presence that still had some hope, some resilience. . . .

And then, abruptly and shockingly amid the frozen silence, one of the dungeon doors on the left of the corridor was flung open and screams echoed out of it.

"No, no, I'm half-blood, I'm half-blood, I tell you! My father was a wizard, he *was,* look him up, Arkie Alderton, he's a well-known broomstick designer, look him up, I tell you — get your hands off me, get your hands off —"

"This is your final warning," said Umbridge's soft voice, magically magnified so that it sounded clearly over the man's desperate screams. "If you struggle, you will be subjected to the Dementor's Kiss."

The man's screams subsided, but dry sobs echoed through the corridor.

"Take him away," said Umbridge.

Two dementors appeared in the doorway of the courtroom, their rotting, scabbed hands clutching the upper arms of a wizard who appeared to be fainting. They glided away down the corridor with him, and the darkness they trailed behind them swallowed him from sight.

"Next — Mary Cattermole," called Umbridge.

A small woman stood up; she was trembling from head to foot. Her dark hair was smoothed back into a bun and she wore long, plain robes. Her face was completely bloodless. As she passed the dementors, Harry saw her shudder.

He did it instinctively, without any sort of plan, because he hated the sight of her walking alone into the dungeon: As the door began to swing closed, he slipped into the courtroom behind her.

It was not the same room in which he had once been interrogated for improper use of magic. This one was much smaller, though the ceiling was quite as high; it gave the claustrophobic sense of being stuck at the bottom of a deep well.

There were more dementors in here, casting their freezing aura over the place; they stood like faceless sentinels in the corners farthest from the high, raised platform. Here, behind a balustrade, sat

Umbridge, with Yaxley on one side of her, and Hermione, quite as white-faced as Mrs. Cattermole, on the other. At the foot of the platform, a bright-silver, long-haired cat prowled up and down, up and down, and Harry realized that it was there to protect the prosecutors from the despair that emanated from the dementors: That was for the accused to feel, not the accusers.

"Sit down," said Umbridge in her soft, silky voice.

Mrs. Cattermole stumbled to the single seat in the middle of the floor beneath the raised platform. The moment she had sat down, chains clinked out of the arms of the chair and bound her there.

"You are Mary Elizabeth Cattermole?" asked Umbridge.

Mrs. Cattermole gave a single, shaky nod.

"Married to Reginald Cattermole of the Magical Maintenance Department?"

Mrs. Cattermole burst into tears.

"I don't know where he is, he was supposed to meet me here!"

Umbridge ignored her.

"Mother to Maisie, Ellie, and Alfred Cattermole?"

Mrs. Cattermole sobbed harder than ever.

"They're frightened, they think I might not come home —"

"Spare us," spat Yaxley. "The brats of Mudbloods do not stir our sympathies."

Mrs. Cattermole's sobs masked Harry's footsteps as he made his way carefully toward the steps that led up to the raised platform. The moment he had passed the place where the Patronus cat patrolled, he felt the change in temperature: It was warm and comfortable here. The Patronus, he was sure, was Umbridge's, and it glowed brightly because she was so happy here, in her element, upholding the twisted laws she had helped to write. Slowly and very carefully he edged his way along the platform behind Umbridge, Yaxley, and Hermione, taking a seat behind the latter. He was worried about making Hermione jump. He thought of casting the *Muffliato* charm upon Umbridge and Yaxley, but even murmuring the word might cause Hermione alarm. Then Umbridge raised her voice to address Mrs. Cattermole, and Harry seized his chance.

"I'm behind you," he whispered into Hermione's ear.

As he had expected, she jumped so violently she nearly overturned the bottle of ink with which she was supposed to be recording the interview, but both Umbridge and Yaxley were concentrating upon Mrs. Cattermole, and this went unnoticed.

"A wand was taken from you upon your arrival at the Ministry today, Mrs. Cattermole," Umbridge was saying. "Eight-and-three-quarter inches, cherry, unicorn-hair core. Do you recognize that description?"

Mrs. Cattermole nodded, mopping her eyes on her sleeve.

"Could you please tell us from which witch or wizard you took that wand?"

"T-took?" sobbed Mrs. Cattermole. "I didn't t-take it from anybody. I b-bought it when I was eleven years old. It — it — it — *chose* me."

She cried harder than ever.

Umbridge laughed a soft girlish laugh that made Harry want to attack her. She leaned forward over the barrier, the better to observe her victim, and something gold swung forward too, and dangled over the void: the locket.

Hermione had seen it; she let out a little squeak, but Umbridge and Yaxley, still intent upon their prey, were deaf to everything else.

"No," said Umbridge, "no, I don't think so, Mrs. Cattermole. Wands only choose witches or wizards. You are not a witch. I have your responses to the questionnaire that was sent to you here — Mafalda, pass them to me."

Umbridge held out a small hand: She looked so toadlike at that moment that Harry was quite surprised not to see webs between the stubby fingers. Hermione's hands were shaking with shock. She fumbled in a pile of documents balanced on the chair beside her, finally withdrawing a sheaf of parchment with Mrs. Cattermole's name on it.

"That's — that's pretty, Dolores," she said, pointing at the pendant gleaming in the ruffled folds of Umbridge's blouse.

"What?" snapped Umbridge, glancing down. "Oh yes — an old family heirloom," she said, patting the locket lying on her large bosom. "The *S* stands for Selwyn. . . . I am related to the Selwyns. . . . Indeed, there are few pure-blood families to whom I am not related. . . . A pity," she continued in a louder voice, flicking through Mrs. Cattermole's questionnaire, "that the same cannot be said for you. *'Parents' professions: greengrocers.'*"

Yaxley laughed jeeringly. Below, the fluffy silver cat patrolled up and down, and the dementors stood waiting in the corners.

It was Umbridge's lie that brought the blood surging into Harry's brain and obliterated his sense of caution — that the locket she had taken as a bribe from a petty criminal was being used to bolster her own pure-blood credentials. He raised his wand, not even troubling to keep it concealed beneath the Invisibility Cloak, and said, *"Stupefy!"*

There was a flash of red light; Umbridge crumpled and her forehead hit the edge of the balustrade: Mrs. Cattermole's papers slid off her lap onto the floor and, down below, the prowling silver cat vanished. Ice-cold air hit them like an oncoming wind: Yaxley, confused, looked around for the source of the trouble and saw Harry's disembodied hand and wand pointing at him. He tried to draw his own wand, but too late: *"Stupefy!"*

Yaxley slid to the ground to lie curled on the floor.

"Harry!"

"Hermione, if you think I was going to sit here and let her pretend —"

"Harry, Mrs. Cattermole!"

Harry whirled around, throwing off the Invisibility Cloak; down below, the dementors had moved out of their corners; they were gliding toward the woman chained to the chair: Whether because the Patronus had vanished or because they sensed that their masters were no longer in control, they seemed to have abandoned restraint. Mrs. Cattermole let out a terrible scream of fear as a slimy, scabbed hand grasped her chin and forced her face back.

"EXPECTO PATRONUM!"

The silver stag soared from the tip of Harry's wand and leaped toward the dementors, which fell back and melted into the dark shadows again. The stag's light, more powerful and more warming than the cat's protection, filled the whole dungeon as it cantered around and around the room.

"Get the Horcrux," Harry told Hermione.

He ran back down the steps, stuffing the Invisibility Cloak back into his bag, and approached Mrs. Cattermole.

"You?" she whispered, gazing into his face. "But — but Reg said you were the one who submitted my name for questioning!"

"Did I?" muttered Harry, tugging at the chains binding her arms.

"Well, I've had a change of heart. *Diffindo!*" Nothing happened. "Hermione, how do I get rid of these chains?"

"Wait, I'm trying something up here —"

"Hermione, we're surrounded by dementors!"

"I know that, Harry, but if she wakes up and the locket's gone — I need to duplicate it — *Geminio!* There . . . That should fool her. . . ."

Hermione came running downstairs.

"Let's see. . . . *Relashio!*"

The chains clinked and withdrew into the arms of the chair. Mrs. Cattermole looked just as frightened as ever before.

"I don't understand," she whispered.

"You're going to leave here with us," said Harry, pulling her to her feet. "Go home, grab your children, and get out, get out of the country if you've got to. Disguise yourselves and run. You've seen how it is, you won't get anything like a fair hearing here."

"Harry," said Hermione, "how are we going to get out of here with all those dementors outside the door?"

"Patronuses," said Harry, pointing his wand at his own: The stag slowed and walked, still gleaming brightly, toward the door. "As many as we can muster; do yours, Hermione."

"*Expec — Expecto patronum,*" said Hermione. Nothing happened.

"It's the only spell she ever has trouble with," Harry told a completely bemused Mrs. Cattermole. "Bit unfortunate, really . . . Come on, Hermione. . . ."

"*Expecto patronum!*"

A silver otter burst from the end of Hermione's wand and swam gracefully through the air to join the stag.

"C'mon," said Harry, and he led Hermione and Mrs. Cattermole to the door.

When the Patronuses glided out of the dungeon there were cries of shock from the people waiting outside. Harry looked around; the dementors were falling back on both sides of them, melding into the darkness, scattering before the silver creatures.

"It's been decided that you should all go home and go into hiding with your families," Harry told the waiting Muggle-borns, who were dazzled by the light of the Patronuses and still cowering slightly. "Go abroad if you can. Just get well away from the Ministry. That's the — er — new official position. Now, if you'll just follow the Patronuses, you'll be able to leave from the Atrium."

They managed to get up the stone steps without being intercepted, but as they approached the lifts Harry started to have misgivings. If they emerged into the Atrium with a silver stag, an otter soaring alongside it, and twenty or so people, half of them accused Muggle-borns, he could not help feeling that they would attract unwanted attention. He had just reached this unwelcome conclusion when the lift clanged to a halt in front of them.

"Reg!" screamed Mrs. Cattermole, and she threw herself into Ron's arms. "Runcorn let me out, he attacked Umbridge and Yaxley, and he's told all of us to leave the country, I think we'd better do it, Reg, I really do, let's hurry home and fetch the children and — why are you so wet?"

"Water," muttered Ron, disengaging himself. "Harry, they know there are intruders inside the Ministry, something about a hole in Umbridge's office door, I reckon we've got five minutes if that —"

Hermione's Patronus vanished with a *pop* as she turned a horror-struck face to Harry.

"Harry, if we're trapped here — !"

"We won't be if we move fast," said Harry. He addressed the silent group behind them, who were all gawping at him.

"Who's got wands?"

About half of them raised their hands.

"Okay, all of you who haven't got wands need to attach yourself to somebody who has. We'll need to be fast before they stop us. Come on."

They managed to cram themselves into two lifts. Harry's Patronus stood sentinel before the golden grilles as they shut and the lifts began to rise.

"Level eight," said the witch's cool voice, "Atrium."

Harry knew at once that they were in trouble. The Atrium was full of people moving from fireplace to fireplace, sealing them off.

"Harry!" squeaked Hermione. "What are we going to — ?"

"STOP!" Harry thundered, and the powerful voice of Runcorn echoed through the Atrium: The wizards sealing the fireplaces froze. "Follow me," he whispered to the group of terrified Muggleborns, who moved forward in a huddle, shepherded by Ron and Hermione.

"What's up, Albert?" said the same balding wizard who had followed Harry out of the fireplace earlier. He looked nervous.

"This lot need to leave before you seal the exits," said Harry with all the authority he could muster.

The group of wizards in front of him looked at one another.

"We've been told to seal all exits and not let anyone —"

"Are you contradicting me?" Harry blustered. "Would you like me to have your family tree examined, like I had Dirk Cresswell's?"

"Sorry!" gasped the balding wizard, backing away. "I didn't mean nothing, Albert, but I thought . . . I thought they were in for questioning and . . ."

"Their blood is pure," said Harry, and his deep voice echoed impressively through the hall. "Purer than many of yours, I daresay. Off you go," he boomed to the Muggle-borns, who scurried forward into the fireplaces and began to vanish in pairs. The Ministry wizards hung back, some looking confused, others scared and resentful. Then:

"Mary!"

Mrs. Cattermole looked over her shoulder. The real Reg Cattermole, no longer vomiting but pale and wan, had just come running out of a lift.

"R-Reg?"

She looked from her husband to Ron, who swore loudly.

The balding wizard gaped, his head turning ludicrously from one Reg Cattermole to the other.

"Hey — what's going on? What is this?"

"Seal the exit! SEAL IT!"

Yaxley had burst out of another lift and was running toward the group beside the fireplaces, into which all of the Muggle-borns but Mrs. Cattermole had now vanished. As the balding wizard lifted his wand, Harry raised an enormous fist and punched him, sending him flying through the air.

"He's been helping Muggle-borns escape, Yaxley!" Harry shouted.

The balding wizard's colleagues set up an uproar, under cover of which Ron grabbed Mrs. Cattermole, pulled her into the still-open fireplace, and disappeared. Confused, Yaxley looked from Harry to the punched wizard, while the real Reg Cattermole screamed, "My wife! Who was that with my wife? What's going on?"

Harry saw Yaxley's head turn, saw an inkling of the truth dawn in that brutish face.

"Come on!" Harry shouted at Hermione; he seized her hand and they jumped into the fireplace together as Yaxley's curse sailed over Harry's head. They spun for a few seconds before shooting up out of a toilet into a cubicle. Harry flung open the door; Ron was standing there beside the sinks, still wrestling with Mrs. Cattermole.

"Reg, I don't understand —"

"Let go, I'm not your husband, you've got to go home!"

There was a noise in the cubicle behind them; Harry looked around; Yaxley had just appeared.

"LET'S GO!" Harry yelled. He seized Hermione by the hand and Ron by the arm and turned on the spot.

Darkness engulfed them, along with the sensation of compressing bands, but something was wrong. . . . Hermione's hand seemed to be sliding out of his grip. . . .

He wondered whether he was going to suffocate; he could not breathe or see and the only solid things in the world were Ron's arm and Hermione's fingers, which were slowly slipping away. . . .

And then he saw the door of number twelve, Grimmauld Place, with its serpent door knocker, but before he could draw breath, there was a scream and a flash of purple light; Hermione's hand was suddenly vicelike upon his and everything went dark again.

THE THIEF

arry opened his eyes and was dazzled by gold and green; he had no idea what had happened, he only knew that he was lying on what seemed to be leaves and twigs. Struggling to draw breath into lungs that felt flattened, he blinked and realized that the gaudy glare was sunlight streaming through a canopy of leaves far above him. Then an object twitched close to his face. He pushed himself onto his hands and knees, ready to face some small, fierce creature, but saw that the object was Ron's foot. Looking around, Harry saw that they and Hermione were lying on a forest floor, apparently alone.

Harry's first thought was of the Forbidden Forest, and for a moment, even though he knew how foolish and dangerous it would be for them to appear in the grounds of Hogwarts, his heart leapt at the thought of sneaking through the trees to Hagrid's hut. However, in the few moments it took for Ron to give a low groan and Harry to start crawling toward him, he realized that this was not the

Forbidden Forest: The trees looked younger, they were more widely spaced, the ground clearer.

He met Hermione, also on her hands and knees, at Ron's head. The moment his eyes fell upon Ron, all other concerns fled Harry's mind, for blood drenched the whole of Ron's left side and his face stood out, grayish-white, against the leaf-strewn earth. The Polyjuice Potion was wearing off now: Ron was halfway between Cattermole and himself in appearance, his hair turning redder and redder as his face drained of the little color it had left.

"What's happened to him?"

"Splinched," said Hermione, her fingers already busy at Ron's sleeve, where the blood was wettest and darkest.

Harry watched, horrified, as she tore open Ron's shirt. He had always thought of Splinching as something comical, but this . . . His insides crawled unpleasantly as Hermione laid bare Ron's upper arm, where a great chunk of flesh was missing, scooped cleanly away as though by a knife.

"Harry, quickly, in my bag, there's a small bottle labeled 'Essence of Dittany'—"

"Bag — right —"

Harry sped to the place where Hermione had landed, seized the tiny beaded bag, and thrust his hand inside it. At once, object after object began presenting itself to his touch: He felt the leather spines of books, woolly sleeves of jumpers, heels of shoes —

"Quickly!"

He grabbed his wand from the ground and pointed it into the depths of the magical bag.

"Accio Dittany!"

A small brown bottle zoomed out of the bag; he caught it and hastened back to Hermione and Ron, whose eyes were now half-closed, strips of white eyeball all that were visible between his lids.

"He's fainted," said Hermione, who was also rather pale; she no longer looked like Mafalda, though her hair was still gray in places. "Unstopper it for me, Harry, my hands are shaking."

Harry wrenched the stopper off the little bottle, Hermione took it and poured three drops of the potion onto the bleeding wound. Greenish smoke billowed upward and when it had cleared, Harry saw that the bleeding had stopped. The wound now looked several days old; new skin stretched over what had just been open flesh.

"Wow," said Harry.

"It's all I feel safe doing," said Hermione shakily. "There are spells that would put him completely right, but I daren't try in case I do them wrong and cause more damage. . . . He's lost so much blood already. . . ."

"How did he get hurt? I mean" — Harry shook his head, trying to clear it, to make sense of whatever had just taken place — "why are we here? I thought we were going back to Grimmauld Place?"

Hermione took a deep breath. She looked close to tears.

"Harry, I don't think we're going to be able to go back there."

"What d'you — ?"

"As we Disapparated, Yaxley caught hold of me and I couldn't get rid of him, he was too strong, and he was still holding on when we arrived at Grimmauld Place, and then — well, I think he must have seen the door, and thought we were stopping there, so he slackened his grip and I managed to shake him off and I brought us here instead!"

"But then, where's he? Hang on. . . . You don't mean he's at Grimmauld Place? He can't get in there?"

Her eyes sparkled with unshed tears as she nodded.

"Harry, I think he can. I — I forced him to let go with a Revulsion Jinx, but I'd already taken him inside the Fidelius Charm's protection. Since Dumbledore died, we're Secret-Keepers, so I've given him the secret, haven't I?"

There was no pretending; Harry was sure she was right. It was a serious blow. If Yaxley could now get inside the house, there was no way that they could return. Even now, he could be bringing other Death Eaters in there by Apparition. Gloomy and oppressive though the house was, it had been their one safe refuge: even, now that Kreacher was so much happier and friendlier, a kind of home. With a twinge of regret that had nothing to do with food, Harry imagined the house-elf busying himself over the steak-and-kidney pie that Harry, Ron, and Hermione would never eat.

"Harry, I'm sorry, I'm so sorry!"

"Don't be stupid, it wasn't your fault! If anything, it was mine. . . ."

Harry put his hand in his pocket and drew out Mad-Eye's eye. Hermione recoiled, looking horrified.

"Umbridge had stuck it to her office door, to spy on people. I couldn't leave it there . . . but that's how they knew there were intruders."

Before Hermione could answer, Ron groaned and opened his eyes. He was still gray and his face glistened with sweat.

"How d'you feel?" Hermione whispered.

"Lousy," croaked Ron, wincing as he felt his injured arm. "Where are we?"

"In the woods where they held the Quidditch World Cup," said Hermione. "I wanted somewhere enclosed, undercover, and this was —"

"— the first place you thought of," Harry finished for her, glancing around at the apparently deserted glade. He could not help remembering what had happened the last time they had Apparated to the first place Hermione had thought of — how Death Eaters had found them within minutes. Had it been Legilimency? Did Voldemort or his henchmen know, even now, where Hermione had taken them?

"D'you reckon we should move on?" Ron asked Harry, and Harry could tell by the look on Ron's face that he was thinking the same.

"I dunno."

Ron still looked pale and clammy. He had made no attempt to sit up and it looked as though he was too weak to do so. The prospect of moving him was daunting.

"Let's stay here for now," Harry said.

Looking relieved, Hermione sprang to her feet.

"Where are you going?" asked Ron.

"If we're staying, we should put some protective enchantments around the place," she replied, and raising her wand, she began to walk in a wide circle around Harry and Ron, murmuring incantations as she went. Harry saw little disturbances in the surrounding air: It was as if Hermione had cast a heat haze upon their clearing.

"*Salvio Hexia . . . Protego Totalum . . . Repello Muggletum . . . Muffliato . . .* You could get out the tent, Harry. . . ."

"Tent?"

"In the bag!"

"In the . . . of course," said Harry.

He did not bother to grope inside it this time, but used another

Summoning Charm. The tent emerged in a lumpy mass of canvas, rope, and poles. Harry recognized it, partly because of the smell of cats, as the same tent in which they had slept on the night of the Quidditch World Cup.

"I thought this belonged to that bloke Perkins at the Ministry?" he asked, starting to disentangle the tent pegs.

"Apparently he didn't want it back, his lumbago's so bad," said Hermione, now performing complicated figure-of-eight movements with her wand, "so Ron's dad said I could borrow it. *Erecto!*" she added, pointing her wand at the misshapen canvas, which in one fluid motion rose into the air and settled, fully constructed, onto the ground before Harry, out of whose startled hands a tent peg soared, to land with a final thud at the end of a guy rope.

"*Cave Inimicum,*" Hermione finished with a skyward flourish. "That's as much as I can do. At the very least, we should know they're coming, I can't guarantee it will keep out Vol —"

"Don't say the name!" Ron cut across her, his voice harsh.

Harry and Hermione looked at each other.

"I'm sorry," Ron said, moaning a little as he raised himself to look at them, "but it feels like a — a jinx or something. Can't we call him You-Know-Who — please?"

"Dumbledore said fear of a name —" began Harry.

"In case you hadn't noticed, mate, calling You-Know-Who by his name didn't do Dumbledore much good in the end," Ron snapped back. "Just — just show You-Know-Who some respect, will you?"

"*Respect?*" Harry repeated, but Hermione shot him a warning look; apparently he was not to argue with Ron while the latter was in such a weakened condition.

Harry and Hermione half carried, half dragged Ron through

the entrance of the tent. The interior was exactly as Harry remembered it: a small flat, complete with bathroom and tiny kitchen. He shoved aside an old armchair and lowered Ron carefully onto the lower berth of a bunk bed. Even this very short journey had turned Ron whiter still, and once they had settled him on the mattress he closed his eyes again and did not speak for a while.

"I'll make some tea," said Hermione breathlessly, pulling kettle and mugs from the depths of her bag and heading toward the kitchen.

Harry found the hot drink as welcome as the firewhisky had been on the night that Mad-Eye had died; it seemed to burn away a little of the fear fluttering in his chest. After a minute or two, Ron broke the silence.

"What d'you reckon happened to the Cattermoles?"

"With any luck, they'll have got away," said Hermione, clutching her hot mug for comfort. "As long as Mr. Cattermole had his wits about him, he'll have transported Mrs. Cattermole by Side-Along-Apparition and they'll be fleeing the country right now with their children. That's what Harry told her to do."

"Blimey, I hope they escaped," said Ron, leaning back on his pillows. The tea seemed to be doing him good; a little of his color had returned. "I didn't get the feeling Reg Cattermole was all that quick-witted, though, the way everyone was talking to me when I was him. God, I hope they made it. . . . If they both end up in Azkaban because of us . . ."

Harry looked over at Hermione and the question he had been about to ask — about whether Mrs. Cattermole's lack of a wand would prevent her Apparating alongside her husband — died in his throat. Hermione was watching Ron fret over the fate of the Cattermoles, and there was such tenderness in her expression that

Harry felt almost as if he had surprised her in the act of kissing him.

"So, have you got it?" Harry asked her, partly to remind her that he was there.

"Got — got what?" she said with a little start.

"What did we just go through all that for? The locket! Where's the locket?"

"*You got it?*" shouted Ron, raising himself a little higher on his pillows. "No one tells me anything! Blimey, you could have mentioned it!"

"Well, we were running for our lives from the Death Eaters, weren't we?" said Hermione. "Here."

And she pulled the locket out of the pocket of her robes and handed it to Ron.

It was as large as a chicken's egg. An ornate letter *S,* inlaid with many small green stones, glinted dully in the diffused light shining through the tent's canvas roof.

"There isn't any chance someone's destroyed it since Kreacher had it?" asked Ron hopefully. "I mean, are we sure it's still a Horcrux?"

"I think so," said Hermione, taking it back from him and looking at it closely. "There'd be some sign of damage if it had been magically destroyed."

She passed it to Harry, who turned it over in his fingers. The thing looked perfect, pristine. He remembered the mangled remains of the diary, and how the stone in the Horcrux ring had been cracked open when Dumbledore destroyed it.

"I reckon Kreacher's right," said Harry. "We're going to have to work out how to open this thing before we can destroy it."

Sudden awareness of what he was holding, of what lived behind the little golden doors, hit Harry as he spoke. Even after all their efforts to find it, he felt a violent urge to fling the locket from him. Mastering himself again, he tried to prise the locket apart with his fingers, then attempted the charm Hermione had used to open Regulus's bedroom door. Neither worked. He handed the locket back to Ron and Hermione, each of whom did their best, but were no more successful at opening it than he had been.

"Can you feel it, though?" Ron asked in a hushed voice, as he held it tight in his clenched fist.

"What d'you mean?"

Ron passed the Horcrux to Harry. After a moment or two, Harry thought he knew what Ron meant. Was it his own blood pulsing through his veins that he could feel, or was it something beating inside the locket, like a tiny metal heart?

"What are we going to do with it?" Hermione asked.

"Keep it safe till we work out how to destroy it," Harry replied, and, little though he wanted to, he hung the chain around his own neck, dropping the locket out of sight beneath his robes, where it rested against his chest beside the pouch Hagrid had given him.

"I think we should take it in turns to keep watch outside the tent," he added to Hermione, standing up and stretching. "And we'll need to think about some food as well. You stay there," he added sharply, as Ron attempted to sit up and turned a nasty shade of green.

With the Sneakoscope Hermione had given Harry for his birthday set carefully upon the table in the tent, Harry and Hermione spent the rest of the day sharing the role of lookout. However, the Sneakoscope remained silent and still upon its point all day, and whether because of the protective enchantments and Muggle-repelling charms Hermione had spread around them, or because people rarely ventured this way, their patch of wood remained deserted, apart from occasional birds and squirrels. Evening brought no change; Harry lit his wand as he swapped places with Hermione at ten o'clock, and looked out upon a deserted scene, noting the bats fluttering high above him across the single patch of starry sky visible from their protected clearing.

He felt hungry now, and a little light-headed. Hermione had not packed any food in her magical bag, as she had assumed that they would be returning to Grimmauld Place that night, so they had had nothing to eat except some wild mushrooms that Hermione had collected from amongst the nearest trees and stewed in a billycan. After a couple of mouthfuls Ron had pushed his portion away, looking queasy; Harry had only persevered so as not to hurt Hermione's feelings.

The surrounding silence was broken by odd rustlings and what sounded like crackings of twigs: Harry thought that they were caused by animals rather than people, yet he kept his wand held tight at the ready. His insides, already uncomfortable due to their inadequate helping of rubbery mushrooms, tingled with unease.

He had thought that he would feel elated if they managed to steal back the Horcrux, but somehow he did not; all he felt as he sat looking out at the darkness, of which his wand lit only a tiny part, was worry about what would happen next. It was as though he had been hurtling toward this point for weeks, months, maybe even years, but now he had come to an abrupt halt, run out of road.

There were other Horcruxes out there somewhere, but he did not have the faintest idea where they could be. He did not even know what all of them were. Meanwhile he was at a loss to know how to destroy the only one that they had found, the Horcrux that currently lay against the bare flesh of his chest. Curiously, it had not taken heat from his body, but lay so cold against his skin it might just have emerged from icy water. From time to time Harry thought, or perhaps imagined, that he could feel the tiny heartbeat ticking irregularly alongside his own.

Nameless forebodings crept upon him as he sat there in the dark: He tried to resist them, push them away, yet they came at him relentlessly. *Neither can live while the other survives.* Ron and Hermione, now talking softly behind him in the tent, could walk away if they wanted to: He could not. And it seemed to Harry as he sat there trying to master his own fear and exhaustion, that the Horcrux against his chest was ticking away the time he had left. . . . *Stupid idea,* he told himself, *don't think that. . . .*

His scar was starting to prickle again. He was afraid that he was making it happen by having these thoughts, and tried to direct them into another channel. He thought of poor Kreacher, who had expected them home and had received Yaxley instead. Would the elf keep silent or would he tell the Death Eater everything he knew? Harry wanted to believe that Kreacher had changed toward him in the past month, that he would be loyal now, but who knew what would happen? What if the Death Eaters tortured the elf? Sick images swarmed into Harry's head and he tried to push these away too, for there was nothing he could do for Kreacher: He and Hermione had already decided against trying to summon him; what if someone from the Ministry came too? They could not count on elfish Apparition being free from the same flaw that had taken Yaxley to Grimmauld Place on the hem of Hermione's sleeve.

Harry's scar was burning now. He thought that there was so much they did not know: Lupin had been right about magic they had never encountered or imagined. Why hadn't Dumbledore explained more? Had he thought that there would be time; that he would live for years, for centuries perhaps, like his friend Nicolas Flamel? If so, he had been wrong. . . . Snape had seen to that. . . . Snape, the sleeping snake, who had struck at the top of the tower . . .

And Dumbledore had fallen . . . fallen . . .

"Give it to me, Gregorovitch."

Harry's voice was high, clear, and cold, his wand held in front of him by a long-fingered white hand. The man at whom he was pointing was suspended upside down in midair, though there were no ropes holding him; he swung there, invisibly and eerily bound, his limbs wrapped about him, his terrified face, on a level with Harry's, ruddy due to the blood that had rushed to his head. He had pure-white hair and a thick, bushy beard: a trussed-up Father Christmas.

"I have it not, I have it no more! It was, many years ago, stolen from me!"

"Do not lie to Lord Voldemort, Gregorovitch. He knows. . . . He always knows."

The hanging man's pupils were wide, dilated with fear, and they seemed to swell, bigger and bigger until their blackness swallowed Harry whole —

And now Harry was hurrying along a dark corridor in stout little Gregorovitch's wake as he held a lantern aloft: Gregorovitch burst into the room at the end of the passage and his lantern illuminated what looked like a workshop; wood shavings and gold gleamed in the swinging pool of light, and there on the window ledge sat perched, like a giant bird, a young man with golden hair. In the split second that the lantern's light illuminated him, Harry saw the delight upon his handsome face, then the intruder shot a Stunning Spell from his wand and jumped neatly backward out of the window with a crow of laughter.

And Harry was hurtling back out of those wide, tunnellike pupils and Gregorovitch's face was stricken with terror.

"Who was the thief, Gregorovitch?" said the high cold voice.

"I do not know, I never knew, a young man — no — please — PLEASE!"

A scream that went on and on and then a burst of green light —

"Harry!"

He opened his eyes, panting, his forehead throbbing. He had passed out against the side of the tent, had slid sideways down the canvas, and was sprawled on the ground. He looked up at Hermione, whose bushy hair obscured the tiny patch of sky visible through the dark branches high above them.

"Dream," he said, sitting up quickly and attempting to meet Hermione's glower with a look of innocence. "Must've dozed off, sorry."

"I know it was your scar! I can tell by the look on your face! You were looking into Vol —"

"Don't say his name!" came Ron's angry voice from the depths of the tent.

"Fine," retorted Hermione. *"You-Know-Who's* mind, then!"

"I didn't mean it to happen!" Harry said. "It was a dream! Can *you* control what you dream about, Hermione?"

"If you just learned to apply Occlumency —"

But Harry was not interested in being told off; he wanted to discuss what he had just seen.

"He's found Gregorovitch, Hermione, and I think he's killed him, but before he killed him he read Gregorovitch's mind and I saw —"

"I think I'd better take over the watch if you're so tired you're falling asleep," said Hermione coldly.

"I can finish the watch!"

"No, you're obviously exhausted. Go and lie down."

She dropped down in the mouth of the tent, looking stubborn. Angry, but wishing to avoid a row, Harry ducked back inside.

Ron's still-pale face was poking out from the lower bunk; Harry climbed into the one above him, lay down, and looked up at the dark canvas ceiling. After several moments, Ron spoke in a voice so low that it would not carry to Hermione, huddled in the entrance.

"What's You-Know-Who doing?"

Harry screwed up his eyes in the effort to remember every detail, then whispered into the darkness.

"He found Gregorovitch. He had him tied up, he was torturing him."

"How's Gregorovitch supposed to make him a new wand if he's tied up?"

"I dunno. . . . It's weird, isn't it?"

Harry closed his eyes, thinking of all he had seen and heard. The more he recalled, the less sense it made. . . . Voldemort had said nothing about Harry's wand, nothing about the twin cores, nothing about Gregorovitch making a new and more powerful wand to beat Harry's. . . .

"He wanted something from Gregorovitch," Harry said, eyes still closed tight. "He asked him to hand it over, but Gregorovitch said it had been stolen from him . . . and then . . . then . . ."

He remembered how he, as Voldemort, had seemed to hurtle through Gregorovitch's eyes, into his memories. . . .

"He read Gregorovitch's mind, and I saw this young bloke perched on a windowsill, and he fired a curse at Gregorovitch and jumped out of sight. He stole it, he stole whatever You-Know-Who's after. And I . . . I think I've seen him somewhere. . . ."

Harry wished he could have another glimpse of the laughing boy's face. The theft had happened many years ago, according to Gregorovitch. Why did the young thief look familiar?

The noises of the surrounding woods were muffled inside the tent; all Harry could hear was Ron's breathing. After a while, Ron whispered, "Couldn't you see what the thief was holding?"

"No . . . it must've been something small."

"Harry?"

The wooden slats of Ron's bunk creaked as he repositioned himself in bed.

"Harry, you don't reckon You-Know-Who's after something else to turn into a Horcrux?"

"I don't know," said Harry slowly. "Maybe. But wouldn't it be dangerous for him to make another one? Didn't Hermione say he had pushed his soul to the limit already?"

"Yeah, but maybe he doesn't know that."

"Yeah . . . maybe," said Harry.

He had been sure that Voldemort had been looking for a way around the problem of the twin cores, sure that Voldemort sought a solution from the old wandmaker . . . and yet he had killed him, apparently without asking him a single question about wandlore.

What was Voldemort trying to find? Why, with the Ministry of Magic and the Wizarding world at his feet, was he far away, intent on the pursuit of an object that Gregorovitch had once owned, and which had been stolen by the unknown thief?

Harry could still see the blond-haired youth's face; it was merry, wild; there was a Fred and George-ish air of triumphant trickery about him. He had soared from the windowsill like a bird, and Harry had seen him before, but he could not think where. . . .

With Gregorovitch dead, it was the merry-faced thief who was in danger now, and it was on him that Harry's thoughts dwelled, as Ron's snores began to rumble from the lower bunk and as he himself drifted slowly into sleep once more.

THE GOBLIN'S REVENGE

Early next morning, before the other two were awake, Harry left the tent to search the woods around them for the oldest, most gnarled, and resilient-looking tree he could find. There in its shadow he buried Mad-Eye Moody's eye and marked the spot by gouging a small cross in the bark with his wand. It was not much, but Harry felt that Mad-Eye would have much preferred this to being stuck on Dolores Umbridge's door. Then he returned to the tent to wait for the others to wake, and discuss what they were going to do next.

Harry and Hermione felt that it was best not to stay anywhere too long, and Ron agreed, with the sole proviso that their next move took them within reach of a bacon sandwich. Hermione therefore removed the enchantments she had placed around the clearing, while Harry and Ron obliterated all the marks and impressions on the ground that might show they had camped there. Then they Disapparated to the outskirts of a small market town.

Once they had pitched the tent in the shelter of a small copse of trees and surrounded it with freshly cast defensive enchantments, Harry ventured out under the Invisibility Cloak to find sustenance. This, however, did not go as planned. He had barely entered the town when an unnatural chill, a descending mist, and a sudden darkening of the skies made him freeze where he stood.

"But you can make a brilliant Patronus!" protested Ron, when Harry arrived back at the tent empty-handed, out of breath, and mouthing the single word, *dementors.*

"I couldn't . . . make one," he panted, clutching the stitch in his side. "Wouldn't . . . come."

Their expressions of consternation and disappointment made Harry feel ashamed. It had been a nightmarish experience, seeing the dementors gliding out of the mist in the distance and realizing, as the paralyzing cold choked his lungs and a distant screaming filled his ears, that he was not going to be able to protect himself. It had taken all Harry's willpower to uproot himself from the spot and run, leaving the eyeless dementors to glide amongst the Muggles who might not be able to see them, but would assuredly feel the despair they cast wherever they went.

"So we still haven't got any food."

"Shut up, Ron," snapped Hermione. "Harry, what happened? Why do you think you couldn't make your Patronus? You managed perfectly yesterday!"

"I don't know."

He sat low in one of Perkins's old armchairs, feeling more humiliated by the moment. He was afraid that something had gone wrong inside him. Yesterday seemed a long time ago: Today he might have been thirteen years old again, the only one who collapsed on the Hogwarts Express.

Ron kicked a chair leg.

"What?" he snarled at Hermione. "I'm starving! All I've had since I bled half to death is a couple of toadstools!"

"You go and fight your way through the dementors, then," said Harry, stung.

"I would, but my arm's in a sling, in case you hadn't noticed!"

"That's convenient."

"And what's that supposed to — ?"

"Of course!" cried Hermione, clapping a hand to her forehead and startling both of them into silence. "Harry, give me the locket! Come on," she said impatiently, clicking her fingers at him when he did not react, "the Horcrux, Harry, you're still wearing it!"

She held out her hands, and Harry lifted the golden chain over his head. The moment it parted contact with Harry's skin he felt free and oddly light. He had not even realized that he was clammy or that there was a heavy weight pressing on his stomach until both sensations lifted.

"Better?" asked Hermione.

"Yeah, loads better!"

"Harry," she said, crouching down in front of him and using the kind of voice he associated with visiting the very sick, "you don't think you've been possessed, do you?"

"What? No!" he said defensively. "I remember everything we've done while I've been wearing it. I wouldn't know what I'd done if I'd been possessed, would I? Ginny told me there were times when she couldn't remember anything."

"Hmm," said Hermione, looking down at the heavy gold locket. "Well, maybe we ought not to wear it. We can just keep it in the tent."

"We are not leaving that Horcrux lying around," Harry stated firmly. "If we lose it, if it gets stolen —"

"Oh, all right, all right," said Hermione, and she placed it around her own neck and tucked it out of sight down the front of her shirt. "But we'll take turns wearing it, so nobody keeps it on too long."

"Great," said Ron irritably, "and now we've sorted that out, can we please get some food?"

"Fine, but we'll go somewhere else to find it," said Hermione with half a glance at Harry. "There's no point staying where we know dementors are swooping around."

In the end they settled down for the night in a far-flung field belonging to a lonely farm, from which they had managed to obtain eggs and bread.

"It's not stealing, is it?" asked Hermione in a troubled voice, as they devoured scrambled eggs on toast. "Not if I left some money under the chicken coop?"

Ron rolled his eyes and said, with his cheeks bulging, "'Er-my-nee, 'oo worry 'oo much. 'Elax!"

And, indeed, it was much easier to relax when they were comfortably well fed: The argument about the dementors was forgotten in laughter that night, and Harry felt cheerful, even hopeful, as he took the first of the three night watches.

This was their first encounter with the fact that a full stomach meant good spirits; an empty one, bickering and gloom. Harry was least surprised by this, because he had suffered periods of near starvation at the Dursleys'. Hermione bore up reasonably well on those nights when they managed to scavenge nothing but berries or stale biscuits, her temper perhaps a little shorter than usual and her silences rather dour. Ron, however, had always been used to three delicious meals a day, courtesy of his mother or of the Hogwarts house-elves, and hunger made him both unreasonable and irascible. Whenever lack of food coincided with Ron's turn to wear the Horcrux, he became downright unpleasant.

"So where next?" was his constant refrain. He did not seem to have any ideas himself, but expected Harry and Hermione to come up with plans while he sat and brooded over the low food supplies. Accordingly Harry and Hermione spent fruitless hours trying to decide where they might find the other Horcruxes, and how to destroy the one they had already got, their conversations becoming increasingly repetitive as they had no new information.

As Dumbledore had told Harry that he believed Voldemort had hidden the Horcruxes in places important to him, they kept reciting, in a sort of dreary litany, those locations they knew that Voldemort had lived or visited. The orphanage where he had been born and raised; Hogwarts, where he had been educated; Borgin and Burkes, where he had worked after completing school; then Albania, where he had spent his years of exile: These formed the basis of their speculations.

"Yeah, let's go to Albania. Shouldn't take more than an afternoon to search an entire country," said Ron sarcastically.

"There can't be anything there. He'd already made five of his Horcruxes before he went into exile, and Dumbledore was certain the snake is the sixth," said Hermione. "We know the snake's not in Albania, it's usually with Vol —"

"*Didn't I ask you to stop saying that?*"

"Fine! The snake is usually with *You-Know-Who* — happy?"

"Not particularly."

"I can't see him hiding anything at Borgin and Burkes," said

Harry, who had made this point many times before, but said it again simply to break the nasty silence. "Borgin and Burke were experts at Dark objects, they would've recognized a Horcrux straightaway."

Ron yawned pointedly. Repressing a strong urge to throw something at him, Harry plowed on, "I still reckon he might have hidden something at Hogwarts."

Hermione sighed.

"But Dumbledore would have found it, Harry!"

Harry repeated the argument he kept bringing out in favor of this theory.

"Dumbledore said in front of me that he never assumed he knew all of Hogwarts's secrets. I'm telling you, if there was one place Vol —"

"Oi!"

"YOU-KNOW-WHO, then!" Harry shouted, goaded past endurance. "If there was one place that was really important to You-Know-Who, it was Hogwarts!"

"Oh, come on," scoffed Ron. "His *school*?"

"Yeah, his school! It was his first real home, the place that meant he was special; it meant everything to him, and even after he left —"

"This is You-Know-Who we're talking about, right? Not you?" inquired Ron. He was tugging at the chain of the Horcrux around his neck: Harry was visited by a desire to seize it and throttle him.

"You told us that You-Know-Who asked Dumbledore to give him a job after he left," said Hermione.

"That's right," said Harry.

"And Dumbledore thought he only wanted to come back to try and find something, probably another founder's object, to make into another Horcrux?"

"Yeah," said Harry.

"But he didn't get the job, did he?" said Hermione. "So he never got the chance to find a founder's object there and hide it in the school!"

"Okay, then," said Harry, defeated. "Forget Hogwarts."

Without any other leads, they traveled into London and, hidden beneath the Invisibility Cloak, searched for the orphanage in which Voldemort had been raised. Hermione stole into a library and discovered from their records that the place had been demolished many years before. They visited its site and found a tower block of offices.

"We could try digging in the foundations?" Hermione suggested halfheartedly.

"He wouldn't have hidden a Horcrux here," Harry said. He had known it all along: The orphanage had been the place Voldemort had been determined to escape; he would never have hidden a part of his soul there. Dumbledore had shown Harry that Voldemort sought grandeur or mystique in his hiding places; this dismal gray corner of London was as far removed as you could imagine from Hogwarts or the Ministry or a building like Gringotts, the Wizarding bank, with its golden doors and marble floors.

Even without any new ideas, they continued to move through the countryside, pitching the tent in a different place each night for security. Every morning they made sure that they had removed all clues to their presence, then set off to find another lonely and secluded spot, traveling by Apparition to more woods, to the shadowy crevices of cliffs, to purple moors, gorse-covered mountainsides, and once a sheltered and pebbly cove. Every twelve hours or so they passed the Horcrux between them as though they were playing some perverse, slow-motion game of pass-the-parcel, where they dreaded the music stopping because the reward was twelve hours of increased fear and anxiety.

Harry's scar kept prickling. It happened most often, he noticed, when he was wearing the Horcrux. Sometimes he could not stop himself reacting to the pain.

"What? What did you see?" demanded Ron, whenever he noticed Harry wince.

"A face," muttered Harry, every time. "The same face. The thief who stole from Gregorovitch."

And Ron would turn away, making no effort to hide his disappointment. Harry knew that Ron was hoping to hear news of his family or of the rest of the Order of the Phoenix, but after all, he, Harry, was not a television aerial; he could only see what Voldemort was thinking at the time, not tune in to whatever took his fancy. Apparently Voldemort was dwelling endlessly on the unknown youth with the gleeful face, whose name and whereabouts, Harry felt sure, Voldemort knew no better than he did. As Harry's scar continued to burn and the merry, blond-haired boy swam tantalizingly in his memory, he learned to suppress any sign of pain or discomfort, for the other two showed nothing but impatience at the mention of the thief. He could not entirely blame them, when they were so desperate for a lead on the Horcruxes.

As the days stretched into weeks, Harry began to suspect that Ron and Hermione were having conversations without, and about, him. Several times they stopped talking abruptly when Harry entered the tent, and twice he came accidentally upon them, huddled a little distance away, heads together and talking fast; both times they fell silent when they realized he was approaching them and hastened to appear busy collecting wood or water.

Harry could not help wondering whether they had only agreed to come on what now felt like a pointless and rambling journey because they thought he had some secret plan that they would learn in due course. Ron was making no effort to hide his bad mood, and Harry was starting to fear that Hermione too was disappointed by his poor leadership. In desperation he tried to think of further Horcrux locations, but the only one that continued to occur to him was Hogwarts, and as neither of the others thought this at all likely, he stopped suggesting it.

Autumn rolled over the countryside as they moved through it: They were now pitching the tent on mulches of fallen leaves. Natural mists joined those cast by the dementors; wind and rain added to their troubles. The fact that Hermione was getting better at identifying edible fungi could not altogether compensate for their continuing isolation, the lack of other people's company, or their total ignorance of what was going on in the war against Voldemort.

"My mother," said Ron one night, as they sat in the tent on a riverbank in Wales, "can make good food appear out of thin air."

He prodded moodily at the lumps of charred gray fish on his plate. Harry glanced automatically at Ron's neck and saw, as he had expected, the golden chain of the Horcrux glinting there. He managed to fight down the impulse to swear at Ron, whose attitude would, he knew, improve slightly when the time came to take off the locket.

"Your mother can't produce food out of thin air," said Hermione. "No one can. Food is the first of the five Principal Exceptions to Gamp's Law of Elemental Transfigur —"

"Oh, speak English, can't you?" Ron said, prising a fish bone out from between his teeth.

"It's impossible to make good food out of nothing! You can Summon it if you know where it is, you can transform it, you can increase the quantity if you've already got some —"

"Well, don't bother increasing this, it's disgusting," said Ron.

"Harry caught the fish and I did my best with it! I notice I'm always the one who ends up sorting out the food, because I'm a *girl,* I suppose!"

"No, it's because you're supposed to be the best at magic!" shot back Ron.

Hermione jumped up and bits of roast pike slid off her tin plate onto the floor.

"*You* can do the cooking tomorrow, Ron, *you* can find the ingredients and try and charm them into something worth eating, and I'll sit here and pull faces and moan and you can see how you —"

"Shut up!" said Harry, leaping to his feet and holding up both hands. "Shut up *now!*"

Hermione looked outraged.

"How can you side with him, he hardly ever does the cook —"

"Hermione, be quiet, I can hear someone!"

He was listening hard, his hands still raised, warning them not to talk. Then, over the rush and gush of the dark river beside them, he heard voices again. He looked around at the Sneakoscope. It was not moving.

"You cast the Muffliato charm over us, right?" he whispered to Hermione.

"I did everything," she whispered back, "Muffliato, Muggle-Repelling and Disillusionment Charms, all of it. They shouldn't be able to hear or see us, whoever they are."

Heavy scuffing and scraping noises, plus the sound of dislodged stones and twigs, told them that several people were clambering down the steep, wooded slope that descended to the narrow bank where they had pitched the tent. They drew their wands, waiting. The enchantments they had cast around themselves ought to be sufficient, in the near total darkness, to shield them from the notice of Muggles and normal witches and wizards. If these were Death Eaters, then perhaps their defenses were about to be tested by Dark Magic for the first time.

The voices became louder but no more intelligible as the group of men reached the bank. Harry estimated that their owners were fewer than twenty feet away, but the cascading river made it impossible to tell for sure. Hermione snatched up the beaded bag and started to rummage; after a moment she drew out three Extendable Ears and threw one each to Harry and Ron, who hastily inserted the ends of the flesh-colored strings into their ears and fed the other ends out of the tent entrance.

Within seconds Harry heard a weary male voice.

"There ought to be a few salmon in here, or d'you reckon it's too early in the season? *Accio Salmon!*"

There were several distinct splashes and then the slapping sounds of fish against flesh. Somebody grunted appreciatively. Harry pressed the Extendable Ear deeper into his own: Over the murmur of the river he could make out more voices, but they were not speaking English or any human language he had ever heard. It was a rough and unmelodious tongue, a string of rattling, guttural noises, and there seemed to be two speakers, one with a slightly lower, slower voice than the other.

A fire danced into life on the other side of the canvas; large shadows passed between tent and flames. The delicious smell of baking

salmon wafted tantalizingly in their direction. Then came the clinking of cutlery on plates, and the first man spoke again.

"Here, Griphook, Gornuk."

Goblins! Hermione mouthed at Harry, who nodded.

"Thank you," said the goblins together in English.

"So, you three have been on the run how long?" asked a new,
mellow, and pleasant voice; it was vaguely familiar to Harry, who
pictured a round-bellied, cheerful-faced man.

"Six weeks . . . seven . . . I forget," said the tired man. "Met up
with Griphook in the first couple of days and joined forces with
Gornuk not long after. Nice to have a bit of company." There was
a pause, while knives scraped plates and tin mugs were picked up
and replaced on the ground. "What made you leave, Ted?" continued the man.

"Knew they were coming for me," replied mellow-voiced Ted, and
Harry suddenly knew who he was: Tonks's father. "Heard Death
Eaters were in the area last week and decided I'd better run for it.
Refused to register as a Muggle-born on principle, see, so I knew
it was a matter of time, knew I'd have to leave in the end. My wife
should be okay, she's pure-blood. And then I met Dean here, what,
a few days ago, son?"

"Yeah," said another voice, and Harry, Ron, and Hermione stared
at each other, silent but beside themselves with excitement, sure they
recognized the voice of Dean Thomas, their fellow Gryffindor.

"Muggle-born, eh?" asked the first man.

"Not sure," said Dean. "My dad left my mum when I was a kid.
I've got no proof he was a wizard, though."

There was silence for a while, except for the sounds of munching;
then Ted spoke again.

"I've got to say, Dirk, I'm surprised to run into you. Pleased, but surprised. Word was you'd been caught."

"I was," said Dirk. "I was halfway to Azkaban when I made a break for it, Stunned Dawlish, and nicked his broom. It was easier than you'd think; I don't reckon he's quite right at the moment. Might be Confunded. If so, I'd like to shake the hand of the witch or wizard who did it, probably saved my life."

There was another pause in which the fire crackled and the river rushed on. Then Ted said, "And where do you two fit in? I, er, had the impression the goblins were for You-Know-Who, on the whole."

"You had a false impression," said the higher-voiced of the goblins. "We take no sides. This is a wizards' war."

"How come you're in hiding, then?"

"I deemed it prudent," said the deeper-voiced goblin. "Having refused what I considered an impertinent request, I could see that my personal safety was in jeopardy."

"What did they ask you to do?" asked Ted.

"Duties ill-befitting the dignity of my race," replied the goblin, his voice rougher and less human as he said it. "I am not a house-elf."

"What about you, Griphook?"

"Similar reasons," said the higher-voiced goblin. "Gringotts is no longer under the sole control of my race. I recognize no Wizarding master."

He added something under his breath in Gobbledegook, and Gornuk laughed.

"What's the joke?" asked Dean.

"He said," replied Dirk, "that there are things wizards don't recognize, either."

There was a short pause.

"I don't get it," said Dean.

"I had my small revenge before I left," said Griphook in English.

"Good man — goblin, I should say," amended Ted hastily. "Didn't manage to lock a Death Eater up in one of the old high-security vaults, I suppose?"

"If I had, the sword would not have helped him break out," replied Griphook. Gornuk laughed again and even Dirk gave a dry chuckle.

"Dean and I are still missing something here," said Ted.

"So is Severus Snape, though he does not know it," said Griphook, and the two goblins roared with malicious laughter. Inside the tent Harry's breathing was shallow with excitement: He and Hermione stared at each other, listening as hard as they could.

"Didn't you hear about that, Ted?" asked Dirk. "About the kids who tried to steal Gryffindor's sword out of Snape's office at Hogwarts?"

An electric current seemed to course through Harry, jangling his every nerve as he stood rooted to the spot.

"Never heard a word," said Ted. "Not in the *Prophet,* was it?"

"Hardly," chortled Dirk. "Griphook here told me, he heard about it from Bill Weasley who works for the bank. One of the kids who tried to take the sword was Bill's younger sister."

Harry glanced toward Hermione and Ron, both of whom were clutching the Extendable Ears as tightly as lifelines.

"She and a couple of friends got into Snape's office and smashed open the glass case where he was apparently keeping the sword. Snape caught them as they were trying to smuggle it down the staircase."

"Ah, God bless 'em," said Ted. "What did they think, that they'd be able to use the sword on You-Know-Who? Or on Snape himself?"

"Well, whatever they thought they were going to do with it, Snape decided the sword wasn't safe where it was," said Dirk. "Couple of days later, once he'd got the say-so from You-Know-Who, I imagine, he sent it down to London to be kept in Gringotts instead."

The goblins started to laugh again.

"I'm still not seeing the joke," said Ted.

"It's a fake," rasped Griphook.

"The sword of Gryffindor!"

"Oh yes. It is a copy — an excellent copy, it is true — but it was Wizard-made. The original was forged centuries ago by goblins and had certain properties only goblin-made armor possesses. Wherever the genuine sword of Gryffindor is, it is not in a vault at Gringotts bank."

"I see," said Ted. "And I take it you didn't bother telling the Death Eaters this?"

"I saw no reason to trouble them with the information," said Griphook smugly, and now Ted and Dean joined in Gornuk and Dirk's laughter.

Inside the tent, Harry closed his eyes, willing someone to ask the question he needed answered, and after a minute that seemed ten, Dean obliged; he was (Harry remembered with a jolt) an ex-boyfriend of Ginny's too.

"What happened to Ginny and the others? The ones who tried to steal it?"

"Oh, they were punished, and cruelly," said Griphook indifferently.

"They're okay, though?" asked Ted quickly. "I mean, the Weasleys don't need any more of their kids injured, do they?"

"They suffered no serious injury, as far as I am aware," said Griphook.

"Lucky for them," said Ted. "With Snape's track record I suppose we should just be glad they're still alive."

"You believe that story, then, do you, Ted?" asked Dirk. "You believe Snape killed Dumbledore?"

"'Course I do," said Ted. "You're not going to sit there and tell me you think Potter had anything to do with it?"

"Hard to know what to believe these days," muttered Dirk.

"I know Harry Potter," said Dean. "And I reckon he's the real thing — the Chosen One, or whatever you want to call it."

"Yeah, there's a lot would like to believe he's that, son," said Dirk, "me included. But where is he? Run for it, by the looks of things. You'd think, if he knew anything we don't, or had anything special going for him, he'd be out there now fighting, rallying resistance, instead of hiding. And you know, the *Prophet* made a pretty good case against him —"

"The *Prophet*?" scoffed Ted. "You deserve to be lied to if you're still reading that muck, Dirk. You want the facts, try the *Quibbler*."

There was a sudden explosion of choking and retching, plus a good deal of thumping; by the sound of it, Dirk had swallowed a fish bone. At last he spluttered, "The *Quibbler*? That lunatic rag of Xeno Lovegood's?"

"It's not so lunatic these days," said Ted. "You want to give it a look. Xeno is printing all the stuff the *Prophet*'s ignoring, not a single mention of Crumple-Horned Snorkacks in the last issue. How long they'll let him get away with it, mind, I don't know. But

Xeno says, front page of every issue, that any wizard who's against You-Know-Who ought to make helping Harry Potter their number-one priority."

"Hard to help a boy who's vanished off the face of the earth," said Dirk.

"Listen, the fact that they haven't caught him yet's one hell of an achievement," said Ted. "I'd take tips from him gladly; it's what we're trying to do, stay free, isn't it?"

"Yeah, well, you've got a point there," said Dirk heavily. "With the whole of the Ministry and all their informers looking for him I'd have expected him to be caught by now. Mind, who's to say they haven't already caught and killed him without publicizing it?"

"Ah, don't say that, Dirk," murmured Ted.

There was a long pause filled with more clattering of knives and forks. When they spoke again it was to discuss whether they ought to sleep on the bank or retreat back up the wooded slope. Deciding the trees would give better cover, they extinguished their fire, then clambered back up the incline, their voices fading away.

Harry, Ron, and Hermione reeled in the Extendable Ears. Harry, who had found the need to remain silent increasingly difficult the longer they eavesdropped, now found himself unable to say more than, "Ginny — the sword —"

"I know!" said Hermione.

She lunged for the tiny beaded bag, this time sinking her arm in it right up to the armpit.

"Here . . . we . . . are . . ." she said between gritted teeth, and she pulled at something that was evidently in the depths of the bag. Slowly the edge of an ornate picture frame came into sight. Harry hurried to help her. As they lifted the empty portrait of Phineas

Nigellus free of Hermione's bag, she kept her wand pointing at it, ready to cast a spell at any moment.

"If somebody swapped the real sword for the fake while it was in Dumbledore's office," she panted, as they propped the painting against the side of the tent, "Phineas Nigellus would have seen it happen, he hangs right beside the case!"

"Unless he was asleep," said Harry, but he still held his breath as Hermione knelt down in front of the empty canvas, her wand directed at its center, cleared her throat, then said:

"Er — Phineas? Phineas Nigellus?"

Nothing happened.

"Phineas Nigellus?" said Hermione again. "Professor Black? Please could we talk to you? Please?"

"'Please' always helps," said a cold, snide voice, and Phineas Nigellus slid into his portrait. At once, Hermione cried:

"Obscuro!"

A black blindfold appeared over Phineas Nigellus's clever, dark eyes, causing him to bump into the frame and shriek with pain.

"What — how dare — what are you — ?"

"I'm very sorry, Professor Black," said Hermione, "but it's a necessary precaution!"

"Remove this foul addition at once! Remove it, I say! You are ruining a great work of art! Where am I? What is going on?"

"Never mind where we are," said Harry, and Phineas Nigellus froze, abandoning his attempts to peel off the painted blindfold.

"Can that possibly be the voice of the elusive Mr. Potter?"

"Maybe," said Harry, knowing that this would keep Phineas Nigellus's interest. "We've got a couple of questions to ask you — about the sword of Gryffindor."

"Ah," said Phineas Nigellus, now turning his head this way and that in an effort to catch sight of Harry, "yes. That silly girl acted most unwisely there —"

"Shut up about my sister," said Ron roughly. Phineas Nigellus raised supercilious eyebrows.

"Who else is here?" he asked, turning his head from side to side. "Your tone displeases me! The girl and her friends were foolhardy in the extreme. Thieving from the headmaster!"

"They weren't thieving," said Harry. "That sword isn't Snape's."

"It belongs to Professor Snape's school," said Phineas Nigellus. "Exactly what claim did the Weasley girl have upon it? She deserved her punishment, as did the idiot Longbottom and the Lovegood oddity!"

"Neville is not an idiot and Luna is not an oddity!" said Hermione.

"Where am I?" repeated Phineas Nigellus, starting to wrestle with the blindfold again. "Where have you brought me? Why have you removed me from the house of my forebears?"

"Never mind that! How did Snape punish Ginny, Neville, and Luna?" asked Harry urgently.

"*Professor* Snape sent them into the Forbidden Forest, to do some work for the oaf, Hagrid."

"Hagrid's not an oaf!" said Hermione shrilly.

"And Snape might've thought that was a punishment," said Harry, "but Ginny, Neville, and Luna probably had a good laugh with Hagrid. The Forbidden Forest . . . they've faced plenty worse than the Forbidden Forest, big deal!"

He felt relieved; he had been imagining horrors, the Cruciatus Curse at the very least.

"What we really wanted to know, Professor Black, is whether anyone else has, um, taken out the sword at all? Maybe it's been taken away for cleaning or — or something?"

Phineas Nigellus paused again in his struggles to free his eyes and sniggered.

"*Muggle-borns,*" he said. "Goblin-made armor does not require cleaning, simple girl. Goblins' silver repels mundane dirt, imbibing only that which strengthens it."

"Don't call Hermione simple," said Harry.

"I grow weary of contradiction," said Phineas Nigellus. "Perhaps it is time for me to return to the headmaster's office?"

Still blindfolded, he began groping the side of his frame, trying to feel his way out of his picture and back into the one at Hogwarts. Harry had a sudden inspiration.

"Dumbledore! Can't you bring us Dumbledore?"

"I beg your pardon?" asked Phineas Nigellus.

"Professor Dumbledore's portrait — couldn't you bring him along, here, into yours?"

Phineas Nigellus turned his face in the direction of Harry's voice.

"Evidently it is not only Muggle-borns who are ignorant, Potter. The portraits of Hogwarts may commune with each other, but they cannot travel outside the castle except to visit a painting of themselves hanging elsewhere. Dumbledore cannot come here with me, and after the treatment I have received at your hands, I can assure you that I shall not be making a return visit!"

Slightly crestfallen, Harry watched Phineas redouble his attempts to leave his frame.

"Professor Black," said Hermione, "couldn't you just tell us, *please,* when was the last time the sword was taken out of its case? Before Ginny took it out, I mean?"

Phineas snorted impatiently.

"I believe that the last time I saw the sword of Gryffindor leave its case was when Professor Dumbledore used it to break open a ring."

Hermione whipped around to look at Harry. Neither of them dared say more in front of Phineas Nigellus, who had at last managed to locate the exit.

"Well, good night to you," he said a little waspishly, and he began to move out of sight again. Only the edge of his hat brim remained in view when Harry gave a sudden shout.

"Wait! Have you told Snape you saw this?"

Phineas Nigellus stuck his blindfolded head back into the picture.

"Professor Snape has more important things on his mind than the many eccentricities of Albus Dumbledore. *Good-bye,* Potter!"

And with that, he vanished completely, leaving behind him nothing but his murky backdrop.

"Harry!" Hermione cried.

"I know!" Harry shouted. Unable to contain himself, he punched the air; it was more than he had dared to hope for. He strode up and down the tent, feeling that he could have run a mile; he did not even feel hungry anymore. Hermione was squashing Phineas Nigellus's portrait back into the beaded bag; when she had fastened the clasp she threw the bag aside and raised a shining face to Harry.

"The sword can destroy Horcruxes! Goblin-made blades imbibe only that which strengthen them — Harry, that sword's impregnated with basilisk venom!"

"And Dumbledore didn't give it to me because he still needed it, he wanted to use it on the locket —"

"— and he must have realized they wouldn't let you have it if he put it in his will —"

"— so he made a copy —"

"— and put a fake in the glass case —"

"— and he left the real one — where?"

They gazed at each other; Harry felt that the answer was dangling invisibly in the air above them, tantalizingly close. Why hadn't Dumbledore told him? Or had he, in fact, told Harry, but Harry had not realized it at the time?

"Think!" whispered Hermione. "Think! Where would he have left it?"

"Not at Hogwarts," said Harry, resuming his pacing.

"Somewhere in Hogsmeade?" suggested Hermione.

"The Shrieking Shack?" said Harry. "Nobody ever goes in there."

"But Snape knows how to get in, wouldn't that be a bit risky?"

"Dumbledore trusted Snape," Harry reminded her.

"Not enough to tell him that he had swapped the swords," said Hermione.

"Yeah, you're right!" said Harry, and he felt even more cheered at the thought that Dumbledore had had some reservations, however faint, about Snape's trustworthiness. "So, would he have hidden the sword well away from Hogsmeade, then? What d'you reckon, Ron? Ron?"

Harry looked around. For one bewildered moment he thought that Ron had left the tent, then realized that Ron was lying in the shadow of a lower bunk, looking stony.

"Oh, remembered me, have you?" he said.

"What?"

Ron snorted as he stared up at the underside of the upper bunk.

"You two carry on. Don't let me spoil your fun."

Perplexed, Harry looked to Hermione for help, but she shook her head, apparently as nonplussed as he was.

"What's the problem?" asked Harry.

"Problem? There's no problem," said Ron, still refusing to look at Harry. "Not according to you, anyway."

There were several *plunks* on the canvas over their heads. It had started to rain.

"Well, you've obviously got a problem," said Harry. "Spit it out, will you?"

Ron swung his long legs off the bed and sat up. He looked mean, unlike himself.

"All right, I'll spit it out. Don't expect me to skip up and down the tent because there's some other damn thing we've got to find. Just add it to the list of stuff you don't know."

"I don't know?" repeated Harry. "*I* don't know?"

Plunk, plunk, plunk. The rain was falling harder and heavier; it pattered on the leaf-strewn bank all around them and into the river chattering through the dark. Dread doused Harry's jubilation: Ron was saying exactly what he had suspected and feared him to be thinking.

"It's not like I'm not having the time of my life here," said Ron, "you know, with my arm mangled and nothing to eat and freezing my backside off every night. I just hoped, you know, after we'd been running round a few weeks, we'd have achieved something."

"Ron," Hermione said, but in such a quiet voice that Ron could pretend not to have heard it over the loud tattoo the rain was now beating on the tent.

"I thought you knew what you'd signed up for," said Harry.

"Yeah, I thought I did too."

"So what part of it isn't living up to your expectations?" asked Harry. Anger was coming to his defense now. "Did you think we'd be staying in five-star hotels? Finding a Horcrux every other day? Did you think you'd be back to Mummy by Christmas?"

"We thought you knew what you were doing!" shouted Ron, standing up, and his words pierced Harry like scalding knives. "We thought Dumbledore had told you what to do, we thought you had a real plan!"

"Ron!" said Hermione, this time clearly audible over the rain thundering on the tent roof, but again, he ignored her.

"Well, sorry to let you down," said Harry, his voice quite calm even though he felt hollow, inadequate. "I've been straight with you from the start, I told you everything Dumbledore told me. And in case you haven't noticed, we've found one Horcrux —"

"Yeah, and we're about as near getting rid of it as we are to finding the rest of them — nowhere effing near, in other words!"

"Take off the locket, Ron," Hermione said, her voice unusually high. "Please take it off. You wouldn't be talking like this if you hadn't been wearing it all day."

"Yeah, he would," said Harry, who did not want excuses made for Ron. "D'you think I haven't noticed the two of you whispering behind my back? D'you think I didn't guess you were thinking this stuff?"

"Harry, we weren't —"

"Don't lie!" Ron hurled at her. "You said it too, you said you were disappointed, you said you'd thought he had a bit more to go on than —"

"I didn't say it like that — Harry, I didn't!" she cried.

The rain was pounding the tent, tears were pouring down Hermione's face, and the excitement of a few minutes before had vanished as if it had never been, a short-lived firework that had flared and died, leaving everything dark, wet, and cold. The sword of Gryffindor was hidden they knew not where, and they were three teenagers in a tent whose only achievement was not, yet, to be dead.

"So why are you still here?" Harry asked Ron.

"Search me," said Ron.

"Go home then," said Harry.

"Yeah, maybe I will!" shouted Ron, and he took several steps toward Harry, who did not back away. "Didn't you hear what they said about my sister? But you don't give a rat's fart, do you, it's only the Forbidden Forest, Harry *I've-Faced-Worse* Potter doesn't care what happens to her in here — well, I do, all right, giant spiders and mental stuff —"

"I was only saying — she was with the others, they were with Hagrid —"

"Yeah, I get it, you don't care! And what about the rest of my family, 'the Weasleys don't need another kid injured,' did you hear that?"

"Yeah, I —"

"Not bothered what it meant, though?"

"Ron!" said Hermione, forcing her way between them. "I don't think it means anything new has happened, anything we don't know about; think, Ron, Bill's already scarred, plenty of people

must have seen that George has lost an ear by now, and you're supposed to be on your deathbed with spattergroit, I'm sure that's all
he meant —"

"Oh, you're sure, are you? Right then, well, I won't bother myself about them. It's all right for you two, isn't it, with your parents
safely out of the way —"

"My parents are *dead*!" Harry bellowed.

"And mine could be going the same way!" yelled Ron.

"Then GO!" roared Harry. "Go back to them, pretend you've
got over your spattergroit and Mummy'll be able to feed you up
and —"

Ron made a sudden movement: Harry reacted, but before either wand was clear of its owner's pocket, Hermione had raised her
own.

"Protego!" she cried, and an invisible shield expanded between
her and Harry on the one side and Ron on the other; all of them
were forced backward a few steps by the strength of the spell, and
Harry and Ron glared from either side of the transparent barrier as
though they were seeing each other clearly for the first time. Harry
felt a corrosive hatred toward Ron: Something had broken between
them.

"Leave the Horcrux," Harry said.

Ron wrenched the chain from over his head and cast the locket
into a nearby chair. He turned to Hermione.

"What are you doing?"

"What do you mean?"

"Are you staying, or what?"

"I . . ." She looked anguished. "Yes — yes, I'm staying. Ron, we
said we'd go with Harry, we said we'd help —"

"I get it. You choose him."

"Ron, no — please — come back, come back!"

She was impeded by her own Shield Charm; by the time she had removed it he had already stormed into the night. Harry stood quite still and silent, listening to her sobbing and calling Ron's name amongst the trees.

After a few minutes she returned, her sopping hair plastered to her face.

"He's g-g-gone! Disapparated!"

She threw herself into a chair, curled up, and started to cry.

Harry felt dazed. He stooped, picked up the Horcrux, and placed it around his own neck. He dragged blankets off Ron's bunk and threw them over Hermione. Then he climbed onto his own bed and stared up at the dark canvas roof, listening to the pounding of the rain.

GODRIC'S HOLLOW

When Harry woke the following day it was several seconds before he remembered what had happened. Then he hoped, childishly, that it had been a dream, that Ron was still there and had never left. Yet by turning his head on his pillow he could see Ron's deserted bunk. It was like a dead body in the way it seemed to draw his eyes. Harry jumped down from his own bed, keeping his eyes averted from Ron's. Hermione, who was already busy in the kitchen, did not wish Harry good morning, but turned her face away quickly as he went by.

He's gone, Harry told himself. *He's gone.* He had to keep thinking it as he washed and dressed, as though repetition would dull the shock of it. *He's gone and he's not coming back.* And that was the simple truth of it, Harry knew, because their protective enchantments meant that it would be impossible, once they vacated this spot, for Ron to find them again.

He and Hermione ate breakfast in silence. Hermione's eyes were

puffy and red; she looked as if she had not slept. They packed up
their things, Hermione dawdling. Harry knew why she wanted to
spin out their time on the riverbank; several times he saw her look
up eagerly, and he was sure she had deluded herself into thinking
that she heard footsteps through the heavy rain, but no red-haired
figure appeared between the trees. Every time Harry imitated her,
looked around (for he could not help hoping a little, himself) and
saw nothing but rain-swept woods, another little parcel of fury
exploded inside him. He could hear Ron saying, *"We thought you
knew what you were doing!"*, and he resumed packing with a hard
knot in the pit of his stomach.

The muddy river beside them was rising rapidly and would soon
spill over onto their bank. They had lingered a good hour after they
would usually have departed their campsite. Finally having entirely
repacked the beaded bag three times, Hermione seemed unable
to find any more reasons to delay: She and Harry grasped hands
and Disapparated, reappearing on a windswept heather-covered
hillside.

The instant they arrived, Hermione dropped Harry's hand and
walked away from him, finally sitting down on a large rock, her face
on her knees, shaking with what he knew were sobs. He watched
her, supposing that he ought to go and comfort her, but something
kept him rooted to the spot. Everything inside him felt cold and
tight: Again he saw the contemptuous expression on Ron's face.
Harry strode off through the heather, walking in a large circle with
the distraught Hermione at its center, casting the spells she usually
performed to ensure their protection.

They did not discuss Ron at all over the next few days. Harry was
determined never to mention his name again, and Hermione seemed

to know that it was no use forcing the issue, although sometimes at night when she thought he was sleeping, he would hear her crying. Meanwhile Harry had started bringing out the Marauder's Map and examining it by wandlight. He was waiting for the moment when Ron's labeled dot would reappear in the corridors of Hogwarts, proving that he had returned to the comfortable castle, protected by his status of pureblood. However, Ron did not appear on the map, and after a while Harry found himself taking it out simply to stare at Ginny's name in the girls' dormitory, wondering whether the intensity with which he gazed at it might break into her sleep, that she would somehow know he was thinking about her, hoping that she was all right.

By day, they devoted themselves to trying to determine the possible locations of Gryffindor's sword, but the more they talked about the places in which Dumbledore might have hidden it, the more desperate and far-fetched their speculation became. Cudgel his brains though he might, Harry could not remember Dumbledore ever mentioning a place in which he might hide something. There were moments when he did not know whether he was angrier with Ron or with Dumbledore. *We thought you knew what you were doing. . . . We thought Dumbledore had told you what to do. . . . We thought you had a real plan!*

He could not hide it from himself: Ron had been right. Dumbledore had left him with virtually nothing. They had discovered one Horcrux, but they had no means of destroying it: The others were as unattainable as they had ever been. Hopelessness threatened to engulf him. He was staggered now to think of his own presumption in accepting his friends' offers to accompany him on this meandering, pointless journey. He knew nothing, he had no ideas, and he was constantly, painfully on the alert for any indication that Hermione too was about to tell him that she had had enough, that she was leaving.

They were spending many evenings in near silence, and Hermione took to bringing out Phineas Nigellus's portrait and propping it up in a chair, as though he might fill part of the gaping hole left by Ron's departure. Despite his previous assertion that he would never visit them again, Phineas Nigellus did not seem able to resist the chance to find out more about what Harry was up to, and consented to reappear, blindfolded, every few days or so. Harry was even glad to see him, because he was company, albeit of a snide and taunting kind. They relished any news about what was happening at Hogwarts, though Phineas Nigellus was not an ideal informer. He venerated Snape, the first Slytherin headmaster since he himself had controlled the school, and they had to be careful not to criticize or ask impertinent questions about Snape, or Phineas Nigellus would instantly leave his painting.

However, he did let drop certain snippets. Snape seemed to be facing a constant, low level of mutiny from a hard core of students. Ginny had been banned from going into Hogsmeade. Snape had reinstated Umbridge's old decree forbidding gatherings of three or more students or any unofficial student societies.

From all of these things, Harry deduced that Ginny, and probably Neville and Luna along with her, had been doing their best to continue Dumbledore's Army. This scant news made Harry want to see Ginny so badly it felt like a stomachache; but it also made him think of Ron again, and of Dumbledore, and of Hogwarts itself, which he missed nearly as much as his ex-girlfriend. Indeed, as Phineas Nigellus talked about Snape's crackdown, Harry experienced a split second of madness when he imagined simply going back to school to join the destabilization of Snape's regime: Being fed, and having a soft bed, and other people being in charge, seemed the most wonderful prospect in the world at that moment. But then he remembered that he was Undesirable Number One, that there was a ten-thousand-Galleon price on his head, and that to walk into Hogwarts these days was just as dangerous as walking into the Ministry of Magic. Indeed, Phineas Nigellus inadvertently emphasized this fact by slipping in leading questions about Harry and Hermione's whereabouts. Hermione shoved him back inside the beaded bag every time he did this, and Phineas Nigellus invariably refused to reappear for several days after these unceremonious good-byes.

The weather grew colder and colder. They did not dare remain in any one area too long, so rather than staying in the south of England, where a hard ground frost was the worst of their worries, they continued to meander up and down the country, braving a mountainside, where sleet pounded the tent; a wide, flat marsh, where the tent was flooded with chill water; and a tiny island in the middle of a Scottish loch, where snow half buried the tent in the night.

They had already spotted Christmas trees twinkling from several sitting room windows before there came an evening when Harry resolved to suggest, again, what seemed to him the only unexplored avenue left to them. They had just eaten an unusually good meal: Hermione had been to a supermarket under the Invisibility Cloak (scrupulously dropping the money into an open till as she left), and Harry thought that she might be more persuadable than usual on a stomach full of spaghetti Bolognese and tinned pears. He had also had the foresight to suggest that they take a few hours' break from wearing the Horcrux, which was hanging over the end of the bunk beside him.

"Hermione?"

"Hmm?" She was curled up in one of the sagging armchairs with *The Tales of Beedle the Bard*. He could not imagine how much more she could get out of the book, which was not, after all, very long; but evidently she was still deciphering something in it, because *Spellman's Syllabary* lay open on the arm of the chair.

Harry cleared his throat. He felt exactly as he had done on the occasion, several years previously, when he had asked Professor McGonagall whether he could go into Hogsmeade, despite the fact that he had not persuaded the Dursleys to sign his permission slip.

"Hermione, I've been thinking, and —"

"Harry, could you help me with something?"

Apparently she had not been listening to him. She leaned forward and held out *The Tales of Beedle the Bard*.

"Look at that symbol," she said, pointing to the top of a page. Above what Harry assumed was the title of the story (being unable to read runes, he could not be sure), there was a picture of what looked like a triangular eye, its pupil crossed with a vertical line.

"I never took Ancient Runes, Hermione."

"I know that, but it isn't a rune and it's not in the syllabary, either. All along I thought it was a picture of an eye, but I don't think it is! It's been inked in, look, somebody's drawn it there, it isn't really part of the book. Think, have you ever seen it before?"

"No . . . No, wait a moment." Harry looked closer. "Isn't it the same symbol Luna's dad was wearing round his neck?"

"Well, that's what I thought too!"

"Then it's Grindelwald's mark."

She stared at him, openmouthed.

"*What?*"

"Krum told me . . ."

He recounted the story that Viktor Krum had told him at the wedding. Hermione looked astonished.

"*Grindelwald's* mark?"

She looked from Harry to the weird symbol and back again. "I've never heard that Grindelwald had a mark. There's no mention of it in anything I've ever read about him."

"Well, like I say, Krum reckoned that symbol was carved on a wall at Durmstrang, and Grindelwald put it there."

She fell back into the old armchair, frowning.

"That's very odd. If it's a symbol of Dark Magic, what's it doing in a book of children's stories?"

"Yeah, it is weird," said Harry. "And you'd think Scrimgeour would have recognized it. He was Minister, he ought to have been expert on Dark stuff."

"I know. . . . Perhaps he thought it was an eye, just like I did. All the other stories have little pictures over the titles."

She did not speak, but continued to pore over the strange mark. Harry tried again.

"Hermione?"

"Hmm?"

"I've been thinking. I — I want to go to Godric's Hollow."

She looked up at him, but her eyes were unfocused, and he was sure she was still thinking about the mysterious mark on the book.

"Yes," she said. "Yes, I've been wondering that too. I really think we'll have to."

"Did you hear me right?" he asked.

"Of course I did. You want to go to Godric's Hollow. I agree, I think we should. I mean, I can't think of anywhere else it could be either. It'll be dangerous, but the more I think about it, the more likely it seems it's there."

"Er — *what's* there?" asked Harry.

At that, she looked just as bewildered as he felt.

"Well, the sword, Harry! Dumbledore must have known you'd want to go back there, and I mean, Godric's Hollow is Godric Gryffindor's birthplace —"

"Really? Gryffindor came from Godric's Hollow?"

"Harry, did you ever even open *A History of Magic*?"

"Erm," he said, smiling for what felt like the first time in months: The muscles in his face felt oddly stiff. "I might've opened it, you know, when I bought it . . . just the once. . . ."

"Well, as the village is named after him I'd have thought you might have made the connection," said Hermione. She sounded much more like her old self than she had done of late; Harry half expected her to announce that she was off to the library. "There's a bit about the village in *A History of Magic*, wait . . ."

She opened the beaded bag and rummaged for a while, finally extracting her copy of their old school textbook, *A History of Magic* by Bathilda Bagshot, which she thumbed through until finding the page she wanted.

"*'Upon the signature of the International Statute of Secrecy in 1689, wizards went into hiding for good. It was natural, perhaps, that they formed their own small communities within a community. Many small villages and hamlets attracted several magical families, who banded together for mutual support and protection. The villages of Tinworth in Cornwall, Upper Flagley in Yorkshire, and Ottery St. Catchpole on the south coast of England were notable homes to knots of Wizarding families who lived alongside tolerant and sometimes Confunded Muggles. Most celebrated of these half-magical dwelling places is, perhaps, Godric's Hollow, the West Country village where the great wizard Godric Gryffindor was born, and where Bowman Wright, Wizarding smith, forged the first Golden Snitch. The graveyard is full of the names of ancient magical families, and this accounts, no doubt, for the stories of hauntings that have dogged the little church beside it for many centuries.'*

"You and your parents aren't mentioned," Hermione said, closing the book, "because Professor Bagshot doesn't cover anything later than the end of the nineteenth century. But you see? Godric's Hollow, Godric Gryffindor, Gryffindor's sword; don't you think Dumbledore would have expected you to make the connection?"

"Oh yeah . . ."

Harry did not want to admit that he had not been thinking about the sword at all when he suggested they go to Godric's Hollow. For him, the lure of the village lay in his parents' graves, the house where he had narrowly escaped death, and in the person of Bathilda Bagshot.

"Remember what Muriel said?" he asked eventually.

"Who?"

"You know," he hesitated: He did not want to say Ron's name. "Ginny's great-aunt. At the wedding. The one who said you had skinny ankles."

"Oh," said Hermione. It was a sticky moment: Harry knew that she had sensed Ron's name in the offing. He rushed on:

"She said Bathilda Bagshot still lives in Godric's Hollow."

"Bathilda Bagshot," murmured Hermione, running her index finger over Bathilda's embossed name on the front cover of *A History of Magic.* "Well, I suppose —"

She gasped so dramatically that Harry's insides turned over; he drew his wand, looking around at the entrance, half expecting to see a hand forcing its way through the entrance flap, but there was nothing there.

"What?" he said, half angry, half relieved. "What did you do that for? I thought you'd seen a Death Eater unzipping the tent, at least —"

"Harry, *what if Bathilda's got the sword?* What if Dumbledore entrusted it to her?"

Harry considered this possibility. Bathilda would be an extremely old woman by now, and according to Muriel, she was "gaga." Was it likely that Dumbledore would have hidden the sword of Gryffindor with her? If so, Harry felt that Dumbledore had left a great deal to chance: Dumbledore had never revealed that he had replaced the sword with a fake, nor had he so much as mentioned a friendship with Bathilda. Now, however, was not the moment to cast doubt on Hermione's theory, not when she was so surprisingly willing to fall in with Harry's dearest wish.

"Yeah, he might have done! So, are we going to go to Godric's Hollow?"

"Yes, but we'll have to think it through carefully, Harry." She was sitting up now, and Harry could tell that the prospect of having a plan again had lifted her mood as much as his. "We'll need to practice Disapparating together under the Invisibility Cloak for a start, and perhaps Disillusionment Charms would be sensible too, unless you think we should go the whole hog and use Polyjuice

Potion? In that case we'll need to collect hair from somebody. I actually think we'd better do that, Harry, the thicker our disguises the better. . . ."

Harry let her talk, nodding and agreeing whenever there was a pause, but his mind had left the conversation. For the first time since he had discovered that the sword in Gringotts was a fake, he felt excited.

He was about to go home, about to return to the place where he had had a family. It was in Godric's Hollow that, but for Voldemort, he would have grown up and spent every school holiday. He could have invited friends to his house. . . . He might even have had brothers and sisters. . . . It would have been his mother who had made his seventeenth birthday cake. The life he had lost had hardly ever seemed so real to him as at this moment, when he knew he was about to see the place where it had been taken from him. After Hermione had gone to bed that night, Harry quietly extracted his rucksack from Hermione's beaded bag, and from inside it, the photograph album Hagrid had given him so long ago. For the first time in months, he perused the old pictures of his parents, smiling and waving up at him from the images, which were all he had left of them now.

Harry would gladly have set out for Godric's Hollow the following day, but Hermione had other ideas. Convinced as she was that Voldemort would expect Harry to return to the scene of his parents' deaths, she was determined that they would set off only after they had ensured that they had the best disguises possible. It was therefore a full week later — once they had surreptitiously obtained hairs from innocent Muggles who were Christmas shopping, and had practiced Apparating and Disapparating while underneath the Invisibility Cloak together — that Hermione agreed to make the journey.

They were to Apparate to the village under cover of darkness, so it was late afternoon when they finally swallowed Polyjuice Potion, Harry transforming into a balding, middle-aged Muggle man, Hermione into his small and rather mousy wife. The beaded bag containing all of their possessions (apart from the Horcrux, which Harry was wearing around his neck) was tucked into an inside pocket of Hermione's buttoned-up coat. Harry lowered the Invisibility Cloak over them, then they turned into the suffocating darkness once again.

Heart beating in his throat, Harry opened his eyes. They were standing hand in hand in a snowy lane under a dark blue sky, in which the night's first stars were already glimmering feebly. Cottages stood on either side of the narrow road, Christmas decorations twinkling in their windows. A short way ahead of them, a glow of golden streetlights indicated the center of the village.

"All this snow!" Hermione whispered beneath the cloak. "Why didn't we think of snow? After all our precautions, we'll leave prints! We'll just have to get rid of them — you go in front, I'll do it —"

Harry did not want to enter the village like a pantomime horse, trying to keep themselves concealed while magically covering their traces.

"Let's take off the Cloak," said Harry, and when she looked frightened, "Oh, come on, we don't look like us and there's no one around."

He stowed the Cloak under his jacket and they made their way forward unhampered, the icy air stinging their faces as they passed more cottages: Any one of them might have been the one in which James and Lily had once lived or where Bathilda lived now. Harry gazed at the front doors, their snow-burdened roofs, and their front porches, wondering whether he remembered any of them, knowing deep inside that it was impossible, that he had been little more than a year old when he had left this place forever. He was not even sure whether he would be able to see the cottage at all; he did not know what happened when the subjects of a Fidelius Charm died. Then the little lane along which they were walking curved to the left and the heart of the village, a small square, was revealed to them.

Strung all around with colored lights, there was what looked like a war memorial in the middle, partly obscured by a windblown Christmas tree. There were several shops, a post office, a pub, and a little church whose stained-glass windows were glowing jewel-bright across the square.

The snow here had become impacted: It was hard and slippery where people had trodden on it all day. Villagers were crisscrossing in front of them, their figures briefly illuminated by streetlamps. They heard a snatch of laughter and pop music as the pub door opened and closed; then they heard a carol start up inside the little church.

"Harry, I think it's Christmas Eve!" said Hermione.

"Is it?"

He had lost track of the date; they had not seen a newspaper for weeks.

"I'm sure it is," said Hermione, her eyes upon the church. "They . . . they'll be in there, won't they? Your mum and dad? I can see the graveyard behind it."

Harry felt a thrill of something that was beyond excitement, more like fear. Now that he was so near, he wondered whether he wanted to see after all. Perhaps Hermione knew how he was feeling, because she reached for his hand and took the lead for the first time, pulling him forward. Halfway across the square, however, she stopped dead.

"Harry, look!"

She was pointing at the war memorial. As they had passed it, it had transformed. Instead of an obelisk covered in names, there was a statue of three people: a man with untidy hair and glasses, a woman with long hair and a kind, pretty face, and a baby boy sitting in his mother's arms. Snow lay upon all their heads, like fluffy white caps.

Harry drew closer, gazing up into his parents' faces. He had never imagined that there would be a statue. . . . How strange it was to see himself represented in stone, a happy baby without a scar on his forehead. . . .

"C'mon," said Harry, when he had looked his fill, and they turned again toward the church. As they crossed the road, he glanced over his shoulder; the statue had turned back into the war memorial.

The singing grew louder as they approached the church. It made Harry's throat constrict, it reminded him so forcefully of Hogwarts, of Peeves bellowing rude versions of carols from inside suits of armor, of the Great Hall's twelve Christmas trees, of Dumbledore wearing a bonnet he had won in a cracker, of Ron in a hand-knitted sweater. . . .

There was a kissing gate at the entrance to the graveyard. Hermione pushed it open as quietly as possible and they edged through it. On either side of the slippery path to the church doors, the snow lay deep and untouched. They moved off through the snow, carving deep trenches behind them as they walked around the building, keeping to the shadows beneath the brilliant windows.

Behind the church, row upon row of snowy tombstones protruded from a blanket of pale blue that was flecked with dazzling red, gold, and green wherever the reflections from the stained glass hit the snow. Keeping his hand closed tightly on the wand in his jacket pocket, Harry moved toward the nearest grave.

"Look at this, it's an Abbott, could be some long-lost relation of Hannah's!"

"Keep your voice down," Hermione begged him.

They waded deeper and deeper into the graveyard, gouging dark tracks into the snow behind them, stooping to peer at the words on old headstones, every now and then squinting into the surrounding darkness to make absolutely sure that they were unaccompanied.

"Harry, here!"

Hermione was two rows of tombstones away; he had to wade back to her, his heart positively banging in his chest.

"Is it — ?"

"No, but look!"

She pointed to the dark stone. Harry stooped down and saw, upon the frozen, lichen-spotted granite, the words KENDRA DUM-BLEDORE and, a short way below her dates of birth and death, AND HER DAUGHTER ARIANA. There was also a quotation:

Where your treasure is, there will your heart be also.

So Rita Skeeter and Muriel had got some of their facts right. The Dumbledore family had indeed lived here, and part of it had died here.

Seeing the grave was worse than hearing about it. Harry could not help thinking that he and Dumbledore both had deep roots in this graveyard, and that Dumbledore ought to have told him so, yet he had never thought to share the connection. They could have visited the place together; for a moment Harry imagined coming here with Dumbledore, of what a bond that would have been, of how much it would have meant to him. But it seemed that to Dumbledore, the fact that their families lay side by side in the same graveyard had been an unimportant coincidence, irrelevant, perhaps, to the job he wanted Harry to do.

Hermione was looking at Harry, and he was glad that his face was hidden in shadow. He read the words on the tombstone again. *Where your treasure is, there will your heart be also.* He did not understand what these words meant. Surely Dumbledore had chosen them, as the eldest member of the family once his mother had died.

"Are you sure he never mentioned — ?" Hermione began.

"No," said Harry curtly, then, "let's keep looking," and he turned away, wishing he had not seen the stone: He did not want his excited trepidation tainted with resentment.

"Here!" cried Hermione again a few moments later from out of the darkness. "Oh no, sorry! I thought it said Potter."

She was rubbing at a crumbling, mossy stone, gazing down at it, a little frown on her face.

"Harry, come back a moment."

He did not want to be sidetracked again, and only grudgingly made his way back through the snow toward her.

"What?"

"Look at this!"

The grave was extremely old, weathered so that Harry could hardly make out the name. Hermione showed him the symbol beneath it.

"Harry, that's the mark in the book!"

He peered at the place she indicated: The stone was so worn that it was hard to make out what was engraved there, though there did seem to be a triangular mark beneath the nearly illegible name.

"Yeah . . . it could be. . . ."

Hermione lit her wand and pointed it at the name on the headstone.

"It says Ig — Ignotus, I think. . . ."

"I'm going to keep looking for my parents, all right?" Harry told her, a slight edge to his voice, and he set off again, leaving her crouched beside the old grave.

Every now and then he recognized a surname that, like Abbott, he had met at Hogwarts. Sometimes there were several generations of the same Wizarding family represented in the graveyard: Harry could tell from the dates that it had either died out, or the current members had moved away from Godric's Hollow. Deeper and deeper amongst the graves he went, and every time he reached a new headstone he felt a little lurch of apprehension and anticipation.

The darkness and the silence seemed to become, all of a sudden, much deeper. Harry looked around, worried, thinking of dementors, then realized that the carols had finished, that the chatter and flurry of churchgoers were fading away as they made their way back into the square. Somebody inside the church had just turned off the lights.

Then Hermione's voice came out of the blackness for the third time, sharp and clear from a few yards away.

"Harry, they're here . . . right here."

And he knew by her tone that it was his mother and father this time: He moved toward her, feeling as if something heavy were pressing on his chest, the same sensation he had had right after

Dumbledore had died, a grief that had actually weighed on his heart and lungs.

The headstone was only two rows behind Kendra and Ariana's. It was made of white marble, just like Dumbledore's tomb, and this made it easy to read, as it seemed to shine in the dark. Harry did not need to kneel or even approach very close to it to make out the words engraved upon it.

JAMES POTTER   LILY POTTER

BORN 27 MARCH 1960   BORN 30 JANUARY 1960
DIED 31 OCTOBER 1981   DIED 31 OCTOBER 1981

The last enemy that shall be destroyed is death.

Harry read the words slowly, as though he would have only one chance to take in their meaning, and he read the last of them aloud.

"'The last enemy that shall be destroyed is death' . . ." A horrible thought came to him, and with it a kind of panic. "Isn't that a Death Eater idea? Why is that there?"

"It doesn't mean defeating death in the way the Death Eaters mean it, Harry," said Hermione, her voice gentle. "It means . . . you know . . . living beyond death. Living after death."

But they were not living, thought Harry: They were gone. The empty words could not disguise the fact that his parents' moldering remains lay beneath snow and stone, indifferent, unknowing. And tears came before he could stop them, boiling hot then instantly freezing on his face, and what was the point in wiping them off or pretending? He let them fall, his lips pressed hard together, looking down at the thick snow hiding from his eyes the place where the last of Lily and James lay, bones now, surely, or dust, not knowing or caring that their living son stood so near, his heart still beating, alive because of their sacrifice and close to wishing, at this moment, that he was sleeping under the snow with them.

Hermione had taken his hand again and was gripping it tightly. He could not look at her, but returned the pressure, now taking deep, sharp gulps of the night air, trying to steady himself, trying to regain control. He should have brought something to give them, and he had not thought of it, and every plant in the graveyard was leafless and frozen. But Hermione raised her wand, moved it in a circle through the air, and a wreath of Christmas roses blossomed before them. Harry caught it and laid it on his parents' grave.

As soon as he stood up he wanted to leave: He did not think he could stand another moment there. He put his arm around Hermione's shoulders, and she put hers around his waist, and they turned in silence and walked away through the snow, past Dumbledore's mother and sister, back toward the dark church and the out-of-sight kissing gate.

BATHILDA'S SECRET

"Harry, stop."

"What's wrong?"

They had only just reached the grave of the unknown Abbott.

"There's someone there. Someone watching us. I can tell. There, over by the bushes."

They stood quite still, holding on to each other, gazing at the dense black boundary of the graveyard. Harry could not see anything.

"Are you sure?"

"I saw something move, I could have sworn I did. . . ."

She broke from him to free her wand arm.

"We look like Muggles," Harry pointed out.

"Muggles who've just been laying flowers on your parents' grave! Harry, I'm sure there's someone over there!"

Harry thought of *A History of Magic*; the graveyard was supposed to be haunted: what if — ? But then he heard a rustle and saw a little eddy of dislodged snow in the bush to which Hermione had pointed. Ghosts could not move snow.

"It's a cat," said Harry, after a second or two, "or a bird. If it was a Death Eater we'd be dead by now. But let's get out of here, and we can put the Cloak back on."

They glanced back repeatedly as they made their way out of the graveyard. Harry, who did not feel as sanguine as he had pretended when reassuring Hermione, was glad to reach the gate and the slippery pavement. They pulled the Invisibility Cloak back over themselves. The pub was fuller than before: Many voices inside it were now singing the carol that they had heard as they approached the church. For a moment Harry considered suggesting they take refuge inside it, but before he could say anything Hermione murmured, "Let's go this way," and pulled him down the dark street leading out of the village in the opposite direction from which they had entered. Harry could make out the point where the cottages ended and the lane turned into open country again. They walked as quickly as they dared, past more windows sparkling with multicolored lights, the outlines of Christmas trees dark through the curtains.

"How are we going to find Bathilda's house?" asked Hermione, who was shivering a little and kept glancing back over her shoulder. "Harry? What do you think? Harry?"

She tugged at his arm, but Harry was not paying attention. He was looking toward the dark mass that stood at the very end of this row of houses. Next moment he had sped up, dragging Hermione along with him; she slipped a little on the ice.

"Harry —"

"Look. . . . Look at it, Hermione. . . ."

"I don't . . . oh!"

He could see it; the Fidelius Charm must have died with James and Lily. The hedge had grown wild in the sixteen years since Hagrid had taken Harry from the rubble that lay scattered amongst the waist-high grass. Most of the cottage was still standing, though entirely covered in dark ivy and snow, but the right side of the top floor had been blown apart; that, Harry was sure, was where the curse had backfired. He and Hermione stood at the gate, gazing up at the wreck of what must once have been a cottage just like those that flanked it.

"I wonder why nobody's ever rebuilt it?" whispered Hermione.

"Maybe you can't rebuild it?" Harry replied. "Maybe it's like the injuries from Dark Magic and you can't repair the damage?"

He slipped a hand from beneath the Cloak and grasped the snowy and thickly rusted gate, not wishing to open it, but simply to hold some part of the house.

"You're not going to go inside? It looks unsafe, it might — oh, Harry, look!"

His touch on the gate seemed to have done it. A sign had risen out of the ground in front of them, up through the tangles of nettles and weeds, like some bizarre, fast-growing flower, and in golden letters upon the wood it said:

On this spot, on the night of 31 October 1981,
Lily and James Potter lost their lives.
Their son, Harry, remains the only wizard
ever to have survived the Killing Curse.
This house, invisible to Muggles, has been left
in its ruined state as a monument to the Potters

and as a reminder of the violence
that tore apart their family.

And all around these neatly lettered words, scribbles had been
added by other witches and wizards who had come to see the place
where the Boy Who Lived had escaped. Some had merely signed
their names in Everlasting Ink; others had carved their initials into
the wood, still others had left messages. The most recent of these,
shining brightly over sixteen years' worth of magical graffiti, all said
similar things.

Good luck, Harry, wherever you are.
If you read this, Harry, we're all behind you!
Long live Harry Potter.

"They shouldn't have written on the sign!" said Hermione,
indignant.

But Harry beamed at her.

"It's brilliant. I'm glad they did. I . . ."

He broke off. A heavily muffled figure was hobbling up the lane
toward them, silhouetted by the bright lights in the distant square.
Harry thought, though it was hard to judge, that the figure was a
woman. She was moving slowly, possibly frightened of slipping on
the snowy ground. Her stoop, her stoutness, her shuffling gait all
gave an impression of extreme age. They watched in silence as she
drew nearer. Harry was waiting to see whether she would turn into
any of the cottages she was passing, but he knew instinctively that
she would not. At last she came to a halt a few yards from them and
simply stood there in the middle of the frozen road, facing them.

He did not need Hermione's pinch to his arm. There was next to no chance that this woman was a Muggle: She was standing there gazing at a house that ought to have been completely invisible to her, if she was not a witch. Even assuming that she *was* a witch, however, it was odd behavior to come out on a night this cold, simply to look at an old ruin. By all the rules of normal magic, meanwhile, she ought not to be able to see Hermione and him at all. Nevertheless, Harry had the strangest feeling that she knew that they were there, and also who they were. Just as he had reached this uneasy conclusion, she raised a gloved hand and beckoned.

Hermione moved closer to him under the Cloak, her arm pressed against his.

"How does she know?"

He shook his head. The woman beckoned again, more vigorously. Harry could think of many reasons not to obey the summons, and yet his suspicions about her identity were growing stronger every moment that they stood facing each other in the deserted street.

Was it possible that she had been waiting for them all these long months? That Dumbledore had told her to wait, and that Harry would come in the end? Was it not likely that it was she who had moved in the shadows in the graveyard and had followed them to this spot? Even her ability to sense them suggested some Dumbledore-ish power that he had never encountered before.

Finally Harry spoke, causing Hermione to gasp and jump.

"Are you Bathilda?"

The muffled figure nodded and beckoned again.

Beneath the Cloak Harry and Hermione looked at each other. Harry raised his eyebrows; Hermione gave a tiny, nervous nod.

They stepped toward the woman and, at once, she turned and hobbled off back the way they had come. Leading them past several houses, she turned in at a gate. They followed her up the front path through a garden nearly as overgrown as the one they had just left. She fumbled for a moment with a key at the front door, then opened it and stepped back to let them pass.

She smelled bad, or perhaps it was her house: Harry wrinkled his nose as they sidled past her and pulled off the Cloak. Now that he was beside her, he realized how tiny she was; bowed down with age, she came barely level with his chest. She closed the door behind them, her knuckles blue and mottled against the peeling paint, then turned and peered into Harry's face. Her eyes were thick with cataracts and sunken into folds of transparent skin, and her whole face was dotted with broken veins and liver spots. He wondered whether she could make him out at all; even if she could, it was the balding Muggle whose identity he had stolen that she would see.

The odor of old age, of dust, of unwashed clothes and stale food intensified as she unwound a moth-eaten black shawl, revealing a head of scant white hair through which the scalp showed clearly.

"Bathilda?" Harry repeated.

She nodded again. Harry became aware of the locket against his skin; the thing inside it that sometimes ticked or beat had woken; he could feel it pulsing through the cold gold. Did it know, could it sense, that the thing that would destroy it was near?

Bathilda shuffled past them, pushing Hermione aside as though she had not seen her, and vanished into what seemed to be a sitting room.

"Harry, I'm not sure about this," breathed Hermione.

"Look at the size of her; I think we could overpower her if we had to," said Harry. "Listen, I should have told you, I knew she wasn't all there. Muriel called her 'gaga.'"

"Come!" called Bathilda from the next room.

Hermione jumped and clutched Harry's arm.

"It's okay," said Harry reassuringly, and he led the way into the sitting room.

Bathilda was tottering around the place lighting candles, but it was still very dark, not to mention extremely dirty. Thick dust crunched beneath their feet, and Harry's nose detected, underneath the dank and mildewed smell, something worse, like meat gone bad. He wondered when was the last time anyone had been inside Bathilda's house to check whether she was coping. She seemed to have forgotten that she could do magic, too, for she lit the candles clumsily by hand, her trailing lace cuff in constant danger of catching fire.

"Let me do that," offered Harry, and he took the matches from her. She stood watching him as he finished lighting the candle stubs that stood on saucers around the room, perched precariously on stacks of books and on side tables crammed with cracked and moldy cups.

The last surface on which Harry spotted a candle was a bow-fronted chest of drawers on which there stood a large number of photographs. When the flame danced into life, its reflection wavered on their dusty glass and silver. He saw a few tiny movements from the pictures. As Bathilda fumbled with logs for the fire, he muttered *"Tergeo"*: The dust vanished from the photographs, and he saw at once that half a dozen were missing from the largest and most ornate frames. He wondered whether Bathilda or somebody else had removed them. Then the sight of a photograph near the back of the collection caught his eye, and he snatched it up.

It was the golden-haired, merry-faced thief, the young man who had perched on Gregorovitch's windowsill, smiling lazily up at Harry out of the silver frame. And it came to Harry instantly where he had seen the boy before: in *The Life and Lies of Albus Dumbledore,* arm in arm with the teenage Dumbledore, and that must be where all the missing photographs were: in Rita's book.

"Mrs. — Miss — Bagshot?" he said, and his voice shook slightly. "Who is this?"

Bathilda was standing in the middle of the room watching Hermione light the fire for her.

"Miss Bagshot?" Harry repeated, and he advanced with the picture in his hands as the flames burst into life in the fireplace. Bathilda looked up at his voice, and the Horcrux beat faster upon his chest.

"Who is this person?" Harry asked her, pushing the picture forward.

She peered at it solemnly, then up at Harry.

"Do you know who this is?" he repeated in a much slower and louder voice than usual. "This man? Do you know him? What's he called?"

Bathilda merely looked vague. Harry felt an awful frustration. How had Rita Skeeter unlocked Bathilda's memories?

"Who is this man?" he repeated loudly.

"Harry, what are you doing?" asked Hermione.

"This picture, Hermione, it's the thief, the thief who stole from Gregorovitch! Please!" he said to Bathilda. "Who is this?"

But she only stared at him.

"Why did you ask us to come with you, Mrs. — Miss — Bagshot?" asked Hermione, raising her own voice. "Was there something you wanted to tell us?"

Giving no sign that she had heard Hermione, Bathilda now shuffled a few steps closer to Harry. With a little jerk of her head she looked back into the hall.

"You want us to leave?" he asked.

She repeated the gesture, this time pointing firstly at him, then at herself, then at the ceiling.

"Oh, right . . . Hermione, I think she wants me to go upstairs with her."

"All right," said Hermione, "let's go."

But when Hermione moved, Bathilda shook her head with surprising vigor, once more pointing first at Harry, then to herself.

"She wants me to go with her, alone."

"Why?" asked Hermione, and her voice rang out sharp and clear in the candlelit room; the old lady shook her head a little at the loud noise.

"Maybe Dumbledore told her to give the sword to me, and only to me?"

"Do you really think she knows who you are?"

"Yes," said Harry, looking down into the milky eyes fixed upon his own, "I think she does."

"Well, okay then, but be quick, Harry."

"Lead the way," Harry told Bathilda.

She seemed to understand, because she shuffled around him toward the door. Harry glanced back at Hermione with a reassuring smile, but he was not sure she had seen it; she stood hugging herself in the midst of the candlelit squalor, looking toward the bookcase. As Harry walked out of the room, unseen by both Hermione and Bathilda, he slipped the silver-framed photograph of the unknown thief inside his jacket.

The stairs were steep and narrow: Harry was half tempted to place his hands on stout Bathilda's backside to ensure that she did not topple over backward on top of him, which seemed only too likely. Slowly, wheezing a little, she climbed to the upper landing, turned immediately right, and led him into a low-ceilinged bedroom.

It was pitch-black and smelled horrible: Harry had just made out a chamber pot protruding from under the bed before Bathilda closed the door and even that was swallowed by the darkness.

"*Lumos*," said Harry, and his wand ignited. He gave a start: Bathilda had moved close to him in those few seconds of darkness, and he had not heard her approach.

"You are Potter?" she whispered.

"Yes, I am."

She nodded slowly, solemnly. Harry felt the Horcrux beating fast, faster than his own heart: It was an unpleasant, agitating sensation.

"Have you got anything for me?" Harry asked, but she seemed distracted by his lit wand-tip.

"Have you got anything for me?" he repeated.

Then she closed her eyes and several things happened at once: Harry's scar prickled painfully; the Horcrux twitched so that the front of his sweater actually moved; the dark, fetid room dissolved momentarily. He felt a leap of joy and spoke in a high, cold voice: *Hold him!*

Harry swayed where he stood: The dark, foul-smelling room seemed to close around him again; he did not know what had just happened.

"Have you got anything for me?" he asked for a third time, much louder.

"Over here," she whispered, pointing to the corner. Harry raised his wand and saw the outline of a cluttered dressing table beneath the curtained window.

This time she did not lead him. Harry edged between her and the unmade bed, his wand raised. He did not want to look away from her.

"What is it?" he asked as he reached the dressing table, which was heaped high with what looked and smelled like dirty laundry.

"There," she said, pointing at the shapeless mass.

And in the instant that he looked away, his eyes raking the tangled mess for a sword hilt, a ruby, she moved weirdly: He saw it out of the corner of his eye; panic made him turn and horror paralyzed him as he saw the old body collapsing and the great snake pouring from the place where her neck had been.

The snake struck as he raised his wand: The force of the bite to his forearm sent the wand spinning up toward the ceiling; its light swung dizzyingly around the room and was extinguished: Then a powerful blow from the tail to his midriff knocked the breath out of him: He fell backward onto the dressing table, into the mound of filthy clothing —

He rolled sideways, narrowly avoiding the snake's tail, which thrashed down upon the table where he had been a second earlier: Fragments of the glass surface rained upon him as he hit the floor. From below he heard Hermione call, "Harry?"

He could not get enough breath into his lungs to call back: Then a heavy smooth mass smashed him to the floor and he felt it slide over him, powerful, muscular —

"No!" he gasped, pinned to the floor.

"*Yes,*" whispered the voice. "*Yesss . . . hold you . . . hold you . . .*"

"Accio . . . Accio Wand . . ."

But nothing happened and he needed his hands to try to force the snake from him as it coiled itself around his torso, squeezing the air from him, pressing the Horcrux hard into his chest, a circle of ice that throbbed with life, inches from his own frantic heart, and his brain was flooding with cold, white light, all thought obliterated, his own breath drowned, distant footsteps, everything going. . . .

A metal heart was banging outside his chest, and now he was flying, flying with triumph in his heart, without need of broomstick or thestral. . . .

He was abruptly awake in the sour-smelling darkness; Nagini had released him. He scrambled up and saw the snake outlined against the landing light: It struck, and Hermione dived aside with a shriek; her deflected curse hit the curtained window, which shattered. Frozen air filled the room as Harry ducked to avoid another shower of broken glass and his foot slipped on a pencil-like something — his wand —

He bent and snatched it up, but now the room was full of the snake, its tail thrashing; Hermione was nowhere to be seen and for a moment Harry thought the worst, but then there was a loud bang and a flash of red light, and the snake flew into the air, smacking Harry hard in the face as it went, coil after heavy coil rising up to the ceiling. Harry raised his wand, but as he did so, his scar seared more painfully, more powerfully than it had done in years.

"He's coming! *Hermione, he's coming!*"

As he yelled the snake fell, hissing wildly. Everything was chaos: It smashed shelves from the wall, and splintered china flew everywhere as Harry jumped over the bed and seized the dark shape he knew to be Hermione —

She shrieked with pain as he pulled her back across the bed: The snake reared again, but Harry knew that worse than the snake was coming, was perhaps already at the gate, his head was going to split open with the pain from his scar —

The snake lunged as he took a running leap, dragging Hermione with him; as it struck, Hermione screamed, *"Confringo!"* and her spell flew around the room, exploding the wardrobe mirror and ricocheting back at them, bouncing from floor to ceiling; Harry felt the heat of it sear the back of his hand. Glass cut his cheek as, pulling Hermione with him, he leapt from bed to broken dressing table and then straight out of the smashed window into nothingness, her scream reverberating through the night as they twisted in midair. . . .

And then his scar burst open and he was Voldemort and he was running across the fetid bedroom, his long white hands clutching at the windowsill as he glimpsed the bald man and the little woman twist and vanish, and he screamed with rage, a scream that mingled with the girl's, that echoed across the dark gardens over the church bells ringing in Christmas Day. . . .

And his scream was Harry's scream, his pain was Harry's pain . . . that it could happen here, where it had happened before . . . here, within sight of that house where he had come so close to knowing what it was to die . . . to die. . . . The pain was so terrible . . . ripped from his body. . . . But if he had no body, why did his head hurt so badly; if he was dead, how could he feel so unbearably, didn't pain cease with death, didn't it go . . .

The night wet and windy, two children dressed as pumpkins wad-
dling across the square, and the shop windows covered in paper spiders,
all the tawdry Muggle trappings of a world in which they did not
believe. . . . And he was gliding along, that sense of purpose and power

and rightness in him that he always knew on these occasions. . . . Not anger . . . that was for weaker souls than he . . . but triumph, yes. . . . He had waited for this, he had hoped for it. . . .

"Nice costume, mister!"

He saw the small boy's smile falter as he ran near enough to see beneath the hood of the cloak, saw the fear cloud his painted face: Then the child turned and ran away. . . . Beneath the robe he fingered the handle of his wand. . . . One simple movement and the child would never reach his mother . . . but unnecessary, quite unnecessary. . . .

And along a new and darker street he moved, and now his destination was in sight at last, the Fidelius Charm broken, though they did not know it yet. . . . And he made less noise than the dead leaves slithering along the pavement as he drew level with the dark hedge, and stared over it. . . .

They had not drawn the curtains; he saw them quite clearly in their little sitting room, the tall black-haired man in his glasses, making puffs of colored smoke erupt from his wand for the amusement of the small black-haired boy in his blue pajamas. The child was laughing and trying to catch the smoke, to grab it in his small fist. . . .

A door opened and the mother entered, saying words he could not hear, her long dark-red hair falling over her face. Now the father scooped up the son and handed him to the mother. He threw his wand down upon the sofa and stretched, yawning. . . .

The gate creaked a little as he pushed it open, but James Potter did not hear. His white hand pulled out the wand beneath his cloak and pointed it at the door, which burst open.

He was over the threshold as James came sprinting into the hall. It was easy, too easy, he had not even picked up his wand. . . .

"Lily, take Harry and go! It's him! Go! Run! I'll hold him off!"

Hold him off, without a wand in his hand! . . . He laughed before casting the curse. . . .

"Avada Kedavra!"

The green light filled the cramped hallway, it lit the pram pushed against the wall, it made the banisters glare like lightning rods, and James Potter fell like a marionette whose strings were cut. . . .

He could hear her screaming from the upper floor, trapped, but as long as she was sensible, she, at least, had nothing to fear. . . . He climbed the steps, listening with faint amusement to her attempts to barricade herself in. . . . She had no wand upon her either. . . . How stupid they were, and how trusting, thinking that their safety lay in friends, that weapons could be discarded even for moments. . . .

He forced the door open, cast aside the chair and boxes hastily piled against it with one lazy wave of his wand . . . and there she stood, the child in her arms. At the sight of him, she dropped her son into the crib behind her and threw her arms wide, as if this would help, as if in shielding him from sight she hoped to be chosen instead. . . .

"Not Harry, not Harry, please not Harry!"

"Stand aside, you silly girl . . . stand aside, now."

"Not Harry, please no, take me, kill me instead —"

"This is my last warning —"

"Not Harry! Please . . . have mercy . . . have mercy. . . . Not Harry! Not Harry! Please — I'll do anything —"

"Stand aside. Stand aside, girl!"

He could have forced her away from the crib, but it seemed more prudent to finish them all. . . .

The green light flashed around the room and she dropped like her husband. The child had not cried all this time: He could stand, clutching the bars of his crib, and he looked up into the intruder's face with a kind of bright interest, perhaps thinking that it was his father who hid beneath the cloak, making more pretty lights, and his mother would pop up any moment, laughing —

He pointed the wand very carefully into the boy's face: He wanted to see it happen, the destruction of this one, inexplicable danger. The child began to cry: It had seen that he was not James. He did not like it crying, he had never been able to stomach the small ones whining in the orphanage —

"Avada Kedavra!"

And then he broke: He was nothing, nothing but pain and terror, and he must hide himself, not here in the rubble of the ruined house, where the child was trapped and screaming, but far away . . . far away. . . .

"No," he moaned.

The snake rustled on the filthy, cluttered floor, and he had killed the boy, and yet he was the boy. . . .

"No . . ."

And now he stood at the broken window of Bathilda's house, immersed in memories of his greatest loss, and at his feet the great snake slithered over broken china and glass. . . . He looked down and saw something . . . something incredible. . . .

"No . . ."

"Harry, it's all right, you're all right!"

He stooped down and picked up the smashed photograph. There he was, the unknown thief, the thief he was seeking. . . .

"No . . . I dropped it. . . . I dropped it. . . ."

"Harry, it's okay, wake up, wake up!"

He was Harry. . . . Harry, not Voldemort . . . and the thing that was rustling was not a snake. . . . He opened his eyes.

"Harry," Hermione whispered. "Do you feel all — all right?"

"Yes," he lied.

He was in the tent, lying on one of the lower bunks beneath a heap of blankets. He could tell that it was almost dawn by the stillness and the quality of the cold, flat light beyond the canvas ceiling. He was drenched in sweat; he could feel it on the sheets and blankets.

"We got away."

"Yes," said Hermione. "I had to use a Hover Charm to get you into your bunk, I couldn't lift you. You've been . . . Well, you haven't been quite . . ."

There were purple shadows under her brown eyes and he noticed a small sponge in her hand: She had been wiping his face.

"You've been ill," she finished. "Quite ill."

"How long ago did we leave?"

"Hours ago. It's nearly morning."

"And I've been . . . what, unconscious?"

"Not exactly," said Hermione uncomfortably. "You've been shouting and moaning and . . . things," she added in a tone that made Harry feel uneasy. What had he done? Screamed curses like Voldemort, cried like the baby in the crib?

"I couldn't get the Horcrux off you," Hermione said, and he knew she wanted to change the subject. "It was stuck, stuck to your chest. You've got a mark; I'm sorry, I had to use a Severing Charm to get it away. The snake bit you too, but I've cleaned the wound and put some dittany on it. . . ."

He pulled the sweaty T-shirt he was wearing away from himself and looked down. There was a scarlet oval over his heart where the locket had burned him. He could also see the half-healed puncture marks to his forearm.

"Where've you put the Horcrux?"

"In my bag. I think we should keep it off for a while."

He lay back on his pillows and looked into her pinched gray face.

"We shouldn't have gone to Godric's Hollow. It's my fault, it's all my fault, Hermione, I'm sorry."

"It's not your fault. I wanted to go too; I really thought Dumbledore might have left the sword there for you."

"Yeah, well . . . we got that wrong, didn't we?"

"What happened, Harry? What happened when she took you upstairs? Was the snake hiding somewhere? Did it just come out and kill her and attack you?"

"No," he said. "*She* was the snake . . . or the snake was her . . . all along."

"W-what?"

He closed his eyes. He could still smell Bathilda's house on him: It made the whole thing horribly vivid.

"Bathilda must've been dead a while. The snake was . . . was inside her. You-Know-Who put it there in Godric's Hollow, to wait. You were right. He knew I'd go back."

"The snake was *inside* her?"

He opened his eyes again: Hermione looked revolted, nauseated.

"Lupin said there would be magic we'd never imagined," Harry said. "She didn't want to talk in front of you, because it was Parseltongue, all Parseltongue, and I didn't realize, but of course I could understand her. Once we were up in the room, the snake sent a message to You-Know-Who, I heard it happen inside my head, I felt him get excited, he said to keep me there . . . and then . . ."

He remembered the snake coming out of Bathilda's neck: Hermione did not need to know the details.

". . . she changed, changed into the snake, and attacked."

He looked down at the puncture marks.

"It wasn't supposed to kill me, just keep me there till You-Know-Who came."

If he had only managed to kill the snake, it would have been worth it, all of it. . . . Sick at heart, he sat up and threw back the covers.

"Harry, no, I'm sure you ought to rest!"

"You're the one who needs sleep. No offense, but you look terrible. I'm fine. I'll keep watch for a while. Where's my wand?"

She did not answer, she merely looked at him.

"Where's my wand, Hermione?"

She was biting her lip, and tears swam in her eyes.

"Harry . . ."

"Where's my wand?"

She reached down beside the bed and held it out to him.

The holly and phoenix wand was nearly severed in two. One fragile strand of phoenix feather kept both pieces hanging together. The wood had splintered apart completely. Harry took it into his hands as though it was a living thing that had suffered a terrible injury. He could not think properly: Everything was a blur of panic and fear. Then he held out the wand to Hermione.

"Mend it. Please."

"Harry, I don't think, when it's broken like this —"

"Please, Hermione, try!"

"R-Reparo."

The dangling half of the wand resealed itself. Harry held it up.

"Lumos!"

The wand sparked feebly, then went out. Harry pointed it at Hermione.

"Expelliarmus!"

Hermione's wand gave a little jerk, but did not leave her hand. The feeble attempt at magic was too much for Harry's wand, which split into two again. He stared at it, aghast, unable to take in what he was seeing . . . the wand that had survived so much . . .

"Harry," Hermione whispered so quietly he could hardly hear her. "I'm so, so sorry. I think it was me. As we were leaving, you know, the snake was coming for us, and so I cast a Blasting Curse, and it rebounded everywhere, and it must have — must have hit —"

"It was an accident," said Harry mechanically. He felt empty, stunned. "We'll — we'll find a way to repair it."

"Harry, I don't think we're going to be able to," said Hermione, the tears trickling down her face. "Remember . . . remember Ron? When he broke his wand, crashing the car? It was never the same again, he had to get a new one."

Harry thought of Ollivander, kidnapped and held hostage by Voldemort; of Gregorovitch, who was dead. How was he supposed to find himself a new wand?

"Well," he said, in a falsely matter-of-fact voice, "well, I'll just borrow yours for now, then. While I keep watch."

Her face glazed with tears, Hermione handed over her wand, and he left her sitting beside his bed, desiring nothing more than to get away from her.

THE LIFE AND LIES OF ALBUS DUMBLEDORE

The sun was coming up: The pure, colorless vastness of the sky stretched over him, indifferent to him and his suffering. Harry sat down in the tent entrance and took a deep breath of clean air. Simply to be alive to watch the sun rise over the sparkling snowy hillside ought to have been the greatest treasure on earth, yet he could not appreciate it: His senses had been spiked by the calamity of losing his wand. He looked out over a valley blanketed in snow, distant church bells chiming through the glittering silence.

Without realizing it, he was digging his fingers into his arms as if he were trying to resist physical pain. He had spilled his own blood more times than he could count; he had lost all the bones in his right arm once; this journey had already given him scars to his chest and forearm to join those on his hand and forehead, but never, until this moment, had he felt himself to be fatally weakened, vulnerable, and naked, as though the best part of his magical power had been torn from him. He knew exactly what Hermione would say if he expressed any of this: The wand is only as good as the wizard. But she was wrong, his case was different. She had not felt the wand spin like the needle of a compass and shoot golden flames at his enemy. He had lost the protection of the twin cores, and only now that it was gone did he realize how much he had been counting upon it.

He pulled the pieces of the broken wand out of his pocket and, without looking at them, tucked them away in Hagrid's pouch around his neck. The pouch was now too full of broken and use-less objects to take any more. Harry's hand brushed the old Snitch through the mokeskin and for a moment he had to fight the temp-tation to pull it out and throw it away. Impenetrable, unhelpful, useless, like everything else Dumbledore had left behind —

And his fury at Dumbledore broke over him now like lava, scorching him inside, wiping out every other feeling. Out of sheer desperation they had talked themselves into believing that Godric's Hollow held answers, convinced themselves that they were supposed to go back, that it was all part of some secret path laid out for them by Dumbledore; but there was no map, no plan. Dumbledore had left them to grope in the darkness, to wrestle with unknown and undreamed-of terrors, alone and unaided: Nothing was explained, nothing was given freely, they had no sword, and now, Harry had no wand. And he had dropped the photograph of the thief, and it would surely be easy now for Voldemort to find out who he was. . . . Voldemort had all the information now. . . .

"Harry?"

Hermione looked frightened that he might curse her with her own wand. Her face streaked with tears, she crouched down beside him, two cups of tea trembling in her hands and something bulky under her arm.

"Thanks," he said, taking one of the cups.

"Do you mind if I talk to you?"

"No," he said because he did not want to hurt her feelings.

"Harry, you wanted to know who that man in the picture was. Well . . . I've got the book."

Timidly she pushed it onto his lap, a pristine copy of *The Life and Lies of Albus Dumbledore.*

"Where — how — ?"

"It was in Bathilda's sitting room, just lying there. . . . This note was sticking out of the top of it."

Hermione read the few lines of spiky, acid-green writing aloud.

"*'Dear Batty, Thanks for your help. Here's a copy of the book, hope you like it. You said everything, even if you don't remember it. Rita.'* I think it must have arrived while the real Bathilda was alive, but perhaps she wasn't in any fit state to read it?"

"No, she probably wasn't."

Harry looked down upon Dumbledore's face and experienced a surge of savage pleasure: Now he would know all the things that Dumbledore had never thought it worth telling him, whether Dumbledore wanted him to or not.

"You're still really angry at me, aren't you?" said Hermione; he looked up to see fresh tears leaking out of her eyes, and knew that his anger must have shown in his face.

"No," he said quietly. "No, Hermione, I know it was an accident. You were trying to get us out of there alive, and you were incredible. I'd be dead if you hadn't been there to help me."

He tried to return her watery smile, then turned his attention to the book. Its spine was stiff; it had clearly never been opened before. He riffled through the pages, looking for photographs. He came across the one he sought almost at once, the young Dumbledore and his handsome companion, roaring with laughter at some long-forgotten joke. Harry dropped his eyes to the caption.

Albus Dumbledore, shortly after his mother's death,
with his friend Gellert Grindelwald.

Harry gaped at the last word for several long moments. Grindelwald. His friend Grindelwald. He looked sideways at Hermione, who was still contemplating the name as though she could not believe her eyes. Slowly she looked up at Harry.

"*Grindelwald?*"

Ignoring the remainder of the photographs, Harry searched the pages around them for a recurrence of that fatal name. He soon discovered it and read greedily, but became lost: It was necessary to go further back to make sense of it all, and eventually he found himself at the start of a chapter entitled "The Greater Good." Together, he and Hermione started to read:

Now approaching his eighteenth birthday, Dumbledore left Hogwarts in a blaze of glory — Head Boy, Prefect, Winner of the Barnabus Finkley Prize for Exceptional Spell-Casting, British Youth Representative to the Wizengamot, Gold Medal-Winner for Ground-Breaking Contribution to the International Alchemical Conference in Cairo. Dumbledore intended, next, to take a Grand Tour with Elphias "Dogbreath" Doge, the dim-witted but devoted sidekick he had picked up at school.

The two young men were staying at the Leaky Cauldron in London, preparing to depart for Greece the following morning, when an owl arrived bearing news of Dumbledore's mother's death. "Dogbreath" Doge, who refused to be interviewed for this book, has given the public his own sentimental version of what happened next. He represents Kendra's death as a tragic blow, and Dumbledore's decision to give up his expedition as an act of noble self-sacrifice.

Certainly Dumbledore returned to Godric's Hollow at once, supposedly to "care" for his younger brother and sister. But how much care did he actually give them?

"He were a head case, that Aberforth," says Enid Smeek, whose family lived on the outskirts of Godric's Hollow at that time. "Ran wild. 'Course, with his mum and dad gone you'd have felt sorry for him, only he kept chucking goat dung at my head. I don't think Albus was fussed about him, I never saw them together, anyway."

So what was Albus doing, if not comforting his wild young brother? The answer, it seems, is ensuring the continued imprisonment of his sister. For, though her first jailer had died, there was no change in the pitiful condition of Ariana Dumbledore. Her very existence continued to be known only to those few outsiders who, like "Dogbreath" Doge, could be counted upon to believe in the story of her "ill health."

Another such easily satisfied friend of the family was Bathilda Bagshot, the celebrated magical historian who has lived in Godric's Hollow for many years. Kendra, of course, had rebuffed Bathilda when she first attempted to welcome the family to the village. Several years later, however, the author sent an owl to Albus at Hogwarts, having been favorably impressed by his paper on trans-species transformation in *Transfiguration Today*. This initial contact led to acquaintance with the entire Dumbledore family. At the time of Kendra's death, Bathilda was the only person in Godric's Hollow who was on speaking terms with Dumbledore's mother.

Unfortunately, the brilliance that Bathilda exhibited earlier in her life has now dimmed. "The fire's lit, but the cauldron's empty," as Ivor Dillonsby put it to me, or, in Enid Smeek's slightly earthier phrase, "She's nutty as squirrel poo." Nevertheless, a combination of tried-and-tested reporting techniques enabled me to extract enough nuggets of hard fact to string together the whole scandalous story.

Like the rest of the Wizarding world, Bathilda puts Kendra's premature death down to a backfiring charm, a story repeated by Albus and Aberforth in later years. Bathilda also parrots the family line on Ariana, calling her "frail" and "delicate." On one subject, however, Bathilda is well worth the effort I put into procuring Veritaserum, for she, and she alone, knows the full story of the best-kept secret of Albus Dumbledore's life. Now revealed for the first time, it calls into question everything that his admirers believed of Dumbledore: his supposed hatred of the Dark Arts, his opposition to the oppression of Muggles, even his devotion to his own family.

The very same summer that Dumbledore went home to Godric's Hollow, now an orphan and head of the family, Bathilda Bagshot agreed to accept into her home her great-nephew, Gellert Grindelwald.

The name of Grindelwald is justly famous: In a list of Most Dangerous Dark Wizards of All Time, he would miss out on the top spot only because You-Know-Who arrived, a generation later, to steal his crown. As Grindelwald never extended his campaign of terror to Britain, however, the details of his rise to power are not widely known here.

Educated at Durmstrang, a school famous even then for its unfortunate tolerance of the Dark Arts, Grindelwald showed himself quite as precociously brilliant as Dumbledore. Rather than channel his abilities into the attainment of awards and prizes, however, Gellert Grindelwald devoted himself to other pursuits. At sixteen years old, even Durmstrang felt it could no longer turn a blind eye to the twisted experiments of Gellert Grindelwald, and he was expelled.

Hitherto, all that has been known of Grindelwald's next movements is that he "traveled abroad for some months." It can now be revealed that Grindelwald chose to visit his great-aunt in Godric's Hollow, and that there, intensely shocking though it will be for many to hear it, he struck up a close friendship with none other than Albus Dumbledore.

"He seemed a charming boy to me," babbles Bathilda, "whatever he became later. Naturally I introduced him to poor Albus, who was missing the company of lads his own age. The boys took to each other at once."

They certainly did. Bathilda shows me a letter, kept by her, that Albus Dumbledore sent Gellert Grindelwald in the dead of night.

"Yes, even after they'd spent all day in discussion — both such brilliant young boys, they got on like a cauldron on fire — I'd sometimes hear an owl tapping at Gellert's bedroom window, delivering a letter from Albus! An idea would have struck him, and he had to let Gellert know immediately!"

And what ideas they were. Profoundly shocking though

Albus Dumbledore's fans will find it, here are the thoughts of their seventeen-year-old hero, as relayed to his new best friend. (A copy of the original letter may be seen on page 463.)

> *Gellert —*
>
> *Your point about Wizard dominance being* FOR THE MUGGLES' OWN GOOD *— this, I think, is the crucial point. Yes, we have been given power and yes, that power gives us the right to rule, but it also gives us responsibilities over the ruled. We must stress this point, it will be the foundation stone upon which we build. Where we are opposed, as we surely will be, this must be the basis of all our counterarguments. We seize control* FOR THE GREATER GOOD. *And from this it follows that where we meet resistance, we must use only the force that is necessary and no more. (This was your mistake at Durmstrang! But I do not complain, because if you had not been expelled, we would never have met.)*
>
> *Albus*

Astonished and appalled though his many admirers will be, this letter constitutes proof that Albus Dumbledore once dreamed of overthrowing the Statute of Secrecy and establishing Wizard rule over Muggles. What a blow for those who have always portrayed Dumbledore as the Muggle-borns' greatest champion! How hollow those speeches promoting Muggle rights seem in the light of this damning new evidence! How despicable does Albus Dumbledore appear, busy plotting his rise to power when he should have been mourning his mother and caring for his sister!

No doubt those determined to keep Dumbledore on his crumbling pedestal will bleat that he did not, after all, put his plans into action, that he must have suffered a change of heart, that he came to his senses. However, the truth seems altogether more shocking.

Barely two months into their great new friendship, Dumbledore and Grindelwald parted, never to see each other again until they met for their legendary duel (for more, see chapter 22). What caused this abrupt rupture? *Had* Dumbledore come to his senses? Had he told Grindelwald he wanted no more part in his plans? Alas, no.

"It was poor little Ariana dying, I think, that did it," says Bathilda. "It came as an awful shock. Gellert was there in the house when it happened, and he came back to my house all of a dither, told me he wanted to go home the next day. Terribly distressed, you know. So I arranged a Portkey and that was the last I saw of him.

"Albus was beside himself at Ariana's death. It was so dreadful for those two brothers. They had lost everybody except each other. No wonder tempers ran a little high. Aberforth blamed Albus, you know, as people will under these dreadful circumstances. But Aberforth always talked a little madly, poor boy. All the same, breaking Albus's nose at the funeral was not decent. It would have destroyed Kendra to see her sons fighting like that, across her daughter's body. A shame Gellert could not have stayed for the funeral. . . . He would have been a comfort to Albus, at least. . . ."

This dreadful coffin-side brawl, known only to those few who attended Ariana Dumbledore's funeral, raises several questions. Why exactly did Aberforth Dumbledore blame Albus for his sister's death? Was it, as "Batty" pretends, a mere effusion of grief? Or could there have been some more concrete reason for his fury? Grindelwald, expelled from Durmstrang for near-fatal attacks upon fellow students, fled the country hours after the girl's death, and Albus (out of shame or fear?) never saw him again, not until forced to do so by the pleas of the Wizarding world.

Neither Dumbledore nor Grindelwald ever seems to have referred to this brief boyhood friendship in later life. However, there can be no doubt that Dumbledore delayed, for some five years of turmoil, fatalities, and disappearances, his attack upon Gellert Grindelwald. Was it lingering affection for the man or fear of exposure as his once best friend that caused Dumbledore to hesitate? Was it only reluctantly that Dumbledore set out to capture the man he was once so delighted he had met?

And how did the mysterious Ariana die? Was she the inadvertent victim of some Dark rite? Did she stumble across something she ought not to have done, as the two young men sat practicing for their attempt at glory and domination? Is it possible that Ariana Dumbledore was the first person to die "for the greater good"?

The chapter ended here and Harry looked up. Hermione had reached the bottom of the page before him. She tugged the book out of Harry's hands, looking a little alarmed by his expression, and closed it without looking at it, as though hiding something indecent.

"Harry —"

But he shook his head. Some inner certainty had crashed down inside him; it was exactly as he had felt after Ron left. He had trusted Dumbledore, believed him the embodiment of goodness and wisdom. All was ashes: How much more could he lose? Ron, Dumbledore, the phoenix wand . . .

"Harry." She seemed to have heard his thoughts. "Listen to me. It — it doesn't make very nice reading —"

"Yeah, you could say that —"

"— but don't forget, Harry, this is Rita Skeeter writing."

"You did read that letter to Grindelwald, didn't you?"

"Yes, I — I did." She hesitated, looking upset, cradling her tea in her cold hands. "I think that's the worst bit. I know Bathilda thought it was all just talk, but 'For the Greater Good' became Grindelwald's slogan, his justification for all the atrocities he committed later. And . . . from that . . . it looks like Dumbledore gave him the idea. They say 'For the Greater Good' was even carved over the entrance to Nurmengard."

"What's Nurmengard?"

"The prison Grindelwald had built to hold his opponents. He ended up in there himself, once Dumbledore had caught him. Anyway, it's — it's an awful thought that Dumbledore's ideas helped Grindelwald rise to power. But on the other hand, even Rita can't pretend that they knew each other for more than a few months one summer when they were both really young, and —"

"I thought you'd say that," said Harry. He did not want to let his anger spill out at her, but it was hard to keep his voice steady. "I thought you'd say 'They were young.' They were the same age as we are now. And here we are, risking our lives to fight the Dark Arts, and there he was, in a huddle with his new best friend, plotting their rise to power over the Muggles."

His temper would not remain in check much longer: He stood up and walked around, trying to work some of it off.

"I'm not trying to defend what Dumbledore wrote," said Hermione. "All that 'right to rule' rubbish, it's 'Magic Is Might' all over again. But Harry, his mother had just died, he was stuck alone in the house —"

"Alone? He wasn't alone! He had his brother and sister for company, his Squib sister he was keeping locked up —"

"I don't believe it," said Hermione. She stood up too. "Whatever was wrong with that girl, I don't think she was a Squib. The Dumbledore we knew would never, ever have allowed —"

"The Dumbledore we thought we knew didn't want to conquer Muggles by force!" Harry shouted, his voice echoing across the empty hilltop, and several blackbirds rose into the air, squawking and spiraling against the pearly sky.

"He changed, Harry, he changed! It's as simple as that! Maybe he did believe these things when he was seventeen, but the whole of the rest of his life was devoted to fighting the Dark Arts! Dumbledore was the one who stopped Grindelwald, the one who always voted for Muggle protection and Muggle-born rights, who fought You-Know-Who from the start, and who died trying to bring him down!"

Rita's book lay on the ground between them, so that the face of Albus Dumbledore smiled dolefully at both.

"Harry, I'm sorry, but I think the real reason you're so angry is that Dumbledore never told you any of this himself."

"Maybe I am!" Harry bellowed, and he flung his arms over his head, hardly knowing whether he was trying to hold in his anger or protect himself from the weight of his own disillusionment. "Look what he asked from me, Hermione! Risk your life, Harry! And again! And again! And don't expect me to explain everything, just trust me blindly, trust that I know what I'm doing, trust me even though I don't trust you! Never the whole truth! Never!"

His voice cracked with the strain, and they stood looking at each other in the whiteness and the emptiness, and Harry felt they were as insignificant as insects beneath that wide sky.

"He loved you," Hermione whispered. "I know he loved you."

Harry dropped his arms.

"I don't know who he loved, Hermione, but it was never me. This isn't love, the mess he's left me in. He shared a damn sight more of what he was really thinking with Gellert Grindelwald than he ever shared with me."

Harry picked up Hermione's wand, which he had dropped in the snow, and sat back down in the entrance of the tent.

"Thanks for the tea. I'll finish the watch. You get back in the warm."

She hesitated, but recognized the dismissal. She picked up the book and then walked back past him into the tent, but as she did so, she brushed the top of his head lightly with her hand. He closed his eyes at her touch, and hated himself for wishing that what she said was true: that Dumbledore had really cared.

THE SILVER DOE

It was snowing by the time Hermione took over the watch at midnight. Harry's dreams were confused and disturbing: Nagini wove in and out of them, first through a gigantic, cracked ring, then through a wreath of Christmas roses. He woke repeatedly, panicky, convinced that somebody had called out to him in the distance, imagining that the wind whipping around the tent was footsteps or voices.

Finally he got up in the darkness and joined Hermione, who was huddled in the entrance to the tent reading *A History of Magic* by the light of her wand. The snow was still falling thickly, and she greeted with relief his suggestion of packing up early and moving on.

"We'll go somewhere more sheltered," she agreed, shivering as she pulled on a sweatshirt over her pajamas. "I kept thinking I could hear people moving outside. I even thought I saw somebody once or twice."

Harry paused in the act of pulling on a jumper and glanced at the silent, motionless Sneakoscope on the table.

"I'm sure I imagined it," said Hermione, looking nervous. "The snow in the dark, it plays tricks on your eyes. . . . But perhaps we ought to Disapparate under the Invisibility Cloak, just in case?"

Half an hour later, with the tent packed, Harry wearing the Horcrux, and Hermione clutching the beaded bag, they Disapparated. The usual tightness engulfed them; Harry's feet parted company with the snowy ground, then slammed hard onto what felt like frozen earth covered with leaves.

"Where are we?" he asked, peering around at a fresh mass of trees as Hermione opened the beaded bag and began tugging out tent poles.

"The Forest of Dean," she said. "I came camping here once with my mum and dad."

Here too snow lay on the trees all around and it was bitterly cold, but they were at least protected from the wind. They spent most of the day inside the tent, huddled for warmth around the useful bright blue flames that Hermione was so adept at producing, and which could be scooped up and carried around in a jar. Harry felt as though he was recuperating from some brief but severe illness, an impression reinforced by Hermione's solicitousness. That afternoon fresh flakes drifted down upon them, so that even their sheltered clearing had a fresh dusting of powdery snow.

After two nights of little sleep, Harry's senses seemed more alert than usual. Their escape from Godric's Hollow had been so narrow that Voldemort seemed somehow closer than before, more threatening. As darkness drew in again Harry refused Hermione's offer to keep watch and told her to go to bed.

Harry moved an old cushion into the tent mouth and sat down, wearing all the sweaters he owned but even so, still shivery. The darkness deepened with the passing hours until it was virtually impenetrable. He was on the point of taking out the Marauder's Map, so as to watch Ginny's dot for a while, before he remembered that it was the Christmas holidays and that she would be back at the Burrow.

Every tiny movement seemed magnified in the vastness of the forest. Harry knew that it must be full of living creatures, but he wished they would all remain still and silent so that he could separate their innocent scurryings and prowlings from noises that might proclaim other, sinister movements. He remembered the sound of a cloak slithering over dead leaves many years ago, and at once thought he heard it again before mentally shaking himself. Their protective enchantments had worked for weeks; why should they break now? And yet he could not throw off the feeling that something was different tonight.

Several times he jerked upright, his neck aching because he had fallen asleep, slumped at an awkward angle against the side of the tent. The night reached such a depth of velvety blackness that he might have been suspended in limbo between Disapparition and Apparition. He had just held up a hand in front of his face to see whether he could make out his fingers when it happened.

A bright silver light appeared right ahead of him, moving through the trees. Whatever the source, it was moving soundlessly. The light seemed simply to drift toward him.

He jumped to his feet, his voice frozen in his throat, and raised Hermione's wand. He screwed up his eyes as the light became blinding, the trees in front of it pitch-black in silhouette, and still the thing came closer. . . .

And then the source of the light stepped out from behind an oak. It was a silver-white doe, moon-bright and dazzling, picking her way over the ground, still silent, and leaving no hoofprints in the fine powdering of snow. She stepped toward him, her beautiful head with its wide, long-lashed eyes held high.

Harry stared at the creature, filled with wonder, not at her strangeness, but at her inexplicable familiarity. He felt that he had been waiting for her to come, but that he had forgotten, until this moment, that they had arranged to meet. His impulse to shout for Hermione, which had been so strong a moment ago, had gone. He knew, he would have staked his life on it, that she had come for him, and him alone.

They gazed at each other for several long moments and then she turned and walked away.

"No," he said, and his voice was cracked with lack of use. "Come back!"

She continued to step deliberately through the trees, and soon her brightness was striped by their thick black trunks. For one trembling second he hesitated. Caution murmured it could be a trick, a lure, a trap. But instinct, overwhelming instinct, told him that this was not Dark Magic. He set off in pursuit.

Snow crunched beneath his feet, but the doe made no noise as she passed through the trees, for she was nothing but light. Deeper and deeper into the forest she led him, and Harry walked quickly, sure that when she stopped, she would allow him to approach her properly. And then she would speak and the voice would tell him what he needed to know.

At last, she came to a halt. She turned her beautiful head toward him once more, and he broke into a run, a question burning in him, but as he opened his lips to ask it, she vanished.

Though the darkness had swallowed her whole, her burnished image was still imprinted on his retinas; it obscured his vision, brightening when he lowered his eyelids, disorienting him. Now fear came: Her presence had meant safety.

"Lumos!" he whispered, and the wand-tip ignited.

The imprint of the doe faded away with every blink of his eyes as he stood there, listening to the sounds of the forest, to distant crackles of twigs, soft swishes of snow. Was he about to be attacked? Had she enticed him into an ambush? Was he imagining that somebody stood beyond the reach of the wandlight, watching him?

He held the wand higher. Nobody ran out at him, no flash of green light burst from behind a tree. Why, then, had she led him to this spot?

Something gleamed in the light of the wand, and Harry spun about, but all that was there was a small, frozen pool, its cracked black surface glittering as he raised the wand higher to examine it.

He moved forward rather cautiously and looked down. The ice reflected his distorted shadow and the beam of wandlight, but deep below the thick, misty gray carapace, something else glinted. A great silver cross . . .

His heart skipped into his mouth: He dropped to his knees at the pool's edge and angled the wand so as to flood the bottom of the pool with as much light as possible. A glint of deep red . . . It was a sword with glittering rubies in its hilt. . . . The sword of Gryffindor was lying at the bottom of the forest pool.

Barely breathing, he stared down at it. How was this possible?

How could it have come to be lying in a forest pool, this close to the place where they were camping? Had some unknown magic drawn Hermione to this spot, or was the doe, which he had taken to be a Patronus, some kind of guardian of the pool? Or had the sword been put into the pool after they had arrived, precisely because they were here? In which case, where was the person who had wanted to pass it to Harry? Again he directed the wand at the surrounding trees and bushes, searching for a human outline, for the glint of an eye, but he could not see anyone there. All the same, a little more fear leavened his exhilaration as he returned his attention to the sword reposing upon the bottom of the frozen pool.

He pointed the wand at the silvery shape and murmured, *"Accio Sword."*

It did not stir. He had not expected it to. If it had been that easy, the sword would have lain on the ground for him to pick up, not in the depths of a frozen pool. He set off around the circle of ice, thinking hard about the last time the sword had delivered itself to him. He had been in terrible danger then, and had asked for help.

"Help," he murmured, but the sword remained upon the pool bottom, indifferent, motionless.

What was it, Harry asked himself (walking again), that Dumbledore had told him the last time he had retrieved the sword? *Only a true Gryffindor could have pulled* that *out of the hat.* And what were the qualities that defined a Gryffindor? A small voice inside Harry's head answered him: *Their daring, nerve, and chivalry set Gryffindors apart.*

Harry stopped walking and let out a long sigh, his smoky breath dispersing rapidly upon the frozen air. He knew what he had to do. If he was honest with himself, he had thought it might come to this from the moment he had spotted the sword through the ice.

He glanced around at the surrounding trees again, but was convinced now that nobody was going to attack him. They had had their chance as he walked alone through the forest, had had plenty of opportunity as he examined the pool. The only reason to delay at this point was because the immediate prospect was so deeply uninviting.

With fumbling fingers Harry started to remove his many layers of clothing. Where "chivalry" entered into this, he thought ruefully, he was not entirely sure, unless it counted as chivalrous that he was not calling for Hermione to do it in his stead.

An owl hooted somewhere as he stripped off, and he thought with a pang of Hedwig. He was shivering now, his teeth chattering horribly, and yet he continued to strip off until at last he stood there in his underwear, barefooted in the snow. He placed the pouch containing his wand, his mother's letter, the shard of Sirius's mirror, and the old Snitch on top of his clothes, then he pointed Hermione's wand at the ice.

"*Diffindo.*"

It cracked with a sound like a bullet in the silence: The surface of the pool broke and chunks of dark ice rocked on the ruffled water. As far as Harry could judge, it was not deep, but to retrieve the sword he would have to submerge himself completely.

Contemplating the task ahead would not make it easier or the water warmer. He stepped to the pool's edge and placed Hermione's wand on the ground, still lit. Then, trying not to imagine how much colder he was about to become or how violently he would soon be shivering, he jumped.

Every pore of his body screamed in protest: The very air in his lungs seemed to freeze solid as he was submerged to his shoulders in the frozen water. He could hardly breathe; trembling so violently the water lapped over the edges of the pool, he felt for the blade with his numb feet. He only wanted to dive once.

Harry put off the moment of total submersion from second to second, gasping and shaking, until he told himself that it must be done, gathered all his courage, and dived.

The cold was agony: It attacked him like fire. His brain itself seemed to have frozen as he pushed through the dark water to the bottom and reached out, groping for the sword. His fingers closed around the hilt; he pulled it upward.

Then something closed tight around his neck. He thought of water weeds, though nothing had brushed him as he dived, and raised his empty hand to free himself. It was not weed: The chain of the Horcrux had tightened and was slowly constricting his windpipe.

Harry kicked out wildly, trying to push himself back to the surface, but merely propelled himself into the rocky side of the pool. Thrashing, suffocating, he scrabbled at the strangling chain, his frozen fingers unable to loosen it, and now little lights were popping inside his head, and he was going to drown, there was nothing left, nothing he could do, and the arms that closed around his chest were surely Death's. . . .

Choking and retching, soaking and colder than he had ever been in his life, he came to facedown in the snow. Somewhere close by, another person was panting and coughing and staggering around. Hermione had come again, as she had come when the snake attacked. . . . Yet it did not sound like her, not with those deep coughs, not judging by the weight of the footsteps. . . .

Harry had no strength to lift his head and see his savior's identity. All he could do was raise a shaking hand to his throat and feel the place where the locket had cut tightly into his flesh. It was gone:

Someone had cut him free. Then a panting voice spoke from over his head.

"Are — you — *mental?*"

Nothing but the shock of hearing that voice could have given Harry the strength to get up. Shivering violently, he staggered to his feet. There before him stood Ron, fully dressed but drenched to the skin, his hair plastered to his face, the sword of Gryffindor in one hand and the Horcrux dangling from its broken chain in the other.

"Why the *hell*," panted Ron, holding up the Horcrux, which swung backward and forward on its shortened chain in some parody of hypnosis, "didn't you take this thing off before you dived?"

Harry could not answer. The silver doe was nothing, nothing compared with Ron's reappearance; he could not believe it. Shuddering with cold, he caught up the pile of clothes still lying at the water's edge and began to pull them on. As he dragged sweater after sweater over his head, Harry stared at Ron, half expecting him to have disappeared every time he lost sight of him, and yet he had to be real: He had just dived into the pool, he had saved Harry's life.

"It was y-you?" Harry said at last, his teeth chattering, his voice weaker than usual due to his near-strangulation.

"Well, yeah," said Ron, looking slightly confused.

"Y-you cast that doe?"

"What? No, of course not! I thought it was you doing it!"

"My Patronus is a stag."

"Oh yeah. I thought it looked different. No antlers."

Harry put Hagrid's pouch back around his neck, pulled on a final sweater, stooped to pick up Hermione's wand, and faced Ron again.

"How come you're here?"

Apparently Ron had hoped that this point would come up later, if at all.

"Well, I've — you know — I've come back. If —" He cleared his throat. "You know. You still want me."

There was a pause, in which the subject of Ron's departure seemed to rise like a wall between them. Yet he was here. He had returned. He had just saved Harry's life.

Ron looked down at his hands. He seemed momentarily surprised to see the things he was holding.

"Oh yeah, I got it out," he said, rather unnecessarily, holding up the sword for Harry's inspection. "That's why you jumped in, right?"

"Yeah," said Harry. "But I don't understand. How did you get here? How did you find us?"

"Long story," said Ron. "I've been looking for you for hours, it's a big forest, isn't it? And I was just thinking I'd have to kip under a tree and wait for morning when I saw that deer coming and you following."

"You didn't see anyone else?"

"No," said Ron. "I —"

But he hesitated, glancing at two trees growing close together some yards away.

"I did think I saw something move over there, but I was running to the pool at the time, because you'd gone in and you hadn't come up, so I wasn't going to make a detour to — hey!"

Harry was already hurrying to the place Ron had indicated. The two oaks grew close together; there was a gap of only a few inches between the trunks at eye level, an ideal place to see but not be seen.

The ground around the roots, however, was free of snow, and Harry could see no sign of footprints. He walked back to where Ron stood waiting, still holding the sword and the Horcrux.

"Anything there?" Ron asked.

"No," said Harry.

"So how did the sword get in that pool?"

"Whoever cast the Patronus must have put it there."

They both looked at the ornate silver sword, its rubied hilt glinting a little in the light from Hermione's wand.

"You reckon this is the real one?" asked Ron.

"One way to find out, isn't there?" said Harry.

The Horcrux was still swinging from Ron's hand. The locket was twitching slightly. Harry knew that the thing inside it was agitated again. It had sensed the presence of the sword and had tried to kill Harry rather than let him possess it. Now was not the time for long discussions; now was the moment to destroy the locket once and for all. Harry looked around, holding Hermione's wand high, and saw the place: a flattish rock lying in the shadow of a sycamore tree.

"Come here," he said, and he led the way, brushed snow from the rock's surface, and held out his hand for the Horcrux. When Ron offered the sword, however, Harry shook his head.

"No, you should do it."

"Me?" said Ron, looking shocked. "Why?"

"Because you got the sword out of the pool. I think it's supposed to be you."

He was not being kind or generous. As certainly as he had known that the doe was benign, he knew that Ron had to be the one to wield the sword. Dumbledore had at least taught Harry something about certain kinds of magic, of the incalculable power of certain acts.

"I'm going to open it," said Harry, "and you stab it. Straightaway, okay? Because whatever's in there will put up a fight. The bit of Riddle in the diary tried to kill me."

"How are you going to open it?" asked Ron. He looked terrified.

"I'm going to ask it to open, using Parseltongue," said Harry. The answer came so readily to his lips that he thought that he had always known it deep down: Perhaps it had taken his recent encounter with Nagini to make him realize it. He looked at the serpentine *S*, inlaid with glittering green stones: It was easy to visualize it as a minuscule snake, curled upon the cold rock.

"No!" said Ron. "No, don't open it! I'm serious!"

"Why not?" asked Harry. "Let's get rid of the damn thing, it's been months —"

"I can't, Harry, I'm serious — you do it —"

"But why?"

"Because that thing's bad for me!" said Ron, backing away from the locket on the rock. "I can't handle it! I'm not making excuses, Harry, for what I was like, but it affects me worse than it affected you and Hermione, it made me think stuff — stuff I was thinking anyway, but it made everything worse, I can't explain it, and then I'd take it off and I'd get my head on straight again, and then I'd have to put the effing thing back on — I can't do it, Harry!"

He had backed away, the sword dragging at his side, shaking his head.

"You can do it," said Harry, "you can! You've just got the sword, I know it's supposed to be you who uses it. Please, just get rid of it, Ron."

The sound of his name seemed to act like a stimulant. Ron swallowed, then, still breathing hard through his long nose, moved back toward the rock.

"Tell me when," he croaked.

"On three," said Harry, looking back down at the locket and narrowing his eyes, concentrating on the letter *S,* imagining a serpent, while the contents of the locket rattled like a trapped cockroach. It would have been easy to pity it, except that the cut around Harry's neck still burned.

"One . . . two . . . three . . . *open.*"

The last word came as a hiss and a snarl and the golden doors of the locket swung wide with a little click.

Behind both of the glass windows within blinked a living eye, dark and handsome as Tom Riddle's eyes had been before he turned them scarlet and slit-pupiled.

"Stab," said Harry, holding the locket steady on the rock.

Ron raised the sword in his shaking hands: The point dangled over the frantically swiveling eyes, and Harry gripped the locket tightly, bracing himself, already imagining blood pouring from the empty windows.

Then a voice hissed from out of the Horcrux.

"I have seen your heart, and it is mine."

"Don't listen to it!" Harry said harshly. "Stab it!"

"I have seen your dreams, Ronald Weasley, and I have seen your fears. All you desire is possible, but all that you dread is also possible. . . ."

"Stab!" shouted Harry; his voice echoed off the surrounding trees, the sword point trembled, and Ron gazed down into Riddle's eyes.

"Least loved, always, by the mother who craved a daughter . . . Least

loved, now, by the girl who prefers your friend . . . Second best, always, eternally overshadowed . . ."

"Ron, stab it now!" Harry bellowed: He could feel the locket quivering in his grip and was scared of what was coming. Ron raised the sword still higher, and as he did so, Riddle's eyes gleamed scarlet.

Out of the locket's two windows, out of the eyes, there bloomed, like two grotesque bubbles, the heads of Harry and Hermione, weirdly distorted.

Ron yelled in shock and backed away as the figures blossomed out of the locket, first chests, then waists, then legs, until they stood in the locket, side by side like trees with a common root, swaying over Ron and the real Harry, who had snatched his fingers away from the locket as it burned, suddenly, white-hot.

"Ron!" he shouted, but the Riddle-Harry was now speaking with Voldemort's voice and Ron was gazing, mesmerized, into its face.

"Why return? We were better without you, happier without you, glad of your absence. . . . We laughed at your stupidity, your cowardice, your presumption —"

"Presumption!" echoed the Riddle-Hermione, who was more beautiful and yet more terrible than the real Hermione: She swayed, cackling, before Ron, who looked horrified yet transfixed, the sword hanging pointlessly at his side. *"Who could look at you, who would ever look at you, beside Harry Potter? What have you ever done, compared with the Chosen One? What are you, compared with the Boy Who Lived?"*

"Ron, stab it, STAB IT!" Harry yelled, but Ron did not move: His eyes were wide, and the Riddle-Harry and the Riddle-Hermione were reflected in them, their hair swirling like flames, their eyes shining red, their voices lifted in an evil duet.

"Your mother confessed," sneered Riddle-Harry, while Riddle-Hermione jeered, *"that she would have preferred me as a son, would be glad to exchange . . ."*

"Who wouldn't prefer him, what woman would take you, you are nothing, nothing, nothing to him," crooned Riddle-Hermione, and she stretched like a snake and entwined herself around Riddle-Harry, wrapping him in a close embrace: Their lips met.

On the ground in front of them, Ron's face filled with anguish. He raised the sword high, his arms shaking.

"Do it, Ron!" Harry yelled.

Ron looked toward him, and Harry thought he saw a trace of scarlet in his eyes.

"Ron — ?"

The sword flashed, plunged: Harry threw himself out of the way, there was a clang of metal and a long, drawn-out scream. Harry whirled around, slipping in the snow, wand held ready to defend himself: but there was nothing to fight.

The monstrous versions of himself and Hermione were gone: There was only Ron, standing there with the sword held slackly in his hand, looking down at the shattered remains of the locket on the flat rock.

Slowly, Harry walked back to him, hardly knowing what to say or do. Ron was breathing heavily: His eyes were no longer red at all, but their normal blue; they were also wet.

Harry stooped, pretending he had not seen, and picked up the broken Horcrux. Ron had pierced the glass in both windows:

Riddle's eyes were gone, and the stained silk lining of the locket was smoking slightly. The thing that had lived in the Horcrux had vanished; torturing Ron had been its final act.

The sword clanged as Ron dropped it. He had sunk to his knees, his head in his arms. He was shaking, but not, Harry realized, from cold. Harry crammed the broken locket into his pocket, knelt down beside Ron, and placed a hand cautiously on his shoulder. He took it as a good sign that Ron did not throw it off.

"After you left," he said in a low voice, grateful for the fact that Ron's face was hidden, "she cried for a week. Probably longer, only she didn't want me to see. There were loads of nights when we never even spoke to each other. With you gone . . ."

He could not finish; it was only now that Ron was here again that Harry fully realized how much his absence had cost them.

"She's like my sister," he went on. "I love her like a sister and I reckon she feels the same way about me. It's always been like that. I thought you knew."

Ron did not respond, but turned his face away from Harry and wiped his nose noisily on his sleeve. Harry got to his feet again and walked to where Ron's enormous rucksack lay yards away, discarded as Ron had run toward the pool to save Harry from drowning. He hoisted it onto his own back and walked back to Ron, who clambered to his feet as Harry approached, eyes bloodshot but otherwise composed.

"I'm sorry," he said in a thick voice. "I'm sorry I left. I know I was a — a —"

He looked around at the darkness, as if hoping a bad enough word would swoop down upon him and claim him.

"You've sort of made up for it tonight," said Harry. "Getting the sword. Finishing off the Horcrux. Saving my life."

"That makes me sound a lot cooler than I was," Ron mumbled.

"Stuff like that always sounds cooler than it really was," said Harry. "I've been trying to tell you that for years."

Simultaneously they walked forward and hugged, Harry gripping the still-sopping back of Ron's jacket.

"And now," said Harry as they broke apart, "all we've got to do is find the tent again."

But it was not difficult. Though the walk through the dark forest with the doe had seemed lengthy, with Ron by his side the journey back seemed to take a surprisingly short time. Harry could not wait to wake Hermione, and it was with quickening excitement that he entered the tent, Ron lagging a little behind him.

It was gloriously warm after the pool and the forest, the only illumination the bluebell flames still shimmering in a bowl on the floor. Hermione was fast asleep, curled up under her blankets, and did not move until Harry had said her name several times.

"Hermione!"

She stirred, then sat up quickly, pushing her hair out of her face.

"What's wrong? Harry? Are you all right?"

"It's okay, everything's fine. More than fine. I'm great. There's someone here."

"What do you mean? Who — ?"

She saw Ron, who stood there holding the sword and dripping onto the threadbare carpet. Harry backed into a shadowy corner, slipped off Ron's rucksack, and attempted to blend in with the canvas.

Hermione slid out of her bunk and moved like a sleepwalker

toward Ron, her eyes upon his pale face. She stopped right in front of him, her lips slightly parted, her eyes wide. Ron gave a weak, hopeful smile and half raised his arms.

Hermione launched herself forward and started punching every inch of him that she could reach.

"Ouch — ow — gerroff! What the — ? Hermione — OW!"

"You — complete — *arse* — Ronald — Weasley!"

She punctuated every word with a blow: Ron backed away, shielding his head as Hermione advanced.

"You — crawl — back — here — after — weeks — and — weeks — oh, *where's my wand?*"

She looked as though ready to wrestle it out of Harry's hands and he reacted instinctively.

"Protego!"

The invisible shield erupted between Ron and Hermione: The force of it knocked her backward onto the floor. Spitting hair out of her mouth, she leapt up again.

"Hermione!" said Harry. "Calm —"

"I will not calm down!" she screamed. Never before had he seen her lose control like this; she looked quite demented. "Give me back my wand! *Give it back to me!*"

"Hermione, will you please —"

"Don't you tell me what to do, Harry Potter!" she screeched. "Don't you dare! Give it back now! And YOU!"

She was pointing at Ron in dire accusation: It was like a malediction, and Harry could not blame Ron for retreating several steps.

"I came running after you! I called you! I begged you to come back!"

"I know," Ron said, "Hermione, I'm sorry, I'm really —"

"Oh, you're *sorry*!"

She laughed, a high-pitched, out-of-control sound; Ron looked at Harry for help, but Harry merely grimaced his helplessness.

"You come back after weeks — *weeks* — and you think it's all going to be all right if you just say *sorry*?"

"Well, what else can I say?" Ron shouted, and Harry was glad that Ron was fighting back.

"Oh, I don't know!" yelled Hermione with awful sarcasm. "Rack your brains, Ron, that should only take a couple of seconds —"

"Hermione," interjected Harry, who considered this a low blow, "he just saved my —"

"I don't care!" she screamed. "I don't care what he's done! Weeks and weeks, we could have been *dead* for all he knew —"

"I knew you weren't dead!" bellowed Ron, drowning her voice for the first time, and approaching as close as he could with the Shield Charm between them. "Harry's all over the *Prophet*, all over the radio, they're looking for you everywhere, all these rumors and mental stories, I knew I'd hear straight off if you were dead, you don't know what it's been like —"

"What it's been like for *you*?"

Her voice was now so shrill only bats would be able to hear it soon, but she had reached a level of indignation that rendered her temporarily speechless, and Ron seized his opportunity.

"I wanted to come back the minute I'd Disapparated, but I walked straight into a gang of Snatchers, Hermione, and I couldn't go anywhere!"

"A gang of what?" asked Harry, as Hermione threw herself down into a chair with her arms and legs crossed so tightly it seemed unlikely that she would unravel them for several years.

"Snatchers," said Ron. "They're everywhere — gangs trying to earn gold by rounding up Muggle-borns and blood traitors, there's a reward from the Ministry for everyone captured. I was on my own and I look like I might be school age; they got really excited, thought I was a Muggle-born in hiding. I had to talk fast to get out of being dragged to the Ministry."

"What did you say to them?"

"Told them I was Stan Shunpike. First person I could think of."

"And they believed that?"

"They weren't the brightest. One of them was definitely part troll, the smell off him. . . ."

Ron glanced at Hermione, clearly hopeful she might soften at this small instance of humor, but her expression remained stony above her tightly knotted limbs.

"Anyway, they had a row about whether I was Stan or not. It was a bit pathetic to be honest, but there were still five of them and only one of me and they'd taken my wand. Then two of them got into a fight and while the others were distracted I managed to hit the one holding me in the stomach, grabbed his wand, Disarmed the bloke holding mine, and Disapparated. I didn't do it so well, Splinched myself again" — Ron held up his right hand to show two missing fingernails; Hermione raised her eyebrows coldly — "and I came out miles from where you were. By the time I got back to that bit of riverbank where we'd been . . . you'd gone."

"Gosh, what a gripping story," Hermione said in the lofty voice she adopted when wishing to wound. "You must have been simply terrified. Meanwhile we went to Godric's Hollow and, let's think, what happened there, Harry? Oh yes, You-Know-Who's snake turned up, it nearly killed both of us, and then You-Know-Who himself arrived and missed us by about a second."

"What?" Ron said, gaping from her to Harry, but Hermione ignored him.

"Imagine losing fingernails, Harry! That really puts our sufferings into perspective, doesn't it?"

"Hermione," said Harry quietly, "Ron just saved my life."

She appeared not to have heard him.

"One thing I would like to know, though," she said, fixing her eyes on a spot a foot over Ron's head. "How exactly did you find us tonight? That's important. Once we know, we'll be able to make sure we're not visited by anyone else we don't want to see."

Ron glared at her, then pulled a small silver object from his jeans pocket.

"This."

She had to look at Ron to see what he was showing them.

"The Deluminator?" she asked, so surprised she forgot to look cold and fierce.

"It doesn't just turn the lights on and off," said Ron. "I don't know how it works or why it happened then and not any other time, because I've been wanting to come back ever since I left. But I was listening to the radio really early on Christmas morning and I heard . . . I heard you."

He was looking at Hermione.

"You heard me on the radio?" she asked incredulously.

"No, I heard you coming out of my pocket. Your voice," he held up the Deluminator again, "came out of this."

"And what exactly did I say?" asked Hermione, her tone somewhere between skepticism and curiosity.

"My name. 'Ron.' And you said . . . something about a wand. . . ."

Hermione turned a fiery shade of scarlet. Harry remembered: It had been the first time Ron's name had been said aloud by either of them since the day he had left; Hermione had mentioned it when talking about repairing Harry's wand.

"So I took it out," Ron went on, looking at the Deluminator, "and it didn't seem different or anything, but I was sure I'd heard you. So I clicked it. And the light went out in my room, but another light appeared right outside the window."

Ron raised his empty hand and pointed in front of him, his eyes focused on something neither Harry nor Hermione could see.

"It was a ball of light, kind of pulsing, and bluish, like that light you get around a Portkey, you know?"

"Yeah," said Harry and Hermione together automatically.

"I knew this was it," said Ron. "I grabbed my stuff and packed it, then I put on my rucksack and went out into the garden.

"The little ball of light was hovering there, waiting for me, and when I came out it bobbed along a bit and I followed it behind the shed and then it . . . well, it went inside me."

"Sorry?" said Harry, sure he had not heard correctly.

"It sort of floated toward me," said Ron, illustrating the movement with his free index finger, "right to my chest, and then — it just went straight through. It was here," he touched a point close to his heart, "I could feel it, it was hot. And once it was inside me I knew what I was supposed to do, I knew it would take me where

I needed to go. So I Disapparated and came out on the side of a hill. There was snow everywhere. . . ."

"We were there," said Harry. "We spent two nights there, and the second night I kept thinking I could hear someone moving around in the dark and calling out!"

"Yeah, well, that would've been me," said Ron. "Your protective spells work, anyway, because I couldn't see you and I couldn't hear you. I was sure you were around, though, so in the end I got in my sleeping bag and waited for one of you to appear. I thought you'd have to show yourselves when you packed up the tent."

"No, actually," said Hermione. "We've been Disapparating under the Invisibility Cloak as an extra precaution. And we left really early, because, as Harry says, we'd heard somebody blundering around."

"Well, I stayed on that hill all day," said Ron. "I kept hoping you'd appear. But when it started to get dark I knew I must have missed you, so I clicked the Deluminator again, the blue light came out and went inside me, and I Disapparated and arrived here in these woods. I still couldn't see you, so I just had to hope one of you would show yourselves in the end — and Harry did. Well, I saw the doe first, obviously."

"You saw the what?" said Hermione sharply.

They explained what had happened, and as the story of the silver doe and the sword in the pool unfolded, Hermione frowned from one to the other of them, concentrating so hard she forgot to keep her limbs locked together.

"But it must have been a Patronus!" she said. "Couldn't you see who was casting it? Didn't you see anyone? And it led you to the sword! I can't believe this! Then what happened?"

Ron explained how he had watched Harry jump into the pool and had waited for him to resurface; how he had realized that something was wrong, dived in, and saved Harry, then returned for the sword. He got as far as the opening of the locket, then hesitated, and Harry cut in.

"— and Ron stabbed it with the sword."

"And . . . and it went? Just like that?" she whispered.

"Well, it — it screamed," said Harry with half a glance at Ron. "Here."

He threw the locket into her lap; gingerly she picked it up and examined its punctured windows.

Deciding that it was at last safe to do so, Harry removed the Shield Charm with a wave of Hermione's wand and turned to Ron.

"Did you just say you got away from the Snatchers with a spare wand?"

"What?" said Ron, who had been watching Hermione examining the locket. "Oh — oh yeah."

He tugged open a buckle on his rucksack and pulled a short, dark wand out of its pocket. "Here. I figured it's always handy to have a backup."

"You were right," said Harry, holding out his hand. "Mine's broken."

"You're kidding?" Ron said, but at that moment Hermione got to her feet, and he looked apprehensive again.

Hermione put the vanquished Horcrux into the beaded bag, then climbed back into her bed and settled down without another word.

Ron passed Harry the new wand.

"About the best you could hope for, I think," murmured Harry.

"Yeah," said Ron. "Could've been worse. Remember those birds she set on me?"

"I still haven't ruled it out," came Hermione's muffled voice from beneath her blankets, but Harry saw Ron smiling slightly as he pulled his maroon pajamas out of his rucksack.

XENOPHILIUS LOVEGOOD

Harry had not expected Hermione's anger to abate overnight, and was therefore unsurprised that she communicated mainly by dirty looks and pointed silences the next morning. Ron responded by maintaining an unnaturally somber demeanor in her presence as an outward sign of continuing remorse. In fact, when all three of them were together Harry felt like the only non-mourner at a poorly attended funeral. During those few moments he spent alone with Harry, however (collecting water and searching the undergrowth for mushrooms), Ron became shamelessly cheery.

"Someone helped us," he kept saying. "Someone sent that doe. Someone's on our side. One Horcrux down, mate!"

Bolstered by the destruction of the locket, they set to debating the possible locations of the other Horcruxes, and even though they had discussed the matter so often before, Harry felt optimistic, certain that more breakthroughs would succeed the first. Hermione's sulkiness could not mar his buoyant spirits: The sudden upswing in their fortunes, the appearance of the mysterious doe, the recovery of Gryffindor's sword, and above all, Ron's return, made Harry so happy that it was quite difficult to maintain a straight face.

Late in the afternoon he and Ron escaped Hermione's baleful presence again, and under the pretense of scouring the bare hedges for nonexistent blackberries, they continued their ongoing exchange of news. Harry had finally managed to tell Ron the whole story of his and Hermione's various wanderings, right up to the full story of what had happened at Godric's Hollow; Ron was now filling Harry in on everything he had discovered about the wider Wizarding world during his weeks away.

". . . and how did you find out about the Taboo?" he asked Harry after explaining the many desperate attempts of Muggle-borns to evade the Ministry.

"The what?"

"You and Hermione have stopped saying You-Know-Who's name!"

"Oh, yeah. Well, it's just a bad habit we've slipped into," said Harry. "But I haven't got a problem calling him V —"

"NO!" roared Ron, causing Harry to jump into the hedge and Hermione (nose buried in a book at the tent entrance) to scowl over at them. "Sorry," said Ron, wrenching Harry back out of the brambles, "but the name's been jinxed, Harry, that's how they track people! Using his name breaks protective enchantments, it causes some kind of magical disturbance — it's how they found us in Tottenham Court Road!"

"Because we used his *name*?"

"Exactly! You've got to give them credit, it makes sense. It was only people who were serious about standing up to him, like Dumbledore, who ever dared use it. Now they've put a Taboo on it, anyone who says it is trackable — quick-and-easy way to find Order members! They nearly got Kingsley —"

"You're kidding?"

"Yeah, a bunch of Death Eaters cornered him, Bill said, but he fought his way out. He's on the run now, just like us." Ron scratched his chin thoughtfully with the end of his wand. "You don't reckon Kingsley could have sent that doe?"

"His Patronus is a lynx, we saw it at the wedding, remember?"

"Oh yeah . . ."

They moved farther along the hedge, away from the tent and Hermione.

"Harry . . . you don't reckon it could've been Dumbledore?"

"Dumbledore what?"

Ron looked a little embarrassed, but said in a low voice, "Dumbledore . . . the doe? I mean," Ron was watching Harry out of the corners of his eyes, "he had the real sword last, didn't he?"

Harry did not laugh at Ron, because he understood too well the longing behind the question. The idea that Dumbledore had managed to come back to them, that he was watching over them, would have been inexpressibly comforting. He shook his head.

"Dumbledore's dead," he said. "I saw it happen, I saw the body. He's definitely gone. Anyway, his Patronus was a phoenix, not a doe."

"Patronuses can change, though, can't they?" said Ron. "Tonks's changed, didn't it?"

"Yeah, but if Dumbledore was alive, why wouldn't he show himself? Why wouldn't he just hand us the sword?"

"Search me," said Ron. "Same reason he didn't give it to you while he was alive? Same reason he left you an old Snitch and Hermione a book of kids' stories?"

"Which is what?" asked Harry, turning to look Ron full in the face, desperate for the answer.

"I dunno," said Ron. "Sometimes I've thought, when I've been a bit hacked off, he was having a laugh or — or he just wanted to make it more difficult. But I don't think so, not anymore. He knew what he was doing when he gave me the Deluminator, didn't he? He — well," Ron's ears turned bright red and he became engrossed in a tuft of grass at his feet, which he prodded with his toe, "he must've known I'd run out on you."

"No," Harry corrected him. "He must've known you'd always want to come back."

Ron looked grateful, but still awkward. Partly to change the subject, Harry said, "Speaking of Dumbledore, have you heard what Skeeter wrote about him?"

"Oh yeah," said Ron at once, "people are talking about it quite a lot. 'Course, if things were different, it'd be huge news, Dumbledore being pals with Grindelwald, but now it's just something to laugh about for people who didn't like Dumbledore, and a bit of a slap in the face for everyone who thought he was such a good bloke. I don't know that it's such a big deal, though. He was really young when they —"

"Our age," said Harry, just as he had retorted to Hermione, and something in his face seemed to decide Ron against pursuing the subject.

A large spider sat in the middle of a frosted web in the brambles. Harry took aim at it with the wand Ron had given him the previous night, which Hermione had since condescended to examine, and had decided was made of blackthorn.

"*Engorgio.*"

The spider gave a little shiver, bouncing slightly in the web. Harry tried again. This time the spider grew slightly larger.

"Stop that," said Ron sharply. "I'm sorry I said Dumbledore was young, okay?"

Harry had forgotten Ron's hatred of spiders.

"Sorry — *Reducio.*"

The spider did not shrink. Harry looked down at the blackthorn wand. Every minor spell he had cast with it so far that day had seemed less powerful than those he had produced with his phoenix wand. The new one felt intrusively unfamiliar, like having somebody else's hand sewn to the end of his arm.

"You just need to practice," said Hermione, who had approached them noiselessly from behind and had stood watching anxiously as Harry tried to enlarge and reduce the spider. "It's all a matter of confidence, Harry."

He knew why she wanted it to be all right: She still felt guilty about breaking his wand. He bit back the retort that sprang to his lips, that she could take the blackthorn wand if she thought it made no difference, and he would have hers instead. Keen for them all to be friends again, however, he agreed; but when Ron gave Hermione a tentative smile, she stalked off and vanished behind her book once more.

All three of them returned to the tent when darkness fell, and Harry took first watch. Sitting in the entrance, he tried to make the blackthorn wand levitate small stones at his feet; but his magic still seemed clumsier and less powerful than it had done before.

Hermione was lying on her bunk reading, while Ron, after many nervous glances up at her, had taken a small wooden wireless out of his rucksack and started to try and tune it.

"There's this one program," he told Harry in a low voice, "that tells the news like it really is. All the others are on You-Know-Who's side and are following the Ministry line, but this one . . . you wait till you hear it, it's great. Only they can't do it every night, they have to keep changing locations in case they're raided, and you need a password to tune in. . . . Trouble is, I missed the last one. . . ."

He drummed lightly on the top of the radio with his wand, muttering random words under his breath. He threw Hermione many covert glances, plainly fearing an angry outburst, but for all the notice she took of him he might not have been there. For ten minutes or so Ron tapped and muttered, Hermione turned the pages of her book, and Harry continued to practice with the blackthorn wand.

Finally Hermione climbed down from her bunk. Ron ceased his tapping at once.

"If it's annoying you, I'll stop!" he told Hermione nervously.

Hermione did not deign to respond, but approached Harry.

"We need to talk," she said.

He looked at the book still clutched in her hand. It was *The Life and Lies of Albus Dumbledore.*

"What?" he said apprehensively. It flew through his mind that there was a chapter on him in there; he was not sure he felt up to hearing Rita's version of his relationship with Dumbledore. Hermione's answer, however, was completely unexpected.

"I want to go and see Xenophilius Lovegood."

He stared at her.

"Sorry?"

"Xenophilius Lovegood. Luna's father. I want to go and talk to him!"

"Er — why?"

She took a deep breath, as though bracing herself, and said, "It's that mark, the mark in *Beedle the Bard*. Look at this!"

She thrust *The Life and Lies of Albus Dumbledore* under Harry's unwilling eyes and he saw a photograph of the original letter that Dumbledore had written Grindelwald, with Dumbledore's familiar thin, slanting handwriting. He hated seeing absolute proof that Dumbledore really had written those words, that they had not been Rita's invention.

"The signature," said Hermione. "Look at the signature, Harry!"

He obeyed. For a moment he had no idea what she was talking about, but, looking more closely with the aid of his lit wand, he saw that Dumbledore had replaced the *A* of Albus with a tiny version of the same triangular mark inscribed upon *The Tales of Beedle the Bard*.

"Er — what are you — ?" said Ron tentatively, but Hermione quelled him with a look and turned back to Harry.

"It keeps cropping up, doesn't it?" she said. "I know Viktor said it was Grindelwald's mark, but it was definitely on that old grave in Godric's Hollow, and the dates on the headstone were long before Grindelwald came along! And now this! Well, we can't ask Dumbledore or Grindelwald what it means — I don't even know whether Grindelwald's still alive — but we can ask Mr. Lovegood. He was wearing the symbol at the wedding. I'm sure this is important, Harry!"

Harry did not answer immediately. He looked into her intense, eager face and then out into the surrounding darkness, thinking.

After a long pause he said, "Hermione, we don't need another Godric's Hollow. We talked ourselves into going there, and —"

"But it keeps appearing, Harry! Dumbledore left me *The Tales of Beedle the Bard,* how do you know we're not supposed to find out about the sign?"

"Here we go again!" Harry felt slightly exasperated. "We keep trying to convince ourselves Dumbledore left us secret signs and clues —"

"The Deluminator turned out to be pretty useful," piped up Ron. "I think Hermione's right, I think we ought to go and see Lovegood."

Harry threw him a dark look. He was quite sure that Ron's support of Hermione had little to do with a desire to know the meaning of the triangular rune.

"It won't be like Godric's Hollow," Ron added, "Lovegood's on your side, Harry, *The Quibbler*'s been for you all along, it keeps telling everyone they've got to help you!"

"I'm sure this is important!" said Hermione earnestly.

"But don't you think if it was, Dumbledore would have told me about it before he died?"

"Maybe . . . maybe it's something you need to find out for yourself," said Hermione with a faint air of clutching at straws.

"Yeah," said Ron sycophantically, "that makes sense."

"No, it doesn't," snapped Hermione, "but I still think we ought to talk to Mr. Lovegood. A symbol that links Dumbledore, Grindelwald, and Godric's Hollow? Harry, I'm sure we ought to know about this!"

"I think we should vote on it," said Ron. "Those in favor of going to see Lovegood —"

His hand flew into the air before Hermione's. Her lips quivered suspiciously as she raised her own.

"Outvoted, Harry, sorry," said Ron, clapping him on the back.

"Fine," said Harry, half amused, half irritated. "Only, once we've seen Lovegood, let's try and look for some more Horcruxes, shall we? Where do the Lovegoods live, anyway? Do either of you know?"

"Yeah, they're not far from my place," said Ron. "I dunno exactly where, but Mum and Dad always point toward the hills whenever they mention them. Shouldn't be hard to find."

When Hermione had returned to her bunk, Harry lowered his voice.

"You only agreed to try and get back in her good books."

"All's fair in love and war," said Ron brightly, "and this is a bit of both. Cheer up, it's the Christmas holidays, Luna'll be home!"

They had an excellent view of the village of Ottery St. Catchpole from the breezy hillside to which they Disapparated next morning. From their high vantage point the village looked like a collection of toy houses in the great slanting shafts of sunlight stretching to earth in the breaks between clouds. They stood for a minute or two looking toward the Burrow, their hands shadowing their eyes, but all they could make out were the high hedges and trees of the orchard, which afforded the crooked little house protection from Muggle eyes.

"It's weird, being this near, but not going to visit," said Ron.

"Well, it's not like you haven't just seen them. You were there for Christmas," said Hermione coldly.

"I wasn't at the Burrow!" said Ron with an incredulous laugh. "Do you think I was going to go back there and tell them all I'd walked out on you? Yeah, Fred and George would've been great about it. And Ginny, she'd have been really understanding."

"But where have you been, then?" asked Hermione, surprised.

"Bill and Fleur's new place. Shell Cottage. Bill's always been decent to me. He — he wasn't impressed when he heard what I'd done, but he didn't go on about it. He knew I was really sorry. None of the rest of the family know I was there. Bill told Mum he and Fleur weren't going home for Christmas because they wanted to spend it alone. You know, first holiday after they were married. I don't think Fleur minded. You know how much she hates Celestina Warbeck."

Ron turned his back on the Burrow.

"Let's try up here," he said, leading the way over the top of the hill.

They walked for a few hours, Harry, at Hermione's insistence, hidden beneath the Invisibility Cloak. The cluster of low hills appeared to be uninhabited apart from one small cottage, which seemed deserted.

"Do you think it's theirs, and they've gone away for Christmas?" said Hermione, peering through the window at a neat little kitchen with geraniums on the windowsill. Ron snorted.

"Listen, I've got a feeling you'd be able to tell who lived there if you looked through the Lovegoods' window. Let's try the next lot of hills."

So they Disapparated a few miles farther north.

"Aha!" shouted Ron, as the wind whipped their hair and clothes. Ron was pointing upward, toward the top of the hill on which they had appeared, where a most strange-looking house rose vertically against the sky, a great black cylinder with a ghostly moon hanging behind it in the afternoon sky. "That's got to be Luna's house, who else would live in a place like that? It looks like a giant rook!"

"It's nothing like a bird," said Hermione, frowning at the tower.

"I was talking about a chess rook," said Ron. "A castle to you."

Ron's legs were the longest and he reached the top of the hill first. When Harry and Hermione caught up with him, panting and clutching stitches in their sides, they found him grinning broadly.

"It's theirs," said Ron. "Look."

Three hand-painted signs had been tacked to a broken-down gate. The first read,

THE QUIBBLER. EDITOR: X. LOVEGOOD

the second,

PICK YOUR OWN MISTLETOE

the third,

KEEP OFF THE DIRIGIBLE PLUMS

The gate creaked as they opened it. The zigzagging path leading to the front door was overgrown with a variety of odd plants, including a bush covered in the orange radishlike fruit Luna sometimes wore as earrings. Harry thought he recognized a Snargaluff and gave the wizened stump a wide berth. Two aged crab apple trees, bent with the wind, stripped of leaves but still heavy with berry-sized red fruits and bushy crowns of white-beaded mistletoe, stood sentinel on either side of the front door. A little owl with a slightly flattened, hawklike head peered down at them from one of the branches.

"You'd better take off the Invisibility Cloak, Harry," said Hermione. "It's you Mr. Lovegood wants to help, not us."

He did as she suggested, handing her the Cloak to stow in the beaded bag. She then rapped three times on the thick black door, which was studded with iron nails and bore a knocker shaped like an eagle.

Barely ten seconds passed, then the door was flung open and there stood Xenophilius Lovegood, barefoot and wearing what appeared to be a stained nightshirt. His long white candyfloss hair was dirty and unkempt. Xenophilius had been positively dapper at Bill and Fleur's wedding by comparison.

"What? What is it? Who are you? What do you want?" he cried in a high-pitched, querulous voice, looking first at Hermione, then at Ron, and finally at Harry, upon which his mouth fell open in a perfect, comical O.

"Hello, Mr. Lovegood," said Harry, holding out his hand. "I'm Harry, Harry Potter."

Xenophilius did not take Harry's hand, although the eye that was not pointing inward at his nose slid straight to the scar on Harry's forehead.

"Would it be okay if we came in?" asked Harry. "There's something we'd like to ask you."

"I . . . I'm not sure that's advisable," whispered Xenophilius. He swallowed and cast a quick look around the garden. "Rather a shock . . . My word . . . I . . . I'm afraid I don't really think I ought to —"

"It won't take long," said Harry, slightly disappointed by this less-than-warm welcome.

"I — oh, all right then. Come in, quickly. *Quickly!*"

They were barely over the threshold when Xenophilius slammed the door shut behind them. They were standing in the most peculiar kitchen Harry had ever seen. The room was perfectly circular, so that it felt like being inside a giant pepper pot. Everything was curved to fit the walls — the stove, the sink, and the cupboards — and all of it had been painted with flowers, insects, and birds in bright primary colors. Harry thought he recognized Luna's style: The effect, in such an enclosed space, was slightly overwhelming.

In the middle of the floor, a wrought-iron spiral staircase led to the upper levels. There was a great deal of clattering and banging coming from overhead: Harry wondered what Luna could be doing.

"You'd better come up," said Xenophilius, still looking extremely uncomfortable, and he led the way.

The room above seemed to be a combination of living room and workplace, and as such, was even more cluttered than the kitchen. Though much smaller and entirely round, the room somewhat resembled the Room of Requirement on the unforgettable occasion that it had transformed itself into a gigantic labyrinth comprised of centuries of hidden objects. There were piles upon piles of books and papers on every surface. Delicately made models of creatures Harry did not recognize, all flapping wings or snapping jaws, hung from the ceiling.

Luna was not there: The thing that was making such a racket was a wooden object covered in magically turning cogs and wheels. It looked like the bizarre offspring of a workbench and a set of old shelves, but after a moment Harry deduced that it was an old-fashioned printing press, due to the fact that it was churning out *Quibblers*.

"Excuse me," said Xenophilius, and he strode over to the machine, seized a grubby tablecloth from beneath an immense number of books and papers, which all tumbled onto the floor, and threw it over the press, somewhat muffling the loud bangs and clatters. He then faced Harry.

"Why have you come here?"

Before Harry could speak, however, Hermione let out a small cry of shock.

"Mr. Lovegood — what's that?"

She was pointing at an enormous, gray spiral horn, not unlike that of a unicorn, which had been mounted on the wall, protruding several feet into the room.

"It is the horn of a Crumple-Horned Snorkack," said Xenophilius.

"No it isn't!" said Hermione.

"Hermione," muttered Harry, embarrassed, "now's not the moment —"

"But Harry, it's an Erumpent horn! It's a Class B Tradeable Material and it's an extraordinarily dangerous thing to have in a house!"

"How d'you know it's an Erumpent horn?" asked Ron, edging away from the horn as fast as he could, given the extreme clutter of the room.

"There's a description in *Fantastic Beasts and Where to Find Them*! Mr. Lovegood, you need to get rid of it straightaway, don't you know it can explode at the slightest touch?"

"The Crumple-Horned Snorkack," said Xenophilius very clearly, a mulish look upon his face, "is a shy and highly magical creature, and its horn —"

"Mr. Lovegood, I recognize the grooved markings around the base, that's an Erumpent horn and it's incredibly dangerous — I don't know where you got it —"

"I bought it," said Xenophilius dogmatically, "two weeks ago, from a delightful young wizard who knew of my interest in the exquisite

Snorkack. A Christmas surprise for my Luna. Now," he said, turning to Harry, "why exactly have you come here, Mr. Potter?"

"We need some help," said Harry, before Hermione could start again.

"Ah," said Xenophilius. "Help. Hmm."

His good eye moved again to Harry's scar. He seemed simultaneously terrified and mesmerized.

"Yes. The thing is . . . helping Harry Potter . . . rather dangerous . . ."

"Aren't you the one who keeps telling everyone it's their first duty to help Harry?" said Ron. "In that magazine of yours?"

Xenophilius glanced behind him at the concealed printing press, still banging and clattering beneath the tablecloth.

"Er — yes, I have expressed that view. However —"

"That's for everyone else to do, not you personally?" said Ron.

Xenophilius did not answer. He kept swallowing, his eyes darting between the three of them. Harry had the impression that he was undergoing some painful internal struggle.

"Where's Luna?" asked Hermione. "Let's see what she thinks."

Xenophilius gulped. He seemed to be steeling himself. Finally he said in a shaky voice difficult to hear over the noise of the printing press, "Luna is down at the stream, fishing for Freshwater Plimpies. She . . . she will like to see you. I'll go and call her and then — yes, very well. I shall try to help you."

He disappeared down the spiral staircase and they heard the front door open and close. They looked at each other.

"Cowardly old wart," said Ron. "Luna's got ten times his guts."

"He's probably worried about what'll happen to them if the Death Eaters find out I was here," said Harry.

"Well, I agree with Ron," said Hermione. "Awful old hypocrite, telling everyone else to help you and trying to worm out of it himself. And for heaven's sake keep away from that horn."

Harry crossed to the window on the far side of the room. He could see a stream, a thin, glittering ribbon lying far below them at the base of the hill. They were very high up; a bird fluttered past the window as he stared in the direction of the Burrow, now invisible beyond another line of hills. Ginny was over there somewhere. They were closer to each other today than they had been since Bill and Fleur's wedding, but she could have no idea he was gazing toward her now, thinking of her. He supposed he ought to be glad of it; anyone he came into contact with was in danger, Xenophilius's attitude proved that.

He turned away from the window and his gaze fell upon another peculiar object standing upon the cluttered, curved sideboard: a stone bust of a beautiful but austere-looking witch wearing a most bizarre-looking headdress. Two objects that resembled golden ear trumpets curved out from the sides. A tiny pair of glittering blue wings was stuck to a leather strap that ran over the top of her head, while one of the orange radishes had been stuck to a second strap around her forehead.

"Look at this," said Harry.

"Fetching," said Ron. "Surprised he didn't wear that to the wedding."

They heard the front door close, and a moment later Xenophilius had climbed back up the spiral staircase into the room, his thin legs now encased in Wellington boots, bearing a tray of ill-assorted teacups and a steaming teapot.

"Ah, you have spotted my pet invention," he said, shoving the tray into Hermione's arms and joining Harry at the statue's side. "Modeled, fittingly enough, upon the head of the beautiful Rowena Ravenclaw. *'Wit beyond measure is man's greatest treasure!'"*

He indicated the objects like ear trumpets.

"These are the Wrackspurt siphons — to remove all sources of distraction from the thinker's immediate area. Here," he pointed out the tiny wings, "a billywig propeller, to induce an elevated frame of mind. Finally," he pointed to the orange radish, "the Dirigible Plum, so as to enhance the ability to accept the extraordinary."

Xenophilius strode back to the tea tray, which Hermione had managed to balance precariously on one of the cluttered side tables.

"May I offer you all an infusion of Gurdyroots?" said Xenophilius. "We make it ourselves." As he started to pour out the drink, which was as deeply purple as beetroot juice, he added, "Luna is down beyond Bottom Bridge, she is most excited that you are here. She ought not to be too long, she has caught nearly enough Plimpies to make soup for all of us. Do sit down and help yourselves to sugar.

"Now," he removed a tottering pile of papers from an armchair and sat down, his Wellingtoned legs crossed, "how may I help you, Mr. Potter?"

"Well," said Harry, glancing at Hermione, who nodded encouragingly, "it's about that symbol you were wearing around your neck at Bill and Fleur's wedding, Mr. Lovegood. We wondered what it meant."

Xenophilius raised his eyebrows.

"Are you referring to the sign of the Deathly Hallows?"

THE TALE OF THE THREE BROTHERS

Harry turned to look at Ron and Hermione. Neither of them seemed to have understood what Xenophilius had said either.

"The Deathly Hallows?"

"That's right," said Xenophilius. "You haven't heard of them? I'm not surprised. Very, very few wizards believe. Witness that knuckle-headed young man at your brother's wedding," he nodded at Ron, "who attacked me for sporting the symbol of a well-known Dark wizard! Such ignorance. There is nothing Dark about the Hallows — at least, not in that crude sense. One simply uses the symbol to reveal oneself to other believers, in the hope that they might help one with the Quest."

He stirred several lumps of sugar into his Gurdyroot infusion and drank some.

"I'm sorry," said Harry. "I still don't really understand."

To be polite, he took a sip from his cup too, and almost gagged:

The stuff was quite disgusting, as though someone had liquidized bogey-flavored Every Flavor Beans.

"Well, you see, believers seek the Deathly Hallows," said Xenophilius, smacking his lips in apparent appreciation of the Gurdyroot infusion.

"But what *are* the Deathly Hallows?" asked Hermione.

Xenophilius set aside his empty teacup.

"I assume that you are all familiar with 'The Tale of the Three Brothers'?"

Harry said, "No," but Ron and Hermione both said, "Yes." Xenophilius nodded gravely.

"Well, well, Mr. Potter, the whole thing starts with 'The Tale of the Three Brothers' . . . I have a copy somewhere. . . ."

He glanced vaguely around the room, at the piles of parchment and books, but Hermione said, "I've got a copy, Mr. Lovegood, I've got it right here."

And she pulled out *The Tales of Beedle the Bard* from the small, beaded bag.

"The original?" inquired Xenophilius sharply, and when she nodded, he said, "Well then, why don't you read it aloud? Much the best way to make sure we all understand."

"Er . . . all right," said Hermione nervously. She opened the book, and Harry saw that the symbol they were investigating headed the top of the page as she gave a little cough, and began to read.

"*'There were once three brothers who were traveling along a lonely, winding road at twilight —'*"

"Midnight, our mum always told us," said Ron, who had stretched out, arms behind his head, to listen. Hermione shot him a look of annoyance.

"Sorry, I just think it's a bit spookier if it's midnight!" said Ron.

"Yeah, because we really need a bit more fear in our lives," said Harry before he could stop himself. Xenophilius did not seem to be paying much attention, but was staring out of the window at the sky. "Go on, Hermione."

"*In time, the brothers reached a river too deep to wade through and too dangerous to swim across. However, these brothers were learned in the magical arts, and so they simply waved their wands and made a bridge appear across the treacherous water. They were halfway across it when they found their path blocked by a hooded figure.*

"*And Death spoke to them —*'"

"Sorry," interjected Harry, "but *Death* spoke to them?"

"It's a fairy tale, Harry!"

"Right, sorry. Go on."

"*And Death spoke to them. He was angry that he had been cheated out of three new victims, for travelers usually drowned in the river. But Death was cunning. He pretended to congratulate the three brothers upon their magic, and said that each had earned a prize for having been clever enough to evade him.*

"*So the oldest brother, who was a combative man, asked for a wand more powerful than any in existence: a wand that must always win duels for its owner, a wand worthy of a wizard who had conquered Death! So Death crossed to an elder tree on the banks of the river, fashioned a wand from a branch that hung there, and gave it to the oldest brother.*

"*Then the second brother, who was an arrogant man, decided that he wanted to humiliate Death still further, and asked for the power to recall others from Death. So Death picked up a stone from the riverbank and gave it to the second brother, and told him that the stone would have the power to bring back the dead.*

"'And then Death asked the third and youngest brother what he would like. The youngest brother was the humblest and also the wisest of the brothers, and he did not trust Death. So he asked for something that would enable him to go forth from that place without being followed by Death. And Death, most unwillingly, handed over his own Cloak of Invisibility.'"

"Death's got an Invisibility Cloak?" Harry interrupted again.

"So he can sneak up on people," said Ron. "Sometimes he gets bored of running at them, flapping his arms and shrieking . . . sorry, Hermione."

"'Then Death stood aside and allowed the three brothers to continue on their way, and they did so, talking with wonder of the adventure they had had, and admiring Death's gifts.

"'In due course the brothers separated, each for his own destination.

"'The first brother traveled on for a week or more, and reaching a distant village, sought out a fellow wizard with whom he had a quarrel. Naturally, with the Elder Wand as his weapon, he could not fail to win the duel that followed. Leaving his enemy dead upon the floor, the oldest brother proceeded to an inn, where he boasted loudly of the powerful wand he had snatched from Death himself, and of how it made him invincible.

"'That very night, another wizard crept upon the oldest brother as he lay, wine-sodden, upon his bed. The thief took the wand and, for good measure, slit the oldest brother's throat.

"'And so Death took the first brother for his own.

"'Meanwhile, the second brother journeyed to his own home, where he lived alone. Here he took out the stone that had the power to recall the dead, and turned it thrice in his hand. To his amazement and his

*delight, the figure of the girl he had once hoped to marry, before her
untimely death, appeared at once before him.*

*"'Yet she was sad and cold, separated from him as by a veil. Though
she had returned to the mortal world, she did not truly belong there and
suffered. Finally the second brother, driven mad with hopeless longing,
killed himself so as truly to join her.*

"'And so Death took the second brother for his own.

*"'But though Death searched for the third brother for many years, he
was never able to find him. It was only when he had attained a great
age that the youngest brother finally took off the Cloak of Invisibility
and gave it to his son. And then he greeted Death as an old friend, and
went with him gladly, and, equals, they departed this life.'"*

Hermione closed the book. It was a moment or two before Xenophilius seemed to realize that she had stopped reading, then he withdrew his gaze from the window and said, "Well, there you are."

"Sorry?" said Hermione, sounding confused.

"Those are the Deathly Hallows," said Xenophilius.

He picked up a quill from a packed table at his elbow, and pulled
a torn piece of parchment from between more books.

"The Elder Wand," he said, and he drew a straight vertical line
upon the parchment. "The Resurrection Stone," he said, and he added
a circle on top of the line. "The Cloak of Invisibility," he finished, enclosing both line and circle in a triangle, to make the symbol that so
intrigued Hermione. "Together," he said, "the Deathly Hallows."

"But there's no mention of the words 'Deathly Hallows' in the
story," said Hermione.

"Well, of course not," said Xenophilius, maddeningly smug. "That
is a children's tale, told to amuse rather than to instruct. Those of us

who understand these matters, however, recognize that the ancient story refers to three objects, or Hallows, which, if united, will make the possessor master of Death."

There was a short silence in which Xenophilius glanced out of the window. Already the sun was low in the sky.

"Luna ought to have enough Plimpies soon," he said quietly.

"When you say 'master of Death' —" said Ron.

"Master," said Xenophilius, waving an airy hand. "Conqueror. Vanquisher. Whichever term you prefer."

"But then . . . do you mean . . ." said Hermione slowly, and Harry could tell that she was trying to keep any trace of skepticism out of her voice, "that you believe these objects — these Hallows — actually exist?"

Xenophilius raised his eyebrows again.

"Well, of course."

"But," said Hermione, and Harry could hear her restraint starting to crack, "Mr. Lovegood, how can you *possibly* believe — ?"

"Luna has told me all about you, young lady," said Xenophilius. "You are, I gather, not unintelligent, but painfully limited. Narrow. Close-minded."

"Perhaps you ought to try on the hat, Hermione," said Ron, nodding toward the ludicrous headdress. His voice shook with the strain of not laughing.

"Mr. Lovegood," Hermione began again. "We all know that there are such things as Invisibility Cloaks. They are rare, but they exist. But —"

"Ah, but the Third Hallow is a *true* Cloak of Invisibility, Miss Granger! I mean to say, it is not a traveling cloak imbued with a Disillusionment Charm, or carrying a Bedazzling Hex, or else woven from Demiguise hair, which will hide one initially but fade with the years until it turns opaque. We are talking about a cloak that really and truly renders the wearer completely invisible, and endures eternally, giving constant and impenetrable concealment, no matter what spells are cast at it. How many cloaks have you ever seen like *that*, Miss Granger?"

Hermione opened her mouth to answer, then closed it again, looking more confused than ever. She, Harry, and Ron glanced at one another, and Harry knew that they were all thinking the same thing. It so happened that a cloak exactly like the one Xenophilius had just described was in the room with them at that very moment.

"Exactly," said Xenophilius, as if he had defeated them all in reasoned argument. "None of you have ever seen such a thing. The possessor would be immeasurably rich, would he not?"

He glanced out of the window again. The sky was now tinged with the faintest trace of pink.

"All right," said Hermione, disconcerted. "Say the Cloak existed . . . what about the stone, Mr. Lovegood? The thing you call the Resurrection Stone?"

"What of it?"

"Well, how can that be real?"

"Prove that it is not," said Xenophilius.

Hermione looked outraged.

"But that's — I'm sorry, but that's completely ridiculous! How can I *possibly* prove it doesn't exist? Do you expect me to get hold of — of all the pebbles in the world and test them? I mean, you could claim that *anything's* real if the only basis for believing in it is that nobody's *proved* it doesn't exist!"

"Yes, you could," said Xenophilius. "I am glad to see that you are opening your mind a little."

"So the Elder Wand," said Harry quickly, before Hermione could retort, "you think that exists too?"

"Oh, well, in that case there is endless evidence," said Xenophilius. "The Elder Wand is the Hallow that is most easily traced, because of the way in which it passes from hand to hand."

"Which is what?" asked Harry.

"Which is that the possessor of the wand must capture it from its previous owner, if he is to be truly master of it," said Xenophilius. "Surely you have heard of the way the wand came to Egbert the Egregious, after his slaughter of Emeric the Evil? Of how Godelot died in his own cellar after his son, Hereward, took the wand from him? Of the dreadful Loxias, who took the wand from Barnabas Deverill, whom he had killed? The bloody trail of the Elder Wand is splattered across the pages of Wizarding history."

Harry glanced at Hermione. She was frowning at Xenophilius, but she did not contradict him.

"So where do you think the Elder Wand is now?" asked Ron.

"Alas, who knows?" said Xenophilius, as he gazed out of the window. "Who knows where the Elder Wand lies hidden? The trail goes cold with Arcus and Livius. Who can say which of them really defeated Loxias, and which took the wand? And who can say who may have defeated them? History, alas, does not tell us."

There was a pause. Finally Hermione asked stiffly, "Mr. Lovegood, does the Peverell family have anything to do with the Deathly Hallows?"

Xenophilius looked taken aback as something shifted in Harry's memory, but he could not locate it. Peverell . . . he had heard that name before. . . .

"But you have been misleading me, young woman!" said Xenophilius, now sitting up much straighter in his chair and goggling at Hermione. "I thought you were new to the Hallows Quest! Many of us Questers believe that the Peverells have everything — *everything!* — to do with the Hallows!"

"Who are the Peverells?" asked Ron.

"That was the name on the grave with the mark on it, in Godric's Hollow," said Hermione, still watching Xenophilius. "Ignotus Peverell."

"Exactly!" said Xenophilius, his forefinger raised pedantically. "The sign of the Deathly Hallows on Ignotus's grave is conclusive proof!"

"Of what?" asked Ron.

"Why, that the three brothers in the story were actually the three Peverell brothers, Antioch, Cadmus, and Ignotus! That they were the original owners of the Hallows!"

With another glance at the window he got to his feet, picked up the tray, and headed for the spiral staircase.

"You will stay for dinner?" he called, as he vanished downstairs again. "Everybody always requests our recipe for Freshwater Plimpy soup."

"Probably to show the Poisoning Department at St. Mungo's," said Ron under his breath.

Harry waited until they could hear Xenophilius moving about in the kitchen downstairs before speaking.

"What do you think?" he asked Hermione.

"Oh, Harry," she said wearily, "it's a pile of utter rubbish. This can't be what the sign really means. This must just be his weird take on it. What a waste of time."

"I s'pose this *is* the man who brought us Crumple-Horned Snorkacks," said Ron.

"You don't believe it either?" Harry asked him.

"Nah, that story's just one of those things you tell kids to teach them lessons, isn't it? 'Don't go looking for trouble, don't pick fights, don't go messing around with stuff that's best left alone! Just keep your head down, mind your own business, and you'll be okay.' Come to think of it," Ron added, "maybe that story's why elder wands are supposed to be unlucky."

"What are you talking about?"

"One of those superstitions, isn't it? 'May-born witches will marry Muggles.' 'Jinx by twilight, undone by midnight.' 'Wand of elder, never prosper.' You must've heard them. My mum's full of them."

"Harry and I were raised by Muggles," Hermione reminded him. "We were taught different superstitions." She sighed deeply as a rather pungent smell drifted up from the kitchen. The one good thing about her exasperation with Xenophilius was that it seemed to have made her forget that she was annoyed at Ron. "I think you're right," she told him. "It's just a morality tale, it's obvious which gift is best, which one you'd choose —"

The three of them spoke at the same time; Hermione said, "the Cloak," Ron said, "the wand," and Harry said, "the stone."

They looked at each other, half surprised, half amused.

"You're *supposed* to say the Cloak," Ron told Hermione, "but you wouldn't need to be invisible if you had the wand. *An unbeatable wand,* Hermione, come on!"

"We've already got an Invisibility Cloak," said Harry.

"And it's helped us rather a lot, in case you hadn't noticed!" said Hermione. "Whereas the wand would be bound to attract trouble —"

"Only if you shouted about it," argued Ron. "Only if you were prat enough to go dancing around, waving it over your head, and singing, 'I've got an unbeatable wand, come and have a go if you think you're hard enough.' As long as you kept your trap shut —"

"Yes, but *could* you keep your trap shut?" said Hermione, looking skeptical. "You know, the only true thing he said to us was that there have been stories about extra-powerful wands for hundreds of years."

"There have?" asked Harry.

Hermione looked exasperated: The expression was so endearingly familiar that Harry and Ron grinned at each other.

"The Deathstick, the Wand of Destiny, they crop up under different names through the centuries, usually in the possession of some Dark wizard who's boasting about them. Professor Binns mentioned some of them, but — oh, it's all nonsense. Wands are only as powerful as the wizards who use them. Some wizards just like to boast that theirs are bigger and better than other people's."

"But how do you know," said Harry, "that those wands — the Deathstick and the Wand of Destiny — aren't the same wand, surfacing over the centuries under different names?"

"What, and they're all really the Elder Wand, made by Death?" said Ron.

Harry laughed: The strange idea that had occurred to him was, after all, ridiculous. His wand, he reminded himself, had been of holly, not elder, and it had been made by Ollivander, whatever it had done that night Voldemort had pursued him across the skies. And if it had been unbeatable, how could it have been broken?

"So why would you take the stone?" Ron asked him.

"Well, if you could bring people back, we could have Sirius . . . Mad-Eye . . . Dumbledore . . . my parents. . . ."

Neither Ron nor Hermione smiled.

"But according to Beedle the Bard, they wouldn't want to come back, would they?" said Harry, thinking about the tale they had just heard. "I don't suppose there have been loads of other stories about a stone that can raise the dead, have there?" he asked Hermione.

"No," she replied sadly. "I don't think anyone except Mr. Lovegood could kid themselves that's possible. Beedle probably took the idea from the Sorcerer's Stone; you know, instead of a stone to make you immortal, a stone to reverse death."

The smell from the kitchen was getting stronger: It was something like burning underpants. Harry wondered whether it would be possible to eat enough of whatever Xenophilius was cooking to spare his feelings.

"What about the Cloak, though?" said Ron slowly. "Don't you realize, he's right? I've got so used to Harry's Cloak and how good it is, I never stopped to think. I've never heard of one like Harry's. It's infallible. We've never been spotted under it —"

"Of course not — we're invisible when we're under it, Ron!"

"But all the stuff he said about other cloaks, and they're not exactly ten a Knut, you know, is true! It's never occurred to me before, but I've heard stuff about charms wearing off cloaks when they get old, or them being ripped apart by spells so they've got holes in.

Harry's was owned by his dad, so it's not exactly new, is it, but it's just . . . perfect!"

"Yes, all right, but Ron, the *stone* . . ."

As they argued in whispers, Harry moved around the room, only half listening. Reaching the spiral stair, he raised his eyes absently to the next level and was distracted at once. His own face was looking back at him from the ceiling of the room above.

After a moment's bewilderment, he realized that it was not a mirror, but a painting. Curious, he began to climb the stairs.

"Harry, what are you doing? I don't think you should look around when he's not here!"

But Harry had already reached the next level.

Luna had decorated her bedroom ceiling with five beautifully painted faces: Harry, Ron, Hermione, Ginny, and Neville. They were not moving as the portraits at Hogwarts moved, but there was a certain magic about them all the same: Harry thought they breathed. What appeared to be fine golden chains wove around the pictures, linking them together, but after examining them for a minute or so, Harry realized that the chains were actually one word, repeated a thousand times in golden ink: *friends . . . friends . . . friends . . .*

Harry felt a great rush of affection for Luna. He looked around the room. There was a large photograph beside the bed, of a young Luna and a woman who looked very like her. They were hugging. Luna looked rather better-groomed in this picture than Harry had ever seen her in life. The picture was dusty. This struck Harry as slightly odd. He stared around.

Something was wrong. The pale blue carpet was also thick with dust. There were no clothes in the wardrobe, whose doors stood ajar. The bed had a cold, unfriendly look, as though it had not been slept in for weeks. A single cobweb stretched over the nearest window, across a bloodred sky.

"What's wrong?" Hermione asked as Harry descended the staircase, but before he could respond, Xenophilius reached the top of the stairs from the kitchen, now holding a tray laden with bowls.

"Mr. Lovegood," said Harry. "Where's Luna?"

"Excuse me?"

"Where's Luna?"

Xenophilius halted on the top step.

"I — I've already told you. She is down at Bottom Bridge, fishing for Plimpies."

"So why have you only laid that tray for four?"

Xenophilius tried to speak, but no sound came out. The only noise was the continued chugging of the printing press, and a slight rattle from the tray as Xenophilius's hands shook.

"I don't think Luna's been here for weeks," said Harry. "Her clothes are gone, her bed hasn't been slept in. Where is she? And why do you keep looking out of the window?"

Xenophilius dropped the tray: The bowls bounced and smashed. Harry, Ron, and Hermione drew their wands: Xenophilius froze, his hand about to enter his pocket. At that moment the printing press gave a huge bang and numerous *Quibbler*s came streaming across the floor from underneath the tablecloth; the press fell silent at last.

Hermione stooped down and picked up one of the magazines, her wand still pointing at Mr. Lovegood.

"Harry, look at this."

He strode over to her as quickly as he could through all the clutter. The front of *The Quibbler* carried his own picture, emblazoned with the words UNDESIRABLE NUMBER ONE and captioned with the reward money.

"*The Quibbler*'s going for a new angle, then?" Harry asked coldly, his mind working very fast. "Is that what you were doing when you went into the garden, Mr. Lovegood? Sending an owl to the Ministry?"

Xenophilius licked his lips.

"They took my Luna," he whispered. "Because of what I've been writing. They took my Luna and I don't know where she is, what they've done to her. But they might give her back to me if I — if I —"

"Hand over Harry?" Hermione finished for him.

"No deal," said Ron flatly. "Get out of the way, we're leaving."

Xenophilius looked ghastly, a century old, his lips drawn back into a dreadful leer.

"They will be here at any moment. I must save Luna. I cannot lose Luna. You must not leave."

He spread his arms in front of the staircase, and Harry had a sudden vision of his mother doing the same thing in front of his crib.

"Don't make us hurt you," Harry said. "Get out of the way, Mr. Lovegood."

"HARRY!" Hermione screamed.

Figures on broomsticks were flying past the windows. As the three of them looked away from him, Xenophilius drew his wand. Harry realized their mistake just in time: He launched himself sideways, shoving Ron and Hermione out of harm's way as Xenophilius's Stunning Spell soared across the room and hit the Erumpent horn.

There was a colossal explosion. The sound of it seemed to blow the room apart: Fragments of wood and paper and rubble flew in all directions, along with an impenetrable cloud of thick white dust. Harry flew through the air, then crashed to the floor, unable to see as debris rained upon him, his arms over his head. He heard Hermione's scream, Ron's yell, and a series of sickening metallic thuds, which told him that Xenophilius had been blasted off his feet and fallen backward down the spiral stairs.

Half buried in rubble, Harry tried to raise himself: He could barely breathe or see for dust. Half of the ceiling had fallen in, and the end of Luna's bed was hanging through the hole. The bust of Rowena Ravenclaw lay beside him with half its face missing, fragments of torn parchment were floating through the air, and most of the printing press lay on its side, blocking the top of the staircase to the kitchen. Then another white shape moved close by, and Hermione, coated in dust like a second statue, pressed her finger to her lips.

The door downstairs crashed open.

"Didn't I tell you there was no need to hurry, Travers?" said a rough voice. "Didn't I tell you this nutter was just raving as usual?"

There was a bang and a scream of pain from Xenophilius.

"No . . . no . . . upstairs . . . Potter!"

"I told you last week, Lovegood, we weren't coming back for anything less than some solid information! Remember last week? When you wanted to swap your daughter for that stupid bleeding headdress? And the week before" — another bang, another squeal — "when you thought we'd give her back if you offered us proof there are Crumple" — *bang* — "Headed" — *bang* — "Snorkacks?"

"No — no — I beg you!" sobbed Xenophilius. "It really is Potter! Really!"

"And now it turns out you only called us here to try and blow us up!" roared the Death Eater, and there was a volley of bangs interspersed with squeals of agony from Xenophilius.

"The place looks like it's about to fall in, Selwyn," said a cool second voice, echoing up the mangled staircase. "The stairs are completely blocked. Could try clearing it? Might bring the place down."

"You lying piece of filth," shouted the wizard named Selwyn. "You've never seen Potter in your life, have you? Thought you'd lure us here to kill us, did you? And you think you'll get your girl back like this?"

"I swear . . . I swear . . . Potter's upstairs!"

"*Homenum revelio,*" said the voice at the foot of the stairs.

Harry heard Hermione gasp, and he had the odd sensation that something was swooping low over him, immersing his body in its shadow.

"There's someone up there all right, Selwyn," said the second man sharply.

"It's Potter, I tell you, it's Potter!" sobbed Xenophilius. "Please . . . please . . . give me Luna, just let me have Luna. . . ."

"You can have your little girl, Lovegood," said Selwyn, "if you get up those stairs and bring me down Harry Potter. But if this is a plot, if it's a trick, if you've got an accomplice waiting up there to ambush us, we'll see if we can spare a bit of your daughter for you to bury."

Xenophilius gave a wail of fear and despair. There were scurryings and scrapings: Xenophilius was trying to get through the debris on the stairs.

"Come on," Harry whispered, "we've got to get out of here."

He started to dig himself out under cover of all the noise Xenophilius was making on the staircase. Ron was buried deepest: Harry and Hermione climbed, as quietly as they could, over all the wreckage to where he lay, trying to prise a heavy chest of drawers off his legs. While Xenophilius's banging and scraping drew nearer and nearer, Hermione managed to free Ron with the use of a Hover Charm.

"All right," breathed Hermione, as the broken printing press blocking the top of the stairs began to tremble; Xenophilius was feet away from them. She was still white with dust. "Do you trust me, Harry?"

Harry nodded.

"Okay then," Hermione whispered, "give me the Invisibility Cloak. Ron, you're going to put it on."

"Me? But Harry —"

"*Please, Ron!* Harry, hold on tight to my hand, Ron, grab my shoulder."

Harry held out his left hand. Ron vanished beneath the Cloak. The printing press blocking the stairs was vibrating: Xenophilius was trying to shift it using a Hover Charm. Harry did not know what Hermione was waiting for.

"Hold tight," she whispered. "Hold tight . . . any second . . ."

Xenophilius's paper-white face appeared over the top of the sideboard.

"*Obliviate!*" cried Hermione, pointing her wand first into his face, then at the floor beneath them. "*Deprimo!*"

She had blasted a hole in the sitting room floor. They fell like boulders, Harry still holding onto her hand for dear life; there was a scream from below, and he glimpsed two men trying to get out of the way as vast quantities of rubble and broken furniture rained all around them from the shattered ceiling. Hermione twisted in midair and the thundering of the collapsing house rang in Harry's ears as she dragged him once more into darkness.

THE DEATHLY HALLOWS

Harry fell, panting, onto grass and scrambled up at once. They seemed to have landed in the corner of a field at dusk; Hermione was already running in a circle around them, waving her wand.

"*Protego Totalum . . . Salvio Hexia . . .*"

"That treacherous old bleeder!" Ron panted, emerging from beneath the Invisibility Cloak and throwing it to Harry. "Hermione, you're a genius, a total genius, I can't believe we got out of that!"

"*Cave Inimicum . . .* Didn't I *say* it was an Erumpent horn, didn't I tell him? And now his house has been blown apart!"

"Serves him right," said Ron, examining his torn jeans and the cuts to his legs. "What d'you reckon they'll do to him?"

"Oh, I hope they don't kill him!" groaned Hermione. "That's why I wanted the Death Eaters to get a glimpse of Harry before we left, so they knew Xenophilius hadn't been lying!"

"Why hide me, though?" asked Ron.

"You're supposed to be in bed with spattergroit, Ron! They've kidnapped Luna because her father supported Harry! What would happen to your family if they knew you're with him?"

"But what about *your* mum and dad?"

"They're in Australia," said Hermione. "They should be all right. They don't know anything."

"You're a genius," Ron repeated, looking awed.

"Yeah, you are, Hermione," agreed Harry fervently. "I don't know what we'd do without you."

She beamed, but became solemn at once.

"What about Luna?"

"Well, if they're telling the truth and she's still alive —" began Ron.

"Don't say that, don't say it!" squealed Hermione. "She must be alive, she must!"

"Then she'll be in Azkaban, I expect," said Ron. "Whether she survives the place, though . . . Loads don't. . . ."

"She will," said Harry. He could not bear to contemplate the alternative. "She's tough, Luna, much tougher than you'd think. She's probably teaching all the inmates about Wrackspurts and Nargles."

"I hope you're right," said Hermione. She passed a hand over her eyes. "I'd feel so sorry for Xenophilius if —"

"— if he hadn't just tried to sell us to the Death Eaters, yeah," said Ron.

They put up the tent and retreated inside it, where Ron made them tea. After their narrow escape, the chilly, musty old place felt like home: safe, familiar, and friendly.

"Oh, why did we go there?" groaned Hermione after a few minutes' silence. "Harry, you were right, it was Godric's Hollow all over again, a complete waste of time! The Deathly Hallows . . . such rubbish . . . although actually," a sudden thought seemed to have struck her, "he might have made it all up, mightn't he? He probably doesn't believe in the Deathly Hallows at all, he just wanted to keep us talking until the Death Eaters arrived!"

"I don't think so," said Ron. "It's a damn sight harder making stuff up when you're under stress than you'd think. I found that out when the Snatchers caught me. It was much easier pretending to be Stan, because I knew a bit about him, than inventing a whole new person. Old Lovegood was under loads of pressure, trying to make sure we stayed put. I reckon he told us the truth, or what he thinks is the truth, just to keep us talking."

"Well, I don't suppose it matters," sighed Hermione. "Even if he was being honest, I never heard such a lot of nonsense in all my life."

"Hang on, though," said Ron. "The Chamber of Secrets was supposed to be a myth, wasn't it?"

"But the Deathly Hallows *can't* exist, Ron!"

"You keep saying that, but one of them can," said Ron. "Harry's Invisibility Cloak —"

"'The Tale of the Three Brothers' is a story," said Hermione firmly. "A story about how humans are frightened of death. If surviving was as simple as hiding under the Invisibility Cloak, we'd have everything we need already!"

"I don't know. We could do with an unbeatable wand," said Harry, turning the blackthorn wand he so disliked over in his fingers.

"There's no such thing, Harry!"

"You said there have been loads of wands — the Deathstick and whatever they were called —"

"All right, even if you want to kid yourself the Elder Wand's real, what about the Resurrection Stone?" Her fingers sketched quotation marks around the name, and her tone dripped sarcasm. "No magic can raise the dead, and that's that!"

"When my wand connected with You-Know-Who's, it made my mum and dad appear . . . and Cedric . . ."

"But they weren't really back from the dead, were they?" said Hermione. "Those kinds of — of pale imitations aren't the same as truly bringing someone back to life."

"But she, the girl in the tale, didn't really come back, did she? The story says that once people are dead, they belong with the dead. But the second brother still got to see her and talk to her, didn't he? He even lived with her for a while. . . ."

He saw concern and something less easily definable in Hermione's expression. Then, as she glanced at Ron, Harry realized that it was fear: He had scared her with his talk of living with dead people.

"So that Peverell bloke who's buried in Godric's Hollow," he said hastily, trying to sound robustly sane, "you don't know anything about him, then?"

"No," she replied, looking relieved at the change of subject. "I looked him up after I saw the mark on his grave; if he'd been any-one famous or done anything important, I'm sure he'd be in one of our books. The only place I've managed to find the name 'Peverell' is *Nature's Nobility: A Wizarding Genealogy.* I borrowed it from Kreacher," she explained as Ron raised his eyebrows. "It lists the pure-blood families that are now extinct in the male line. Apparently the Peverells were one of the earliest families to vanish."

"'Extinct in the male line'?" repeated Ron.

"It means the name's died out," said Hermione, "centuries ago, in the case of the Peverells. They could still have descendants, though, they'd just be called something different."

And then it came to Harry in one shining piece, the memory that had stirred at the sound of the name "Peverell": a filthy old man brandishing an ugly ring in the face of a Ministry official, and he cried aloud, "Marvolo Gaunt!"

"Sorry?" said Ron and Hermione together.

"*Marvolo Gaunt!* You-Know-Who's grandfather! In the Pensieve! With Dumbledore! Marvolo Gaunt said he was descended from the Peverells!"

Ron and Hermione looked bewildered.

"The ring, the ring that became the Horcrux, Marvolo Gaunt said it had the Peverell coat of arms on it! I saw him waving it in the bloke from the Ministry's face, he nearly shoved it up his nose!"

"The Peverell coat of arms?" said Hermione sharply. "Could you see what it looked like?"

"Not really," said Harry, trying to remember. "There was nothing fancy on there, as far as I could see; maybe a few scratches. I only ever saw it really close up after it had been cracked open."

Harry saw Hermione's comprehension in the sudden widening of her eyes. Ron was looking from one to the other, astonished.

"Blimey . . . You reckon it was this sign again? The sign of the Hallows?"

"Why not?"said Harry excitedly. "Marvolo Gaunt was an ignorant old git who lived like a pig, all he cared about was his ancestry. If that ring had been passed down through the centuries, he might not have known what it really was. There were no books in that house, and trust me, he wasn't the type to read fairy tales to his kids. He'd have loved to think the scratches on the stone were a coat of arms, because as far as he was concerned, having pure blood made you practically royal."

"Yes . . . and that's all very interesting," said Hermione cautiously, "but Harry, if you're thinking what I think you're think —"

"Well, why not? *Why not?*" said Harry, abandoning caution. "It was a stone, wasn't it?" He looked at Ron for support. "What if it was the Resurrection Stone?"

Ron's mouth fell open.

"Blimey — but would it still work if Dumbledore broke — ?"

"Work? *Work?* Ron, it never worked! *There's no such thing as a Resurrection Stone!*"

Hermione had leapt to her feet, looking exasperated and angry. "Harry, you're trying to fit everything into the Hallows story —"

"*Fit everything in?*" he repeated. "Hermione, it fits of its own accord! I know the sign of the Deathly Hallows was on that stone! Gaunt said he was descended from the Peverells!"

"A minute ago you told us you never saw the mark on the stone properly!"

"Where d'you reckon the ring is now?" Ron asked Harry. "What did Dumbledore do with it after he broke it open?"

But Harry's imagination was racing ahead, far beyond Ron and Hermione's. . . .

Three objects, or Hallows, which, if united, will make the possessor master of Death . . . Master . . . Conqueror . . . Vanquisher . . . The last enemy that shall be destroyed is death. . . .

And he saw himself, possessor of the Hallows, facing Voldemort, whose Horcruxes were no match . . . *Neither can live while the other survives. . . .* Was this the answer? Hallows versus Horcruxes? Was there a way, after all, to ensure that he was the one who triumphed? If he were the master of the Deathly Hallows, would he be safe?

"Harry?"

But he scarcely heard Hermione: He had pulled out his Invisibility Cloak and was running it through his fingers, the cloth supple as water, light as air. He had never seen anything to equal it in his nearly seven years in the Wizarding world. The Cloak was exactly what Xenophilius had described: *A cloak that really and truly renders the wearer completely invisible, and endures eternally, giving constant and impenetrable concealment, no matter what spells are cast at it. . . .*

And then, with a gasp, he remembered —

"Dumbledore had my Cloak the night my parents died!"

His voice shook and he could feel the color in his face, but he did not care.

"My mum told Sirius that Dumbledore borrowed the Cloak! This is why! He wanted to examine it, because he thought it was the third Hallow! Ignotus Peverell is buried in Godric's Hollow. . . ." Harry was walking blindly around the tent, feeling as though great new vistas of truth were opening all around him. "He's my ancestor! I'm descended from the third brother! It all makes sense!"

He felt armed in certainty, in his belief in the Hallows, as if the mere idea of possessing them was giving him protection, and he felt joyous as he turned back to the other two.

"Harry," said Hermione again, but he was busy undoing the pouch around his neck, his fingers shaking hard.

"Read it," he told her, pushing his mother's letter into her hand. "Read it! Dumbledore had the Cloak, Hermione! Why else would he want it? He didn't need a Cloak, he could perform a Disillusionment

Charm so powerful that he made himself completely invisible without one!"

Something fell to the floor and rolled, glittering, under a chair: He had dislodged the Snitch when he pulled out the letter. He stooped to pick it up, and then the newly tapped spring of fabulous discoveries threw him another gift, and shock and wonder erupted inside him so that he shouted out.

"IT'S IN HERE! He left me the ring — it's in the Snitch!"

"You — you reckon?"

He could not understand why Ron looked taken aback. It was so obvious, so clear to Harry: Everything fit, everything. . . . His Cloak was the third Hallow, and when he discovered how to open the Snitch he would have the second, and then all he needed to do was find the first Hallow, the Elder Wand, and then —

But it was as though a curtain fell on a lit stage: All his excitement, all his hope and happiness were extinguished at a stroke, and he stood alone in the darkness, and the glorious spell was broken.

"That's what he's after."

The change in his voice made Ron and Hermione look even more scared.

"You-Know-Who's after the Elder Wand."

He turned his back on their strained, incredulous faces. He knew it was the truth. It all made sense. Voldemort was not seeking a new wand; he was seeking an old wand, a very old wand indeed. Harry walked to the entrance of the tent, forgetting about Ron and Hermione as he looked out into the night, thinking. . . .

Voldemort had been raised in a Muggle orphanage. Nobody could have told him *The Tales of Beedle the Bard* when he was a child, any more than Harry had heard them. Hardly any wizards believed in the Deathly Hallows. Was it likely that Voldemort knew about them?

Harry gazed into the darkness. . . . If Voldemort had known about the Deathly Hallows, surely he would have sought them, done anything to possess them: three objects that made the possessor master of Death? If he had known about the Deathly Hallows, he might not have needed Horcruxes in the first place. Didn't the simple fact that he had taken a Hallow, and turned it into a Horcrux, demonstrate that he did not know this last great Wizarding secret?

Which meant that Voldemort sought the Elder Wand without realizing its full power, without understanding that it was one of three . . . for the wand was the Hallow that could not be hidden, whose existence was best known. . . . *The bloody trail of the Elder Wand is splattered across the pages of Wizarding history . . .*

Harry watched the cloudy sky, curves of smoke-gray and silver sliding over the face of the white moon. He felt lightheaded with amazement at his discoveries.

He turned back into the tent. It was a shock to see Ron and Hermione standing exactly where he had left them, Hermione still holding Lily's letter, Ron at her side looking slightly anxious. Didn't they realize how far they had traveled in the last few minutes?

"This is it," Harry said, trying to bring them inside the glow of his own astonished certainty. "This explains everything. The Deathly Hallows are real, and I've got one — maybe two —"

He held up the Snitch.

"— and You-Know-Who's chasing the third, but he doesn't realize . . . he just thinks it's a powerful wand —"

"Harry," said Hermione, moving across to him and handing him back Lily's letter, "I'm sorry, but I think you've got this wrong, all wrong."

"But don't you see? It all fits —"

"No, it doesn't," she said. "It *doesn't,* Harry, you're just getting carried away. Please," she said as he started to speak, "please just answer me this: If the Deathly Hallows really existed, and Dumbledore knew about them, knew that the person who possessed all three of them would be master of Death — Harry, why wouldn't he have told you? Why?"

He had his answer ready.

"But you said it, Hermione! You've got to find out about them for yourself! It's a Quest!"

"But I only said that to try and persuade you to come to the Lovegoods'!" cried Hermione in exasperation. "I didn't really believe it!"

Harry took no notice.

"Dumbledore usually let me find out stuff for myself. He let me try my strength, take risks. This feels like the kind of thing he'd do."

"Harry, this isn't a game, this isn't practice! This is the real thing, and Dumbledore left you very clear instructions: Find and destroy the Horcruxes! That symbol doesn't mean anything, forget the Deathly Hallows, we can't afford to get sidetracked —"

Harry was barely listening to her. He was turning the Snitch over and over in his hands, half expecting it to break open, to reveal the Resurrection Stone, to prove to Hermione that he was right, that the Deathly Hallows were real.

She appealed to Ron.

"You don't believe in this, do you?"

Harry looked up. Ron hesitated.

"I dunno . . . I mean . . . bits of it sort of fit together," said Ron awkwardly. "But when you look at the whole thing . . ." He took a deep breath. "I think we're supposed to get rid of Horcruxes, Harry. That's what Dumbledore told us to do. Maybe . . . maybe we should forget about this Hallows business."

"Thank you, Ron," said Hermione. "I'll take first watch."

And she strode past Harry and sat down in the tent entrance, bringing the action to a fierce full stop.

But Harry hardly slept that night. The idea of the Deathly Hallows had taken possession of him, and he could not rest while agitating thoughts whirled through his mind: the wand, the stone, and the Cloak, if he could just possess them all. . . .

I open at the close. . . . But what was 'the close'? Why couldn't he have the stone now? If only he had the stone, he could ask Dumbledore these questions in person . . . and Harry murmured words to the Snitch in the darkness, trying everything, even Parseltongue, but the golden ball would not open. . . .

And the wand, the Elder Wand, where was that hidden? Where was Voldemort searching now? Harry wished his scar would burn and show him Voldemort's thoughts, because for the first time ever, he and Voldemort were united in wanting the very same thing. . . . Hermione would not like that idea, of course. . . . But then, she did not believe . . . Xenophilius had been right, in a way . . . *Limited. Narrow. Close-minded.* The truth was that she was scared of the idea of the Deathly Hallows, especially of the Resurrection Stone . . . and Harry pressed his mouth again to the Snitch, kissing it, nearly swallowing it, but the cold metal did not yield. . . .

It was nearly dawn when he remembered Luna, alone in a cell in Azkaban, surrounded by dementors, and he suddenly felt ashamed of himself. He had forgotten all about her in his feverish contemplation of the Hallows. If only they could rescue her; but dementors in those numbers would be virtually unassailable. Now he came to think about it, he had not yet tried casting a Patronus with the blackthorn wand. . . . He must try that in the morning. . . .

If only there was a way of getting a better wand . . .

And desire for the Elder Wand, the Deathstick, unbeatable, invincible, swallowed him once more. . . .

They packed up the tent next morning and moved on through a dreary shower of rain. The downpour pursued them to the coast, where they pitched the tent that night, and persisted through the whole week, through sodden landscapes that Harry found bleak and depressing. He could think only of the Deathly Hallows. It was as though a flame had been lit inside him that nothing, not Hermione's flat disbelief nor Ron's persistent doubts, could extinguish. And yet the fiercer the longing for the Hallows burned inside him, the less joyful it made him. He blamed Ron and Hermione: Their determined indifference was as bad as the relentless rain for dampening his spirits, but neither could erode his certainty, which remained absolute. Harry's belief in and longing for the Hallows consumed him so much that he felt quite isolated from the other two and their obsession with the Horcruxes.

"Obsession?" said Hermione in a low fierce voice, when Harry was careless enough to use the word one evening, after Hermione had told him off for his lack of interest in locating more Horcruxes. "We're not the ones with an obsession, Harry! We're the ones trying to do what Dumbledore wanted us to do!"

But he was impervious to the veiled criticism. Dumbledore had left the sign of the Hallows for Hermione to decipher, and he had also, Harry remained convinced of it, left the Resurrection Stone hidden in the golden Snitch. *Neither can live while the other survives. . . . master of Death* . . . Why didn't Ron and Hermione understand?

"*'The last enemy that shall be destroyed is death,'*" Harry quoted calmly.

"I thought it was You-Know-Who we were supposed to be fighting?" Hermione retorted, and Harry gave up on her.

Even the mystery of the silver doe, which the other two insisted on discussing, seemed less important to Harry now, a vaguely interesting sideshow. The only other thing that mattered to him was that his scar had begun to prickle again, although he did all he could to hide this fact from the other two. He sought solitude whenever it happened, but was disappointed by what he saw. The visions he and Voldemort were sharing had changed in quality; they had become blurred, shifting as though they were moving in and out of focus. Harry was just able to make out the indistinct features of an object that looked like a skull, and something like a mountain that was more shadow than substance. Used to images sharp as reality, Harry was disconcerted by the change. He was worried that the connection between himself and Voldemort had been damaged, a connection that he both feared and, whatever he had told Hermione, prized. Somehow Harry connected these unsatisfying, vague images with the destruction of his wand, as if it was the blackthorn wand's fault that he could no longer see into Voldemort's mind as well as before.

As the weeks crept on, Harry could not help but notice, even through his new self-absorption, that Ron seemed to be taking charge. Perhaps because he was determined to make up for having walked out on them, perhaps because Harry's descent into listlessness galvanized his dormant leadership qualities, Ron was the one now encouraging and exhorting the other two into action.

"Three Horcruxes left," he kept saying. "We need a plan of action, come on! Where haven't we looked? Let's go through it again. The orphanage . . ."

Diagon Alley, Hogwarts, the Riddle House, Borgin and Burkes, Albania, every place that they knew Tom Riddle had ever lived or worked, visited or murdered, Ron and Hermione raked over them again, Harry joining in only to stop Hermione pestering him. He would have been happy to sit alone in silence, trying to read Voldemort's thoughts, to find out more about the Elder Wand, but Ron insisted on journeying to ever more unlikely places simply, Harry was aware, to keep them moving.

"You never know," was Ron's constant refrain. "Upper Flagley is a Wizarding village, he might've wanted to live there. Let's go and have a poke around."

These frequent forays into Wizarding territory brought them within occasional sight of Snatchers.

"Some of them are supposed to be as bad as Death Eaters," said Ron. "The lot that got me were a bit pathetic, but Bill reckons some of them are really dangerous. They said on *Potterwatch* —"

"On what?" said Harry.

"*Potterwatch,* didn't I tell you that's what it was called? The program I keep trying to get on the radio, the only one that tells the truth about what's going on! Nearly all the programs are following You-Know-Who's line, all except *Potterwatch.* I really want you to hear it, but it's tricky tuning in. . . ."

Ron spent evening after evening using his wand to beat out various rhythms on top of the wireless while the dials whirled. Occasionally they would catch snatches of advice on how to treat dragon pox, and once a few bars of "A Cauldron Full of Hot Strong Love." While he tapped, Ron continued to try to hit on the correct password, muttering strings of random words under his breath.

"They're normally something to do with the Order," he told them. "Bill had a real knack for guessing them. I'm bound to get one in the end. . . ."

But not until March did luck favor Ron at last. Harry was sitting in the tent entrance, on guard duty, staring idly at a clump of grape hyacinths that had forced their way through the chilly ground, when Ron shouted excitedly from inside the tent.

"I've got it, I've got it! Password was 'Albus'! Get in here, Harry!"

Roused for the first time in days from his contemplation of the Deathly Hallows, Harry hurried back inside the tent to find Ron and Hermione kneeling on the floor beside the little radio. Hermione, who had been polishing the sword of Gryffindor just for something to do, was sitting open-mouthed, staring at the tiny speaker, from which a most familiar voice was issuing.

". . . apologize for our temporary absence from the airwaves, which was due to a number of house calls in our area by those charming Death Eaters."

"But that's Lee Jordan!" said Hermione.

"I know!" beamed Ron. "Cool, eh?"

". . . now found ourselves another secure location," Lee was saying, "and I'm pleased to tell you that two of our regular contributors have joined me here this evening. Evening, boys!"

"Hi."

"Evening, River."

"'River,' that's Lee," Ron explained. "They've all got code names, but you can usually tell —"

"Shh!" said Hermione.

"But before we hear from Royal and Romulus," Lee went on, "let's take a moment to report those deaths that the *Wizarding Wireless Network News* and *Daily Prophet* don't think important enough to mention. It is with great regret that we inform our listeners of the murders of Ted Tonks and Dirk Cresswell."

Harry felt a sick, swooping in his belly. He, Ron, and Hermione gazed at one another in horror.

"A goblin by the name of Gornuk was also killed. It is believed that Muggle-born Dean Thomas and a second goblin, both believed to have been traveling with Tonks, Cresswell, and Gornuk, may have escaped. If Dean is listening, or if anyone has any knowledge of his whereabouts, his parents and sisters are desperate for news.

"Meanwhile, in Gaddley, a Muggle family of five has been found dead in their home. Muggle authorities are attributing the deaths to a gas leak, but members of the Order of the Phoenix inform me that it was the Killing Curse — more evidence, as if it were needed, of the fact that Muggle slaughter is becoming little more than a recreational sport under the new regime.

"Finally, we regret to inform our listeners that the remains of Bathilda Bagshot have been discovered in Godric's Hollow. The evidence is that she died several months ago. The Order of the Phoenix informs us that her body showed unmistakable signs of injuries inflicted by Dark Magic.

"Listeners, I'd like to invite you now to join us in a minute's silence in memory of Ted Tonks, Dirk Cresswell, Bathilda Bagshot, Gornuk, and the unnamed, but no less regretted, Muggles murdered by the Death Eaters."

Silence fell, and Harry, Ron, and Hermione did not speak. Half of Harry yearned to hear more, half of him was afraid of what might come next. It was the first time he had felt fully connected to the outside world for a long time.

"Thank you," said Lee's voice. "And now we turn to regular contributor Royal, for an update on how the new Wizarding order is affecting the Muggle world."

"Thanks, River," said an unmistakable voice, deep, measured, reassuring.

"Kingsley!" burst out Ron.

"We know!" said Hermione, hushing him.

"Muggles remain ignorant of the source of their suffering as they continue to sustain heavy casualties," said Kingsley. "However, we continue to hear truly inspirational stories of wizards and witches risking their own safety to protect Muggle friends and neighbors, often without the Muggles' knowledge. I'd like to appeal to all our listeners to emulate their example, perhaps by casting a protective charm over any Muggle dwellings in your street. Many lives could be saved if such simple measures are taken."

"And what would you say, Royal, to those listeners who reply that in these dangerous times, it should be 'Wizards first'?" asked Lee.

"I'd say that it's one short step from 'Wizards first' to 'Purebloods first,' and then to 'Death Eaters,'" replied Kingsley. "We're all human, aren't we? Every human life is worth the same, and worth saving."

"Excellently put, Royal, and you've got my vote for Minister of

Magic if ever we get out of this mess," said Lee. "And now, over to Romulus for our popular feature 'Pals of Potter.'"

"Thanks, River," said another very familiar voice; Ron started to speak, but Hermione forestalled him in a whisper.

"We know it's Lupin!"

"Romulus, do you maintain, as you have every time you've appeared on our program, that Harry Potter is still alive?"

"I do," said Lupin firmly. "There is no doubt at all in my mind that his death would be proclaimed as widely as possible by the Death Eaters if it had happened, because it would strike a deadly blow at the morale of those resisting the new regime. 'The Boy Who Lived' remains a symbol of everything for which we are fighting: the triumph of good, the power of innocence, the need to keep resisting."

A mixture of gratitude and shame welled up in Harry. Had Lupin forgiven him, then, for the terrible things he had said when they had last met?

"And what would you say to Harry if you knew he was listening, Romulus?"

"I'd tell him we're all with him in spirit," said Lupin, then hesitated slightly. "And I'd tell him to follow his instincts, which are good and nearly always right."

Harry looked at Hermione, whose eyes were full of tears.

"Nearly always right," she repeated.

"Oh, didn't I tell you?" said Ron in surprise. "Bill told me Lupin's living with Tonks again! And apparently she's getting pretty big too. . . ."

" . . . and our usual update on those friends of Harry Potter's who are suffering for their allegiance?" Lee was saying.

"Well, as regular listeners will know, several of the more outspoken supporters of Harry Potter have now been imprisoned, including Xenophilius Lovegood, erstwhile editor of *The Quibbler*," said Lupin.

"At least he's still alive!" muttered Ron.

"We have also heard within the last few hours that Rubeus Hagrid" — all three of them gasped, and so nearly missed the rest of the sentence — "well-known gamekeeper at Hogwarts School, has narrowly escaped arrest within the grounds of Hogwarts, where he is rumored to have hosted a 'Support Harry Potter' party in his house. However, Hagrid was not taken into custody, and is, we believe, on the run."

"I suppose it helps, when escaping from Death Eaters, if you've got a sixteen-foot-high half brother?" asked Lee.

"It would tend to give you an edge," agreed Lupin gravely. "May I just add that while we here at *Potterwatch* applaud Hagrid's spirit, we would urge even the most devoted of Harry's supporters against following Hagrid's lead. 'Support Harry Potter' parties are unwise in the present climate."

"Indeed they are, Romulus," said Lee, "so we suggest that you continue to show your devotion to the man with the lightning scar by listening to *Potterwatch*! And now let's move to news concerning the wizard who is proving just as elusive as Harry Potter. We like to refer to him as the Chief Death Eater, and here to give his views on some of the more insane rumors circulating about him, I'd like to introduce a new correspondent: Rodent."

"*'Rodent'?*" said yet another familiar voice, and Harry, Ron, and Hermione cried out together:

"Fred!"

"No — is it George?"

"It's Fred, I think," said Ron, leaning in closer, as whichever twin it was said,

"I'm not being 'Rodent,' no way, I told you I wanted to be 'Rapier'!"

"Oh, all right then. 'Rapier,' could you please give us your take on the various stories we've been hearing about the Chief Death Eater?"

"Yes, River, I can," said Fred. "As our listeners will know, unless they've taken refuge at the bottom of a garden pond or somewhere similar, You-Know-Who's strategy of remaining in the shadows is creating a nice little climate of panic. Mind you, if all the alleged sightings of him are genuine, we must have a good nineteen You-Know-Whos running around the place."

"Which suits him, of course," said Kingsley. "The air of mystery is creating more terror than actually showing himself."

"Agreed," said Fred. "So, people, let's try and calm down a bit. Things are bad enough without inventing stuff as well. For instance, this new idea that You-Know-Who can kill with a single glance from his eyes. That's a *basilisk,* listeners. One simple test: Check whether the thing that's glaring at you has got legs. If it has, it's safe to look into its eyes, although if it really is You-Know-Who, that's still likely to be the last thing you ever do."

For the first time in weeks and weeks, Harry was laughing: He could feel the weight of tension leaving him.

"And the rumors that he keeps being sighted abroad?" asked Lee.

"Well, who wouldn't want a nice little holiday after all the hard work he's been putting in?" asked Fred. "Point is, people, don't get lulled into a false sense of security, thinking he's out of the country. Maybe he is, maybe he isn't, but the fact remains he can move faster than Severus Snape confronted with shampoo when he wants to, so don't count on him being a long way away if you're planning on taking any risks. I never thought I'd hear myself say it, but safety first!"

"Thank you very much for those wise words, Rapier," said Lee. "Listeners, that brings us to the end of another *Potterwatch*. We don't know when it will be possible to broadcast again, but you can be sure we shall be back. Keep twiddling those dials: The next password will be 'Mad-Eye.' Keep each other safe: Keep faith. Good night."

The radio's dial twirled and the lights behind the tuning panel went out. Harry, Ron, and Hermione were still beaming. Hearing familiar, friendly voices was an extraordinary tonic; Harry had become so used to their isolation he had nearly forgotten that other people were resisting Voldemort. It was like waking from a long sleep.

"Good, eh?" said Ron happily.

"Brilliant," said Harry.

"It's so brave of them," sighed Hermione admiringly. "If they were found . . ."

"Well, they keep on the move, don't they?" said Ron. "Like us."

"But did you hear what Fred said?" asked Harry excitedly; now the broadcast was over, his thoughts turned again toward his all-consuming obsession. "He's abroad! He's still looking for the Wand, I knew it!"

"Harry —"

"Come on, Hermione, why are you so determined not to admit it? Vol —"

"HARRY, NO!"

"— demort's after the Elder Wand!"

"The name's Taboo!" Ron bellowed, leaping to his feet as a loud crack sounded outside the tent. "I told you, Harry, I told you, we can't say it anymore — we've got to put the protection back around us — quickly — it's how they find —"

But Ron stopped talking, and Harry knew why. The Sneakoscope on the table had lit up and begun to spin; they could hear voices coming nearer and nearer: rough, excited voices. Ron pulled the Deluminator out of his pocket and clicked it: Their lamps went out.

"Come out of there with your hands up!" came a rasping voice through the darkness. "We know you're in there! You've got half a dozen wands pointing at you and we don't care who we curse!"

MALFOY MANOR

Harry looked around at the other two, now mere outlines in the darkness. He saw Hermione point her wand, not toward the outside, but into his face; there was a bang, a burst of white light, and he buckled in agony, unable to see. He could feel his face swelling rapidly under his hands as heavy footfalls surrounded him.

"Get up, vermin."

Unknown hands dragged Harry roughly off the ground. Before he could stop them, someone had rummaged through his pockets and removed the blackthorn wand. Harry clutched at his excruciatingly painful face, which felt unrecognizable beneath his fingers, tight, swollen, and puffy as though he had suffered some violent allergic reaction. His eyes had been reduced to slits through which he could barely see; his glasses fell off as he was bundled out of the tent; all he could make out were the blurred shapes of four or five people wrestling Ron and Hermione outside too.

"Get — off — her!" Ron shouted. There was the unmistakable sound of knuckles hitting flesh: Ron grunted in pain and Hermione screamed, "No! Leave him alone, leave him alone!"

"Your boyfriend's going to have worse than that done to him if he's on my list," said the horribly familiar, rasping voice. "Delicious girl . . . What a treat . . . I do enjoy the softness of the skin. . . ."

Harry's stomach turned over. He knew who this was: Fenrir Greyback, the werewolf who was permitted to wear Death Eater robes in return for his hired savagery.

"Search the tent!" said another voice.

Harry was thrown facedown onto the ground. A thud told him that Ron had been cast down beside him. They could hear footsteps and crashes; the men were pushing over chairs inside the tent as they searched.

"Now, let's see who we've got," said Greyback's gloating voice from overhead, and Harry was rolled over onto his back. A beam of wandlight fell into his face and Greyback laughed.

"I'll be needing butterbeer to wash this one down. What happened to you, ugly?"

Harry did not answer immediately.

"I *said*," repeated Greyback, and Harry received a blow to the diaphragm that made him double over in pain, "what happened to you?"

"Stung," Harry muttered. "Been stung."

"Yeah, looks like it," said a second voice.

"What's your name?" snarled Greyback.

"Dudley," said Harry.

"And your first name?"

"I — Vernon. Vernon Dudley."

"Check the list, Scabior," said Greyback, and Harry heard him move sideways to look down at Ron, instead. "And what about you, ginger?"

"Stan Shunpike," said Ron.

"Like 'ell you are," said the man called Scabior. "We know Stan Shunpike, 'e's put a bit of work our way."

There was another thud.

"I'b Bardy," said Ron, and Harry could tell that his mouth was full of blood. "Bardy Weadley."

"A Weasley?" rasped Greyback. "So you're related to blood traitors even if you're not a Mudblood. And lastly, your pretty little friend . . ." The relish in his voice made Harry's flesh crawl.

"Easy, Greyback," said Scabior over the jeering of the others.

"Oh, I'm not going to bite just yet. We'll see if she's a bit quicker at remembering her name than Barny. Who are you, girly?"

"Penelope Clearwater," said Hermione. She sounded terrified, but convincing.

"What's your blood status?"

"Half-blood," said Hermione.

"Easy enough to check," said Scabior. "But the 'ole lot of 'em look like they could still be 'ogwarts age —"

"We'b lebt," said Ron.

"Left, 'ave you, ginger?" said Scabior. "And you decided to go camping? And you thought, just for a laugh, you'd use the Dark Lord's name?"

"Nod a laugh," said Ron. "Aggiden."

"Accident?" There was more jeering laughter.

"You know who used to like using the Dark Lord's name,

Weasley?" growled Greyback. "The Order of the Phoenix. Mean anything to you?"

"Doh."

"Well, they don't show the Dark Lord proper respect, so the name's been Tabooed. A few Order members have been tracked that way. We'll see. Bind them up with the other two prisoners!"

Someone yanked Harry up by the hair, dragged him a short way, pushed him down into a sitting position, then started binding him back-to-back with other people. Harry was still half blind, barely able to see anything through his puffed-up eyes. When at last the man tying them had walked away, Harry whispered to the other prisoners.

"Anyone still got a wand?"

"No," said Ron and Hermione from either side of him.

"This is all my fault. I said the name, I'm sorry —"

"Harry?"

It was a new, but familiar, voice, and it came from directly behind Harry, from the person tied to Hermione's left.

"*Dean?*"

"It *is* you! If they find out who they've got — ! They're Snatchers, they're only looking for truants to sell for gold —"

"Not a bad little haul for one night," Greyback was saying, as a pair of hobnailed boots marched close by Harry and they heard more crashes from inside the tent. "A Mudblood, a runaway goblin, and three truants. You checked their names on the list yet, Scabior?" he roared.

"Yeah. There's no Vernon Dudley on 'ere, Greyback."

"Interesting," said Greyback. "That's interesting."

He crouched down beside Harry, who saw, through the infinitesimal gap left between his swollen eyelids, a face covered in matted gray hair and whiskers, with pointed brown teeth and sores at the corners of his mouth. Greyback smelled as he had done at the top of the tower where Dumbledore had died: of dirt, sweat, and blood.

"So you aren't wanted, then, Vernon? Or are you on that list under a different name? What House were you in at Hogwarts?"

"Slytherin," said Harry automatically.

"Funny 'ow they all thinks we wants to 'ear that," jeered Scabior out of the shadows. "But none of 'em can tell us where the common room is."

"It's in the dungeons," said Harry clearly. "You enter through the wall. It's full of skulls and stuff and it's under the lake, so the light's all green."

There was a short pause.

"Well, well, looks like we really 'ave caught a little Slytherin," said Scabior. "Good for you, Vernon, 'cause there ain't a lot of Mudblood Slytherins. Who's your father?"

"He works at the Ministry," Harry lied. He knew that his whole story would collapse with the smallest investigation, but on the other hand, he only had until his face regained its usual appearance before the game was up in any case. "Department of Magical Accidents and Catastrophes."

"You know what, Greyback," said Scabior. "I think there *is* a Dudley in there."

Harry could barely breathe: Could luck, sheer luck, get them safely out of this?

"Well, well," said Greyback, and Harry could hear the tiniest note of trepidation in that callous voice, and knew that Greyback was wondering whether he had indeed just attacked and bound the son of a Ministry official. Harry's heart was pounding against the ropes around his ribs; he would not have been surprised to know that Greyback could see it. "If you're telling the truth, ugly, you've got nothing to fear from a trip to the Ministry. I expect your father'll reward us just for picking you up."

"But," said Harry, his mouth bone dry, "if you just let us —"

"Hey!" came a shout from inside the tent. "Look at this, Greyback!"

A dark figure came bustling toward them, and Harry saw a glint of silver in the light of their wands. They had found Gryffindor's sword.

"Ve-e-ry nice," said Greyback appreciatively, taking it from his companion. "Oh, very nice indeed. Looks goblin-made, that. Where did you get something like this?"

"It's my father's," Harry lied, hoping against hope that it was too dark for Greyback to see the name etched just below the hilt. "We borrowed it to cut firewood —"

"'ang on a minute, Greyback! Look at this, in the *Prophet*!"

As Scabior said it, Harry's scar, which was stretched tight across his distended forehead, burned savagely. More clearly than he could make out anything around him, he saw a towering building, a grim fortress, jet-black and forbidding; Voldemort's thoughts had suddenly become razor-sharp again; he was gliding toward the gigantic building with a sense of calmly euphoric purpose. . . .

So close . . . So close . . .

With a huge effort of will Harry closed his mind to Voldemort's thoughts, pulling himself back to where he sat, tied to Ron, Hermione, Dean, and Griphook in the darkness, listening to Greyback and Scabior.

"*'ermione Granger,'*" Scabior was saying, "*the Mudblood who is known to be traveling with 'arry Potter.'*"

Harry's scar burned in the silence, but he made a supreme effort to keep himself present, not to slip into Voldemort's mind. He heard the creak of Greyback's boots as he crouched down in front of Hermione.

"You know what, little girly? This picture looks a hell of a lot like you."

"It isn't! It isn't me!"

Hermione's terrified squeak was as good as a confession.

"*. . . known to be traveling with Harry Potter,'*" repeated Greyback quietly.

A stillness had settled over the scene. Harry's scar was exquisitely painful, but he struggled with all his strength against the pull of Voldemort's thoughts: It had never been so important to remain in his own right mind.

"Well, this changes things, doesn't it?" whispered Greyback. Nobody spoke: Harry sensed the gang of Snatchers watching, frozen, and felt Hermione's arm trembling against his. Greyback got up and took a couple of steps to where Harry sat, crouching down again to stare closely at his misshapen features.

"What's that on your forehead, Vernon?" he asked softly, his breath foul in Harry's nostrils as he pressed a filthy finger to the taut scar.

"Don't touch it!" Harry yelled; he could not stop himself; he thought he might be sick from the pain of it.

"I thought you wore glasses, Potter?" breathed Greyback.

"I found glasses!" yelped one of the Snatchers skulking in the background. "There was glasses in the tent, Greyback, wait —"

And seconds later Harry's glasses had been rammed back onto his face. The Snatchers were closing in now, peering at him.

"It is!" rasped Greyback. "We've caught Potter!"

They all took several steps backward, stunned by what they had done. Harry, still fighting to remain present inside his own splitting head, could think of nothing to say: Fragmented visions were breaking across the surface of his mind —

— *He was gliding around the high walls of the black fortress —*

No, he was Harry, tied up and wandless, in grave danger —

— *looking up, up to the topmost window, the highest tower —*

He was Harry, and they were discussing his fate in low voices —

— *Time to fly . . .*

". . . to the Ministry?"

"To hell with the Ministry," growled Greyback. "They'll take the credit, and we won't get a look in. I say we take him straight to You-Know-Who."

"Will you summon 'im? 'ere?" said Scabior, sounding awed, terrified.

"No," snarled Greyback, "I haven't got — they say he's using the Malfoys' place as a base. We'll take the boy there."

Harry thought he knew why Greyback was not calling Voldemort. The werewolf might be allowed to wear Death Eater robes when they wanted to use him, but only Voldemort's inner circle were branded with the Dark Mark: Greyback had not been granted this highest honor.

Harry's scar seared again —

— and he rose into the night, flying straight up to the window at the very top of the tower —

". . . completely sure it's him? 'Cause if it ain't, Greyback, we're dead."

"Who's in charge here?" roared Greyback, covering his moment of inadequacy. "I say that's Potter, and him plus his wand, that's two hundred thousand Galleons right there! But if you're too gutless to come along, any of you, it's all for me, and with any luck, I'll get the girl thrown in!"

— The window was the merest slit in the black rock, not big enough for a man to enter. . . . A skeletal figure was just visible through it, curled beneath a blanket. . . . Dead, or sleeping . . . ?

"All right!" said Scabior. "All right, we're in! And what about the rest of 'em, Greyback, what'll we do with 'em?"

"Might as well take the lot. We've got two Mudbloods, that's another ten Galleons. Give me the sword as well. If they're rubies, that's another small fortune right there."

The prisoners were dragged to their feet. Harry could hear Hermione's breathing, fast and terrified.

"Grab hold and make it tight. I'll do Potter!" said Greyback, seizing a fistful of Harry's hair; Harry could feel his long yellow nails scratching his scalp. "On three! One — two — three —"

They Disapparated, pulling the prisoners with them. Harry struggled, trying to throw off Greyback's hand, but it was hopeless: Ron and Hermione were squeezed tightly against him on either side, he could not separate from the group, and as the breath was squeezed out of him his scar seared more painfully still —

— as he forced himself through the slit of a window like a snake and landed, lightly as vapor, inside the cell-like room —

The prisoners lurched into one another as they landed in a country lane. Harry's eyes, still puffy, took a moment to acclimatize, then he saw a pair of wrought-iron gates at the foot of what looked like a long drive. He experienced the tiniest trickle of relief. The worst had not happened yet: Voldemort was not here. He was, Harry knew, for he was fighting to resist the vision, in some strange, fortresslike place, at the top of a tower. How long it would take Voldemort to get to this place, once he knew that Harry was here, was another matter. . . .

One of the Snatchers strode to the gates and shook them.

"How do we get in? They're locked, Greyback, I can't — blimey!"

He whipped his hands away in fright. The iron was contorting, twisting itself out of the abstract furls and coils into a frightening face, which spoke in a clanging, echoing voice: "State your purpose!"

"We've got Potter!" Greyback roared triumphantly. "We've captured Harry Potter!"

The gates swung open.

"Come on!" said Greyback to his men, and the prisoners were shunted through the gates and up the drive, between high hedges that muffled their footsteps. Harry saw a ghostly white shape above him, and realized it was an albino peacock. He stumbled and was dragged onto his feet by Greyback; now he was staggering along sideways, tied back-to-back to the four other prisoners. Closing his puffy eyes, he allowed the pain in his scar to overcome him for a moment, wanting to know what Voldemort was doing, whether he knew yet that Harry was caught. . . .

The emaciated figure stirred beneath its thin blanket and rolled over toward him, eyes opening in a skull of a face. . . . The frail man sat up, great sunken eyes fixed upon him, upon Voldemort, and then he smiled. Most of his teeth were gone. . . .

"So, you have come. I thought you would . . . one day. But your journey was pointless. I never had it."

"You lie!"

As Voldemort's anger throbbed inside him, Harry's scar threatened to burst with pain, and he wrenched his mind back to his own body, fighting to remain present as the prisoners were pushed over gravel.

Light spilled out over all of them.

"What is this?" said a woman's cold voice.

"We're here to see He-Who-Must-Not-Be-Named!" rasped Greyback.

"Who are you?"

"You know me!" There was resentment in the werewolf's voice. "Fenrir Greyback! We've caught Harry Potter!"

Greyback seized Harry and dragged him around to face the light, forcing the other prisoners to shuffle around too.

"I know 'e's swollen, ma'am, but it's 'im!" piped up Scabior. "If you look a bit closer, you'll see 'is scar. And this 'ere, see the girl? The Mudblood who's been traveling around with 'im, ma'am. There's no doubt it's 'im, and we've got 'is wand as well! 'Ere, ma'am —"

Through his puffy eyelids Harry saw Narcissa Malfoy scrutinizing his swollen face. Scabior thrust the blackthorn wand at her. She raised her eyebrows.

"Bring them in," she said.

Harry and the others were shoved and kicked up broad stone steps into a hallway lined with portraits.

"Follow me," said Narcissa, leading the way across the hall. "My son, Draco, is home for his Easter holidays. If that is Harry Potter, he will know."

The drawing room dazzled after the darkness outside; even with his eyes almost closed Harry could make out the wide proportions of the room. A crystal chandelier hung from the ceiling, more portraits against the dark purple walls. Two figures rose from chairs in front of an ornate marble fireplace as the prisoners were forced into the room by the Snatchers.

"What is this?"

The dreadfully familiar, drawling voice of Lucius Malfoy fell on Harry's ears. He was panicking now: He could see no way out, and it was easier, as his fear mounted, to block out Voldemort's thoughts, though his scar was still burning.

"They say they've got Potter," said Narcissa's cold voice. "Draco, come here."

Harry did not dare look directly at Draco, but saw him obliquely: a figure slightly taller than he was, rising from an armchair, his face a pale and pointed blur beneath white-blond hair.

Greyback forced the prisoners to turn again so as to place Harry directly beneath the chandelier.

"Well, boy?" rasped the werewolf.

Harry was facing a mirror over the fireplace, a great gilded thing in an intricately scrolled frame. Through the slits of his eyes he saw his own reflection for the first time since leaving Grimmauld Place.

His face was huge, shiny, and pink, every feature distorted by Hermione's jinx. His black hair reached his shoulders and there was a dark shadow around his jaw. Had he not known that it was he who stood there, he would have wondered who was wearing his glasses. He resolved not to speak, for his voice was sure to give him away; yet he still avoided eye contact with Draco as the latter approached.

"Well, Draco?" said Lucius Malfoy. He sounded avid. "Is it? Is it Harry Potter?"

"I can't — I can't be sure," said Draco. He was keeping his distance from Greyback, and seemed as scared of looking at Harry as Harry was of looking at him.

"But look at him carefully, look! Come closer!"

Harry had never heard Lucius Malfoy so excited.

"Draco, if we are the ones who hand Potter over to the Dark Lord, everything will be forgiv —"

"Now, we won't be forgetting who actually caught him, I hope, Mr. Malfoy?" said Greyback menacingly.

"Of course not, of course not!" said Lucius impatiently. He approached Harry himself, came so close that Harry could see the usually languid, pale face in sharp detail even through his swollen eyes. With his face a puffy mask, Harry felt as though he was peering out from between the bars of a cage.

"What did you do to him?" Lucius asked Greyback. "How did he get into this state?"

"That wasn't us."

"Looks more like a Stinging Jinx to me," said Lucius.

His gray eyes raked Harry's forehead.

"There's something there," he whispered, "it could be the scar, stretched tight. . . . Draco, come here, look properly! What do you think?"

Harry saw Draco's face up close now, right beside his father's. They were extraordinarily alike, except that while his father looked beside himself with excitement, Draco's expression was full of reluctance, even fear.

"I don't know," he said, and he walked away toward the fireplace where his mother stood watching.

"We had better be certain, Lucius," Narcissa called to her husband in her cold, clear voice. "Completely sure that it is Potter, before we summon the Dark Lord . . . They say this is his" — she was looking closely at the blackthorn wand — "but it does not resemble Ollivander's description. . . . If we are mistaken, if we call the Dark Lord here for nothing . . . Remember what he did to Rowle and Dolohov?"

"What about the Mudblood, then?" growled Greyback. Harry was nearly thrown off his feet as the Snatchers forced the prisoners to swivel around again, so that the light fell on Hermione instead.

"Wait," said Narcissa sharply. "Yes — yes, she was in Madam Malkin's with Potter! I saw her picture in the *Prophet*! Look, Draco, isn't it the Granger girl?"

"I . . . maybe . . . yeah."

"But then, that's the Weasley boy!" shouted Lucius, striding around the bound prisoners to face Ron. "It's them, Potter's friends — Draco, look at him, isn't it Arthur Weasley's son, what's his name — ?"

"Yeah," said Draco again, his back to the prisoners. "It could be."

The drawing room door opened behind Harry. A woman spoke,

and the sound of the voice wound Harry's fear to an even higher pitch.

"What is this? What's happened, Cissy?"

Bellatrix Lestrange walked slowly around the prisoners, and stopped on Harry's right, staring at Hermione through her heavily lidded eyes.

"But surely," she said quietly, "this is the Mudblood girl? This is Granger?"

"Yes, yes, it's Granger!" cried Lucius. "And beside her, we think, Potter! Potter and his friends, caught at last!"

"Potter?" shrieked Bellatrix, and she backed away, the better to take in Harry. "Are you sure? Well then, the Dark Lord must be informed at once!"

She dragged back her left sleeve: Harry saw the Dark Mark burned into the flesh of her arm, and knew that she was about to touch it, to summon her beloved master —

"I was about to call him!" said Lucius, and his hand actually closed upon Bellatrix's wrist, preventing her from touching the Mark. "*I* shall summon him, Bella, Potter has been brought to my house, and it is therefore upon my authority —"

"Your authority!" she sneered, attempting to wrench her hand from his grasp. "You lost your authority when you lost your wand, Lucius! How dare you! Take your hands off me!"

"This is nothing to do with you, you did not capture the boy —"

"Begging your pardon, *Mr.* Malfoy," interjected Greyback, "but it's us that caught Potter, and it's us that'll be claiming the gold —"

"Gold!" laughed Bellatrix, still attempting to throw off her brother-in-law, her free hand groping in her pocket for her wand. "Take your gold, filthy scavenger, what do I want with gold? I seek only the honor of his — of —"

She stopped struggling, her dark eyes fixed upon something Harry could not see. Jubilant at her capitulation, Lucius threw her hand from him and ripped up his own sleeve —

"STOP!" shrieked Bellatrix. "Do not touch it, we shall all perish if the Dark Lord comes now!"

Lucius froze, his index finger hovering over his own Mark. Bellatrix strode out of Harry's limited line of vision.

"What is that?" he heard her say.

"Sword," grunted an out-of-sight Snatcher.

"Give it to me."

"It's not yorn, missus, it's mine, I reckon I found it."

There was a bang and a flash of red light: Harry knew that the Snatcher had been Stunned. There was a roar of anger from his fellows: Scabior drew his wand.

"What d'you think you're playing at, woman?"

"*Stupefy!*" she screamed. "*Stupefy!*"

They were no match for her, even though there were four of them against one of her: She was a witch, as Harry knew, with prodigious skill and no conscience. They fell where they stood, all except Greyback, who had been forced into a kneeling position, his arms outstretched. Out of the corners of his eyes Harry saw Bellatrix bearing down upon the werewolf, the sword of Gryffindor gripped tightly in her hand, her face waxen.

"Where did you get this sword?" she whispered to Greyback as she pulled his wand out of his unresisting grip.

"How dare you?" he snarled, his mouth the only thing that could move as he was forced to gaze up at her. He bared his pointed teeth. "Release me, woman!"

"Where did you find this sword?" she repeated, brandishing it in his face. "Snape sent it to my vault in Gringotts!"

"It was in their tent," rasped Greyback. "Release me, I say!"

She waved her wand, and the werewolf sprang to his feet, but appeared too wary to approach her. He prowled behind an armchair, his filthy curved nails clutching its back.

"Draco, move this scum outside," said Bellatrix, indicating the unconscious men. "If you haven't got the guts to finish them, then leave them in the courtyard for me."

"Don't you dare speak to Draco like —" said Narcissa furiously, but Bellatrix screamed,

"Be quiet! The situation is graver than you can possibly imagine, Cissy! We have a very serious problem!"

She stood, panting slightly, looking down at the sword, examining its hilt. Then she turned to look at the silent prisoners.

"If it is indeed Potter, he must not be harmed," she muttered, more to herself than to the others. "The Dark Lord wishes to dispose of Potter himself. . . . But if he finds out . . . I must . . . I must know. . . ."

She turned back to her sister again.

"The prisoners must be placed in the cellar, while I think what to do!"

"This is my house, Bella, you don't give orders in my —"

"Do it! You have no idea of the danger we are in!" shrieked Bellatrix. She looked frightening, mad; a thin stream of fire issued from her wand and burned a hole in the carpet.

Narcissa hesitated for a moment, then addressed the werewolf.

"Take these prisoners down to the cellar, Greyback."

"Wait," said Bellatrix sharply. "All except . . . except for the Mudblood."

Greyback gave a grunt of pleasure.

"No!" shouted Ron. "You can have me, keep me!"

Bellatrix hit him across the face; the blow echoed around the room.

"If she dies under questioning, I'll take you next," she said. "Blood traitor is next to Mudblood in my book. Take them downstairs, Greyback, and make sure they are secure, but do nothing more to them — yet."

She threw Greyback's wand back to him, then took a short silver knife from under her robes. She cut Hermione free from the other prisoners, then dragged her by the hair into the middle of the room, while Greyback forced the rest of them to shuffle across to another door, into a dark passageway, his wand held out in front of him, projecting an invisible and irresistible force.

"Reckon she'll let me have a bit of the girl when she's finished with her?" Greyback crooned as he forced them along the corridor. "I'd say I'll get a bite or two, wouldn't you, ginger?"

Harry could feel Ron shaking. They were forced down a steep flight of stairs, still tied back-to-back and in danger of slipping and breaking their necks at any moment. At the bottom was a heavy door. Greyback unlocked it with a tap of his wand, then forced them into a dank and musty room and left them in total darkness. The echoing bang of the slammed cellar door had not died away before there was a terrible, drawn-out scream from directly above them.

"HERMIONE!" Ron bellowed, and he started to writhe and

struggle against the ropes tying them together, so that Harry staggered. "HERMIONE!"

"Be quiet!" Harry said. "Shut up, Ron, we need to work out a way —"

"HERMIONE! HERMIONE!"

"We need a plan, stop yelling — we need to get these ropes off —"

"Harry?" came a whisper through the darkness. "Ron? Is that you?"

Ron stopped shouting. There was a sound of movement close by them, then Harry saw a shadow moving closer.

"Harry? Ron?"

"Luna?"

"Yes, it's me! Oh no, I didn't want you to be caught!"

"Luna, can you help us get these ropes off?" said Harry.

"Oh yes, I expect so. . . . There's an old nail we use if we need to break anything. . . . Just a moment . . ."

Hermione screamed again from overhead, and they could hear Bellatrix screaming too, but her words were inaudible, for Ron shouted again, "HERMIONE! HERMIONE!"

"Mr. Ollivander?" Harry could hear Luna saying. "Mr. Ollivander, have you got the nail? If you just move over a little bit . . . I think it was beside the water jug. . . ."

She was back within seconds.

"You'll need to stay still," she said.

Harry could feel her digging at the rope's tough fibers to work the knots free. From upstairs they heard Bellatrix's voice.

"I'm going to ask you again! Where did you get this sword? *Where?*"

"We found it — we found it — PLEASE!" Hermione screamed again; Ron struggled harder than ever, and the rusty nail slipped onto Harry's wrist.

"Ron, please stay still!" Luna whispered. "I can't see what I'm doing —"

"My pocket!" said Ron. "In my pocket, there's a Deluminator, and it's full of light!"

A few seconds later, there was a click, and the luminescent spheres the Deluminator had sucked from the lamps in the tent flew into the cellar: Unable to rejoin their sources, they simply hung there, like tiny suns, flooding the underground room with light. Harry saw Luna, all eyes in her white face, and the motionless figure of Ollivander the wandmaker, curled up on the floor in the corner. Craning around, he caught sight of their fellow prisoners: Dean and Griphook the goblin, who seemed barely conscious, kept standing by the ropes that bound him to the humans.

"Oh, that's much easier, thanks, Ron," said Luna, and she began hacking at their bindings again. "Hello, Dean!"

From above came Bellatrix's voice.

"You are lying, filthy Mudblood, and I know it! You have been inside my vault at Gringotts! Tell the truth, *tell the truth!*"

Another terrible scream —

"HERMIONE!"

"What else did you take? What else have you got? Tell me the truth or, I swear, I shall run you through with this knife!"

"There!"

Harry felt the ropes fall away and turned, rubbing his wrists, to see Ron running around the cellar, looking up at the low ceiling, searching for a trapdoor. Dean, his face bruised and bloody, said

"Thanks" to Luna and stood there, shivering, but Griphook sank onto the cellar floor, looking groggy and disoriented, many welts across his swarthy face.

Ron was now trying to Disapparate without a wand.

"There's no way out, Ron," said Luna, watching his fruitless efforts. "The cellar is completely escape-proof. I tried, at first. Mr. Ollivander has been here for a long time, he's tried everything."

Hermione was screaming again: The sound went through Harry like physical pain. Barely conscious of the fierce prickling of his scar, he too started to run around the cellar, feeling the walls for he hardly knew what, knowing in his heart that it was useless.

"What else did you take, what else? ANSWER ME! *CRUCIO!*"

Hermione's screams echoed off the walls upstairs, Ron was half sobbing as he pounded the walls with his fists, and Harry in utter desperation seized Hagrid's pouch from around his neck and groped inside it: He pulled out Dumbledore's Snitch and shook it, hoping for he did not know what — nothing happened — he waved the broken halves of the phoenix wand, but they were lifeless — the mirror fragment fell sparkling to the floor, and he saw a gleam of brightest blue —

Dumbledore's eye was gazing at him out of the mirror.

"Help us!" he yelled at it in mad desperation. "We're in the cellar of Malfoy Manor, help us!"

The eye blinked and was gone.

Harry was not even sure that it had really been there. He tilted the shard of mirror this way and that, and saw nothing reflected there but the walls and ceiling of their prison, and upstairs Hermione was screaming worse than ever, and next to him Ron was bellowing, "HERMIONE! HERMIONE!"

"How did you get into my vault?" they heard Bellatrix scream. "Did that dirty little goblin in the cellar help you?"

"We only met him tonight!" Hermione sobbed. "We've never been inside your vault. . . . It isn't the real sword! It's a copy, just a copy!"

"A copy?" screeched Bellatrix. "Oh, a likely story!"

"But we can find out easily!" came Lucius's voice. "Draco, fetch the goblin, he can tell us whether the sword is real or not!"

Harry dashed across the cellar to where Griphook was huddled on the floor.

"Griphook," he whispered into the goblin's pointed ear, "you must tell them that sword's a fake, they mustn't know it's the real one, Griphook, please —"

He could hear someone scuttling down the cellar steps; next moment, Draco's shaking voice spoke from behind the door.

"Stand back. Line up against the back wall. Don't try anything, or I'll kill you!"

They did as they were bidden; as the lock turned, Ron clicked the Deluminator and the lights whisked back into his pocket, restoring the cellar's darkness. The door flew open; Malfoy marched inside, wand held out in front of him, pale and determined. He seized the little goblin by the arm and backed out again, dragging Griphook with him. The door slammed shut and at the same moment a loud *crack* echoed inside the cellar.

Ron clicked the Deluminator. Three balls of light flew back into the air from his pocket, revealing Dobby the house-elf, who had just Apparated into their midst.

"DOB — !"

Harry hit Ron on the arm to stop him shouting, and Ron looked terrified at his mistake. Footsteps crossed the ceiling overhead: Draco marching Griphook to Bellatrix.

Dobby's enormous, tennis-ball-shaped eyes were wide; he was trembling from his feet to the tips of his ears. He was back in the home of his old masters, and it was clear that he was petrified.

"Harry Potter," he squeaked in the tiniest quiver of a voice, "Dobby has come to rescue you."

"But how did you — ?"

An awful scream drowned Harry's words: Hermione was being tortured again. He cut to the essentials.

"You can Disapparate out of this cellar?" he asked Dobby, who nodded, his ears flapping.

"And you can take humans with you?"

Dobby nodded again.

"Right. Dobby, I want you to grab Luna, Dean, and Mr. Ollivander, and take them — take them to —"

"Bill and Fleur's," said Ron. "Shell Cottage on the outskirts of Tinworth!"

The elf nodded for a third time.

"And then come back," said Harry. "Can you do that, Dobby?"

"Of course, Harry Potter," whispered the little elf. He hurried over to Mr. Ollivander, who appeared to be barely conscious. He took one of the wandmaker's hands in his own, then held out the other to Luna and Dean, neither of whom moved.

"Harry, we want to help you!" Luna whispered.

"We can't leave you here," said Dean.

"Go, both of you! We'll see you at Bill and Fleur's."

As Harry spoke, his scar burned worse than ever, and for a few seconds he looked down, not upon the wandmaker, but on another man who was just as old, just as thin, but laughing scornfully.

"Kill me, then, Voldemort, I welcome death! But my death will not bring you what you seek. . . . There is so much you do not understand. . . ."

He felt Voldemort's fury, but as Hermione screamed again he shut it out, returning to the cellar and the horror of his own present.

"Go!" Harry beseeched Luna and Dean. "Go! We'll follow, just go!"

They caught hold of the elf's outstretched fingers. There was another loud *crack,* and Dobby, Luna, Dean, and Ollivander vanished.

"What was that?" shouted Lucius Malfoy from over their heads. "Did you hear that? What was that noise in the cellar?"

Harry and Ron stared at each other.

"Draco — no, call Wormtail! Make him go and check!"

Footsteps crossed the room overhead, then there was silence. Harry knew that the people in the drawing room were listening for more noises from the cellar.

"We're going to have to try and tackle him," he whispered to Ron. They had no choice: The moment anyone entered the room and saw the absence of three prisoners, they were lost. "Leave the lights on," Harry added, and as they heard someone descending the steps outside the door, they backed against the wall on either side of it.

"Stand back," came Wormtail's voice. "Stand away from the door. I am coming in."

The door flew open. For a split second Wormtail gazed into the apparently empty cellar, ablaze with light from the three miniature suns floating in midair. Then Harry and Ron launched themselves upon him. Ron seized Wormtail's wand arm and forced it upward; Harry slapped a hand to his mouth, muffling his voice. Silently they struggled: Wormtail's wand emitted sparks; his silver hand closed around Harry's throat.

"What is it, Wormtail?" called Lucius Malfoy from above.

"Nothing!" Ron called back, in a passable imitation of Wormtail's wheezy voice. "All fine!"

Harry could barely breathe.

"You're going to kill me?" Harry choked, attempting to prise off the metal fingers. "After I saved your life? You owe me, Wormtail!"

The silver fingers slackened. Harry had not expected it: He wrenched himself free, astonished, keeping his hand over Wormtail's mouth. He saw the ratlike man's small watery eyes widen with fear and surprise: He seemed just as shocked as Harry at what his hand had done, at the tiny, merciful impulse it had betrayed, and he continued to struggle more powerfully, as though to undo that moment of weakness.

"And we'll have that," whispered Ron, tugging Wormtail's wand from his other hand.

Wandless, helpless, Pettigrew's pupils dilated in terror. His eyes had slid from Harry's face to something else. His own silver fingers were moving inexorably toward his own throat.

"No —"

Without pausing to think, Harry tried to drag back the hand, but there was no stopping it. The silver tool that Voldemort had given his most cowardly servant had turned upon its disarmed and useless owner; Pettigrew was reaping his reward for his hesitation, his moment of pity; he was being strangled before their eyes.

"No!"

Ron had released Wormtail too, and together he and Harry tried to pull the crushing metal fingers from around Wormtail's throat, but it was no use. Pettigrew was turning blue.

"Relashio!" said Ron, pointing the wand at the silver hand, but nothing happened; Pettigrew dropped to his knees, and at the same moment, Hermione gave a dreadful scream from overhead. Wormtail's eyes rolled upward in his purple face; he gave a last twitch, and was still.

Harry and Ron looked at each other, then leaving Wormtail's body on the floor behind them, ran up the stairs and back into the shadowy passageway leading to the drawing room. Cautiously they crept along it until they reached the drawing room door, which was ajar. Now they had a clear view of Bellatrix looking down at Griphook, who was holding Gryffindor's sword in his long-fingered hands. Hermione was lying at Bellatrix's feet. She was barely stirring.

"Well?" Bellatrix said to Griphook. "Is it the true sword?"

Harry waited, holding his breath, fighting against the prickling of his scar.

"No," said Griphook. "It is a fake."

"Are you sure?" panted Bellatrix. "Quite sure?"

"Yes," said the goblin.

Relief broke across her face, all tension drained from it.

"Good," she said, and with a casual flick of her wand she slashed another deep cut into the goblin's face, and he dropped with a yell at her feet. She kicked him aside. "And now," she said in a voice that burst with triumph, "we call the Dark Lord!"

And she pushed back her sleeve and touched her forefinger to the Dark Mark.

At once, Harry's scar felt as though it had split open again. His true surroundings vanished: He was Voldemort, and the skeletal wizard before him was laughing toothlessly at him; he was enraged at the summons he felt — he had warned them, he had told them to summon him for nothing less than Potter. If they were mistaken . . .

"Kill me, then!" demanded the old man. *"You will not win, you cannot win! That wand will never, ever be yours —"*

And Voldemort's fury broke: A burst of green light filled the prison room and the frail old body was lifted from its hard bed and then fell back, lifeless, and Voldemort returned to the window, his wrath barely controllable. . . . They would suffer his retribution if they had no good reason for calling him back. . . .

"And I think," said Bellatrix's voice, "we can dispose of the Mudblood. Greyback, take her if you want her."

"NOOOOOOOOOOOOO!"

Ron had burst into the drawing room; Bellatrix looked around, shocked; she turned her wand to face Ron instead —

"Expelliarmus!" he roared, pointing Wormtail's wand at Bellatrix, and hers flew into the air and was caught by Harry, who had sprinted after Ron. Lucius, Narcissa, Draco, and Greyback wheeled about; Harry yelled, *"Stupefy!"* and Lucius Malfoy collapsed onto the hearth. Jets of light flew from Draco's, Narcissa's, and Greyback's wands; Harry threw himself to the floor, rolling behind a sofa to avoid them.

"STOP OR SHE DIES!"

Panting, Harry peered around the edge of the sofa. Bellatrix was supporting Hermione, who seemed to be unconscious, and was holding her short silver knife to Hermione's throat.

"Drop your wands," she whispered. "Drop them, or we'll see exactly how filthy her blood is!"

Ron stood rigid, clutching Wormtail's wand. Harry straightened up, still holding Bellatrix's.

"I said, drop them!" she screeched, pressing the blade into Hermione's throat: Harry saw beads of blood appear there.

"All right!" he shouted, and he dropped Bellatrix's wand onto the floor at his feet. Ron did the same with Wormtail's. Both raised their hands to shoulder height.

"Good!" she leered. "Draco, pick them up! The Dark Lord is coming, Harry Potter! Your death approaches!"

Harry knew it; his scar was bursting with the pain of it, and he could feel Voldemort flying through the sky from far away, over a dark and stormy sea, and soon he would be close enough to Apparate to them, and Harry could see no way out.

"Now," said Bellatrix softly, as Draco hurried back to her with the wands, "Cissy, I think we ought to tie these little heroes up again, while Greyback takes care of Miss Mudblood. I am sure the Dark Lord will not begrudge you the girl, Greyback, after what you have done tonight."

At the last word there was a peculiar grinding noise from above. All of them looked upward in time to see the crystal chandelier tremble; then, with a creak and an ominous jingling, it began to fall. Bellatrix was directly beneath it; dropping Hermione, she threw herself aside with a scream. The chandelier crashed to the floor in an explosion of crystal and chains, falling on top of Hermione and the goblin, who still clutched the sword of Gryffindor. Glittering shards of crystal flew in all directions: Draco doubled over, his hands covering his bloody face.

As Ron ran to pull Hermione out of the wreckage, Harry took his chance: He leapt over an armchair and wrested the three wands from Draco's grip, pointed all of them at Greyback, and yelled, *"Stupefy!"* The werewolf was lifted off his feet by the triple spell, flew up to the ceiling, and then smashed to the ground.

As Narcissa dragged Draco out of the way of further harm, Bellatrix sprang to her feet, her hair flying as she brandished the silver knife; but Narcissa had directed her wand at the doorway.

"Dobby!" she screamed, and even Bellatrix froze. "You! *You* dropped the chandelier — ?"

The tiny elf trotted into the room, his shaking finger pointing at his old mistress.

"You must not hurt Harry Potter," he squeaked.

"Kill him, Cissy!" shrieked Bellatrix, but there was another loud *crack,* and Narcissa's wand too flew into the air and landed on the other side of the room.

"You dirty little monkey!" bawled Bellatrix. "How dare you take a witch's wand, how dare you defy your masters?"

"Dobby has no master!" squealed the elf. "Dobby is a free elf, and Dobby has come to save Harry Potter and his friends!"

Harry's scar was blinding him with pain. Dimly he knew that they had moments, seconds before Voldemort was with them.

"Ron, catch — and GO!" he yelled, throwing one of the wands to him; then he bent down to tug Griphook out from under the chandelier. Hoisting the groaning goblin, who still clung to the sword, over one shoulder, Harry seized Dobby's hand and spun on the spot to Disapparate.

As he turned into darkness he caught one last view of the drawing room: of the pale, frozen figures of Narcissa and Draco, of the streak of red that was Ron's hair, and a blur of flying silver, as Bellatrix's knife flew across the room at the place where he was vanishing —

Bill and Fleur's . . . Shell Cottage . . . Bill and Fleur's . . .

He had disappeared into the unknown; all he could do was repeat the name of the destination and hope that it would suffice to take him there. The pain in his forehead pierced him, and the weight of the goblin bore down upon him; he could feel the blade of Gryffindor's sword bumping against his back; Dobby's hand jerked in his; he wondered whether the elf was trying to take charge, to pull them in the right direction, and tried, by squeezing the fingers, to indicate that that was fine with him. . . .

And then they hit solid earth and smelled salty air. Harry fell to his knees, relinquished Dobby's hand, and attempted to lower Griphook gently to the ground.

"Are you all right?" he said as the goblin stirred, but Griphook merely whimpered.

Harry squinted around through the darkness. There seemed to be a cottage a short way away under the wide starry sky, and he thought he saw movement outside it.

"Dobby, is this Shell Cottage?" he whispered, clutching the two wands he had brought from the Malfoys', ready to fight if he needed to. "Have we come to the right place? Dobby?"

He looked around. The little elf stood feet from him.

"DOBBY!"

The elf swayed slightly, stars reflected in his wide, shining eyes. Together, he and Harry looked down at the silver hilt of the knife protruding from the elf's heaving chest.

"Dobby — no — HELP!" Harry bellowed toward the cottage, toward the people moving there. "HELP!"

He did not know or care whether they were wizards or Muggles, friends or foes; all he cared about was that a dark stain was spreading across Dobby's front, and that he had stretched out his thin arms to Harry with a look of supplication. Harry caught him and laid him sideways on the cool grass.

"Dobby, no, don't die, don't die —"

The elf's eyes found him, and his lips trembled with the effort to form words.

"Harry . . . Potter . . ."

And then with a little shudder the elf became quite still, and his eyes were nothing more than great glassy orbs, sprinkled with light from the stars they could not see.

THE WANDMAKER

I t was like sinking into an old nightmare; for an instant Harry knelt again beside Dumbledore's body at the foot of the tallest tower at Hogwarts, but in reality he was staring at a tiny body curled upon the grass, pierced by Bellatrix's silver knife. Harry's voice was still saying, "Dobby . . . *Dobby* . . ." even though he knew that the elf had gone where he could not call him back.

After a minute or so he realized that they had, after all, come to the right place, for here were Bill and Fleur, Dean and Luna, gathering around him as he knelt over the elf.

"Hermione?" he said suddenly. "Where is she?"

"Ron's taken her inside," said Bill. "She'll be all right."

Harry looked back down at Dobby. He stretched out a hand and pulled the sharp blade from the elf's body, then dragged off his own jacket and covered Dobby in it like a blanket.

The sea was rushing against rock somewhere nearby; Harry listened to it while the others talked, discussing matters in which he could take no interest, making decisions. Dean carried the injured Griphook into the house, Fleur hurrying with them; now Bill was making suggestions about burying the elf. Harry agreed without really knowing what he was saying. As he did so, he gazed down at the tiny body, and his scar prickled and burned, and in one part of his mind, viewed as if from the wrong end of a long telescope, he saw Voldemort punishing those they had left behind at Malfoy Manor. His rage was dreadful and yet Harry's grief for Dobby seemed to diminish it, so that it became a distant storm that reached Harry from across a vast, silent ocean.

"I want to do it properly," were the first words of which Harry was fully conscious of speaking. "Not by magic. Have you got a spade?"

And shortly afterward he had set to work, alone, digging the grave in the place that Bill had shown him at the end of the garden, between bushes. He dug with a kind of fury, relishing the manual work, glorying in the non-magic of it, for every drop of his sweat and every blister felt like a gift to the elf who had saved their lives.

His scar burned, but he was master of the pain; he felt it, yet was apart from it. He had learned control at last, learned to shut his mind to Voldemort, the very thing Dumbledore had wanted him to learn from Snape. Just as Voldemort had not been able to possess Harry while Harry was consumed with grief for Sirius, so his thoughts could not penetrate Harry now, while he mourned Dobby. Grief, it seemed, drove Voldemort out . . . though Dumbledore, of course, would have said that it was love. . . .

On Harry dug, deeper and deeper into the hard, cold earth, subsuming his grief in sweat, denying the pain in his scar. In the darkness, with nothing but the sound of his own breath and the rushing sea to keep him company, the things that had happened at the Malfoys' returned to him, the things he had heard came back to him, and understanding blossomed in the darkness. . . .

The steady rhythm of his arms beat time with his thoughts. Hallows . . . Horcruxes . . . Hallows . . . Horcruxes . . . Yet he no longer burned with that weird, obsessive longing. Loss and fear had snuffed it out: He felt as though he had been slapped awake again.

Deeper and deeper Harry sank into the grave, and he knew where Voldemort had been tonight, and whom he had killed in the topmost cell of Nurmengard, and why. . . .

And he thought of Wormtail, dead because of one small unconscious impulse of mercy. . . . Dumbledore had foreseen that. . . . How much more had he known?

Harry lost track of time. He knew only that the darkness had lightened a few degrees when he was rejoined by Ron and Dean.

"How's Hermione?"

"Better," said Ron. "Fleur's looking after her."

Harry had his retort ready for when they asked him why he had not simply created a perfect grave with his wand, but he did not need it. They jumped down into the hole he had made with spades of their own, and together they worked in silence until the hole seemed deep enough.

Harry wrapped the elf more snugly in his jacket. Ron sat on the edge of the grave and stripped off his shoes and socks, which he placed upon the elf's bare feet. Dean produced a woolen hat, which Harry placed carefully upon Dobby's head, muffling his batlike ears.

"We should close his eyes."

Harry had not heard the others coming through the darkness.

Bill was wearing a traveling cloak, Fleur a large white apron, from the pocket of which protruded a bottle of what Harry recognized to be Skele-Gro. Hermione was wrapped in a borrowed dressing gown, pale and unsteady on her feet; Ron put an arm around her when she reached him. Luna, who was huddled in one of Fleur's coats, crouched down and placed her fingers tenderly upon each of the elf's eyelids, sliding them over his glassy stare.

"There," she said softly. "Now he could be sleeping."

Harry placed the elf into the grave, arranged his tiny limbs so that he might have been resting, then climbed out and gazed for the last time upon the little body. He forced himself not to break down as he remembered Dumbledore's funeral, and the rows and rows of golden chairs, and the Minister of Magic in the front row, the recitation of Dumbledore's achievements, the stateliness of the white marble tomb. He felt that Dobby deserved just as grand a funeral, and yet here the elf lay between bushes in a roughly dug hole.

"I think we ought to say something," piped up Luna. "I'll go first, shall I?"

And as everybody looked at her, she addressed the dead elf at the bottom of the grave.

"Thank you so much, Dobby, for rescuing me from that cellar. It's so unfair that you had to die, when you were so good and brave. I'll always remember what you did for us. I hope you're happy now."

She turned and looked expectantly at Ron, who cleared his throat and said in a thick voice, "Yeah . . . thanks, Dobby."

"Thanks," muttered Dean.

Harry swallowed.

"Good-bye, Dobby," he said. It was all he could manage, but Luna had said it all for him. Bill raised his wand, and the pile of earth beside the grave rose up into the air and fell neatly upon it, a small, reddish mound.

"D'you mind if I stay here a moment?" he asked the others.

They murmured words he did not catch; he felt gentle pats upon his back, and then they all traipsed back toward the cottage, leaving Harry alone beside the elf.

He looked around: There were a number of large white stones, smoothed by the sea, marking the edge of the flower beds. He picked up one of the largest and laid it, pillowlike, over the place where Dobby's head now rested. He then felt in his pocket for a wand.

There were two in there. He had forgotten, lost track; he could not now remember whose wands these were; he seemed to remember wrenching them out of someone's hand. He selected the shorter of the two, which felt friendlier in his hand, and pointed it at the rock.

Slowly, under his murmured instruction, deep cuts appeared upon the rock's surface. He knew that Hermione could have done it more neatly, and probably more quickly, but he wanted to mark the spot as he had wanted to dig the grave. When Harry stood up again, the stone read:

HERE LIES DOBBY, A FREE ELF.

He looked down at his handiwork for a few more seconds, then walked away, his scar still prickling a little, and his mind full of those things that had come to him in the grave, ideas that had taken shape in the darkness, ideas both fascinating and terrible.

They were all sitting in the living room when he entered the little hall, their attention focused upon Bill, who was talking. The room was light-colored, pretty, with a small fire of driftwood burning brightly in the fireplace. Harry did not want to drop mud upon the carpet, so he stood in the doorway, listening.

". . . lucky that Ginny's on holiday. If she'd been at Hogwarts, they could have taken her before we reached her. Now we know she's safe too."

He looked around and saw Harry standing there.

"I've been getting them all out of the Burrow," he explained. "Moved them to Muriel's. The Death Eaters know Ron's with you now, they're bound to target the family — don't apologize," he added at the sight of Harry's expression. "It was always a matter of time, Dad's been saying so for months. We're the biggest blood-traitor family there is."

"How are they protected?" asked Harry.

"Fidelius Charm. Dad's Secret-Keeper. And we've done it on this cottage too; I'm Secret-Keeper here. None of us can go to work, but that's hardly the most important thing now. Once Ollivander and Griphook are well enough, we'll move them to Muriel's too. There isn't much room here, but she's got plenty. Griphook's legs are on the mend, Fleur's given him Skele-Gro; we could probably move them in an hour or —"

"No," Harry said, and Bill looked startled. "I need both of them here. I need to talk to them. It's important."

He heard the authority in his own voice, the conviction, the sense of purpose that had come to him as he dug Dobby's grave. All of their faces were turned toward him, looking puzzled.

"I'm going to wash," Harry told Bill, looking down at his hands, still covered in mud and Dobby's blood. "Then I'll need to see them, straightaway."

He walked into the little kitchen, to the basin beneath a window overlooking the sea. Dawn was breaking over the horizon, shell pink and faintly gold, as he washed, again following the train of thought that had come to him in the dark garden. . . .

Dobby would never be able to tell them who had sent him to the cellar, but Harry knew what he had seen. A piercing blue eye had looked out of the mirror fragment, and then help had come. *Help will always be given at Hogwarts to those who ask for it.*

Harry dried his hands, impervious to the beauty of the scene outside the window and to the murmuring of the others in the sitting room. He looked out over the ocean and felt closer, this dawn, than ever before, closer to the heart of it all.

And still his scar prickled, and he knew that Voldemort was getting there too. Harry understood and yet did not understand. His instinct was telling him one thing, his brain quite another. The Dumbledore in Harry's head smiled, surveying Harry over the tips of his fingers, pressed together as if in prayer.

You gave Ron the Deluminator. You understood him. . . . You gave him a way back. . . .

And you understood Wormtail too. . . . You knew there was a bit of regret there, somewhere. . . .

And if you knew them . . . What did you know about me, Dumbledore?

Am I meant to know, but not to seek? Did you know how hard I'd find that? Is that why you made it this difficult? So I'd have time to work that out?

Harry stood quite still, eyes glazed, watching the place where a bright gold rim of dazzling sun was rising over the horizon. Then he looked down at his clean hands and was momentarily surprised to see the cloth he was holding in them. He set it down and returned to the hall, and as he did so, he felt his scar pulse angrily, and there flashed across his mind, swift as the reflection of a dragonfly over water, the outline of a building he knew extremely well.

Bill and Fleur were standing at the foot of the stairs.

"I need to speak to Griphook and Ollivander," Harry said.

"No," said Fleur. "You will 'ave to wait, 'Arry. Zey are both ill, tired —"

"I'm sorry," he said without heat, "but it can't wait. I need to talk to them now. Privately — and separately. It's urgent."

"Harry, what the hell's going on?" asked Bill. "You turn up here with a dead house-elf and a half-conscious goblin, Hermione looks as though she's been tortured, and Ron's just refused to tell me anything —"

"We can't tell you what we're doing," said Harry flatly. "You're in the Order, Bill, you know Dumbledore left us a mission. We're not supposed to talk about it to anyone else."

Fleur made an impatient noise, but Bill did not look at her; he was staring at Harry. His deeply scarred face was hard to read. Finally Bill said, "All right. Who do you want to talk to first?"

Harry hesitated. He knew what hung on his decision. There was hardly any time left; now was the moment to decide: Horcruxes or Hallows?

"Griphook," Harry said. "I'll speak to Griphook first."

His heart was racing as if he had been sprinting and had just cleared an enormous obstacle.

"Up here, then," said Bill, leading the way.

Harry had walked up several steps before stopping and looking back.

"I need you two as well!" he called to Ron and Hermione, who had been skulking, half concealed, in the doorway of the sitting room.

They both moved into the light, looking oddly relieved.

"How are you?" Harry asked Hermione. "You were amazing — coming up with that story when she was hurting you like that —"

Hermione gave a weak smile as Ron gave her a one-armed squeeze.

"What are we doing now, Harry?" he asked.

"You'll see. Come on."

Harry, Ron, and Hermione followed Bill up the steep stairs onto a small landing. Three doors led off it.

"In here," said Bill, opening the door into his and Fleur's room. It too had a view of the sea, now flecked with gold in the sunrise. Harry moved to the window, turned his back on the spectacular view, and waited, his arms folded, his scar prickling. Hermione took the chair beside the dressing table; Ron sat on the arm.

Bill reappeared, carrying the little goblin, whom he set down carefully upon the bed. Griphook grunted thanks, and Bill left, closing the door upon them all.

"I'm sorry to take you out of bed," said Harry. "How are your legs?"

"Painful," replied the goblin. "But mending."

He was still clutching the sword of Gryffindor, and wore a strange look: half truculent, half intrigued. Harry noted the goblin's sallow skin, his long thin fingers, his black eyes. Fleur had removed his shoes: His long feet were dirty. He was larger than a house-elf, but not by much. His domed head was much bigger than a human's.

"You probably don't remember —" Harry began.

"— that I was the goblin who showed you to your vault, the first time you ever visited Gringotts?" said Griphook. "I remember, Harry Potter. Even amongst goblins, you are very famous."

Harry and the goblin looked at each other, sizing each other up. Harry's scar was still prickling. He wanted to get through this interview with Griphook quickly, and at the same time was afraid of making a false move. While he tried to decide on the best way to approach his request, the goblin broke the silence.

"You buried the elf," he said, sounding unexpectedly rancorous. "I watched you from the window of the bedroom next door."

"Yes," said Harry.

Griphook looked at him out of the corners of his slanting black eyes.

"You are an unusual wizard, Harry Potter."

"In what way?" asked Harry, rubbing his scar absently.

"You dug the grave."

"So?"

Griphook did not answer. Harry rather thought he was being sneered at for acting like a Muggle, but it did not much matter to him whether Griphook approved of Dobby's grave or not. He gathered himself for the attack.

"Griphook, I need to ask —"

"You also rescued a goblin."

"What?"

"You brought me here. Saved me."

"Well, I take it you're not sorry?" said Harry a little impatiently.

"No, Harry Potter," said Griphook, and with one finger he twisted the thin black beard upon his chin, "but you are a very odd wizard."

"Right," said Harry. "Well, I need some help, Griphook, and you can give it to me."

The goblin made no sign of encouragement, but continued to frown at Harry as though he had never seen anything like him.

"I need to break into a Gringotts vault."

Harry had not meant to say it so baldly; the words were forced from him as pain shot through his lightning scar and he saw, again, the outline of Hogwarts. He closed his mind firmly. He needed to deal with Griphook first. Ron and Hermione were staring at Harry as though he had gone mad.

"Harry —" said Hermione, but she was cut off by Griphook.

"Break into a Gringotts vault?" repeated the goblin, wincing a little as he shifted his position upon the bed. "It is impossible."

"No, it isn't," Ron contradicted him. "It's been done."

"Yeah," said Harry. "The same day I first met you, Griphook. My birthday, seven years ago."

"The vault in question was empty at the time," snapped the goblin, and Harry understood that even though Griphook had left Gringotts, he was offended at the idea of its defenses being breached. "Its protection was minimal."

"Well, the vault we need to get into isn't empty, and I'm guessing its protection will be pretty powerful," said Harry. "It belongs to the Lestranges."

He saw Hermione and Ron look at each other, astonished, but there would be time enough to explain after Griphook had given his answer.

"You have no chance," said Griphook flatly. "No chance at all. *If you seek beneath our floors, a treasure that was never yours —*"

"*Thief, you have been warned, beware* — yeah, I know, I remember," said Harry. "But I'm not trying to get myself any treasure, I'm not trying to take anything for personal gain. Can you believe that?"

The goblin looked slantwise at Harry, and the lightning scar on Harry's forehead prickled, but he ignored it, refusing to acknowledge its pain or its invitation.

"If there was a wizard of whom I would believe that they did not seek personal gain," said Griphook finally, "it would be you, Harry Potter. Goblins and elves are not used to the protection or the respect that you have shown this night. Not from wand-carriers."

"Wand-carriers," repeated Harry: The phrase fell oddly upon his ears as his scar prickled, as Voldemort turned his thoughts northward, and as Harry burned to question Ollivander next door.

"The right to carry a wand," said the goblin quietly, "has long been contested between wizards and goblins."

"Well, goblins can do magic without wands," said Ron.

"That is immaterial! Wizards refuse to share the secrets of wand-lore with other magical beings, they deny us the possibility of extending our powers!"

"Well, goblins won't share any of their magic either," said Ron. "You won't tell us how to make swords and armor the way you do. Goblins know how to work metal in a way wizards have never —"

"It doesn't matter," said Harry, noting Griphook's rising color. "This isn't about wizards versus goblins or any other sort of magical creature —"

Griphook gave a nasty laugh.

"But it is, it is about precisely that! As the Dark Lord becomes ever more powerful, your race is set still more firmly above mine!

Gringotts falls under Wizarding rule, house-elves are slaughtered, and who amongst the wand-carriers protests?"

"We do!" said Hermione. She had sat up straight, her eyes bright. "We protest! And I'm hunted quite as much as any goblin or elf, Griphook! I'm a Mudblood!"

"Don't call yourself —" Ron muttered.

"Why shouldn't I?" said Hermione. "Mudblood, and proud of it! I've got no higher position under this new order than you have, Griphook! It was me they chose to torture, back at the Malfoys'!"

As she spoke, she pulled aside the neck of the dressing gown to reveal the thin cut Bellatrix had made, scarlet against her throat.

"Did you know that it was Harry who set Dobby free?" she asked. "Did you know that we've wanted elves to be freed for years?" (Ron fidgeted uncomfortably on the arm of Hermione's chair.) "You can't want You-Know-Who defeated more than we do, Griphook!"

The goblin gazed at Hermione with the same curiosity he had shown Harry.

"What do you seek within the Lestranges' vault?" he asked abruptly. "The sword that lies inside it is a fake. This is the real one." He looked from one to the other of them. "I think that you already know this. You asked me to lie for you back there."

"But the fake sword isn't the only thing in that vault, is it?" asked Harry. "Perhaps you've seen the other things in there?"

His heart was pounding harder than ever. He redoubled his efforts to ignore the pulsing of his scar.

The goblin twisted his beard around his finger again.

"It is against our code to speak of the secrets of Gringotts. We are the guardians of fabulous treasures. We have a duty to the objects placed in our care, which were, so often, wrought by our fingers."

The goblin stroked the sword, and his black eyes roved from Harry to Hermione to Ron and then back again.

"So young," he said finally, "to be fighting so many."

"Will you help us?" said Harry. "We haven't got a hope of breaking in without a goblin's help. You're our one chance."

"I shall . . . think about it," said Griphook maddeningly.

"But —" Ron started angrily; Hermione nudged him in the ribs.

"Thank you," said Harry.

The goblin bowed his great domed head in acknowledgement, then flexed his short legs.

"I think," he said, settling himself ostentatiously upon Bill and Fleur's bed, "that the Skele-Gro has finished its work. I may be able to sleep at last. Forgive me. . . ."

"Yeah, of course," said Harry, but before leaving the room he leaned forward and took the sword of Gryffindor from beside the goblin. Griphook did not protest, but Harry thought he saw resentment in the goblin's eyes as he closed the door upon him.

"Little git," whispered Ron. "He's enjoying keeping us hanging."

"Harry," whispered Hermione, pulling them both away from the door, into the middle of the still-dark landing, "are you saying what I think you're saying? Are you saying there's a Horcrux in the Lestranges' vault?"

"Yes," said Harry. "Bellatrix was terrified when she thought we'd been in there, she was beside herself. Why? What did she think we'd seen, what else did she think we might have taken? Something she was petrified You-Know-Who would find out about."

"But I thought we were looking for places You-Know-Who's been, places he's done something important?" said Ron, looking baffled. "Was he ever inside the Lestranges' vault?"

"I don't know whether he was ever inside Gringotts," said Harry. "He never had gold there when he was younger, because nobody left him anything. He would have seen the bank from the outside, though, the first time he ever went to Diagon Alley."

Harry's scar throbbed, but he ignored it; he wanted Ron and Hermione to understand about Gringotts before they spoke to Ollivander.

"I think he would have envied anyone who had a key to a Gringotts vault. I think he'd have seen it as a real symbol of belonging to the Wizarding world. And don't forget, he trusted Bellatrix and her husband. They were his most devoted servants before he fell, and they went looking for him after he vanished. He said it the night he came back, I heard him."

Harry rubbed his scar.

"I don't think he'd have told Bellatrix it was a Horcrux, though. He never told Lucius Malfoy the truth about the diary. He probably told her it was a treasured possession and asked her to place it in her vault. The safest place in the world for anything you want to hide, Hagrid told me . . . except for Hogwarts."

When Harry had finished speaking, Ron shook his head.

"You really understand him."

"Bits of him," said Harry. "Bits . . . I just wish I'd understood Dumbledore as much. But we'll see. Come on — Ollivander now."

Ron and Hermione looked bewildered but impressed as they followed him across the little landing and knocked upon the door opposite Bill and Fleur's. A weak "Come in!" answered them.

The wandmaker was lying on the twin bed farthest from the window. He had been held in the cellar for more than a year, and tortured, Harry knew, on at least one occasion. He was emaciated, the bones of his face sticking out sharply against the yellowish skin. His great silver eyes seemed vast in their sunken sockets. The hands that lay upon the blanket could have belonged to a skeleton. Harry sat down on the empty bed, beside Ron and Hermione. The rising sun was not visible here. The room faced the cliff-top garden and the freshly dug grave.

"Mr. Ollivander, I'm sorry to disturb you," Harry said.

"My dear boy." Ollivander's voice was feeble. "You rescued us. I thought we would die in that place. I can never thank you . . . *never* thank you . . . enough."

"We were glad to do it."

Harry's scar throbbed. He knew, he was certain, that there was hardly any time left in which to beat Voldemort to his goal, or else to attempt to thwart him. He felt a flutter of panic . . . yet he had made his decision when he chose to speak to Griphook first. Feigning a calm he did not feel, he groped in the pouch around his neck and took out the two halves of his broken wand.

"Mr. Ollivander, I need some help."

"Anything. Anything," said the wandmaker weakly.

"Can you mend this? Is it possible?"

Ollivander held out a trembling hand, and Harry placed the two barely connected halves into his palm.

"Holly and phoenix feather," said Ollivander in a tremulous voice. "Eleven inches. Nice and supple."

"Yes," said Harry. "Can you — ?"

"No," whispered Ollivander. "I am sorry, very sorry, but a wand that has suffered this degree of damage cannot be repaired by any means that I know of."

Harry had been braced to hear it, but it was a blow nevertheless. He took the wand halves back and replaced them in the pouch around his neck. Ollivander stared at the place where the shattered wand had vanished, and did not look away until Harry had taken from his pocket the two wands he had brought from the Malfoys'.

"Can you identify these?" Harry asked.

The wandmaker took the first of the wands and held it close to his faded eyes, rolling it between his knobble-knuckled fingers, flexing it slightly.

"Walnut and dragon heartstring," he said. "Twelve-and-three-quarter inches. Unyielding. This wand belonged to Bellatrix Lestrange."

"And this one?"

Ollivander performed the same examination.

"Hawthorn and unicorn hair. Ten inches precisely. Reasonably springy. This was the wand of Draco Malfoy."

"Was?" repeated Harry. "Isn't it still his?"

"Perhaps not. If you took it —"

"— I did —"

"— then it may be yours. Of course, the manner of taking matters. Much also depends upon the wand itself. In general, however, where a wand has been won, its allegiance will change."

There was silence in the room, except for the distant rushing of the sea.

"You talk about wands like they've got feelings," said Harry, "like they can think for themselves."

"The wand chooses the wizard," said Ollivander. "That much has always been clear to those of us who have studied wandlore."

"A person can still use a wand that hasn't chosen them, though?" asked Harry.

"Oh yes, if you are any wizard at all you will be able to channel your magic through almost any instrument. The best results, however, must always come where there is the strongest affinity between wizard and wand. These connections are complex. An initial attraction, and then a mutual quest for experience, the wand learning from the wizard, the wizard from the wand."

The sea gushed forward and backward; it was a mournful sound.

"I took this wand from Draco Malfoy by force," said Harry. "Can I use it safely?"

"I think so. Subtle laws govern wand ownership, but the conquered wand will usually bend its will to its new master."

"So I should use this one?" said Ron, pulling Wormtail's wand out of his pocket and handing it to Ollivander.

"Chestnut and dragon heartstring. Nine-and-a-quarter inches. Brittle. I was forced to make this shortly after my kidnapping, for Peter Pettigrew. Yes, if you won it, it is more likely to do your bidding, and do it well, than another wand."

"And this holds true for all wands, does it?" asked Harry.

"I think so," replied Ollivander, his protuberant eyes upon Harry's face. "You ask deep questions, Mr. Potter. Wandlore is a complex and mysterious branch of magic."

"So, it isn't necessary to kill the previous owner to take true possession of a wand?" asked Harry.

Ollivander swallowed.

"Necessary? No, I should not say that it is necessary to kill."

"There are legends, though," said Harry, and as his heart rate quickened, the pain in his scar became more intense; he was sure that Voldemort had decided to put his idea into action. "Legends about a wand — or wands — that have passed from hand to hand by murder."

Ollivander turned pale. Against the snowy pillow he was light gray, and his eyes were enormous, bloodshot, and bulging with what looked like fear.

"Only one wand, I think," he whispered.

"And You-Know-Who is interested in it, isn't he?" asked Harry.

"I — how?" croaked Ollivander, and he looked appealingly at Ron and Hermione for help. "How do you know this?"

"He wanted you to tell him how to overcome the connection between our wands," said Harry.

Ollivander looked terrified.

"He tortured me, you must understand that! The Cruciatus Curse, I — I had no choice but to tell him what I knew, what I guessed!"

"I understand," said Harry. "You told him about the twin cores? You said he just had to borrow another wizard's wand?"

Ollivander looked horrified, transfixed, by the amount that Harry knew. He nodded slowly.

"But it didn't work," Harry went on. "Mine still beat the borrowed wand. Do you know why that is?"

Ollivander shook his head as slowly as he had just nodded.

"I had . . . never heard of such a thing. Your wand performed something unique that night. The connection of the twin cores is incredibly rare, yet why your wand should have snapped the borrowed wand, I do not know. . . ."

"We were talking about the other wand, the wand that changes hands by murder. When You-Know-Who realized my wand had done something strange, he came back and asked about that other wand, didn't he?"

"How do you know this?"

Harry did not answer.

"Yes, he asked," whispered Ollivander. "He wanted to know everything I could tell him about the wand variously known as the Deathstick, the Wand of Destiny, or the Elder Wand."

Harry glanced sideways at Hermione. She looked flabbergasted.

"The Dark Lord," said Ollivander in hushed and frightened tones, "had always been happy with the wand I made him — yew and phoenix feather, thirteen-and-a-half inches — until he discovered the connection of the twin cores. Now he seeks another, more powerful wand, as the only way to conquer yours."

"But he'll know soon, if he doesn't already, that mine's broken beyond repair," said Harry quietly.

"No!" said Hermione, sounding frightened. "He can't know that, Harry, how could he — ?"

"Priori Incantatem," said Harry. "We left your wand and the blackthorn wand at the Malfoys', Hermione. If they examine them properly, make them re-create the spells they've cast lately, they'll see that yours broke mine, they'll see that you tried and failed to mend it, and they'll realize that I've been using the blackthorn one ever since."

The little color she had regained since their arrival had drained from her face. Ron gave Harry a reproachful look, and said, "Let's not worry about that now —"

But Mr. Ollivander intervened.

"The Dark Lord no longer seeks the Elder Wand only for your destruction, Mr. Potter. He is determined to possess it because he believes it will make him truly invulnerable."

"And will it?"

"The owner of the Elder Wand must always fear attack," said Ollivander, "but the idea of the Dark Lord in possession of the Deathstick is, I must admit . . . formidable."

Harry was suddenly reminded of how he had been unsure, when they first met, of how much he liked Ollivander. Even now, having been tortured and imprisoned by Voldemort, the idea of the Dark wizard in possession of this wand seemed to enthrall him as much as it repulsed him.

"You — you really think this wand exists, then, Mr. Ollivander?" asked Hermione.

"Oh yes," said Ollivander. "Yes, it is perfectly possible to trace the wand's course through history. There are gaps, of course, and long ones, where it vanishes from view, temporarily lost or hidden; but always it resurfaces. It has certain identifying characteristics that those who are learned in wandlore recognize. There are written accounts, some of them obscure, that I and other wandmakers have made it our business to study. They have the ring of authenticity."

"So you — you don't think it can be a fairy tale or a myth?" Hermione asked hopefully.

"No," said Ollivander. "Whether it *needs* to pass by murder, I do not know. Its history is bloody, but that may be simply due to the fact that it is such a desirable object, and arouses such passions in wizards. Immensely powerful, dangerous in the wrong hands, and an object of incredible fascination to all of us who study the power of wands."

"Mr. Ollivander," said Harry, "you told You-Know-Who that Gregorovitch had the Elder Wand, didn't you?"

Ollivander turned, if possible, even paler. He looked ghostly as he gulped.

"But how — how do you — ?"

"Never mind how I know it," said Harry, closing his eyes momentarily as his scar burned and he saw, for mere seconds, a vision of the main street in Hogsmeade, still dark, because it was so much farther north. "You told You-Know-Who that Gregorovitch had the wand?"

"It was a rumor," whispered Ollivander. "A rumor, years and years ago, long before you were born! I believe Gregorovitch himself started it. You can see how good it would be for business: that he was studying and duplicating the qualities of the Elder Wand!"

"Yes, I can see that," said Harry. He stood up. "Mr. Ollivander, one last thing, and then we'll let you get some rest. What do you know about the Deathly Hallows?"

"The — the what?" asked the wandmaker, looking utterly bewildered.

"The Deathly Hallows."

"I'm afraid I don't know what you're talking about. Is this still something to do with wands?"

Harry looked into the sunken face and believed that Ollivander was not acting. He did not know about the Hallows.

"Thank you," said Harry. "Thank you very much. We'll leave you to get some rest now."

Ollivander looked stricken.

"He was torturing me!" he gasped. "The Cruciatus Curse . . . you have no idea. . . ."

"I do," said Harry. "I really do. Please get some rest. Thank you for telling me all of this."

He led Ron and Hermione down the staircase. Harry caught a glimpse of Bill, Fleur, Luna, and Dean sitting at the table in the kitchen, cups of tea in front of them. They all looked up at Harry as he appeared in the doorway, but he merely nodded to them and continued into the garden, Ron and Hermione behind him. The reddish mound of earth that covered Dobby lay ahead, and Harry walked back to it, as the pain in his head built more and more powerfully. It was a huge effort now to close down the visions that were forcing themselves upon him, but he knew that he would have to resist only a little longer. He would yield very soon, because he needed to know that his theory was right. He must make only one more short effort, so that he could explain to Ron and Hermione.

"Gregorovitch had the Elder Wand a long time ago," he said. "I saw You-Know-Who trying to find him. When he tracked him down, he found that Gregorovitch didn't have it anymore: It was stolen from him by Grindelwald. How Grindelwald found out that Gregorovitch had it, I don't know — but if Gregorovitch was stupid enough to spread the rumor, it can't have been that difficult."

Voldemort was at the gates of Hogwarts; Harry could see him standing there, and see too the lamp bobbing in the pre-dawn, coming closer and closer.

"And Grindelwald used the Elder Wand to become powerful. And at the height of his power, when Dumbledore knew he was the only one who could stop him, he dueled Grindelwald and beat him, and he took the Elder Wand."

"*Dumbledore* had the Elder Wand?" said Ron. "But then — where is it now?"

"At Hogwarts," said Harry, fighting to remain with them in the cliff-top garden.

"But then, let's go!" said Ron urgently. "Harry, let's go and get it before he does!"

"It's too late for that," said Harry. He could not help himself, but clutched his head, trying to help it resist. "He knows where it is. He's there now."

"Harry!" Ron said furiously. "How long have you known this — why have we been wasting time? Why did you talk to Griphook first? We could have gone — we could still go —"

"No," said Harry, and he sank to his knees in the grass. "Hermione's right. Dumbledore didn't want me to have it. He didn't want me to take it. He wanted me to get the Horcruxes."

"The unbeatable wand, Harry!" moaned Ron.

"I'm not supposed to . . . I'm supposed to get the Horcruxes. . . ."

And now everything was cool and dark: The sun was barely visible over the horizon as he glided alongside Snape, up through the grounds toward the lake.

"I shall join you in the castle shortly," he said in his high, cold voice. "Leave me now."

Snape bowed and set off back up the path, his black cloak billowing behind him. Harry walked slowly, waiting for Snape's figure to disappear. It would not do for Snape, or indeed anyone else, to see where he was going. But there were no lights in the castle windows, and he could conceal himself . . . and in a second he had cast upon himself a Disillusionment Charm that hid him even from his own eyes.

And he walked on, around the edge of the lake, taking in the outlines of the beloved castle, his first kingdom, his birthright. . . .

And here it was, beside the lake, reflected in the dark waters. The white marble tomb, an unnecessary blot on the familiar landscape. He felt again that rush of controlled euphoria, that heady sense of purpose in destruction. He raised the old yew wand: How fitting that this would be its last great act.

The tomb split open from head to foot. The shrouded figure was as long and thin as it had been in life. He raised the wand again.

The wrappings fell open. The face was translucent, pale, sunken, yet almost perfectly preserved. They had left his spectacles on the crooked nose: He felt amused derision. Dumbledore's hands were folded upon his chest, and there it lay, clutched beneath them, buried with him.

Had the old fool imagined that marble or death would protect the wand? Had he thought that the Dark Lord would be scared to violate his tomb? The spiderlike hand swooped and pulled the wand from Dumbledore's grasp, and as he took it, a shower of sparks flew from its tip, sparkling over the corpse of its last owner, ready to serve a new master at last.

SHELL COTTAGE

Bill and Fleur's cottage stood alone on a cliff overlooking the sea, its walls embedded with shells and whitewashed. It was a lonely and beautiful place. Wherever Harry went inside the tiny cottage or its garden, he could hear the constant ebb and flow of the sea, like the breathing of some great, slumbering creature. He spent much of the next few days making excuses to escape the crowded cottage, craving the cliff-top view of open sky and wide, empty sea, and the feel of cold, salty wind on his face.

The enormity of his decision not to race Voldemort to the wand still scared Harry. He could not remember, ever before, choosing *not* to act. He was full of doubts, doubts that Ron could not help voicing whenever they were together.

"What if Dumbledore wanted us to work out the symbol in time to get the wand?" "What if working out what the symbol meant made you 'worthy' to get the Hallows?" "Harry, if that really is the Elder Wand, how the hell are we supposed to finish off You-Know-Who?"

Harry had no answers: There were moments when he wondered whether it had been outright madness not to try to prevent Voldemort breaking open the tomb. He could not even explain satisfactorily why he had decided against it: Every time he tried to reconstruct the internal arguments that had led to his decision, they sounded feebler to him.

The odd thing was that Hermione's support made him feel just as confused as Ron's doubts. Now forced to accept that the Elder Wand was real, she maintained that it was an evil object, and that the way Voldemort had taken possession of it was repellent, not to be considered.

"You could never have done that, Harry," she said again and again. "You couldn't have broken into Dumbledore's grave."

But the idea of Dumbledore's corpse frightened Harry much less than the possibility that he might have misunderstood the living Dumbledore's intentions. He felt that he was still groping in the dark; he had chosen his path but kept looking back, wondering whether he had misread the signs, whether he should not have taken the other way. From time to time, anger at Dumbledore crashed over him again, powerful as the waves slamming themselves against the cliff beneath the cottage, anger that Dumbledore had not explained before he died.

"But *is* he dead?" said Ron, three days after they had arrived at the cottage. Harry had been staring out over the wall that separated the cottage garden from the cliff when Ron and Hermione had found him; he wished they had not, having no wish to join in with their argument.

"Yes, he is, Ron, *please* don't start that again!"

"Look at the facts, Hermione," said Ron, speaking across Harry, who continued to gaze at the horizon. "The silver doe. The sword. The eye Harry saw in the mirror —"

"Harry admits he could have imagined the eye! Don't you, Harry?"

"I could have," said Harry without looking at her.

"But you don't think you did, do you?" asked Ron.

"No, I don't," said Harry.

"There you go!" said Ron quickly, before Hermione could carry on. "If it wasn't Dumbledore, explain how Dobby knew we were in the cellar, Hermione?"

"I can't — but can you explain how Dumbledore sent him to us if he's lying in a tomb at Hogwarts?"

"I dunno, it could've been his ghost!"

"Dumbledore wouldn't come back as a ghost," said Harry. There was little about Dumbledore he was sure of now, but he knew that much. "He would have gone on."

"What d'you mean, 'gone on'?" asked Ron, but before Harry could say any more, a voice behind them said, "'Arry?"

Fleur had come out of the cottage, her long silver hair flying in the breeze.

"'Arry, Grip'ook would like to speak to you. 'E eez in ze smallest bedroom, 'e says 'e does not want to be over'eard."

Her dislike of the goblin sending her to deliver messages was clear; she looked irritable as she walked back around the house.

Griphook was waiting for them, as Fleur had said, in the tiniest of the cottage's three bedrooms, in which Hermione and Luna slept by night. He had drawn the red cotton curtains against the bright, cloudy sky, which gave the room a fiery glow at odds with the rest of the airy, light cottage.

"I have reached my decision, Harry Potter," said the goblin, who was sitting cross-legged in a low chair, drumming its arms with his spindly fingers. "Though the goblins of Gringotts will consider it base treachery, I have decided to help you —"

"That's great!" said Harry, relief surging through him. "Griphook, thank you, we're really —"

"— in return," said the goblin firmly, "for payment."

Slightly taken aback, Harry hesitated.

"How much do you want? I've got gold."

"Not gold," said Griphook. "I have gold."

His black eyes glittered; there were no whites to his eyes.

"I want the sword. The sword of Godric Gryffindor."

Harry's spirits plummeted.

"You can't have that," he said. "I'm sorry."

"Then," said the goblin softly, "we have a problem."

"We can give you something else," said Ron eagerly. "I'll bet the Lestranges have got loads of stuff, you can take your pick once we get into the vault."

He had said the wrong thing. Griphook flushed angrily.

"I am not a thief, boy! I am not trying to procure treasures to which I have no right!"

"The sword's ours —"

"It is not," said the goblin.

"We're Gryffindors, and it was Godric Gryffindor's —"

"And before it was Gryffindor's, whose was it?" demanded the goblin, sitting up straight.

"No one's," said Ron. "It was made for him, wasn't it?"

"No!" cried the goblin, bristling with anger as he pointed a long finger at Ron. "Wizarding arrogance again! That sword was Ragnuk the First's, taken from him by Godric Gryffindor! It is a lost treasure, a masterpiece of goblinwork! It belongs with the goblins! The sword is the price of my hire, take it or leave it!"

Griphook glared at them. Harry glanced at the other two, then said, "We need to discuss this, Griphook, if that's all right. Could you give us a few minutes?"

The goblin nodded, looking sour.

Downstairs in the empty sitting room, Harry walked to the fireplace, brow furrowed, trying to think what to do. Behind him, Ron said, "He's having a laugh. We can't let him have that sword."

"It is true?" Harry asked Hermione. "Was the sword stolen by Gryffindor?"

"I don't know," she said hopelessly. "Wizarding history often skates over what the wizards have done to other magical races, but there's no account that I know of that says Gryffindor stole the sword."

"It'll be one of those goblin stories," said Ron, "about how the wizards are always trying to get one over on them. I suppose we should think ourselves lucky he hasn't asked for one of our wands."

"Goblins have got good reason to dislike wizards, Ron," said Hermione. "They've been treated brutally in the past."

"Goblins aren't exactly fluffy little bunnies, though, are they?" said Ron. "They've killed plenty of us. They've fought dirty too."

"But arguing with Griphook about whose race is most underhanded and violent isn't going to make him more likely to help us, is it?"

There was a pause while they tried to think of a way around the problem. Harry looked out of the window at Dobby's grave. Luna was arranging sea lavender in a jam jar beside the headstone.

"Okay," said Ron, and Harry turned back to face him, "how's

this? We tell Griphook we need the sword until we get inside the vault, and then he can have it. There's a fake in there, isn't there? We switch them, and give him the fake."

"Ron, he'd know the difference better than we would!" said Hermione. "He's the only one who realized there had been a swap!"

"Yeah, but we could scarper before he realizes —"

He quailed beneath the look Hermione was giving him.

"That," she said quietly, "is despicable. Ask for his help, then double-cross him? And you wonder why goblins don't like wizards, Ron?"

Ron's ears had turned red.

"All right, all right! It was the only thing I could think of! What's your solution, then?"

"We need to offer him something else, something just as valuable."

"Brilliant. I'll go and get one of our other ancient goblin-made swords and you can gift wrap it."

Silence fell between them again. Harry was sure that the goblin would accept nothing but the sword, even if they had something as valuable to offer him. Yet the sword was their one, indispensable weapon against the Horcruxes.

He closed his eyes for a moment or two and listened to the rush of the sea. The idea that Gryffindor might have stolen the sword was unpleasant to him: He had always been proud to be a Gryffindor; Gryffindor had been the champion of Muggle-borns, the wizard who had clashed with the pureblood-loving Slytherin. . . .

"Maybe he's lying," Harry said, opening his eyes again. "Griphook. Maybe Gryffindor didn't take the sword. How do we know the goblin version of history's right?"

"Does it make a difference?" asked Hermione.

"Changes how I feel about it," said Harry.

He took a deep breath.

"We'll tell him he can have the sword after he's helped us get into that vault — but we'll be careful to avoid telling him exactly *when* he can have it."

A grin spread slowly across Ron's face. Hermione, however, looked alarmed.

"Harry, we can't —"

"He can have it," Harry went on, "after we've used it on all of the Horcruxes. I'll make sure he gets it then. I'll keep my word."

"But that could be years!" said Hermione.

"I know that, but *he* needn't. I won't be lying . . . really."

Harry met her eyes with a mixture of defiance and shame. He remembered the words that had been engraved over the gateway to Nurmengard: FOR THE GREATER GOOD. He pushed the idea away. What choice did they have?

"I don't like it," said Hermione.

"Nor do I, much," Harry admitted.

"Well, I think it's genius," said Ron, standing up again. "Let's go and tell him."

Back in the smallest bedroom, Harry made the offer, careful to phrase it so as not to give any definite time for the handover of the sword. Hermione frowned at the floor while he was speaking; he felt irritated at her, afraid that she might give the game away. However, Griphook had eyes for nobody but Harry.

"I have your word, Harry Potter, that you will give me the sword of Gryffindor if I help you?"

"Yes," said Harry.

"Then shake," said the goblin, holding out his hand.

Harry took it and shook. He wondered whether those black eyes saw any misgivings in his own. Then Griphook relinquished him, clapped his hands together, and said, "So. We begin!"

It was like planning to break into the Ministry all over again. They settled to work in the smallest bedroom, which was kept, according to Griphook's preference, in semidarkness.

"I have visited the Lestranges' vault only once," Griphook told them, "on the occasion I was told to place inside it the false sword. It is one of the most ancient chambers. The oldest Wizarding families store their treasures at the deepest level, where the vaults are largest and best protected. . . ."

They remained shut in the cupboardlike room for hours at a time. Slowly the days stretched into weeks. There was problem after problem to overcome, not least of which was that their store of Polyjuice Potion was greatly depleted.

"There's really only enough left for one of us," said Hermione, tilting the thick mudlike potion against the lamplight.

"That'll be enough," said Harry, who was examining Griphook's hand-drawn map of the deepest passageways.

The other inhabitants of Shell Cottage could hardly fail to notice that something was going on now that Harry, Ron, and Hermione only emerged for mealtimes. Nobody asked questions, although Harry often felt Bill's eyes on the three of them at the table, thoughtful, concerned.

The longer they spent together, the more Harry realized that he did not much like the goblin. Griphook was unexpectedly bloodthirsty, laughed at the idea of pain in lesser creatures, and seemed to relish the possibility that they might have to hurt other wizards to reach the Lestranges' vault. Harry could tell that his distaste was shared by the other two, but they did not discuss it: They needed Griphook.

The goblin ate only grudgingly with the rest of them. Even after his legs had mended, he continued to request trays of food in his room, like the still-frail Ollivander, until Bill (following an angry outburst from Fleur) went upstairs to tell him that the arrangement could not continue. Thereafter Griphook joined them at the over-crowded table, although he refused to eat the same food, insisting, instead, on lumps of raw meat, roots, and various fungi.

Harry felt responsible: It was, after all, he who had insisted that the goblin remain at Shell Cottage so that he could question him; his fault that the whole Weasley family had been driven into hiding, that Bill, Fred, George, and Mr. Weasley could no longer work.

"I'm sorry," he told Fleur, one blustery April evening as he helped her prepare dinner. "I never meant you to have to deal with all of this."

She had just set some knives to work, chopping up steaks for Griphook and Bill, who had preferred his meat bloody ever since he had been attacked by Greyback. While the knives sliced away behind her, her somewhat irritable expression softened.

"'Arry, you saved my sister's life, I do not forget."

This was not, strictly speaking, true, but Harry decided against reminding her that Gabrielle had never been in real danger.

"Anyway," Fleur went on, pointing her wand at a pot of sauce on the stove, which began to bubble at once, "Mr. Ollivander leaves for Muriel's zis evening. Zat will make zings easier. Ze goblin," she scowled a little at the mention of him, "can move downstairs, and you, Ron, and Dean can take zat room."

"We don't mind sleeping in the living room," said Harry, who knew that Griphook would think poorly of having to sleep on the sofa; keeping Griphook happy was essential to their plans. "Don't worry about us." And when she tried to protest he went on, "We'll be off your hands soon too, Ron, Hermione, and I. We won't need to be here much longer."

"But what do you mean?" she said, frowning at him, her wand pointing at the casserole dish now suspended in midair. "Of course you must not leave, you are safe 'ere!"

She looked rather like Mrs. Weasley as she said it, and he was glad that the back door opened at that moment. Luna and Dean entered, their hair damp from the rain outside and their arms full of driftwood.

". . . and tiny little ears," Luna was saying, "a bit like a hippo's, Daddy says, only purple and hairy. And if you want to call them, you have to hum; they prefer a waltz, nothing too fast. . . ."

Looking uncomfortable, Dean shrugged at Harry as he passed, following Luna into the combined dining and sitting room where Ron and Hermione were laying the dinner table. Seizing the chance to escape Fleur's questions, Harry grabbed two jugs of pumpkin juice and followed them.

". . . and if you ever come to our house I'll be able to show you the horn, Daddy wrote to me about it but I haven't seen it yet, because the Death Eaters took me from the Hogwarts Express and I never got home for Christmas," Luna was saying, as she and Dean relaid the fire.

"Luna, we told you," Hermione called over to her. "That horn exploded. It came from an Erumpent, not a Crumple-Horned Snorkack —"

"No, it was definitely a Snorkack horn," said Luna serenely. "Daddy told me. It will probably have re-formed by now, they mend themselves, you know."

Hermione shook her head and continued laying down forks as Bill appeared, leading Mr. Ollivander down the stairs. The wandmaker still looked exceptionally frail, and he clung to Bill's arm as the latter supported him, carrying a large suitcase.

"I'm going to miss you, Mr. Ollivander," said Luna, approaching the old man.

"And I you, my dear," said Ollivander, patting her on the shoulder. "You were an inexpressible comfort to me in that terrible place."

"So, *au revoir,* Mr. Ollivander," said Fleur, kissing him on both cheeks. "And I wonder whezzer you could oblige me by delivering a package to Bill's Auntie Muriel? I never returned 'er tiara."

"It will be an honor," said Ollivander with a little bow, "the very least I can do in return for your generous hospitality."

Fleur drew out a worn velvet case, which she opened to show the wandmaker. The tiara sat glittering and twinkling in the light from the low-hanging lamp.

"Moonstones and diamonds," said Griphook, who had sidled into the room without Harry noticing. "Made by goblins, I think?"

"And paid for by wizards," said Bill quietly, and the goblin shot him a look that was both furtive and challenging.

A strong wind gusted against the cottage windows as Bill and Ollivander set off into the night. The rest of them squeezed in around the table; elbow to elbow and with barely enough room to move, they started to eat. The fire crackled and popped in the grate beside them. Fleur, Harry noticed, was merely playing with her food; she glanced at the window every few minutes; however, Bill returned before they had finished their first course, his long hair tangled by the wind.

"Everything's fine," he told Fleur. "Ollivander settled in, Mum and Dad say hello. Ginny sends you all her love. Fred and George are driving Muriel up the wall, they're still operating an Owl-Order business out of her back room. It cheered her up to have her tiara back, though. She said she thought we'd stolen it."

"Ah, she eez *charmante,* your aunt," said Fleur crossly, waving her wand and causing the dirty plates to rise and form a stack in midair. She caught them and marched out of the room.

"Daddy's made a tiara," piped up Luna. "Well, more of a crown, really."

Ron caught Harry's eye and grinned; Harry knew that he was remembering the ludicrous headdress they had seen on their visit to Xenophilius.

"Yes, he's trying to re-create the lost diadem of Ravenclaw. He thinks he's identified most of the main elements now. Adding the billywig wings really made a difference —"

There was a bang on the front door. Everyone's head turned toward it. Fleur came running out of the kitchen, looking frightened; Bill jumped to his feet, his wand pointing at the door; Harry, Ron, and Hermione did the same. Silently Griphook slipped beneath the table, out of sight.

"Who is it?" Bill called.

"It is I, Remus John Lupin!" called a voice over the howling wind. Harry experienced a thrill of fear; what had happened? "I am a werewolf, married to Nymphadora Tonks, and you, the Secret-Keeper of Shell Cottage, told me the address and bade me come in an emergency!"

"Lupin," muttered Bill, and he ran to the door and wrenched it open.

Lupin fell over the threshold. He was white-faced, wrapped in a traveling cloak, his graying hair windswept. He straightened up, looked around the room, making sure of who was there, then cried aloud, "It's a boy! We've named him Ted, after Dora's father!"

Hermione shrieked.

"Wha — ? Tonks — Tonks has had the baby?"

"Yes, yes, she's had the baby!" shouted Lupin. All around the table came cries of delight, sighs of relief: Hermione and Fleur both squealed, "Congratulations!" and Ron said, "Blimey, a baby!" as if he had never heard of such a thing before.

"Yes — yes — a boy," said Lupin again, who seemed dazed by his own happiness. He strode around the table and hugged Harry; the scene in the basement of Grimmauld Place might never have happened.

"You'll be godfather?" he said as he released Harry.

"M-me?" stammered Harry.

"You, yes, of course — Dora quite agrees, no one better —"

"I — yeah — blimey —"

Harry felt overwhelmed, astonished, delighted; now Bill was hurrying to fetch wine, and Fleur was persuading Lupin to join them for a drink.

"I can't stay long, I must get back," said Lupin, beaming around at them all. He looked years younger than Harry had ever seen him. "Thank you, thank you, Bill."

Bill had soon filled all of their goblets, they stood and raised them high in a toast.

"To Teddy Remus Lupin," said Lupin, "a great wizard in the making!"

"'Oo does 'e look like?" Fleur inquired.

"I think he looks like Dora, but she thinks he is like me. Not much hair. It looked black when he was born, but I swear it's turned ginger in the hour since. Probably be blond by the time I get back. Andromeda says Tonks's hair started changing color the day that she was born." He drained his goblet. "Oh, go on then, just one more," he added, beaming, as Bill made to fill it again.

The wind buffeted the little cottage and the fire leapt and crackled, and Bill was soon opening another bottle of wine. Lupin's news seemed to have taken them out of themselves, removed them for a while from their state of siege: Tidings of new life were exhilarating. Only the goblin seemed untouched by the suddenly festive atmosphere, and after a while he slunk back to the bedroom he now occupied alone. Harry thought he was the only one who had noticed this, until he saw Bill's eyes following the goblin up the stairs.

"No . . . no . . . I really must get back," said Lupin at last, declining yet another goblet of wine. He got to his feet and pulled his traveling cloak back around himself.

"Good-bye, good-bye — I'll try and bring some pictures in a few days' time — they'll all be so glad to know that I've seen you —"

He fastened his cloak and made his farewells, hugging the women and grasping hands with the men, then, still beaming, returned into the wild night.

"Godfather, Harry!" said Bill as they walked into the kitchen together, helping clear the table. "A real honor! Congratulations!"

As Harry set down the empty goblets he was carrying, Bill pulled the door behind him closed, shutting out the still-voluble voices of the others, who were continuing to celebrate even in Lupin's absence.

"I wanted a private word, actually, Harry. It hasn't been easy to get an opportunity with the cottage this full of people."

Bill hesitated.

"Harry, you're planning something with Griphook."

It was a statement, not a question, and Harry did not bother to deny it. He merely looked at Bill, waiting.

"I know goblins," said Bill. "I've worked for Gringotts ever since I left Hogwarts. As far as there can be friendship between wizards and goblins, I have goblin friends — or, at least, goblins I know well, and like." Again, Bill hesitated.

"Harry, what do you want from Griphook, and what have you promised him in return?"

"I can't tell you that," said Harry. "Sorry, Bill."

The kitchen door opened behind them; Fleur was trying to bring through more empty goblets.

"Wait," Bill told her. "Just a moment."

She backed out and he closed the door again.

"Then I have to say this," Bill went on. "If you have struck any kind of bargain with Griphook, and most particularly if that bargain involves treasure, you must be exceptionally careful. Goblin notions of ownership, payment, and repayment are not the same as human ones."

Harry felt a slight squirm of discomfort, as though a small snake had stirred inside him.

"What do you mean?" he asked.

"We are talking about a different breed of being," said Bill.

"Dealings between wizards and goblins have been fraught for centuries — but you'll know all that from History of Magic. There has been fault on both sides, I would never claim that wizards have been innocent. However, there is a belief among some goblins, and those at Gringotts are perhaps most prone to it, that wizards cannot be trusted in matters of gold and treasure, that they have no respect for goblin ownership."

"I respect —" Harry began, but Bill shook his head.

"You don't understand, Harry, nobody could understand unless they have lived with goblins. To a goblin, the rightful and true master of any object is the maker, not the purchaser. All goblin-made objects are, in goblin eyes, rightfully theirs."

"But if it was bought —"

"— then they would consider it rented by the one who had paid the money. They have, however, great difficulty with the idea of goblin-made objects passing from wizard to wizard. You saw Griphook's face when the tiara passed under his eyes. He disapproves. I believe he thinks, as do the fiercest of his kind, that it ought to have been returned to the goblins once the original purchaser died. They consider our habit of keeping goblin-made objects, passing them from wizard to wizard without further payment, little more than theft."

Harry had an ominous feeling now; he wondered whether Bill guessed more than he was letting on.

"All I am saying," said Bill, setting his hand on the door back into the sitting room, "is to be very careful what you promise goblins, Harry. It would be less dangerous to break into Gringotts than to renege on a promise to a goblin."

"Right," said Harry as Bill opened the door, "yeah. Thanks. I'll bear that in mind."

As he followed Bill back to the others a wry thought came to him, born no doubt of the wine he had drunk. He seemed set on course to become just as reckless a godfather to Teddy Lupin as Sirius Black had been to him.

GRINGOTTS

Their plans were made, their preparations complete; in the smallest bedroom a single long, coarse black hair (plucked from the sweater Hermione had been wearing at Malfoy Manor) lay curled in a small glass phial on the mantelpiece.

"And you'll be using her actual wand," said Harry, nodding toward the walnut wand, "so I reckon you'll be pretty convincing."

Hermione looked frightened that the wand might sting or bite her as she picked it up.

"I hate this thing," she said in a low voice. "I really hate it. It feels all wrong, it doesn't work properly for me. . . . It's like a bit of *her*."

Harry could not help but remember how Hermione had dismissed his loathing of the blackthorn wand, insisting that he was imagining things when it did not work as well as his own, telling him to simply practice. He chose not to repeat her own advice back to her, however; the eve of their attempted assault on Gringotts felt like the wrong moment to antagonize her.

"It'll probably help you get in character, though," said Ron. "Think what that wand's done!"

"But that's my point!" said Hermione. "This is the wand that tortured Neville's mum and dad, and who knows how many other people? This is the wand that killed Sirius!"

Harry had not thought of that: He looked down at the wand and was visited by a brutal urge to snap it, to slice it in half with Gryffindor's sword, which was propped against the wall beside him.

"I miss *my* wand," Hermione said miserably. "I wish Mr. Ollivander could have made me another one too."

Mr. Ollivander had sent Luna a new wand that morning. She was out on the back lawn at that moment, testing its capabilities in the late afternoon sun. Dean, who had lost his wand to the Snatchers, was watching rather gloomily.

Harry looked down at the hawthorn wand that had once belonged to Draco Malfoy. He had been surprised, but pleased, to discover that it worked for him at least as well as Hermione's had done. Remembering what Ollivander had told them of the secret workings of wands, Harry thought he knew what Hermione's problem was: She had not won the walnut wand's allegiance by taking it personally from Bellatrix.

The door of the bedroom opened and Griphook entered. Harry reached instinctively for the hilt of the sword and drew it close to him, but regretted his action at once: He could tell that the goblin had noticed. Seeking to gloss over the sticky moment, he said, "We've just been checking the last-minute stuff, Griphook. We've told Bill and Fleur we're leaving tomorrow, and we've told them not to get up to see us off."

They had been firm on this point, because Hermione would need to transform into Bellatrix before they left, and the less that Bill and Fleur knew or suspected about what they were about to do, the better. They had also explained that they would not be returning. As they had lost Perkins's old tent on the night that the Snatchers caught them, Bill had lent them another one. It was now packed inside the beaded bag, which, Harry was impressed to learn, Hermione had protected from the Snatchers by the simple expedient of stuffing it down her sock.

Though he would miss Bill, Fleur, Luna, and Dean, not to mention the home comforts they had enjoyed over the last few weeks, Harry was looking forward to escaping the confinement of Shell Cottage. He was tired of trying to make sure that they were not overheard, tired of being shut in the tiny, dark bedroom. Most of all, he longed to be rid of Griphook. However, precisely how and when they were to part from the goblin without handing over Gryffindor's sword remained a question to which Harry had no answer. It had been impossible to decide how they were going to do it, because the goblin rarely left Harry, Ron, and Hermione alone together for more than five minutes at a time: "He could give my mother lessons," growled Ron, as the goblin's long fingers kept appearing around the edges of doors. With Bill's warning in mind, Harry could not help suspecting that Griphook was on the watch for possible skulduggery. Hermione disapproved so heartily of the planned double-cross that Harry had given up attempting to pick her brains on how best to do it; Ron, on the rare occasions that they had been able to snatch a few Griphook-free moments, had come up with nothing better than "We'll just have to wing it, mate."

Harry slept badly that night. Lying awake in the early hours, he thought back to the way he had felt the night before they had infiltrated the Ministry of Magic and remembered a determination, almost an excitement. Now he was experiencing jolts of anxiety, nagging doubts: He could not shake off the fear that it was all going to go wrong. He kept telling himself that their plan was good, that Griphook knew what they were facing, that they were well-prepared for all the difficulties they were likely to encounter, yet still he felt uneasy. Once or twice he heard Ron stir and was sure that he too was awake, but they were sharing the sitting room with Dean, so Harry did not speak.

It was a relief when six o'clock arrived and they could slip out of their sleeping bags, dress in the semidarkness, then creep out into the garden, where they were to meet Hermione and Griphook. The dawn was chilly, but there was little wind now that it was May. Harry looked up at the stars still glimmering palely in the dark sky and listened to the sea washing backward and forward against the cliff: He was going to miss the sound.

Small green shoots were forcing their way up through the red earth of Dobby's grave now; in a year's time the mound would be covered in flowers. The white stone that bore the elf's name had already acquired a weathered look. He realized now that they could hardly have laid Dobby to rest in a more beautiful place, but Harry ached with sadness to think of leaving him behind. Looking down on the grave, he wondered yet again how the elf had known where to come to rescue them. His fingers moved absentmindedly to the little pouch still strung around his neck, through which he could feel the jagged mirror fragment in which he had been sure he had seen Dumbledore's eye. Then the sound of a door opening made him look around.

Bellatrix Lestrange was striding across the lawn toward them, accompanied by Griphook. As she walked, she was tucking the small, beaded bag into the inside pocket of another set of the old robes they had taken from Grimmauld Place. Though Harry knew perfectly well that it was really Hermione, he could not suppress a shiver of loathing. She was taller than he was, her long black hair rippling down her back, her heavily lidded eyes disdainful as they rested upon him; but then she spoke, and he heard Hermione through Bellatrix's low voice.

"She tasted *disgusting,* worse than Gurdyroots! Okay, Ron, come here so I can do you. . . ."

"Right, but remember, I don't like the beard too long —"

"Oh, for heaven's sake, this isn't about looking handsome —"

"It's not that, it gets in the way! But I liked my nose a bit shorter, try and do it the way you did last time."

Hermione sighed and set to work, muttering under her breath as she transformed various aspects of Ron's appearance. He was to be given a completely fake identity, and they were trusting to the malevolent aura cast by Bellatrix to protect him. Meanwhile Harry and Griphook were to be concealed under the Invisibility Cloak.

"There," said Hermione, "how does he look, Harry?"

It was just possible to discern Ron under his disguise, but only, Harry thought, because he knew him so well. Ron's hair was now long and wavy; he had a thick brown beard and mustache, no freckles, a short, broad nose, and heavy eyebrows.

"Well, he's not my type, but he'll do," said Harry. "Shall we go, then?"

All three of them glanced back at Shell Cottage, lying dark and silent under the fading stars, then turned and began to walk toward the point, just beyond the boundary wall, where the Fidelius Charm stopped working and they would be able to Disapparate. Once past the gate, Griphook spoke.

"I should climb up now, Harry Potter, I think?"

Harry bent down and the goblin clambered onto his back, his hands linked in front of Harry's throat. He was not heavy, but Harry disliked the feeling of the goblin and the surprising strength with which he clung on. Hermione pulled the Invisibility Cloak out of the beaded bag and threw it over them both.

"Perfect," she said, bending down to check Harry's feet. "I can't see a thing. Let's go."

Harry turned on the spot, with Griphook on his shoulders, concentrating with all his might on the Leaky Cauldron, the inn that was the entrance to Diagon Alley. The goblin clung even tighter as they moved into the compressing darkness, and seconds later Harry's feet found pavement and he opened his eyes on Charing Cross Road. Muggles bustled past wearing the hangdog expressions of early morning, quite unconscious of the little inn's existence.

The bar of the Leaky Cauldron was nearly deserted. Tom, the stooped and toothless landlord, was polishing glasses behind the bar counter; a couple of warlocks having a muttered conversation in the far corner glanced at Hermione and drew back into the shadows.

"Madam Lestrange," murmured Tom, and as Hermione passed he inclined his head subserviently.

"Good morning," said Hermione, and as Harry crept past, still carrying Griphook piggyback under the Cloak, he saw Tom look surprised.

"Too polite," Harry whispered in Hermione's ear as they passed out of the inn into the tiny backyard. "You need to treat people like they're scum!"

"Okay, okay!"

Hermione drew out Bellatrix's wand and tapped a brick in the nondescript wall in front of them. At once the bricks began to whirl and spin: A hole appeared in the middle of them, which grew wider and wider, finally forming an archway onto the narrow cobbled street that was Diagon Alley.

It was quiet, barely time for the shops to open, and there were hardly any shoppers abroad. The crooked, cobbled street was much altered now from the bustling place Harry had visited before his first term at Hogwarts so many years before. More shops than ever were boarded up, though several new establishments dedicated to the Dark Arts had been created since his last visit. Harry's own face glared down at him from posters plastered over many windows, always captioned with the words UNDESIRABLE NUMBER ONE.

A number of ragged people sat huddled in doorways. He heard them moaning to the few passersby, pleading for gold, insisting that they were really wizards. One man had a bloody bandage over his eye.

As they set off along the street, the beggars glimpsed Hermione. They seemed to melt away before her, drawing hoods over their faces and fleeing as fast as they could. Hermione looked after them curiously, until the man with the bloodied bandage came staggering right across her path.

"My children!" he bellowed, pointing at her. His voice was cracked, high-pitched; he sounded distraught. "Where are my children? What has he done with them? You know, *you know*!"

"I — I really —" stammered Hermione.

The man lunged at her, reaching for her throat: Then, with a bang and a burst of red light he was thrown backward onto the ground, unconscious. Ron stood there, his wand still outstretched and a look of shock visible behind his beard. Faces appeared at the windows on either side of the street, while a little knot of prosperous-looking passersby gathered their robes about them and broke into gentle trots, keen to vacate the scene.

Their entrance into Diagon Alley could hardly have been more conspicuous; for a moment Harry wondered whether it might not be better to leave now and try to think of a different plan. Before they could move or consult one another, however, they heard a cry from behind them.

"Why, Madam Lestrange!"

Harry whirled around and Griphook tightened his hold around Harry's neck: A tall, thin wizard with a crown of bushy gray hair and a long, sharp nose was striding toward them.

"It's Travers," hissed the goblin into Harry's ear, but at that moment Harry could not think who Travers was. Hermione had drawn herself up to her fullest height and said with as much contempt as she could muster:

"And what do you want?"

Travers stopped in his tracks, clearly affronted.

"He's another Death Eater!" breathed Griphook, and Harry sidled sideways to repeat the information into Hermione's ear.

"I merely sought to greet you," said Travers coolly, "but if my presence is not welcome . . ."

Harry recognized his voice now; Travers was one of the Death Eaters who had been summoned to Xenophilius's house.

"No, no, not at all, Travers," said Hermione quickly, trying to cover up her mistake. "How are you?"

"Well, I confess I am surprised to see you out and about, Bellatrix."

"Really? Why?" asked Hermione.

"Well," Travers coughed, "I *heard* that the inhabitants of Malfoy Manor were confined to the house, after the . . . ah . . . *escape.*"

Harry willed Hermione to keep her head. If this was true, and Bellatrix was not supposed to be out in public —

"The Dark Lord forgives those who have served him most faithfully in the past," said Hermione in a magnificent imitation of Bellatrix's most contemptuous manner. "Perhaps your credit is not as good with him as mine is, Travers."

Though the Death Eater looked offended, he also seemed less suspicious. He glanced down at the man Ron had just Stunned.

"How did it offend you?"

"It does not matter, it will not do so again," said Hermione coolly.

"Some of these wandless can be troublesome," said Travers. "While they do nothing but beg I have no objection, but one of them actually asked me to plead her case at the Ministry last week. *I'm a witch, sir, I'm a witch, let me prove it to you!*'" he said in a squeaky impersonation. "As if I was going to give her my wand — but whose wand," said Travers curiously, "are you using at the moment, Bellatrix? I heard that your own was —"

"I have my wand here," said Hermione coldly, holding up Bellatrix's wand. "I don't know what rumors you have been listening to, Travers, but you seem sadly misinformed."

Travers seemed a little taken aback at that, and he turned instead to Ron.

"Who is your friend? I do not recognize him."

"This is Dragomir Despard," said Hermione; they had decided that a fictional foreigner was the safest cover for Ron to assume. "He speaks very little English, but he is in sympathy with the Dark Lord's aims. He has traveled here from Transylvania to see our new regime."

"Indeed? How do you do, Dragomir?"

"'Ow you?" said Ron, holding out his hand.

Travers extended two fingers and shook Ron's hand as though frightened of dirtying himself.

"So what brings you and your — ah — sympathetic friend to Diagon Alley this early?" asked Travers.

"I need to visit Gringotts," said Hermione.

"Alas, I also," said Travers. "Gold, filthy gold! We cannot live without it, yet I confess I deplore the necessity of consorting with our long-fingered friends."

Harry felt Griphook's clasped hands tighten momentarily around his neck.

"Shall we?" said Travers, gesturing Hermione forward.

Hermione had no choice but to fall into step beside him and head along the crooked, cobbled street toward the place where the snowy-white Gringotts stood towering over the other little shops. Ron sloped along beside them, and Harry and Griphook followed.

A watchful Death Eater was the very last thing they needed, and the worst of it was, with Travers marching at what he believed to be Bellatrix's side, there was no means for Harry to communicate with Hermione or Ron. All too soon they arrived at the foot of the marble steps leading up to the great bronze doors. As Griphook had already warned them, the liveried goblins who usually flanked the entrance had been replaced by two wizards, both of whom were clutching long thin golden rods.

"Ah, Probity Probes," sighed Travers theatrically, "so crude — but effective!"

And he set off up the steps, nodding left and right to the wizards, who raised the golden rods and passed them up and down his body. The Probes, Harry knew, detected spells of concealment and hidden magical objects. Knowing that he had only seconds, Harry pointed Draco's wand at each of the guards in turn and murmured, *"Confundo"* twice. Unnoticed by Travers, who was looking through the bronze doors at the inner hall, each of the guards gave a little start as the spells hit them.

Hermione's long black hair rippled behind her as she climbed the steps.

"One moment, madam," said the guard, raising his Probe.

"But you've just done that!" said Hermione in Bellatrix's commanding, arrogant voice. Travers looked around, eyebrows raised. The guard was confused. He stared down at the thin golden Probe and then at his companion, who said in a slightly dazed voice,

"Yeah, you've just checked them, Marius."

Hermione swept forward, Ron by her side, Harry and Griphook trotting invisibly behind them. Harry glanced back as they crossed the threshold: The wizards were both scratching their heads.

Two goblins stood before the inner doors, which were made of silver and which carried the poem warning of dire retribution to potential thieves. Harry looked up at it, and all of a sudden a knife-sharp memory came to him: standing on this very spot on the day that he had turned eleven, the most wonderful birthday of his life, and Hagrid standing beside him saying, *"Like I said, yeh'd be mad ter try an' rob it."* Gringotts had seemed a place of wonder that day, the enchanted repository of a trove of gold he had never known he possessed, and never for an instant could he have dreamed that he would return to steal. . . . But within seconds they were standing in the vast marble hall of the bank.

The long counter was manned by goblins sitting on high stools, serving the first customers of the day. Hermione, Ron, and Travers headed toward an old goblin who was examining a thick gold coin through an eyeglass. Hermione allowed Travers to step ahead of her on the pretext of explaining features of the hall to Ron.

The goblin tossed the coin he was holding aside, said to nobody in particular, "Leprechaun," and then greeted Travers, who passed over a tiny golden key, which was examined and given back to him.

Hermione stepped forward.

"Madam Lestrange!" said the goblin, evidently startled. "Dear me! How — how may I help you today?"

"I wish to enter my vault," said Hermione.

The old goblin seemed to recoil a little. Harry glanced around. Not only was Travers hanging back, watching, but several other goblins had looked up from their work to stare at Hermione.

"You have . . . identification?" asked the goblin.

"Identification? I — I have never been asked for identification before!" said Hermione.

"They know!" whispered Griphook in Harry's ear. *"They must have been warned there might be an impostor!"*

"Your wand will do, madam," said the goblin. He held out a slightly trembling hand, and in a dreadful blast of realization Harry knew that the goblins of Gringotts were aware that Bellatrix's wand had been stolen.

"Act now, act now," whispered Griphook in Harry's ear, *"the Imperius Curse!"*

Harry raised the hawthorn wand beneath the cloak, pointed it at the old goblin, and whispered, for the first time in his life, *"Imperio!"*

A curious sensation shot down Harry's arm, a feeling of tingling warmth that seemed to flow from his mind, down the sinews and veins connecting him to the wand and the curse it had just cast. The goblin took Bellatrix's wand, examined it closely, and then said, "Ah, you have had a new wand made, Madam Lestrange!"

"What?" said Hermione. "No, no, that's mine —"

"A new wand?" said Travers, approaching the counter again; still the goblins all around were watching. "But how could you have done, which wandmaker did you use?"

Harry acted without thinking: Pointing his wand at Travers, he muttered, *"Imperio!"* once more.

"Oh yes, I see," said Travers, looking down at Bellatrix's wand, "yes, very handsome. And is it working well? I always think wands require a little breaking in, don't you?"

Hermione looked utterly bewildered, but to Harry's enormous relief she accepted the bizarre turn of events without comment.

The old goblin behind the counter clapped his hands and a younger goblin approached.

"I shall need the Clankers," he told the goblin, who dashed away and returned a moment later with a leather bag that seemed to be full of jangling metal, which he handed to his senior. "Good, good! So, if you will follow me, Madam Lestrange," said the old goblin, hopping down off his stool and vanishing from sight, "I shall take you to your vault."

He appeared around the end of the counter, jogging happily toward them, the contents of the leather bag still jingling. Travers was now standing quite still with his mouth hanging wide open. Ron was drawing attention to this odd phenomenon by regarding Travers with confusion.

"Wait — Bogrod!"

Another goblin came scurrying around the counter.

"We have instructions," he said with a bow to Hermione. "Forgive me, Madam, but there have been special orders regarding the vault of Lestrange."

He whispered urgently in Bogrod's ear, but the Imperiused goblin shook him off.

"I am aware of the instructions. Madam Lestrange wishes to visit her vault. . . . Very old family . . . old clients . . . This way, please . . ."

And, still clanking, he hurried toward one of the many doors leading off the hall. Harry looked back at Travers, who was still rooted to the spot looking abnormally vacant, and made his decision: With a flick of his wand he made Travers come with them, walking meekly in their wake as they reached the door and passed into the rough stone passageway beyond, which was lit with flaming torches.

"We're in trouble; they suspect," said Harry as the door slammed behind them and he pulled off the Invisibility Cloak. Griphook jumped down from his shoulders; neither Travers nor Bogrod showed the slightest surprise at the sudden appearance of Harry Potter in their midst. "They're Imperiused," he added, in response to Hermione and Ron's confused queries about Travers and Bogrod, who were both now standing there looking blank. "I don't think I did it strongly enough, I don't know. . . ."

And another memory darted through his mind, of the real Bellatrix Lestrange shrieking at him when he had first tried to use an Unforgivable Curse: "You need to *mean* them, Potter!"

"What do we do?" asked Ron. "Shall we get out now, while we can?"

"If we can," said Hermione, looking back toward the door into the main hall, beyond which who knew what was happening.

"We've got this far, I say we go on," said Harry.

"Good!" said Griphook. "So, we need Bogrod to control the cart; I no longer have the authority. But there will not be room for the wizard."

Harry pointed his wand at Travers.

"Imperio!"

The wizard turned and set off along the dark track at a smart pace.

"What are you making him do?"

"Hide," said Harry as he pointed his wand at Bogrod, who whistled to summon a little cart that came trundling along the tracks toward them out of the darkness. Harry was sure he could hear shouting behind them in the main hall as they all clambered into it, Bogrod in front with Griphook, Harry, Ron, and Hermione crammed together in the back.

With a jerk the cart moved off, gathering speed: They hurtled past Travers, who was wriggling into a crack in the wall, then the cart began twisting and turning through the labyrinthine passages, sloping downward all the time. Harry could not hear anything over the rattling of the cart on the tracks: His hair flew behind him as they swerved between stalactites, flying ever deeper into the earth, but he kept glancing back. They might as well have left enormous footprints behind them; the more he thought about it, the more foolish it seemed to have disguised Hermione as Bellatrix, to have brought along Bellatrix's wand, when the Death Eaters knew who had stolen it —

They were deeper than Harry had ever penetrated within Gringotts; they took a hairpin bend at speed and saw ahead of them, with seconds to spare, a waterfall pounding over the track. Harry heard Griphook shout, "No!" but there was no braking: They zoomed through it. Water filled Harry's eyes and mouth: He could not see or breathe: Then, with an awful lurch, the cart flipped over and they were all thrown out of it. Harry heard the cart smash into pieces against the passage wall, heard Hermione shriek something, and felt himself glide back toward the ground as though weightless, landing painlessly on the rocky passage floor.

"C-Cushioning Charm," Hermione spluttered, as Ron pulled her to her feet, but to Harry's horror he saw that she was no longer Bellatrix; instead she stood there in overlarge robes, sopping wet and completely herself; Ron was red-haired and beardless again. They were realizing it as they looked at each other, feeling their own faces.

"The Thief's Downfall!" said Griphook, clambering to his feet and looking back at the deluge onto the tracks, which, Harry knew now, had been more than water. "It washes away all enchantment, all magical concealment! They know there are impostors in Gringotts, they have set off defenses against us!"

Harry saw Hermione checking that she still had the beaded bag, and hurriedly thrust his own hand under his jacket to make sure he had not lost the Invisibility Cloak. Then he turned to see Bogrod shaking his head in bewilderment: The Thief's Downfall seemed to have lifted the Imperius Curse.

"We need him," said Griphook, "we cannot enter the vault without a Gringotts goblin. And we need the Clankers!"

"Imperio!" Harry said again; his voice echoed through the stone passage as he felt again the sense of heady control that flowed from brain to wand. Bogrod submitted once more to his will, his befuddled expression changing to one of polite indifference, as Ron hurried to pick up the leather bag of metal tools.

"Harry, I think I can hear people coming!" said Hermione, and she pointed Bellatrix's wand at the waterfall and cried, *"Protego!"* They saw the Shield Charm break the flow of enchanted water as it flew up the passageway.

"Good thinking," said Harry. "Lead the way, Griphook!"

"How are we going to get out again?" Ron asked as they hurried on foot into the darkness after the goblin, Bogrod panting in their wake like an old dog.

"Let's worry about that when we have to," said Harry. He was trying to listen: He thought he could hear something clanking and moving around nearby. "Griphook, how much farther?"

"Not far, Harry Potter, not far . . ."

And they turned a corner and saw the thing for which Harry had been prepared, but which still brought all of them to a halt.

A gigantic dragon was tethered to the ground in front of them, barring access to four or five of the deepest vaults in the place. The beast's scales had turned pale and flaky during its long incarceration under the ground; its eyes were milkily pink; both rear legs bore heavy cuffs from which chains led to enormous pegs driven deep into the rocky floor. Its great spiked wings, folded close to its body, would have filled the chamber if it spread them, and when it turned its ugly head toward them, it roared with a noise that made the rock tremble, opened its mouth, and spat a jet of fire that sent them running back up the passageway.

"It is partially blind," panted Griphook, "but even more savage for that. However, we have the means to control it. It has learned what to expect when the Clankers come. Give them to me."

Ron passed the bag to Griphook, and the goblin pulled out a number of small metal instruments that when shaken made a loud, ringing noise like miniature hammers on anvils. Griphook handed them out: Bogrod accepted his meekly.

"You know what to do," Griphook told Harry, Ron, and Hermione. "It will expect pain when it hears the noise: It will retreat, and Bogrod must place his palm upon the door of the vault."

They advanced around the corner again, shaking the Clankers, and the noise echoed off the rocky walls, grossly magnified, so that the inside of Harry's skull seemed to vibrate with the din. The dragon let out another hoarse roar, then retreated. Harry could see it trembling, and as they drew nearer he saw the scars made by vicious slashes across its face, and guessed that it had been taught to fear hot swords when it heard the sound of the Clankers.

"Make him press his hand to the door!" Griphook urged Harry, who turned his wand again upon Bogrod. The old goblin obeyed, pressing his palm to the wood, and the door of the vault melted away to reveal a cavelike opening crammed from floor to ceiling with golden coins and goblets, silver armor, the skins of strange creatures — some with long spines, others with drooping wings — potions in jeweled flasks, and a skull still wearing a crown.

"Search, fast!" said Harry as they all hurried inside the vault.

He had described Hufflepuff's cup to Ron and Hermione, but if it was the other, unknown Horcrux that resided in this vault, he did not know what it looked like. He barely had time to glance around, however, before there was a muffled clunk from behind them: The door had reappeared, sealing them inside the vault, and they were plunged into total darkness.

"No matter, Bogrod will be able to release us!" said Griphook as Ron gave a shout of surprise. "Light your wands, can't you? And hurry, we have very little time!"

"*Lumos!*"

Harry shone his lit wand around the vault: Its beam fell upon glittering jewels; he saw the fake sword of Gryffindor lying on a high shelf amongst a jumble of chains. Ron and Hermione had lit their wands too, and were now examining the piles of objects surrounding them.

"Harry, could this be — ? Aargh!"

Hermione screamed in pain, and Harry turned his wand on her in time to see a jeweled goblet tumbling from her grip. But as it fell, it split, became a shower of goblets, so that a second later, with a great clatter, the floor was covered in identical cups rolling in every direction, the original impossible to discern amongst them.

"It burned me!" moaned Hermione, sucking her blistered fingers.

"They have added Gemino and Flagrante Curses!" said Griphook. "Everything you touch will burn and multiply, but the copies are worthless — and if you continue to handle the treasure, you will eventually be crushed to death by the weight of expanding gold!"

"Okay, don't touch anything!" said Harry desperately, but even as he said it, Ron accidentally nudged one of the fallen goblets with his foot, and twenty more exploded into being while Ron hopped on the spot, part of his shoe burned away by contact with the hot metal.

"Stand still, don't move!" said Hermione, clutching at Ron.

"Just look around!" said Harry. "Remember, the cup's small and gold, it's got a badger engraved on it, two handles — otherwise see if you can spot Ravenclaw's symbol anywhere, the eagle —"

They directed their wands into every nook and crevice, turning cautiously on the spot. It was impossible not to brush up against anything; Harry sent a great cascade of fake Galleons onto the ground where they joined the goblets, and now there was scarcely room to place their feet, and the glowing gold blazed with heat, so that the vault felt like a furnace. Harry's wandlight passed over shields and goblin-made helmets set on shelves rising to the ceiling; higher and higher he raised the beam, until suddenly it found an object that made his heart skip and his hand tremble.

"It's there, it's up there!"

Ron and Hermione pointed their wands at it too, so that the little golden cup sparkled in a three-way spotlight: the cup that had belonged to Helga Hufflepuff, which had passed into the possession of Hepzibah Smith, from whom it had been stolen by Tom Riddle.

"And how the hell are we going to get up there without touching anything?" asked Ron.

"Accio Cup!" cried Hermione, who had evidently forgotten in her desperation what Griphook had told them during their planning sessions.

"No use, no use!" snarled the goblin.

"Then what do we do?" said Harry, glaring at the goblin. "If you want the sword, Griphook, then you'll have to help us more than — wait! Can I touch stuff with the sword? Hermione, give it here!"

Hermione fumbled inside her robes, drew out the beaded bag, rummaged for a few seconds, then removed the shining sword. Harry seized it by its rubied hilt and touched the tip of the blade to a silver flagon nearby, which did not multiply.

"If I can just poke the sword through a handle — but how am I going to get up there?"

The shelf on which the cup reposed was out of reach for any of them, even Ron, who was tallest. The heat from the enchanted treasure rose in waves, and sweat ran down Harry's face and back as he struggled to think of a way up to the cup; and then he heard the dragon roar on the other side of the vault door, and the sound of clanking growing louder and louder.

They were truly trapped now: There was no way out except through the door, and a horde of goblins seemed to be approaching on the other side. Harry looked at Ron and Hermione and saw terror in their faces.

"Hermione," said Harry as the clanking grew louder, "I've got to get up there, we've got to get rid of it —"

She raised her wand, pointed it at Harry, and whispered, *"Levicorpus."*

Hoisted into the air by his ankle, Harry hit a suit of armor and replicas burst out of it like white-hot bodies, filling the cramped space. With screams of pain Ron, Hermione, and the two goblins were knocked aside into other objects, which also began to replicate. Half buried in a rising tide of red-hot treasure, they struggled and yelled as Harry thrust the sword through the handle of Hufflepuff's cup, hooking it onto the blade.

"Impervius!" screeched Hermione in an attempt to protect herself, Ron, and the goblins from the burning metal.

Then the worst scream yet made Harry look down: Ron and Hermione were waist-deep in treasure, struggling to keep Bogrod from slipping beneath the rising tide, but Griphook had sunk out of sight and nothing but the tips of a few long fingers were left in view.

Harry seized Griphook's fingers and pulled. The blistered goblin emerged by degrees, howling.

"Liberacorpus!" yelled Harry, and with a crash he and Griphook landed on the surface of the swelling treasure, and the sword flew out of Harry's hand.

"Get it!" Harry yelled, fighting the pain of the hot metal on his skin, as Griphook clambered onto his shoulders again, determined to avoid the swelling mass of red-hot objects. "Where's the sword? It had the cup on it!"

The clanking on the other side of the door was growing deafening — it was too late —

"There!"

It was Griphook who had seen it and Griphook who lunged, and in that instant Harry knew that the goblin had never expected them to keep their word. One hand holding tightly to a fistful of Harry's hair, to make sure he did not fall into the heaving sea of burning gold, Griphook seized the hilt of the sword and swung it high out of Harry's reach.

The tiny golden cup, skewered by the handle on the sword's blade, was flung into the air. The goblin still astride him, Harry dived and caught it, and although he could feel it scalding his flesh he did not relinquish it, even while countless Hufflepuff cups burst from his fist, raining down upon him as the entrance of the vault opened up again and he found himself sliding uncontrollably on an expanding avalanche of fiery gold and silver that bore him, Ron, and Hermione into the outer chamber.

Hardly aware of the pain from the burns covering his body, and still borne along on the swell of replicating treasure, Harry shoved the cup into his pocket and reached up to retrieve the sword, but Griphook was gone. Sliding from Harry's shoulders the moment he could, he had sprinted for cover amongst the surrounding goblins, brandishing the sword and crying, "Thieves! Thieves! Help! Thieves!" He vanished into the midst of the advancing crowd, all of whom were holding daggers and who accepted him without question.

Slipping on the hot metal, Harry struggled to his feet and knew that the only way out was through.

"*Stupefy!*" he bellowed, and Ron and Hermione joined in: Jets of red light flew into the crowd of goblins, and some toppled over, but others advanced, and Harry saw several wizard guards running around the corner.

The tethered dragon let out a roar, and a gush of flame flew over the goblins: The wizards fled, doubled-up, back the way they had come, and inspiration, or madness, came to Harry. Pointing his wand at the thick cuffs chaining the beast to the floor, he yelled, "*Relashio!*"

The cuffs broke open with loud bangs.

"This way!" Harry yelled, and still shooting Stunning Spells at the advancing goblins, he sprinted toward the blind dragon.

"Harry — Harry — what are you doing?" cried Hermione.

"Get up, climb up, come on —"

The dragon had not realized that it was free: Harry's foot found the crook of its hind leg and he pulled himself up onto its back.

The scales were hard as steel; it did not even seem to feel him. He stretched out an arm; Hermione hoisted herself up; Ron climbed on behind them, and a second later the dragon became aware that it was untethered.

With a roar it reared: Harry dug in his knees, clutching as tightly as he could to the jagged scales as the wings opened, knocking the shrieking goblins aside like skittles, and it soared into the air. Harry, Ron, and Hermione, flat on its back, scraped against the ceiling as it dived toward the passage opening, while the pursuing goblins hurled daggers that glanced off its flanks.

"We'll never get out, it's too big!" Hermione screamed, but the dragon opened its mouth and belched flame again, blasting the tunnel, whose floors and ceiling cracked and crumbled. By sheer force the dragon clawed and fought its way through. Harry's eyes were shut tight against the heat and dust: Deafened by the crashing of rock and the dragon's roars, he could only cling to its back, expecting to be shaken off at any moment; then he heard Hermione yelling, *"Defodio!"*

She was helping the dragon enlarge the passageway, carving out the ceiling as it struggled upward toward the fresher air, away from the shrieking and clanking goblins: Harry and Ron copied her, blasting the ceiling apart with more gouging spells. They passed the underground lake, and the great crawling, snarling beast seemed to sense freedom and space ahead of it, and behind them the passage was full of the dragon's thrashing, spiked tail, of great lumps of rock, gigantic fractured stalactites, and the clanking of the goblins seemed to be growing more muffled, while ahead, the dragon's fire kept their progress clear —

And then at last, by the combined force of their spells and the dragon's brute strength, they had blasted their way out of the passage into the marble hallway. Goblins and wizards shrieked and ran for cover, and finally the dragon had room to stretch its wings: Turning its horned head toward the cool outside air it could smell beyond the entrance, it took off, and with Harry, Ron, and Hermione still clinging to its back, it forced its way through the metal doors, leaving them buckled and hanging from their hinges, as it staggered into Diagon Alley and launched itself into the sky.

THE FINAL
HIDING PLACE

There was no means of steering; the dragon could not see where it was going, and Harry knew that if it turned sharply or rolled in midair they would find it impossible to cling onto its broad back. Nevertheless, as they climbed higher and higher, London unfurling below them like a gray-and-green map, Harry's overwhelming feeling was of gratitude for an escape that had seemed impossible. Crouching low over the beast's neck, he clung tight to the metallic scales, and the cool breeze was soothing on his burned and blistered skin, the dragon's wings beating the air like the sails of a windmill. Behind him, whether from delight or fear he could not tell, Ron kept swearing at the top of his voice, and Hermione seemed to be sobbing.

After five minutes or so, Harry lost some of his immediate dread that the dragon was going to throw them off, for it seemed intent on nothing but getting as far away from its underground prison as possible; but the question of how and when they were to dismount remained rather frightening. He had no idea how long dragons could fly without landing, nor how this particular dragon, which could barely see, would locate a good place to put down. He glanced around constantly, imagining that he could feel his scar prickling. . . .

How long would it be before Voldemort knew that they had broken into the Lestranges' vault? How soon would the goblins of Gringotts notify Bellatrix? How quickly would they realize what had been taken? And then, when they discovered that the golden cup was missing? Voldemort would know, at last, that they were hunting Horcruxes. . . .

The dragon seemed to crave cooler and fresher air: It climbed steadily until they were flying through wisps of chilly cloud, and Harry could no longer make out the little colored dots which were cars pouring in and out of the capital. On and on they flew, over countryside parceled out in patches of green and brown, over roads and rivers winding through the landscape like strips of matte and glossy ribbon.

"What do you reckon it's looking for?" Ron yelled as they flew farther and farther north.

"No idea," Harry bellowed back. His hands were numb with cold but he did not dare attempt to shift his grip. He had been wondering for some time what they would do if they saw the coast sail beneath them, if the dragon headed for open sea; he was cold and numb, not to mention desperately hungry and thirsty. When, he wondered, had the beast itself last eaten? Surely it would need sustenance before long? And what if, at that point, it realized it had three highly edible humans sitting on its back?

The sun slipped lower in the sky, which was turning indigo; and still the dragon flew, cities and towns gliding out of sight beneath them, its enormous shadow sliding over the earth like a great dark cloud. Every part of Harry ached with the effort of holding on to the dragon's back.

"Is it my imagination," shouted Ron after a considerable stretch of silence, "or are we losing height?"

Harry looked down and saw deep green mountains and lakes, coppery in the sunset. The landscape seemed to grow larger and more detailed as he squinted over the side of the dragon, and he wondered whether it had divined the presence of fresh water by the flashes of reflected sunlight.

Lower and lower the dragon flew, in great spiraling circles, honing in, it seemed, upon one of the smaller lakes.

"I say we jump when it gets low enough!" Harry called back to the others. "Straight into the water before it realizes we're here!"

They agreed, Hermione a little faintly, and now Harry could see the dragon's wide yellow underbelly rippling in the surface of the water.

"NOW!"

He slithered over the side of the dragon and plummeted feetfirst toward the surface of the lake; the drop was greater than he had estimated and he hit the water hard, plunging like a stone into a freezing, green, reed-filled world. He kicked toward the surface and emerged, panting, to see enormous ripples emanating in circles from the places where Ron and Hermione had fallen. The dragon did not seem to have noticed anything: It was already fifty feet away, swooping low over the lake to scoop up water in its scarred snout. As Ron and Hermione emerged, spluttering and gasping, from the depths of the lake, the dragon flew on, its wings beating hard, and landed at last on a distant bank.

Harry, Ron, and Hermione struck out for the opposite shore. The lake did not seem to be deep: Soon it was more a question of fighting their way through reeds and mud than swimming, and at last they flopped, sodden, panting, and exhausted, onto slippery grass.

Hermione collapsed, coughing and shuddering. Though Harry could have happily lain down and slept, he staggered to his feet, drew out his wand, and started casting the usual protective spells around them.

When he had finished, he joined the others. It was the first time that he had seen them properly since escaping from the vault. Both had angry red burns all over their faces and arms, and their clothing was singed away in places. They were wincing as they dabbed essence of dittany onto their many injuries. Hermione handed Harry the bottle, then pulled out three bottles of pumpkin juice she had brought from Shell Cottage and clean, dry robes for all of them. They changed and then gulped down the juice.

"Well, on the upside," said Ron finally, who was sitting watching the skin on his hands regrow, "we got the Horcrux. On the downside —"

"— no sword," said Harry through gritted teeth, as he dripped dittany through the singed hole in his jeans onto the angry burn beneath.

"No sword," repeated Ron. "That double-crossing little scab . . ."

Harry pulled the Horcrux from the pocket of the wet jacket he had just taken off and set it down on the grass in front of them. Glinting in the sun, it drew their eyes as they swigged their bottles of juice.

"At least we can't wear it this time, that'd look a bit weird hanging round our necks," said Ron, wiping his mouth on the back of his hand.

Hermione looked across the lake to the far bank, where the dragon was still drinking.

"What'll happen to it, do you think?" she asked. "Will it be all right?"

"You sound like Hagrid," said Ron. "It's a dragon, Hermione, it can look after itself. It's us we need to worry about."

"What do you mean?"

"Well, I don't know how to break this to you," said Ron, "but I think they *might* have noticed we broke into Gringotts."

All three of them started to laugh, and once started, it was difficult to stop. Harry's ribs ached, he felt lightheaded with hunger, but he lay back on the grass beneath the reddening sky and laughed until his throat was raw.

"What are we going to do, though?" said Hermione finally, hiccuping herself back to seriousness. "He'll know, won't he? You-Know-Who will know we know about his Horcruxes!"

"Maybe they'll be too scared to tell him?" said Ron hopefully. "Maybe they'll cover up —"

The sky, the smell of lake water, the sound of Ron's voice were extinguished: Pain cleaved Harry's head like a sword stroke. He was standing in a dimly lit room, and a semicircle of wizards faced him, and on the floor at his feet knelt a small, quaking figure.

"What did you say to me?" His voice was high and cold, but fury and fear burned inside him. The one thing he had dreaded — but it could not be true, he could not see how . . .

The goblin was trembling, unable to meet the red eyes high above his.

"Say it again!" murmured Voldemort. *"Say it again!"*

"M-my Lord," stammered the goblin, its black eyes wide with terror, "m-my Lord . . . we t-tried t-to st-stop them. . . . Im-impostors, my Lord . . . broke — broke into the — into the Lestranges' v-vault. . . ."

"Impostors? What impostors? I thought Gringotts had ways of revealing impostors? Who were they?"

"It was . . . it was . . . the P-Potter b-boy and t-two accomplices. . . ."

"And they took?" he said, his voice rising, a terrible fear gripping him. "Tell me! *What did they take?"*

"A . . . a s-small golden c-cup, m-my Lord . . ."

The scream of rage, of denial left him as if it were a stranger's: He was crazed, frenzied, it could not be true, it was impossible, nobody had ever known: How was it possible that the boy could have discovered his secret?

The Elder Wand slashed through the air and green light erupted through the room; the kneeling goblin rolled over, dead; the watching wizards scattered before him, terrified: Bellatrix and Lucius Malfoy threw others behind them in their race for the door, and again and again his wand fell, and those who were left were slain, all of them, for bringing him this news, for hearing about the golden cup —

Alone amongst the dead he stormed up and down, and they passed before him in vision: his treasures, his safeguards, his anchors to immortality — the diary was destroyed and the cup was stolen: What if, *what if,* the boy knew about the others? Could he know, had he already acted, had he traced more of them? Was Dumbledore at the root of this? Dumbledore, who had always suspected him; Dumbledore, dead on his orders; Dumbledore, whose wand was his now, yet who reached out from the ignominy of death through the boy, *the boy* —

But surely if the boy had destroyed any of his Horcruxes, he, Lord Voldemort, would have known, would have felt it? He, the greatest wizard of them all; he, the most powerful; he, the killer of Dumbledore and of how many other worthless, nameless men: How could Lord Voldemort not have known, if he, himself, most important and precious, had been attacked, mutilated?

True, he had not felt it when the diary had been destroyed, but he had thought that was because he had no body to feel, being less than ghost. . . . No, surely, the rest were safe. . . . The other Horcruxes must be intact. . . .

But he must know, he must be sure. . . . He paced the room, kicking aside the goblin's corpse as he passed, and the pictures blurred and burned in his boiling brain: the lake, the shack, and Hogwarts —

A modicum of calm cooled his rage now: How could the boy know that he had hidden the ring in the Gaunt shack? No one had ever known him to be related to the Gaunts, he had hidden the connection, the killings had never been traced to him: The ring, surely, was safe.

And how could the boy, or anybody else, know about the cave or penetrate its protection? The idea of the locket being stolen was absurd. . . .

As for the school: He alone knew where in Hogwarts he had stowed the Horcrux, because he alone had plumbed the deepest secrets of that place. . . .

And there was still Nagini, who must remain close now, no longer sent to do his bidding, under his protection. . . .

But to be sure, to be utterly sure, he must return to each of his hiding places, he must redouble protection around each of his Horcruxes. . . . A job, like the quest for the Elder Wand, that he must undertake alone . . .

Which should he visit first, which was in most danger? An old unease flickered inside him. Dumbledore had known his middle name. . . . Dumbledore might have made the connection with the Gaunts. . . . Their abandoned home was, perhaps, the least secure of his hiding places, it was there that he would go first. . . .

The lake, surely impossible . . . though was there a slight possibility that Dumbledore might have known some of his past misdeeds, through the orphanage.

And Hogwarts . . . but he knew that his Horcrux there was safe; it would be impossible for Potter to enter Hogsmeade without detection, let alone the school. Nevertheless, it would be prudent to alert Snape to the fact that the boy might try to reenter the castle. . . . To tell Snape why the boy might return would be foolish, of course; it had been a grave mistake to trust Bellatrix and Malfoy: Didn't their stupidity and carelessness prove how unwise it was ever to trust?

He would visit the Gaunt shack first, then, and take Nagini with him: He would not be parted from the snake anymore . . . and he strode from the room, through the hall, and out into the dark garden where the fountain played; he called the snake in Parseltongue and it slithered out to join him like a long shadow. . . .

Harry's eyes flew open as he wrenched himself back to the present: He was lying on the bank of the lake in the setting sun, and Ron and Hermione were looking down at him. Judging by their worried looks, and by the continued pounding of his scar, his sudden excursion into Voldemort's mind had not passed unnoticed. He struggled up, shivering, vaguely surprised that he was still wet to his skin, and saw the cup lying innocently in the grass before him, and the lake, deep blue shot with gold in the failing sun.

"He knows." His own voice sounded strange and low after Voldemort's high screams. "He knows, and he's going to check where the others are, and the last one," he was already on his feet, "is at Hogwarts. I knew it. I *knew* it."

"What?"

Ron was gaping at him; Hermione sat up, looking worried.

"But what did you see? How do you know?"

"I saw him find out about the cup, I — I was in his head, he's" — Harry remembered the killings — "he's seriously angry, and scared too, he can't understand how we knew, and now he's going to check the others are safe, the ring first. He thinks the Hogwarts one is safest, because Snape's there, because it'll be so hard not to be seen getting in, I think he'll check that one last, but he could still be there within hours —"

"Did you see where in Hogwarts it is?" asked Ron, now scrambling to his feet too.

"No, he was concentrating on warning Snape, he didn't think about exactly where it is —"

"Wait, *wait!*" cried Hermione as Ron caught up the Horcrux and Harry pulled out the Invisibility Cloak again. "We can't just *go,* we haven't got a plan, we need to —"

"We need to get going," said Harry firmly. He had been hoping to sleep, looking forward to getting into the new tent, but that was impossible now. "Can you imagine what he's going to do once he realizes the ring and the locket are gone? What if he moves the Hogwarts Horcrux, decides it isn't safe enough?"

"But how are we going to get in?"

"We'll go to Hogsmeade," said Harry, "and try to work something out once we see what the protection around the school's like. Get under the Cloak, Hermione, I want to stick together this time."

"But we don't really fit —"

"It'll be dark, no one's going to notice our feet."

The flapping of enormous wings echoed across the black water: The dragon had drunk its fill and risen into the air. They paused in their preparations to watch it climb higher and higher, now black against the rapidly darkening sky, until it vanished over a nearby mountain. Then Hermione walked forward and took her place between the other two. Harry pulled the Cloak down as far as it would go, and together they turned on the spot into the crushing darkness.

THE MISSING MIRROR

arry's feet touched road. He saw the achingly familiar Hogsmeade High Street: dark shop fronts, and the outline of black mountains beyond the village, and the curve in the road ahead that led off toward Hogwarts, and light spilling from the windows of the Three Broomsticks, and with a lurch of the heart he remembered, with piercing accuracy, how he had landed here nearly a year before, supporting a desperately weak Dumbledore; all this in a second, upon landing — and then, even as he relaxed his grip upon Ron's and Hermione's arms, it happened.

The air was rent by a scream that sounded like Voldemort's when he had realized the cup had been stolen: It tore at every nerve in Harry's body, and he knew immediately that their appearance had caused it. Even as he looked at the other two beneath the Cloak, the door of the Three Broomsticks burst open and a dozen cloaked and hooded Death Eaters dashed into the street, their wands aloft.

Harry seized Ron's wrist as he raised his wand; there were too many of them to Stun: Even attempting it would give away their position. One of the Death Eaters waved his wand and the scream stopped, still echoing around the distant mountains.

"Accio Cloak!" roared one of the Death Eaters.

Harry seized its folds, but it made no attempt to escape: The Summoning Charm had not worked on it.

"Not under your wrapper, then, Potter?" yelled the Death Eater who had tried the charm, and then to his fellows, "Spread out. He's here."

Six of the Death Eaters ran toward them: Harry, Ron, and Hermione backed as quickly as possible down the nearest side street, and the Death Eaters missed them by inches. They waited in the darkness, listening to the footsteps running up and down, beams of light flying along the street from the Death Eaters' searching wands.

"Let's just leave!" Hermione whispered. "Disapparate now!"

"Great idea," said Ron, but before Harry could reply a Death Eater shouted,

"We know you're here, Potter, and there's no getting away! We'll find you!"

"They were ready for us," whispered Harry. "They set up that spell to tell them we'd come. I reckon they've done something to keep us here, trap us —"

"What about dementors?" called another Death Eater. "Let 'em have free rein, they'd find him quick enough!"

"The Dark Lord wants Potter dead by no hand but his —"

"— an' dementors won't kill him! The Dark Lord wants Potter's life, not his soul. He'll be easier to kill if he's been Kissed first!"

There were noises of agreement. Dread filled Harry: To repel dementors they would have to produce Patronuses, which would give them away immediately.

"We're going to have to try to Disapparate, Harry!" Hermione whispered.

Even as she said it, he felt the unnatural cold begin to steal over the street. Light was sucked from the environment right up to the stars, which vanished. In the pitch-blackness, he felt Hermione take hold of his arm and together, they turned on the spot.

The air through which they needed to move seemed to have become solid: They could not Disapparate; the Death Eaters had cast their charms well. The cold was biting deeper and deeper into Harry's flesh. He, Ron, and Hermione retreated down the side street, groping their way along the wall, trying not to make a sound. Then, around the corner, gliding noiselessly, came dementors, ten or more of them, visible because they were of a denser darkness than their surroundings, with their black cloaks and their scabbed and rotting hands. Could they sense fear in the vicinity? Harry was sure of it: They seemed to be coming more quickly now, taking those dragging, rattling breaths he detested, tasting despair on the air, closing in —

He raised his wand: He could not, would not, suffer the Dementor's Kiss, whatever happened afterward. It was of Ron and Hermione that he thought as he whispered, *"Expecto Patronum!"*

The silver stag burst from his wand and charged: The dementors scattered and there was a triumphant yell from somewhere out of sight.

"It's him, down there, down there, I saw his Patronus, it was a stag!"

The dementors had retreated, the stars were popping out again, and the footsteps of the Death Eaters were becoming louder; but before Harry in his panic could decide what to do, there was a grinding of bolts nearby, a door opened on the left-hand side of the narrow street, and a rough voice said, "Potter, in here, quick!"

He obeyed without hesitation: The three of them hurtled through the open doorway.

"Upstairs, keep the Cloak on, keep quiet!" muttered a tall figure, passing them on his way into the street and slamming the door behind him.

Harry had had no idea where they were, but now he saw, by the stuttering light of a single candle, the grubby, sawdust-strewn bar of the Hog's Head Inn. They ran behind the counter and through a second doorway, which led to a rickety wooden staircase that they climbed as fast as they could. The stairs opened onto a sitting room with a threadbare carpet and a small fireplace, above which hung a single large oil painting of a blonde girl who gazed out at the room with a kind of vacant sweetness.

Shouts reached them from the street below. Still wearing the Invisibility Cloak, they crept toward the grimy window and looked down. Their savior, whom Harry now recognized as the Hog's Head's barman, was the only person not wearing a hood.

"So what?" he was bellowing into one of the hooded faces. "So what? You send dementors down my street, I'll send a Patronus back at 'em! I'm not having 'em near me, I've told you that, I'm not having it!"

"That wasn't your Patronus!" said a Death Eater. "That was a stag, it was Potter's!"

"Stag!" roared the barman, and he pulled out a wand. "Stag! You idiot — *Expecto Patronum!*"

Something huge and horned erupted from the wand: Head down, it charged toward the High Street and out of sight.

"That's not what I saw —" said the Death Eater, though with less certainty.

"Curfew's been broken, you heard the noise," one of his companions told the barman. "Someone was out in the street against regulations —"

"If I want to put my cat out, I will, and be damned to your curfew!"

"*You* set off the Caterwauling Charm?"

"What if I did? Going to cart me off to Azkaban? Kill me for sticking my nose out my own front door? Do it, then, if you want to! But I hope for your sakes you haven't pressed your little Dark Marks and summoned him. He's not going to like being called here for me and my old cat, is he, now?"

"Don't you worry about us," said one of the Death Eaters, "worry about yourself, breaking curfew!"

"And where will you lot traffick potions and poisons when my pub's closed down? What'll happen to your little sidelines then?"

"Are you threatening — ?"

"I keep my mouth shut, it's why you come here, isn't it?"

"I still say I saw a stag Patronus!" shouted the first Death Eater.

"Stag?" roared the barman. "It's a *goat*, idiot!"

"All right, we made a mistake," said the second Death Eater. "Break curfew again and we won't be so lenient!"

The Death Eaters strode back toward the High Street. Hermione moaned with relief, wove out from under the Cloak, and sat down on a wobble-legged chair. Harry drew the curtains tight shut, then pulled the Cloak off himself and Ron. They could hear the barman down below, rebolting the door of the bar, then climbing the stairs.

Harry's attention was caught by something on the mantelpiece: a small, rectangular mirror propped on top of it, right beneath the portrait of the girl.

The barman entered the room.

"You bloody fools," he said gruffly, looking from one to the other of them. "What were you thinking, coming here?"

"Thank you," said Harry. "We can't thank you enough. You saved our lives."

The barman grunted. Harry approached him, looking up into the face, trying to see past the long, stringy, wire-gray hair and beard. He wore spectacles. Behind the dirty lenses, the eyes were a piercing, brilliant blue.

"It's your eye I've been seeing in the mirror."

There was silence in the room. Harry and the barman looked at each other.

"You sent Dobby."

The barman nodded and looked around for the elf.

"Thought he'd be with you. Where've you left him?"

"He's dead," said Harry. "Bellatrix Lestrange killed him."

The barman's face was impassive. After a few moments he said, "I'm sorry to hear it. I liked that elf."

He turned away, lighting lamps with prods of his wand, not looking at any of them.

"You're Aberforth," said Harry to the man's back.

He neither confirmed nor denied it, but bent to light the fire.

"How did you get this?" Harry asked, walking across to Sirius's mirror, the twin of the one he had broken nearly two years before.

"Bought it from Dung 'bout a year ago," said Aberforth. "Albus told me what it was. Been trying to keep an eye out for you."

Ron gasped.

"The silver doe!" he said excitedly. "Was that you too?"

"What are you talking about?" said Aberforth.

"Someone sent a doe Patronus to us!"

"Brains like that, you could be a Death Eater, son. Haven't I just proved my Patronus is a goat?"

"Oh," said Ron. "Yeah . . . well, I'm hungry!" he added defensively as his stomach gave an enormous rumble.

"I got food," said Aberforth, and he sloped out of the room, reappearing moments later with a large loaf of bread, some cheese, and a pewter jug of mead, which he set upon a small table in front of the fire. Ravenous, they ate and drank, and for a while there was silence but for the crackle of the fire, the clink of goblets, and the sound of chewing.

"Right then," said Aberforth when they had eaten their fill, and Harry and Ron sat slumped dozily in their chairs. "We need to think of the best way to get you out of here. Can't be done by night, you heard what happens if anyone moves outdoors during darkness: Caterwauling Charm's set off, they'll be onto you like bowtruckles on doxy eggs. I don't reckon I'll be able to pass off a stag as a goat a second time. Wait for daybreak when curfew lifts, then you can put your Cloak back on and set out on foot. Get right out of Hogsmeade, up into the mountains, and you'll be able to Disapparate there. Might see Hagrid. He's been hiding in a cave up there with Grawp ever since they tried to arrest him."

"We're not leaving," said Harry. "We need to get into Hogwarts."

"Don't be stupid, boy," said Aberforth.

"We've got to," said Harry.

"What you've got to do," said Aberforth, leaning forward, "is to get as far from here as you can."

"You don't understand. There isn't much time. We've got to get into the castle. Dumbledore — I mean, your brother — wanted us —"

The firelight made the grimy lenses of Aberforth's glasses momentarily opaque, a bright flat white, and Harry remembered the blind eyes of the giant spider, Aragog.

"My brother Albus wanted a lot of things," said Aberforth, "and people had a habit of getting hurt while he was carrying out his grand plans. You get away from this school, Potter, and out of the country if you can. Forget my brother and his clever schemes. He's gone where none of this can hurt him, and you don't owe him anything."

"You don't understand," said Harry again.

"Oh, don't I?" said Aberforth quietly. "You don't think I understood my own brother? Think you knew Albus better than I did?"

"I didn't mean that," said Harry, whose brain felt sluggish with exhaustion and from the surfeit of food and wine. "It's . . . he left me a job."

"Did he now?" said Aberforth. "Nice job, I hope? Pleasant? Easy? Sort of thing you'd expect an unqualified wizard kid to be able to do without overstretching themselves?"

Ron gave a rather grim laugh. Hermione was looking strained.

"I-it's not easy, no," said Harry. "But I've got to —"

"'Got to'? Why 'got to'? He's dead, isn't he?" said Aberforth roughly. "Let it go, boy, before you follow him! Save yourself!"

"I can't."

"Why not?"

"I —" Harry felt overwhelmed; he could not explain, so he took the offensive instead. "But you're fighting too, you're in the Order of the Phoenix —"

"I was," said Aberforth. "The Order of the Phoenix is finished. You-Know-Who's won, it's over, and anyone who's pretending different's kidding themselves. It'll never be safe for you here, Potter, he wants you too badly. So go abroad, go into hiding, save yourself. Best take these two with you." He jerked a thumb at Ron and Hermione. "They'll be in danger long as they live now everyone knows they've been working with you."

"I can't leave," said Harry. "I've got a job —"

"Give it to someone else!"

"I can't. It's got to be me, Dumbledore explained it all —"

"Oh, did he now? And did he tell you everything, was he honest with you?"

Harry wanted with all his heart to say "Yes," but somehow the simple word would not rise to his lips. Aberforth seemed to know what he was thinking.

"I knew my brother, Potter. He learned secrecy at our mother's knee. Secrets and lies, that's how we grew up, and Albus . . . he was a natural."

The old man's eyes traveled to the painting of the girl over the mantelpiece. It was, now Harry looked around properly, the only picture in the room. There was no photograph of Albus Dumbledore, nor of anyone else.

"Mr. Dumbledore?" said Hermione rather timidly. "Is that your sister? Ariana?"

"Yes," said Aberforth tersely. "Been reading Rita Skeeter, have you, missy?"

Even by the rosy light of the fire it was clear that Hermione had turned red.

"Elphias Doge mentioned her to us," said Harry, trying to spare Hermione.

"That old berk," muttered Aberforth, taking another swig of mead. "Thought the sun shone out of my brother's every orifice, he did. Well, so did plenty of people, you three included, by the looks of it."

Harry kept quiet. He did not want to express the doubts and uncertainties about Dumbledore that had riddled him for months now. He had made his choice while he dug Dobby's grave, he had decided to continue along the winding, dangerous path indicated for him by Albus Dumbledore, to accept that he had not been told everything that he wanted to know, but simply to trust. He had no desire to doubt again; he did not want to hear anything that would deflect him from his purpose. He met Aberforth's gaze, which was so strikingly like his brother's: The bright blue eyes gave the same impression that they were X-raying the object of their scrutiny, and Harry thought that Aberforth knew what he was thinking and despised him for it.

"Professor Dumbledore cared about Harry, very much," said Hermione in a low voice.

"Did he now?" said Aberforth. "Funny thing, how many of the people my brother cared about very much ended up in a worse state than if he'd left 'em well alone."

"What do you mean?" asked Hermione breathlessly.

"Never you mind," said Aberforth.

"But that's a really serious thing to say!" said Hermione. "Are you — are you talking about your sister?"

Aberforth glared at her: His lips moved as if he were chewing the words he was holding back. Then he burst into speech.

"When my sister was six years old, she was attacked, set upon, by three Muggle boys. They'd seen her doing magic, spying through the back garden hedge: She was a kid, she couldn't control it, no witch or wizard can at that age. What they saw scared them, I expect. They forced their way through the hedge, and when she couldn't show them the trick, they got a bit carried away trying to stop the little freak doing it."

Hermione's eyes were huge in the firelight; Ron looked slightly sick. Aberforth stood up, tall as Albus, and suddenly terrible in his anger and the intensity of his pain.

"It destroyed her, what they did: She was never right again. She wouldn't use magic, but she couldn't get rid of it; it turned inward and drove her mad, it exploded out of her when she couldn't control it, and at times she was strange and dangerous. But mostly she was sweet and scared and harmless.

"And my father went after the bastards that did it," said Aberforth, "and attacked them. And they locked him up in Azkaban for it. He never said why he'd done it, because if the Ministry had known what Ariana had become, she'd have been locked up in St. Mungo's for good. They'd have seen her as a serious threat to the International Statute of Secrecy, unbalanced like she was, with magic exploding out of her at moments when she couldn't keep it in any longer.

"We had to keep her safe and quiet. We moved house, put it about she was ill, and my mother looked after her, and tried to keep her calm and happy.

"*I* was her favorite," he said, and as he said it, a grubby schoolboy seemed to look out through Aberforth's wrinkles and tangled beard. "Not Albus, he was always up in his bedroom when he was home, reading his books and counting his prizes, keeping up with his correspondence with 'the most notable magical names of the day,'" Aberforth sneered. "*He* didn't want to be bothered with her. She liked me best. I could get her to eat when she wouldn't do it for my mother, I could get her to calm down when she was in one of her rages, and when she was quiet, she used to help me feed the goats.

"Then, when she was fourteen . . . See, I wasn't there," said Aberforth. "If I'd been there, I could have calmed her down. She had one of her rages, and my mother wasn't as young as she was, and . . . it was an accident. Ariana couldn't control it. But my mother was killed."

Harry felt a horrible mixture of pity and repulsion; he did not want to hear any more, but Aberforth kept talking, and Harry wondered how long it had been since he had spoken about this; whether, in fact, he had ever spoken about it.

"So that put paid to Albus's trip round the world with little Doge. The pair of 'em came home for my mother's funeral and then Doge went off on his own, and Albus settled down as head of the family. Ha!"

Aberforth spat into the fire.

"I'd have looked after her, I told him so, I didn't care about school, I'd have stayed home and done it. He told me I had to finish my education and *he'd* take over from my mother. Bit of a comedown for Mr. Brilliant, there's no prizes for looking after your half-mad sister, stopping her blowing up the house every other day. But he did all right for a few weeks . . . till he came."

And now a positively dangerous look crept over Aberforth's face.

"Grindelwald. And at last, my brother had an *equal* to talk to, someone just as bright and talented as *he* was. And looking after Ariana took a backseat then, while they were hatching all their plans for a new Wizarding order, and looking for *Hallows,* and whatever else it was they were so interested in. Grand plans for the benefit of all Wizardkind, and if one young girl got neglected, what did that matter, when Albus was working for *the greater good*?

"But after a few weeks of it, I'd had enough, I had. It was nearly time for me to go back to Hogwarts, so I told 'em, both of 'em, face-to-face, like I am to you, now," and Aberforth looked down at Harry, and it took little imagination to see him as a teenager, wiry and angry, confronting his elder brother. "I told him, you'd better give it up now. You can't move her, she's in no fit state, you can't take her with you, wherever it is you're planning to go, when you're making your clever speeches, trying to whip yourselves up a following. He didn't like that," said Aberforth, and his eyes were briefly occluded by the firelight on the lenses of his glasses: They shone white and blind again. "Grindelwald didn't like that at all. He got angry. He told me what a stupid little boy I was, trying to stand in the way of him and my brilliant brother. . . . Didn't I *understand,* my poor sister wouldn't *have* to be hidden once they'd changed the world, and led the wizards out of hiding, and taught the Muggles their place?

"And there was an argument . . . and I pulled out my wand, and he pulled out his, and I had the Cruciatus Curse used on me by my brother's best friend — and Albus was trying to stop him, and then all three of us were dueling, and the flashing lights and the bangs set her off, she couldn't stand it —"

The color was draining from Aberforth's face as though he had suffered a mortal wound.

"— and I think she wanted to help, but she didn't really know what she was doing, and I don't know which of us did it, it could have been any of us — and she was dead."

His voice broke on the last word and he dropped down into the nearest chair. Hermione's face was wet with tears, and Ron was almost as pale as Aberforth. Harry felt nothing but revulsion: He wished he had not heard it, wished he could wash his mind clean of it.

"I'm so . . . I'm so sorry," Hermione whispered.

"Gone," croaked Aberforth. "Gone forever."

He wiped his nose on his cuff and cleared his throat.

"'Course, Grindelwald scarpered. He had a bit of a track record already, back in his own country, and he didn't want Ariana set to his account too. And Albus was free, wasn't he? Free of the burden of his sister, free to become the greatest wizard of the —"

"He was never free," said Harry.

"I beg your pardon?" said Aberforth.

"Never," said Harry. "The night that your brother died, he drank a potion that drove him out of his mind. He started screaming, pleading with someone who wasn't there. 'Don't hurt them, please . . . hurt me instead.'"

Ron and Hermione were staring at Harry. He had never gone into details about what had happened on the island on the lake: The events that had taken place after he and Dumbledore had returned to Hogwarts had eclipsed it so thoroughly.

"He thought he was back there with you and Grindelwald, I know he did," said Harry, remembering Dumbledore whimpering, pleading. "He thought he was watching Grindelwald hurting you and Ariana. . . . It was torture to him, if you'd seen him then, you wouldn't say he was free."

Aberforth seemed lost in contemplation of his own knotted and veined hands. After a long pause he said, "How can you be sure, Potter, that my brother wasn't more interested in the greater good than in you? How can you be sure you aren't dispensable, just like my little sister?"

A shard of ice seemed to pierce Harry's heart.

"I don't believe it. Dumbledore loved Harry," said Hermione.

"Why didn't he tell him to hide, then?" shot back Aberforth. "Why didn't he say to him, 'Take care of yourself, here's how to survive'?"

"Because," said Harry before Hermione could answer, "sometimes you've *got* to think about more than your own safety! Sometimes you've *got* to think about the greater good! This is war!"

"You're seventeen, boy!"

"I'm of age, and I'm going to keep fighting even if you've given up!"

"Who says I've given up?"

"'The Order of the Phoenix is finished,'" Harry repeated. "'You-Know-Who's won, it's over, and anyone who's pretending different's kidding themselves.'"

"I don't say I like it, but it's the truth!"

"No, it isn't," said Harry. "Your brother knew how to finish You-Know-Who and he passed the knowledge on to me. I'm going to keep going until I succeed — or I die. Don't think I don't know how this might end. I've known it for years."

He waited for Aberforth to jeer or to argue, but he did not. He merely scowled.

"We need to get into Hogwarts," said Harry again. "If you can't help us, we'll wait till daybreak, leave you in peace, and try to find a way in ourselves. If you *can* help us — well, now would be a great time to mention it."

Aberforth remained fixed in his chair, gazing at Harry with the eyes that were so extraordinarily like his brother's. At last he cleared his throat, got to his feet, walked around the little table, and approached the portrait of Ariana.

"You know what to do," he said.

She smiled, turned, and walked away, not as people in portraits usually did, out of the sides of their frames, but along what seemed to be a long tunnel painted behind her. They watched her slight figure retreating until finally she was swallowed by the darkness.

"Er — what — ?" began Ron.

"There's only one way in now," said Aberforth. "You must know they've got all the old secret passageways covered at both ends, dementors all around the boundary walls, regular patrols inside the school from what my sources tell me. The place has never been so heavily guarded. How you expect to do anything once you get inside it, with Snape in charge and the Carrows as his deputies . . . well, that's your lookout, isn't it? You say you're prepared to die."

"But what . . . ?" said Hermione, frowning at Ariana's picture.

A tiny white dot had reappeared at the end of the painted tunnel, and now Ariana was walking back toward them, growing bigger and bigger as she came. But there was somebody else with her now, someone taller than she was, who was limping along, looking excited. His hair was longer than Harry had ever seen it: He appeared to have suffered several gashes to his face and his clothes were ripped and torn. Larger and larger the two figures grew, until only their heads and shoulders filled the portrait. Then the whole thing swung forward on the wall like a little door, and the entrance to a real tunnel was revealed. And out of it, his hair overgrown, his face cut, his robes ripped, clambered the real Neville Longbottom, who gave a roar of delight, leapt down from the mantelpiece, and yelled, "I knew you'd come! *I knew it, Harry!*"

THE LOST DIADEM

Neville — what the — how — ?"

But Neville had spotted Ron and Hermione, and with yells of delight was hugging them too. The longer Harry looked at Neville, the worse he appeared: One of his eyes was swollen yellow and purple, there were gouge marks on his face, and his general air of unkemptness suggested that he had been living rough. Nevertheless, his battered visage shone with happiness as he let go of Hermione and said again, "I knew you'd come! Kept telling Seamus it was a matter of time!"

"Neville, what's happened to you?"

"What? This?" Neville dismissed his injuries with a shake of the head. "This is nothing. Seamus is worse. You'll see. Shall we get going then? Oh," he turned to Aberforth, "Ab, there might be a couple more people on the way."

"Couple more?" repeated Aberforth ominously. "What d'you

mean, a couple more, Longbottom? There's a curfew and a Cater-wauling Charm on the whole village!"

"I know, that's why they'll be Apparating directly into the bar," said Neville. "Just send them down the passage when they get here, will you? Thanks a lot."

Neville held out his hand to Hermione and helped her to climb up onto the mantelpiece and into the tunnel; Ron followed, then Neville. Harry addressed Aberforth.

"I don't know how to thank you. You've saved our lives twice."

"Look after 'em, then," said Aberforth gruffly. "I might not be able to save 'em a third time."

Harry clambered up onto the mantelpiece and through the hole behind Ariana's portrait. There were smooth stone steps on the other side: It looked as though the passageway had been there for years. Brass lamps hung from the walls and the earthy floor was worn and smooth; as they walked, their shadows rippled, fanlike, across the wall.

"How long's this been here?" Ron asked as they set off. "It isn't on the Marauder's Map, is it, Harry? I thought there were only seven passages in and out of school?"

"They sealed off all of those before the start of the year," said Neville. "There's no chance of getting through any of them now, not with curses over the entrances and Death Eaters and demen-tors waiting at the exits." He started walking backward, beaming, drinking them in. "Never mind that stuff. . . . Is it true? Did you break into Gringotts? Did you escape on a dragon? It's everywhere, everyone's talking about it, Terry Boot got beaten up by Carrow for yelling about it in the Great Hall at dinner!"

"Yeah, it's true," said Harry.

Neville laughed gleefully.

"What did you do with the dragon?"

"Released it into the wild," said Ron. "Hermione was all for keeping it as a pet —"

"Don't exaggerate, Ron —"

"But what have you been doing? People have been saying you've just been on the run, Harry, but I don't think so. I think you've been up to something."

"You're right," said Harry, "but tell us about Hogwarts, Neville, we haven't heard anything."

"It's been . . . well, it's not really like Hogwarts anymore," said Neville, the smile fading from his face as he spoke. "Do you know about the Carrows?"

"Those two Death Eaters who teach here?"

"They do more than teach," said Neville. "They're in charge of all discipline. They like punishment, the Carrows."

"Like Umbridge?"

"Nah, they make her look tame. The other teachers are all supposed to refer us to the Carrows if we do anything wrong. They don't, though, if they can avoid it. You can tell they all hate them as much as we do.

"Amycus, the bloke, he teaches what used to be Defense Against the Dark Arts, except now it's just the Dark Arts. We're supposed to practice the Cruciatus Curse on people who've earned detentions —"

"*What?*"

Harry, Ron, and Hermione's united voices echoed up and down the passage.

"Yeah," said Neville. "That's how I got this one," he pointed at a particularly deep gash in his cheek, "I refused to do it. Some people are into it, though; Crabbe and Goyle love it. First time they've ever been top in anything, I expect.

"Alecto, Amycus's sister, teaches Muggle Studies, which is compulsory for everyone. We've all got to listen to her explain how Muggles are like animals, stupid and dirty, and how they drove wizards into hiding by being vicious toward them, and how the natural order is being reestablished. I got this one," he indicated another slash to his face, "for asking her how much Muggle blood she and her brother have got."

"Blimey, Neville," said Ron, "there's a time and a place for getting a smart mouth."

"You didn't hear her," said Neville. "You wouldn't have stood it either. The thing is, it helps when people stand up to them, it gives everyone hope. I used to notice that when you did it, Harry."

"But they've used you as a knife sharpener," said Ron, wincing slightly as they passed a lamp and Neville's injuries were thrown into even greater relief.

Neville shrugged.

"Doesn't matter. They don't want to spill too much pure blood, so they'll torture us a bit if we're mouthy but they won't actually kill us."

Harry did not know what was worse, the things that Neville was saying or the matter-of-fact tone in which he said them.

"The only people in real danger are the ones whose friends and relatives on the outside are giving trouble. They get taken hostage. Old Xeno Lovegood was getting a bit too outspoken in *The Quibbler,* so they dragged Luna off the train on the way back for Christmas."

"Neville, she's all right, we've seen her —"

"Yeah, I know, she managed to get a message to me."

From his pocket he pulled a golden coin, and Harry recognized it as one of the fake Galleons that Dumbledore's Army had used to send one another messages.

"These have been great," said Neville, beaming at Hermione. "The Carrows never rumbled how we were communicating, it drove them mad. We used to sneak out at night and put graffiti on the walls: *Dumbledore's Army, Still Recruiting,* stuff like that. Snape hated it."

"You *used to?*" said Harry, who had noticed the past tense.

"Well, it got more difficult as time went on," said Neville. "We lost Luna at Christmas, and Ginny never came back after Easter, and the three of us were sort of the leaders. The Carrows seemed to know I was behind a lot of it, so they started coming down on me hard, and then Michael Corner went and got caught releasing a first-year they'd chained up, and they tortured him pretty badly. That scared people off."

"No kidding," muttered Ron, as the passage began to slope upward.

"Yeah, well, I couldn't ask people to go through what Michael did, so we dropped those kinds of stunts. But we were still fighting, doing underground stuff, right up until a couple of weeks ago. That's when they decided there was only one way to stop me, I suppose, and they went for Gran."

"They *what?*" said Harry, Ron, and Hermione together.

"Yeah," said Neville, panting a little now, because the passage was climbing so steeply, "well, you can see their thinking. It had worked really well, kidnapping kids to force their relatives to behave,

I s'pose it was only a matter of time before they did it the other way around. Thing was," he faced them, and Harry was astonished to see that he was grinning, "they bit off a bit more than they could chew with Gran. Little old witch living alone, they probably thought they didn't need to send anyone particularly powerful. Anyway," Neville laughed, "Dawlish is still in St. Mungo's and Gran's on the run. She sent me a letter," he clapped a hand to the breast pocket of his robes, "telling me she was proud of me, that I'm my parents' son, and to keep it up."

"Cool," said Ron.

"Yeah," said Neville happily. "Only thing was, once they realized they had no hold over me, they decided Hogwarts could do without me after all. I don't know whether they were planning to kill me or send me to Azkaban; either way, I knew it was time to disappear."

"But," said Ron, looking thoroughly confused, "aren't — aren't we heading straight back into Hogwarts?"

"'Course," said Neville. "You'll see. We're here."

They turned a corner and there ahead of them was the end of the passage. Another short flight of steps led to a door just like the one hidden behind Ariana's portrait. Neville pushed it open and climbed through. As Harry followed, he heard Neville call out to unseen people:

"Look who it is! Didn't I tell you?"

As Harry emerged into the room beyond the passage, there were several screams and yells: "HARRY!" "It's Potter, it's POTTER!" "Ron!" *"Hermione!"*

He had a confused impression of colored hangings, of lamps and many faces. The next moment, he, Ron, and Hermione were engulfed, hugged, pounded on the back, their hair ruffled, their hands shaken, by what seemed to be more than twenty people: They might just have won a Quidditch final.

"Okay, okay, calm down!" Neville called, and as the crowd backed away, Harry was able to take in their surroundings.

He did not recognize the room at all. It was enormous, and looked rather like the interior of a particularly sumptuous tree house, or perhaps a gigantic ship's cabin. Multicolored hammocks were strung from the ceiling and from a balcony that ran around the dark wood-paneled and windowless walls, which were covered in bright tapestry hangings: Harry saw the gold Gryffindor lion, emblazoned on scarlet; the black badger of Hufflepuff, set against yellow; and the bronze eagle of Ravenclaw, on blue. The silver and green of Slytherin alone were absent. There were bulging bookcases, a few broomsticks propped against the walls, and in the corner, a large wooden-cased wireless.

"Where are we?"

"Room of Requirement, of course!" said Neville. "Surpassed itself, hasn't it? The Carrows were chasing me, and I knew I had just one chance for a hideout: I managed to get through the door and this is what I found! Well, it wasn't exactly like this when I arrived, it was a load smaller, there was only one hammock and just Gryffindor hangings. But it's expanded as more and more of the D.A. have arrived."

"And the Carrows can't get in?" asked Harry, looking around for the door.

"No," said Seamus Finnigan, whom Harry had not recognized until he spoke: Seamus's face was bruised and puffy. "It's a proper hideout, as long as one of us stays in here, they can't get at us, the door won't open. It's all down to Neville. He really *gets* this room.

You've got to ask it for *exactly* what you need — like, 'I don't want any Carrow supporters to be able to get in' — and it'll do it for you! You've just got to make sure you close the loopholes! Neville's the man!"

"It's quite straightforward, really," said Neville modestly. "I'd been in here about a day and a half, and getting really hungry, and wishing I could get something to eat, and that's when the passage to the Hog's Head opened up. I went through it and met Aberforth. He's been providing us with food, because for some reason, that's the one thing the room doesn't really do."

"Yeah, well, food's one of the five exceptions to Gamp's Law of Elemental Transfiguration," said Ron to general astonishment.

"So we've been hiding out here for nearly two weeks," said Seamus, "and it just makes more hammocks every time we need them, and it even sprouted a pretty good bathroom once girls started turning up —"

"— and thought they'd quite like to wash, yes," supplied Lavender Brown, whom Harry had not noticed until that point. Now that he looked around properly, he recognized many familiar faces. Both Patil twins were there, as were Terry Boot, Ernie Macmillan, Anthony Goldstein, and Michael Corner.

"Tell us what you've been up to, though," said Ernie. "There've been so many rumors, we've been trying to keep up with you on *Potterwatch*." He pointed at the wireless. "You didn't break into Gringotts?"

"They did!" said Neville. "And the dragon's true too!"

There was a smattering of applause and a few whoops; Ron took a bow.

"What were you after?" asked Seamus eagerly.

Before any of them could parry the question with one of their own, Harry felt a terrible, scorching pain in the lightning scar. As he turned his back hastily on the curious and delighted faces, the Room of Requirement vanished, and he was standing inside a ruined stone shack, and the rotting floorboards were ripped apart at his feet, a disinterred golden box lay open and empty beside the hole, and Voldemort's scream of fury vibrated inside his head.

With an enormous effort he pulled out of Voldemort's mind again, back to where he stood, swaying, in the Room of Requirement, sweat pouring from his face and Ron holding him up.

"Are you all right, Harry?" Neville was saying. "Want to sit down? I expect you're tired, aren't — ?"

"No," said Harry. He looked at Ron and Hermione, trying to tell them without words that Voldemort had just discovered the loss of one of the other Horcruxes. Time was running out fast: If Voldemort chose to visit Hogwarts next, they would miss their chance.

"We need to get going," he said, and their expressions told him that they understood.

"What are we going to do, then, Harry?" asked Seamus. "What's the plan?"

"Plan?" repeated Harry. He was exercising all his willpower to prevent himself succumbing again to Voldemort's rage: His scar was still burning. "Well, there's something we — Ron, Hermione, and I — need to do, and then we'll get out of here."

Nobody was laughing or whooping anymore. Neville looked confused.

"What d'you mean, 'get out of here'?"

"We haven't come back to stay," said Harry, rubbing his scar, trying to soothe the pain. "There's something important we need to do —"

"What is it?"

"I — I can't tell you."

There was a ripple of muttering at this: Neville's brows contracted.

"Why can't you tell us? It's something to do with fighting You-Know-Who, right?"

"Well, yeah —"

"Then we'll help you."

The other members of Dumbledore's Army were nodding, some enthusiastically, others solemnly. A couple of them rose from their chairs to demonstrate their willingness for immediate action.

"You don't understand." Harry seemed to have said that a lot in the last few hours. "We — we can't tell you. We've got to do it — alone."

"Why?" asked Neville.

"Because . . ." In his desperation to start looking for the missing Horcrux, or at least to have a private discussion with Ron and Hermione about where they might commence their search, Harry found it difficult to gather his thoughts. His scar was still searing. "Dumbledore left the three of us a job," he said carefully, "and we weren't supposed to tell — I mean, he wanted us to do it, just the three of us."

"We're his army," said Neville. "Dumbledore's Army. We were all in it together, we've been keeping it going while you three have been off on your own —"

"It hasn't exactly been a picnic, mate," said Ron.

"I never said it had, but I don't see why you can't trust us. Everyone in this room's been fighting and they've been driven in here because the Carrows were hunting them down. Everyone in here's proven they're loyal to Dumbledore — loyal to you."

"Look," Harry began, without knowing what he was going to say, but it did not matter: The tunnel door had just opened behind him.

"We got your message, Neville! Hello you three, I thought you must be here!"

It was Luna and Dean. Seamus gave a great roar of delight and ran to hug his best friend.

"Hi, everyone!" said Luna happily. "Oh, it's great to be back!"

"Luna," said Harry distractedly, "what are you doing here? How did you — ?"

"I sent for her," said Neville, holding up the fake Galleon. "I promised her and Ginny that if you turned up I'd let them know. We all thought that if you came back, it would mean revolution. That we were going to overthrow Snape and the Carrows."

"Of course that's what it means," said Luna brightly. "Isn't it, Harry? We're going to fight them out of Hogwarts?"

"Listen," said Harry with a rising sense of panic, "I'm sorry, but that's not what we came back for. There's something we've got to do, and then —"

"You're going to leave us in this mess?" demanded Michael Corner.

"No!" said Ron. "What we're doing will benefit everyone in the end, it's all about trying to get rid of You-Know-Who —"

"Then let us help!" said Neville angrily. "We want to be a part of it!"

There was another noise behind them, and Harry turned. His heart seemed to fail: Ginny was now climbing through the hole in the wall, closely followed by Fred, George, and Lee Jordan. Ginny gave Harry a radiant smile: He had forgotten, or had never fully appreciated, how beautiful she was, but he had never been less pleased to see her.

"Aberforth's getting a bit annoyed," said Fred, raising his hand in answer to several cries of greeting. "He wants a kip, and his bar's turned into a railway station."

Harry's mouth fell open. Right behind Lee Jordan came Harry's old girlfriend, Cho Chang. She smiled at him.

"I got the message," she said, holding up her own fake Galleon, and she walked over to sit beside Michael Corner.

"So what's the plan, Harry?" said George.

"There isn't one," said Harry, still disoriented by the sudden appearance of all these people, unable to take everything in while his scar was still burning so fiercely.

"Just going to make it up as we go along, are we? My favorite kind," said Fred.

"You've got to stop this!" Harry told Neville. "What did you call them all back for? This is insane —"

"We're fighting, aren't we?" said Dean, taking out his fake Galleon. "The message said Harry was back, and we were going to fight! I'll have to get a wand, though —"

"You haven't got a *wand* — ?" began Seamus.

Ron turned suddenly to Harry.

"Why can't they help?"

"What?"

"They can help." He dropped his voice and said, so that none of them could hear but Hermione, who stood between them, "We don't know where it is. We've got to find it fast. We don't have to tell them it's a Horcrux."

Harry looked from Ron to Hermione, who murmured, "I think Ron's right. We don't even know what we're looking for, we need them." And when Harry looked unconvinced, "You don't have to do everything alone, Harry."

Harry thought fast, his scar still prickling, his head threatening to split again. Dumbledore had warned him against telling anyone but Ron and Hermione about the Horcruxes. *Secrets and lies, that's how we grew up, and Albus . . . he was a natural. . . .* Was he turning into Dumbledore, keeping his secrets clutched to his chest, afraid to trust? But Dumbledore had trusted Snape, and where had that led? To murder at the top of the highest tower . . .

"All right," he said quietly to the other two. "Okay," he called to the room at large, and all noise ceased: Fred and George, who had been cracking jokes for the benefit of those nearest, fell silent, and all of them looked alert, excited.

"There's something we need to find," Harry said. "Something — something that'll help us overthrow You-Know-Who. It's here at Hogwarts, but we don't know where. It might have belonged to Ravenclaw. Has anyone heard of an object like that? Has anyone ever come across something with her eagle on it, for instance?"

He looked hopefully toward the little group of Ravenclaws, to

Padma, Michael, Terry, and Cho, but it was Luna who answered, perched on the arm of Ginny's chair.

"Well, there's her lost diadem. I told you about it, remember, Harry? The lost diadem of Ravenclaw? Daddy's trying to duplicate it."

"Yeah, but the lost diadem," said Michael Corner, rolling his eyes, "is *lost*, Luna. That's sort of the point."

"When was it lost?" asked Harry.

"Centuries ago, they say," said Cho, and Harry's heart sank. "Professor Flitwick says the diadem vanished with Ravenclaw herself. People have looked, but," she appealed to her fellow Ravenclaws, "nobody's ever found a trace of it, have they?"

They all shook their heads.

"Sorry, but what *is* a diadem?" asked Ron.

"It's a kind of crown," said Terry Boot. "Ravenclaw's was supposed to have magical properties, enhance the wisdom of the wearer."

"Yes, Daddy's Wrackspurt siphons —"

But Harry cut across Luna.

"And none of you have ever seen anything that looks like it?"

They all shook their heads again. Harry looked at Ron and Hermione and his own disappointment was mirrored back at him. An object that had been lost this long, and apparently without trace, did not seem like a good candidate for the Horcrux hidden in the castle. . . . Before he could formulate a new question, however, Cho spoke again.

"If you'd like to see what the diadem's supposed to look like, I could take you up to our common room and show you, Harry? Ravenclaw's wearing it in her statue."

Harry's scar scorched again: For a moment the Room of Requirement swam before him, and he saw instead the dark earth soaring beneath him and felt the great snake wrapped around his shoulders. Voldemort was flying again, whether to the underground lake or here, to the castle, he did not know: Either way, there was hardly any time left.

"He's on the move," he said quietly to Ron and Hermione. He glanced at Cho and then back at them. "Listen, I know it's not much of a lead, but I'm going to go and look at this statue, at least find out what the diadem looks like. Wait for me here and keep, you know — the other one — safe."

Cho had got to her feet, but Ginny said rather fiercely, "No, Luna will take Harry, won't you, Luna?"

"Oooh, yes, I'd like to," said Luna happily, and Cho sat down again, looking disappointed.

"How do we get out?" Harry asked Neville.

"Over here."

He led Harry and Luna to a corner, where a small cupboard opened onto a steep staircase.

"It comes out somewhere different every day, so they've never been able to find it," he said. "Only trouble is, we never know exactly where we're going to end up when we go out. Be careful, Harry, they're always patrolling the corridors at night."

"No problem," said Harry. "See you in a bit."

He and Luna hurried up the staircase, which was long, lit by torches, and turned corners in unexpected places. At last they reached what appeared to be solid wall.

"Get under here," Harry told Luna, pulling out the Invisibility Cloak and throwing it over both of them. He gave the wall a little push.

It melted away at his touch and they slipped outside: Harry glanced back and saw that it had resealed itself at once. They were standing in a dark corridor: Harry pulled Luna back into the shadows, fumbled in the pouch around his neck, and took out the Marauder's Map. Holding it close to his nose he searched, and located his and Luna's dots at last.

"We're up on the fifth floor," he whispered, watching Filch moving away from them, a corridor ahead. "Come on, this way."

They crept off.

Harry had prowled the castle at night many times before, but never had his heart hammered this fast, never had so much depended on his safe passage through the place. Through squares of moonlight upon the floor, past suits of armor whose helmets creaked at the sound of their soft footsteps, around corners beyond which who knew what lurked, Harry and Luna walked, checking the Marauder's Map whenever light permitted, twice pausing to allow a ghost to pass without drawing attention to themselves. He expected to encounter an obstacle at any moment; his worst fear was Peeves, and he strained his ears with every step to hear the first, telltale signs of the poltergeist's approach.

"This way, Harry," breathed Luna, plucking his sleeve and pulling him toward a spiral staircase.

They climbed in tight, dizzying circles; Harry had never been up here before. At last they reached a door. There was no handle and no keyhole: nothing but a plain expanse of aged wood, and a bronze knocker in the shape of an eagle.

Luna reached out a pale hand, which looked eerie floating in midair, unconnected to arm or body. She knocked once, and in the silence it sounded to Harry like a cannon blast. At once the beak of the eagle opened, but instead of a bird's call, a soft, musical voice said, "Which came first, the phoenix or the flame?"

"Hmm . . . What do you think, Harry?" said Luna, looking thoughtful.

"What? Isn't there just a password?"

"Oh no, you've got to answer a question," said Luna.

"What if you get it wrong?"

"Well, you have to wait for somebody who gets it right," said Luna. "That way you learn, you see?"

"Yeah . . . Trouble is, we can't really afford to wait for anyone else, Luna."

"No, I see what you mean," said Luna seriously. "Well then, I think the answer is that a circle has no beginning."

"Well reasoned," said the voice, and the door swung open.

The deserted Ravenclaw common room was a wide, circular room, airier than any Harry had ever seen at Hogwarts. Graceful arched windows punctuated the walls, which were hung with blue-and-bronze silks: By day, the Ravenclaws would have a spectacular view of the surrounding mountains. The ceiling was domed and painted with stars, which were echoed in the midnight-blue carpet. There were tables, chairs, and bookcases, and in a niche opposite the door stood a tall statue of white marble.

Harry recognized Rowena Ravenclaw from the bust he had seen at Luna's house. The statue stood beside a door that led, he guessed, to dormitories above. He strode right up to the marble woman, and she seemed to look back at him with a quizzical half smile on her face, beautiful yet slightly intimidating. A delicate-looking circlet had been reproduced in marble on top of her head. It was not unlike the tiara Fleur had worn at her wedding. There were tiny words etched into it. Harry stepped out from under the Cloak and climbed up onto Ravenclaw's plinth to read them.

"'Wit beyond measure is man's greatest treasure.'"

"Which makes you pretty skint, witless," said a cackling voice.

Harry whirled around, slipped off the plinth, and landed on the floor. The sloping-shouldered figure of Alecto Carrow was standing before him, and even as Harry raised his wand, she pressed a stubby forefinger to the skull and snake branded on her forearm.

THE SACKING OF
SEVERUS SNAPE

The moment her finger touched the Mark, Harry's scar burned savagely, the starry room vanished from sight, and he was standing upon an outcrop of rock beneath a cliff, and the sea was washing around him and there was triumph in his heart — *They have the boy.*

A loud *bang* brought Harry back to where he stood: Disoriented, he raised his wand, but the witch before him was already falling forward; she hit the ground so hard that the glass in the bookcases tinkled.

"I've never Stunned anyone except in our D.A. lessons," said Luna, sounding mildly interested. "That was noisier than I thought it would be."

And sure enough, the ceiling had begun to tremble. Scurrying, echoing footsteps were growing louder from behind the door leading to the dormitories: Luna's spell had woken Ravenclaws sleeping above.

"Luna, where are you? I need to get under the Cloak!"

Luna's feet appeared out of nowhere; he hurried to her side and she let the Cloak fall back over them as the door opened and a stream of Ravenclaws, all in their nightclothes, flooded into the common room. There were gasps and cries of surprise as they saw Alecto lying there unconscious. Slowly they shuffled in around her, a savage beast that might wake at any moment and attack them. Then one brave little first-year darted up to her and prodded her backside with his big toe.

"I think she might be dead!" he shouted with delight.

"Oh, look," whispered Luna happily, as the Ravenclaws crowded in around Alecto. "They're pleased!"

"Yeah . . . great . . ."

Harry closed his eyes, and as his scar throbbed he chose to sink again into Voldemort's mind. . . . He was moving along the tunnel into the first cave. . . . He had chosen to make sure of the locket before coming . . . but that would not take him long. . . .

There was a rap on the common room door and every Ravenclaw froze. From the other side, Harry heard the soft, musical voice that issued from the eagle door knocker: "Where do Vanished objects go?"

"I dunno, do I? Shut it!" snarled an uncouth voice that Harry knew was that of the Carrow brother, Amycus. "Alecto? *Alecto?* Are you there? Have you got him? Open the door!"

The Ravenclaws were whispering amongst themselves, terrified. Then, without warning, there came a series of loud bangs, as though somebody was firing a gun into the door.

"*ALECTO!* If he comes, and we haven't got Potter — d'you want to go the same way as the Malfoys? ANSWER ME!" Amycus bellowed, shaking the door for all he was worth, but still it did not open. The Ravenclaws were all backing away, and some of the most frightened began scampering back up the staircase to their beds. Then, just as Harry was wondering whether he ought not to blast open the door and Stun Amycus before the Death Eater could do anything else, a second, most familiar voice rang out beyond the door.

"May I ask what you are doing, Professor Carrow?"

"Trying — to get — through this damned — door!" shouted Amycus. "Go and get Flitwick! Get him to open it, now!"

"But isn't your sister in there?" asked Professor McGonagall. "Didn't Professor Flitwick let her in earlier this evening, at your urgent request? Perhaps she could open the door for you? Then you needn't wake up half the castle."

"She ain't answering, you old besom! *You* open it! Garn! Do it, now!"

"Certainly, if you wish it," said Professor McGonagall, with awful coldness. There was a genteel tap of the knocker and the musical voice asked again,

"Where do Vanished objects go?"

"Into nonbeing, which is to say, everything," replied Professor McGonagall.

"Nicely phrased," replied the eagle door knocker, and the door swung open.

The few Ravenclaws who had remained behind sprinted for the stairs as Amycus burst over the threshold, brandishing his wand. Hunched like his sister, he had a pallid, doughy face and tiny eyes, which fell at once on Alecto, sprawled motionless on the floor. He let out a yell of fury and fear.

"What've they done, the little whelps?" he screamed. "I'll Cruciate the lot of 'em till they tell me who did it — and what's the Dark Lord going to say?" he shrieked, standing over his sister and smacking himself on the forehead with his fist. "We haven't got him, and they've gorn and killed her!"

"She's only Stunned," said Professor McGonagall impatiently, who had stooped down to examine Alecto. "She'll be perfectly all right."

"No she bludgering well won't!" bellowed Amycus. "Not after the Dark Lord gets hold of her! She's gorn and sent for him, I felt me Mark burn, and he thinks we've got Potter!"

"'Got Potter'?" said Professor McGonagall sharply. "What do you mean, 'got Potter'?"

"He told us Potter might try and get inside Ravenclaw Tower, and to send for him if we caught him!"

"Why would Harry Potter try to get inside Ravenclaw Tower? Potter belongs in my House!"

Beneath the disbelief and anger, Harry heard a little strain of pride in her voice, and affection for Minerva McGonagall gushed up inside him.

"We was told he might come in here!" said Carrow. "I dunno why, do I?"

Professor McGonagall stood up and her beady eyes swept the room. Twice they passed right over the place where Harry and Luna stood.

"We can push it off on the kids," said Amycus, his piglike face suddenly crafty. "Yeah, that's what we'll do. We'll say Alecto was ambushed by the kids, them kids up there" — he looked up at the starry ceiling toward the dormitories — "and we'll say they forced her to press her Mark, and that's why he got a false alarm. . . . He can punish them. Couple of kids more or less, what's the difference?"

"Only the difference between truth and lies, courage and cowardice," said Professor McGonagall, who had turned pale, "a difference, in short, which you and your sister seem unable to appreciate. But let me make one thing very clear. You are not going to pass off your many ineptitudes on the students of Hogwarts. I shall not permit it."

"Excuse me?"

Amycus moved forward until he was offensively close to Professor McGonagall, his face within inches of hers. She refused to back away, but looked down at him as if he were something disgusting she had found stuck to a lavatory seat.

"It's not a case of what *you'll* permit, Minerva McGonagall. Your time's over. It's us what's in charge here now, and you'll back me up or you'll pay the price."

And he spat in her face.

Harry pulled the Cloak off himself, raised his wand, and said, "You shouldn't have done that."

As Amycus spun around, Harry shouted, *"Crucio!"*

The Death Eater was lifted off his feet. He writhed through the air like a drowning man, thrashing and howling in pain, and then, with a crunch and a shattering of glass, he smashed into the front of a bookcase and crumpled, insensible, to the floor.

"I see what Bellatrix meant," said Harry, the blood thundering through his brain, "you need to really mean it."

"Potter!" whispered Professor McGonagall, clutching her heart. "Potter — you're here! What — ? How — ?" She struggled to pull herself together. "Potter, that was foolish!"

"He spat at you," said Harry.

"Potter, I — that was very — very *gallant* of you — but don't you realize — ?"

"Yeah, I do," Harry assured her. Somehow her panic steadied him. "Professor McGonagall, Voldemort's on the way."

"Oh, are we allowed to say the name now?" asked Luna with an air of interest, pulling off the Invisibility Cloak. This appearance of a second outlaw seemed to overwhelm Professor McGonagall, who staggered backward and fell into a nearby chair, clutching at the neck of her old tartan dressing gown.

"I don't think it makes any difference what we call him," Harry told Luna. "He already knows where I am."

In a distant part of Harry's brain, that part connected to the angry, burning scar, he could see Voldemort sailing fast over the dark lake in the ghostly green boat. . . . He had nearly reached the island where the stone basin stood. . . .

"You must flee," whispered Professor McGonagall. "Now, Potter, as quickly as you can!"

"I can't," said Harry. "There's something I need to do. Professor, do you know where the diadem of Ravenclaw is?"

"The d-diadem of Ravenclaw? Of course not — hasn't it been lost for centuries?" She sat up a little straighter. "Potter, it was madness, utter madness, for you to enter this castle —"

"I had to," said Harry. "Professor, there's something hidden here that I'm supposed to find, and it *could* be the diadem — if I could just speak to Professor Flitwick —"

There was a sound of movement, of clinking glass: Amycus was coming round. Before Harry or Luna could act, Professor McGonagall rose to her feet, pointed her wand at the groggy Death Eater, and said, *"Imperio."*

Amycus got up, walked over to his sister, picked up her wand, then shuffled obediently to Professor McGonagall and handed it over along with his own. Then he lay down on the floor beside Alecto. Professor McGonagall waved her wand again, and a length of shimmering silver rope appeared out of thin air and snaked around the Carrows, binding them tightly together.

"Potter," said Professor McGonagall, turning to face him again with superb indifference to the Carrows' predicament, "if He-Who-Must-Not-Be-Named does indeed know that you are here —"

As she said it, a wrath that was like physical pain blazed through Harry, setting his scar on fire, and for a second he looked down upon a basin whose potion had turned clear, and saw that no golden locket lay safe beneath the surface —

"Potter, are you all right?" said a voice, and Harry came back: He was clutching Luna's shoulder to steady himself.

"Time's running out, Voldemort's getting nearer. Professor, I'm acting on Dumbledore's orders, I must find what he wanted me to find! But we've got to get the students out while I'm searching the castle — it's me Voldemort wants, but he won't care about killing a few more or less, not now —" *not now he knows I'm attacking Horcruxes,* Harry finished the sentence in his head.

"You're acting on *Dumbledore's* orders?" she repeated with a look of dawning wonder. Then she drew herself up to her fullest height.

"We shall secure the school against He-Who-Must-Not-Be-Named while you search for this — this object."

"Is that possible?"

"I think so," said Professor McGonagall dryly, "we teachers are rather good at magic, you know. I am sure we will be able to hold him off for a while if we all put our best efforts into it. Of course, something will have to be done about Professor Snape —"

"Let me —"

"— and if Hogwarts is about to enter a state of siege, with the Dark Lord at the gates, it would indeed be advisable to take as many innocent people out of the way as possible. With the Floo Network under observation, and Apparition impossible within the grounds —"

"There's a way," said Harry quickly, and he explained about the passageway leading into the Hog's Head.

"Potter, we're talking about hundreds of students —"

"I know, Professor, but if Voldemort and the Death Eaters are concentrating on the school boundaries they won't be interested in anyone who's Disapparating out of the Hog's Head."

"There's something in that," she agreed. She pointed her wand at the Carrows, and a silver net fell upon their bound bodies, tied itself around them, and hoisted them into the air, where they dangled beneath the blue-and-gold ceiling like two large, ugly sea creatures. "Come. We must alert the other Heads of House. You'd better put that Cloak back on."

She marched toward the door, and as she did so she raised her wand. From the tip burst three silver cats with spectacle markings around their eyes. The Patronuses ran sleekly ahead, filling the spiral staircase with silvery light, as Professor McGonagall, Harry, and Luna hurried back down.

Along the corridors they raced, and one by one the Patronuses left them; Professor McGonagall's tartan dressing gown rustled over the floor, and Harry and Luna jogged behind her under the Cloak.

They had descended two more floors when another set of quiet footsteps joined theirs. Harry, whose scar was still prickling, heard them first: He felt in the pouch around his neck for the Marauder's Map, but before he could take it out, McGonagall too seemed to become aware of their company. She halted, raised her wand ready to duel, and said, "Who's there?"

"It is I," said a low voice.

From behind a suit of armor stepped Severus Snape.

Hatred boiled up in Harry at the sight of him: He had forgotten the details of Snape's appearance in the magnitude of his crimes, forgotten how his greasy black hair hung in curtains around his thin face, how his black eyes had a dead, cold look. He was not wearing nightclothes, but was dressed in his usual black cloak, and he too was holding his wand ready for a fight.

"Where are the Carrows?" he asked quietly.

"Wherever you told them to be, I expect, Severus," said Professor McGonagall.

Snape stepped nearer, and his eyes flitted over Professor McGonagall into the air around her, as if he knew that Harry was there. Harry held his wand up too, ready to attack.

"I was under the impression," said Snape, "that Alecto had apprehended an intruder."

"Really?" said Professor McGonagall. "And what gave you that impression?"

Snape made a slight flexing movement of his left arm, where the Dark Mark was branded into his skin.

"Oh, but naturally," said Professor McGonagall. "You Death Eaters have your own private means of communication, I forgot."

Snape pretended not to have heard her. His eyes were still probing the air all about her, and he was moving gradually closer, with an air of hardly noticing what he was doing.

"I did not know that it was your night to patrol the corridors, Minerva."

"You have some objection?"

"I wonder what could have brought you out of your bed at this late hour?"

"I thought I heard a disturbance," said Professor McGonagall.

"Really? But all seems calm."

Snape looked into her eyes.

"Have you seen Harry Potter, Minerva? Because if you have, I must insist —"

Professor McGonagall moved faster than Harry could have believed: Her wand slashed through the air and for a split second Harry thought that Snape must crumple, unconscious, but the swiftness of his Shield Charm was such that McGonagall was thrown off balance. She brandished her wand at a torch on the wall and it flew out of its bracket: Harry, about to curse Snape, was forced to pull Luna out of the way of the descending flames, which became a ring of fire that filled the corridor and flew like a lasso at Snape —

Then it was no longer fire, but a great black serpent that McGonagall blasted to smoke, which re-formed and solidified in seconds to become a swarm of pursuing daggers: Snape avoided them only by forcing the suit of armor in front of him, and with echoing clangs the daggers sank, one after another, into its breast —

"Minerva!" said a squeaky voice, and looking behind him, still shielding Luna from flying spells, Harry saw Professors Flitwick and Sprout sprinting up the corridor toward them in their nightclothes, with the enormous Professor Slughorn panting along at the rear.

"No!" squealed Flitwick, raising his wand. "You'll do no more murder at Hogwarts!"

Flitwick's spell hit the suit of armor behind which Snape had taken shelter: With a clatter it came to life. Snape struggled free of the crushing arms and sent it flying back toward his attackers: Harry and Luna had to dive sideways to avoid it as it smashed into the wall and shattered. When Harry looked up again, Snape was in full flight, McGonagall, Flitwick, and Sprout all thundering after him: He hurtled through a classroom door and, moments later, he heard McGonagall cry, "Coward! *COWARD!*"

"What's happened, what's happened?" asked Luna.

Harry dragged her to her feet and they raced along the corridor, trailing the Invisibility Cloak behind them, into the deserted classroom where Professors McGonagall, Flitwick, and Sprout were standing at a smashed window.

"He jumped," said Professor McGonagall as Harry and Luna ran into the room.

"You mean he's *dead*?" Harry sprinted to the window, ignoring Flitwick's and Sprout's yells of shock at his sudden appearance.

"No, he's not dead," said McGonagall bitterly. "Unlike Dumbledore, he was still carrying a wand . . . and he seems to have learned a few tricks from his master."

With a tingle of horror, Harry saw in the distance a huge, batlike shape flying through the darkness toward the perimeter wall.

There were heavy footfalls behind them, and a great deal of puffing: Slughorn had just caught up.

"Harry!" he panted, massaging his immense chest beneath his

emerald-green silk pajamas. "My dear boy . . . what a surprise . . . Minerva, do please explain. . . . Severus . . . what . . . ?"

"Our headmaster is taking a short break," said Professor McGonagall, pointing at the Snape-shaped hole in the window.

"Professor!" Harry shouted, his hands at his forehead. He could see the Inferi-filled lake sliding beneath him, and he felt the ghostly green boat bump into the underground shore, and Voldemort leapt from it with murder in his heart —

"Professor, we've got to barricade the school, he's coming now!"

"Very well. He-Who-Must-Not-Be-Named is coming," she told the other teachers. Sprout and Flitwick gasped; Slughorn let out a low groan. "Potter has work to do in the castle on Dumbledore's orders. We need to put in place every protection of which we are capable while Potter does what he needs to do."

"You realize, of course, that nothing we do will be able to keep out You-Know-Who indefinitely?" squeaked Flitwick.

"But we can hold him up," said Professor Sprout.

"Thank you, Pomona," said Professor McGonagall, and between the two witches there passed a look of grim understanding. "I suggest we establish basic protection around the place, then gather our students and meet in the Great Hall. Most must be evacuated, though if any of those who are over age wish to stay and fight, I think they ought to be given the chance."

"Agreed," said Professor Sprout, already hurrying toward the door. "I shall meet you in the Great Hall in twenty minutes with my House."

And as she jogged out of sight, they could hear her muttering, "Tentacula. Devil's Snare. And Snargaluff pods . . . yes, I'd like to see the Death Eaters fighting those."

"I can act from here," said Flitwick, and although he could barely see out of it, he pointed his wand through the smashed window and started muttering incantations of great complexity. Harry heard a weird rushing noise, as though Flitwick had unleashed the power of the wind into the grounds.

"Professor," Harry said, approaching the little Charms master, "Professor, I'm sorry to interrupt, but this is important. Have you got any idea where the diadem of Ravenclaw is?"

"— *Protego Horribilis* — the diadem of Ravenclaw?" squeaked Flitwick. "A little extra wisdom never goes amiss, Potter, but I hardly think it would be much use in *this* situation!"

"I only meant — do you know where it is? Have you ever seen it?"

"Seen it? Nobody has seen it in living memory! Long since lost, boy!"

Harry felt a mixture of desperate disappointment and panic. What, then, was the Horcrux?

"We shall meet you and your Ravenclaws in the Great Hall, Filius!" said Professor McGonagall, beckoning to Harry and Luna to follow her.

They had just reached the door when Slughorn rumbled into speech.

"My word," he puffed, pale and sweaty, his walrus mustache aquiver. "What a to-do! I'm not at all sure whether this is wise, Minerva. He is bound to find a way in, you know, and anyone who has tried to delay him will be in most grievous peril —"

"I shall expect you and the Slytherins in the Great Hall in twenty minutes, also," said Professor McGonagall. "If you wish to leave with your students, we shall not stop you. But if any of you attempt to sabotage our resistance or take up arms against us within this castle, then, Horace, we duel to kill."

"Minerva!" he said, aghast.

"The time has come for Slytherin House to decide upon its loyalties," interrupted Professor McGonagall. "Go and wake your students, Horace."

Harry did not stay to watch Slughorn splutter: He and Luna ran after Professor McGonagall, who had taken up a position in the middle of the corridor and raised her wand.

"*Piertotum* — oh, for heaven's sake, Filch, not *now* —"

The aged caretaker had just come hobbling into view, shouting, "Students out of bed! Students in the corridors!"

"They're supposed to be, you blithering idiot!" shouted McGonagall. "Now go and do something constructive! Find Peeves!"

"P-Peeves?" stammered Filch as though he had never heard the name before.

"Yes, *Peeves,* you fool, *Peeves!* Haven't you been complaining about him for a quarter of a century? Go and fetch him, at once!"

Filch evidently thought Professor McGonagall had taken leave of her senses, but hobbled away, hunch-shouldered, muttering under his breath.

"And now — *Piertotum Locomotor!*" cried Professor McGonagall.

And all along the corridor the statues and suits of armor jumped down from their plinths, and from the echoing crashes from the floors above and below, Harry knew that their fellows throughout the castle had done the same.

"Hogwarts is threatened!" shouted Professor McGonagall. "Man the boundaries, protect us, do your duty to our school!"

Clattering and yelling, the horde of moving statues stampeded past Harry: some of them smaller, others larger, than life. There were animals too, and the clanking suits of armor brandished swords and spiked balls on chains.

"Now, Potter," said McGonagall, "you and Miss Lovegood had better return to your friends and bring them to the Great Hall — I shall rouse the other Gryffindors."

They parted at the top of the next staircase, Harry and Luna running back toward the concealed entrance to the Room of Requirement. As they ran, they met crowds of students, most wearing traveling cloaks over their pajamas, being shepherded down to the Great Hall by teachers and prefects.

"That was Potter!"

"Harry Potter!"

"It was him, I swear, I just saw him!"

But Harry did not look back, and at last they reached the entrance to the Room of Requirement. Harry leaned against the enchanted wall, which opened to admit them, and he and Luna sped back down the steep staircase.

"Wh — ?"

As the room came into view, Harry slipped down a few stairs in shock. It was packed, far more crowded than when he had last been in there. Kingsley and Lupin were looking up at him, as were Oliver Wood, Katie Bell, Angelina Johnson and Alicia Spinnet, Bill and Fleur, and Mr. and Mrs. Weasley.

"Harry, what's happening?" said Lupin, meeting him at the foot of the stairs.

"Voldemort's on his way, they're barricading the school — Snape's run for it — What are you doing here? How did you know?"

"We sent messages to the rest of Dumbledore's Army," Fred

explained. "You couldn't expect everyone to miss the fun, Harry, and the D.A. let the Order of the Phoenix know, and it all kind of snowballed."

"What first, Harry?" called George. "What's going on?"

"They're evacuating the younger kids and everyone's meeting in the Great Hall to get organized," Harry said. "We're fighting."

There was a great roar and a surge toward the foot of the stairs; he was pressed back against the wall as they ran past him, the mingled members of the Order of the Phoenix, Dumbledore's Army, and Harry's old Quidditch team, all with their wands drawn, heading up into the main castle.

"Come on, Luna," Dean called as he passed, holding out his free hand; she took it and followed him back up the stairs.

The crowd was thinning: Only a little knot of people remained below in the Room of Requirement, and Harry joined them. Mrs. Weasley was struggling with Ginny. Around them stood Lupin, Fred, George, Bill, and Fleur.

"You're underage!" Mrs. Weasley shouted at her daughter as Harry approached. "I won't permit it! The boys, yes, but you, you've got to go home!"

"I won't!"

Ginny's hair flew as she pulled her arm out of her mother's grip.

"I'm in Dumbledore's Army —"

"A teenagers' gang!"

"A teenagers' gang that's about to take him on, which no one else has dared to do!" said Fred.

"She's sixteen!" shouted Mrs. Weasley. "She's not old enough! What you two were thinking, bringing her with you —"

Fred and George looked slightly ashamed of themselves.

"Mum's right, Ginny," said Bill gently. "You can't do this. Everyone underage will have to leave, it's only right."

"I can't go home!" Ginny shouted, angry tears sparkling in her eyes. "My whole family's here, I can't stand waiting there alone and not knowing and —"

Her eyes met Harry's for the first time. She looked at him beseechingly, but he shook his head and she turned away bitterly.

"Fine," she said, staring at the entrance to the tunnel back to the Hog's Head. "I'll say good-bye now, then, and —"

There was a scuffling and a great thump: Someone else had clambered out of the tunnel, overbalanced slightly, and fallen. He pulled himself up on the nearest chair, looked around through lopsided horn-rimmed glasses, and said, "Am I too late? Has it started? I only just found out, so I — I —"

Percy spluttered into silence. Evidently he had not expected to run into most of his family. There was a long moment of astonishment, broken by Fleur turning to Lupin and saying, in a wildly transparent attempt to break the tension, "So — 'ow eez leetle Teddy?"

Lupin blinked at her, startled. The silence between the Weasleys seemed to be solidifying, like ice.

"I — oh yes — he's fine!" Lupin said loudly. "Yes, Tonks is with him — at her mother's —"

Percy and the other Weasleys were still staring at one another, frozen.

"Here, I've got a picture!" Lupin shouted, pulling a photograph from inside his jacket and showing it to Fleur and Harry, who saw a tiny baby with a tuft of bright turquoise hair, waving fat fists at the camera.

"I was a fool!" Percy roared, so loudly that Lupin nearly dropped his photograph. "I was an idiot, I was a pompous prat, I was a — a —"

"Ministry-loving, family-disowning, power-hungry moron," said Fred.

Percy swallowed.

"Yes, I was!"

"Well, you can't say fairer than that," said Fred, holding out his hand to Percy.

Mrs. Weasley burst into tears. She ran forward, pushed Fred aside, and pulled Percy into a strangling hug, while he patted her on the back, his eyes on his father.

"I'm sorry, Dad," Percy said.

Mr. Weasley blinked rather rapidly, then he too hurried to hug his son.

"What made you see sense, Perce?" inquired George.

"It's been coming on for a while," said Percy, mopping his eyes under his glasses with a corner of his traveling cloak. "But I had to find a way out and it's not so easy at the Ministry, they're imprisoning traitors all the time. I managed to make contact with Aberforth and he tipped me off ten minutes ago that Hogwarts was going to make a fight of it, so here I am."

"Well, we do look to our prefects to take a lead at times such as these," said George in a good imitation of Percy's most pompous manner. "Now let's get upstairs and fight, or all the good Death Eaters'll be taken."

"So, you're my sister-in-law now?" said Percy, shaking hands with Fleur as they hurried off toward the staircase with Bill, Fred, and George.

"Ginny!" barked Mrs. Weasley.

Ginny had been attempting, under cover of the reconciliation, to sneak upstairs too.

"Molly, how about this," said Lupin. "Why doesn't Ginny stay here, then at least she'll be on the scene and know what's going on, but she won't be in the middle of the fighting?"

"I —"

"That's a good idea," said Mr. Weasley firmly. "Ginny, you stay in this room, you hear me?"

Ginny did not seem to like the idea much, but under her father's unusually stern gaze, she nodded. Mr. and Mrs. Weasley and Lupin headed off for the stairs as well.

"Where's Ron?" asked Harry. "Where's Hermione?"

"They must have gone up to the Great Hall already," Mr. Weasley called over his shoulder.

"I didn't see them pass me," said Harry.

"They said something about a bathroom," said Ginny, "not long after you left."

"A bathroom?"

Harry strode across the room to an open door leading off the Room of Requirement and checked the bathroom beyond. It was empty.

"You're sure they said bath — ?"

But then his scar seared and the Room of Requirement vanished: He was looking through the high wrought-iron gates with winged boars on pillars at either side, looking through the dark grounds toward the castle, which was ablaze with lights. Nagini lay draped over his shoulders. He was possessed of that cold, cruel sense of purpose that preceded murder.

THE BATTLE OF HOGWARTS

The enchanted ceiling of the Great Hall was dark and scattered with stars, and below it the four long House tables were lined with disheveled students, some in traveling cloaks, others in dressing gowns. Here and there shone the pearly white figures of the school ghosts. Every eye, living and dead, was fixed upon Professor McGonagall, who was speaking from the raised platform at the top of the Hall. Behind her stood the remaining teachers, including the palomino centaur, Firenze, and the members of the Order of the Phoenix who had arrived to fight.

". . . evacuation will be overseen by Mr. Filch and Madam Pomfrey. Prefects, when I give the word, you will organize your House and take your charges, in an orderly fashion, to the evacuation point."

Many of the students looked petrified. However, as Harry skirted the walls, scanning the Gryffindor table for Ron and Hermione, Ernie Macmillan stood up at the Hufflepuff table and shouted, "And what if we want to stay and fight?"

There was a smattering of applause.

"If you are of age, you may stay," said Professor McGonagall.

"What about our things?" called a girl at the Ravenclaw table. "Our trunks, our owls?"

"We have no time to collect possessions," said Professor McGonagall. "The important thing is to get you out of here safely."

"Where's Professor Snape?" shouted a girl from the Slytherin table.

"He has, to use the common phrase, done a bunk," replied Professor McGonagall, and a great cheer erupted from the Gryffindors, Hufflepuffs, and Ravenclaws.

Harry moved up the Hall alongside the Gryffindor table, still looking for Ron and Hermione. As he passed, faces turned in his direction, and a great deal of whispering broke out in his wake.

"We have already placed protection around the castle," Professor McGonagall was saying, "but it is unlikely to hold for very long unless we reinforce it. I must ask you, therefore, to move quickly and calmly, and do as your prefects —"

But her final words were drowned as a different voice echoed throughout the Hall. It was high, cold, and clear: There was no telling from where it came; it seemed to issue from the walls themselves. Like the monster it had once commanded, it might have lain dormant there for centuries.

"I know that you are preparing to fight." There were screams amongst the students, some of whom clutched each other, looking around in terror for the source of the sound. "Your efforts are futile. You cannot fight me. I do not want to kill you. I have great respect for the teachers of Hogwarts. I do not want to spill magical blood."

There was silence in the Hall now, the kind of silence that presses against the eardrums, that seems too huge to be contained by walls.

"Give me Harry Potter," said Voldemort's voice, "and none shall be harmed. Give me Harry Potter, and I shall leave the school untouched. Give me Harry Potter, and you will be rewarded.

"You have until midnight."

The silence swallowed them all again. Every head turned, every eye in the place seemed to have found Harry, to hold him frozen in the glare of thousands of invisible beams. Then a figure rose from the Slytherin table and he recognized Pansy Parkinson as she raised a shaking arm and screamed, "But he's there! Potter's *there*! Someone grab him!"

Before Harry could speak, there was a massive movement. The Gryffindors in front of him had risen and stood facing, not Harry, but the Slytherins. Then the Hufflepuffs stood, and almost at the same moment, the Ravenclaws, all of them with their backs to Harry, all of them looking toward Pansy instead, and Harry, awestruck and overwhelmed, saw wands emerging everywhere, pulled from beneath cloaks and from under sleeves.

"Thank you, Miss Parkinson," said Professor McGonagall in a clipped voice. "You will leave the Hall first with Mr. Filch. If the rest of your House could follow."

Harry heard the grinding of benches and then the sound of the Slytherins trooping out on the other side of the Hall.

"Ravenclaws, follow on!" cried Professor McGonagall.

Slowly the four tables emptied. The Slytherin table was completely deserted, but a number of older Ravenclaws remained seated while their fellows filed out; even more Hufflepuffs stayed behind, and half of Gryffindor remained in their seats, necessitating Professor McGonagall's descent from the teachers' platform to chivvy the underage on their way.

"Absolutely not, Creevey, go! *And* you, Peakes!"

Harry hurried over to the Weasleys, all sitting together at the Gryffindor table.

"Where are Ron and Hermione?"

"Haven't you found — ?" began Mr. Weasley, looking worried.

But he broke off as Kingsley had stepped forward on the raised platform to address those who had remained behind.

"We've only got half an hour until midnight, so we need to act fast! A battle plan has been agreed between the teachers of Hogwarts and the Order of the Phoenix. Professors Flitwick, Sprout, and McGonagall are going to take groups of fighters up to the three highest towers — Ravenclaw, Astronomy, and Gryffindor — where they'll have a good overview, excellent positions from which to work spells. Meanwhile Remus" — he indicated Lupin — "Arthur" — he pointed toward Mr. Weasley, sitting at the Gryffindor table — "and I will take groups into the grounds. We'll need somebody to organize defense of the entrances of the passageways into the school —"

"Sounds like a job for us," called Fred, indicating himself and George, and Kingsley nodded his approval.

"All right, leaders up here and we'll divide up the troops!"

"Potter," said Professor McGonagall, hurrying up to him, as students flooded the platform, jostling for position, receiving instructions, *"Aren't you supposed to be looking for something?"*

"What? Oh," said Harry, "oh yeah!"

He had almost forgotten about the Horcrux, almost forgotten that the battle was being fought so that he could search for it: The inexplicable absence of Ron and Hermione had momentarily driven every other thought from his mind.

"Then go, Potter, go!"

"Right — yeah —"

He sensed eyes following him as he ran out of the Great Hall again, into the entrance hall still crowded with evacuating students. He allowed himself to be swept up the marble staircase with them, but at the top he hurried off along a deserted corridor. Fear and panic were clouding his thought processes. He tried to calm himself, to concentrate on finding the Horcrux, but his thoughts buzzed as frantically and fruitlessly as wasps trapped beneath a glass. Without Ron and Hermione to help him he could not seem to marshal his ideas. He slowed down, coming to a halt halfway along an empty passage, where he sat down upon the plinth of a departed statue and pulled the Marauder's Map out of the pouch around his neck. He could not see Ron's or Hermione's names anywhere on it, though the density of the crowd of dots now making its way to the Room of Requirement might, he thought, be concealing them. He put the map away, pressed his hands over his face, and closed his eyes, trying to concentrate. . . .

Voldemort thought I'd go to Ravenclaw Tower.

There it was: a solid fact, the place to start. Voldemort had stationed Alecto Carrow in the Ravenclaw common room, and there could only be one explanation: Voldemort feared that Harry already knew his Horcrux was connected to that House.

But the only object anyone seemed to associate with Ravenclaw was the lost diadem . . . and how could the Horcrux be the diadem? How was it possible that Voldemort, the Slytherin, had found the diadem that had eluded generations of Ravenclaws? Who could have told him where to look, when nobody had seen the diadem in living memory?

In living memory . . .

Beneath his fingers, Harry's eyes flew open again. He leapt up from the plinth and tore back the way he had come, now in pursuit of his one last hope. The sound of hundreds of people marching toward the Room of Requirement grew louder and louder as he returned to the marble stairs. Prefects were shouting instructions, trying to keep track of the students in their own Houses; there was much pushing and shoving; Harry saw Zacharias Smith bowling over first-years to get to the front of the queue; here and there younger students were in tears, while older ones called desperately for friends or siblings. . . .

Harry caught sight of a pearly white figure drifting across the entrance hall below and yelled as loudly as he could over the clamor.

"Nick! NICK! I need to talk to you!"

He forced his way back through the tide of students, finally reaching the bottom of the stairs, where Nearly Headless Nick, ghost of Gryffindor Tower, stood waiting for him.

"Harry! My dear boy!"

Nick made to grasp Harry's hands with both of his own: Harry's felt as though they had been thrust into icy water.

"Nick, you've got to help me. Who's the ghost of Ravenclaw Tower?"

Nearly Headless Nick looked surprised and a little offended.

"The Gray Lady, of course; but if it is ghostly services you require — ?"

"It's got to be her — d'you know where she is?"

"Let's see. . . ."

Nick's head wobbled a little on his ruff as he turned hither and thither, peering over the heads of the swarming students.

"That's her over there, Harry, the young woman with the long hair."

Harry looked in the direction of Nick's transparent, pointing finger and saw a tall ghost who caught sight of Harry looking at her, raised her eyebrows, and drifted away through a solid wall.

Harry ran after her. Once through the door of the corridor into which she had disappeared, he saw her at the very end of the passage, still gliding smoothly away from him.

"Hey — wait — come back!"

She consented to pause, floating a few inches from the ground. Harry supposed that she was beautiful, with her waist-length hair and floor-length cloak, but she also looked haughty and proud. Close to, he recognized her as a ghost he had passed several times in the corridor, but to whom he had never spoken.

"You're the Gray Lady?"

She nodded but did not speak.

"The ghost of Ravenclaw Tower?"

"That is correct."

Her tone was not encouraging.

"Please: I need some help. I need to know anything you can tell me about the lost diadem."

A cold smile curved her lips.

"I am afraid," she said, turning to leave, "that I cannot help you."

"WAIT!"

He had not meant to shout, but anger and panic were threatening to overwhelm him. He glanced at his watch as she hovered in front of him: It was a quarter to midnight.

"This is urgent," he said fiercely. "If that diadem's at Hogwarts, I've got to find it, fast."

"You are hardly the first student to covet the diadem," she said disdainfully. "Generations of students have badgered me —"

"This isn't about trying to get better marks!" Harry shouted at her. "It's about Voldemort — defeating Voldemort — or aren't you interested in that?"

She could not blush, but her transparent cheeks became more opaque, and her voice was heated as she replied, "Of course I — how dare you suggest — ?"

"Well, help me, then!"

Her composure was slipping.

"It — it is not a question of —" she stammered. "My mother's diadem —"

"Your *mother's*?"

She looked angry with herself.

"When I lived," she said stiffly, "I was Helena Ravenclaw."

"You're her *daughter*? But then, you must know what happened to it!"

"While the diadem bestows wisdom," she said with an obvious effort to pull herself together, "I doubt that it would greatly increase your chances of defeating the wizard who calls himself Lord —"

"Haven't I just told you, I'm not interested in wearing it!" Harry said fiercely. "There's no time to explain — but if you care about Hogwarts, if you want to see Voldemort finished, you've got to tell me anything you know about the diadem!"

She remained quite still, floating in midair, staring down at him, and a sense of hopelessness engulfed Harry. Of course, if she had known anything, she would have told Flitwick or Dumbledore, who had surely asked her the same question. He had shaken his head and made to turn away when she spoke in a low voice.

"I stole the diadem from my mother."

"You — you did what?"

"I stole the diadem," repeated Helena Ravenclaw in a whisper. "I sought to make myself cleverer, more important than my mother. I ran away with it."

He did not know how he had managed to gain her confidence, and did not ask; he simply listened, hard, as she went on:

"My mother, they say, never admitted that the diadem was gone, but pretended that she had it still. She concealed her loss, my dreadful betrayal, even from the other founders of Hogwarts.

"Then my mother fell ill — fatally ill. In spite of my perfidy, she was desperate to see me one more time. She sent a man who had long loved me, though I spurned his advances, to find me. She knew that he would not rest until he had done so."

Harry waited. She drew a deep breath and threw back her head.

"He tracked me to the forest where I was hiding. When I refused to return with him, he became violent. The Baron was always a hot-tempered man. Furious at my refusal, jealous of my freedom, he stabbed me."

"The *Baron*? You mean — ?"

"The Bloody Baron, yes," said the Gray Lady, and she lifted aside the cloak she wore to reveal a single dark wound in her white chest. "When he saw what he had done, he was overcome with remorse. He took the weapon that had claimed my life, and used it to kill himself. All these centuries later, he wears his chains as an act of penitence . . . as he should," she added bitterly.

"And . . . and the diadem?"

"It remained where I had hidden it when I heard the Baron blundering through the forest toward me. Concealed inside a hollow tree."

"A hollow tree?" repeated Harry. "What tree? Where was this?"

"A forest in Albania. A lonely place I thought was far beyond my mother's reach."

"Albania," repeated Harry. Sense was emerging miraculously from confusion, and now he understood why she was telling him what she had denied Dumbledore and Flitwick. "You've already told someone this story, haven't you? Another student?"

She closed her eyes and nodded.

"I had . . . no idea. . . . He was . . . flattering. He seemed to . . . to understand . . . to sympathize. . . ."

Yes, Harry thought, Tom Riddle would certainly have understood Helena Ravenclaw's desire to possess fabulous objects to which she had little right.

"Well, you weren't the first person Riddle wormed things out of," Harry muttered. "He could be charming when he wanted. . . ."

So Voldemort had managed to wheedle the location of the lost diadem out of the Gray Lady. He had traveled to that far-flung forest and retrieved the diadem from its hiding place, perhaps as soon as he left Hogwarts, before he even started work at Borgin and Burkes.

And wouldn't those secluded Albanian woods have seemed an excellent refuge when, so much later, Voldemort had needed a place to lie low, undisturbed, for ten long years?

But the diadem, once it became his precious Horcrux, had not been left in that lowly tree. . . . No, the diadem had been returned secretly to its true home, and Voldemort must have put it there —

"— the night he asked for a job!" said Harry, finishing his thought.

"I beg your pardon?"

"He hid the diadem in the castle, the night he asked Dumbledore to let him teach!" said Harry. Saying it out loud enabled him to make sense of it all. "He must've hidden the diadem on his way up to, or down from, Dumbledore's office! But it was still worth trying to get the job — then he might've got the chance to nick Gryffindor's sword as well — thank you, thanks!"

Harry left her floating there, looking utterly bewildered. As he rounded the corner back into the entrance hall, he checked his watch. It was five minutes until midnight, and though he now knew *what* the last Horcrux was, he was no closer to discovering *where* it was. . . .

Generations of students had failed to find the diadem; that suggested that it was not in Ravenclaw Tower — but if not there, where? What hiding place had Tom Riddle discovered inside Hogwarts Castle, that he believed would remain secret forever?

Lost in desperate speculation, Harry turned a corner, but he had taken only a few steps down the new corridor when the window to his left broke open with a deafening, shattering crash. As he leapt aside, a gigantic body flew in through the window and hit the opposite wall. Something large and furry detached itself, whimpering, from the new arrival and flung itself at Harry.

"Hagrid!" Harry bellowed, fighting off Fang the boarhound's attentions as the enormous bearded figure clambered to his feet. "What the — ?"

"Harry, yer here! *Yer here!*"

Hagrid stooped down, bestowed upon Harry a cursory and rib-cracking hug, then ran back to the shattered window.

"Good boy, Grawpy!" he bellowed through the hole in the window. "I'll see yer in a moment, there's a good lad!"

Beyond Hagrid, out in the dark night, Harry saw bursts of light in the distance and heard a weird, keening scream. He looked down at his watch: It was midnight. The battle had begun.

"Blimey, Harry," panted Hagrid, "this is it, eh? Time ter fight?"

"Hagrid, where have you come from?"

"Heard You-Know-Who from up in our cave," said Hagrid grimly. "Voice carried, didn' it? 'Yeh got till midnight ter gimme Potter.' Knew yeh mus' be here, knew what mus' be happenin'. Get *down*, Fang. So we come ter join in, me an' Grawpy an' Fang. Smashed our way through the boundary by the forest, Grawpy was carryin' us, Fang an' me. Told him ter let me down at the castle, so he shoved me through the window, bless him. Not exac'ly what I meant, bu' — where's Ron an' Hermione?"

"That," said Harry, "is a really good question. Come on."

They hurried together along the corridor, Fang lolloping beside them. Harry could hear movement through the corridors all around: running footsteps, shouts; through the windows, he could see more flashes of light in the dark grounds.

"Where're we goin'?" puffed Hagrid, pounding along at Harry's heels, making the floorboards quake.

"I dunno exactly," said Harry, making another random turn, "but Ron and Hermione must be around here somewhere. . . ."

The first casualties of the battle were already strewn across the passage ahead: The two stone gargoyles that usually guarded the entrance to the staffroom had been smashed apart by a jinx that had sailed through another broken window. Their remains stirred feebly on the floor, and as Harry leapt over one of their disembodied heads, it moaned faintly, "Oh, don't mind me . . . I'll just lie here and crumble. . . ."

Its ugly stone face made Harry think suddenly of the marble bust of Rowena Ravenclaw at Xenophilius's house, wearing that mad headdress — and then of the statue in Ravenclaw Tower, with the stone diadem upon her white curls. . . .

And as he reached the end of the passage, the memory of a third stone effigy came back to him: that of an ugly old warlock, onto whose head Harry himself had placed a wig and a battered old tiara. The shock shot through Harry with the heat of firewhisky, and he nearly stumbled.

He knew, at last, where the Horcrux sat waiting for him. . . .

Tom Riddle, who confided in no one and operated alone, might have been arrogant enough to assume that he, and only he, had penetrated the deepest mysteries of Hogwarts Castle. Of course, Dumbledore and Flitwick, those model pupils, had never set foot in that particular place, but he, Harry, had strayed off the beaten track in his time at school — here at last was a secret he and Voldemort knew, that Dumbledore had never discovered —

He was roused by Professor Sprout, who was thundering past followed by Neville and half a dozen others, all of them wearing earmuffs and carrying what appeared to be large potted plants.

"Mandrakes!" Neville bellowed at Harry over his shoulder as he ran. "Going to lob them over the walls — they won't like this!"

Harry knew now where to go: He sped off, with Hagrid and Fang galloping behind him. They passed portrait after portrait, and the painted figures raced alongside them, wizards and witches in ruffs and breeches, in armor and cloaks, cramming themselves into each others' canvases, screaming news from other parts of the castle. As they reached the end of this corridor, the whole castle shook, and Harry knew, as a gigantic vase blew off its plinth with explosive force, that it was in the grip of enchantments more sinister than those of the teachers and the Order.

"It's all righ', Fang — it's all righ'!" yelled Hagrid, but the great boarhound had taken flight as slivers of china flew like shrapnel through the air, and Hagrid pounded off after the terrified dog, leaving Harry alone.

He forged on through the trembling passages, his wand at the ready, and for the length of one corridor the little painted knight, Sir Cadogan, rushed from painting to painting beside him, clanking along in his armor, screaming encouragement, his fat little pony cantering behind him.

"Braggarts and rogues, dogs and scoundrels, drive them out, Harry Potter, see them off!"

Harry hurtled around a corner and found Fred and a small knot of students, including Lee Jordan and Hannah Abbott, standing beside another empty plinth, whose statue had concealed a secret passageway. Their wands were drawn and they were listening at the concealed hole.

"Nice night for it!" Fred shouted as the castle quaked again, and Harry sprinted by, elated and terrified in equal measure. Along yet another corridor he dashed, and then there were owls everywhere, and Mrs. Norris was hissing and trying to bat them with her paws, no doubt to return them to their proper place. . . .

"Potter!"

Aberforth Dumbledore stood blocking the corridor ahead, his wand held ready.

"I've had hundreds of kids thundering through my pub, Potter!"

"I know, we're evacuating," Harry said, "Voldemort's —"

"— attacking because they haven't handed you over, yeah," said Aberforth, "I'm not deaf, the whole of Hogsmeade heard him. And it never occurred to any of you to keep a few Slytherins hostage? There are kids of Death Eaters you've just sent to safety. Wouldn't it have been a bit smarter to keep 'em here?"

"It wouldn't stop Voldemort," said Harry, "and your brother would never have done it."

Aberforth grunted and tore away in the opposite direction.

Your brother would never have done it. . . . Well, it was the truth, Harry thought as he ran on again; Dumbledore, who had defended Snape for so long, would never have held students ransom. . . .

And then he skidded around a final corner and with a yell of mingled relief and fury he saw them: Ron and Hermione, both with their arms full of large, curved, dirty yellow objects, Ron with a broomstick under his arm.

"Where the *hell* have you been?" Harry shouted.

"Chamber of Secrets," said Ron.

"Chamber — *what*?" said Harry, coming to an unsteady halt before them.

"It was Ron, all Ron's idea!" said Hermione breathlessly. "Wasn't it absolutely brilliant? There we were, after you left, and I said to Ron, even if we find the other one, how are we going to get rid of it? We still hadn't got rid of the cup! And then he thought of it! The basilisk!"

"What the — ?"

"Something to get rid of Horcruxes," said Ron simply.

Harry's eyes dropped to the objects clutched in Ron and Hermione's arms: great curved fangs, torn, he now realized, from the skull of a dead basilisk.

"But how did you get in there?" he asked, staring from the fangs to Ron. "You need to speak Parseltongue!"

"He did!" whispered Hermione. "Show him, Ron!"

Ron made a horrible strangled hissing noise.

"It's what you did to open the locket," he told Harry apologetically. "I had to have a few goes to get it right, but," he shrugged modestly, "we got there in the end."

"He was *amazing*!" said Hermione. "Amazing!"

"So . . ." Harry was struggling to keep up. "So . . ."

"So we're another Horcrux down," said Ron, and from under his jacket he pulled the mangled remains of Hufflepuff's cup. "Hermione stabbed it. Thought she should. She hasn't had the pleasure yet."

"Genius!" yelled Harry.

"It was nothing," said Ron, though he looked delighted with himself. "So what's new with you?"

As he said it, there was an explosion from overhead: All three of them looked up as dust fell from the ceiling and they heard a distant scream.

"I know what the diadem looks like, and I know where it is," said Harry, talking fast. "He hid it exactly where I hid my old Potions book, where everyone's been hiding stuff for centuries. He thought he was the only one to find it. Come on."

As the walls trembled again, he led the other two back through the concealed entrance and down the staircase into the Room of

Requirement. It was empty except for three women: Ginny, Tonks, and an elderly witch wearing a moth-eaten hat, whom Harry recognized immediately as Neville's grandmother.

"Ah, Potter," she said crisply as if she had been waiting for him. "You can tell us what's going on."

"Is everyone okay?" said Ginny and Tonks together.

"'S far as we know," said Harry. "Are there still people in the passage to the Hog's Head?"

He knew that the room would not be able to transform while there were still users inside it.

"I was the last to come through," said Mrs. Longbottom. "I sealed it, I think it unwise to leave it open now Aberforth has left his pub. Have you seen my grandson?"

"He's fighting," said Harry.

"Naturally," said the old lady proudly. "Excuse me, I must go and assist him."

With surprising speed she trotted off toward the stone steps.

Harry looked at Tonks.

"I thought you were supposed to be with Teddy at your mother's?"

"I couldn't stand not knowing —" Tonks looked anguished. "She'll look after him — have you seen Remus?"

"He was planning to lead a group of fighters into the grounds —"

Without another word, Tonks sped off.

"Ginny," said Harry, "I'm sorry, but we need you to leave too. Just for a bit. Then you can come back in."

Ginny looked simply delighted to leave her sanctuary.

"And then you can come back in!" he shouted after her as she ran up the steps after Tonks. *"You've got to come back in!"*

"Hang on a moment!" said Ron sharply. "We've forgotten someone!"

"Who?" asked Hermione.

"The house-elves, they'll all be down in the kitchen, won't they?"

"You mean we ought to get them fighting?" asked Harry.

"No," said Ron seriously, "I mean we should tell them to get out. We don't want any more Dobbies, do we? We can't order them to die for us —"

There was a clatter as the basilisk fangs cascaded out of Hermione's arms. Running at Ron, she flung them around his neck and kissed him full on the mouth. Ron threw away the fangs and broomstick he was holding and responded with such enthusiasm that he lifted Hermione off her feet.

"Is this the moment?" Harry asked weakly, and when nothing happened except that Ron and Hermione gripped each other still more firmly and swayed on the spot, he raised his voice. "OI! There's a war going on here!"

Ron and Hermione broke apart, their arms still around each other.

"I know, mate," said Ron, who looked as though he had recently been hit on the back of the head with a Bludger, "so it's now or never, isn't it?"

"Never mind that, what about the Horcrux?" Harry shouted. "D'you think you could just — just hold it in until we've got the diadem?"

"Yeah — right — sorry —" said Ron, and he and Hermione set about gathering up fangs, both pink in the face.

It was clear, as the three of them stepped back into the corridor upstairs, that in the minutes that they had spent in the Room of Requirement the situation within the castle had deteriorated severely: The walls and ceiling were shaking worse than ever; dust filled the air, and through the nearest window, Harry saw bursts of green and red light so close to the foot of the castle that he knew the Death Eaters must be very near to entering the place. Looking down, Harry saw Grawp the giant meandering past, swinging what looked like a stone gargoyle torn from the roof and roaring his displeasure.

"Let's hope he steps on some of them!" said Ron as more screams echoed from close by.

"As long as it's not any of our lot!" said a voice: Harry turned and saw Ginny and Tonks, both with their wands drawn at the next window, which was missing several panes. Even as he watched, Ginny sent a well-aimed jinx into a crowd of fighters below.

"Good girl!" roared a figure running through the dust toward them, and Harry saw Aberforth again, his gray hair flying as he led a small group of students past. "They look like they might be breaching the north battlements, they've brought giants of their own!"

"Have you seen Remus?" Tonks called after him.

"He was dueling Dolohov," shouted Aberforth, "haven't seen him since!"

"Tonks," said Ginny, "Tonks, I'm sure he's okay —"

But Tonks had run off into the dust after Aberforth.

Ginny turned, helpless, to Harry, Ron, and Hermione.

"They'll be all right," said Harry, though he knew they were empty words. "Ginny, we'll be back in a moment, just keep out of the way, keep safe — come on!" he said to Ron and Hermione, and they ran back to the stretch of wall beyond which the Room of Requirement was waiting to do the bidding of the next entrant.

I need the place where everything is hidden, Harry begged of it inside his head, and the door materialized on their third run past.

The furor of the battle died the moment they crossed the threshold and closed the door behind them: All was silent. They were in a place the size of a cathedral with the appearance of a city, its towering walls built of objects hidden by thousands of long-gone students.

"And he never realized *anyone* could get in?" said Ron, his voice echoing in the silence.

"He thought he was the only one," said Harry. "Too bad for him I've had to hide stuff in my time . . . this way," he added, "I think it's down here. . . ."

He passed the stuffed troll and the Vanishing Cabinet Draco Malfoy had mended last year with such disastrous consequences, then hesitated, looking up and down aisles of junk; he could not remember where to go next. . . .

"Accio Diadem!" cried Hermione in desperation, but nothing flew through the air toward them. It seemed that, like the vault at Gringotts, the room would not yield its hidden objects that easily.

"Let's split up," Harry told the other two. "Look for a stone bust of an old man wearing a wig and a tiara! It's standing on a cupboard and it's definitely somewhere near here. . . ."

They sped off up adjacent aisles; Harry could hear the others' footsteps echoing through the towering piles of junk, of bottles, hats, crates, chairs, books, weapons, broomsticks, bats. . . .

"Somewhere near here," Harry muttered to himself. "Some-where . . . somewhere . . ."

Deeper and deeper into the labyrinth he went, looking for objects he recognized from his one previous trip into the room. His breath was loud in his ears, and then his very soul seemed to shiver: There it was, right ahead, the blistered old cupboard in which he had hidden his old Potions book, and on top of it, the pockmarked stone warlock wearing a dusty old wig and what looked like an ancient, discolored tiara.

He had already stretched out his hand, though he remained ten feet away, when a voice behind him said, "Hold it, Potter."

He skidded to a halt and turned around. Crabbe and Goyle were standing behind him, shoulder to shoulder, wands pointing right at Harry. Through the small space between their jeering faces he saw Draco Malfoy.

"That's my wand you're holding, Potter," said Malfoy, pointing his own through the gap between Crabbe and Goyle.

"Not anymore," panted Harry, tightening his grip on the haw-thorn wand. "Winners, keepers, Malfoy. Who's lent you theirs?"

"My mother," said Draco.

Harry laughed, though there was nothing very humorous about the situation. He could not hear Ron or Hermione anymore. They seemed to have run out of earshot, searching for the diadem.

"So how come you three aren't with Voldemort?" asked Harry.

"We're gonna be rewarded," said Crabbe: His voice was surprisingly soft for such an enormous person; Harry had hardly ever heard him speak before. Crabbe was smiling like a small child promised a large bag of sweets. "We 'ung back, Potter. We decided not to go. Decided to bring you to 'im."

"Good plan," said Harry in mock admiration. He could not believe that he was this close, and was going to be thwarted by Malfoy, Crabbe, and Goyle. He began edging slowly backward toward the place where the Horcrux sat lopsided upon the bust. If he could just get his hands on it before the fight broke out . . .

"So how did you get in here?" he asked, trying to distract them.

"I virtually lived in the Room of Hidden Things all last year," said Malfoy, his voice brittle. "I know how to get in."

"We was hiding in the corridor outside," grunted Goyle. "We can do Diss-lusion Charms now! And then," his face split into a gormless grin, "you turned up right in front of us and said you was looking for a die-dum! What's a die-dum?"

"Harry?" Ron's voice echoed suddenly from the other side of the wall to Harry's right. "Are you talking to someone?"

With a whiplike movement, Crabbe pointed his wand at the fifty-foot mountain of old furniture, of broken trunks, of old books and robes and unidentifiable junk, and shouted, *"Descendo!"*

The wall began to totter, then the top third crumbled into the aisle next door where Ron stood.

"Ron!" Harry bellowed, as somewhere out of sight Hermione screamed, and Harry heard innumerable objects crashing to the floor on the other side of the destabilized wall: He pointed his wand at the rampart, cried, *"Finite!"* and it steadied.

"No!" shouted Malfoy, staying Crabbe's arm as the latter made to repeat his spell. "If you wreck the room you might bury this diadem thing!"

"What's that matter?" said Crabbe, tugging himself free. "It's Potter the Dark Lord wants, who cares about a die-dum?"

"Potter came in here to get it," said Malfoy with ill-disguised impatience at the slow-wittedness of his colleagues, "so that must mean —"

"'Must mean'?" Crabbe turned on Malfoy with undisguised ferocity. "Who cares what you think? I don't take your orders no more, *Draco.* You an' your dad are finished."

"Harry?" shouted Ron again, from the other side of the junk wall. "What's going on?"

"Harry?" mimicked Crabbe. "What's going — *no,* Potter! *Crucio!*"

Harry had lunged for the tiara; Crabbe's curse missed him but hit the stone bust, which flew into the air; the diadem soared upward and then dropped out of sight in the mass of objects on which the bust had rested.

"STOP!" Malfoy shouted at Crabbe, his voice echoing through the enormous room. "The Dark Lord wants him alive —"

"So? I'm not killing him, am I?" yelled Crabbe, throwing off Malfoy's restraining arm. "But if I can, I will, the Dark Lord wants him dead anyway, what's the diff — ?"

A jet of scarlet light shot past Harry by inches: Hermione had run around the corner behind him and sent a Stunning Spell straight at Crabbe's head. It only missed because Malfoy pulled him out of the way.

"It's that Mudblood! *Avada Kedavra!*"

Harry saw Hermione dive aside, and his fury that Crabbe had aimed to kill wiped all else from his mind. He shot a Stunning Spell at Crabbe, who lurched out of the way, knocking Malfoy's wand out of his hand; it rolled out of sight beneath a mountain of broken furniture and boxes.

"Don't kill him! DON'T KILL HIM!" Malfoy yelled at Crabbe

and Goyle, who were both aiming at Harry: Their split second's hesitation was all Harry needed.

"Expelliarmus!"

Goyle's wand flew out of his hand and disappeared into the bulwark of objects beside him; Goyle leapt foolishly on the spot, trying to retrieve it; Malfoy jumped out of range of Hermione's second Stunning Spell, and Ron, appearing suddenly at the end of the aisle, shot a full Body-Bind Curse at Crabbe, which narrowly missed.

Crabbe wheeled around and screamed, *"Avada Kedavra!"* again. Ron leapt out of sight to avoid the jet of green light. The wandless Malfoy cowered behind a three-legged wardrobe as Hermione charged toward them, hitting Goyle with a Stunning Spell as she came.

"It's somewhere here!" Harry yelled at her, pointing at the pile of junk into which the old tiara had fallen. "Look for it while I go and help R —"

"HARRY!" she screamed.

A roaring, billowing noise behind him gave him a moment's warning. He turned and saw both Ron and Crabbe running as hard as they could up the aisle toward them.

"Like it hot, scum?" roared Crabbe as he ran.

But he seemed to have no control over what he had done. Flames of abnormal size were pursuing them, licking up the sides of the junk bulwarks, which were crumbling to soot at their touch.

"Aguamenti!" Harry bawled, but the jet of water that soared from the tip of his wand evaporated in the air.

"RUN!"

Malfoy grabbed the Stunned Goyle and dragged him along; Crabbe outstripped all of them, now looking terrified; Harry, Ron, and Hermione pelted along in his wake, and the fire pursued them. It was not normal fire; Crabbe had used a curse of which Harry had no knowledge: As they turned a corner the flames chased them as though they were alive, sentient, intent upon killing them. Now the fire was mutating, forming a gigantic pack of fiery beasts: Flaming serpents, chimaeras, and dragons rose and fell and rose again, and the detritus of centuries on which they were feeding was thrown up in the air into their fanged mouths, tossed high on clawed feet, before being consumed by the inferno.

Malfoy, Crabbe, and Goyle had vanished from view: Harry, Ron, and Hermione stopped dead; the fiery monsters were circling them, drawing closer and closer, claws and horns and tails lashed, and the heat was solid as a wall around them.

"What can we do?" Hermione screamed over the deafening roars of the fire. "What can we do?"

"Here!"

Harry seized a pair of heavy-looking broomsticks from the nearest pile of junk and threw one to Ron, who pulled Hermione onto it behind him. Harry swung his leg over the second broom and, with hard kicks to the ground, they soared up into the air, missing by feet the horned beak of a flaming raptor that snapped its jaws at them. The smoke and heat were becoming overwhelming: Below them the cursed fire was consuming the contraband of generations of hunted students, the guilty outcomes of a thousand banned experiments, the secrets of the countless souls who had sought refuge in the room. Harry could not see a trace of Malfoy, Crabbe, or Goyle anywhere: He swooped as low as he dared over the marauding monsters of flame to try to find them, but there was nothing but fire: What a terrible way to die. . . . He had never wanted this. . . .

"Harry, let's get out, let's get out!" bellowed Ron, though it was impossible to see where the door was through the black smoke.

And then Harry heard a thin, piteous human scream from amidst the terrible commotion, the thunder of devouring flame.

"It's — too — dangerous — !" Ron yelled, but Harry wheeled in the air. His glasses giving his eyes some small protection from the smoke, he raked the firestorm below, seeking a sign of life, a limb or a face that was not yet charred like wood. . . .

And he saw them: Malfoy with his arms around the unconscious Goyle, the pair of them perched on a fragile tower of charred desks, and Harry dived. Malfoy saw him coming and raised one arm, but even as Harry grasped it he knew at once that it was no good: Goyle was too heavy and Malfoy's hand, covered in sweat, slid instantly out of Harry's —

"IF WE DIE FOR THEM, I'LL KILL YOU, HARRY!" roared Ron's voice, and, as a great flaming chimaera bore down upon them, he and Hermione dragged Goyle onto their broom and rose, rolling and pitching, into the air once more as Malfoy clambered up behind Harry.

"The door, get to the door, the door!" screamed Malfoy in Harry's ear, and Harry sped up, following Ron, Hermione, and Goyle through the billowing black smoke, hardly able to breathe: and all around them the last few objects unburned by the devouring flames were flung into the air, as the creatures of the cursed fire cast them high in celebration: cups and shields, a sparkling necklace, and an old, discolored tiara —

"What are you doing, what are you doing, the door's that way!" screamed Malfoy, but Harry made a hairpin swerve and dived. The diadem seemed to fall in slow motion, turning and glittering as it

dropped toward the maw of a yawning serpent, and then he had it, caught it around his wrist —

Harry swerved again as the serpent lunged at him; he soared upward and straight toward the place where, he prayed, the door stood open: Ron, Hermione, and Goyle had vanished; Malfoy was screaming and holding Harry so tightly it hurt. Then, through the smoke, Harry saw a rectangular patch on the wall and steered the broom at it, and moments later clean air filled his lungs and they collided with the wall in the corridor beyond.

Malfoy fell off the broom and lay facedown, gasping, coughing, and retching. Harry rolled over and sat up: The door to the Room of Requirement had vanished, and Ron and Hermione sat panting on the floor beside Goyle, who was still unconscious.

"C-Crabbe," choked Malfoy as soon as he could speak. "C-Crabbe . . ."

"He's dead," said Ron harshly.

There was silence, apart from panting and coughing. Then a number of huge bangs shook the castle, and a great cavalcade of transparent figures galloped past on horses, their heads screaming with bloodlust under their arms. Harry staggered to his feet when the Headless Hunt had passed and looked around: The battle was still going on all around him. He could hear more screams than those of the retreating ghosts. Panic flared within him.

"Where's Ginny?" he said sharply. "She was here. She was supposed to be going back into the Room of Requirement."

"Blimey, d'you reckon it'll still work after that fire?" asked Ron, but he too got to his feet, rubbing his chest and looking left and right. "Shall we split up and look — ?"

"No," said Hermione, getting to her feet too. Malfoy and Goyle remained slumped hopelessly on the corridor floor; neither of them had wands. "Let's stick together. I say we go — Harry, what's that on your arm?"

"What? Oh yeah —"

He pulled the diadem from his wrist and held it up. It was still hot, blackened with soot, but as he looked at it closely he was just able to make out the tiny words etched upon it: WIT BEYOND MEASURE IS MAN'S GREATEST TREASURE.

A bloodlike substance, dark and tarry, seemed to be leaking from the diadem. Suddenly Harry felt the thing vibrate violently, then break apart in his hands, and as it did so, he thought he heard the faintest, most distant scream of pain, echoing not from the grounds or the castle, but from the thing that had just fragmented in his fingers.

"It must have been Fiendfyre!" whimpered Hermione, her eyes on the broken pieces.

"Sorry?"

"Fiendfyre — cursed fire — it's one of the substances that destroy Horcruxes, but I would never, ever have dared use it, it's so dangerous — how did Crabbe know how to — ?"

"Must've learned from the Carrows," said Harry grimly.

"Shame he wasn't concentrating when they mentioned how to stop it, really," said Ron, whose hair, like Hermione's, was singed, and whose face was blackened. "If he hadn't tried to kill us all, I'd be quite sorry he was dead."

"But don't you realize?" whispered Hermione. "This means, if we can just get the snake —"

But she broke off as yells and shouts and the unmistakable noises of dueling filled the corridor. Harry looked around and his heart seemed to fail: Death Eaters had penetrated Hogwarts. Fred and Percy had just backed into view, both of them dueling masked and hooded men.

Harry, Ron, and Hermione ran forward to help: Jets of light flew in every direction and the man dueling Percy backed off, fast: Then his hood slipped and they saw a high forehead and streaked hair —

"Hello, Minister!" bellowed Percy, sending a neat jinx straight at Thicknesse, who dropped his wand and clawed at the front of his robes, apparently in awful discomfort. "Did I mention I'm resigning?"

"You're joking, Perce!" shouted Fred as the Death Eater he was battling collapsed under the weight of three separate Stunning Spells. Thicknesse had fallen to the ground with tiny spikes erupting all over him; he seemed to be turning into some form of sea urchin. Fred looked at Percy with glee.

"You actually *are* joking, Perce. . . . I don't think I've heard you joke since you were —"

The air exploded. They had been grouped together, Harry, Ron, Hermione, Fred, and Percy, the two Death Eaters at their feet, one Stunned, the other Transfigured; and in that fragment of a moment, when danger seemed temporarily at bay, the world was rent apart. Harry felt himself flying through the air, and all he could do was hold as tightly as possible to that thin stick of wood that was his one and only weapon, and shield his head in his arms: He heard the screams and yells of his companions without a hope of knowing what had happened to them —

And then the world resolved itself into pain and semidarkness: He was half buried in the wreckage of a corridor that had been

subjected to a terrible attack. Cold air told him that the side of the
castle had been blown away, and hot stickiness on his cheek told
him that he was bleeding copiously. Then he heard a terrible cry that
pulled at his insides, that expressed agony of a kind neither flame
nor curse could cause, and he stood up, swaying, more frightened
than he had been that day, more frightened, perhaps, than he had
been in his life. . . .

And Hermione was struggling to her feet in the wreckage, and
three redheaded men were grouped on the ground where the wall
had blasted apart. Harry grabbed Hermione's hand as they staggered
and stumbled over stone and wood.

"No — no — no!" someone was shouting. "No! Fred! No!"

And Percy was shaking his brother, and Ron was kneeling beside
them, and Fred's eyes stared without seeing, the ghost of his last
laugh still etched upon his face.

THE ELDER WAND

T he world had ended, so why had the battle not ceased, the castle fallen silent in horror, and every combatant laid down their arms? Harry's mind was in free fall, spinning out of control, unable to grasp the impossibility, because Fred Weasley could not be dead, the evidence of all his senses must be lying —

And then a body fell past the hole blown into the side of the school, and curses flew in at them from the darkness, hitting the wall behind their heads.

"Get down!" Harry shouted, as more curses flew through the night: He and Ron had both grabbed Hermione and pulled her to the floor, but Percy lay across Fred's body, shielding it from further harm, and when Harry shouted, "Percy, come on, we've got to move!" he shook his head.

"Percy!" Harry saw tear tracks streaking the grime coating Ron's face as he seized his elder brother's shoulders and pulled, but Percy would not budge. "Percy, you can't do anything for him! We're going to —"

Hermione screamed, and Harry, turning, did not need to ask why. A monstrous spider the size of a small car was trying to climb through the huge hole in the wall: One of Aragog's descendants had joined the fight.

Ron and Harry shouted together; their spells collided and the monster was blown backward, its legs jerking horribly, and vanished into the darkness.

"It brought friends!" Harry called to the others, glancing over the edge of the castle through the hole in the wall the curses had blasted: More giant spiders were climbing the side of the building, liberated from the Forbidden Forest, into which the Death Eaters must have penetrated. Harry fired Stunning Spells down upon them, knocking the lead monster into its fellows, so that they rolled back down the building and out of sight. Then more curses came soaring over Harry's head, so close he felt the force of them blow his hair.

"Let's move, NOW!"

Pushing Hermione ahead of him with Ron, Harry stooped to seize Fred's body under the armpits. Percy, realizing what Harry was trying to do, stopped clinging to the body and helped; together, crouching low to avoid the curses flying at them from the grounds, they hauled Fred out of the way.

"Here," said Harry, and they placed him in a niche where a suit of armor had stood earlier. He could not bear to look at Fred a second longer than he had to, and after making sure that the body was well hidden, he took off after Ron and Hermione. Malfoy and Goyle had vanished, but at the end of the corridor, which was now full of dust and falling masonry, glass long gone from the windows, he saw many people running backward and forward, whether friends or foes he could not tell. Rounding the corner, Percy let out a bull-like roar: "ROOKWOOD!" and sprinted off in the direction of a tall man, who was pursuing a couple of students.

"Harry, in here!" Hermione screamed.

She had pulled Ron behind a tapestry: They seemed to be wrestling together, and for one mad second Harry thought that they were embracing again; then he saw that Hermione was trying to restrain Ron, to stop him running after Percy.

"Listen to me — LISTEN, RON!"

"I wanna help — I wanna kill Death Eaters —"

His face was contorted, smeared with dust and smoke, and he was shaking with rage and grief.

"Ron, we're the only ones who can end it! Please — Ron — we need the snake, we've got to kill the snake!" said Hermione.

But Harry knew how Ron felt: Pursuing another Horcrux could not bring the satisfaction of revenge; he too wanted to fight, to punish them, the people who had killed Fred, and he wanted to find the other Weasleys, and above all make sure, make quite sure, that Ginny was not — but he could not permit that idea to form in his mind —

"We will fight!" Hermione said. "We'll have to, to reach the snake! But let's not lose sight now of what we're supposed to be d-doing! We're the only ones who can end it!"

She was crying too, and she wiped her face on her torn and singed sleeve as she spoke, but she took great heaving breaths to calm herself as, still keeping a tight hold on Ron, she turned to Harry.

"You need to find out where Voldemort is, because he'll have the snake with him, won't he? Do it, Harry — look inside him!"

Why was it so easy? Because his scar had been burning for hours, yearning to show him Voldemort's thoughts? He closed his eyes on her command, and at once, the screams and the bangs and all the discordant sounds of the battle were drowned until they became distant, as though he stood far, far away from them. . . .

He was standing in the middle of a desolate but strangely familiar room, with peeling paper on the walls and all the windows boarded except for one. The sounds of the assault on the castle were muffled and distant. The single unblocked window revealed distant bursts of light where the castle stood, but inside the room it was dark except for a solitary oil lamp.

He was rolling his wand between his fingers, watching it, his thoughts on the room in the castle, the secret room only he had ever found, the room, like the Chamber, that you had to be clever and cunning and inquisitive to discover. . . . He was confident that the boy would not find the diadem . . . although Dumbledore's puppet had come much farther than he had ever expected . . . too far. . . .

"My Lord," said a voice, desperate and cracked. He turned: There was Lucius Malfoy sitting in the darkest corner, ragged and still bearing the marks of the punishment he had received after the boy's last escape. One of his eyes remained closed and puffy. "My Lord . . . please . . . my son . . ."

"If your son is dead, Lucius, it is not my fault. He did not come and join me, like the rest of the Slytherins. Perhaps he has decided to befriend Harry Potter?"

"No — never," whispered Malfoy.

"You must hope not."

"Aren't — aren't you afraid, my Lord, that Potter might die at another hand but yours?" asked Malfoy, his voice shaking. "Wouldn't
it be . . . forgive me . . . more prudent to call off this battle, enter
the castle, and seek him y-yourself?"

"Do not pretend, Lucius. You wish the battle to cease so that you
can discover what has happened to your son. And I do not need to seek
Potter. Before the night is out, Potter will have come to find me."

Voldemort dropped his gaze once more to the wand in his fingers.
It troubled him . . . and those things that troubled Lord Voldemort
needed to be rearranged. . . .

"Go and fetch Snape."

"Snape, m-my Lord?"

"Snape. Now. I need him. There is a — service — I require from
him. Go."

Frightened, stumbling a little through the gloom, Lucius left
the room. Voldemort continued to stand there, twirling the wand
between his fingers, staring at it.

"It is the only way, Nagini," he whispered, and he looked around,
and there was the great thick snake, now suspended in midair, twisting gracefully within the enchanted, protected space he had made
for her, a starry, transparent sphere somewhere between glittering
cage and tank.

With a gasp, Harry pulled back and opened his eyes; at the same
moment his ears were assaulted with the screeches and cries, the
smashes and bangs of battle.

"He's in the Shrieking Shack. The snake's with him, it's got some
sort of magical protection around it. He's just sent Lucius Malfoy
to find Snape."

"Voldemort's sitting in the Shrieking Shack?" said Hermione, outraged. "He's not — he's not even *fighting*?"

"He doesn't think he needs to fight," said Harry. "He thinks I'm going to go to him."

"But why?"

"He knows I'm after Horcruxes — he's keeping Nagini close beside him — obviously I'm going to have to go to him to get near the thing —"

"Right," said Ron, squaring his shoulders. "So you can't go, that's what he wants, what he's expecting. You stay here and look after Hermione, and I'll go and get it —"

Harry cut across Ron.

"You two stay here, I'll go under the Cloak and I'll be back as soon as I —"

"No," said Hermione, "it makes much more sense if I take the Cloak and —"

"Don't even think about it," Ron snarled at her.

Before Hermione could get farther than "Ron, I'm just as capable —" the tapestry at the top of the staircase on which they stood was ripped open.

"POTTER!"

Two masked Death Eaters stood there, but even before their wands were fully raised, Hermione shouted, *"Glisseo!"*

The stairs beneath their feet flattened into a chute and she, Harry, and Ron hurtled down it, unable to control their speed but so fast that the Death Eaters' Stunning Spells flew far over their heads. They shot through the concealing tapestry at the bottom and spun onto the floor, hitting the opposite wall.

"Duro!" cried Hermione, pointing her wand at the tapestry, and

there were two loud, sickening crunches as the tapestry turned to stone and the Death Eaters pursuing them crumpled against it.

"Get back!" shouted Ron, and he, Harry, and Hermione flattened themselves against a door as a herd of galloping desks thundered past, shepherded by a sprinting Professor McGonagall. She appeared not to notice them: Her hair had come down and there was a gash on her cheek. As she turned the corner, they heard her scream, "CHARGE!"

"Harry, you get the Cloak on," said Hermione. "Never mind us —"

But he threw it over all three of them; large though they were, he doubted anyone would see their disembodied feet through the dust that clogged the air, the falling stone, the shimmer of spells.

They ran down the next staircase and found themselves in a corridor full of duelers. The portraits on either side of the fighters were crammed with figures screaming advice and encouragement, while Death Eaters, both masked and unmasked, dueled students and teachers. Dean had won himself a wand, for he was face-to-face with Dolohov, Parvati with Travers. Harry, Ron, and Hermione raised their wands at once, ready to strike, but the duelers were weaving and darting around so much that there was a strong likelihood of hurting one of their own side if they cast curses. Even as they stood braced, looking for the opportunity to act, there came a great *"Wheeeeeeeeeeee!"* and, looking up, Harry saw Peeves zooming over them, dropping Snargaluff pods down onto the Death Eaters, whose heads were suddenly engulfed in wriggling green tubers like fat worms.

"Argh!"

A fistful of tubers had hit the Cloak over Ron's head; the slimy green roots were suspended improbably in midair as Ron tried to shake them loose.

"Someone's invisible there!" shouted a masked Death Eater, pointing.

Dean made the most of the Death Eater's momentary distraction, knocking him out with a Stunning Spell; Dolohov attempted to retaliate and Parvati shot a Body-Bind Curse at him.

"LET'S GO!" Harry yelled, and he, Ron, and Hermione gathered the Cloak tightly around themselves and pelted, heads down, through the midst of the fighters, slipping a little in pools of Snargaluff juice, toward the top of the marble staircase into the entrance hall.

"I'm Draco Malfoy, I'm Draco, I'm on your side!"

Draco was on the upper landing, pleading with another masked Death Eater. Harry Stunned the Death Eater as they passed: Malfoy looked around, beaming, for his savior, and Ron punched him from under the Cloak. Malfoy fell backward on top of the Death Eater, his mouth bleeding, utterly bemused.

"And that's the second time we've saved your life tonight, you two-faced bastard!" Ron yelled.

There were more duelers all over the stairs and in the hall, Death Eaters everywhere Harry looked: Yaxley, close to the front doors, in combat with Flitwick, a masked Death Eater dueling Kingsley right beside them. Students ran in every direction, some carrying or dragging injured friends. Harry directed a Stunning Spell toward the masked Death Eater; it missed but nearly hit Neville, who had emerged from nowhere brandishing armfuls of Venomous Tentacula, which looped itself happily around the nearest Death Eater and began reeling him in.

Harry, Ron, and Hermione sped down the marble staircase: Glass shattered to their left, and the Slytherin hourglass that had recorded House points spilled its emeralds everywhere, so that people slipped and staggered as they ran. Two bodies fell from the balcony overhead as they reached the ground, and a gray blur that Harry took for an animal sped four-legged across the hall to sink its teeth into one of the fallen.

"NO!" shrieked Hermione, and with a deafening blast from her wand, Fenrir Greyback was thrown backward from the feebly stirring body of Lavender Brown. He hit the marble banisters and struggled to return to his feet. Then, with a bright white flash and a crack, a crystal ball fell on top of his head, and he crumpled to the ground and did not move.

"I have more!" shrieked Professor Trelawney from over the banisters. "More for any who want them! Here —"

And with a movement like a tennis serve, she heaved another enormous crystal sphere from her bag, waved her wand through the air, and caused the ball to speed across the hall and smash through a window. At the same moment, the heavy wooden front doors burst open, and more of the gigantic spiders forced their way into the entrance hall.

Screams of terror rent the air: The fighters scattered, Death Eaters and Hogwartians alike, and red and green jets of light flew into the midst of the oncoming monsters, which shuddered and reared, more terrifying than ever.

"How do we get out?" yelled Ron over all the screaming, but before either Harry or Hermione could answer they were bowled aside: Hagrid had come thundering down the stairs, brandishing his flowery pink umbrella.

"Don't hurt 'em, don't hurt 'em!" he yelled.

"HAGRID, NO!"

Harry forgot everything else: He sprinted out from under the Cloak, running bent double to avoid the curses illuminating the whole hall.

"HAGRID, COME BACK!"

But he was not even halfway to Hagrid when he saw it happen: Hagrid vanished amongst the spiders, and with a great scurrying, a foul swarming movement, they retreated under the onslaught of spells, Hagrid buried in their midst.

"HAGRID!"

Harry heard someone calling his own name, whether friend or foe he did not care: He was sprinting down the front steps into the dark grounds, and the spiders were swarming away with their prey, and he could see nothing of Hagrid at all.

"HAGRID!"

He thought he could make out an enormous arm waving from the midst of the spider swarm, but as he made to chase after them, his way was impeded by a monumental foot, which swung down out of the darkness and made the ground on which he stood shudder. He looked up: A giant stood before him, twenty feet high, its head hidden in shadow, nothing but its treelike, hairy shins illuminated by light from the castle doors. With one brutal, fluid movement, it smashed a massive fist through an upper window, and glass rained down upon Harry, forcing him back under the shelter of the doorway.

"Oh my — !" shrieked Hermione, as she and Ron caught up with Harry and gazed upward at the giant now trying to seize people through the window above.

"DON'T!" Ron yelled, grabbing Hermione's hand as she raised her wand. "Stun him and he'll crush half the castle —"

"HAGGER?"

Grawp came lurching around the corner of the castle; only now did Harry realize that Grawp was, indeed, an undersized giant. The gargantuan monster trying to crush people on the upper floors looked around and let out a roar. The stone steps trembled as he stomped toward his smaller kin, and Grawp's lopsided mouth fell open, showing yellow, half-brick-sized teeth; and then they launched themselves at each other with the savagery of lions.

"RUN!" Harry roared; the night was full of hideous yells and blows as the giants wrestled, and he seized Hermione's hand and tore down the steps into the grounds, Ron bringing up the rear. Harry had not lost hope of finding and saving Hagrid; he ran so fast that they were halfway toward the forest before they were brought up short again.

The air around them had frozen: Harry's breath caught and solidified in his chest. Shapes moved out in the darkness, swirling figures of concentrated blackness, moving in a great wave toward the castle, their faces hooded and their breath rattling. . . .

Ron and Hermione closed in beside him as the sounds of fighting behind them grew suddenly muted, deadened, because a silence only dementors could bring was falling thickly through the night, and Fred was gone, and Hagrid was surely dying or already dead. . . .

"Come on, Harry!" said Hermione's voice from a very long way away. "Patronuses, Harry, come on!"

He raised his wand, but a dull hopelessness was spreading through him: How many more lay dead that he did not yet know about; he felt as though his soul had already half left his body. . . .

"HARRY, COME ON!" screamed Hermione.

A hundred dementors were advancing, gliding toward them, sucking their way closer to Harry's despair, which was like a promise of a feast. . . .

He saw Ron's silver terrier burst into the air, flicker feebly, and expire; he saw Hermione's otter twist in midair and fade; and his own wand trembled in his hand, and he almost welcomed the oncoming oblivion, the promise of nothing, of no feeling. . . .

And then a silver hare, a boar, and a fox soared past Harry, Ron, and Hermione's heads: The dementors fell back before the creatures' approach. Three more people had arrived out of the darkness to stand beside them, their wands outstretched, continuing to cast their Patronuses: Luna, Ernie, and Seamus.

"That's right," said Luna encouragingly, as if they were back in the Room of Requirement and this was simply spell practice for the D.A. "That's right, Harry . . . come on, think of something happy. . . ."

"Something happy?" he said, his voice cracked.

"We're all still here," she whispered, "we're still fighting. Come on, now. . . ."

There was a silver spark, then a wavering light, and then, with the greatest effort it had ever cost him, the stag burst from the end of Harry's wand. It cantered forward, and now the dementors scattered in earnest, and immediately the night was mild again, but the sounds of the surrounding battle were loud in his ears.

"Can't thank you enough," said Ron shakily, turning to Luna, Ernie, and Seamus, "you just saved —"

With a roar and an earth-quaking tremor, another giant came lurching out of the darkness from the direction of the forest, brandishing a club taller than any of them.

"RUN!" Harry shouted again, but the others needed no telling: They all scattered, and not a second too soon, for next moment the creature's vast foot had fallen exactly where they had been standing. Harry looked round: Ron and Hermione were following him, but the other three had vanished back into the battle.

"Let's get out of range!" yelled Ron as the giant swung its club again and its bellows echoed through the night, across the grounds where bursts of red and green light continued to illuminate the darkness.

"The Whomping Willow," said Harry, "go!"

Somehow he walled it all up in his mind, crammed it into a small space into which he could not look now: Thoughts of Fred and Hagrid, and his terror for all the people he loved, scattered in and outside the castle, must all wait, because they had to run, had to reach the snake and Voldemort, because that was, as Hermione said, the only way to end it —

He sprinted, half believing he could outdistance death itself, ignoring the jets of light flying in the darkness all around him, and the sound of the lake crashing like the sea, and the creaking of the Forbidden Forest though the night was windless; through grounds that seemed themselves to have risen in rebellion, he ran faster than he had ever moved in his life, and it was he who saw the great tree first, the Willow that protected the secret at its roots with whiplike, slashing branches.

Panting and gasping, Harry slowed down, skirting the Willow's swiping branches, peering through the darkness toward its thick trunk, trying to see the single knot in the bark of the old tree that would paralyze it. Ron and Hermione caught up, Hermione so out of breath she could not speak.

"How — how're we going to get in?" panted Ron. "I can — see the place — if we just had — Crookshanks again —"

"Crookshanks?" wheezed Hermione, bent double, clutching her chest. *"Are you a wizard, or what?"*

"Oh — right — yeah —"

Ron looked around, then directed his wand at a twig on the ground and said, *"Wingardium Leviosa!"* The twig flew up from the ground, spun through the air as if caught by a gust of wind, then zoomed directly at the trunk through the Willow's ominously swaying branches. It jabbed at a place near the roots, and at once, the writhing tree became still.

"Perfect!" panted Hermione.

"Wait."

For one teetering second, while the crashes and booms of the battle filled the air, Harry hesitated. Voldemort wanted him to do this, wanted him to come. . . . Was he leading Ron and Hermione into a trap?

But then the reality seemed to close upon him, cruel and plain: The only way forward was to kill the snake, and the snake was where Voldemort was, and Voldemort was at the end of this tunnel. . . .

"Harry, we're coming, just get in there!" said Ron, pushing him forward.

Harry wriggled into the earthy passage hidden in the tree's roots. It was a much tighter squeeze than it had been the last time they had entered it. The tunnel was low-ceilinged: They had had to double up to move through it nearly four years previously; now there was nothing for it but to crawl. Harry went first, his wand illuminated, expecting at any moment to meet barriers, but none came. They moved in silence, Harry's gaze fixed upon the swinging beam of the wand held in his fist.

At last the tunnel began to slope upward and Harry saw a sliver of light ahead. Hermione tugged at his ankle.

"The Cloak!" she whispered. "Put the Cloak on!"

He groped behind him and she forced the bundle of slippery cloth into his free hand. With difficulty he dragged it over himself, murmured, *"Nox,"* extinguishing his wandlight, and continued on his hands and knees, as silently as possible, all his senses straining, expecting every second to be discovered, to hear a cold clear voice, see a flash of green light.

And then he heard voices coming from the room directly ahead of them, only slightly muffled by the fact that the opening at the end of the tunnel had been blocked up by what looked like an old crate. Hardly daring to breathe, Harry edged right up to the opening and peered through a tiny gap left between crate and wall.

The room beyond was dimly lit, but he could see Nagini, swirling and coiling like a serpent underwater, safe in her enchanted, starry sphere, which floated unsupported in midair. He could see the edge of a table, and a long-fingered white hand toying with a wand. Then Snape spoke, and Harry's heart lurched: Snape was inches away from where he crouched, hidden.

". . . my Lord, their resistance is crumbling —"

"— and it is doing so without your help," said Voldemort in his high, clear voice. "Skilled wizard though you are, Severus, I do not think you will make much difference now. We are almost there . . . almost."

"Let me find the boy. Let me bring you Potter. I know I can find him, my Lord. Please."

Snape strode past the gap, and Harry drew back a little, keeping his eyes fixed upon Nagini, wondering whether there was any spell that might penetrate the protection surrounding her, but he could not think of anything. One failed attempt, and he would give away his position. . . .

Voldemort stood up. Harry could see him now, see the red eyes, the flattened, serpentine face, the pallor of him gleaming slightly in the semidarkness.

"I have a problem, Severus," said Voldemort softly.

"My Lord?" said Snape.

Voldemort raised the Elder Wand, holding it as delicately and precisely as a conductor's baton.

"Why doesn't it work for me, Severus?"

In the silence Harry imagined he could hear the snake hissing slightly as it coiled and uncoiled — or was it Voldemort's sibilant sigh lingering on the air?

"My — my Lord?" said Snape blankly. "I do not understand. You — you have performed extraordinary magic with that wand."

"No," said Voldemort. "I have performed my usual magic. I am extraordinary, but this wand . . . no. It has not revealed the wonders it has promised. I feel no difference between this wand and the one I procured from Ollivander all those years ago."

Voldemort's tone was musing, calm, but Harry's scar had begun to throb and pulse: Pain was building in his forehead, and he could feel that controlled sense of fury building inside Voldemort.

"No difference," said Voldemort again.

Snape did not speak. Harry could not see his face: He wondered whether Snape sensed danger, was trying to find the right words to reassure his master.

Voldemort started to move around the room: Harry lost sight of him for seconds as he prowled, speaking in that same measured voice, while the pain and fury mounted in Harry.

"I have thought long and hard, Severus. . . . Do you know why I have called you back from the battle?"

And for a moment Harry saw Snape's profile: His eyes were fixed upon the coiling snake in its enchanted cage.

"No, my Lord, but I beg you will let me return. Let me find Potter."

"You sound like Lucius. Neither of you understands Potter as I do. He does not need finding. Potter will come to me. I know his weakness, you see, his one great flaw. He will hate watching the others struck down around him, knowing that it is for him that it happens. He will want to stop it at any cost. He will come."

"But my Lord, he might be killed accidentally by one other than yourself —"

"My instructions to my Death Eaters have been perfectly clear. Capture Potter. Kill his friends — the more, the better — but do not kill him.

"But it is of you that I wished to speak, Severus, not Harry Potter. You have been very valuable to me. Very valuable."

"My Lord knows I seek only to serve him. But — let me go and find the boy, my Lord. Let me bring him to you. I know I can —"

"I have told you, no!" said Voldemort, and Harry caught the glint of red in his eyes as he turned again, and the swishing of his cloak was like the slithering of a snake, and he felt Voldemort's impatience in his burning scar. "My concern at the moment, Severus, is what will happen when I finally meet the boy!"

"My Lord, there can be no question, surely — ?"

"— but there *is* a question, Severus. There is."

Voldemort halted, and Harry could see him plainly again as he slid the Elder Wand through his white fingers, staring at Snape.

"Why did both the wands I have used fail when directed at Harry Potter?"

"I — I cannot answer that, my Lord."

"Can't you?"

The stab of rage felt like a spike driven through Harry's head: He forced his own fist into his mouth to stop himself from crying out in pain. He closed his eyes, and suddenly he was Voldemort, looking into Snape's pale face.

"My wand of yew did everything of which I asked it, Severus, except to kill Harry Potter. Twice it failed. Ollivander told me under torture of the twin cores, told me to take another's wand. I did so, but Lucius's wand shattered upon meeting Potter's."

"I — I have no explanation, my Lord."

Snape was not looking at Voldemort now. His dark eyes were still fixed upon the coiling serpent in its protective sphere.

"I sought a third wand, Severus. The Elder Wand, the Wand of Destiny, the Deathstick. I took it from its previous master. I took it from the grave of Albus Dumbledore."

And now Snape looked at Voldemort, and Snape's face was like a death mask. It was marble white and so still that when he spoke, it was a shock to see that anyone lived behind the blank eyes.

"My Lord — let me go to the boy —"

"All this long night, when I am on the brink of victory, I have sat here," said Voldemort, his voice barely louder than a whisper, "wondering, wondering, why the Elder Wand refuses to be what it ought to be, refuses to perform as legend says it must perform for its rightful owner . . . and I think I have the answer."

Snape did not speak.

"Perhaps you already know it? You are a clever man, after all, Severus. You have been a good and faithful servant, and I regret what must happen."

"My Lord —"

"The Elder Wand cannot serve me properly, Severus, because I am not its true master. The Elder Wand belongs to the wizard who killed its last owner. You killed Albus Dumbledore. While you live, Severus, the Elder Wand cannot be truly mine."

"My Lord!" Snape protested, raising his wand.

"It cannot be any other way," said Voldemort. "I must master the wand, Severus. Master the wand, and I master Potter at last."

And Voldemort swiped the air with the Elder Wand. It did nothing to Snape, who for a split second seemed to think he had been reprieved: But then Voldemort's intention became clear. The snake's cage was rolling through the air, and before Snape could do anything more than yell, it had encased him, head and shoulders, and Voldemort spoke in Parseltongue.

"Kill."

There was a terrible scream. Harry saw Snape's face losing the little color it had left; it whitened as his black eyes widened, as the snake's fangs pierced his neck, as he failed to push the enchanted cage off himself, as his knees gave way and he fell to the floor.

"I regret it," said Voldemort coldly.

He turned away; there was no sadness in him, no remorse. It was time to leave this shack and take charge, with a wand that would now do his full bidding. He pointed it at the starry cage holding the snake, which drifted upward, off Snape, who fell sideways onto the floor, blood gushing from the wounds in his neck. Voldemort swept from the room without a backward glance, and the great serpent floated after him in its huge protective sphere.

Back in the tunnel and his own mind, Harry opened his eyes: He had drawn blood biting down on his knuckles in the effort not to shout out. Now he was looking through the tiny crack between crate and wall, watching a foot in a black boot trembling on the floor.

"Harry!" breathed Hermione behind him, but he had already pointed his wand at the crate blocking his view. It lifted an inch into the air and drifted sideways silently. As quietly as he could, he pulled himself up into the room.

He did not know why he was doing it, why he was approaching the dying man: He did not know what he felt as he saw Snape's white face, and the fingers trying to staunch the bloody wound at his neck. Harry took off the Invisibility Cloak and looked down upon the man he hated, whose widening black eyes found Harry as he tried to speak. Harry bent over him, and Snape seized the front of his robes and pulled him close.

A terrible rasping, gurgling noise issued from Snape's throat.

"Take . . . it. . . . Take . . . it. . . ."

Something more than blood was leaking from Snape. Silvery blue, neither gas nor liquid, it gushed from his mouth and his ears and his eyes, and Harry knew what it was, but did not know what to do —

A flask, conjured from thin air, was thrust into his shaking hands by Hermione. Harry lifted the silvery substance into it with his wand. When the flask was full to the brim, and Snape looked as though there was no blood left in him, his grip on Harry's robes slackened.

"Look . . . at . . . me. . . ." he whispered.

The green eyes found the black, but after a second, something in the depths of the dark pair seemed to vanish, leaving them fixed, blank, and empty. The hand holding Harry thudded to the floor, and Snape moved no more.

THE PRINCE'S TALE

arry remained kneeling at Snape's side, simply staring down at him, until quite suddenly a high, cold voice spoke so close to them that Harry jumped to his feet, the flask gripped tightly in his hands, thinking that Voldemort had reentered the room.

Voldemort's voice reverberated from the walls and floor, and Harry realized that he was talking to Hogwarts and to all the surrounding area, that the residents of Hogsmeade and all those still fighting in the castle would hear him as clearly as if he stood beside them, his breath on the back of their necks, a deathblow away.

"You have fought," said the high, cold voice, "valiantly. Lord Voldemort knows how to value bravery.

"Yet you have sustained heavy losses. If you continue to resist me, you will all die, one by one. I do not wish this to happen. Every drop of magical blood spilled is a loss and a waste.

"Lord Voldemort is merciful. I command my forces to retreat immediately.

"You have one hour. Dispose of your dead with dignity. Treat your injured.

"I speak now, Harry Potter, directly to you. You have permitted your friends to die for you rather than face me yourself. I shall wait for one hour in the Forbidden Forest. If, at the end of that hour, you have not come to me, have not given yourself up, then battle recommences. This time, I shall enter the fray myself, Harry Potter, and I shall find you, and I shall punish every last man, woman, and child who has tried to conceal you from me. One hour."

Both Ron and Hermione shook their heads frantically, looking at Harry.

"Don't listen to him," said Ron.

"It'll be all right," said Hermione wildly. "Let's — let's get back to the castle, if he's gone to the forest we'll need to think of a new plan —"

She glanced at Snape's body, then hurried back to the tunnel entrance. Ron followed her. Harry gathered up the Invisibility Cloak, then looked down at Snape. He did not know what to feel, except shock at the way Snape had been killed, and the reason for which it had been done. . . .

They crawled back through the tunnel, none of them talking, and Harry wondered whether Ron and Hermione could still hear Voldemort ringing in their heads, as he could.

You have permitted your friends to die for you rather than face me yourself. I shall wait for one hour in the Forbidden Forest. . . . One hour. . . .

Small bundles seemed to litter the lawn at the front of the castle. It could only be an hour or so from dawn, yet it was pitch-black. The three of them hurried toward the stone steps. A lone clog, the

size of a small boat, lay abandoned in front of them. There was no
other sign of Grawp or of his attacker.

The castle was unnaturally silent. There were no flashes of light
now, no bangs or screams or shouts. The flagstones of the deserted
entrance hall were stained with blood. Emeralds were still scattered
all over the floor, along with pieces of marble and splintered wood.
Part of the banisters had been blown away.

"Where is everyone?" whispered Hermione.

Ron led the way to the Great Hall. Harry stopped in the
doorway.

The House tables were gone and the room was crowded. The
survivors stood in groups, their arms around each other's necks.
The injured were being treated upon the raised platform by Madam
Pomfrey and a group of helpers. Firenze was amongst the injured; his
flank poured blood and he shook where he lay, unable to stand.

The dead lay in a row in the middle of the Hall. Harry could not
see Fred's body, because his family surrounded him. George was
kneeling at his head; Mrs. Weasley was lying across Fred's chest, her
body shaking, Mr. Weasley stroking her hair while tears cascaded
down his cheeks.

Without a word to Harry, Ron and Hermione walked away.
Harry saw Hermione approach Ginny, whose face was swollen and
blotchy, and hug her. Ron joined Bill, Fleur, and Percy, who flung an
arm around Ron's shoulders. As Ginny and Hermione moved closer
to the rest of the family, Harry had a clear view of the bodies lying
next to Fred: Remus and Tonks, pale and still and peaceful-looking,
apparently asleep beneath the dark, enchanted ceiling.

The Great Hall seemed to fly away, become smaller, shrink,
as Harry reeled backward from the doorway. He could not draw

breath. He could not bear to look at any of the other bodies, to see who else had died for him. He could not bear to join the Weasleys, could not look into their eyes, when if he had given himself up in the first place, Fred might never have died. . . .

He turned away and ran up the marble staircase. Lupin, Tonks . . . He yearned not to feel. . . . He wished he could rip out his heart, his innards, everything that was screaming inside him. . . .

The castle was completely empty; even the ghosts seemed to have joined the mass mourning in the Great Hall. Harry ran without stopping, clutching the crystal flask of Snape's last thoughts, and he did not slow down until he reached the stone gargoyle guarding the headmaster's office.

"Password?"

"Dumbledore!" said Harry without thinking, because it was he whom he yearned to see, and to his surprise the gargoyle slid aside, revealing the spiral staircase behind.

But when Harry burst into the circular office he found a change. The portraits that hung all around the walls were empty. Not a single headmaster or headmistress remained to see him; all, it seemed, had flitted away, charging through the paintings that lined the castle, so that they could have a clear view of what was going on.

Harry glanced hopelessly at Dumbledore's deserted frame, which hung directly behind the headmaster's chair, then turned his back on it. The stone Pensieve lay in the cabinet where it had always been: Harry heaved it onto the desk and poured Snape's memories into the wide basin with its runic markings around the edge. To escape into someone else's head would be a blessed relief. . . . Nothing that even Snape had left him could be worse than his own thoughts. The memories swirled, silver white and strange, and without hesitating,

with a feeling of reckless abandonment, as though this would assuage his torturing grief, Harry dived.

He fell headlong into sunlight, and his feet found warm ground.
When he straightened up, he saw that he was in a nearly deserted
playground. A single huge chimney dominated the distant skyline.
Two girls were swinging backward and forward, and a skinny boy
was watching them from behind a clump of bushes. His black hair
was overlong and his clothes were so mismatched that it looked
deliberate: too short jeans, a shabby, overlarge coat that might have
belonged to a grown man, an odd smocklike shirt.

Harry moved closer to the boy. Snape looked no more than nine
or ten years old, sallow, small, stringy. There was undisguised greed
in his thin face as he watched the younger of the two girls swinging
higher and higher than her sister.

"Lily, don't do it!" shrieked the elder of the two.

But the girl had let go of the swing at the very height of its arc
and flown into the air, quite literally flown, launched herself skyward with a great shout of laughter, and instead of crumpling on
the playground asphalt, she soared like a trapeze artist through the
air, staying up far too long, landing far too lightly.

"Mummy told you not to!"

Petunia stopped her swing by dragging the heels of her sandals
on the ground, making a crunching, grinding sound, then leapt
up, hands on hips.

"Mummy said you weren't allowed, Lily!"

"But I'm fine," said Lily, still giggling. "Tuney, look at this. Watch
what I can do."

Petunia glanced around. The playground was deserted apart from
themselves and, though the girls did not know it, Snape. Lily had

picked up a fallen flower from the bush behind which Snape lurked. Petunia advanced, evidently torn between curiosity and disapproval. Lily waited until Petunia was near enough to have a clear view, then held out her palm. The flower sat there, opening and closing its petals, like some bizarre, many-lipped oyster.

"Stop it!" shrieked Petunia.

"It's not hurting you," said Lily, but she closed her hand on the blossom and threw it back to the ground.

"It's not right," said Petunia, but her eyes had followed the flower's flight to the ground and lingered upon it. "How do you do it?" she added, and there was definite longing in her voice.

"It's obvious, isn't it?" Snape could no longer contain himself, but had jumped out from behind the bushes. Petunia shrieked and ran backward toward the swings, but Lily, though clearly startled, remained where she was. Snape seemed to regret his appearance. A dull flush of color mounted the sallow cheeks as he looked at Lily.

"What's obvious?" asked Lily.

Snape had an air of nervous excitement. With a glance at the distant Petunia, now hovering beside the swings, he lowered his voice and said, "I know what you are."

"What do you mean?"

"You're . . . you're a witch," whispered Snape.

She looked affronted.

"*That's* not a very nice thing to say to somebody!"

She turned, nose in the air, and marched off toward her sister.

"No!" said Snape. He was highly colored now, and Harry wondered why he did not take off the ridiculously large coat, unless it was because he did not want to reveal the smock beneath it. He flapped after the girls, looking ludicrously batlike, like his older self.

The sisters considered him, united in disapproval, both holding on to one of the swing poles as though it was the safe place in tag.

"You *are*," said Snape to Lily. "You *are* a witch. I've been watching you for a while. But there's nothing wrong with that. My mum's one, and I'm a wizard."

Petunia's laugh was like cold water.

"Wizard!" she shrieked, her courage returned now that she had recovered from the shock of his unexpected appearance. "*I* know who *you* are. You're that Snape boy! They live down Spinner's End by the river," she told Lily, and it was evident from her tone that she considered the address a poor recommendation. "Why have you been spying on us?"

"Haven't been spying," said Snape, hot and uncomfortable and dirty-haired in the bright sunlight. "Wouldn't spy on *you*, anyway," he added spitefully, "*you're* a Muggle."

Though Petunia evidently did not understand the word, she could hardly mistake the tone.

"Lily, come on, we're leaving!" she said shrilly. Lily obeyed her sister at once, glaring at Snape as she left. He stood watching them as they marched through the playground gate, and Harry, the only one left to observe him, recognized Snape's bitter disappointment, and understood that Snape had been planning this moment for a while, and that it had all gone wrong. . . .

The scene dissolved, and before Harry knew it, re-formed around him. He was now in a small thicket of trees. He could see a sunlit river glittering through their trunks. The shadows cast by the trees made a basin of cool green shade. Two children sat facing each other, cross-legged on the ground. Snape had removed his coat now; his odd smock looked less peculiar in the half light.

". . . and the Ministry can punish you if you do magic outside school, you get letters."

"But I *have* done magic outside school!"

"We're all right. We haven't got wands yet. They let you off when you're a kid and you can't help it. But once you're eleven," he nodded importantly, "and they start training you, then you've got to go careful."

There was a little silence. Lily had picked up a fallen twig and twirled it in the air, and Harry knew that she was imagining sparks trailing from it. Then she dropped the twig, leaned in toward the boy, and said, "It *is* real, isn't it? It's not a joke? Petunia says you're lying to me. Petunia says there isn't a Hogwarts. It *is* real, isn't it?"

"It's real for us," said Snape. "Not for her. But we'll get the letter, you and me."

"Really?" whispered Lily.

"Definitely," said Snape, and even with his poorly cut hair and his odd clothes, he struck an oddly impressive figure sprawled in front of her, brimful of confidence in his destiny.

"And will it really come by owl?" Lily whispered.

"Normally," said Snape. "But you're Muggle-born, so someone from the school will have to come and explain to your parents."

"Does it make a difference, being Muggle-born?"

Snape hesitated. His black eyes, eager in the greenish gloom, moved over the pale face, the dark red hair.

"No," he said. "It doesn't make any difference."

"Good," said Lily, relaxing: It was clear that she had been worrying.

"You've got loads of magic," said Snape. "I saw that. All the time I was watching you . . ."

His voice trailed away; she was not listening, but had stretched out on the leafy ground and was looking up at the canopy of leaves overhead. He watched her as greedily as he had watched her in the playground.

"How are things at your house?" Lily asked.

A little crease appeared between his eyes.

"Fine," he said.

"They're not arguing anymore?"

"Oh yes, they're arguing," said Snape. He picked up a fistful of leaves and began tearing them apart, apparently unaware of what he was doing. "But it won't be that long and I'll be gone."

"Doesn't your dad like magic?"

"He doesn't like anything, much," said Snape.

"Severus?"

A little smile twisted Snape's mouth when she said his name.

"Yeah?"

"Tell me about the dementors again."

"What d'you want to know about them for?"

"If I use magic outside school —"

"They wouldn't give you to the dementors for that! Dementors are for people who do really bad stuff. They guard the wizard prison, Azkaban. You're not going to end up in Azkaban, you're too —"

He turned red again and shredded more leaves. Then a small

rustling noise behind Harry made him turn: Petunia, hiding behind a tree, had lost her footing.

"Tuney!" said Lily, surprise and welcome in her voice, but Snape had jumped to his feet.

"Who's spying now?" he shouted. "What d'you want?"

Petunia was breathless, alarmed at being caught. Harry could see her struggling for something hurtful to say.

"What is that you're wearing, anyway?" she said, pointing at Snape's chest. "Your mum's blouse?"

There was a *crack*: A branch over Petunia's head had fallen. Lily screamed: The branch caught Petunia on the shoulder, and she staggered backward and burst into tears.

"Tuney!"

But Petunia was running away. Lily rounded on Snape.

"Did you make that happen?"

"No." He looked both defiant and scared.

"You did!" She was backing away from him. "You *did*! You hurt her!"

"No — no I didn't!"

But the lie did not convince Lily: After one last burning look, she ran from the little thicket, off after her sister, and Snape looked miserable and confused. . . .

And the scene re-formed. Harry looked around: He was on platform nine and three-quarters, and Snape stood beside him, slightly hunched, next to a thin, sallow-faced, sour-looking woman who greatly resembled him. Snape was staring at a family of four a short distance away. The two girls stood a little apart from their parents. Lily seemed to be pleading with her sister; Harry moved closer to listen.

". . . I'm sorry, Tuney, I'm sorry! Listen —" She caught her sister's hand and held tight to it, even though Petunia tried to pull it away. "Maybe once I'm there — no, listen, Tuney! Maybe once I'm there, I'll be able to go to Professor Dumbledore and persuade him to change his mind!"

"I don't — want — to — go!" said Petunia, and she dragged her hand back out of her sister's grasp. "You think I want to go to some stupid castle and learn to be a — a —"

Her pale eyes roved over the platform, over the cats mewling in their owners' arms, over the owls fluttering and hooting at each other in cages, over the students, some already in their long black robes, loading trunks onto the scarlet steam engine or else greeting one another with glad cries after a summer apart.

"— you think I want to be a — a freak?"

Lily's eyes filled with tears as Petunia succeeded in tugging her hand away.

"I'm not a freak," said Lily. "That's a horrible thing to say."

"That's where you're going," said Petunia with relish. "A special school for freaks. You and that Snape boy . . . weirdos, that's what you two are. It's good you're being separated from normal people. It's for our safety."

Lily glanced toward her parents, who were looking around the platform with an air of wholehearted enjoyment, drinking in the scene. Then she looked back at her sister, and her voice was low and fierce.

"You didn't think it was such a freak's school when you wrote to the headmaster and begged him to take you."

Petunia turned scarlet.

"Beg? I didn't beg!"

"I saw his reply. It was very kind."

"You shouldn't have read —" whispered Petunia, "that was my private — how could you — ?"

Lily gave herself away by half-glancing toward where Snape stood nearby. Petunia gasped.

"That boy found it! You and that boy have been sneaking in my room!"

"No — not sneaking —" Now Lily was on the defensive. "Severus saw the envelope, and he couldn't believe a Muggle could have contacted Hogwarts, that's all! He says there must be wizards working undercover in the postal service who take care of —"

"Apparently wizards poke their noses in everywhere!" said Petunia, now as pale as she had been flushed. *"Freak!"* she spat at her sister, and she flounced off to where her parents stood. . . .

The scene dissolved again. Snape was hurrying along the corridor of the Hogwarts Express as it clattered through the countryside. He had already changed into his school robes, had perhaps taken the first opportunity to take off his dreadful Muggle clothes. At last he stopped, outside a compartment in which a group of rowdy boys were talking. Hunched in a corner seat beside the window was Lily, her face pressed against the windowpane.

Snape slid open the compartment door and sat down opposite Lily. She glanced at him and then looked back out of the window. She had been crying.

"I don't want to talk to you," she said in a constricted voice.

"Why not?"

"Tuney h-hates me. Because we saw that letter from Dumbledore."

"So what?"

She threw him a look of deep dislike.

"So she's my sister!"

"She's only a —" He caught himself quickly; Lily, too busy trying to wipe her eyes without being noticed, did not hear him.

"But we're going!" he said, unable to suppress the exhilaration in his voice. "This is it! We're off to Hogwarts!"

She nodded, mopping her eyes, but in spite of herself, she half smiled.

"You'd better be in Slytherin," said Snape, encouraged that she had brightened a little.

"Slytherin?"

One of the boys sharing the compartment, who had shown no interest at all in Lily or Snape until that point, looked around at the word, and Harry, whose attention had been focused entirely on the two beside the window, saw his father: slight, black-haired like Snape, but with that indefinable air of having been well-cared-for, even adored, that Snape so conspicuously lacked.

"Who wants to be in Slytherin? I think I'd leave, wouldn't you?" James asked the boy lounging on the seats opposite him, and with a jolt, Harry realized that it was Sirius. Sirius did not smile.

"My whole family have been in Slytherin," he said.

"Blimey," said James, "and I thought you seemed all right!"

Sirius grinned.

"Maybe I'll break the tradition. Where are you heading, if you've got the choice?"

James lifted an invisible sword.

"'Gryffindor, where dwell the brave at heart!' Like my dad."

Snape made a small, disparaging noise. James turned on him.

"Got a problem with that?"

"No," said Snape, though his slight sneer said otherwise. "If you'd rather be brawny than brainy —"

"Where're you hoping to go, seeing as you're neither?" interjected Sirius.

James roared with laughter. Lily sat up, rather flushed, and looked from James to Sirius in dislike.

"Come on, Severus, let's find another compartment."

"Oooooo . . ."

James and Sirius imitated her lofty voice; James tried to trip Snape as he passed.

"See ya, Snivellus!" a voice called, as the compartment door slammed. . . .

And the scene dissolved once more. . . .

Harry was standing right behind Snape as they faced the candlelit House tables, lined with rapt faces. Then Professor McGonagall said, "Evans, Lily!"

He watched his mother walk forward on trembling legs and sit down upon the rickety stool. Professor McGonagall dropped the Sorting Hat onto her head, and barely a second after it had touched the dark red hair, the hat cried, *"Gryffindor!"*

Harry heard Snape let out a tiny groan. Lily took off the hat, handed it back to Professor McGonagall, then hurried toward the cheering Gryffindors, but as she went she glanced back at Snape, and there was a sad little smile on her face. Harry saw Sirius move up the bench to make room for her. She took one look at him, seemed to recognize him from the train, folded her arms, and firmly turned her back on him.

The roll call continued. Harry watched Lupin, Pettigrew, and his father join Lily and Sirius at the Gryffindor table. At last, when only a dozen students remained to be sorted, Professor McGonagall called Snape.

Harry walked with him to the stool, watched him place the hat upon his head. *"Slytherin!"* cried the Sorting Hat.

And Severus Snape moved off to the other side of the Hall, away from Lily, to where the Slytherins were cheering him, to where Lucius Malfoy, a prefect badge gleaming upon his chest, patted Snape on the back as he sat down beside him. . . .

And the scene changed. . . .

Lily and Snape were walking across the castle courtyard, evidently arguing. Harry hurried to catch up with them, to listen in. As he reached them, he realized how much taller they both were: A few years seemed to have passed since their Sorting.

". . . thought we were supposed to be friends?" Snape was saying. "Best friends?"

"We *are,* Sev, but I don't like some of the people you're hanging round with! I'm sorry, but I detest Avery and Mulciber! *Mulciber!* What do you see in him, Sev, he's creepy! D'you know what he tried to do to Mary Macdonald the other day?"

Lily had reached a pillar and leaned against it, looking up into the thin, sallow face.

"That was nothing," said Snape. "It was a laugh, that's all —"

"It was Dark Magic, and if you think that's funny —"

"What about the stuff Potter and his mates get up to?" demanded Snape. His color rose again as he said it, unable, it seemed, to hold in his resentment.

"What's Potter got to do with anything?" said Lily.

"They sneak out at night. There's something weird about that Lupin. Where does he keep going?"

"He's ill," said Lily. "They say he's ill —"

"Every month at the full moon?" said Snape.

"I know your theory," said Lily, and she sounded cold. "Why are you so obsessed with them anyway? Why do you care what they're doing at night?"

"I'm just trying to show you they're not as wonderful as everyone seems to think they are."

The intensity of his gaze made her blush.

"They don't use Dark Magic, though." She dropped her voice. "And you're being really ungrateful. I heard what happened the other night. You went sneaking down that tunnel by the Whomping Willow, and James Potter saved you from whatever's down there —"

Snape's whole face contorted and he spluttered, "Saved? Saved? You think he was playing the hero? He was saving his neck and his friends' too! You're not going to — I won't let you —"

"*Let* me? *Let* me?"

Lily's bright green eyes were slits. Snape backtracked at once.

"I didn't mean — I just don't want to see you made a fool of — He fancies you, James Potter fancies you!" The words seemed wrenched from him against his will. "And he's not . . . everyone thinks . . . big Quidditch hero —" Snape's bitterness and dislike were rendering him incoherent, and Lily's eyebrows were traveling farther and farther up her forehead.

"I know James Potter's an arrogant toerag," she said, cutting across Snape. "I don't need you to tell me that. But Mulciber's and Avery's idea of humor is just evil. *Evil,* Sev. I don't understand how you can be friends with them."

Harry doubted that Snape had even heard her strictures on Mulciber and Avery. The moment she had insulted James Potter, his whole body had relaxed, and as they walked away there was a new spring in Snape's step. . . .

And the scene dissolved. . . .

Harry watched again as Snape left the Great Hall after sitting his O.W.L. in Defense Against the Dark Arts, watched as he wandered away from the castle and strayed inadvertently close to the place beneath the beech tree where James, Sirius, Lupin, and Pettigrew sat together. But Harry kept his distance this time, because he knew what happened after James had hoisted Severus into the air and taunted him; he knew what had been done and said, and it gave him no pleasure to hear it again. . . . He watched as Lily joined the group and went to Snape's defense. Distantly he heard Snape shout at her in his humiliation and his fury, the unforgivable word: *"Mudblood."*

The scene changed. . . .

"I'm sorry."

"I'm not interested."

"I'm sorry!"

"Save your breath."

It was nighttime. Lily, who was wearing a dressing gown, stood with her arms folded in front of the portrait of the Fat Lady, at the entrance to Gryffindor Tower.

"I only came out because Mary told me you were threatening to sleep here."

"I was. I would have done. I never meant to call you Mudblood, it just —"

"Slipped out?" There was no pity in Lily's voice. "It's too late. I've made excuses for you for years. None of my friends can understand why I even talk to you. You and your precious little Death Eater friends — you see, you don't even deny it! You don't even deny that's what you're all aiming to be! You can't wait to join You-Know-Who, can you?"

He opened his mouth, but closed it without speaking.

"I can't pretend anymore. You've chosen your way, I've chosen mine."

"No — listen, I didn't mean —"

"— to call me Mudblood? But you call everyone of my birth Mudblood, Severus. Why should I be any different?"

He struggled on the verge of speech, but with a contemptuous look she turned and climbed back through the portrait hole. . . .

The corridor dissolved, and the scene took a little longer to re-form: Harry seemed to fly through shifting shapes and colors until his surroundings solidified again and he stood on a hilltop, forlorn and cold in the darkness, the wind whistling through the branches of a few leafless trees. The adult Snape was panting, turning on the spot, his wand gripped tightly in his hand, waiting for something or for someone. . . . His fear infected Harry too, even though he knew that he could not be harmed, and he looked over his shoulder, wondering what it was that Snape was waiting for —

Then a blinding, jagged jet of white light flew through the air: Harry thought of lightning, but Snape had dropped to his knees and his wand had flown out of his hand.

"Don't kill me!"

"That was not my intention."

Any sound of Dumbledore Apparating had been drowned by the sound of the wind in the branches. He stood before Snape with his robes whipping around him, and his face was illuminated from below in the light cast by his wand.

"Well, Severus? What message does Lord Voldemort have for me?"

"No — no message — I'm here on my own account!"

Snape was wringing his hands: He looked a little mad, with his straggling black hair flying around him.

"I — I come with a warning — no, a request — please —"

Dumbledore flicked his wand. Though leaves and branches still flew through the night air around them, silence fell on the spot where he and Snape faced each other.

"What request could a Death Eater make of me?"

"The — the prophecy . . . the prediction . . . Trelawney . . ."

"Ah, yes," said Dumbledore. "How much did you relay to Lord Voldemort?"

"Everything — everything I heard!" said Snape. "That is why — it is for that reason — he thinks it means Lily Evans!"

"The prophecy did not refer to a woman," said Dumbledore. "It spoke of a boy born at the end of July —"

"You know what I mean! He thinks it means her son, he is going to hunt her down — kill them all —"

"If she means so much to you," said Dumbledore, "surely Lord Voldemort will spare her? Could you not ask for mercy for the mother, in exchange for the son?"

"I have — I have asked him —"

"You disgust me," said Dumbledore, and Harry had never heard so much contempt in his voice. Snape seemed to shrink a little. "You do not care, then, about the deaths of her husband and child? They can die, as long as you have what you want?"

Snape said nothing, but merely looked up at Dumbledore.

"Hide them all, then," he croaked. "Keep her — them — safe. Please."

"And what will you give me in return, Severus?"

"In — in return?" Snape gaped at Dumbledore, and Harry expected him to protest, but after a long moment he said, "Anything."

The hilltop faded, and Harry stood in Dumbledore's office, and something was making a terrible sound, like a wounded animal. Snape was slumped forward in a chair and Dumbledore was standing over him, looking grim. After a moment or two, Snape raised his face, and he looked like a man who had lived a hundred years of misery since leaving the wild hilltop.

"I thought . . . you were going . . . to keep her . . . safe. . . ."

"She and James put their faith in the wrong person," said Dumbledore. "Rather like you, Severus. Weren't you hoping that Lord Voldemort would spare her?"

Snape's breathing was shallow.

"Her boy survives," said Dumbledore.

With a tiny jerk of the head, Snape seemed to flick off an irksome fly.

"Her son lives. He has her eyes, precisely her eyes. You remember the shape and color of Lily Evans's eyes, I am sure?"

"DON'T!" bellowed Snape. "Gone . . . dead . . ."

"Is this remorse, Severus?"

"I wish . . . I wish *I* were dead. . . ."

"And what use would that be to anyone?" said Dumbledore coldly. "If you loved Lily Evans, if you truly loved her, then your way forward is clear."

Snape seemed to peer through a haze of pain, and Dumbledore's words appeared to take a long time to reach him.

"What — what do you mean?"

"You know how and why she died. Make sure it was not in vain. Help me protect Lily's son."

"He does not need protection. The Dark Lord has gone —"

"The Dark Lord will return, and Harry Potter will be in terrible danger when he does."

There was a long pause, and slowly Snape regained control of himself, mastered his own breathing. At last he said, "Very well. Very well. But never — never tell, Dumbledore! This must be between us! Swear it! I cannot bear . . . especially Potter's son . . . I want your word!"

"My word, Severus, that I shall never reveal the best of you?" Dumbledore sighed, looking down into Snape's ferocious, anguished face. "If you insist . . ."

The office dissolved but re-formed instantly. Snape was pacing up and down in front of Dumbledore.

"— mediocre, arrogant as his father, a determined rule-breaker, delighted to find himself famous, attention-seeking and impertinent —"

"You see what you expect to see, Severus," said Dumbledore, without raising his eyes from a copy of *Transfiguration Today*. "Other teachers report that the boy is modest, likable, and reasonably talented. Personally, I find him an engaging child."

Dumbledore turned a page, and said, without looking up, "Keep an eye on Quirrell, won't you?"

A whirl of color, and now everything darkened, and Snape and Dumbledore stood a little apart in the entrance hall, while the last stragglers from the Yule Ball passed them on their way to bed.

"Well?" murmured Dumbledore.

"Karkaroff's Mark is becoming darker too. He is panicking, he fears retribution; you know how much help he gave the Ministry after the Dark Lord fell." Snape looked sideways at Dumbledore's crooked-nosed profile. "Karkaroff intends to flee if the Mark burns."

"Does he?" said Dumbledore softly, as Fleur Delacour and Roger Davies came giggling in from the grounds. "And are you tempted to join him?"

"No," said Snape, his black eyes on Fleur's and Roger's retreating figures. "I am not such a coward."

"No," agreed Dumbledore. "You are a braver man by far than Igor Karkaroff. You know, I sometimes think we Sort too soon. . . ."

He walked away, leaving Snape looking stricken. . . .

And now Harry stood in the headmaster's office yet again. It was nighttime, and Dumbledore sagged sideways in the thronelike chair behind the desk, apparently semiconscious. His right hand dangled over the side, blackened and burned. Snape was muttering incantations, pointing his wand at the wrist of the hand, while with his left hand he tipped a goblet full of thick golden potion down Dumbledore's throat. After a moment or two, Dumbledore's eyelids fluttered and opened.

"Why," said Snape, without preamble, "*why* did you put on that ring? It carries a curse, surely you realized that. Why even touch it?"

Marvolo Gaunt's ring lay on the desk before Dumbledore. It was cracked; the sword of Gryffindor lay beside it.

Dumbledore grimaced.

"I . . . was a fool. Sorely tempted . . ."

"Tempted by what?"

Dumbledore did not answer.

"It is a miracle you managed to return here!" Snape sounded furious. "That ring carried a curse of extraordinary power, to contain it is all we can hope for; I have trapped the curse in one hand for the time being —"

Dumbledore raised his blackened, useless hand, and examined it with the expression of one being shown an interesting curio.

"You have done very well, Severus. How long do you think I have?"

Dumbledore's tone was conversational; he might have been asking for a weather forecast. Snape hesitated, and then said, "I cannot tell. Maybe a year. There is no halting such a spell forever. It will spread eventually, it is the sort of curse that strengthens over time."

Dumbledore smiled. The news that he had less than a year to live seemed a matter of little or no concern to him.

"I am fortunate, extremely fortunate, that I have you, Severus."

"If you had only summoned me a little earlier, I might have been able to do more, buy you more time!" said Snape furiously. He looked down at the broken ring and the sword. "Did you think that breaking the ring would break the curse?"

"Something like that . . . I was delirious, no doubt. . . ." said Dumbledore. With an effort he straightened himself in his chair. "Well, really, this makes matters much more straightforward."

Snape looked utterly perplexed. Dumbledore smiled.

"I refer to the plan Lord Voldemort is revolving around me. His plan to have the poor Malfoy boy murder me."

Snape sat down in the chair Harry had so often occupied, across the desk from Dumbledore. Harry could tell that he wanted to say more on the subject of Dumbledore's cursed hand, but the other held it up in polite refusal to discuss the matter further. Scowling, Snape said, "The Dark Lord does not expect Draco to succeed. This is merely punishment for Lucius's recent failures. Slow torture for Draco's parents, while they watch him fail and pay the price."

"In short, the boy has had a death sentence pronounced upon him as surely as I have," said Dumbledore. "Now, I should have thought the natural successor to the job, once Draco fails, is yourself?"

There was a short pause.

"That, I think, is the Dark Lord's plan."

"Lord Voldemort foresees a moment in the near future when he will not need a spy at Hogwarts?"

"He believes the school will soon be in his grasp, yes."

"And if it does fall into his grasp," said Dumbledore, almost, it seemed, as an aside, "I have your word that you will do all in your power to protect the students of Hogwarts?"

Snape gave a stiff nod.

"Good. Now then. Your first priority will be to discover what Draco is up to. A frightened teenage boy is a danger to others as well as to himself. Offer him help and guidance, he ought to accept, he likes you —"

"— much less since his father has lost favor. Draco blames me, he thinks I have usurped Lucius's position."

"All the same, try. I am concerned less for myself than for accidental victims of whatever schemes might occur to the boy. Ultimately, of course, there is only one thing to be done if we are to save him from Lord Voldemort's wrath."

Snape raised his eyebrows and his tone was sardonic as he asked, "Are you intending to let him kill you?"

"Certainly not. *You* must kill me."

There was a long silence, broken only by an odd clicking noise. Fawkes the phoenix was gnawing a bit of cuttlebone.

"Would you like me to do it now?" asked Snape, his voice heavy with irony. "Or would you like a few moments to compose an epitaph?"

"Oh, not quite yet," said Dumbledore, smiling. "I daresay the moment will present itself in due course. Given what has happened tonight," he indicated his withered hand, "we can be sure that it will happen within a year."

"If you don't mind dying," said Snape roughly, "why not let Draco do it?"

"That boy's soul is not yet so damaged," said Dumbledore. "I would not have it ripped apart on my account."

"And my soul, Dumbledore? Mine?"

"You alone know whether it will harm your soul to help an old man avoid pain and humiliation," said Dumbledore. "I ask this one great favor of you, Severus, because death is coming for me as surely as the Chudley Cannons will finish bottom of this year's league. I confess I should prefer a quick, painless exit to the protracted and messy affair it will be if, for instance, Greyback is involved — I hear Voldemort has recruited him? Or dear Bellatrix, who likes to play with her food before she eats it."

His tone was light, but his blue eyes pierced Snape as they had frequently pierced Harry, as though the soul they discussed was visible to him. At last Snape gave another curt nod.

Dumbledore seemed satisfied.

"Thank you, Severus . . ."

The office disappeared, and now Snape and Dumbledore were strolling together in the deserted castle grounds by twilight.

"What are you doing with Potter, all these evenings you are closeted together?" Snape asked abruptly.

Dumbledore looked weary.

"Why? You aren't trying to give him *more* detentions, Severus? The boy will soon have spent more time in detention than out."

"He is his father over again —"

"In looks, perhaps, but his deepest nature is much more like his mother's. I spend time with Harry because I have things to discuss with him, information I must give him before it is too late."

"Information," repeated Snape. "You trust him . . . you do not trust me."

"It is not a question of trust. I have, as we both know, limited time. It is essential that I give the boy enough information for him to do what he needs to do."

"And why may I not have the same information?"

"I prefer not to put all of my secrets in one basket, particularly not a basket that spends so much time dangling on the arm of Lord Voldemort."

"Which I do on your orders!"

"And you do it extremely well. Do not think that I underestimate the constant danger in which you place yourself, Severus. To give Voldemort what appears to be valuable information while withholding the essentials is a job I would entrust to nobody but you."

"Yet you confide much more in a boy who is incapable of Occlumency, whose magic is mediocre, and who has a direct connection into the Dark Lord's mind!"

"Voldemort fears that connection," said Dumbledore. "Not so long ago he had one small taste of what truly sharing Harry's mind means to him. It was pain such as he has never experienced. He will not try to possess Harry again, I am sure of it. Not in that way."

"I don't understand."

"Lord Voldemort's soul, maimed as it is, cannot bear close contact with a soul like Harry's. Like a tongue on frozen steel, like flesh in flame —"

"Souls? We were talking of minds!"

"In the case of Harry and Lord Voldemort, to speak of one is to speak of the other."

Dumbledore glanced around to make sure that they were alone. They were close by the Forbidden Forest now, but there was no sign of anyone near them.

"After you have killed me, Severus —"

"You refuse to tell me everything, yet you expect that small service of me!" snarled Snape, and real anger flared in the thin face now. "You take a great deal for granted, Dumbledore! Perhaps I have changed my mind!"

"You gave me your word, Severus. And while we are talking about services you owe me, I thought you agreed to keep a close eye on our young Slytherin friend?"

Snape looked angry, mutinous. Dumbledore sighed.

"Come to my office tonight, Severus, at eleven, and you shall not complain that I have no confidence in you. . . ."

They were back in Dumbledore's office, the windows dark, and Fawkes sat silent as Snape sat quite still, as Dumbledore walked around him, talking.

"Harry must not know, not until the last moment, not until it is necessary, otherwise how could he have the strength to do what must be done?"

"But what must he do?"

"That is between Harry and me. Now listen closely, Severus. There will come a time — after my death — do not argue, do not interrupt! There will come a time when Lord Voldemort will seem to fear for the life of his snake."

"For Nagini?" Snape looked astonished.

"Precisely. If there comes a time when Lord Voldemort stops sending that snake forth to do his bidding, but keeps it safe beside him under magical protection, then, I think, it will be safe to tell Harry."

"Tell him what?"

Dumbledore took a deep breath and closed his eyes.

"Tell him that on the night Lord Voldemort tried to kill him, when Lily cast her own life between them as a shield, the Killing Curse rebounded upon Lord Voldemort, and a fragment of Voldemort's soul was blasted apart from the whole, and latched itself onto the only living soul left in that collapsing building. Part of Lord Voldemort lives inside Harry, and it is that which gives him the power of speech with snakes, and a connection with Lord Voldemort's mind that he has never understood. And while that fragment of soul, unmissed by Voldemort, remains attached to and protected by Harry, Lord Voldemort cannot die."

Harry seemed to be watching the two men from one end of a long tunnel, they were so far away from him, their voices echoing strangely in his ears.

"So the boy . . . the boy must die?" asked Snape quite calmly.

"And Voldemort himself must do it, Severus. That is essential."

Another long silence. Then Snape said, "I thought . . . all these years . . . that we were protecting him for her. For Lily."

"We have protected him because it has been essential to teach him, to raise him, to let him try his strength," said Dumbledore, his eyes still tight shut. "Meanwhile, the connection between them grows ever stronger, a parasitic growth: Sometimes I have thought he suspects it himself. If I know him, he will have arranged matters so that when he does set out to meet his death, it will truly mean the end of Voldemort."

Dumbledore opened his eyes. Snape looked horrified.

"You have kept him alive so that he can die at the right moment?"

"Don't be shocked, Severus. How many men and women have you watched die?"

"Lately, only those whom I could not save," said Snape. He stood up. "You have used me."

"Meaning?"

"I have spied for you and lied for you, put myself in mortal danger for you. Everything was supposed to be to keep Lily Potter's son safe. Now you tell me you have been raising him like a pig for slaughter —"

"But this is touching, Severus," said Dumbledore seriously. "Have you grown to care for the boy, after all?"

"For *him*?" shouted Snape. *"Expecto Patronum!"*

From the tip of his wand burst the silver doe: She landed on the office floor, bounded once across the office, and soared out of the window. Dumbledore watched her fly away, and as her silvery glow faded he turned back to Snape, and his eyes were full of tears.

"After all this time?"

"Always," said Snape.

And the scene shifted. Now, Harry saw Snape talking to the portrait of Dumbledore behind his desk.

"You will have to give Voldemort the correct date of Harry's departure from his aunt and uncle's," said Dumbledore. "Not to do so will raise suspicion, when Voldemort believes you so well informed. However, you must plant the idea of decoys; that, I think, ought to ensure Harry's safety. Try Confunding Mundungus Fletcher. And Severus, if you are forced to take part in the chase, be sure to act your part convincingly. . . . I am counting upon you to remain in Lord Voldemort's good books as long as possible, or Hogwarts will be left to the mercy of the Carrows. . . ."

Now Snape was head to head with Mundungus in an unfamiliar tavern, Mundungus's face looking curiously blank, Snape frowning in concentration.

"You will suggest to the Order of the Phoenix," Snape murmured, "that they use decoys. Polyjuice Potion. Identical Potters. It is the only thing that might work. You will forget that I have suggested this. You will present it as your own idea. You understand?"

"I understand," murmured Mundungus, his eyes unfocused. . . .

Now Harry was flying alongside Snape on a broomstick through a clear dark night: He was accompanied by other hooded Death Eaters, and ahead were Lupin and a Harry who was really George. . . . A Death Eater moved ahead of Snape and raised his wand, pointing it directly at Lupin's back —

"*Sectumsempra!*" shouted Snape.

But the spell, intended for the Death Eater's wand hand, missed and hit George instead —

And next, Snape was kneeling in Sirius's old bedroom. Tears were dripping from the end of his hooked nose as he read the old letter from Lily. The second page carried only a few words:

could ever have been friends with Gellert Grindelwald. I think her mind's going, personally!
    Lots of love,

    Lily

    Snape took the page bearing Lily's signature, and her love, and tucked it inside his robes. Then he ripped in two the photograph he was also holding, so that he kept the part from which Lily laughed, throwing the portion showing James and Harry back onto the floor, under the chest of drawers. . . .

    And now Snape stood again in the headmaster's study as Phineas Nigellus came hurrying into his portrait.

    "Headmaster! They are camping in the Forest of Dean! The Mudblood —"

    "Do not use that word!"

    "— the Granger girl, then, mentioned the place as she opened her bag and I heard her!"

    "Good. Very good!" cried the portrait of Dumbledore behind the headmaster's chair. "Now, Severus, the sword! Do not forget that it must be taken under conditions of need and valor — and he must not know that you give it! If Voldemort should read Harry's mind and see you acting for him —"

    "I know," said Snape curtly. He approached the portrait of Dumbledore and pulled at its side. It swung forward, revealing a hidden cavity behind it from which he took the sword of Gryffindor.

"And you still aren't going to tell me why it's so important to give Potter the sword?" said Snape as he swung a traveling cloak over his robes.

"No, I don't think so," said Dumbledore's portrait. "He will know what to do with it. And Severus, be very careful, they may not take kindly to your appearance after George Weasley's mishap —"

Snape turned at the door.

"Don't worry, Dumbledore," he said coolly. "I have a plan. . . ."

And Snape left the room. Harry rose up out of the Pensieve, and moments later he lay on the carpeted floor in exactly the same room: Snape might just have closed the door.

THE FOREST AGAIN

Finally, the truth. Lying with his face pressed into the dusty carpet of the office where he had once thought he was learning the secrets of victory, Harry understood at last that he was not supposed to survive. His job was to walk calmly into Death's welcoming arms. Along the way, he was to dispose of Voldemort's remaining links to life, so that when at last he flung himself across Voldemort's path, and did not raise a wand to defend himself, the end would be clean, and the job that ought to have been done in Godric's Hollow would be finished: Neither would live, neither could survive.

He felt his heart pounding fiercely in his chest. How strange that in his dread of death, it pumped all the harder, valiantly keeping him alive. But it would have to stop, and soon. Its beats were numbered. How many would there be time for, as he rose and walked through the castle for the last time, out into the grounds and into the forest?

Terror washed over him as he lay on the floor, with that funeral drum pounding inside him. Would it hurt to die? All those times he had thought that it was about to happen and escaped, he had never really thought of the thing itself: His will to live had always been so much stronger than his fear of death. Yet it did not occur to him now to try to escape, to outrun Voldemort. It was over, he knew it, and all that was left was the thing itself: dying.

If he could only have died on that summer's night when he had left number four, Privet Drive, for the last time, when the noble phoenix-feather wand had saved him! If he could only have died like Hedwig, so quickly he would not have known it had happened! Or if he could have launched himself in front of a wand to save someone he loved. . . . He envied even his parents' deaths now. This cold-blooded walk to his own destruction would require a different kind of bravery. He felt his fingers trembling slightly and made an effort to control them, although no one could see him; the portraits on the walls were all empty.

Slowly, very slowly, he sat up, and as he did so he felt more alive and more aware of his own living body than ever before. Why had he never appreciated what a miracle he was, brain and nerve and bounding heart? It would all be gone . . . or at least, he would be gone from it. His breath came slow and deep, and his mouth and throat were completely dry, but so were his eyes.

Dumbledore's betrayal was almost nothing. Of course there had been a bigger plan; Harry had simply been too foolish to see it, he realized that now. He had never questioned his own assumption that Dumbledore wanted him alive. Now he saw that his life span had always been determined by how long it took to eliminate all the Horcruxes. Dumbledore had passed the job of destroying them to

him, and obediently he had continued to chip away at the bonds tying not only Voldemort, but himself, to life! How neat, how elegant,
not to waste any more lives, but to give the dangerous task to the
boy who had already been marked for slaughter, and whose death
would not be a calamity, but another blow against Voldemort.

And Dumbledore had known that Harry would not duck out,
that he would keep going to the end, even though it was *his* end,
because he had taken trouble to get to know him, hadn't he? Dumbledore knew, as Voldemort knew, that Harry would not let anyone else
die for him now that he had discovered it was in his power to stop
it. The images of Fred, Lupin, and Tonks lying dead in the Great
Hall forced their way back into his mind's eye, and for a moment
he could hardly breathe: Death was impatient. . . .

But Dumbledore had overestimated him. He had failed: The
snake survived. One Horcrux remained to bind Voldemort to the
earth, even after Harry had been killed. True, that would mean an
easier job for somebody. He wondered who would do it. . . . Ron
and Hermione would know what needed to be done, of course. . . .
That would have been why Dumbledore wanted him to confide in
two others . . . so that if he fulfilled his true destiny a little early,
they could carry on. . . .

Like rain on a cold window, these thoughts pattered against the
hard surface of the incontrovertible truth, which was that he must
die. *I must die.* It must end.

Ron and Hermione seemed a long way away, in a far-off country;
he felt as though he had parted from them long ago. There would
be no good-byes and no explanations, he was determined of that.
This was a journey they could not take together, and the attempts
they would make to stop him would waste valuable time. He looked

down at the battered gold watch he had received on his seventeenth birthday. Nearly half of the hour allotted by Voldemort for his surrender had elapsed.

He stood up. His heart was leaping against his ribs like a frantic bird. Perhaps it knew it had little time left, perhaps it was determined to fulfill a lifetime's beats before the end. He did not look back as he closed the office door.

The castle was empty. He felt ghostly striding through it alone, as if he had already died. The portrait people were still missing from their frames; the whole place was eerily still, as if all its remaining lifeblood were concentrated in the Great Hall where the dead and the mourners were crammed.

Harry pulled the Invisibility Cloak over himself and descended through the floors, at last walking down the marble staircase into the entrance hall. Perhaps some tiny part of him hoped to be sensed, to be seen, to be stopped, but the Cloak was, as ever, impenetrable, perfect, and he reached the front doors easily.

Then Neville nearly walked into him. He was one half of a pair that was carrying a body in from the grounds. Harry glanced down and felt another dull blow to his stomach: Colin Creevey, though underage, must have sneaked back just as Malfoy, Crabbe, and Goyle had done. He was tiny in death.

"You know what? I can manage him alone, Neville," said Oliver Wood, and he heaved Colin over his shoulder in a fireman's lift and carried him into the Great Hall.

Neville leaned against the door frame for a moment and wiped his forehead with the back of his hand. He looked like an old man. Then he set off down the steps again into the darkness to recover more bodies.

Harry took one glance back at the entrance of the Great Hall. People were moving around, trying to comfort each other, drinking, kneeling beside the dead, but he could not see any of the people he loved, no hint of Hermione, Ron, Ginny, or any of the other Weasleys, no Luna. He felt he would have given all the time remaining to him for just one last look at them; but then, would he ever have the strength to stop looking? It was better like this.

He moved down the steps and out into the darkness. It was nearly four in the morning, and the deathly stillness of the grounds felt as though they were holding their breath, waiting to see whether he could do what he must.

Harry moved toward Neville, who was bending over another body.

"Neville."

"Blimey, Harry, you nearly gave me heart failure!"

Harry had pulled off the Cloak: The idea had come to him out of nowhere, born out of a desire to make absolutely sure.

"Where are you going, alone?" Neville asked suspiciously.

"It's all part of the plan," said Harry. "There's something I've got to do. Listen — Neville —"

"Harry!" Neville looked suddenly scared. "Harry, you're not thinking of handing yourself over?"

"No," Harry lied easily. " 'Course not . . . this is something else. But I might be out of sight for a while. You know Voldemort's snake, Neville? He's got a huge snake. . . . Calls it Nagini . . ."

"I've heard, yeah. . . . What about it?"

"It's got to be killed. Ron and Hermione know that, but just in case they —"

The awfulness of that possibility smothered him for a moment,

made it impossible to keep talking. But he pulled himself together
again: This was crucial, he must be like Dumbledore, keep a cool
head, make sure there were backups, others to carry on. Dumbledore
had died knowing that three people still knew about the Horcruxes;
now Neville would take Harry's place: There would still be three
in the secret.

"Just in case they're — busy — and you get the chance —"

"Kill the snake?"

"Kill the snake," Harry repeated.

"All right, Harry. You're okay, are you?"

"I'm fine. Thanks, Neville."

But Neville seized his wrist as Harry made to move on.

"We're all going to keep fighting, Harry. You know that?"

"Yeah, I —"

The suffocating feeling extinguished the end of the sentence; he
could not go on. Neville did not seem to find it strange. He patted
Harry on the shoulder, released him, and walked away to look for
more bodies.

Harry swung the Cloak back over himself and walked on. Someone else was moving not far away, stooping over another prone
figure on the ground. He was feet away from her when he realized
it was Ginny.

He stopped in his tracks. She was crouching over a girl who was
whispering for her mother.

"It's all right," Ginny was saying. "It's okay. We're going to get
you inside."

"But I want to go *home*," whispered the girl. "I don't want to
fight anymore!"

"I know," said Ginny, and her voice broke. "It's going to be all right."

Ripples of cold undulated over Harry's skin. He wanted to shout out to the night, he wanted Ginny to know that he was there, he wanted her to know where he was going. He wanted to be stopped, to be dragged back, to be sent back home. . . .

But he *was* home. Hogwarts was the first and best home he had known. He and Voldemort and Snape, the abandoned boys, had all found home here. . . .

Ginny was kneeling beside the injured girl now, holding her hand. With a huge effort Harry forced himself on. He thought he saw Ginny look around as he passed, and wondered whether she had sensed someone walking nearby, but he did not speak, and he did not look back.

Hagrid's hut loomed out of the darkness. There were no lights, no sound of Fang scrabbling at the door, his bark booming in welcome. All those visits to Hagrid, and the gleam of the copper kettle on the fire, and rock cakes and giant grubs, and his great bearded face, and Ron vomiting slugs, and Hermione helping him save Norbert . . .

He moved on, and now he reached the edge of the forest, and he stopped.

A swarm of dementors was gliding amongst the trees; he could feel their chill, and he was not sure he would be able to pass safely through it. He had no strength left for a Patronus. He could no longer control his own trembling. It was not, after all, so easy to die. Every second he breathed, the smell of the grass, the cool air on his face, was so precious: To think that people had years and years, time to waste, so much time it dragged, and he was clinging to each second. At the same time he thought that he would not be able to go on, and knew that he must. The long game was ended, the Snitch had been caught, it was time to leave the air. . . .

The Snitch. His nerveless fingers fumbled for a moment with the pouch at his neck and he pulled it out.

I open at the close.

Breathing fast and hard, he stared down at it. Now that he wanted time to move as slowly as possible, it seemed to have sped up, and understanding was coming so fast it seemed to have bypassed thought. This was the close. This was the moment.

He pressed the golden metal to his lips and whispered, "I am about to die."

The metal shell broke open. He lowered his shaking hand, raised Draco's wand beneath the Cloak, and murmured, *"Lumos."*

The black stone with its jagged crack running down the center sat in the two halves of the Snitch. The Resurrection Stone had cracked down the vertical line representing the Elder Wand. The triangle and circle representing the Cloak and the stone were still discernible.

And again Harry understood without having to think. It did not matter about bringing them back, for he was about to join them. He was not really fetching them: They were fetching him.

He closed his eyes and turned the stone over in his hand three times.

He knew it had happened, because he heard slight movements around him that suggested frail bodies shifting their footing on the earthy, twig-strewn ground that marked the outer edge of the forest. He opened his eyes and looked around.

They were neither ghost nor truly flesh, he could see that. They resembled most closely the Riddle that had escaped from the diary so long ago, and he had been memory made nearly solid. Less substantial than living bodies, but much more than ghosts, they moved toward him, and on each face, there was the same loving smile.

James was exactly the same height as Harry. He was wearing the clothes in which he had died, and his hair was untidy and ruffled, and his glasses were a little lopsided, like Mr. Weasley's.

Sirius was tall and handsome, and younger by far than Harry had seen him in life. He loped with an easy grace, his hands in his pockets and a grin on his face.

Lupin was younger too, and much less shabby, and his hair was thicker and darker. He looked happy to be back in this familiar place, scene of so many adolescent wanderings.

Lily's smile was widest of all. She pushed her long hair back as she drew close to him, and her green eyes, so like his, searched his face hungrily, as though she would never be able to look at him enough.

"You've been so brave."

He could not speak. His eyes feasted on her, and he thought that he would like to stand and look at her forever, and that would be enough.

"You are nearly there," said James. "Very close. We are . . . so proud of you."

"Does it hurt?"

The childish question had fallen from Harry's lips before he could stop it.

"Dying? Not at all," said Sirius. "Quicker and easier than falling asleep."

"And he will want it to be quick. He wants it over," said Lupin.

"I didn't want you to die," Harry said. These words came without his volition. "Any of you. I'm sorry —"

He addressed Lupin more than any of them, beseeching him.

"— right after you'd had your son . . . Remus, I'm sorry —"

"I am sorry too," said Lupin. "Sorry I will never know him . . . but he will know why I died and I hope he will understand. I was trying to make a world in which he could live a happier life."

A chilly breeze that seemed to emanate from the heart of the forest lifted the hair at Harry's brow. He knew that they would not tell him to go, that it would have to be his decision.

"You'll stay with me?"

"Until the very end," said James.

"They won't be able to see you?" asked Harry.

"We are part of you," said Sirius. "Invisible to anyone else."

Harry looked at his mother.

"Stay close to me," he said quietly.

And he set off. The dementors' chill did not overcome him; he passed through it with his companions, and they acted like Patronuses to him, and together they marched through the old trees that grew closely together, their branches tangled, their roots gnarled and twisted underfoot. Harry clutched the Cloak tightly around him in the darkness, traveling deeper and deeper into the forest, with no idea where exactly Voldemort was, but sure that he would find him. Beside him, making scarcely a sound, walked James, Sirius, Lupin, and Lily, and their presence was his courage, and the reason he was able to keep putting one foot in front of the other.

His body and mind felt oddly disconnected now, his limbs working without conscious instruction, as if he were passenger, not driver, in the body he was about to leave. The dead who walked beside him through the forest were much more real to him now than the living back at the castle: Ron, Hermione, Ginny, and all the others were the ones who felt like ghosts as he stumbled and slipped toward the end of his life, toward Voldemort. . . .

A thud and a whisper: Some other living creature had stirred close by. Harry stopped under the Cloak, peering around, listening, and his mother and father, Lupin and Sirius stopped too.

"Someone there," came a rough whisper close at hand. "He's got an Invisibility Cloak. Could it be — ?"

Two figures emerged from behind a nearby tree: Their wands flared, and Harry saw Yaxley and Dolohov peering into the darkness, directly at the place Harry, his mother and father and Sirius and Lupin stood. Apparently they could not see anything.

"Definitely heard something," said Yaxley. "Animal, d'you reckon?"

"That head case Hagrid kept a whole bunch of stuff in here," said Dolohov, glancing over his shoulder.

Yaxley looked down at his watch.

"Time's nearly up. Potter's had his hour. He's not coming."

"And he was sure he'd come! He won't be happy."

"Better go back," said Yaxley. "Find out what the plan is now."

He and Dolohov turned and walked deeper into the forest. Harry followed them, knowing that they would lead him exactly where he wanted to go. He glanced sideways, and his mother smiled at him, and his father nodded encouragement.

They had traveled on mere minutes when Harry saw light ahead, and Yaxley and Dolohov stepped out into a clearing that Harry

knew had been the place where the monstrous Aragog had once
lived. The remnants of his vast web were there still, but the swarm
of descendants he had spawned had been driven out by the Death
Eaters, to fight for their cause.

A fire burned in the middle of the clearing, and its flickering light
fell over a crowd of completely silent, watchful Death Eaters. Some
of them were still masked and hooded; others showed their faces.
Two giants sat on the outskirts of the group, casting massive shadows over the scene, their faces cruel, rough-hewn like rock. Harry
saw Fenrir, skulking, chewing his long nails; the great blond Rowle
was dabbing at his bleeding lip. He saw Lucius Malfoy, who looked
defeated and terrified, and Narcissa, whose eyes were sunken and
full of apprehension.

Every eye was fixed upon Voldemort, who stood with his head
bowed, and his white hands folded over the Elder Wand in front of
him. He might have been praying, or else counting silently in his
mind, and Harry, standing still on the edge of the scene, thought
absurdly of a child counting in a game of hide-and-seek. Behind
his head, still swirling and coiling, the great snake Nagini floated
in her glittering, charmed cage, like a monstrous halo.

When Dolohov and Yaxley rejoined the circle, Voldemort
looked up.

"No sign of him, my Lord," said Dolohov.

Voldemort's expression did not change. The red eyes seemed to
burn in the firelight. Slowly he drew the Elder Wand between his
long fingers.

"My Lord —"

Bellatrix had spoken: She sat closest to Voldemort, disheveled,
her face a little bloody but otherwise unharmed.

Voldemort raised his hand to silence her, and she did not speak another word, but eyed him in worshipful fascination.

"I thought he would come," said Voldemort in his high, clear voice, his eyes on the leaping flames. "I expected him to come."

Nobody spoke. They seemed as scared as Harry, whose heart was now throwing itself against his ribs as though determined to escape the body he was about to cast aside. His hands were sweating as he pulled off the Invisibility Cloak and stuffed it beneath his robes, with his wand. He did not want to be tempted to fight.

"I was, it seems . . . mistaken," said Voldemort.

"You weren't."

Harry said it as loudly as he could, with all the force he could muster: He did not want to sound afraid. The Resurrection Stone slipped from between his numb fingers, and out of the corner of his eyes he saw his parents, Sirius, and Lupin vanish as he stepped forward into the firelight. At that moment he felt that nobody mattered but Voldemort. It was just the two of them.

The illusion was gone as soon as it had come. The giants roared as the Death Eaters rose together, and there were many cries, gasps, even laughter. Voldemort had frozen where he stood, but his red eyes had found Harry, and he stared as Harry moved toward him, with nothing but the fire between them.

Then a voice yelled: "HARRY! NO!"

He turned: Hagrid was bound and trussed, tied to a tree nearby. His massive body shook the branches overhead as he struggled, desperate.

"NO! NO! HARRY, WHAT'RE YEH — ?"

"QUIET!" shouted Rowle, and with a flick of his wand Hagrid was silenced.

Bellatrix, who had leapt to her feet, was looking eagerly from Voldemort to Harry, her breast heaving. The only things that moved were the flames and the snake, coiling and uncoiling in the glittering cage behind Voldemort's head.

Harry could feel his wand against his chest, but he made no attempt to draw it. He knew that the snake was too well protected, knew that if he managed to point the wand at Nagini, fifty curses would hit him first. And still, Voldemort and Harry looked at each other, and now Voldemort tilted his head a little to the side, considering the boy standing before him, and a singularly mirthless smile curled the lipless mouth.

"Harry Potter," he said very softly. His voice might have been part of the spitting fire. "The Boy Who Lived."

None of the Death Eaters moved. They were waiting: Everything was waiting. Hagrid was struggling, and Bellatrix was panting, and Harry thought inexplicably of Ginny, and her blazing look, and the feel of her lips on his —

Voldemort had raised his wand. His head was still tilted to one side, like a curious child, wondering what would happen if he proceeded. Harry looked back into the red eyes, and wanted it to happen now, quickly, while he could still stand, before he lost control, before he betrayed fear —

He saw the mouth move and a flash of green light, and everything was gone.

KING'S CROSS

He lay facedown, listening to the silence. He was perfectly alone. Nobody was watching. Nobody else was there. He was not perfectly sure that he was there himself.

A long time later, or maybe no time at all, it came to him that he must exist, must be more than disembodied thought, because he was lying, definitely lying, on some surface. Therefore he had a sense of touch, and the thing against which he lay existed too.

Almost as soon as he had reached this conclusion, Harry became conscious that he was naked. Convinced as he was of his total solitude, this did not concern him, but it did intrigue him slightly. He wondered whether, as he could feel, he would be able to see. In opening them, he discovered that he had eyes.

He lay in a bright mist, though it was not like mist he had ever experienced before. His surroundings were not hidden by cloudy vapor; rather the cloudy vapor had not yet formed into surroundings. The floor on which he lay seemed to be white, neither warm nor cold, but simply there, a flat, blank something on which to be.

He sat up. His body appeared unscathed. He touched his face. He was not wearing glasses anymore.

Then a noise reached him through the unformed nothingness that surrounded him: the small soft thumpings of something that flapped, flailed, and struggled. It was a pitiful noise, yet also slightly indecent. He had the uncomfortable feeling that he was eavesdropping on something furtive, shameful.

For the first time, he wished he were clothed.

Barely had the wish formed in his head than robes appeared a short distance away. He took them and pulled them on: They were soft, clean, and warm. It was extraordinary how they had appeared, just like that, the moment he had wanted them. . . .

He stood up, looking around. Was he in some great Room of Requirement? The longer he looked, the more there was to see. A great domed glass roof glittered high above him in sunlight. Perhaps it was a palace. All was hushed and still, except for those odd thumping and whimpering noises coming from somewhere close by in the mist. . . .

Harry turned slowly on the spot, and his surroundings seemed to invent themselves before his eyes. A wide-open space, bright and clean, a hall larger by far than the Great Hall, with that clear, domed glass ceiling. It was quite empty. He was the only person there, except for —

He recoiled. He had spotted the thing that was making the noises. It had the form of a small, naked child, curled on the ground, its skin raw and rough, flayed-looking, and it lay shuddering under a seat where it had been left, unwanted, stuffed out of sight, struggling for breath.

He was afraid of it. Small and fragile and wounded though it was, he did not want to approach it. Nevertheless he drew slowly nearer, ready to jump back at any moment. Soon he stood near enough to touch it, yet he could not bring himself to do it. He felt like a coward. He ought to comfort it, but it repulsed him.

"You cannot help."

He spun around. Albus Dumbledore was walking toward him, sprightly and upright, wearing sweeping robes of midnight blue.

"Harry." He spread his arms wide, and his hands were both whole and white and undamaged. "You wonderful boy. You brave, brave man. Let us walk."

Stunned, Harry followed as Dumbledore strode away from where the flayed child lay whimpering, leading him to two seats that Harry had not previously noticed, set some distance away under that high, sparkling ceiling. Dumbledore sat down in one of them, and Harry fell into the other, staring at his old headmaster's face. Dumbledore's long silver hair and beard, the piercingly blue eyes behind half-moon spectacles, the crooked nose: Everything was as he had remembered it. And yet . . .

"But you're dead," said Harry.

"Oh yes," said Dumbledore matter-of-factly.

"Then . . . I'm dead too?"

"Ah," said Dumbledore, smiling still more broadly. "That is the question, isn't it? On the whole, dear boy, I think not."

They looked at each other, the old man still beaming.

"Not?" repeated Harry.

"Not," said Dumbledore.

"But . . ." Harry raised his hand instinctively toward the lightning scar. It did not seem to be there. "But I should have died — I didn't defend myself! I meant to let him kill me!"

"And that," said Dumbledore, "will, I think, have made all the difference."

Happiness seemed to radiate from Dumbledore like light, like fire: Harry had never seen the man so utterly, so palpably content.

"Explain," said Harry.

"But you already know," said Dumbledore. He twiddled his thumbs together.

"I let him kill me," said Harry. "Didn't I?"

"You did," said Dumbledore, nodding. "Go on!"

"So the part of his soul that was in me . . ."

Dumbledore nodded still more enthusiastically, urging Harry onward, a broad smile of encouragement on his face.

". . . has it gone?"

"Oh yes!" said Dumbledore. "Yes, he destroyed it. Your soul is whole, and completely your own, Harry."

"But then . . ."

Harry glanced over his shoulder to where the small, maimed creature trembled under the chair.

"What is that, Professor?"

"Something that is beyond either of our help," said Dumbledore.

"But if Voldemort used the Killing Curse," Harry started again, "and nobody died for me this time — how can I be alive?"

"I think you know," said Dumbledore. "Think back. Remember what he did, in his ignorance, in his greed and his cruelty."

Harry thought. He let his gaze drift over his surroundings. If it was indeed a palace in which they sat, it was an odd one, with chairs set in little rows and bits of railing here and there, and still, he and Dumbledore and the stunted creature under the chair were the only beings there. Then the answer rose to his lips easily, without effort.

"He took my blood," said Harry.

"Precisely!" said Dumbledore. "He took your blood and rebuilt his living body with it! Your blood in his veins, Harry, Lily's protection inside both of you! He tethered you to life while he lives!"

"I live . . . while he lives? But I thought . . . I thought it was the other way round! I thought we both had to die? Or is it the same thing?"

He was distracted by the whimpering and thumping of the agonized creature behind them and glanced back at it yet again.

"Are you sure we can't do anything?"

"There is no help possible."

"Then explain . . . more," said Harry, and Dumbledore smiled.

"You were the seventh Horcrux, Harry, the Horcrux he never meant to make. He had rendered his soul so unstable that it broke apart when he committed those acts of unspeakable evil, the murder of your parents, the attempted killing of a child. But what escaped from that room was even less than he knew. He left more than his body behind. He left part of himself latched to you, the would-be victim who had survived.

"And his knowledge remained woefully incomplete, Harry! That which Voldemort does not value, he takes no trouble to comprehend. Of house-elves and children's tales, of love, loyalty, and innocence, Voldemort knows and understands nothing. *Nothing.* That they all have a power beyond his own, a power beyond the reach of any magic, is a truth he has never grasped.

"He took your blood believing it would strengthen him. He took into his body a tiny part of the enchantment your mother laid upon you when she died for you. His body keeps her sacrifice alive, and while that enchantment survives, so do you and so does Voldemort's one last hope for himself."

Dumbledore smiled at Harry, and Harry stared at him.

"And you knew this? You knew — all along?"

"I guessed. But my guesses have usually been good," said Dumbledore happily, and they sat in silence for what seemed like a long time, while the creature behind them continued to whimper and tremble.

"There's more," said Harry. "There's more to it. Why did my wand break the wand he borrowed?"

"As to that, I cannot be sure."

"Have a guess, then," said Harry, and Dumbledore laughed.

"What you must understand, Harry, is that you and Lord Voldemort have journeyed together into realms of magic hitherto unknown and untested. But here is what I think happened, and it is unprecedented, and no wandmaker could, I think, ever have predicted it or explained it to Voldemort.

"Without meaning to, as you now know, Lord Voldemort doubled the bond between you when he returned to a human form. A part of his soul was still attached to yours, and, thinking to strengthen himself, he took a part of your mother's sacrifice into himself. If he could only have understood the precise and terrible power of that sacrifice, he would not, perhaps, have dared to touch your blood. . . . But then, if he had been able to understand, he could not be Lord Voldemort, and might never have murdered at all.

"Having ensured this two-fold connection, having wrapped your destinies together more securely than ever two wizards were joined in history, Voldemort proceeded to attack you with a wand that shared a core with yours. And now something very strange happened, as we know. The cores reacted in a way that Lord Voldemort, who never knew that your wand was twin of his, had never expected.

"He was more afraid than you were that night, Harry. You had accepted, even embraced, the possibility of death, something Lord Voldemort has never been able to do. Your courage won, your wand overpowered his. And in doing so, something happened between those wands, something that echoed the relationship between their masters.

"I believe that your wand imbibed some of the power and qualities of Voldemort's wand that night, which is to say that it contained a little of Voldemort himself. So your wand recognized him when he pursued you, recognized a man who was both kin and mortal enemy, and it regurgitated some of his own magic against him, magic much more powerful than anything Lucius's wand had ever performed. Your wand now contained the power of your enormous courage and of Voldemort's own deadly skill: What chance did that poor stick of Lucius Malfoy's stand?"

"But if my wand was so powerful, how come Hermione was able to break it?" asked Harry.

"My dear boy, its remarkable effects were directed only at Voldemort, who had tampered so ill-advisedly with the deepest laws of magic. Only toward him was that wand abnormally powerful. Otherwise it was a wand like any other . . . though a good one, I am sure," Dumbledore finished kindly.

Harry sat in thought for a long time, or perhaps seconds. It was very hard to be sure of things like time, here.

"He killed me with your wand."

"He *failed* to kill you with my wand," Dumbledore corrected Harry. "I think we can agree that you are not dead — though, of course," he added, as if fearing he had been discourteous, "I do not minimize your sufferings, which I am sure were severe."

"I feel great at the moment, though," said Harry, looking down at his clean, unblemished hands. "Where are we, exactly?"

"Well, I was going to ask you that," said Dumbledore, looking around. "Where would you say that we are?"

Until Dumbledore had asked, Harry had not known. Now, however, he found that he had an answer ready to give.

"It looks," he said slowly, "like King's Cross station. Except a lot cleaner and empty, and there are no trains as far as I can see."

"King's Cross station!" Dumbledore was chuckling immoderately. "Good gracious, really?"

"Well, where do you think we are?" asked Harry, a little defensively.

"My dear boy, I have no idea. This is, as they say, *your* party."

Harry had no idea what this meant; Dumbledore was being infuriating. He glared at him, then remembered a much more pressing question than that of their current location.

"The Deathly Hallows," he said, and he was glad to see that the words wiped the smile from Dumbledore's face.

"Ah, yes," he said. He even looked a little worried.

"Well?"

For the first time since Harry had met Dumbledore, he looked less than an old man, much less. He looked fleetingly like a small boy caught in wrongdoing.

"Can you forgive me?" he said. "Can you forgive me for not trusting you? For not telling you? Harry, I only feared that you would fail as I had failed. I only dreaded that you would make my mistakes. I crave your pardon, Harry. I have known, for some time now, that you are the better man."

"What are you talking about?" asked Harry, startled by Dumbledore's tone, by the sudden tears in his eyes.

"The Hallows, the Hallows," murmured Dumbledore. "A desperate man's dream!"

"But they're real!"

"Real, and dangerous, and a lure for fools," said Dumbledore. "And I was such a fool. But you know, don't you? I have no secrets from you anymore. You know."

"What do I know?"

Dumbledore turned his whole body to face Harry, and tears still sparkled in the brilliantly blue eyes.

"Master of death, Harry, master of Death! Was I better, ultimately, than Voldemort?"

"Of course you were," said Harry. "Of course — how can you ask that? You never killed if you could avoid it!"

"True, true," said Dumbledore, and he was like a child seeking reassurance. "Yet I too sought a way to conquer death, Harry."

"Not the way he did," said Harry. After all his anger at Dumbledore, how odd it was to sit here, beneath the high, vaulted ceiling, and defend Dumbledore from himself. "Hallows, not Horcruxes."

"Hallows," murmured Dumbledore, "not Horcruxes. Precisely."

There was a pause. The creature behind them whimpered, but Harry no longer looked around.

"Grindelwald was looking for them too?" he asked.

Dumbledore closed his eyes for a moment and nodded.

"It was the thing, above all, that drew us together," he said quietly. "Two clever, arrogant boys with a shared obsession. He wanted to come to Godric's Hollow, as I am sure you have guessed, because of the grave of Ignotus Peverell. He wanted to explore the place the third brother had died."

"So it's true?" asked Harry. "All of it? The Peverell brothers —"

"— were the three brothers of the tale," said Dumbledore, nodding. "Oh yes, I think so. Whether they met Death on a lonely road . . . I think it more likely that the Peverell brothers were simply gifted, dangerous wizards who succeeded in creating those powerful objects. The story of them being Death's own Hallows seems to me the sort of legend that might have sprung up around such creations.

"The Cloak, as you know now, traveled down through the ages, father to son, mother to daughter, right down to Ignotus's last living descendant, who was born, as Ignotus was, in the village of Godric's Hollow."

Dumbledore smiled at Harry.

"Me?"

"You. You have guessed, I know, why the Cloak was in my possession on the night your parents died. James had showed it to me just a few days previously. It explained much of his undetected wrongdoing at school! I could hardly believe what I was seeing. I asked to borrow it, to examine it. I had long since given up my dream of uniting the Hallows, but I could not resist, could not help taking a closer look. . . . It was a Cloak the likes of which I had never seen, immensely old, perfect in every respect . . . and then your father died, and I had two Hallows at last, all to myself!"

His tone was unbearably bitter.

"The Cloak wouldn't have helped them survive, though," Harry said quickly. "Voldemort knew where my mum and dad were. The Cloak couldn't have made them curse-proof."

"True," sighed Dumbledore. "True."

Harry waited, but Dumbledore did not speak, so he prompted him.

"So you'd given up looking for the Hallows when you saw the Cloak?"

"Oh yes," said Dumbledore faintly. It seemed that he forced himself to meet Harry's eyes. "You know what happened. You know. You cannot despise me more than I despise myself."

"But I don't despise you —"

"Then you should," said Dumbledore. He drew a deep breath. "You know the secret of my sister's ill health, what those Muggles did, what she became. You know how my poor father sought revenge, and paid the price, died in Azkaban. You know how my mother gave up her own life to care for Ariana.

"I resented it, Harry."

Dumbledore stated it baldly, coldly. He was looking now over the top of Harry's head, into the distance.

"I was gifted, I was brilliant. I wanted to escape. I wanted to shine. I wanted glory.

"Do not misunderstand me," he said, and pain crossed the face so that he looked ancient again. "I loved them. I loved my parents, I loved my brother and my sister, but I was selfish, Harry, more selfish than you, who are a remarkably selfless person, could possibly imagine.

"So that, when my mother died, and I was left the responsibility of a damaged sister and a wayward brother, I returned to my village in anger and bitterness. Trapped and wasted, I thought! And then, of course, he came. . . ."

Dumbledore looked directly into Harry's eyes again.

"Grindelwald. You cannot imagine how his ideas caught me, Harry, inflamed me. Muggles forced into subservience. We wizards triumphant. Grindelwald and I, the glorious young leaders of the revolution.

"Oh, I had a few scruples. I assuaged my conscience with empty words. It would all be for the greater good, and any harm done would be repaid a hundredfold in benefits for wizards. Did I know, in my heart of hearts, what Gellert Grindelwald was? I think I did, but I closed my eyes. If the plans we were making came to fruition, all my dreams would come true.

"And at the heart of our schemes, the Deathly Hallows! How they fascinated him, how they fascinated both of us! The unbeatable wand, the weapon that would lead us to power! The Resurrection Stone — to him, though I pretended not to know it, it meant an army of Inferi! To me, I confess, it meant the return of my parents, and the lifting of all responsibility from my shoulders.

"And the Cloak . . . somehow, we never discussed the Cloak much, Harry. Both of us could conceal ourselves well enough without the Cloak, the true magic of which, of course, is that it can be used to protect and shield others as well as its owner. I thought that, if we ever found it, it might be useful in hiding Ariana, but our interest in the Cloak was mainly that it completed the trio, for the legend said that the man who united all three objects would then be truly master of death, which we took to mean 'invincible.'

"Invincible masters of death, Grindelwald and Dumbledore! Two months of insanity, of cruel dreams, and neglect of the only two members of my family left to me.

"And then . . . you know what happened. Reality returned in the form of my rough, unlettered, and infinitely more admirable brother. I did not want to hear the truths he shouted at me. I did not want to hear that I could not set forth to seek Hallows with a fragile and unstable sister in tow.

"The argument became a fight. Grindelwald lost control. That which I had always sensed in him, though I pretended not to, now sprang into terrible being. And Ariana . . . after all my mother's care and caution . . . lay dead upon the floor."

Dumbledore gave a little gasp and began to cry in earnest. Harry reached out and was glad to find that he could touch him: He gripped his arm tightly and Dumbledore gradually regained control.

"Well, Grindelwald fled, as anyone but I could have predicted. He vanished, with his plans for seizing power, and his schemes for Muggle torture, and his dreams of the Deathly Hallows, dreams in which I had encouraged him and helped him. He ran, while I was left to bury my sister, and learn to live with my guilt and my terrible grief, the price of my shame.

"Years passed. There were rumors about him. They said he had procured a wand of immense power. I, meanwhile, was offered the post of Minister of Magic, not once, but several times. Naturally, I refused. I had learned that I was not to be trusted with power."

"But you'd have been better, much better, than Fudge or Scrimgeour!" burst out Harry.

"Would I?" asked Dumbledore heavily. "I am not so sure. I had proven, as a very young man, that power was my weakness and my temptation. It is a curious thing, Harry, but perhaps those who are best suited to power are those who have never sought it. Those who, like you, have leadership thrust upon them, and take up the mantle because they must, and find to their own surprise that they wear it well.

"I was safer at Hogwarts. I think I was a good teacher —"

"You were the best —"

"— you are very kind, Harry. But while I busied myself with the training of young wizards, Grindelwald was raising an army. They say he feared me, and perhaps he did, but less, I think, than I feared him.

"Oh, not death," said Dumbledore, in answer to Harry's questioning look. "Not what he could do to me magically. I knew that we were evenly matched, perhaps that I was a shade more skillful. It was the truth I feared. You see, I never knew which of us, in that last, horrific fight, had actually cast the curse that killed my sister. You may call me cowardly: You would be right. Harry, I dreaded beyond all things the knowledge that it had been I who brought about her death, not merely through my arrogance and stupidity, but that I actually struck the blow that snuffed out her life.

"I think he knew it, I think he knew what frightened me. I delayed meeting him until finally, it would have been too shameful to resist any longer. People were dying and he seemed unstoppable, and I had to do what I could.

"Well, you know what happened next. I won the duel. I won the wand."

Another silence. Harry did not ask whether Dumbledore had ever found out who struck Ariana dead. He did not want to know, and even less did he want Dumbledore to have to tell him. At last he knew what Dumbledore would have seen when he looked in the Mirror of Erised, and why Dumbledore had been so understanding of the fascination it had exercised over Harry.

They sat in silence for a long time, and the whimperings of the creature behind them barely disturbed Harry anymore.

At last he said, "Grindelwald tried to stop Voldemort going after the wand. He lied, you know, pretended he had never had it."

Dumbledore nodded, looking down at his lap, tears still glittering on the crooked nose.

"They say he showed remorse in later years, alone in his cell at Nurmengard. I hope that it is true. I would like to think he did feel the horror and shame of what he had done. Perhaps that lie to Voldemort was his attempt to make amends . . . to prevent Voldemort from taking the Hallow . . ."

". . . or maybe from breaking into your tomb?" suggested Harry, and Dumbledore dabbed his eyes.

After another short pause Harry said, "You tried to use the Resurrection Stone."

Dumbledore nodded.

"When I discovered it, after all those years, buried in the abandoned home of the Gaunts — the Hallow I had craved most of all, though in my youth I had wanted it for very different reasons — I lost my head, Harry. I quite forgot that it was now a Horcrux, that the ring was sure to carry a curse. I picked it up, and I put it on, and for a second I imagined that I was about to see Ariana, and my mother, and my father, and to tell them how very, very sorry I was. . . .

"I was such a fool, Harry. After all those years I had learned nothing. I was unworthy to unite the Deathly Hallows, I had proved it time and again, and here was final proof."

"Why?" said Harry. "It was natural! You wanted to see them again. What's wrong with that?"

"Maybe a man in a million could unite the Hallows, Harry. I was fit only to possess the meanest of them, the least extraordinary. I was fit to own the Elder Wand, and not to boast of it, and not to kill with it. I was permitted to tame and to use it, because I took it, not for gain, but to save others from it.

"But the Cloak, I took out of vain curiosity, and so it could never have worked for me as it works for you, its true owner. The stone I would have used in an attempt to drag back those who are at peace, rather than to enable my self-sacrifice, as you did. You are the worthy possessor of the Hallows."

Dumbledore patted Harry's hand, and Harry looked up at the old man and smiled; he could not help himself. How could he remain angry with Dumbledore now?

"Why did you have to make it so difficult?"

Dumbledore's smile was tremulous.

"I am afraid I counted on Miss Granger to slow you up, Harry. I was afraid that your hot head might dominate your good heart. I was scared that, if presented outright with the facts about those tempting objects, you might seize the Hallows as I did, at the wrong time, for the wrong reasons. If you laid hands on them, I wanted you to possess them safely. You are the true master of death, because the true master does not seek to run away from Death. He accepts that he must die, and understands that there are far, far worse things in the living world than dying."

"And Voldemort never knew about the Hallows?"

"I do not think so, because he did not recognize the Resurrection Stone he turned into a Horcrux. But even if he had known about them, Harry, I doubt that he would have been interested in any except the first. He would not think that he needed the Cloak, and as for the stone, whom would he want to bring back from the dead? He fears the dead. He does not love."

"But you expected him to go after the wand?"

"I have been sure that he would try, ever since your wand beat Voldemort's in the graveyard of Little Hangleton. At first, he was afraid that you had conquered him by superior skill. Once he had kidnapped Ollivander, however, he discovered the existence of the twin cores. He thought that explained everything. Yet the borrowed wand did no better against yours! So Voldemort, instead of asking himself what quality it was in you that had made your wand so strong, what gift you possessed that he did not, naturally set out to find the one wand that, they said, would beat any other. For him, the Elder Wand has become an obsession to rival his obsession with you. He believes that the Elder Wand removes his last weakness and makes him truly invincible. Poor Severus . . ."

"If you planned your death with Snape, you meant him to end up with the Elder Wand, didn't you?"

"I admit that was my intention," said Dumbledore, "but it did not work as I intended, did it?"

"No," said Harry. "That bit didn't work out."

The creature behind them jerked and moaned, and Harry and Dumbledore sat without talking for the longest time yet. The realization of what would happen next settled gradually over Harry in the long minutes, like softly falling snow.

"I've got to go back, haven't I?"

"That is up to you."

"I've got a choice?"

"Oh yes." Dumbledore smiled at him. "We are in King's Cross, you say? I think that if you decided not to go back, you would be able to . . . let's say . . . board a train."

"And where would it take me?"

"On," said Dumbledore simply.

Silence again.

"Voldemort's got the Elder Wand."

"True. Voldemort has the Elder Wand."

"But you want me to go back?"

"I think," said Dumbledore, "that if you choose to return, there is a chance that he may be finished for good. I cannot promise it. But I know this, Harry, that you have less to fear from returning here than he does."

Harry glanced again at the raw-looking thing that trembled and choked in the shadow beneath the distant chair.

"Do not pity the dead, Harry. Pity the living, and, above all, those who live without love. By returning, you may ensure that fewer souls are maimed, fewer families are torn apart. If that seems to you a worthy goal, then we say good-bye for the present."

Harry nodded and sighed. Leaving this place would not be nearly as hard as walking into the forest had been, but it was warm and light and peaceful here, and he knew that he was heading back to pain and the fear of more loss. He stood up, and Dumbledore did the same, and they looked for a long moment into each other's faces.

"Tell me one last thing," said Harry. "Is this real? Or has this been happening inside my head?"

Dumbledore beamed at him, and his voice sounded loud and strong in Harry's ears even though the bright mist was descending again, obscuring his figure.

"Of course it is happening inside your head, Harry, but why on earth should that mean that it is not real?"

THE FLAW IN THE PLAN

He was lying facedown on the ground again. The smell of the forest filled his nostrils. He could feel the cold hard ground beneath his cheek, and the hinge of his glasses, which had been knocked sideways by the fall, cutting into his temple. Every inch of him ached, and the place where the Killing Curse had hit him felt like the bruise of an iron-clad punch. He did not stir, but remained exactly where he had fallen, with his left arm bent out at an awkward angle and his mouth gaping.

He had expected to hear cheers of triumph and jubilation at his death, but instead hurried footsteps, whispers, and solicitous murmurs filled the air.

"My Lord . . . *my Lord . . .*"

It was Bellatrix's voice, and she spoke as if to a lover. Harry did not dare open his eyes, but allowed his other senses to explore his predicament. He knew that his wand was still stowed beneath his robes because he could feel it pressed between his chest and the ground. A slight cushioning effect in the area of his stomach told him that the Invisibility Cloak was also there, stuffed out of sight.

"My Lord . . ."

"That will do," said Voldemort's voice.

More footsteps: Several people were backing away from the same spot. Desperate to see what was happening and why, Harry opened his eyes by a millimeter.

Voldemort seemed to be getting to his feet. Various Death Eaters were hurrying away from him, returning to the crowd lining the clearing. Bellatrix alone remained behind, kneeling beside Voldemort.

Harry closed his eyes again and considered what he had seen. The Death Eaters had been huddled around Voldemort, who seemed to have fallen to the ground. Something had happened when he had hit Harry with the Killing Curse. Had Voldemort too collapsed? It seemed like it. And both of them had fallen briefly unconscious and both of them had now returned. . . .

"My Lord, let me —"

"I do not require assistance," said Voldemort coldly, and though he could not see it, Harry pictured Bellatrix withdrawing a helpful hand. "The boy . . . Is he dead?"

There was complete silence in the clearing. Nobody approached Harry, but he felt their concentrated gaze; it seemed to press him harder into the ground, and he was terrified a finger or an eyelid might twitch.

"You," said Voldemort, and there was a bang and a small shriek of pain. "Examine him. Tell me whether he is dead."

Harry did not know who had been sent to verify. He could only lie there, with his heart thumping traitorously, and wait to be examined, but at the same time noting, small comfort though it was, that Voldemort was wary of approaching him, that Voldemort suspected that all had not gone to plan. . . .

Hands, softer than he had been expecting, touched Harry's face, pulled back an eyelid, crept beneath his shirt, down to his chest, and felt his heart. He could hear the woman's fast breathing, her long hair tickled his face. He knew that she could feel the steady pounding of life against his ribs.

"Is Draco alive? Is he in the castle?"

The whisper was barely audible; her lips were an inch from his ear, her head bent so low that her long hair shielded his face from the onlookers.

"Yes," he breathed back.

He felt the hand on his chest contract; her nails pierced him. Then it was withdrawn. She had sat up.

"He is dead!" Narcissa Malfoy called to the watchers.

And now they shouted, now they yelled in triumph and stamped their feet, and through his eyelids, Harry saw bursts of red and silver light shoot into the air in celebration.

Still feigning death on the ground, he understood. Narcissa knew that the only way she would be permitted to enter Hogwarts, and find her son, was as part of the conquering army. She no longer cared whether Voldemort won.

"You see?" screeched Voldemort over the tumult. "Harry Potter is dead by my hand, and no man alive can threaten me now! Watch! *Crucio!*"

Harry had been expecting it, knew his body would not be allowed to remain unsullied upon the forest floor; it must be subjected to humiliation to prove Voldemort's victory. He was lifted into the air, and it took all his determination to remain limp, yet the pain he expected did not come. He was thrown once, twice, three times into the air: His glasses flew off and he felt his wand slide a little beneath his robes, but he kept himself floppy and lifeless, and when he fell to the ground for the last time, the clearing echoed with jeers and shrieks of laughter.

"Now," said Voldemort, "we go to the castle, and show them what has become of their hero. Who shall drag the body? No — Wait —"

There was a fresh outbreak of laughter, and after a few moments Harry felt the ground trembling beneath him.

"You carry him," Voldemort said. "He will be nice and visible in your arms, will he not? Pick up your little friend, Hagrid. And the glasses — put on the glasses — he must be recognizable —"

Someone slammed Harry's glasses back onto his face with deliberate force, but the enormous hands that lifted him into the air were exceedingly gentle. Harry could feel Hagrid's arms trembling with the force of his heaving sobs; great tears splashed down upon him as Hagrid cradled Harry in his arms, and Harry did not dare, by movement or word, to intimate to Hagrid that all was not, yet, lost.

"Move," said Voldemort, and Hagrid stumbled forward, forcing his way through the close-growing trees, back through the forest. Branches caught at Harry's hair and robes, but he lay quiescent, his mouth lolling open, his eyes shut, and in the darkness, while the Death Eaters crowed all around them, and while Hagrid sobbed blindly, nobody looked to see whether a pulse beat in the exposed neck of Harry Potter. . . .

The two giants crashed along behind the Death Eaters; Harry could hear trees creaking and falling as they passed; they made so much din that birds rose shrieking into the sky, and even the jeers of the Death Eaters were drowned. The victorious procession marched on toward the open ground, and after a while Harry could tell, by the lightening of the darkness through his closed eyelids, that the trees were beginning to thin.

"BANE!"

Hagrid's unexpected bellow nearly forced Harry's eyes open. "Happy now, are yeh, that yeh didn' fight, yeh cowardly bunch o' nags? Are yeh happy Harry Potter's — d-dead . . . ?"

Hagrid could not continue, but broke down in fresh tears. Harry wondered how many centaurs were watching their procession pass; he dared not open his eyes to look. Some of the Death Eaters called insults at the centaurs as they left them behind. A little later, Harry sensed, by a freshening of the air, that they had reached the edge of the forest.

"Stop."

Harry thought that Hagrid must have been forced to obey Voldemort's command, because he lurched a little. And now a chill settled over them where they stood, and Harry heard the rasping breath of the dementors that patrolled the outer trees. They would not affect him now. The fact of his own survival burned inside him, a talisman against them, as though his father's stag kept guardian in his heart.

Someone passed close by Harry, and he knew that it was Voldemort himself because he spoke a moment later, his voice magically magnified so that it swelled through the grounds, crashing upon Harry's eardrums.

"Harry Potter is dead. He was killed as he ran away, trying to save himself while you lay down your lives for him. We bring you his body as proof that your hero is gone.

"The battle is won. You have lost half of your fighters. My Death Eaters outnumber you, and the Boy Who Lived is finished. There must be no more war. Anyone who continues to resist, man, woman, or child, will be slaughtered, as will every member of their family. Come out of the castle now, kneel before me, and you shall be spared. Your parents and children, your brothers and sisters will live and be forgiven, and you will join me in the new world we shall build together."

There was silence in the grounds and from the castle. Voldemort was so close to him that Harry did not dare open his eyes again.

"Come," said Voldemort, and Harry heard him move ahead, and Hagrid was forced to follow. Now Harry opened his eyes a fraction, and saw Voldemort striding in front of them, wearing the great snake Nagini around his shoulders, now free of her enchanted cage. But Harry had no possibility of extracting the wand concealed under his robes without being noticed by the Death Eaters, who marched on either side of them through the slowly lightening darkness. . . .

"Harry," sobbed Hagrid. "Oh, Harry . . . Harry . . ."

Harry shut his eyes tight again. He knew that they were approaching the castle and strained his ears to distinguish, above the gleeful voices of the Death Eaters and their tramping footsteps, signs of life from those within.

"Stop."

The Death Eaters came to a halt: Harry heard them spreading out in a line facing the open front doors of the school. He could see, even through his closed lids, the reddish glow that meant light streamed upon him from the entrance hall. He waited. Any moment, the people for whom he had tried to die would see him, lying apparently dead, in Hagrid's arms.

"NO!"

The scream was the more terrible because he had never expected or dreamed that Professor McGonagall could make such a sound. He heard another woman laughing nearby, and knew that Bellatrix gloried in McGonagall's despair. He squinted again for a single second and saw the open doorway filling with people, as the survivors of the battle came out onto the front steps to face their vanquishers and see the truth of Harry's death for themselves. He saw Voldemort standing a little in front of him, stroking Nagini's head with a single white finger. He closed his eyes again.

"No!"

"No!"

"Harry! HARRY!"

Ron's, Hermione's, and Ginny's voices were worse than McGonagall's; Harry wanted nothing more than to call back, yet he made himself lie silent, and their cries acted like a trigger; the crowd of survivors took up the cause, screaming and yelling abuse at the Death Eaters, until —

"SILENCE!" cried Voldemort, and there was a bang and a flash of bright light, and silence was forced upon them all. "It is over! Set him down, Hagrid, at my feet, where he belongs!"

Harry felt himself lowered onto the grass.

"You see?" said Voldemort, and Harry felt him striding backward and forward right beside the place where he lay. "Harry Potter is dead! Do you understand now, deluded ones? He was nothing, ever, but a boy who relied on others to sacrifice themselves for him!"

"He beat you!" yelled Ron, and the charm broke, and the defenders of Hogwarts were shouting and screaming again until a second, more powerful bang extinguished their voices once more.

"He was killed while trying to sneak out of the castle grounds," said Voldemort, and there was relish in his voice for the lie, "killed while trying to save himself —"

But Voldemort broke off: Harry heard a scuffle and a shout, then another bang, a flash of light, and a grunt of pain; he opened his eyes an infinitesimal amount. Someone had broken free of the crowd and charged at Voldemort: Harry saw the figure hit the ground, Disarmed, Voldemort throwing the challenger's wand aside and laughing.

"And who is this?" he said in his soft snake's hiss. "Who has volunteered to demonstrate what happens to those who continue to fight when the battle is lost?"

Bellatrix gave a delighted laugh.

"It is Neville Longbottom, my Lord! The boy who has been giving the Carrows so much trouble! The son of the Aurors, remember?"

"Ah, yes, I remember," said Voldemort, looking down at Neville, who was struggling back to his feet, unarmed and unprotected, standing in the no-man's-land between the survivors and the Death Eaters. "But you are a pureblood, aren't you, my brave boy?" Voldemort asked Neville, who stood facing him, his empty hands curled in fists.

"So what if I am?" said Neville loudly.

"You show spirit and bravery, and you come of noble stock. You will make a very valuable Death Eater. We need your kind, Neville Longbottom."

"I'll join you when hell freezes over," said Neville. "Dumbledore's Army!" he shouted, and there was an answering cheer from the crowd, whom Voldemort's Silencing Charms seemed unable to hold.

"Very well," said Voldemort, and Harry heard more danger in the silkiness of his voice than in the most powerful curse. "If that is your choice, Longbottom, we revert to the original plan. On your head," he said quietly, "be it."

Still watching through his lashes, Harry saw Voldemort wave his wand. Seconds later, out of one of the castle's shattered windows, something that looked like a misshapen bird flew through the half light and landed in Voldemort's hand. He shook the mildewed object by its pointed end and it dangled, empty and ragged: the Sorting Hat.

"There will be no more Sorting at Hogwarts School," said Voldemort. "There will be no more Houses. The emblem, shield, and colors of my noble ancestor, Salazar Slytherin, will suffice for everyone. Won't they, Neville Longbottom?"

He pointed his wand at Neville, who grew rigid and still, then forced the hat onto Neville's head, so that it slipped down below his eyes. There were movements from the watching crowd in front of the castle, and as one, the Death Eaters raised their wands, holding the fighters of Hogwarts at bay.

"Neville here is now going to demonstrate what happens to anyone foolish enough to continue to oppose me," said Voldemort, and with a flick of his wand, he caused the Sorting Hat to burst into flames.

Screams split the dawn, and Neville was aflame, rooted to the spot, unable to move, and Harry could not bear it: He must act —

And then many things happened at the same moment.

They heard uproar from the distant boundary of the school as what sounded like hundreds of people came swarming over the out-of-sight walls and pelted toward the castle, uttering loud war cries.

At the same time, Grawp came lumbering around the side of the castle and yelled, "HAGGER!" His cry was answered by roars from Voldemort's giants: They ran at Grawp like bull elephants, making the earth quake. Then came hooves and the twangs of bows, and arrows were suddenly falling amongst the Death Eaters, who broke ranks, shouting their surprise. Harry pulled the Invisibility Cloak from inside his robes, swung it over himself, and sprang to his feet, as Neville moved too.

In one swift, fluid motion, Neville broke free of the Body-Bind Curse upon him; the flaming hat fell off him and he drew from its depths something silver, with a glittering, rubied handle —

The slash of the silver blade could not be heard over the roar of the oncoming crowd or the sounds of the clashing giants or of the stampeding centaurs, and yet it seemed to draw every eye. With a single stroke Neville sliced off the great snake's head, which spun high into the air, gleaming in the light flooding from the entrance hall, and Voldemort's mouth was open in a scream of fury that nobody could hear, and the snake's body thudded to the ground at his feet —

Hidden beneath the Invisibility Cloak, Harry cast a Shield Charm between Neville and Voldemort before the latter could raise his wand. Then, over the screams and the roars and the thunderous stamps of the battling giants, Hagrid's yell came loudest of all.

"HARRY!" Hagrid shouted. "HARRY — WHERE'S HARRY?"

Chaos reigned. The charging centaurs were scattering the Death Eaters, everyone was fleeing the giants' stamping feet, and nearer and nearer thundered the reinforcements that had come from who knew where; Harry saw great winged creatures soaring around the heads of Voldemort's giants, thestrals and Buckbeak the hippogriff scratching at their eyes while Grawp punched and pummeled them; and now the wizards, defenders of Hogwarts and Death Eaters alike, were being forced back into the castle. Harry was shooting jinxes and curses at any Death Eater he could see, and they crumpled, not knowing what or who had hit them, and their bodies were trampled by the retreating crowd.

Still hidden beneath the Invisibility Cloak, Harry was buffeted into the entrance hall: He was searching for Voldemort and saw him across the room, firing spells from his wand as he backed into the Great Hall, still screaming instructions to his followers as he sent curses flying left and right; Harry cast more Shield Charms, and Voldemort's would-be victims, Seamus Finnigan and Hannah Abbott, darted past him into the Great Hall, where they joined the fight already flourishing inside it.

And now there were more, even more people storming up the front steps, and Harry saw Charlie Weasley overtaking Horace Slughorn, who was still wearing his emerald pajamas. They seemed to have returned at the head of what looked like the families and friends of every Hogwarts student who had remained to fight, along with the shopkeepers and homeowners of Hogsmeade. The centaurs Bane, Ronan, and Magorian burst into the hall with a great clatter of hooves, as behind Harry the door that led to the kitchens was blasted off its hinges.

The house-elves of Hogwarts swarmed into the entrance hall, screaming and waving carving knives and cleavers, and at their head, the locket of Regulus Black bouncing on his chest, was Kreacher, his bullfrog's voice audible even above this din: "Fight! Fight! Fight for my Master, defender of house-elves! Fight the Dark Lord, in the name of brave Regulus! Fight!"

They were hacking and stabbing at the ankles and shins of Death Eaters, their tiny faces alive with malice, and everywhere Harry looked Death Eaters were folding under sheer weight of numbers, overcome by spells, dragging arrows from wounds, stabbed in the leg by elves, or else simply attempting to escape, but swallowed by the oncoming horde.

But it was not over yet: Harry sped between duelers, past struggling prisoners, and into the Great Hall.

Voldemort was in the center of the battle, and he was striking and smiting all within reach. Harry could not get a clear shot, but fought his way nearer, still invisible, and the Great Hall became more and more crowded as everyone who could walk forced their way inside.

Harry saw Yaxley slammed to the floor by George and Lee Jordan, saw Dolohov fall with a scream at Flitwick's hands, saw Walden Macnair thrown across the room by Hagrid, hit the stone wall opposite, and slide unconscious to the ground. He saw Ron and Neville bringing down Fenrir Greyback, Aberforth Stunning Rookwood, Arthur and Percy flooring Thicknesse, and Lucius and Narcissa Malfoy running through the crowd, not even attempting to fight, screaming for their son.

Voldemort was now dueling McGonagall, Slughorn, and Kingsley all at once, and there was cold hatred in his face as they wove and ducked around him, unable to finish him —

Bellatrix was still fighting too, fifty yards away from Voldemort, and like her master she dueled three at once: Hermione, Ginny, and Luna, all battling their hardest, but Bellatrix was equal to them, and Harry's attention was diverted as a Killing Curse shot so close to Ginny that she missed death by an inch —

He changed course, running at Bellatrix rather than Voldemort, but before he had gone a few steps he was knocked sideways.

"NOT MY DAUGHTER, YOU BITCH!"

Mrs. Weasley threw off her cloak as she ran, freeing her arms. Bellatrix spun on the spot, roaring with laughter at the sight of her new challenger.

"OUT OF MY WAY!" shouted Mrs. Weasley to the three girls, and with a swipe of her wand she began to duel. Harry watched with terror and elation as Molly Weasley's wand slashed and twirled, and Bellatrix Lestrange's smile faltered and became a snarl. Jets of light flew from both wands, the floor around the witches' feet became hot and cracked; both women were fighting to kill.

"No!" Mrs. Weasley cried as a few students ran forward, trying to come to her aid. "Get back! *Get back!* She is mine!"

Hundreds of people now lined the walls, watching the two fights, Voldemort and his three opponents, Bellatrix and Molly, and Harry stood, invisible, torn between both, wanting to attack and yet to protect, unable to be sure that he would not hit the innocent.

"What will happen to your children when I've killed you?" taunted Bellatrix, as mad as her master, capering as Molly's curses danced around her. "When Mummy's gone the same way as Freddie?"

"You — will — never — touch — our — children — again!" screamed Mrs. Weasley.

Bellatrix laughed, the same exhilarated laugh her cousin Sirius had given as he toppled backward through the veil, and suddenly Harry knew what was going to happen before it did.

Molly's curse soared beneath Bellatrix's outstretched arm and hit her squarely in the chest, directly over her heart.

Bellatrix's gloating smile froze, her eyes seemed to bulge: For the tiniest space of time she knew what had happened, and then she toppled, and the watching crowd roared, and Voldemort screamed.

Harry felt as though he turned in slow motion; he saw McGonagall, Kingsley, and Slughorn blasted backward, flailing and writhing through the air, as Voldemort's fury at the fall of his last, best lieutenant exploded with the force of a bomb. Voldemort raised his wand and directed it at Molly Weasley.

"Protego!" roared Harry, and the Shield Charm expanded in the middle of the Hall, and Voldemort stared around for the source as Harry pulled off the Invisibility Cloak at last.

The yell of shock, the cheers, the screams on every side of "Harry!" "HE'S ALIVE!" were stifled at once. The crowd was afraid, and silence fell abruptly and completely as Voldemort and Harry looked at each other, and began, at the same moment, to circle each other.

"I don't want anyone else to try to help," Harry said loudly, and in the total silence his voice carried like a trumpet call. "It's got to be like this. It's got to be me."

Voldemort hissed.

"Potter doesn't mean that," he said, his red eyes wide. "That isn't how he works, is it? Who are you going to use as a shield today, Potter?"

"Nobody," said Harry simply. "There are no more Horcruxes. It's just you and me. Neither can live while the other survives, and one of us is about to leave for good. . . ."

"One of us?" jeered Voldemort, and his whole body was taut and his red eyes stared, a snake that was about to strike. "You think it will be you, do you, the boy who has survived by accident, and because Dumbledore was pulling the strings?"

"Accident, was it, when my mother died to save me?" asked Harry. They were still moving sideways, both of them, in that perfect circle, maintaining the same distance from each other, and for Harry no face existed but Voldemort's. "Accident, when I decided to fight in that graveyard? Accident, that I didn't defend myself tonight, and still survived, and returned to fight again?"

"Accidents!" screamed Voldemort, but still he did not strike, and the watching crowd was frozen as if Petrified, and of the hundreds in the Hall, nobody seemed to breathe but they two. "Accident and chance and the fact that you crouched and sniveled behind the skirts of greater men and women, and permitted me to kill them for you!"

"You won't be killing anyone else tonight," said Harry as they circled, and stared into each other's eyes, green into red. "You won't be able to kill any of them ever again. Don't you get it? I was ready to die to stop you from hurting these people —"

"But you did not!"

"— I meant to, and that's what did it. I've done what my mother did. They're protected from you. Haven't you noticed how none of the spells you put on them are binding? You can't torture them. You can't touch them. You don't learn from your mistakes, Riddle, do you?"

"You dare —"

"Yes, I dare," said Harry. "I know things you don't know, Tom Riddle. I know lots of important things that you don't. Want to hear some, before you make another big mistake?"

Voldemort did not speak, but prowled in a circle, and Harry knew that he kept him temporarily mesmerized and at bay, held back by the faintest possibility that Harry might indeed know a final secret. . . .

"Is it love again?" said Voldemort, his snake's face jeering. "Dumbledore's favorite solution, *love,* which he claimed conquered death, though love did not stop him falling from the tower and breaking like an old waxwork? *Love,* which did not prevent me stamping out your Mudblood mother like a cockroach, Potter — and nobody seems to love you enough to run forward this time and take my curse. So what will stop you dying now when I strike?"

"Just one thing," said Harry, and still they circled each other, wrapped in each other, held apart by nothing but the last secret.

"If it is not love that will save you this time," said Voldemort, "you must believe that you have magic that I do not, or else a weapon more powerful than mine?"

"I believe both," said Harry, and he saw shock flit across the snakelike face, though it was instantly dispelled; Voldemort began to laugh, and the sound was more frightening than his screams; humorless and insane, it echoed around the silent Hall.

"You think *you* know more magic than I do?" he said. "Than *I,* than Lord Voldemort, who has performed magic that Dumbledore himself never dreamed of?"

"Oh, he dreamed of it," said Harry, "but he knew more than you, knew enough not to do what you've done."

"You mean he was weak!" screamed Voldemort. "Too weak to dare, too weak to take what might have been his, what will be mine!"

"No, he was cleverer than you," said Harry, "a better wizard, a better man."

"I brought about the death of Albus Dumbledore!"

"You thought you did," said Harry, "but you were wrong."

For the first time, the watching crowd stirred as the hundreds of people around the walls drew breath as one.

"Dumbledore is dead!" Voldemort hurled the words at Harry as though they would cause him unendurable pain. "His body decays in the marble tomb in the grounds of this castle, I have seen it, Potter, and he will not return!"

"Yes, Dumbledore's dead," said Harry calmly, "but you didn't have him killed. He chose his own manner of dying, chose it months before he died, arranged the whole thing with the man you thought was your servant."

"What childish dream is this?" said Voldemort, but still he did not strike, and his red eyes did not waver from Harry's.

"Severus Snape wasn't yours," said Harry. "Snape was Dumbledore's, Dumbledore's from the moment you started hunting down my mother. And you never realized it, because of the thing you can't understand. You never saw Snape cast a Patronus, did you, Riddle?"

Voldemort did not answer. They continued to circle each other like wolves about to tear each other apart.

"Snape's Patronus was a doe," said Harry, "the same as my mother's, because he loved her for nearly all of his life, from the time when they were children. You should have realized," he said as he saw Voldemort's nostrils flare, "he asked you to spare her life, didn't he?"

"He desired her, that was all," sneered Voldemort, "but when she had gone, he agreed that there were other women, and of purer blood, worthier of him —"

"Of course he told you that," said Harry, "but he was Dumbledore's spy from the moment you threatened her, and he's been working against you ever since! Dumbledore was already dying when Snape finished him!"

"It matters not!" shrieked Voldemort, who had followed every word with rapt attention, but now let out a cackle of mad laughter. "It matters not whether Snape was mine or Dumbledore's, or what petty obstacles they tried to put in my path! I crushed them as I crushed your mother, Snape's supposed great *love*! Oh, but it all makes sense, Potter, and in ways that you do not understand!

"Dumbledore was trying to keep the Elder Wand from me! He intended that Snape should be the true master of the wand! But I got there ahead of you, little boy — I reached the wand before you could get your hands on it, I understood the truth before you caught up. I killed Severus Snape three hours ago, and the Elder Wand, the Deathstick, the Wand of Destiny is truly mine! Dumbledore's last plan went wrong, Harry Potter!"

"Yeah, it did," said Harry. "You're right. But before you try to kill me, I'd advise you to think about what you've done. . . . Think, and try for some remorse, Riddle. . . ."

"What is this?"

Of all the things that Harry had said to him, beyond any revelation or taunt, nothing had shocked Voldemort like this. Harry saw his pupils contract to thin slits, saw the skin around his eyes whiten.

"It's your one last chance," said Harry, "it's all you've got left. . . . I've seen what you'll be otherwise. . . . Be a man . . . try . . . Try for some remorse. . . ."

"You dare — ?" said Voldemort again.

"Yes, I dare," said Harry, "because Dumbledore's last plan hasn't backfired on me at all. It's backfired on you, Riddle."

Voldemort's hand was trembling on the Elder Wand, and Harry gripped Draco's very tightly. The moment, he knew, was seconds away.

"That wand still isn't working properly for you because you murdered the wrong person. Severus Snape was never the true master of the Elder Wand. He never defeated Dumbledore."

"He killed —"

"Aren't you listening? *Snape never beat Dumbledore!* Dumbledore's death was planned between them! Dumbledore intended to die undefeated, the wand's last true master! If all had gone as planned, the wand's power would have died with him, because it had never been won from him!"

"But then, Potter, Dumbledore as good as gave me the wand!" Voldemort's voice shook with malicious pleasure. "I stole the wand from its last master's tomb! I removed it against its last master's wishes! Its power is mine!"

"You still don't get it, Riddle, do you? Possessing the wand isn't enough! Holding it, using it, doesn't make it really yours. Didn't you listen to Ollivander? *The wand chooses the wizard.* . . . The Elder Wand recognized a new master before Dumbledore died, someone who never even laid a hand on it. The new master removed the wand from Dumbledore against his will, never realizing exactly what he had done, or that the world's most dangerous wand had given him its allegiance. . . ."

Voldemort's chest rose and fell rapidly, and Harry could feel the curse coming, feel it building inside the wand pointed at his face.

"The true master of the Elder Wand was Draco Malfoy."

Blank shock showed in Voldemort's face for a moment, but then it was gone.

"But what does it matter?" he said softly. "Even if you are right, Potter, it makes no difference to you and me. You no longer have the phoenix wand: We duel on skill alone . . . and after I have killed you, I can attend to Draco Malfoy. . . ."

"But you're too late," said Harry. "You've missed your chance. I got there first. I overpowered Draco weeks ago. I took this wand from him."

Harry twitched the hawthorn wand, and he felt the eyes of everyone in the Hall upon it.

"So it all comes down to this, doesn't it?" whispered Harry. "Does the wand in your hand know its last master was Disarmed? Because if it does . . . I am the true master of the Elder Wand."

A red-gold glow burst suddenly across the enchanted sky above them as an edge of dazzling sun appeared over the sill of the nearest window. The light hit both of their faces at the same time, so that Voldemort's was suddenly a flaming blur. Harry heard the high voice shriek as he too yelled his best hope to the heavens, pointing Draco's wand:

"Avada Kedavra!"

"Expelliarmus!"

The bang was like a cannon blast, and the golden flames that erupted between them, at the dead center of the circle they had been treading, marked the point where the spells collided. Harry saw Voldemort's green jet meet his own spell, saw the Elder Wand fly high, dark against the sunrise, spinning across the enchanted ceiling like the head of Nagini, spinning through the air toward the master it would not kill, who had come to take full possession of it at last. And Harry, with the unerring skill of the Seeker, caught the wand in his free hand as Voldemort fell backward, arms splayed, the slit pupils of the scarlet eyes rolling upward. Tom Riddle hit the floor with a mundane finality, his body feeble and shrunken, the white hands empty, the snakelike face vacant and unknowing. Voldemort was dead, killed by his own rebounding curse, and Harry stood with two wands in his hand, staring down at his enemy's shell.

One shivering second of silence, the shock of the moment suspended: and then the tumult broke around Harry as the screams and the cheers and the roars of the watchers rent the air. The fierce new sun dazzled the windows as they thundered toward him, and the first to reach him were Ron and Hermione, and it was their arms that were wrapped around him, their incomprehensible shouts that deafened him. Then Ginny, Neville, and Luna were there, and then all the Weasleys and Hagrid, and Kingsley and McGonagall and Flitwick and Sprout, and Harry could not hear a word that anyone was shouting, nor tell whose hands were seizing him, pulling him, trying to hug some part of him, hundreds of them pressing in, all of them determined to touch the Boy Who Lived, the reason it was over at last —

The sun rose steadily over Hogwarts, and the Great Hall blazed with life and light. Harry was an indispensable part of the mingled outpourings of jubilation and mourning, of grief and celebration. They wanted him there with them, their leader and symbol, their savior and their guide, and that he had not slept, that he craved the company of only a few of them, seemed to occur to no one. He must speak to the bereaved, clasp their hands, witness their tears, receive their thanks, hear the news now creeping in from every quarter as the morning drew on; that the Imperiused up and down the country had come back to themselves, that Death Eaters were fleeing or else being captured, that the innocent of Azkaban were being released at that very moment, and that Kingsley Shacklebolt had been named temporary Minister of Magic. . . .

They moved Voldemort's body and laid it in a chamber off the Hall, away from the bodies of Fred, Tonks, Lupin, Colin Creevey, and fifty others who had died fighting him. McGonagall had replaced the House tables, but nobody was sitting according to House anymore: All were jumbled together, teachers and pupils, ghosts and parents, centaurs and house-elves, and Firenze lay recovering in a corner, and Grawp peered in through a smashed window, and people were throwing food into his laughing mouth. After a while, exhausted and drained, Harry found himself sitting on a bench beside Luna.

"I'd want some peace and quiet, if it were me," she said.

"I'd love some," he replied.

"I'll distract them all," she said. "Use your Cloak."

And before he could say a word she had cried, "Oooh, look, a Blibbering Humdinger!" and pointed out of the window. Everyone who heard looked around, and Harry slid the Cloak up over himself, and got to his feet.

Now he could move through the Hall without interference. He spotted Ginny two tables away; she was sitting with her head on her mother's shoulder: There would be time to talk later, hours and days and maybe years in which to talk. He saw Neville, the sword of Gryffindor lying beside his plate as he ate, surrounded by a knot of fervent admirers. Along the aisle between the tables he walked, and he spotted the three Malfoys, huddled together as though unsure whether or not they were supposed to be there, but nobody was paying them any attention. Everywhere he looked he saw families reunited, and finally, he saw the two whose company he craved most.

"It's me," he muttered, crouching down between them. "Will you come with me?"

They stood up at once, and together he, Ron, and Hermione left the Great Hall. Great chunks were missing from the marble staircase, part of the balustrade gone, and rubble and bloodstains occurred every few steps as they climbed.

Somewhere in the distance they could hear Peeves zooming through the corridors singing a victory song of his own composition:

> *We did it, we bashed them, wee Potter's the one,*
> *And Voldy's gone moldy, so now let's have fun!*

"Really gives a feeling for the scope and tragedy of the thing, doesn't it?" said Ron, pushing open a door to let Harry and Hermione through.

Happiness would come, Harry thought, but at the moment it was muffled by exhaustion, and the pain of losing Fred and Lupin and Tonks pierced him like a physical wound every few steps. Most of all he felt the most stupendous relief, and a longing to sleep. But first he owed an explanation to Ron and Hermione, who had stuck with him for so long, and who deserved the truth. Painstakingly he recounted what he had seen in the Pensieve and what had happened in the forest, and they had not even begun to express all their shock and amazement when at last they arrived at the place to which they had been walking, though none of them had mentioned their destination.

Since he had last seen it, the gargoyle guarding the entrance to the headmaster's study had been knocked aside; it stood lopsided, looking a little punch-drunk, and Harry wondered whether it would be able to distinguish passwords anymore.

"Can we go up?" he asked the gargoyle.

"Feel free," groaned the statue.

They clambered over him and onto the spiral stone staircase that moved slowly upward like an escalator. Harry pushed open the door at the top.

He had one, brief glimpse of the stone Pensieve on the desk where he had left it, and then an earsplitting noise made him cry out, thinking of curses and returning Death Eaters and the rebirth of Voldemort —

But it was applause. All around the walls, the headmasters and headmistresses of Hogwarts were giving him a standing ovation; they waved their hats and in some cases their wigs, they reached through their frames to grip each other's hands; they danced up and down on the chairs in which they had been painted; Dilys Derwent sobbed unashamedly; Dexter Fortescue was waving his ear-trumpet; and Phineas Nigellus called, in his high, reedy voice, "And let it be noted that Slytherin House played its part! Let our contribution not be forgotten!"

But Harry had eyes only for the man who stood in the largest portrait directly behind the headmaster's chair. Tears were sliding down from behind the half-moon spectacles into the long silver beard, and the pride and the gratitude emanating from him filled Harry with the same balm as phoenix song.

At last, Harry held up his hands, and the portraits fell respectfully silent, beaming and mopping their eyes and waiting eagerly for him to speak. He directed his words at Dumbledore, however, and chose them with enormous care. Exhausted and bleary-eyed though he was, he must make one last effort, seeking one last piece of advice.

"The thing that was hidden in the Snitch," he began, "I dropped it in the forest. I don't know exactly where, but I'm not going to go looking for it again. Do you agree?"

"My dear boy, I do," said Dumbledore, while his fellow pictures looked confused and curious. "A wise and courageous decision, but no less than I would have expected of you. Does anyone else know where it fell?"

"No one," said Harry, and Dumbledore nodded his satisfaction.

"I'm going to keep Ignotus's present, though," said Harry, and Dumbledore beamed.

"But of course, Harry, it is yours forever, until you pass it on!"

"And then there's this."

Harry held up the Elder Wand, and Ron and Hermione looked at it with a reverence that, even in his befuddled and sleep-deprived state, Harry did not like to see.

"I don't want it," said Harry.

"What?" said Ron loudly. "Are you mental?"

"I know it's powerful," said Harry wearily. "But I was happier with mine. So . . ."

He rummaged in the pouch hung around his neck, and pulled out the two halves of holly still just connected by the finest thread of phoenix feather. Hermione had said that they could not be repaired, that the damage was too severe. All he knew was that if this did not work, nothing would.

He laid the broken wand upon the headmaster's desk, touched it with the very tip of the Elder Wand, and said, *"Reparo."*

As his wand resealed, red sparks flew out of its end. Harry knew that he had succeeded. He picked up the holly and phoenix wand and felt a sudden warmth in his fingers, as though wand and hand were rejoicing at their reunion.

"I'm putting the Elder Wand," he told Dumbledore, who was watching him with enormous affection and admiration, "back where it came from. It can stay there. If I die a natural death like Ignotus, its power will be broken, won't it? The previous master will never have been defeated. That'll be the end of it."

Dumbledore nodded. They smiled at each other.

"Are you sure?" said Ron. There was the faintest trace of longing in his voice as he looked at the Elder Wand.

"I think Harry's right," said Hermione quietly.

"That wand's more trouble than it's worth," said Harry. "And quite honestly," he turned away from the painted portraits, thinking now only of the four-poster bed lying waiting for him in Gryffindor Tower, and wondering whether Kreacher might bring him a sandwich there, "I've had enough trouble for a lifetime."

NINETEEN YEARS LATER

NINETEEN YEARS LATER

Autumn seemed to arrive suddenly that year. The morning of the first of September was crisp and golden as an apple, and as the little family bobbed across the rumbling road toward the great sooty station, the fumes of car exhausts and the breath of pedestrians sparkled like cobwebs in the cold air. Two large cages rattled on top of the laden trolleys the parents were pushing; the owls inside them hooted indignantly, and the redheaded girl trailed tearfully behind her brothers, clutching her father's arm.

"It won't be long, and you'll be going too," Harry told her.

"Two years," sniffed Lily. "I want to go *now!*"

The commuters stared curiously at the owls as the family wove its way toward the barrier between platforms nine and ten. Albus's voice drifted back to Harry over the surrounding clamor; his sons had resumed the argument they had started in the car.

"I *won't*! I *won't* be in Slytherin!"

"James, give it a rest!" said Ginny.

"I only said he *might* be," said James, grinning at his younger brother. "There's nothing wrong with that. He *might* be in Slyth —"

But James caught his mother's eye and fell silent. The five Potters approached the barrier. With a slightly cocky look over his shoulder at his younger brother, James took the trolley from his mother and broke into a run. A moment later, he had vanished.

"You'll write to me, won't you?" Albus asked his parents immediately, capitalizing on the momentary absence of his brother.

"Every day, if you want us to," said Ginny.

"Not *every* day," said Albus quickly. "James says most people only get letters from home about once a month."

"We wrote to James three times a week last year," said Ginny.

"And you don't want to believe everything he tells you about Hogwarts," Harry put in. "He likes a laugh, your brother."

Side by side, they pushed the second trolley forward, gathering speed. As they reached the barrier, Albus winced, but no collision came. Instead, the family emerged onto platform nine and three-quarters, which was obscured by thick white steam that was pouring from the scarlet Hogwarts Express. Indistinct figures were swarming through the mist, into which James had already disappeared.

"Where are they?" asked Albus anxiously, peering at the hazy forms they passed as they made their way down the platform.

"We'll find them," said Ginny reassuringly.

But the vapor was dense, and it was difficult to make out anybody's faces. Detached from their owners, voices sounded unnaturally loud. Harry thought he heard Percy discoursing loudly on broomstick regulations, and was quite glad of the excuse not to stop and say hello. . . .

"I think that's them, Al," said Ginny suddenly.

A group of four people emerged from the mist, standing alongside the very last carriage. Their faces only came into focus when Harry, Ginny, Lily, and Albus had drawn right up to them.

"Hi," said Albus, sounding immensely relieved.

Rose, who was already wearing her brand-new Hogwarts robes, beamed at him.

"Parked all right, then?" Ron asked Harry. "I did. Hermione didn't believe I could pass a Muggle driving test, did you? She thought I'd have to Confund the examiner."

"No, I didn't," said Hermione, "I had complete faith in you."

"As a matter of fact, I *did* Confund him," Ron whispered to Harry, as together they lifted Albus's trunk and owl onto the train. "I only forgot to look in the wing mirror, and let's face it, I can use a Supersensory Charm for that."

Back on the platform, they found Lily and Hugo, Rose's younger brother, having an animated discussion about which House they would be sorted into when they finally went to Hogwarts.

"If you're not in Gryffindor, we'll disinherit you," said Ron, "but no pressure."

"*Ron!*"

Lily and Hugo laughed, but Albus and Rose looked solemn.

"He doesn't mean it," said Hermione and Ginny, but Ron was no longer paying attention. Catching Harry's eye, he nodded covertly to a point some fifty yards away. The steam had thinned for a moment, and three people stood in sharp relief against the shifting mist.

"Look who it is."

Draco Malfoy was standing there with his wife and son, a dark coat buttoned up to his throat. His hair was receding somewhat, which emphasized the pointed chin. The new boy resembled Draco as much as Albus resembled Harry. Draco caught sight of Harry, Ron, Hermione, and Ginny staring at him, nodded curtly, and turned away again.

"So that's little Scorpius," said Ron under his breath. "Make sure you beat him in every test, Rosie. Thank God you inherited your mother's brains."

"Ron, for heaven's sake," said Hermione, half stern, half amused. "Don't try to turn them against each other before they've even started school!"

"You're right, sorry," said Ron, but unable to help himself, he added, "Don't get *too* friendly with him, though, Rosie. Granddad Weasley would never forgive you if you married a pureblood."

"Hey!"

James had reappeared; he had divested himself of his trunk, owl, and trolley, and was evidently bursting with news.

"Teddy's back there," he said breathlessly, pointing back over his shoulder into the billowing clouds of steam. "Just seen him! And guess what he's doing? *Snogging Victoire!*"

He gazed up at the adults, evidently disappointed by the lack of reaction.

"*Our* Teddy! *Teddy Lupin!* Snogging *our* Victoire! *Our* cousin! And I asked Teddy what he was doing —"

"You interrupted them?" said Ginny. "You are *so* like Ron —"

"— and he said he'd come to see her off! And then he told me to go away. He's *snogging* her!" James added as though worried he had not made himself clear.

"Oh, it would be lovely if they got married!" whispered Lily ecstatically. "Teddy would *really* be part of the family then!"

"He already comes round for dinner about four times a week," said Harry. "Why don't we just invite him to live with us and have done with it?"

"Yeah!" said James enthusiastically. "I don't mind sharing with Al — Teddy could have my room!"

"No," said Harry firmly, "you and Al will share a room only when I want the house demolished."

He checked the battered old watch that had once been Fabian Prewett's.

"It's nearly eleven, you'd better get on board."

"Don't forget to give Neville our love!" Ginny told James as she hugged him.

"Mum! I can't give a professor *love*!"

"But you *know* Neville —"

James rolled his eyes.

"Outside, yeah, but at school he's Professor Longbottom, isn't he? I can't walk into Herbology and give him *love. . . .*"

Shaking his head at his mother's foolishness, he vented his feelings by aiming a kick at Albus.

"See you later, Al. Watch out for the thestrals."

"I thought they were invisible? *You said they were invisible!*"

But James merely laughed, permitted his mother to kiss him, gave his father a fleeting hug, then leapt onto the rapidly filling train. They saw him wave, then sprint away up the corridor to find his friends.

"Thestrals are nothing to worry about," Harry told Albus. "They're gentle things, there's nothing scary about them. Anyway, you won't be going up to school in the carriages, you'll be going in the boats."

Ginny kissed Albus good-bye.

"See you at Christmas."

"Bye, Al," said Harry as his son hugged him. "Don't forget Hagrid's invited you to tea next Friday. Don't mess with Peeves. Don't duel anyone till you've learned how. And don't let James wind you up."

"What if I'm in Slytherin?"

The whisper was for his father alone, and Harry knew that only the moment of departure could have forced Albus to reveal how great and sincere that fear was.

Harry crouched down so that Albus's face was slightly above his own. Alone of Harry's three children, Albus had inherited Lily's eyes.

"Albus Severus," Harry said quietly, so that nobody but Ginny could hear, and she was tactful enough to pretend to be waving to Rose, who was now on the train, "you were named for two headmasters of Hogwarts. One of them was a Slytherin and he was probably the bravest man I ever knew."

"But *just say* —"

"— then Slytherin House will have gained an excellent student, won't it? It doesn't matter to us, Al. But if it matters to you, you'll be able to choose Gryffindor over Slytherin. The Sorting Hat takes your choice into account."

"Really?"

"It did for me," said Harry.

He had never told any of his children that before, and he saw the wonder in Albus's face when he said it. But now the doors were slamming all along the scarlet train, and the blurred outlines of parents were swarming forward for final kisses, last-minute reminders.

Albus jumped into the carriage and Ginny closed the door behind him. Students were hanging from the windows nearest them. A great number of faces, both on the train and off, seemed to be turned toward Harry.

"Why are they all *staring*?" demanded Albus as he and Rose craned around to look at the other students.

"Don't let it worry you," said Ron. "It's me. I'm extremely famous."

Albus, Rose, Hugo, and Lily laughed. The train began to move, and Harry walked alongside it, watching his son's thin face, already ablaze with excitement. Harry kept smiling and waving, even though it was like a little bereavement, watching his son glide away from him. . . .

The last trace of steam evaporated in the autumn air. The train rounded a corner. Harry's hand was still raised in farewell.

"He'll be all right," murmured Ginny.

As Harry looked at her, he lowered his hand absentmindedly and touched the lightning scar on his forehead.

"I know he will."

The scar had not pained Harry for nineteen years. All was well.

J. K. Rowling began writing stories when she was six years old. She started working on the Harry Potter sequence in 1990, when, she says, "the idea . . . simply fell into my head." The first book, *Harry Potter and the Sorcerer's Stone,* was published in the United Kingdom in 1997 and the United States in 1998. Since then, books in the Harry Potter series have been honored with many prizes, including the Anthony Award, the Hugo Award, the Bram Stoker Award, the Whitbread Children's Book Award, the Nestlé Smarties Book Prize, and the British Book Awards Children's Book of the Year, as well as *New York Times* Notable Book, ALA Notable Children's Book, and ALA Best Book for Young Adults citations. Ms. Rowling has also been named an Officer of the Order of the British Empire.

She lives in Scotland with her family.

Mary GrandPré has illustrated more than twenty beautiful books, including *Henry and Pawl and the Round Yellow Ball,* cowritten with her husband Tom Casmer; *Plum,* a collection of poetry by Tony Mitton; *Lucia and the Light,* by Phyllis Root; and the American editions of all seven Harry Potter novels. Her work has also appeared in *The New Yorker, The Atlantic Monthly,* and *The Wall Street Journal,* and her paintings and pastels have been shown in galleries across the United States.

Ms. GrandPré lives in Sarasota, Florida, with her family.

This

book was

art directed by David

Saylor. The art for both the jacket

and the interior was created using pastels on

toned printmaking paper. The text was set in 12-point

Adobe Garamond, a typeface based on the sixteenth-century type

designs of Claude Garamond, redrawn by Robert Slimbach in 1989. The

book was typeset by Brad Walrod and was printed and bound at

RR Donnelley in Crawfordsville, Indiana. The Managing

Editor was Karyn Browne; the Continuity

Editor was Cheryl Klein; and the

Manufacturing Director

was Angela

Biola.